DAUGHTER AND SKY

The Complete Lost Keepers Series

AR Colbert

Ramsey Street Books

Copyright © 2021 by AR Colbert

All rights reserved

The characters and events portrayed in this book are fictitious. Any similarity to real persons, living or dead, is coincidental and not intended by the author.

No part of this book may be reproduced, or stored in a retrieval system, or transmitted in any form or by any means, electronic, mechanical, photocopying, recording, or otherwise, without express written permission of the publisher.

CONTENTS

A Note From the Author   1

Ancient History   3

Chapter 1   5

Chapter 2   9

Chapter 3   14

Chapter 4   19

Chapter 5   23

Chapter 6   27

Chapter 7   32

Chapter 8   36

Chapter 9   39

Chapter 10   43

Chapter 11   48

Chapter 12   53

Chapter 13   57

Chapter 14   61

Chapter 15	65
The Unseen	69
Prologue	71
Chapter 1	73
Chapter 2	77
Chapter 3	81
Chapter 4	86
Chapter 5	90
Chapter 6	94
Chapter 7	98
Chapter 8	102
Chapter 9	106
Chapter 10	111
Chapter 11	116
Chapter 12	121
The Apothecary	127
Chapter 1	129
Chapter 2	134
Chapter 3	138
Chapter 4	143
Chapter 5	147
Chapter 6	152
Chapter 7	157
Chapter 8	161
Chapter 9	166

Chapter 10	170
Chapter 11	174
Chapter 12	180
Chapter 13	185
Chapter 14	191
In Pursuit	197
Prologue	198
Chapter 1	201
Chapter 2	206
Chapter 3	212
Chapter 4	216
Chapter 5	220
Chapter 6	225
Chapter 7	229
Chapter 8	234
Chapter 9	239
Chapter 10	243
Chapter 11	247
Chapter 12	252
Unraveling	257
Prologue	259
Chapter 1	262
Chapter 2	266
Chapter 3	271
Chapter 4	275

Chapter 5	280
Chapter 6	285
Chapter 7	290
Chapter 8	295
Chapter 9	300
Chapter 10	304
Chapter 11	308
Chapter 12	312
Old Man on the Sea	317
Chapter 1	319
Chapter 2	325
Chapter 3	331
Chapter 4	337
Chapter 5	341
Chapter 6	346
Chapter 7	350
Chapter 8	355
Chapter 9	360
Chapter 10	364
Chapter 11	370
Chapter 12	374
Chapter 13	379
Finding Atlantis	385
Chapter 1	387
Chapter 2	391

Chapter 3	396
Chapter 4	401
Chapter 5	407
Chapter 6	412
Chapter 7	416
Chapter 8	420
Chapter 9	424
Chapter 10	429
Chapter 11	432
Chapter 12	436
Chapter 13	440
Chapter 14	444
The Water Princess	449
Chapter 1	451
Chapter 2	455
Chapter 3	460
Chapter 4	465
Chapter 5	469
Chapter 6	474
Chapter 7	481
Chapter 8	485
Chapter 9	491
Chapter 10	495
Chapter 11	498
Chapter 12	504

Ignited	509
Chapter 1	511
Chapter 2	515
Chapter 3	521
Chapter 4	526
Chapter 5	532
Chapter 6	535
Chapter 7	540
Chapter 8	543
Chapter 9	547
Chapter 10	552
Chapter 11	556
The Center of the Earth	561
Chapter 1	563
Chapter 2	568
Chapter 3	572
Chapter 4	576
Chapter 5	581
Chapter 6	585
Chapter 7	590
Chapter 8	594
Chapter 9	597
Chapter 10	601
Chapter 11	605
Chapter 12	609

Lies in Olympus	613
Chapter 1	615
Chapter 2	618
Chapter 3	621
Chapter 4	625
Chapter 5	630
Chapter 6	635
Chapter 7	639
Chapter 8	643
Chapter 9	648
Chapter 10	652
Chapter 11	655
Chapter 12	660
Chapter 13	664
Chapter 14	668
Deliverance	671
Chapter 1	673
Chapter 2	676
Chapter 3	681
Chapter 4	686
Chapter 5	691
Chapter 6	694
Chapter 7	698
Chapter 8	702
Chapter 9	707

Chapter 10	711
Chapter 11	714
Chapter 12	718
Chapter 13	722
Epilogue	727
A Deeper LOOK	732
New by AR Colbert:	735
About the Author	736

A Note from the Author

Daughter of Sea and Sky is a reformatted version of the original Lost Keepers series. This book was born from the idea of creating a series broken down more like my favorite TV shows than a traditional novel. I wanted each of the original twelve books to feel like an hour-long episode, so you could hit pause between each book or binge the entire series to your heart's content!

They connect together to weave one extra-long epic story arc, but you'll find that this book is still divided into twelve titled sections to keep the original spirit of the series. I hope you will enjoy reading each one as much as I enjoyed writing them!

-AR

Ancient History

CHAPTER 1

I FELT LIKE I was in a movie, mustard stain on my shirt and all. Shoving the last bite of a hot dog into my mouth, I turned to my mom with a grin. "Isn't this amazing?" I asked through a mouthful of half-chewed food.

She quirked an eyebrow at me. "Incredible," she said sarcastically. She dug a napkin out of her bag and passed it my way. "You've got a little something..." She pointed at a spot next to her lips.

I wiped the final evidence of street food from my mouth and sighed. With arms extended fully to both sides I looked up at the sky and spun in a circle. "I can't believe we're really here. Just a couple of gals in the Big Apple. Doin' our thing. Living large."

"Watch it!" A middle-aged man in an ill-fitting business suit barely dodged my swinging arms and scowled as he scurried past.

"Oh! Pardon me, sir. I'm so sorry!"

He turned back over his shoulder with his eyebrows drawn even lower and hissed for good measure. I was mortified, but it elicited a giggle from my mother.

"Oh, Everly."

"I can't help it. It just feels magical here. I don't know what my future holds, but I'm glad New York is going to be a part of it for the next four to six years. It's almost like it's calling to me. I belong here."

"You have a very vivid imagination if you think I'm paying for six years of out-of-state tuition. Four sounds good to me." Mom's smile faded and she turned to me with a serious expression, though her eyes still twinkled with humor. "And by the way, that's not the sound of the city calling to you. It's the sound of that cab honking for you to get out of the way."

"Oh geez!" I hurried across the intersection with a squeal.

I definitely had a few things to learn about life in the city. It was like a different planet from where I was raised. My backwards Oklahoma hometown had little more than a livestock feed shop and a gas station—neither of which had been updated since the early 1980s. We had more cows than people, and all the visual appeal you'd expect from a north forty farmhouse in a field of red dirt, but it was home.

New York was a stimulus overload with flashing lights and blinking advertisements on every surface. The air was fragrant—sometimes leaving my mouth watering from the aroma of street foods and restaurants, and sometimes leaving my eyes watering from the intensity of its odors. Horns and shouts and laughter and music mixed together in a raucous symphony of noise. People brushed past in every direction, everyone in a hurry to get somewhere... or maybe nowhere, but hurrying nonetheless. Some were dressed in suits and ties like Mr. Grumpface who hissed at me, some wore sunglasses that cost more than my car, and some wore next to nothing at all. But I was definitely the only one who dressed like she was from Hibbard, Oklahoma. At least I had on my cute boots.

But as out of place as I was, New York filled some kind of a void I'd never realized I had. It made my heart sing. The city was alive, and it made *me* feel more alive, as well. I was going to like it here.

"Everly?"

I snapped my gaze back toward my mother, who held a slight look of impatience. "Did you say something?"

"You have got to get your head of the clouds, girl." She shook her head. "We have to head back to Millie's place for dinner soon."

"Why the rush? I just ate a hot dog the size of my forearm. I've got a full tank for a while."

"She invited her friend, Claudia, over for dinner. I told her we'd be back by six."

"Claudia with the son who goes to Columbia?"

"That's the one."

"I told her I'm not interested in going to Columbia. She can quit trying to lure me with cute boys."

"Who said he was cute?"

"I just assumed. Otherwise, why would Millie bring him over to tempt me into switching schools?"

Mom pulled me behind her as we navigated through a dense crowd, and continued once it cleared out again. "Hey, I don't blame you for choosing NYU over Columbia. I would probably do the same. But it is such an accomplishment to be accepted into an Ivy League school. I think she just wants you to be sure before you decline something like that."

"Too late." I shrugged. "It's already been declined. So we can eat with Columbia Claudia and her probably cute son, but they can't make me go there."

Mom shook her head and laughed. "I don't think New York is going to know how to handle you."

"Well, they've got six years to figure it out."

She shot a disapproving gaze from the corners of her eyes and held up four fingers in front of me. I took her hand and pushed three of them down, pointing her index finger at a window display up ahead. Then I swung it around to a copper sign with a light patina that read *Rossel & Jude*. Atop the sign, swinging gently with it in the breeze, sat a pure white owl. It looked a bit like the barn owls we had back home, but there wasn't a speck of color on its snowy-white feathers.

"One more stop. I promise we'll be quick." I made puppy dog eyes at her. "Please? It looks so quirky and fun. It says it's a small artist-run gallery, and that print in the window is fabulous. Plus—that squatty little pigeon on the sign said it's worth a look."

I flashed a goofy grin at my mother. The color had drained completely from her face. She almost matched the bird.

"Are you joking? About the owl?" She whispered. She looked seriously disturbed.

"Of course!" I laughed. "I know it's not a pigeon. Weird seeing it hanging out in the middle of the city though, huh? Are you lost, little guy?"

Mom turned me back to face her. "Don't talk to it."

"Okaaay... I was only kidding."

"Let's get back to Millie's."

"Really, though--can we pop in here for a second first? Please? I would really like to see the painting of that print in the window. I promise I won't dilly-dally."

She frowned and glanced back at the owl. It seemed to be watching us. It was honestly a little creepy, but in an intriguing way. I wondered if it was part of the exhibition inside the gallery.

"Fine. Ten minutes, tops."

"Thank you!"

I grabbed her hand, which was frigid and clammy, and pulled her through the door. The gallery was wide open and sparse of furniture. Its tall ceilings revealed black ductwork suspended under a wooden ceiling, and the outer wall was exposed brick with enormous picture windows near the entrance. The rest of the walls were stark white, with no other distractions from the artwork inside.

The space probably wasn't large as far as art galleries went. It had just two main halls. One was essentially void of people other than my mom and me, but the other held a small crowd at the opposite end.

"Oooh, I wonder what's over there," I said, dragging my poor mother along behind me.

"I don't like this," she mumbled under her breath.

As we neared, I noticed an extremely tall young man with broad shoulders propped up against the wall near the rest of the crowd. His skin was a sunkissed bronze, and his hair was tousled into messy perfection, the color of dark chocolate. But his eyes were what really caught my attention. They were an incredible amber, like honey flecked with gold leaf. And they were staring straight at me.

"I wonder if he goes to Columbia," I snickered to my mom. But she gave no witty remark in response. Her eyes were deadlocked on the boy's, and she was practically snarling at him.

"Mom?" I asked. "Is something wrong?"

"We need to go, Everly. Now."

Just then, the crowd parted ahead to reveal the art piece everyone was fawning over. A small girl tugged on her mother's hand and pointed at me with a tiny finger. "It's her, Mama."

The child's mother turned to me with a broad smile. "It's a remarkable piece. Truly breathtaking. The artist captured your essence beautifully."

"Uh, thank you?" I glanced at my mom for help to get away from this crazy woman, but she was still too involved in the staredown with golden eyes to have noticed. The mother and child smiled warmly again as they moved toward the exit, and I stepped forward into their spot in the crowd.

Finally, I saw the piece that had drawn everyone's attention. Hanging on the wall in a gilded golden frame, illuminated by a small spotlight, was a four-foot tall portrait of... *me*.

CHAPTER 2

"MOM?" I BLINDLY PATTED the air behind me, trying to make contact. I needed another set of eyes to confirm what I saw. This couldn't be possible.

The painting was undeniably me. Long caramel waves of hair cascaded over the girl's shoulders, thick and full. I absentmindedly patted down the cowlick to the left of my part as I noticed a matching tuft of hair on the girl in the painting. She even had my eyes—round and blue, except for a pie-shaped third of her left iris, which was a rich brown. *Heterochromia iridum*. I'd learned the term for it when I was a young girl. It was quite a mouthful for saying 'two different colored eyes,' but I'd never forgotten it. My memory was weird like that. I never forgot anything. In fact, my photographic memory was probably the only reason I'd been accepted into Columbia.

But that didn't matter right now. "Mom," I repeated. "Are you seeing this?"

I tilted my head and stepped closer. She... I... *we*? We looked determined. Fierce. The girl in the painting was the tough version of me I'd always wanted to be. Well, her expression and body language were tough, anyway. Her chin was held high, almost defiant, as she leaned forward with her forearms propped on her knees in the seat. On closer examination, I noticed she was missing my scar—the one I'd gotten below my lip when I fell off my horse and landed on a rock in the second grade. Other than that small difference, she could have been my more ferocious twin.

The rest of the scene didn't share the same ferocity. She wore a glimmering golden gown. The chair she sat on more closely resembled a throne. It was an ornate, oversized, high backed Victorian chair, with tufted mauve velvet cushions. I didn't recognize the room she was in. It was vast and open, with arching leaded windows lining the wall that stretched over two stories tall. A plaque below the painting bore the artwork's name: *Deliverance*.

"Mom!"

I had her attention now. Or rather, the painting version of me did. My mom looked less surprised than angry, though. Her jaw worked as she examined the piece before us, then she turned to me. A pink flush was working its way up her neck and into her cheeks, and she was trembling.

"Give me your hair tie," she demanded.

"The one I'm using right now? In my hair?"

"Yes." She impatiently held out her hand.

Unused to seeing my mom worked up in a state like this, I obeyed without further question. I pulled the elastic band from the back of my head and dropped it into her open palm. She pocketed it and immediately began running her fingers through my hair, ruffling it up and pulling it forward to cover my eyes. It hung wildly in my face, tickling my nose and leaving me looking like Cousin Itt.

"Is this necessary?" I reached to push my hair just enough to see through the curtain before my eyes, but my mom swatted my hand back down.

"Don't touch it. Wait right here. I'm going to talk to the artist." She turned on her heels and disappeared through the crowd.

I spun around to follow her and found myself staring into a broad chest covered by a snug fitting navy blue t-shirt. Slowly, my eyes moved up higher, and higher again, past a strong scruffy jawline, full lips twisted into a crooked half-grin, chiseled cheekbones that looked like they'd been carved from granite, and into the glistening golden eyes of the boy who'd watched us walk in.

"Can I have your autograph?" His low, rich, baritone words danced through the air, messing with my senses.

I giggled nervously. "You want me... I mean my, uh... that's not me. You don't want my autograph."

He pushed a section of my untamed hair to the side, and his fingers left my temple tingling where they'd brushed against my skin. He was very forward for a stranger. And if he'd looked like anyone else, I might have balked at him touching me. But this was no ordinary guy. He could touch me all he wanted.

"Are you sure?" One side of his perfect mouth pulled up into that charming crooked grin again. "Because it sure looks like you."

I giggled again. I was acting like a lovestruck pre-teen, but I couldn't help it. The longer I stood near him, the more enamored I became. He must have been a model. This was New York, after all.

"I'm sure," I finally mumbled through a bashful smile. I dropped my chin, allowing my hair to fall forward over the edge of my eye again.

The boy closed his eyes and took a sharp breath before slowly opening them again. He allowed his grin to reach full capacity, displaying a perfect set of white teeth, and I almost swayed in place. I was actually going weak in the knees like some kind of cartoon. What was wrong with me?

"Well, at least tell me your name."

"Everly." It rolled out of my mouth before I could consider otherwise.

"Everly," he repeated. It sounded so much better coming from his lips. Slow and smooth like honey.

"Everly!"

I startled, and turned to face my glowering mother, stomping toward us. When I looked back over my shoulder, the boy was gone.

"What are you doing?" She immediately pulled more of my hair forward when she reached me.

I blew it back out of my face. "Just enjoying the most delightfully bizarre encounter of my life." I sighed.

"I thought I taught you not to talk to strangers." She frowned. I wasn't buying her attempt to be funny. She was still visibly shaken.

"I can't say no to a stranger who looks like that." I grinned. "Speaking of strangers, did you find the artist? I swear I don't know how he painted this. He must have found one of my 4H clippings from the Hibbard Newspaper or something."

"I seriously doubt that. And no." She glanced around the room. "But he's here."

"How do you know?"

Her frown deepened. "I can just feel it."

"If you say so." My mother was starting to sound like she had a few screws loose. Of course, I'd never say that to her face.

She ran her hands up and down the sides of her arms, scanning the room as she did. "Maybe we should just go. Let's get back to Millie's for now, and we can figure this out later."

"It's really not that big of a deal. It's not even me in the picture—it just looks like me. She's missing my scar."

My mom's jaw dropped. "I knew it," she muttered.

I followed her gaze to the lobby, where the early evening sunlight was filtering in through the windows in wide golden rays. Gliding through the sunshine like it was his own personal spotlight came a thin, pale man, probably in his fifties. He stood ramrod straight, like a metal bar held him firmly in place under his clothes, and his feet stepped so softly across the wood floor that he almost appeared to be floating. His hair was stark white and pulled up into a high topknot on his head. He wore all black, which contrasted sharply with his ghostly coloring.

He strode over to the front of our hall and turned to face the crowd of onlookers. A small group meandering toward the exit stopped to compliment him, but he never once looked in their direction. He didn't acknowledge their existence at all. He simply stared straight ahead. Maybe he was blind. Or deaf. Or maybe just stuck up and indifferent.

"Is that the artist?" I asked. Mom didn't answer. She was already walking toward him. *Good luck with that.*

To my surprise, he turned to face her as she approached. It was only then that I saw his eyes. With his fair skin and white hair, I'd expected them to be pale as well. But they were dark. Darker than brown. Almost onyx. I inhaled sharply as his two black holes took in my mother, who by all accounts, looked fearless.

Based on body language alone, I would have guessed she was screaming at him. And with the way her hands waved back and forth in front of her, it was probably very colorful language. But in reality, I couldn't hear a thing. The acoustics in the gallery must have been pretty horrible.

The artist wasn't intimidated. He remained straight-faced as she berated him. His mouth moved in response, but the rest of his face and body were eerily still. A few eyes from passers-by glanced in my direction, clearly associating me with the woman causing a scene. I needed to put some distance between us before I got dragged into the kerfuffle as well.

I glanced around the room again for golden eyes. He was much more fun to talk to than my angry mother. Plus—I hadn't gotten to ask for his name. But he was gone. He'd probably bolted out of there as soon as my mom came unhinged. I couldn't blame him. I wanted to get out there, too.

"Mom?" I called out.

She held one finger out to the side to quiet me and continued speaking to the artist. I tapped my foot impatiently, watching and waiting for my chance to jump in and pull her away. I was sure it was just a coincidence that his painting resembled me. There was no need to carry on like this.

I was so intent on stopping her at my first opportunity, that I failed to see any commotion outside. There were no masked men or grand villainous speeches. No abandoned suitcases or shifty-looking men in the shadows. There was just a *BOOM*.

Then, a thousand things happened at once. Instant chaos. My first indication that something had gone awry was a jolt of pain in my tailbone. I'd fallen. No, I'd been blasted to the ground. I looked up to see shattered glass filling the lobby floor. The white-haired artist reached down and pulled my mom to her feet, then pointed down the opposite hall.

Once the ringing in my ears had quieted down to a shrill hum, I heard the cries of fear. Suddenly it all came together. There had been an explosion on the sidewalk outside of the gallery.

"Go, young lady! What are you waiting for?" An older woman pushed me in the back with her handbag, and I jumped to my feet.

My mom was only a few yards ahead, looking over her shoulder as the artist dragged her toward a doorway down the opposite hall. The rest of the crowd followed closely behind.

"Come on, Everly. It's going to be okay."

CHAPTER 3

I LOOKED UP INTO the enchanting gold-flecked eyes of Mr. Model.

"It's okay," he repeated. "I've got you." Hesitantly, I placed my fingers into his outstretched hand and allowed him to pull me to my feet. Again, my palm came alive where our skin touched. It buzzed with warmth and comfort. And despite the tragedy taking place around us, I felt compelled to giggle again. *Don't be stupid.*

"My mom," I said weakly.

"She's up ahead. We're all going to the same place. They're ushering us into the basement until they can figure out what's going on."

I stepped up on my toes trying to catch a glimpse of my mother ahead, but there were too many people between us. I did spot a snowy-white topknot, however. It was safe to assume she was still with the artist. I released a breath and continued forward, fingers still wrapped in the warm grasp of the tall, handsome stranger beside me.

"Was anyone hurt?"

"I don't think so," he said. "It was probably just some prank, but they've got to clear the area to investigate. The authorities are on the way. We may be stuck here for a while."

He quirked a perfectly arched eyebrow at me and my stomach did a flip. I didn't know how to handle myself around him. We didn't have fine specimens like this back in Oklahoma.

Perhaps sensing my reaction to him, he flashed that crooked grin at me again and I had to look away. He was too dang charming. I couldn't get swept up in a girlish crush when I should be focusing on not stepping on shrapnel from the explosion that had just separated me from my mother in a giant unfamiliar city.

Outside the broken windows in the lobby I noted even more of a mess. A trash can laid on its side in the middle of the sidewalk. In Hibbard, the whole town would have gathered around to check out the scene. They'd be gossiping about it for months, recounting the event and making it larger and more deadly every time they told the story.

But here, it was as though the New Yorkers didn't even notice the smoke still billowing from the metal can. They stepped around the shards of glass, looks of annoyance painting their hurried faces. The lack of response could have convinced me that this was a daily occurrence in their world. Aside from a few people who'd been scraped up by the blast, no one seemed to care much at all. Thankfully there didn't appear to be any major injuries.

I glanced up at the sign again, swaying in the breeze. The owl was gone, leaving only the names of the artists. Rossel & Jude. I wondered which one my mom had scolded.

Finally we reached the door at the opposite end of the other hall. The clean, hip and modern aesthetic of the main gallery did not continue past the doorway. Here the building really showed its age. We funneled into a dark stairwell leading down into the basement. A single flickering bulb lit the way down the creaky wooden steps.

The air was musty and increasingly chilled the further we descended. The odor reminded me of our storm cellar back home. I'd spent way too many spring evenings down there, avoiding tornadoes that never came anywhere near our little farmhouse. Much like right now—I was escaping a prank that had already taken place and similarly posed no real threat. But it was better to be safe than sorry, I supposed. That's what my mom always said during storm season.

On the next step, my foot slipped, knocking me off balance. I reached for the handrails, but there were none on the narrow stairwell. My hand slid across unfinished drywall as I attempted to correct my balance. If I tumbled down these stairs I'd take out ten other people with me, like a human bowling ball.

But two large hands grabbed my waist, effortlessly catching and steadying me on the stairs. Warmth buzzed through my core, like static electricity softly licking its way up my spine. I gasped and turned to face a smiling set of golden eyes. I'd officially made more physical contact with this male model than I had any of the thirteen boys in my graduating class.

"Thanks."

"My pleasure." He grinned. *Oh my stars, I do not need to think about the word 'pleasure' coming from his perfect mouth.*

I turned back to the front and finished my descent. We were two of the last people to reach the basement. It wasn't as musty in the open room below the gallery. Soft light filtered in through a couple of small windows high on the outer wall, and fluorescent lighting illuminated the rest of the room.

Tall metal cabinets lined the perimeter of the room, and a few enclosed glass cases stood in the middle. They contained various vessels of pottery and strange sculptures. I found my mother sitting on the floor next to one and hurried to join her.

She sighed with relief at my arrival, swiping the hair out of my face with both hands and then pulling me into her chest for an embrace. "Oh, Everly. I hoped this would never happen."

I pulled back from her arms, taking in the worry lines etched around her eyes. "Well nobody hopes they'll get to experience an explosion, but all things considered, this wasn't so bad as far as bombs go."

She forced a breathy laugh through her lips and pulled me in again. "You're right. It wasn't a bad bomb."

I allowed her to hold me against her for longer than the situation required before finally prying myself away again. "Mom?"

"Yes, dear?"

I didn't want to offend her, but I'd never been good with delicate situations. "You've been a little... uh... erratic today. Is everything okay?"

She smiled for real this time, but there was still something pained behind it. "I'm sorry I've been acting strange. It's not everyday you stumble into a gallery to find a portrait of your daughter on display."

"Right." Of course that would be startling. It had startled me as well. "But it's not me, remember? No scar."

"Mm." She pressed her lips together and stared off into the distance.

"What did the artist say when you asked him about it?"

She shrugged. "Must be a coincidence."

Well that settled nothing. But whatever. She was in some kind of state right now that I didn't want to deal with. I'd ask more once she had a chance to settle down after dinner.

"Thank you everyone for remaining calm." A thin man stood at the foot of the stairs. He had a colorful silk scarf wrapped around his dainty neck and an air of superiority. "I'm Jude." He glanced around the room, giving us all time to acknowledge that he was one of the gallery's artists. Then, as if that wasn't enough, he added, "I hope you all enjoyed a peek at my work upstairs. Authorities are quickly working to clear the glass and rule out any foul play. I expect we'll only be required to wait here for a short time before they release us. But lucky you! Under these strange circumstances, you now have the honor of previewing more of our art and artifacts from our personal collections—pieces never before exposed to outside eyes." He smiled proudly.

Had he been the one to paint my portrait? I glanced at my mother but saw no recognition in her tired eyes. Whoever he was, he didn't rile her up like the white haired man had. And speaking of good ol' topknot, who must've been Rossel by process of elimination, where had he gone? I looked around the dimly lit space and couldn't find him. I didn't see golden eyes, either.

A doppleganger portrait. A gorgeous guy, finer than any work of art in the gallery, who seemed to take some level of interest in me. A bomb. A shaken mother. An old hipster with black eyes. This day couldn't get any weirder. I loved New York.

Jude continued droning on about his fine collection and I peered through the glass case we were leaning against. There were some really cool pieces in there. I wondered why they would be here, in the basement, rather than on display upstairs, or even in a museum if they were as valuable as Jude led us to believe.

Some of the most interesting items resembled Egyptian drawings I'd seen in school. But they were formed into figurines carved from gold, maybe a foot high. I admired the fine details carved into the metal—the subtle variations in the wings of the humanoid figures, and scales upon their reptilian heads. They were bizarre and captivating.

"Mom look at this stuff."

I turned to see her reaction, but her eyes were closed. Her mouth moved quickly, silently reciting some unknown string of words. "Sorry. Are you praying?"

She didn't respond, so I turned back to look at the pretty collection. My eyes were drawn next to an old coin, the size of a half dollar. It was thin and rubbed almost smooth in spots. But there on the surface of the darkened metal was the outline of an owl, much like the one I'd seen outside of the gallery. I knew he was probably a part of the exhibition somehow. These guys seemed to have a fascination with ancient artifacts and Egyptian history.

I had to admit, it was pretty interesting. I nudged my mom. "Maybe this is what I'll study at NYU. I think these ancient civilizations are incredible. Like, how on earth did they have the technology to create stuff like this?"

Her eyes snapped open. "No." She faced me with a wild ferocity gleaming in her eyes.

"No?" I was taken aback by her forceful response. We'd been trying to come up with ideas for my major all summer. I thought she'd be thrilled that I'd finally found something that interested me.

"There's no money in the field. Jobs are hard to come by. You should look at finance." She blurted the words flippantly. Thoughtlessly.

"I'd rather dig ditches than get into finance." I curled up my lip. "Besides, life isn't all about money. I think this stuff is amazing. I wouldn't mind working for peanuts if it meant I'd get to learn about the way people lived thousands of years ago. Maybe I could even go to Egypt. You know, dig around in the pyramids a little." I nudged her with my elbow again.

"No!" she practically barked at me. Her brows pulled low and her mouth twisted to one side, like she was enduring some kind of internal battle. I'd never seen my mom behave as strangely as she was today. "In fact, maybe New York isn't right for you either. Let's stick to what you know. Oklahoma State has a great Ag Economics program."

That had escalated way too quickly. I was going to have to lay off the sarcasm for a bit. "Where is this coming from, mom? I'm already enrolled. All my stuff—"

"Enough," she whispered harshly. "We're getting you out of New York. Tonight, if we can."

CHAPTER 4

"MATILDA GORDON?" JUDE LOOKED up from the piece of paper held in his hand. "Matilda Gordon," he repeated, glancing around the basement.

Mom's jaw clenched as she looked his way and then back at me.

"Are you going to answer him?" I asked.

"No. I don't know him. He's probably looking for someone else."

"You're right. This basement is probably full of Matilda Gordons."

She pursed her lips and pulled out her phone to check the time. "We should have left already. We're going to be late for dinner."

"I'm sure Millie will understand, given the *bomb* and all."

"Maybe we can create a distraction to get them out of the stairwell so we can get out of here." She looked around for something that might work.

"Mom, what is really going on here?"

"Matilda... Matilda Gordon." Jude looked irritated. He glanced over his shoulder at the man behind him. I hadn't noticed him there earlier, but Rossel stood in the shadows, his white man bun giving him away even in the low light. Jude didn't appear to know who my mother was, but Rossel's dark eyes were pinned on her. His eyes were menacing on their own, but his expression wasn't hardened. It was blank, just as it had been upstairs.

I looked back to my mother who was rubbing her temples with fingers from each hand. She was clearly distressed. She squeezed her eyes shut tight, then opened and fixed them on me. "Everly, I have to tell you something."

The other people in the basement were beginning to murmur amongst themselves, trying to locate the Matilda being summoned by the artists. I supposed they thought the authorities were requesting her. They were probably growing more uncomfortable with each passing second.

I sensed my mother's urgency. "What is it, mom?"

"I—" she hiccuped, and placed her fingers on the front of her throat. She shook her head and tried again, more quickly this time. "I'm fr—"

Again she couldn't complete her thought. She launched into a sudden coughing fit, drawing stares from the rest of the crowd. Her eyes watered, cheeks red. The cough was so intense that it finished with a choking gag-like noise. She wiped her eyes with her knuckles and sighed.

"You're way too worked up, mom. Whatever it is, it's not too big for us. We've handled worse. We can handle this, too." I was really starting to worry now. I'd never seen her like this.

"This is different, sweetheart. This isn't like anything you've ever encountered before. It—" She began dry-heaving. I looked around, panicking, and grabbed a stranger's glittery pink water tumbler, twisting off the lid and shoving it under my mom's face just in time to catch her hot dog from earlier. *Gross.*

I cringed and glanced back at the woman I'd taken the cup from. "Keep it," she said, horrified. "I insist." I shrugged and twisted the lid back into place. Then I turned back to my poor mother.

I knew she wasn't ill. She'd just worked herself into some extreme state of anxiety. "Okay," I said. "No more talking. Do you want some gum?"

Her eyes widened, and she nodded emphatically. She began digging around in her own purse while I retrieved a stick of gum from mine. I passed the minty goodness to her as she victoriously yanked a blue ballpoint pen from the depths of her mom-bag.

She quickly unwrapped the gum and shoved it into her mouth, spreading the wrapper out on her knee and wiping away the powdery residue from the candy. Bringing her pen to the papery lining of the foil wrapper, she paused. Then, as though the words had finally formed in her mind, she began to write.

The only problem was, the lidless pen that had been buried in the bottom of her purse for who knows how long didn't have any ink. She scribbled in circles, trying to make some color appear on the small piece of paper. She tapped the tip rapidly on the cement floor of the basement, and tried once more, grunting as it failed again. She huffed and threw the pen across the room, nearly hitting the elderly woman who had urged me down here with her handbag earlier.

"Mom," I scolded. "Calm down. You're drawing attention." She was. Jude had spotted her, and Rossel had emerged from the shadows. He approached us slowly from the stairwell. Mom shook her head and snatched my bag, shuffling around until she found another pen. Gel, because I was a bit of a pen snob, and there was no better writing utensil.

Clicking it open, she tried to write again. This time she got one letter: I. Then her hand started shaking too violently for her to pen another line. She grabbed her right wrist with her left hand and flexed her fingers gently.

Rossel was close. He'd almost reached us when she attempted to write again. She got an *AT* on the paper, barely legible, before her whole body started convulsing.

"Mom!" I shouted.

Rossel leaned down by her side. He looked at me with those black eyes, but he didn't appear cruel. He was flat and emotionless. "She's having a seizure," he said matter-of-factly in a raspy voice.

"What? She doesn't have seizures!" I put my hands on her shoulders and held her until she stopped moving. Her chest rose and fell several times before she looked at me. She parted her lips to speak, but Rossel shook his head.

"No, Tilly. The oath."

She met his eyes briefly and then looked back over at me as she lifted herself back onto her feet. "I love you, darling." She smiled sadly and studied me for just a moment more before she took Rossel's hand.

"Mom." I stood, too. "Where are you going?"

Jude called out that the mess had been resolved and everyone was free to go. Immediately the room burst into a flurry of activity. The other people trapped in the basement were probably just as anxious to get away from us as they were glad that there was no real threat above.

Ignoring the bodies shuffling around me, I reached out for my mom's arm. "Wait up!"

Rossel paused and looked at my mother. She frowned, then turned back to me. "Don't forget to take your vitamins."

"My vitamins? Mom, what? Hang on—"

Rossel tugged her forward and another group of people shuffled between us, separating us just before I reached the staircase. I practically shoved the man in front of me. He was moving too slowly. My mom was up there being dragged away by some stranger and saying crazy things that sounded an awful lot like goodbye.

But she wasn't leaving me. She wouldn't. Right? Why didn't she fight against him? And how did he know her name? And most importantly, why didn't she wait for me at the top of the stairs?

My heart sank when I finally emerged back up in the hall of the gallery. The glass had been cleaned up, and yellow CAUTION tape was wrapped around the jagged glassless window frames. But my mom was still moving. She was several yards ahead, almost back to the lobby.

"Mom!" I shouted for what felt like the hundredth time. "Please stop!" I jogged ahead and muttered under my breath, "Why are you leaving me?"

One parent abandoning me was enough. I couldn't bear the thought of losing my mother, too. But she didn't turn around. She didn't stop.

CHAPTER 5

"WHY THE LONG FACE?" a deep voice asked from behind me.

I paused just long enough to find golden eyes approaching. "I think there's something wrong with my mom. And she's leaving without me." I wasn't normally the type to spill my guts to strangers, but I didn't have time to chitchat. He placed a warm hand on my back as I turned to catch up to her again. Then he leaned in close.

"She's not leaving. She's just getting a drink."

I followed his gaze over to the lobby and sure enough, she stood with Rossel, swallowing down a glass of water.

I released a lungful of air and smiled. "Oh, thank goodness." I could breathe again. I knew my mother would never abandon me. That's not who she was. But my heart still pounded at the thought of it.

"It's cute the way you look after her," he said.

I turned to face him, lifting my chin to make eye contact. He stood a head taller than me—he had to have been at least six and a half feet tall. And he looked amused, the light from the gallery reflecting off the golden specks in his irises.

"What's your name?"

He raised two dark brows. "My name? You're the celebrity here. Why do you care to know my name?" He flashed a full white grin. The scruff framing his mouth was endearing. With his perfect teeth and impossible eyes, the scruff kept him grounded. Without it he would have been too pretty. Unnaturally attractive. But who was I kidding? He was out of my league either way.

"Because, if we're going to keep running into each other like this, I'd like to be able to address you by your name instead of mentally referring to you as golden eyes."

"Ooh, golden eyes. I like that. It makes me sound mysterious."

"It does," I agreed. "Like a secret agent."

"A man on a mission." He winked.

I laughed. "So agent, are you going to tell me your name or what?"

He raised a brow and dropped his chin. "You can call me Clark. Tate Clark."

"Well, Tate Clark. Mission accomplished. Thank you for helping me stay calm today during some really weird events."

"It was my pleasure. The only payment I request is your autograph."

I felt my cheeks grow warm. "Not that again. I told you that isn't me in the portrait."

He shrugged. "Maybe not. But it's such an enchanting painting." His eyes cut over toward the other hall before settling on me again. He jerked his chin to the wall, motioning for me to follow him off to the side. With one more quick glance at my mother, I joined him.

"I could have sworn it was you when you walked in. I couldn't take my eyes off of you."

My cheeks were on fire now. I had a tendency to get really awkward when complimented. And this was like the greatest compliment in the universe. I didn't know how to respond. "Go on," I said playfully. Internally I groaned at my dumb reaction. But Tate didn't look annoyed. He chuckled and leaned his shoulder against the wall, turning his body inward toward me.

"She looks like a goddess. She's captivating in every way. I just want to be near her." His golden eyes were fixed on mine, and I couldn't look away. It was like an invisible string tethered me to him. "I'm still not convinced it isn't you." His words slowed my breathing. They blocked out any noise or distractions around us. He was just inches away. I could feel the warmth radiating from his chest.

Involuntarily, my chin lifted up and forward. His eyes shot down to my lips, and I held my position, waiting...

Waiting for what? For him to kiss me? What on earth was I doing? He was clearly some playboy who'd swept me up with his magical words. I dropped my chin again and cleared my throat. "Well Agent Clark, I'd better get back to my mom."

So stupid.

I backed away, and he remained propped up by the wall, that charming half grin plastered on his pretty playboy face. "When will I get to see you again, Everly—girl who isn't in the painting?"

"I don't know." I shrugged. "New York is a big city. Probably never." Now several feet away from him, my head seemed to clear and I just wanted to make sure my mom was okay.

He crossed his arms. "I'm sure it'll be sooner than never."

I shot him a skeptical look. "Goodbye Tate. It was nice to meet you."

"See you around." He grinned.

I rounded the corner into the lobby, surprised to find it empty. I rushed through into the only other hall. It was empty, too. The painting of me—or almost me—stared defiantly from the opposite end.

"Mom?" The room was silent. I whirled around back toward Tate, but he was gone, too. What was going on? "Mom!" I yelled again. "Tate?" Everyone had disappeared.

I jumped through one of the now-empty window frames back out onto the busy street, careful not to scrape myself on the glass. I ducked under the caution tape and immediately stepped back into the world of motion that was NYC. The wave of passersby parted around me, ignorant of my panic and too distracted to care. My head swiveled back and forth, scanning the busy streets, but there was no sign of my mom anywhere. No top knots. No tall handsome strangers. It was like I'd dreamed up the whole afternoon.

A police car was parked by the curb in front of the gallery. Two officers sat inside, pounding out notes on an outdated laptop. I ran up and banged on the passenger's window with the palm of my hand.

The officer inside furrowed his brows. He took his time closing up the computer where he typed, and rolled down the window. "Can I help you, Miss?"

"Yes. Were you working the explosion over here?" I gestured toward the gallery.

"Yeah." He looked annoyed. The driver watched our exchange silently, pulling a disposable cup of coffee up to his mouth and taking a long sip.

"Did you happen to see where everyone went?"

"Uh, nope."

I frowned. "One of the artists is a thin man with white hair. He wore it in a bun. You couldn't miss him. He was with my mom, and I can't find them. Are you sure you didn't see them leave?"

He shook his head. "Can't help you. Sorry." The window started moving back up, closing me out.

"Wait!" I slid my hand into the narrow opening, forcing the officer to keep it down a little longer.

"What now?"

"I'd like to file a missing persons report, please."

He rolled his eyes. "We can't file a report for your mommy, sweetheart. Did you check the bathroom? Maybe she's going potty." The driver snorted.

My hands clenched into fists. Why was this officer being such a jerk? Sheriff Halsey back home would never speak to me this way. Couldn't he see I was distressed?

"Fine. I'll file it for myself, then. I'm missing. Can you please return me to my mom?"

He huffed. "How old are you?"

"Eighteen."

"You're a legal adult. Find your own way home." The window began rolling up again, even with my fingers still perched on top of it.

"Hang on!" I cried out, but my plea was ignored. I pulled my hand out at the last second. The officer opened his laptop again and motioned for me to go.

Argghhh! I kicked his tire.

Bloop, bloop. The car chirped at me. The officers sat inside scowling. That was a warning. I'd better watch it or I'd be in even bigger trouble.

I circled back around to the front of the gallery and dropped to the sidewalk, leaning my back against the wall. Surely she was going to come back for me. She wouldn't go back to my aunt's house without me. If I left to search the streets, I'd miss her. And even if she didn't return right away, Rossel would definitely come back at some point, and I could ask him about her then. Fumbling through my bag, I located my phone and dialed the only New York number I knew.

"Millie? Hey, it's Everly. I'm gonna miss dinner tonight."

CHAPTER 6

MILLIE ARRIVED WITHIN MINUTES. Her driver maneuvered a black luxury sedan into a tight spot in front of the gallery, parked, and exited to open my aunt's door for her.

I loved my aunt Millie. I really did. But she was one of the most eccentric women I'd ever encountered. Even the way she exited the vehicle was a bit of a production. She extended one lean leg out of the car first, pointing her toes as though she wanted everyone on the sidewalk to admire the hot pink heel on her foot. Then she stood tall, revealing shiny silver shorts that appeared to be made of mylar, and a pale blue blouse with giant boxy sleeves shaped like milk jugs. Her lipstick matched her heels, and smoky dark lines of kohl rimmed her crystal blue eyes, which were almost the same shade as her shirt.

She was a beautiful woman, but she took the high fashion magazines a little too literally. And she definitely didn't look like your average neighborhood pharmacist. Mom and I always joked that by "pharmacist," Millie was actually telling us she was a drug dealer for the rich and famous. That would better explain her vast wealth, anyway.

But beneath her extreme attire and over-the-top luxurious lifestyle, Millie had a heart of pure gold.

"Everly!" She shuffled through the crowd, heels clicking loudly on the sidewalk, and wrapped me in a hug. "You really called at exactly the perfect moment. We were just returning to the house with some extra cheese for dinner tonight. We were just around the corner there."

"Cheese?"

"Yes, it's a Caciocavallo imported from—never mind. Tell me what happened, dear."

I filled her in with a quick, pared down recount of the afternoon, starting with the painting and finishing with my rejection by the police officers, who were still parked by the curb.

"I see," she said, tapping her foot on the sidewalk. "Go back to the part where you last saw her. She was taking a drink of water? Why didn't you join her then?"

"I was, uh, talking to someone."

"Hmmm..." Millie pursed her lips, a knowing look on her face. Thankfully she didn't push the issue. I was pretty embarrassed about losing track of my mother because I had been too caught up batting my lashes at Tate. Even if he was quite googly-eye-worthy, it wasn't worth it.

"You're right," my aunt continued. "It's not like her to leave. But I can't imagine the artist has any nefarious intentions. Perhaps she found him attractive and they went to get drinks."

"Millie! She would never ditch me to go get drinks with some artist. Besides, I told you she was angry with him. Like, unnecessarily angry. It was honestly a little over the top."

"Not if he was some stalker who'd been following you."

"Stalker? Really?"

"He knew your face well enough to paint it, didn't he?"

"Well, if that were the case, she certainly wouldn't have grabbed drinks with him."

She frowned. "I suppose not. This is strange, indeed." She looked around. "Stay here, I'll be right back."

I watched Millie stride over to the police car with confidence enough to convince them she was the Queen of New York. She stopped with her feet together and folded her body forward at the waist, leaning toward the window with an innocent smile on her lips and a sweet little wave.

"Hi, officers."

The passenger rolled his window down with much more interest than he'd shown me earlier.

"Hello, ma'am." The driver leaned over and waved to her as well. *Don't look too eager, boys.* I rolled my eyes.

"I hate to bother you, but my niece here thinks she may have left something inside the gallery earlier—you know, during all the chaos. And now the owners seem to have vacated the premises." She pouted. "Would you mind if we took a look inside? I promise we won't be long."

"I'm afraid this is private—"

"That would be just fine, ma'am." The officer in the driver's seat unabashedly interrupted the passenger. He grinned, flashing a mouthful of yellowed teeth. "Take all the time you need. We'll even keep a watch out here for you, just to make sure nothing shady is lurking around the corner." He winked at her. Gross.

"Thank you very much. We'll be quick." She returned to her full height and brushed the front of her metallic shorts. "After you," she said to me, gesturing toward the open window.

"Why don't we just take the door?" I asked.

"If you insist." She shrugged and pulled the doors open.

Inside, an eerie silence still hung heavy in the air. "Hello? Rossel? Jude?" No answer. The place was a ghost town. "The painting is over that way." I directed Millie to the hall on the left. "I'm going to check the basement again in case she snuck back down there while I was talking earlier."

Millie gave me a thumbs up, then walked away humming a Beatles tune. Her song and the clicking of her heels were a welcome break in the silence. I turned down the other hall toward the basement door. The same lonely light flickered overhead as I tiptoed down the staircase. "Hello?" I called out again for good measure, but I knew no one would respond.

The basement was empty, just as I'd expected. But with the crowds cleared out, I was able to take a closer look at the room. Drabby filing cabinets lined the walls, though I supposed they might've held some pretty fascinating items behind their dull Band-aid colored exteriors. But the real stars of the show were the glass cabinets. One on the far side of the room was emitting a neon blue glow.

Curious, I decided to take a closer look. Subconsciously, I knew it was wrong to snoop through other people's private collections. My body tried to warn me with the hair rising on end across my arms and the back of my neck. But with every step I took, the light seemed to brighten. It was almost pulsing. Alive. Like it had its own heartbeat, which oddly, was perfectly in sync with my own.

Finally, I reached the cabinet. Inside, among the other figurines and artifacts, lay an ancient clay tablet, inscribed with symbols I couldn't recognize. Deep in the grooves of the tiny symbols, the tablet pulsed with the blue glow that had caught my eye from the doorway. It wasn't large—barely bigger than the size of my hand, but it felt alive, somehow. The thought quickened my pulse, which seemed to quicken the tablet's pulse as well.

"Everly?" Millie's voice called out from the top of the stairs.

"Coming!" I dashed over to join her, suddenly overcome with guilt. I shouldn't have been poking around. Now I'd probably have nightmares about the living tablet in the basement. It was definitely the start of some poorly written horror movie—something was likely stirring in its sarcophagus on the other side of the world now. *Way to go, Everly.*

I was breathless when I reached her at the top of the stairs. Millie tilted her head and glanced over my shoulder down the staircase. "Everything okay down there?"

"Yep. Fine." I smiled too broadly.

She stared at me silently for a moment, then must have decided it wasn't important enough to pursue any further. "Well, I had a look. And that is definitely a painting of you. No one else has eyes like that."

"Sure they do. It's a condition called Heterochromia iridium." I argued. "Plus, if he got such precise details as my eyes, why didn't he include my scar?" I gestured to the obvious raised line under my lip. "It's kind of hard to miss."

"Mm." Millie made the same noise my mom had when I pointed out the scar to her earlier. It was one of the rare moments when I actually remembered they were twins.

Other than their terribly outdated names—Mildred and Matilda, or Millie and Tilly for short—there really weren't many similarities between them. Millie craved the spotlight. She loved to be the center of attention. She lived extravagantly, in a townhome in the upper East Side of Manhattan worth some ridiculous number of millions of dollars.

My mom, on the other hand, was a simple woman. She'd moved me out to the middle of nowhere, Oklahoma after my dad left us when I was just a baby. She said she was tired of people. Tired of the negativity in the world. So she set us up on our own plot of land, complete with a half acre garden, orchard, cattle, horses, chickens, and a pot belly pig named Chorizo.

Physically, they may have looked alike fresh out of the shower. But Millie was always done up with perfect makeup, hair, and nails, while my mom preferred jeans, boots, and a ponytail. Both were beautiful in their own way. They had the same hearty laugh, the same quick wit, and the same clever gleam in their gorgeous crystalline eyes. Somehow those genes had missed me. I took more after my dad, whoever he was.

A flutter of white caught my attention just in time to see the same little white owl from earlier in the day land on the edge of a window frame.

"Hey, little guy. A lot has happened since I last saw you. Sorry to tell you your owners have gone."

"Are you talking to that owl?" Millie asked, eyes wide.

"Yeah. We met earlier."

"Are you kidding me?!" She squeezed my upper arm.

"Ouch! Yes. I'm just kidding. What is it with you two and owls?"

"Your mom saw it too?"

"Of course." I shrugged. "Wait. You're not scared of it are you?"

"Scared? Oh-ho-ho, no. Well," she shifted, uncomfortably. "Yeah, no. I'm not scared of it. But did it... never mind."

"Millie, what is going on?"

She chewed her bottom lip, deliberating before finally speaking again. "It's not the owl I'm afraid of, okay? It's what the owl stands for."

"Is this one of those old wives tales? What was it... if you hear an owl hoot during the day it means death is coming. Was that it?"

"It's not an old wives tale."

"Folklore. Myth. Whatever it is, this sweet little guy doesn't mean us any harm, do ya, buddy?" I walked over to the window, and surprisingly the owl didn't fly away.

"One man's myth is another man's history," Millie said.

"What?" I looked back over my shoulder to see if she was serious.

"Don't talk to the owl. Get in the car. It's time to go."

CHAPTER 7

MILLIE'S DRIVER WAS WAITING patiently for us by the curb, wearing navy blue slacks and a crisp white shirt. He was a tall, broad shouldered man with a youthful, boyish face. He moved to open the back door when he saw us emerge from the gallery. The driver's side door of the police car opened at the same time.

"Did you find what you were looking for, Miss?" The officer sauntered out of the vehicle, his gait clumsy and uncomfortable, like he had sweat running down the back of his pants and he was trying to avoid getting wet. He spoke to Millie, even though he was told *I* was the one looking for something.

"She didn't. But that's okay. We really must get on our way." Millie's patience was gone. Her flirty grin was replaced with unease. That owl must have really gotten to her.

"Well, tell you what... I'm going to give you my number here. You give me a call if you need to get back in, or if there is ever anything else I might be able to help you with." He flashed his yellow teeth again, and it took everything I had not to laugh in his face. Millie was way out of his league. She was out of everyone's league. She'd never married or even *dated* anyone that I could remember.

"Or if you want, I can call you if I find whatever it is you're missing."

"No, no. That's quite alright." She accepted the paper with his number written on it. "I'll keep this handy. Thank you again, officer."

"Anytime," he grinned. "I live to serve."

"He would live to serve you, anyway. Me? He doesn't have time to help me," I mumbled as I climbed into the waiting sedan.

Millie's driver chuckled and closed the door behind me. "Where to?" he asked as he slid into his seat.

"Just take us home, please, Jeeves."

"Jeeves?" The name fell out of my mouth before I could stop myself. I hadn't heard him say more than a couple of words, but he certainly didn't sound like a Jeeves.

The driver laughed again, his tone warm and kind. "That's what I asked her to call me." He glanced over his shoulder with a twinkle in his eye. His voice was rich and thick with a syrupy southern drawl. "She wouldn't let me wear a tux, so I said I at least had to get a cool name if this deal was gonna work."

"I see." I grinned at him. He was probably just five or six years older than me—definitely not the stereotypical New York City driver. Then again, there was nothing stereotypical about Millie's life. I glanced over at her. She was chewing her lip and staring nervously out the window, so I turned my focus back to Jeeves, instead.

"So, tell me who you were before you became Jeeves the tux-less driver."

He laughed again, and his joy was infectious. I couldn't help but smile along with him.

"Well, my mama calls me Brian. But there's a million Brians in the world. There ain't too many Jeeves. I moved up here a few years ago after I graduated from college. I had big dreams. Still do. Not that I don't love bein' Millie's driver—it's just that I've always wanted to be under the lights, and preferably on a stage instead of on a field. Though I did love them Friday night lights..." He quieted for a moment, likely reminiscing. "But it turns out they don't have too many parts available on Broadway for Alabama linebackers, so here I am drivin' instead."

"Do you like it?"

"Shoot yeah, I do! And I couldn't ask for a better boss than Millie. She's got finer taste than all the ladies in the Birmingham Junior League combined! Just wait 'til you try this cheese we picked up."

"I heard about the cheese, and I'm honestly not sure it can live up to the hype. I have a pretty high bar for—" My voice trailed off as I watched a group of pedestrians migrate through the crosswalk in front of our car. Dusk was making an appearance as the sun moved behind the skyline, so the people were just as illuminated by the city's lights as they were the sun. But even through the neon blues and pinks, those golden eyes were unmistakable.

Especially because they were staring straight through the windshield at me.

"Millie." I nudged my aunt. "Do you see that guy in the blue shirt in front of us?"

"Which one?" She directed her eyes to the front of our vehicle.

Tate winked at me, flashed his crooked grin, and moved further into the mass of bodies.

"Right there! The guy who just winked at me."

She squinted and cocked her head to the side. "Sorry, Ev. I didn't see. What about him?"

"Nothing, I guess. He was at the gallery with us earlier, but I don't suppose he would have seen anything either." I chewed at the edge of my thumbnail—a nervous habit I'd never quite been able to kick.

"No, probably not. And I've been thinking about that. Did your mom say anything to you this afternoon? Anything…different?"

"Different from what?"

She sighed. "I don't know. Just, out of the ordinary. Anything that might have sounded a little strange?"

"Everything she did was strange this afternoon. She did say she had something to tell me. She tried a few times, but I think she was literally worried sick. She'd nearly vomit every time she spoke. She tried to write something down, but all I got was an *A* and a *T* before the seizure started."

"*Oh*. Oh my. Okay. This is… *okay*." Millie began fanning herself with her hand.

"What is it, Millie? I feel like I have no idea what is going on today."

She ignored my question, fanning frantically and staring out the window again.

"I'm out of the loop," I said with a dramatic shrug that ended with my hands slapping down on my knees. "It's a lot like Becca Harrison's birthday party in the sixth grade, when I had tissue paper sticking out of my bra and no one thought to tell me about it. Everybody knew it but me. I thought I was getting away with looking mature and cool. *Nope*. I was the fool. They all just giggled at their little secret while I was left clueless and embarrassed at the end of the night."

Jeeves chuckled from the front seat. "Dang, that's rough. Becca Harrison sounds like a real brat."

"You know what? She is a brat, Jeeves. Thank you for that." I turned to my aunt. "Are you being a brat, too, Millie? Are you hiding a secret that's gonna leave me embarrassed at the end of the night?"

"I would never try to embarrass you."

"That's not what I asked." I ground my teeth, frustrated and getting nowhere.

Jeeves rolled to a stop in front of my aunt's mega-million dollar townhouse. I didn't actually know what it cost, but my guess probably wasn't too far off. I pulled the car door handle and stepped out before Jeeves had a chance to get to me.

My eyes grazed over the six story limestone façade of Millie's home. We were less than a block from Fifth Ave. and Central Park, yet the exterior of her spot in the city felt cozy and charming. It wasn't farmhouse-in-the-middle-of-nowhere kind of homey, but still nicer than one might expect living in the largest city in the United States.

She stepped onto the sidewalk, pausing beside me as Jeeves shuffled inside with a bag carrying the famed cheese. Once he disappeared through the brass doors at the entrance, she leaned over and whispered, though she didn't make eye contact.

"Alright. I've decided it's time we let you in on the secret."

"Oh? Color me intrigued." I tried to play down the sarcasm in my tone, but I was getting a little fed up with this nonsense. If this secret could help me figure out what happened to my mom, she should've told me the minute I called her.

Millie inhaled deeply, then finally turned to face me. "Have you ever heard of Atlantis?"

"The lost continent under the sea?"

"Yes." There wasn't an ounce of humor on her face.

"Uh, yeah. What about it?"

She cleared her throat. "That's where we're from—your mother and me. I believe she was trying to tell you that she is Atlantean. And to some degree, you may be as well."

She marched up the steps and through the doorway, leaving me slack-jawed on the sidewalk alone.

CHAPTER 8

I SCURRIED THROUGH THE door after Millie, only to be nearly plowed over by one of the giant beasts who lived with her.

"Lemon Drop, sit." Millie wagged a finger at the English Mastiff who leaned its 200 pound body against my thigh. Another set of gargantuan dog feet galloped across the herringbone wooden floors of Mille's foyer. "Look out, here comes Tiny Tim."

Miraculously, the other dog was even larger than the first. Tiny Tim ran to greet me, his loose, slobbery jowls swinging with each bound until his squishy wet face smooshed right into my gut. "Oof!"

"Tiny, no!" Millie huffed. "Sorry, they're just happy to see you."

"Aww, I'm happy to see you guys, too." I scratched Tiny's head. "But I can't play right now. I have something very serious to discuss with my aunt, who is currently walking away from me. Millie, hang on! You can't drop a sentence like that and then just walk away. What did you mean by —"

"Shhh!" she turned around in the doorway to the kitchen and shot me a stern look. "Not now."

"Not now? But—"

"We have guests coming over for dinner. They'll probably be here any minute now."

I pushed past Tiny Tim and Lemon Drop to follow Millie into her extraordinary kitchen. Her private chef was hard at work preparing hors d'oeuvres as Jeeves pulled the expensive cheese from its packaging and placed it on the marble countertop.

"It's about time," the chef said in an unmistakably French accent. "What took you so long?"

"Sorry, Pierre. We had to stop for Everly. We're probably going to be one person short tonight, too. Only four plates—not five, unless you see my sister arrive." Millie cut her eyes briefly to me and pressed her lips together.

"Oh!" Pierre dramatically placed the back of his hand against his forehead. "Always with the changes."

I muffled a giggle at the sight of her distraught chef, then refocused on my aunt. "Maybe we can go up and prepare the dining room." I shifted my eyes up to the second floor, where her formal dining room was likely already set and decorated beyond my wildest dreams. Millie wasn't a last minute kind of person. But still, I needed to get her alone so we could talk.

She frowned and subtly shook her head. *So much for that plan.* I crossed my arms over my chest. It was so not cool for her to keep me waiting. And the Atlantis thing was obviously a joke. Right? I mean, it didn't exist. But then again, yesterday I might've said the owl, the painting, and the glowing stone tablet couldn't possibly be real, either. I didn't know what to believe anymore.

The doorbell chimed, a cheerful little riff from a Scottish jig. "They're here!" Millie grinned and clapped her hands together.

I followed her back into the grand foyer, doing my best to keep the Mastiffs at bay while Millie opened the door.

"Claudia!" My aunt exchanged side to side air kisses with a petite brunette. Claudia was curvy, and ruffles lining the back of her seafoam green floor length cardigan only drew more attention to her hips. She wore thigh-high black patent boots with spiked heels to add slightly to her height. Her lips were stained a crimson red, her makeup just as perfect as Millie's. They admired each other's outfits before scuttling further inside like a couple of giggling school girls. It was only then that I noticed Claudia's son.

He was lean and wiry. Handsome, as I'd expected, but not in a traditional sense. His hair was a dark auburn, the reddish hue only visible under the lights, and light freckles dotted his nose. His eyes were quite striking—green like the bay. He shoved his hands into his pockets, shoulders tight as he surveyed the room. Landing on me, he offered an apologetic grin.

"Everly, this is my friend Claudia. And this," she gestured proudly to the boy behind them, "is Sean. He'll be starting college this year, too. At Columbia." She dipped her chin for emphasis, already insinuating that I, too, should be attending Columbia.

How could she be thinking about my college choices right now? My mother was missing and she'd just implied that we may be a part of a mythical race of humans.

"I'm so sorry we're late," Claudia said.

"No apologies, necessary." Millie started up the grand staircase that led to the second floor. We all stepped into line behind her, Sean bringing up the rear, and Lemon Drop bounding ahead to the front. "You haven't missed a thing."

She paused and turned back toward us with a conspiratorial glint in her pale blue eyes. "I was just telling Everly about her Atlantean background."

"Wonderful," Claudia said brightly. "Then it sounds like we're just in time."

Sean glanced at me with pity in his eye as he passed me on the stairs. My feet froze in place. Tiny Tim paused beside me, licking my hand with his foamy pink tongue while I watched the others ascend the stairs before me.

"Is this for real?" I asked him quietly. Thankfully he didn't respond. With a day like this, I wouldn't have been all that surprised if he had.

CHAPTER 9

EVERYONE WAS ALREADY SEATED when I entered Millie's dining room. She and Claudia chatted casually about some upcoming fundraiser while Sean sat opposite them, staring down at his napkin. The only other place setting at the table was right beside him.

Thanks a lot, Millie.

He looked up as I pulled out the chair next to him, feigning nonchalance. "So, when did you arrive in New York?"

I had to commend his effort in trying to make me feel comfortable. Any other day it might have worked, but I wasn't in the mood for small talk. It boggled my mind that these people could mention something like descending from Atlantis with such flippancy and move on to dull topics like travel itineraries.

Ignoring his question, I sat down with a huff and pinned him with my glare. "Is this some kind of practical joke? Because I don't think it's funny. I've had kind of a rough day."

The women stopped their conversation and turned to listen.

"I—uh, I don't know about any jokes. No one is joking here." He looked nervously toward his mother for help. She just smiled and gestured for him to continue.

"So what my aunt said about..." I swallowed, rethinking my plan. Perhaps they'd thought she said Atlantan. I could be from Georgia. That was much more reasonable than a sunken continent that didn't exist.

"What I said about you being born from the people of Atlantis." Millie filled in my blank with an encouraging nod.

Okay, so lost continent it is.

"Right. I'm going to need more of an explanation."

Millie's young housemaid arrived then with four dinner salads. They were topped with bleu cheese and candied pecans, and admittedly, looked really delicious. My hot dog from earlier was long forgotten.

We all paused our conversation while the maid was in the room. But the moment she left, I raised my brows expectantly at my aunt. She needed to get to talking.

"This is delightful," Claudia said. "What is this dressing?"

"It's a vinaigrette Pierre makes from scratch. I think it's—"

I loudly cleared my throat. Millie and Claudia both turned to me with the reprimanding looks of a mother. I didn't care if I was being rude. They were, too.

"We can talk about salads later. I have been really patient." My speech was slow, carefully enunciating every syllable. It was a true practice of patience. "I need to know what you're talking about now. You say you're from Atlantis. But surely you can't be referring to *the* Atlantis."

"There is only one."

"Will you please elaborate?"

Millie placed her fork on the table next to her plate. "This world," she gestured broadly, "is more than it seems. You have grown up with the humans in a very one dimensional view of life. But beyond your perception, there is another world."

"An immortal world," Claudia chimed in.

"Immortal?" I nearly choked on my lettuce. "Are you saying you've been around since the beginning of time? And mom?"

"No, dear. Not exactly. But my soul has. It's difficult to explain."

"Alright, talk to me like I'm five. Start at the very beginning. Where is Atlantis?"

Millie sighed, pausing as though she were trying to decide where to begin. "Plato's writings of Atlantis are true, mostly. We were once a great nation. Powerful and advanced. We were placed here to protect the humans, and we served our purpose well."

"Placed here. So you're like guardian angels?"

"Of course not! The angels and demons are in a whole other realm. They usually stay there, and leave us to watch over this one. It's our job to make sure mankind doesn't destroy itself before the battle is complete in the spiritual realm. We are not angels. We are called Keepers."

"Keepers." I chewed on that for a moment. "Keepers of the earth."

"Land, sky, and sea, to be precise." Millie took another bite of her salad.

"Okay. So you're Keepers with immortal souls placed here to protect the humans. But you still haven't told me where Atlantis is."

"Well it used to be in the Mediterranean Sea," she said bitterly. "But our ancestors went and ruined that for us about 12,000 years ago."

"They got a little too big for their britches," Claudia added.

"So now it's at the bottom of the Atlantic."

The maid entered again, removing our salad dishes and replacing them with dinner plates. The scent of individual stuffed cornish hens danced across my palate, making my mouth water. Once the maid left, I spoke again.

"Legend says the gods created some kind of cataclysm that destroyed Atlantis. Is that true?"

"Ha! They wish they were gods." Claudia cut into her meal.

"Humans didn't know what to make of us," Millie said. "They recognized that we were more powerful than they, so they assumed we were gods. Or half-human, half-god. But they were obviously wrong. We're just a different type of being altogether."

"So you destroyed yourselves?" That didn't make sense.

"No. We got into it with some of the other Keepers. Tensions were mounting between the three races, and unfortunately our ancestors enjoyed being thought of as gods by the humans. They took things too far, so the other Keepers had to take matters into their own hands."

"Checks and balances," Claudia added through a mouthful of food.

"So there are three races of Keepers?"

"Yes, my apologies. It's been a century since I've had to review the history with someone. I forget that you were brought up as a human. There are the Atlanteans, that's us, the Keepers of the sea. There are the Olympians, the Keepers of the sky, and there are the Agarthians, Keepers of the land. We were supposed to work together, but even Keepers are susceptible to corruption."

"And egos. Especially those Olympians—they're still on a power trip." Claudia rolled her eyes.

"There's been a rift between the three races for thousands of years. We generally don't associate with one another anymore, except for the annual Order of the Keepers convention. But we each have important roles to play in protecting the humans. And there are laws we must abide by. Which brings me back to your mother."

A pang of guilt stabbed at me. I'd been so caught up in the outrageous story of Keepers that I'd temporarily forgotten the reason I wanted to learn more in the first place.

"Right. My law-abiding, Atlantean mother. Are you suggesting she's gone on some human-saving mission?"

"No, I'm afraid not." Millie rested her fork and frowned. The others stopped eating as well, all eyes fixed on me. "She may be on the other side of the law. Your mother didn't exactly play by the rules."

"What do you mean?" My pulse picked up. Mom *always* played by the rules. I couldn't imagine what the Atlanteans might have disagreed with.

"Well," Claudia spoke now, "she had you."

CHAPTER 10

"ME? WHY IS THAT a crime? Are you not allowed to have children? What about him?" I pointed harshly toward Sean, who raised both hands innocently in the air.

"Of course we can have children, it's just that..." Claudia shifted uncomfortably in her seat. "It's just that there are rules."

"You mentioned that. What did she do wrong?"

"We can't prove that she did anything wrong." Millie set her lips and turned with a pointed stare toward her friend. Claudia gestured toward me but my aunt waved her off. "We don't know anything for sure just yet."

Millie softened her expression and faced me again. "Our kind, the Keepers, have immortal souls, as we mentioned earlier. Our bodies last longer than human bodies, as well. We'll often live for close to a thousand years before our bodies give out. And when that happens, our souls are reincarnated. There are a finite number of Keepers. A finite number of souls."

"So your souls are basically recycled over and over again. Got it. Does that mean you remember life on Atlantis before it was destroyed?" It was an unimportant question, but I couldn't help but ask. If Atlantis was real, I wanted to know everything there was to know about it.

"No. Unfortunately we are unable to keep specific memories. But our collective knowledge as a race grows with each successive generation. And there are certain ties—bonds that can be felt in every generation. The most obvious being our soul mates. You see, every Altantean soul is bonded to another. And in each life, the souls find one another." Millie smiled, though her eyes looked pained. I imagined she may have been thinking of her own soul mate. Or did she have one at all?

"So if an Atlantean has a relationship that results in children with someone from another race, like, I don't know, *humans for example*, then we lose a couple of Atlantean souls." Claudia scowled, and I couldn't help but feel a little guilty under her gaze.

"Forever?" My voice was more timid now.

"Forever." Millie nodded sadly. "A female Keeper can physiologically only have two children in her lifetime. If even one of those children is part human, a soul is lost. Possibly two souls, depending on the genetics."

"What do you mean?"

"Well, the child may have the soul of a Keeper if she takes completely after her mother. She may have the soul of a human if she takes completely after her father..." Millie frowned, and her eyes went distant—lost in a thought she couldn't utter aloud.

"Or she may be fractured, which is what usually happens." Sean, of all people had to finish my aunt's words. The women were too distraught, staring down into their laps.

"What happens to the fractured souls?" My voice was barely a whisper now. Sean locked his eyes on mine, deep green pools of pity. I held his gaze, the silence in the room snuffing out my ability to look away.

"Never you mind that." Millie grinned, snapping back to the present. She tried to improve the mood with overt cheerfulness and failed. We weren't a very cheery bunch at all in that moment.

The maid entered once again, taking my plate before I'd had a chance to finish off my wild rice. I almost objected, but I needed her to leave again so I could get the rest of the story. It seemed they were accusing my mother of hooking up with a mortal, but I would need to hear them say it before I believed it. And I feared what the implications may be if it were true.

A giant slice of turtle cheesecake was placed in front of me next. I resisted the urge to dig right in. First, I needed my aunt to confirm my suspicions. And then I needed to find out how to bail my mom out of Atlantean jail for getting involved with my deadbeat human dad and literally creating some poor lost soul.

Even as I thought the words, doubt clouded my mind. My mother wasn't the type to break rules, especially not rules with such dire consequences.

Finally, the maid retreated with our dirty plates and we were free to speak again. "Okay," I said. "So let's get to the elephant in the room and talk about my dad."

"Yes. Let's." Claudia crossed her arms and shot a smug look at my aunt.

But Millie handled the situation with grace. "This is where things get tricky. Your mother ran away when she found out she was pregnant with you. None of us knew she was in a relationship at all, and when we asked her about it, she panicked and left. It took us years to locate her, and even then we were only able to do so with the help of a seer.

"We found your farm in Oklahoma, but you and your mother lived there alone. Tilly refused to discuss your father. She would get physically ill anytime we pressed her on the matter. I think it was a curse, personally. I think she has been forbidden to speak of your father, which makes me believe he is a very powerful Atlantean, indeed."

"Or," Claudia butted in, "what's more likely, is that your father is a mortal. Tilly would never reveal that information because she'd have to face the courts, and they do not take kindly to the murderers of our souls."

I cringed. My mother a murderer? Surely not.

"So that brings us to you. You're eighteen now, right Everly?" Claudia fixed her blue eyes on me.

"That's right."

"And you have not developed your powers yet." It was a statement more than a question.

"Powers?"

"See?" Claudia sneered at my aunt.

Millie sighed. "There are certain... *perks* that come with being a Keeper. We have abilities beyond what humans are capable of. And generally, they begin to manifest between the ages of sixteen and eighteen. But sometimes there are late bloomers!"

I swallowed. "What kind of powers are we talking about, here?"

"They vary through the different races, and even within the Atlanteans they can manifest in many different ways. I am a healer. The Olympian who helped us locate your mother was a seer. There are warriors, elementals, transporters, guardians, sirens, shifters..." she counted them off on her fingers, each one sounding more exotic than the one before.

"What kind of powers does my mom have?"

"Your mother was a messenger."

"*Was?*"

"Yes. She had her powers bound when she ran away. She gave them up for you—in an attempt to stay hidden." Sadness tugged at Millie's lower lids. I'd never seen my aunt cry. I didn't even know if Atlanteans could cry. But this was as close to losing control of her perfect features as I'd ever seen her.

Whatever powers came with being a "messenger," my mother had sacrificed them. For me. But why? If I were Atlantean, there would be no need to give up her powers and hide. The longer I sat there, the more I conceded that Claudia may be right. I wasn't pure. I was mortal.

As though she could see the thoughts percolating through my mind, Millie continued, trying her best to prove that there was still a chance my mother hadn't broken the rules. That she hadn't lost an Atlantean soul.

"But there are certain commonalities among all Keepers. One of which is a higher level of intelligence. And you, Everly, have an IQ much higher than humans, which is why I'm certain you must be of Atlantean descent on both sides." She crossed her arms and turned toward Claudia with a smug smile, like she'd just won a big court case.

"I'm sorry, Millie. But that's just not true. She could have easily inherited her intelligence from her mother even if her father was mortal. And without any other powers, I'm inclined to believe this is exactly what has happened."

Both women fixed their eyes on me, waiting to see if I could settle their argument. I could memorize facts and take tests like a boss, but that didn't seem all that special. I would never say anything to condemn my mother or the decisions she made, though. Surely there was something I did better than everyone else...

"Is snarkiness a superpower?"

Millie groaned and Claudia frowned. I turned toward Sean, but he wouldn't make eye contact with me. He seemed hesitant to jump into the conversation again. I couldn't blame him. This was awkward for all of us.

"There's still time. She's only just turned eighteen this summer. There's no need to rush into anything, including having my sister tried for a crime she may not have committed. So if you know who has taken her, I really must urge you to have them return her." She eyed Claudia with suspicion heavy in her eyes.

"I told you on the phone earlier, Gregory said he has heard nothing about your sister. If the council sent for her, he would have known about it. And as for Everly, you better hope she's fully Atlantean. Because if she's as smart as you say, then she's not purely mortal. And…" Claudia bit her lip to stop herself from saying any more.

"Unless I get some powers soon, that would mean I have a fractured soul." I finished her thought.

The entire room seemed to darken at my words. Silence hung in the air for longer than was comfortable. It was Lemon Drop who finally broke it with a small whine.

"I'll let her out," I said. "I could use a breath of fresh air right now, too."

CHAPTER 11

MY STEPS WERE QUIET as I slowly led the dogs out of the dining room, but once I hit the stairs, I took off hard and fast, my feet pounding every other step as I sped down to the first floor. Pierre was a blur as I bounded past the kitchen toward the small courtyard off the back of Millie's townhouse.

The cool evening air was a relief for my senses. The air back home would have been hot and muggy, even after the sun went down. I would have relaxed on my back patio and heard the song of cicadas while watching a show of lightning bugs dancing through the air. In NYC, however, I had chill bumps dotting my bare arms in the August evening air. My cicadas were replaced with the sounds of Manhattan nightlife, and my lightning bugs were replaced with street lights. But the outside air was a relief all the same.

Lemon Drop and Tiny Tim were a little worked up. They'd taken my speedy run down the stairs as a signal for play time. "Not now," I said, trying to calm them with open hands. "Go potty." I directed them to the itty-bitty green area designated as their toilet at the back of Millie's first floor outdoor space. They spun excitedly, still under the impression that I was going to throw them a tennis ball or something equally fun.

"You're right," I said. Lemon Drop sat and turned her head sideways. "We're only a block from the park. Let's go." Back inside, I leashed the dogs up and hollered something to Pierre about taking the dogs for a walk.

I didn't fear the New York streets like the other girls from back home. In middle-of-nowhere Oklahoma, we didn't lock doors. We left keys in our cars and didn't even knock before strolling into each other's homes. In comparison, New York was a scary place for them. They'd spewed warnings and stories and words of caution before I left for school here, but I wasn't afraid—it never bothered me too much. And even if it had, I wasn't the least bit nervous with four hundred pounds of dog on my sides.

Millie only lived a short walk away from Central Park, so I wouldn't be long anyway. With leashes wrapped around each fist, my canine companions and I set out for wide open spaces—or as wide and open as we could get in the city.

Locating a paved path, I turned into the park, allowing the dogs to lead me. They'd been here way more than I ever had, so I figured I'd let them take the reins. They weaved off to the right in tandem, as though they visited the area daily. Lights were more sparse here than where we'd entered, and there were fewer people meandering around. A lone jogger passed us on the sidewalk, and then we were alone.

"Alright, guys. Hurry up and go so we can get back home." The longer I stood, watching them sniff the ground, the more uncomfortable I became with my surroundings. Darn those Oklahoma girls for getting into my head!

The dogs continued to sniff and circle, marking various spots as we walked. They may have stayed in the park all night if I'd let them. But I'd had enough. With a gentle tug on their leashes, I called them back. Tiny Tim turned, tongue lolling over the side of his slobbery mouth. With an extra bit of pep, he bounded toward me. I held out my hand to praise him with a pat on the head, but he didn't stop. He kept right on past me, spinning me around with the leash in my hand. I spotted him again behind me, running right up to the tall, dark silhouette of a man.

"Oh my goodness!" I gasped.

The figure strode slowly toward me, shadows still hiding his hooded face. Tiny Tim didn't appear to be concerned, but he was such a gentle giant that he wouldn't recognize danger if it knocked him on the head. And this danger was just close enough to do that.

Lemon Drop joined them now, too. "Watch out. They bite." I made my voice loud and as imposing as I could, but still the figure persisted. I stepped back, tugging at the dogs' leashes with every step the man made toward me. Finally, I entered a ring of yellow light from a street lamp. It cast a long shadow in front of me, leading right up to the feet of the hooded man. He stepped forward once. Twice. And the light struck his shadowy features on the third step.

He pulled down the hood of his gray sweatshirt, revealing the sharp chiseled lines of his handsome face. "What on earth are you doing in Central Park by yourself after dark?"

My breath released with a whoosh as I looked into those golden eyes, twinkling in the light. "I'm not by myself. I have my guard dogs with me."

"They're pretty ineffective guard dogs," he said, scratching a very happy Tiny behind the ears.

"What are you doing here, Tate?" The absurdity of running into the same person three times in one day hit me. That combined with my still-racing heartbeat made my words sound harsher than I'd intended.

"I was out for a run."

His clothing checked out. But still, it was strange. Something told me this wasn't just a coincidence.

"Everly!" Sean's voice called out through the darkness and Lemon Drop tugged excitedly to go meet him. Two guys calling for my attention at the same time—if only middle-school Everly could see me now.

"Over here!" I called back.

Tate shoved his hands into the pockets of his joggers and raised his brows. "Sorry, I didn't realize you were out with your boyfriend."

"He's not my boyfriend." My cheeks flushed at his insinuation. Or was he simply trying to determine whether or not I was available? "We just met tonight. He's the son of a family friend."

Sean finally reached us, approaching with some apprehension. "Your aunt's looking for you." His frown morphed into a scowl as he took in Tate's form across from us. First mom, then Sean. Poor Tate couldn't catch a break. Who knew it was such a hardship to be so beautiful? They hated him on sight.

"Do you know this guy?" Sean gave me a skeptical look.

"Sort of. We met at the gallery earlier."

Sean's eyes widened. He turned again to examine Tate, who stood patiently with a half smirk, still petting Millie's dog.

"We need to get back to the house," he said. Then, to Tate he added, "whatever you're looking for, this isn't it."

What was that supposed to mean? Somewhere behind us, in the shadows of the park, an owl hooted.

Tate crossed his arms and raised his chin a fraction of an inch. "Oh, I think it is."

"Everly, you need to stay away from this guy." Sean narrowed his eyes.

"Why?"

Tate stepped closer to me, sliding his arm casually across the back of my shoulders. The warmth of his touch sent a buzzing feeling down my spine. I wanted to curl in closer and feel his arms wrap around me. We'd only just met, yet I felt comfortable with Tate. Protected. Safe.

"Why would she want to do that? We're friends, aren't we, Everly?"

I tilted my head slightly to look up at his face, my heart pounding in my chest. I met his golden gaze with a lazy grin. Friends? Heck yes, I wanted to be his friend!

"Everly. Everly!"

I snapped my eyes back to a very irritated Sean.

"Come on." His patience was growing thin.

Tate curled his fingers around the edge of my shoulder, and I leaned into him ever so slightly. I didn't want to go anywhere. I wanted to be right here.

"You go ahead," I said. "Tell Millie I'll meet up with you guys soon."

Sean huffed and walked to a grassy area beside the sidewalk, shaking his head. He picked up a stick and waved it in front of the dogs. Then, with a wide swing of his arms, he launched it. "Go get it!" he shouted.

The dogs lunged forward, yanking me from Tate's warm body. I tripped and stumbled, but somehow managed to stay on my feet as I chased the dogs, their leashes still wrapped tightly around my hand. A moment later, Lemon Drop emerged victorious, the stick dangling from her droopy dog lips.

I turned around to see the boys bowed up at each other. They were several yards away now, and I couldn't make out what they were saying, but it looked like one of them might slug the other at any moment.

Why were they so defensive? Or better yet, why had I been so reluctant to leave Tate? With distance between us once again I realized how foolish it would have been for me to stay behind. I still didn't really know him.

"Sean!" I called. "I'm ready now. Let's get back."

"Hang on!" Tate shouted with a frown. He dropped his glare from Sean and jogged over to me. The sight of him running casually over sent another flight of butterflies in my belly. Could he actually be interested in me? I'd always thought love at first sight was just for fairy tales. But maybe... if he was feeling just as woozy around me as I was around him... perhaps this wasn't so foolish after all. Maybe it was meant to be.

"Don't touch her!" Sean yelled, running quickly after him.

The dogs were getting excited again with all the activity. They wanted to play. And it did look like it was all fun and games at first. But no one was having fun after Sean lost his temper.

With surprising swiftness, his heavy fist rose and echoed a dull whack as it collided into Tate's perfect nose.

CHAPTER 12

"WHAT ARE YOU DOING?!"

"I'm protecting you. That's my job." Sean shook out his hand.

"Are you okay?" I rushed over to Tate, who rubbed his jawline, the shadow of a smirk still tugging at the corner of his mouth.

"I'm fine. But let's get you out of here. This guy has lost it."

I prepared to walk away with him. We didn't need that kind of violence in our lives. It was only common sense: Tate made me feel happy and giddy inside. Sean made me feel grumpy, and apparently he had a violent streak.

"Don't do it, Everly." Sean's tone was menacing. "He's messing with you."

I looked back and forth between the two. Yesterday, they'd been strangers to me. Today, they both urged me to leave the other behind, and they were literally fighting over who I should leave with. *Why*? Why would either one give two licks about me?

"Ignore him." Tate reached out and gently rubbed his thumb down the side of my cheek. I practically purred under his touch, forgetting my suspicions from a mere three seconds earlier. Then he was jerked away from me again with a giant shove from Sean.

"What is *wrong* with you?!"

"What is wrong with *you*? I told you he's messing with you. You've fallen for his glamour. He's a siren." Sean pointed an accusing finger at Tate.

"Glamour? He— wh-what?" I turned to see a stone-faced Tate glaring back at him. Then he turned his cold gaze on me. The warmth from his eyes was gone, replaced with something much more sinister. I shivered and ran my hands up and down the sides of my arms. "Are you saying that he's... like *us*?"

"*Us*? That confirms it," Tate sneered. He reached out for my wrist, but this time Tiny Tim stepped between us, letting out a deep, rumbling growl, stopping him in his tracks.

"Good boy," Sean said, patting the dog. "See, even the animals recognize you for what you are. Leave her alone."

"You know I can't do that." Tate crossed his arms. "Now that I know what she is, I can't leave her alone. I can't return unless I've got her with me."

"You don't know what she is. None of us do yet. You can't take her if she's pure, so I suggest you wipe that arrogant grin from your face and run along now."

"Or what?" Tate stepped up to Sean, daring him to hit him again. "She's not pure. Look at her." His lip pulled up in disgust as his eyes scanned up and down my lanky frame. *Ouch*. So much for love at first sight. I was such an idiot.

He stood six inches taller than Sean, but something about the way my new friend held himself made me want to put my money on Sean. He was scrappy. If I didn't fear him damaging Tate's gorgeous face, I might've even liked to see them duke it out.

Then again, now that I knew Tate's gorgeous face was manipulating me and toying with my emotions, maybe it wouldn't be so bad to see it busted up a little bit after all. Especially if he was trying to kidnap me as Sean implied.

"Touch her, and the hunter will become the hunted." Sean said after a silent stare down. I held in a snort. He was being a little melodramatic in my opinion, but it worked. Tate's eyes flashed with fury. "You know what happens if you hunt a mortal."

Tate's lip curled. "I'm still not convinced she's *mortal*, either. And the fractured must be dealt with. You know that as well as I do."

I shook my head emphatically, pushing my hands out in front of myself and flipping them over, as if there was some kind of evidence to prove to him that I was as human as the next girl.

"Totally mortal. See? I'm not fractured." Neither boy glanced in my direction. They were too focused on being the more intimidating man... or whatever kind of beings they were. And maybe that was a good thing. I didn't want to get my mother into deeper trouble by admitting that I was mortal. But I definitely wasn't *immortal*. Ugh. There was no way to win here.

"I'm going to report you," Sean said at last.

"I dare you to draw attention to her. Go ahead. They'll execute her mother and then turn her over to me, anyway."

"She may be pure." Sean insisted again through tightly gritted teeth, practically hissing his words.

"I'll believe it when I see it." Tate winked and blew a kiss in my direction. "And I *will* be seeing more of you, darling." He turned on his heels and jogged off into the shadows.

Tiny's hackles were still raised. I calmed the dog and looked up at Sean, who was still fuming in the low light of the street lamp.

"Well, that was interesting," I said. "I gather he's a Keeper?" Sean shifted his steely gaze to me and I shrugged. "I mean, *I'm* not interested in keeping him. I meant like the being. Like you guys. Obviously, I wouldn't want to keep someone who tried to glamour and kidnap me. Or at least I don't think so. Explain glamour to me? Because if it's what I'm thinking of, like a fairy—"

"You didn't mention that you'd run into an Agarthian during your story earlier." Sean interrupted my nervous rambling. "Is there anything else you conveniently forgot to mention?"

Agarthian? I wanted to argue that I didn't even know what that meant a few hours ago, but Sean definitely wasn't in the mood to argue about the minutiae.

I'd told them about the painting at dinner, but I didn't mention the tablet. Something told me it was sacred. It wasn't something to casually toss out in conversation. Could I trust him to help me figure out what it meant without reporting anything back to his mother?

It really felt like we were on the cusp of figuring out what happened to my mom. She wasn't taken by the Atlantean authorities, according to Claudia. But Tate and the Agarthians didn't seem to be involved with her, either. He had his sights set on me. Maybe the tablet was linked to her disappearance somehow. It was the only stone we'd left unturned, no pun intended.

Ultimately, I didn't have a choice. It wasn't written in a language I understood, but perhaps an Atlantean could. I just hoped he could keep it between us.

"There was one other thing," I said under my breath.

"Yeah? What?" Sean's face was still cold, but I saw curiosity flash behind his jade eyes.

I appraised him again. "I'm not sure if it's something I can explain. Can I show you?"

He took a step back and raised his hands. "Is it something that's gonna get us in trouble?"

I shrugged. "It might. But it might also help me find my mom."

He scratched the back of his head and glanced around the empty park. Finally, he sighed. "Alright, lead the way."

CHAPTER 13

"SO, TELL ME WHAT exactly happened back there." I passed Tiny Tim's leash to Sean as we power-walked past my aunt's street and back toward the gallery.

"What is there to tell?" He shrugged. "You were there."

"I was there, yes. But I have no idea what you and Tate were talking about."

"Tate?" Sean rolled eyes with a sarcastic laugh. "Thaddeus. He's a soul hunter."

I tripped on a crack in the sidewalk. "Uh, that sounds menacing."

"It is. For you, anyway."

"Because he thinks I'm fractured?"

Sean wouldn't look at me or acknowledge my question. Evidently he thought I was some substandard being, just like Tate did. We walked for a few more steps as I considered everything I'd been told about fractured souls.

"So let's say I *am* fractured..." I began after a bit.

Sean looked down at the sidewalk, clearly uncomfortable with the topic.

"That means I'm neither human nor Atlantean, right? But a mix of both. So will I live for a hundred years or a thousand? Or somewhere in between, like maybe five hundred? That could be cool. And will I get any powers?"

"Let's hope not," Sean muttered.

"Hey!" I jabbed him playfully in the ribs with my elbow. "Don't doubt my abilities before I even get them." I tried to lighten his mood, but nothing worked. He stopped in the middle of the sidewalk.

"If you get powers, then yes, it means you are fractured. But no, you will not live to see a hundred. You will not live to see nineteen. That's what the soul hunters are for."

Soul hunters... I swallowed. "Tate's trying to kill me?"

"No. *Thaddeus* is. That's what they do. The Agarthians love to place sirens in the hunter role, because they can lure you in with their glamour. They make you feel good, get you alone, and after your walls are down they convince you to show them your powers. Once they have proof, that's it. You're done. They collect your soul and move on to the next one."

He stomped ahead again, leaving me alone on the sidewalk, trying to catch my breath.

"Wait!" I shouted, finally allowing Lemon Drop to pull me back to the boys. "Hold on. You're stating this like it's a fact. But I don't have any powers."

"That's good for you. Not so good for your mom."

Because then she would be a proven criminal. A murderer. If I were mortal, that would mean my mom would have killed an Atlantean soul. Unless...

"What if my aunt is right? What if mom did hook up with some powerful Atlantean, and she was just too embarrassed to say anything about it? It's possible. Maybe I just haven't gotten my powers yet."

"I doubt it," Sean frowned, and he looked genuinely sad this time. "The bond of soul mates is strong. There would be no need to hide their relationship. In fact, if they'd bonded enough to conceive a child, it would be nearly impossible to keep them apart."

"Maybe he died. That would keep them apart, right? Maybe he was super old when they met, and they could only have me before he passed." I shuddered at the thought of my mom in a relationship with some nine hundred year old man. But who was I kidding? I shuddered to think of her with any man at all. For as long as I'd been alive, it had just been the two of us.

He twisted his mouth to the side, considering it. "Unlikely. But not impossible." I thought I saw him nodding softly from the corner of my eye, probably thinking the scenario through. But the gallery was just ahead on the opposite side of the street, and my thoughts were immediately consumed with what we were about to see.

I became anxious, excited to get to the tablet again. I wanted to be near it, to touch it. The closer we got, the greater the sensation became. It was like I'd left a piece of myself down there in the basement alone, and we both knew I was about to come back for it.

Finally, after what felt like an hour at the crosswalk, we made it to the other side of the street. There were few people out now, so I had a clear view of the metal sign up ahead. "There it is." I pointed.

"Rossel & Jude. Huh. I've never heard of it."

"There are probably thousands of galleries in the city you've never heard of," I said, urging Lemon Drop to move more quickly. I hadn't thought the dog part through. We couldn't leave them out on the street. Maybe we could just bring them inside with us. They weren't exactly easy to hide, but at least they were mostly well-behaved.

"No, I walk this way every day on my route to work. I don't ever recall seeing it here before."

"Sounds like you need to pay better attention to your surroundings."

The glass had been cleaned up from the street, but caution tape still stretched across the windows. I pulled on the door handles, hoping that they were still unlocked. But I'd never been that lucky, and of course, the doors didn't budge.

Sean gestured toward the window. "Let's just climb through."

"Right. Because we're totally discreet with these giant beasts. No one will think twice about a couple of college kids and two English Mastiffs climbing through the windows of an expensive art gallery late at night. They probably won't even notice." I rolled my eyes in case the sarcasm in my tone wasn't evident enough on its own.

Sean didn't see it, though. He was already halfway through the window after Tiny Tim, who jumped through with a surprising amount of grace. I followed them with a groan.

"If the cops show up here again I'm blaming this entirely on you."

"It's New York. No one cares. We could carry these pieces out one at a time and load them into the back of a stolen windowless van if we wanted to, and no one would bat an eye."

"You say that like you've got experience."

"Whoa." Sean stopped dead in his tracks.

"It's this way." I tried to direct him to the basement, but Sean's eyes were locked on one thing, and one thing only.

The lights were off inside the gallery and the halls were dark apart from secondhand light filtering in from the street. But there was one single spotlight, a beacon in the night drawing all attention toward its prized piece—a four foot tall painting of the strong, defiant girl who looked remarkably like me.

CHAPTER 14

SEAN TILTED HIS HEAD, admiring the painting as he moved from side to side, taking it in from every angle. "It's definitely you."

"It's not! Look." I pointed to the scar beneath my lip. "She's missing this. And if you look closely, there's an intensity in her eyes unlike anything I could ever *dream* of possessing."

Sean agreed, "She is much more intimidating than you. But wow. The similarities... if this isn't you, then it's gotta be your identical twin."

Wait a minute. I slapped him on the shoulder. "Sean! You're a genius."

"You have a twin?"

I pointed at the painting. "Obviously."

He raised a brow.

"Look at her. She looks just like me, only...different. Personality-wise. And she's missing the scar. But what if I actually do have an identical twin? Maybe she's living with my long-lost Atlantean father."

That would explain everything. Of course my mom would behave strangely if she saw the painting of my twin after eighteen years of keeping it a secret. And that would be why I'd never met my father—and why she'd never revealed his identity. He'd probably bound his powers and disappeared just like she had!

Visions of the old Parent Trap movie flashed through my mind. "If I can just get to summer camp and trade places with this fierce girl, then maybe we can get our parents to fall back in love."

"I can't deal with you right now." Sean shook his head. Then with a huff, he added, "That's not your twin."

"You can't prove that. It's just as likely that I have a secret twin as it is that some stranger named Rossel coincidentally painted a near-exact likeness of me from the other side of the country."

"Tell me more about Rossel. You saw him right? With your mom?"

"Yeah." I went over everything I'd told him earlier about the white hair and strange mannerisms. I told him about how Rossel knew my mom's nickname, Tilly, and then— "Oh, and I think I forgot to mention this earlier. But he said something about an oath. It didn't really register at the time, but I have no idea what kind of oath he was talking about."

"Interesting." The wheels were really spinning in Sean's brain now. I could tell. "Okay, show me whatever this last surprise is."

"Let's go." The halls grew dark again as we moved away from the painting and back toward the basement door. I thought about pulling out my phone for some illumination, but I'd see light again as soon as we stepped onto the stairs. The tablet was waiting for me, I knew it deep in my bones. I could practically feel it pulsing, emanating the strange blue glow all the way from up here.

The dogs sat at the top of the stairs, refusing to enter the doorway. I tried to coax them in my best sing-songy voice, but they wouldn't budge. And all the while, the urge to get back to the tablet raged harder and harder. "Let's just leave them," I said, getting flustered. "They won't go anywhere."

After a brief hesitation, Sean agreed and followed me into the narrow stairwell. The dogs' collars rang out with faint jingles as they laid in wait for us at the top of the stairs. And we descended.

The blue light became visible almost immediately. I saw it first, but Sean noticed it just a few steps after me. "What is this?" he asked.

"This is what I wanted to show you."

Once we reached the bottom, the light couldn't be ignored any longer. It pulsed along with my rapidly beating heart, brighter now than it had been during the daylight. "Over here." I grabbed Sean's arm and dragged him over to the glass case, a nervous excitement dancing wildly in my belly.

"There." We stood silently for a moment, watching the light emanating from the ancient text carved into the tablet's surface.

"It's almost like it's alive." The wonder in Sean's voice matched what I felt.

"It gets weirder." I took his fingertips and pressed them to the inside of my left wrist. His eyes widened in surprise. "I think it's connected to me somehow. I can't explain it, but I know this has something to do with me, and maybe my mom. Can you read what it says?"

Sean frowned. "I can try, but it's been several years since I practiced the ancient languages. Where's the latch?"

We circled the case, looking for a lock or fixture we could open to access the contents, but we came up short. There didn't appear to be anyway to get inside it. Sean cursed under his breath.

I couldn't give up so easily, though. Even as we stood there, the tablet's call to me grew stronger and stronger. I needed to know what it meant. I paced around the perimeter of the room, searching for some kind of tool I could use to pry the case open, but there wasn't much available. Finally, I settled on a sloppy plan that I would probably come to regret later.

"Stand back."

"Why? Wait! Everly—"

CRASH.

I slammed a fire extinguisher I'd pulled from the wall right into the wide pane of glass enclosing the tablet. I wasn't large for a girl, but I was strong. I could thank eighteen years of farm chores for that.

The shards of glass rained down around us and I waited for some kind of alarm to ring, but there was nothing. It was probably silently alerting the police as we stood there, so we'd have to be quick. I dropped the fire extinguisher and grabbed the tablet.

It was small, and smoother than I'd expected it to be. I ran my fingers gingerly over the edges and traced the engraved symbols with my fingers. Upon closer examination, this looked to be just a small part of a larger message. Several of the symbols along the left side were cut off, incomplete.

"What does it say?" I held it out to Sean.

He reached for it, but immediately pulled his hand back with a faint sizzle. "Ouch! How are you holding that?" He shook his hand as though he'd been stung.

"Did it hurt you?"

"Yes! It's hotter than fire."

I rubbed the smooth surface again. It didn't feel hot to me. "I don't know. It's not burning me. Here, just take a look." I held it in front of me, close to Sean without touching him. He stepped closer and squinted at the small symbols.

I was so focused on the reflection of the blue light in his green eyes, that I didn't hear or see anything else out of place in the dimly lit basement. I didn't know anything was wrong until I felt a strong arm wrap itself around my neck and pull me back into the hard body standing behind me.

CHAPTER 15

"PUT IT DOWN."

I knew it was Tate even before he spoke. I could feel his warmth and a sickening sense of delight even as he attempted to choke me from behind.

Sean immediately launched into action, swinging around to launch a fist into the side of Tate's head, but he missed. Tate held me too close, and Sean likely feared injuring me in the process.

"Why are you following me?" I whispered as he swung me around. Tate kept me between Sean and himself. He was using me as a human body shield. How cowardly. I wanted to tell him to fight like a real man and stop hiding behind me.

"I told you, I can't let you out of my sight." His breath tickled my ear as he whispered his response, sending a trail of chill bumps running down my neck. I elbowed him in the gut.

He grunted, but his grip stayed strong. He was holding me just tight enough to make me immobile without cutting off my ability to breathe. I elbowed him again.

"You've got to stop doing that," he grumbled.

Sean picked up the fire extinguisher I'd dropped earlier and approached with madness shining in his eyes. "Let her go."

"No can do. I've got proof of her broken soul now. I need to finish the job."

"This?" I raised the tablet a few inches into the air. "This isn't proof. The tablet has powers of its own. I'm still just a boring mortal."

"Hand it to me."

I hesitated. Handing this tablet to him would be like giving him a piece of myself. I didn't want to share it, especially not with him. But remembering Sean's reaction to it earlier, maybe it would be able to take care of itself. I said a silent prayer. "Okay. As soon as you let me go."

"I can't let you go."

"Then I can't give you the tablet."

Tate groaned. "I liked it better when you thought I was a charming international spy."

I scoffed. "I wasn't so far off. You've been on a secret mission to eliminate me all along."

"Don't forget the charming part." He pulled me a little closer.

"Your power is charming, maybe. Your personality could use a little work." I elbowed him a third time, irritated that my bony joint wasn't squishing into the softness of his belly but slamming into the rock-hard wall of his abs, instead. And I was irritated even more by the thrill that mental image of his abs gave me.

Shake it off. He's got you under a spell. Glamoured. He might be hot, but he's a jerk.

"Alright, if you insist." His voice took on a song-like quality, a beautiful baritone melody that drew me in and made me want to hear more. "I'll let you go, and you'll hand me the tablet."

Yes, of course I will. Anything you say. I couldn't speak, and my thoughts were no longer my own.

"If I find that you are controlling it somehow with your powers, you will submit to me. Willingly, so I can collect your fractured soul. Though, I promise to make it enjoyable."

Yes. I will submit.

"Everly, snap out of it!" Sean's voice barely registered, and I wished he would just shut up. His voice was so harsh compared to the sublime sound of Tate whispering in my ear. It scratched at the inside of my brain. I needed Tate to speak to me more—to provide a balm for the wretched sound of Sean's words.

"Are you ready?"

"Yes," I whispered.

His grip loosened, but he kept his warm hand tenderly on the back of my neck as I spun to face him. He held out his hand, and I immediately moved to give him the tablet, not of my own control.

"Don't!" Sean's voice called out again from somewhere behind me, but it was too late. I placed the tablet into Tate's open palm.

"Argh!" he dropped it and released me, and we all watched in horror as the tablet fell to the cement basement floor and crumbled into rocks and dust.

My wits crashed back in hard, my soul felt crushed. "No!" I dropped to the floor and swept the broken pieces toward me in a pile.

"What is this?" Tate demanded, his voice back to normal. He rubbed the inside of his injured palm.

"I don't know," Sean said. "But she's not controlling it." the boys both turned thoughtfully toward me. They were just as confused about the tablet as I was.

"It's broken. Help me, please! We've got to get it back together."

"I'm sorry." Sean placed his hand on my shoulder.

"No!" I shrugged him off of me. I wouldn't accept it. It wasn't too late. The pieces began to glow again, ever-so-faintly as I pulled the pieces back into contact with one another.

"Hand that to me," I said, pointing to a large chunk of rock that had bounced several feet away from me.

"I'm not touching that again," Sean said firmly.

To my surprise, it was Tate who moved for it. But instead of picking it up, he kicked it gently with the side of his shoe, sending it gliding back over to where I sat on the dusty floor. And that missing piece was all I needed.

Reunited with the rest of the broken tablet, the pieces began pulsing again. I could feel them, feel the life entering into the inanimate object once again. I sat back and we all watched as the glow became too bright, even for me. We shielded our eyes as the light grew blinding, pulsing faster and faster. And then, darkness.

Once my eyes readjusted to the low light, I reached out for the tablet. It was whole again. Not a single fracture line or crack were left as evidence of the destruction it had endured moments before. And it was cold, no longer pulsing or glowing at all. My heart sank. Our connection, whatever it was, was gone.

"Here," I said, the dejection evident in my voice as I held the object out for Sean. "You can take it now."

He stood, open mouthed, seeing but not believing that the tablet was whole again. "Are you sure?"

"I'm sure."

The sound of a police siren filled the room. Our time was up.

"I'll handle the cops," Tate said, turning for the stairs. I nodded, happy to see him go, but not trusting for a second that his intentions were pure.

"I don't recognize the writing." Sean held the tablet close to his face, squinting hard as he attempted to make out the message.

"Well, we don't have time to decipher it now, anyway. We've got to get out of here. Do you think Millie or your mom might be able to help?"

"I wouldn't show it to them. My mom, especially. She's got a good heart, but she's devoted to my father. And he would be required to report it to the council. Until we know what it might mean, I think it's best if we keep this between us."

"And what about Tate?" I gestured for the stairs.

"Tate has one job. Just one."

"To kill me."

Sean nodded. "But not until he has proof that you're fractured."

"So what now?" I stood and dusted the knees of my pants.

"Now we get the dogs back home to your aunt and pretend nothing happened. Then we make plans. I know someone who may be able to help us figure this out. She's a seer."

"Will she be able to help me find my mom, too?"

"She's got a better chance than we do."

His tone wasn't encouraging, but I didn't see any other option. This tablet was linked to me somehow. There was no denying it. I wouldn't stop searching until I found out what exactly it meant. And I wouldn't stop until I found my mom.

THE UNSEEN

PROLOGUE

TILLY'S HANDS STRUCK THE cool cement floor of the prison cell she'd just been roughly thrown into. She stood, brushing off her pants, and trying not to wince at the stab of pain deep behind her kneecaps. They might bruise, but her body would have them healed by nightfall. Her ego wouldn't heal so quickly. She turned angrily to face the man who had taken her captive.

"There's no need to be so rough," she scolded.

He looked away, feigning indifference. But she knew the guilt he felt. She felt it too. A different flavor, perhaps. Her unlawful act had taken place long ago. It had time to ferment and settle in deep inside her. His guilt was fresh and raw.

She knew Rossel didn't want to take her captive. But he had no choice in the matter. None of them had any choice. They'd done the unthinkable, and there was a price to pay for it.

It looked like Tilly would be paying for it with the rest of her life—another seven hundred years or so.

"You could have at least arranged for me to serve the remainder of my life somewhere more comfortable." She frowned, eyeing the small, sparse room.

"This is the only place suitable for you right now." He lifted his face, revealing the sorrow swirling in his dark eyes.

It was then that she noticed the diamond coating on the steel bars. It shimmered with the king's power. Baerius was the only known Keeper with the ability to render all other powers useless. He'd enchanted this cell to prevent her from teleporting out.

Tilly pursed her lips and held Rossel's gaze. She hoped her silence would encourage him to talk—to tell her the rest of the story, but she had no such luck. After a few breaths of silence, he turned away.

"Wait," she called. He paused, but he didn't look back. "What will you tell Everly?"

"Nothing."

"She'll be afraid. She'll search for me. And it won't be long before—"

"We'll handle it." His hands clenched into fists at his sides.

Tilly gasped. "*No.* You can't hurt her. Tell me you're not going to hurt her!"

Rossel turned slowly back to face her again. His eyes shimmered with unshed tears but his face revealed no other emotion. He'd been practicing this look of resolve for centuries, and he'd mastered it. "My allegiance is to the king. I answer only to him."

"And the prince?"

Rossel's lip curled, exposing receding gums over his ivory teeth. "Don't speak of him."

"He—" Tilly's breath was cut off sharply in her throat as bile rose in her chest. She grabbed at her neck, fighting the urge to panic until it finally calmed enough that she was able to breathe freely once again. The oath prevented her from speaking of the past—even to Rossel.

"You mustn't speak of the prince," Rossel said again. Then he turned on his heels and disappeared from her sight.

The sound of a door slamming shut at the end of the hall signaled his exit, and Tilly slid down the cold concrete wall into a heap on the floor where she wept until her tears had dried and the bruises on her knees had fully healed.

CHAPTER 1

I SWIRLED MY SPOON around the inside of a pretty turquoise bowl, exploring the unknown objects floating in my oatmeal. It smelled delicious, like cinnamon and brown sugar. But there were... other things.

"Pierre?" I called out to my aunt Millie's private chef, who stood at the stove on the opposite side of her giant white marble kitchen island.

"What is it?" he asked in a thick French accent.

"That's what I want to know."

He turned with a frown, rubbing his hands on the white tea towel he held.

"There's something in my oatmeal."

"Oui. Spices and sugar and nuts."

I scooped out a particularly globby offender and it fell off my spoon onto the counter top. "What's that one?"

His frown deepened. "It's a raisin."

"Oh. Do you always put raisins in oatmeal? And why is it yellow?"

"It's not yellow, it's golden."

"I didn't think anyone actually ate golden raisins. They're kind of gr—"

Jeeves, my aunt's driver, tsked from his barstool beside me. "Careful. Don't anger Pierre or he might put worse things than golden raisins in your food." He took a showy, giant spoonful of his own bowl, trying to smile as he chewed a bite and gave the chef a thumbs up. I snorted at his attempt. It was hard to force a smile while chewing a golden raisin.

"You're right. My apologies to the chef. The oatmeal is delicious. Speaking of, *Pierre*," I said with a flourish in a terrible French accent. "What is your real name?"

The chef put his hands on his hips. "What do you mean?" He looked at Jeeves who was still trying to swallow his bite. "What is she talking about?"

"Like Jeeves here," I gestured next to me with my thumb. "His real name is Brian, but he wanted something quirky and funny to go by. You know—like a stereotypical butler."

Jeeves' eyes widened and he shook his head quickly as I spoke.

"And you—" I stuttered over my words as understanding dawned on me. "Y-you are lucky enough to have the perfect name for a French chef without changing anything at all." Jeeves nodded emphatically.

The doorbell rang, mercifully saving me from putting my foot any farther in my mouth. "I'll get it," Jeeves said, hopping to his feet. I bashfully turned my eyes back toward my breakfast until he returned a few moments later with Sean and his mother, Claudia.

"We made it!" Claudia chimed with bright eyes and a smile. "I figured we could take my car since our bags are already in the trunk. Does that work for you? Where's your aunt?"

"Works for me." I passed a nearly empty bowl across the counter to Pierre. All that remained were a few raisins. He shook his head and carried my dish to the sink. I turned back to Claudia, tilting my head at the sound of heels clicking down the wooden stairs around the corner in the foyer. "Sounds like she's coming now."

Millie entered the kitchen, sighing loudly with her cell phone wedged to her ear with her shoulder as she stirred creamer into a coffee mug. "I understand," she said to someone on the other end. "Yes, of course. No, don't worry about it at all. I've got it covered. I hope he gets well soon. Okay, buh-bye."

"Morning! Everything okay?" I asked.

"Yeah," she said with a sad smile. "But I have some bad news. It looks like I'm going to have to skip our trip."

"Why?" Claudia asked. "Should we just reschedule?"

"No!" I said a little too forcefully. "I mean, Sean and I will be preparing for school next weekend. This is probably our last chance to go before classes start."

The truth was that my patience had thinned out to nothing. It had been over a week since my mother disappeared, and I was apparently the only one still concerned about it. Everyone insisted that she was an adult and should be fine. Claudia even had the nerve to suggest that she was on vacation, celebrating me going off to college. It was insulting.

But after our trip to the gallery, Sean was on my side. He knew something bigger was going on. It was actually his idea that we all go to Millie's house in the Hamptons. They had some friends in the area, including a girl who was supposedly a seer, so I was hopeful that we might be able to get some information about my mom. At the very least, I hoped one of his friends may be a little more adept with the ancient languages. We still had no idea what the clay tablet said.

"Everly is right," Millie said. She took a long swig of her coffee and set the mug on the counter. "You all should go. You don't need me there."

"What is so important that you would miss a weekend at the beach?" Claudia asked.

"It's Abby." Millie slid up onto a barstool and Sean rushed to her side.

"What about Abby?" he asked. His tone was a little too urgent, and it drew the eyes of everyone in the room.

"Who's Abby?" I asked with a grin. Sean hadn't mentioned any lady friends. With all the time we'd spent together over the last week, I thought surely he'd have brought up a girlfriend.

"She's an employee down at the shop. Her father has been ill off and on a bit lately, and she just called to say that he's having a particularly rough week. She asked if she could take the weekend off to look after him."

"I'm so sorry to hear that. Does she need any help?" Sean asked.

"I'm sure she'll be just *fine*." I tried to make my words sound firm. I wasn't going to let him back out for some crush. I needed him to introduce me to his seer friend.

Jeeves raised his brows at me, obviously interpreting my irritation for something else. I shook my head softly. *Ew, Jeeves. Sean is totally not my type.*

"Well, I don't want to go without you," Claudia said. "I'm no teenager anymore. I can't keep up with these two." She waved her hand at Sean and me.

"Bring a book. That way they can still squeeze in a vacation before school and you can be there to chaperone."

Claudia gasped and put a hand to her chest. "*Chaperone*? I'm not some third wheel. Besides, they're adults—let them go on without us."

I perked up in my seat. Getting Claudia off my back while I researched the tablet and sought answers about my mom was even better than our original plan. "Yeah, Millie. We'll be totally fine. I promise."

Jeeves smirked at me. *Dangit, this isn't about getting alone with Sean!* I wanted to nudge him in the ribs, but I was too intent on convincing Millie to let us go to pay him any more attention.

"Well, I suppose I don't mind if you two use my house. Just promise me there won't be any wild parties. Hilde next door gets grumpy with even the slightest uptick in volume."

I crossed my heart. "Promise. No noise." Then I turned with a giant grin to Sean, but he didn't return it. In fact, he looked quite distraught.

Millie picked up on it, too. "Abby will be fine," she said with a wink. "I'll swing by and check on her after I close up tonight."

That seemed to appease him. He nodded. "Okay. You sure you don't want to come with us, mom?"

"I'm sure," Claudia said. "You two have fun—but not too much fun. We'll see you in a few days."

Jeeves walked to the foyer to load my bag and unload Claudia's as we said our goodbyes. I thanked my aunt again and turned to follow Sean outside.

"Oh- hang on!" I stopped outside the door. "I forgot my vitamins. I'll be right back!"

I dashed back inside and up the stairs to my room. My mom was pretty laid back about most things, but she had always been an absolute dictator when it came to taking my vitamins. And it was one of the last things she'd said in the gallery before leaving with Rossel. It might have seemed silly to anyone else, but I wanted to smile when I saw her again and let her know I hadn't stopped—even while she was away.

I picked up the giant amber colored bottle and turned it around in my hands. There was no label. My mom special-ordered them for me, and I realized I wouldn't be able to get more without her. I was down to about a quarter of the bottle remaining—about two weeks worth of vitamins. It was just one more painful reminder that she was still missing.

See mom? You've got to come back so you can get me some more.

Shoving the bottle into my purse, I bounded back down the stairs, shouting goodbye again to Jeeves and my aunt as I ran past the kitchen. Sean was already buckled up in the driver's seat of a shiny white Range Rover. I eagerly jumped into the passenger's seat beside him.

"Woo!" I clapped my hands. "Let's do this!"

CHAPTER 2

IT TOOK LONGER THAN I expected to get out of the city, but before long Sean was able to quit cursing at the traffic and roll down the windows. He seemed to relax a bit as we neared the coast.

I turned down the music blasting from his speakers, hoping to chat now that he seemed more at ease. "So... *Abby*." I lifted my brows up and down playfully.

He cut his eyes over sideways at me, then turned back to the road.

I gave him a minute to respond, but it was clear he wasn't interested in offering up any more information than was necessary. "Who is she?" I asked after a beat.

"She works for your aunt."

"I gathered that." I grinned. "But who is she to *you*?"

"Your aunt's employee." He looked over at me again, not even attempting to hide his irritation. I'd learned that Sean wasn't a very open person. He was a pretty flat, cut-to-the-chase kind of guy. If Millie hadn't pushed us together, we probably wouldn't have clicked much as friends at all. But as it stood, we'd been forced to spend our afternoons together.

Once my aunt heard about Tate following me around, Sean was charged with acting as my bodyguard. It was a job neither he nor I was particularly excited about, but Millie insisted. Until we knew for sure whether I had any powers or not, Sean was to stay by my side any time I left Millie's house.

Claudia wasn't very excited about it, either. She might have been my aunt's best friend, but that didn't mean she agreed with Millie's approach to keeping my existence under wraps. She wanted to bring me to her husband, so he could present me in front of the Atlantean council and see if they could determine my true genetics. But knowing that could implicate my mother with the crime of engaging in a relationship with a mortal, Millie resisted. Hard.

So I was left bumbling around New York with Sean until hopefully, I gained some powers of my own. And hopefully, they were strong enough to prove that I had a pure Atlantean soul. Otherwise, Tate would be quick to do away with me.

I hadn't seen him again since the night we nabbed the tablet from the gallery, but I'd felt him. It sounded strange to admit aloud, but every so often while I was out walking the dogs or joining my aunt for lunch, I'd get that familiar tingle of energy running up my spine. It was like my nerves would just come alive. I never saw Tate, but I knew he was watching me.

"So," I said, turning my attention back to a very grumpy looking Sean in the driver's seat. "If Abby works with Millie, does that mean she's Atlantean, too?"

"No."

"Is she Agarthian? Or Olympian?"

"She's human." He frowned. "And I'm done talking about her."

"Okay. Got it." *Sheesh*, evidently I'd hit on a sore spot with him. And it only made me all that much more excited to meet Abby in person when we got back. If Sean was letting a mortal get to him that much, there must have been something special about her.

"Let's change topics then. Tell me about your friends we're going to see."

"I never said they were my friends. I know Gayla through our parents. Her dad is on the Olympian council, so our fathers do business together. We would run around as kids while they met during the annual convention."

"And Gayla is the seer you told me about?"

"Supposedly."

"Supposedly? What does that mean? You don't know for sure?"

Sean huffed. "I haven't seen her in a few years. Once we were old enough to stay home alone, we quit tagging along with our parents to the convention each year. But I heard she got some visionary powers."

I pinched my thumb and forefinger on the bridge of my nose. "You mean we're coming all this way and weekending together on the off chance that you might run into a girl you knew when you were a little boy? And *maybe* she has powers that could *possibly* help me... if she remembers you and has any desire to work with your mortal friend?"

"Do you have a better idea?"

"No."

I crossed my arms over my chest and pouted, staring out the window. As we drove along, the houses grew larger and more spread apart. They were massive, giant mansions sprawled out across the sandy earth, overlooking a deep blue sea. It was basically the antithesis of the scenery I grew up with. Before long, the salty air and balmy wind blowing in from the water eased my sour mood.

I'd been under the impression that Sean's plan was a sure thing. But whether this Gayla remembered him or not, she was our best shot at finding my mom.

Sean slowed his vehicle and turned down a quiet road near the bay. We pulled into a long drive that led to a comparably modest white estate, with an expansive lush green lawn spread out before a charming home with walls of windows.

"Here we are," Sean said. He turned the engine off and hopped out.

The sunshine warmed my cheeks as I joined him. "This place is stunning." I shielded my eyes with a hand to get a better view of the house and yard. "Millie must be one well-connected drug dealer."

I was still snickering at my joke when I noticed an elderly woman with an oversized straw hat scowling at me from the opposite side of a thick green hedge. I waved, and she furrowed her brows.

"Hello, Hilde," Sean called out.

The woman shook her head and continued clipping the bushes that marked the property lines between Millie's house and hers. Boy, I was on a roll with saying the wrong thing at the wrong time today.

Sean grabbed our bags from the trunk of the car, and I followed him up the sidewalk to Millie's gorgeous vacation home. "Are all Atlanteans rich, or just my aunt?"

"We live for a thousand years," Sean said as he entered and flipped on the lights. "That's a long time to amass wealth."

"Compounding interest is a beautiful thing." I ran across the living room to drool over the aqua colored water of the pool out back. And for the first time, I really wondered what could have been so bad to make my mother turn away from the luxuries of the Keepers' lifestyle. Was she really a criminal?

I turned back to Sean, who was searching the fridge for something to drink. "Does your friend Gayla live near here?"

"Not exactly."

"Do you have her number?"

"No."

I groaned. "Come on now. Give me something."

"Most of the younger Keepers hang out at a sports bar in East Hampton—when they're not at the beach anyway."

"Great. Let's go!"

"Right now?" Sean looked disappointed.

"Yes, now. Were you wanting to take a swim first? Kick up your feet for a bit?"

He looked longingly at the pool.

"Sean!" I smacked his arm. "We're not here for fun. We're here for business."

"Alright." He picked up his keys and downed the rest of his water bottle in three gulps. "But remember—I make no promises that she'll be there. And there's no telling who else we might find."

"You mean Tate?" Chill bumps shot up my arm just at the mention of his name.

"No, Thaddeus doesn't ever venture out this far from the city. But he's not the only Agarthian hunter."

"That's okay. He's the only one assigned to me, right? The others would have no reason to believe I'm anything but a mortal. I'm harmless."

Sean shrugged. "If you say so. Let's go."

CHAPTER 3

THE STREETS OF EAST Hampton looked like they were taken directly from the pages of a magazine. Quaint shops filled with cheerful patrons lined the road, which was dotted with simple parks and outdoor seating areas begging me to join in on the fun.

"I love this place." I sighed. "I wish my mom could see it."

"I'm sure she's seen it. This is where the Annual Convention is held each year. Just because she ditched this world when you were born doesn't mean she never took part in it before. In fact, mom said she was very involved. She was one of Maxwell's favorite messengers."

"Who's Maxwell?" *And why was he so enamored with my mother?*

"He's the current leader of the Atlanteans."

"Like your king?"

"We don't call him our king—we're not Olympians for goodness sakes. But yeah, he's a monarch of sorts."

Hmm... a powerful Atlantean who was quite taken by my mother. Could he be a candidate for my father?

"So my mom was one of the king's favorites, huh? Do you know exactly how close they were?"

"No, I wasn't alive then. But don't get any bright ideas. He's bonded with Gloriana and they have two pure Atlantean children." He glanced over in time to catch my frown.

Okay, so I wasn't a princess. But I wasn't sad that I asked. One of these days I might just come across someone who fit the description. My dad had to be out there somewhere.

"Here we are." Sean parallel parked on a side road off the main street. Most of the businesses were back behind us, and all I saw ahead was a dusty line of windows across a strip of abandoned commercial spaces. A brown owl sat perched on the corner of the roof, peering at us through inquisitive yellow eyes.

"This is the sports bar?"

"Yep." Sean climbed out of the vehicle and the sound of the horn as he locked the doors made me jump. "It's called The Keep."

I chuckled. "That's a bit on the nose, isn't it?"

He shrugged. "I guess it's kind of an inside joke. No one out here knows what it means except the people who matter."

"Are you saying humans don't matter?"

"Maybe for a short time. But their lives are over so fast, they don't get the chance to matter for long."

I followed him to the glass doors of the abandoned space. I could see through the window that the place was empty, but Sean pulled open the door and stepped inside anyway. He strode to the back wall, where a painted door blended in perfectly with the neutral beige walls. "This way."

He tugged on the knob and I gasped as the scene on the other side unfolded. The lights were down low, the room illuminated instead by neon signs along the walls advertising various brands of beer and liquor that I'd never heard of. Two pool tables sat in the middle of the room, with low hanging stained glass light fixtures hovering over the green felt surfaces. A shiny lacquered high top bar stretched across one wall, and beside it double doors sat propped open to an outdoor courtyard, hidden entirely from the streets by the brick walls of the building.

A few guys sat propped up at the bar and a couple of tables held small groups of people, but it looked as though most of the crowd was outside. I followed Sean across the floor toward the courtyard, never drawing so much as a curious glance from anyone inside.

Outside was a courtyard half the size of the room we'd left. A green awning covered the space from above, casting an emerald glow across the patio. A hot tub sat in the middle of it all, and it was here where the crowd was centered. Four or five girls sat perched along the edges of the tub, laughing and talking with animated expressions. They could have all been supermodels—with long, lean bodies scantily clad in bikinis and sarongs, lush locks of hair flowing past their shoulders, and million-watt smiles. A group of guys played Cornhole near an exposed brick wall, and other young adults stood coupled or paired up at tables and small seating areas throughout the rest of the space.

"There she is." Sean pointed to the hot tub.

"Of course she's one of the models. Which one?"

"She's the one in purple."

I followed his gaze to a gorgeous girl with long, thick, platinum colored hair and warm, striking dark eyes. She seemed to be at the center of attention in the hot tub, telling some story that had the other girls enthralled. I glanced down at my denim shorts, suddenly feeling very self conscious among these beautiful people.

"Go ahead," Sean said.

"You're not coming with me? I need you to introduce us."

"Nah, I'm good." He shoved his hands into the pockets of his shorts, looking like he would be just fine waiting for hours.

"Sean?" A chipper, slightly raspy voice called out from behind me. "Is that you?"

I turned over my shoulder and saw the stunning blond grinning big enough to show off every single straight white tooth in her mouth.

"Oh my goodness, I can't believe it!" She slid up onto the side of the tub and swung two unfairly long legs over the edge. With a bounce to her step, she hurried over to where we stood and threw both arms around Sean's neck, leaving him with two wet spots on his shirt when she pulled away. His cheeks flushed and I had to stifle my laugh.

"I haven't seen you in ages! How have you been?"

"I've been good, Gayla. How about you?"

"Just dandy." She turned to me. "Who is your friend?"

"Everly Gordon," I said, extending a hand. She brushed past it and hugged me. This time Sean got to laugh as my eyes widened in surprise.

"I'm Gayla. It's so nice to meet you!" She turned back to Sean and whispered something in his ear.

"No, she's not human. She's Atlantean—Millie's niece. She just hasn't gotten her powers yet." He shot me a look that said to play along. Sweet Sean, even if he believed I was fractured, I appreciated him pretending as though I was one of them. It was much easier that way, though I'd have to explain everything to Gayla at some point if she was going to help me find my mom.

I looked around the patio. We'd drawn the attention of a few others now, and they made their way slowly over to where we were standing.

Gayla introduced me to a couple of the guys who had been playing Cornhole and a friend from the hot tub—another pale-haired girl named Dominique, or Dom for short.

The fair-haired friend studied me through narrowed eyes, suspicion twisting her mouth. I felt very exposed under the scrutiny of her stare—as though she somehow knew more than she was letting on.

"Sit down," Gayla said, motioning toward a table on the side. "It's been too long. Let's get some drinks and catch up."

Gayla sat beside Sean, which put me and suspicious Dom together opposite them as the guys got back to their game.

"So I hear you got the finesse genes," Gayla said with a grin.

"Yep," Sean ducked his chin just a smidge, embarrassed but trying to hide it. "Faster, stronger, and better reflexes."

"Just like your dad," she said.

Sean nodded.

"Have you been assigned a role yet? Guardian? Warrior?"

"Not yet." He cut his eyes over to me briefly, but I knew his role of bodyguard for me wasn't an official role for The Keepers. "I'd love either one, though. As long as they don't put me in leadership like my dad."

"I hear you." Gayla sighed.

"Oh—sorry. I forgot. You're a seer, right?"

"Apparently." She shrugged. "Though I don't seem to be a very good one. Even so, the only role for me will be in leadership." She scrunched her nose, trying to show distaste for her future, but honestly just looking adorable. She was too pretty for any expression to actually look ugly. And I loved how uncomfortable it made Sean to look at her. He totally had a crush on her and I couldn't wait to rub it in later.

"What's your power?" Dom cut in suddenly. Her dark brown eyes were focused hard on me.

"She hasn't gotten it yet," Gayla answered for me. She seemed to believe Sean that I would eventually get one. That was good, because I absolutely did not want to lay out the messy backstory of my mother's potential mortal love interest there in the courtyard. And I had no idea if any of the Keepers standing around may have been hunters like Tate. No, I couldn't reveal the truth about myself here. I couldn't reveal it at all until I was certain I could trust Gayla to keep my secret.

"Hmm," Dom said. "Well I'm a telepath. Know what that means?"

I pinched my lips together unable to respond. I knew what I thought that meant, and it wasn't good in this situation.

"It means I can read your thoughts."

I bit my tongue, knowing full well it wouldn't hide the colorful word that just flashed through my mind. Dom smirked. She knew everything.

CHAPTER 4

I KICKED SEAN UNDER the table, hoping he'd wipe the obvious look of shock from his face. He was totally going to give us away.

"Oh, hey," he said, glancing at his watch. "I didn't realize how late it was. We've got to get going."

I nodded gently, trying to play it cool. Dom hadn't peeled her eyes away from me yet, but I didn't have any intentions of explaining myself here.

"Oh no," Gayla frowned. "Already? Well, what are you guys doing later tonight?"

Sean looked at me, asking permission with his eyes. I shrugged. I wasn't opposed to hanging out tonight, we just needed to regroup first. We hadn't anticipated running into a mind-reader, so I wanted to get control of my thoughts and be sure I understood the Keeper laws enough to not get my mom into trouble. And I needed to know that Dom wouldn't rat me out to Tate or anyone else who might want my fractured soul.

"We don't have anything planned yet. What's up?"

"Daddy's throwing a little end of summer party on the boat. You guys should totally come out. You can meet all the other weirdos like us." Gayla winked at me.

I wished I were a weirdo like them. Being mortal sounded completely lame now that I knew there were alternatives. I glanced sideways at Dom, who remained staring at me without any discernible expression on her face. "Sounds fun."

Gayla clapped. "Yay! It's been way too long since the last time we got into trouble." She leaned into Sean, whose cheeks reddened at her touch.

"We'll catch up later then." Sean stood, signaling it was time for us to leave. Dom watched me join his side, and I mentally repeated *clear mind, clear mind, clear mind* so quickly she probably thought I was insane. But at least she wasn't going to get any more information out of me. Not right then, anyway.

With the patio behind us, I searched the dark bar for the door. We were merely steps away from the freedom of setting my mind loose again. I quickened my pace toward the exit, but Sean paused behind me at the sound of someone calling out his name.

"Dude, you too good to say hi?"

I turned to find a handsome guy with dark skin and alluring, ocean colored eyes grinning at Sean. He held his hands out to the side, ready to greet his friend.

Sean didn't disappoint. "Devon!" He laughed as they exchanged some kind of dude hand-shake-back-clap thing. Over their shoulders I saw Dom's thin silhouette in the shadows of the courtyard, silently watching us.

"Uh, Sean..." I approached the guys and tapped him on the shoulder.

"Right," he said. "Sorry. Devon, this is Everly. She just moved here for school. Everly this is Devon—he's one of my good friends from my childhood."

"That's great. Nice to meet you." I tried to stay pleasant but I was starting to panic. I didn't need an introduction to Sean's friend; I just wanted to get out of there. Why couldn't Dom mind her own business? What did she want with me? I glanced back at her cold stare. She was almost smirking now. "I'm gonna go wait outside." I cut Sean a sharp look, urging him to join me, but he seemed oblivious to my rising anxiety.

"Yeah, okay. I'll catch up here in a sec."

Frustrated, I turned and left Sean with Devon. I needed to get out of there. I burst through both sets of doors, dashing through the empty storefront and back out onto the sunny sidewalk. It was only then that I could breathe again. With one last look over my shoulder to be sure I wasn't followed, I turned back to the car.

It was locked. I propped myself up against it for just a minute, watching the horned owl on the roof swivel its ancient looking head back and forth. Its yellow eyes landed on me, and I swore I saw some intelligence there— enough that I had to pull my eyes away. It was making me uncomfortable.

Come on, Sean. Hurry up.

My patience was nearing rock bottom, and the empty street wasn't doing anything for my nerves. With a nod goodbye to the owl, I decided to make my way back to the main road and see what the shops of East Hampton had to offer. Maybe I'd find a cute dress to wear to Gayla's party while Sean was busy gabbing with his buddy.

Small crowds moved up and down the street with carefree ease, blissfully unaware of the beings that lurked just around the corner. Part of me wished I were still ignorant as well—my biggest worry would still be picking a major as I laughed with my mother. Life was grand before we were thrown into the world of the Keepers.

But there was no going back now. Only forward. And with any luck, my situation would improve. I had to hold out hope that mom had a good reason for hiding my lineage. I had to pray that it had nothing to do with broken laws and fractured souls. I had to believe that she was not a criminal, and that I would not be hunted to the death.

Whew. No biggie.

I stepped into line behind a couple of young mothers. One pushed a stroller with two grinning toddlers—twins by the looks of it. The other had a baby strapped to her chest. They strolled slowly enough that I was able to look around and take in the sights of the street. Adorable storefronts lined both sides—quaint cottage-like boutiques interspersed with high-dollar major brands.

I paused to get a closer look at a little shop across the street. A cute purple dress in the window caught my eye. It was a little more adventurous than anything I might've worn back home, but when in New York...

I hurried over to the crosswalk, patiently waiting for my signal to go. A shiny black BMW pulled up to the intersection, and as soon as it passed I'd be clear to cross to the other side. But the vehicle slowed.

Squeak. A small rubber giraffe hit me in the back of the calf with a squeal. I turned to pick it up and return it to the chubby hand of a twin in the stroller.

"I'm so sorry," his mother said. "I'll take it. If you give it back he'll just throw it again." The child whimpered as I changed course and handed his toy to his mother instead. Then I turned back to the street and noticed the BMW was still sitting there in the intersection.

Come on buddy, the light's green.

I looked through the windshield to get the driver's attention, and gasped when I saw that his attention was already on me. He wore dark sunglasses that hid his eyes, but there was no mistaking the man in the car. His white topknot sat perched high on the crown of his head, and his thin arms draped casually over the leather wrapped steering wheel.

"Rossel," I whispered.

The rest of his car was empty—no sign of my mother, but I wouldn't give up that easily. I ran forward to bang on his windows and see what he could tell me about the day she disappeared. He was the last person I saw her with. But as soon as I took one step forward, the engine of Rossel's car roared and he surged forward through a now yellow light.

I cursed under my breath as his red tail lights disappeared down the road, sending pedestrians scurrying out of his way as he flew past them.

The dress would have to wait. I sprinted back the way I'd come, desperate to get back to Sean. We had to follow Rossel and find my mom.

CHAPTER 5

"SO ARE WE GONNA make a plan or what?" Sean leaned against the doorframe of the master bathroom in Millie's vacation home. He was kind enough to give me the big room, and my cosmetics were strewn across her granite counter tops.

"No." I grumbled as I applied a final coat of mascara to my lashes. "There's nothing to plan. Just keep your thoughts quiet so you don't get me killed. Dom is way too eager to dig around in my mind. I'm sure she'll be happy to root around in your stupid brain, too."

"Hey," Sean crossed his arms. "My brain is not stupid. It takes offense to your name calling."

I rolled my eyes and immediately felt guilty for it. Sean had spent the afternoon trying to make me laugh after he refused to engage in the high-speed car chase I'd begged him for.

"He's long gone," Sean had said. *"I wouldn't even know where to begin looking for him."*

I zipped up my makeup bag and threw it on the counter, still frustrated. He was right, of course. Rossel was out of sight long before I got back to Sean's Range Rover. But I was so mad! He was right there in front of me, and I let him get away.

I sighed and turned around to face Sean. "Sorry, brain. I'm just frustrated. I almost had him." But that was okay. We were on to Plan B: Gayla's party.

I spun to show off the dress I'd found in the back of Millie's closet. "Do I look like a rich immortal?" It wasn't as trendy as the purple number I'd spotted in the boutique downtown, but it definitely had that unique Millie flare.

"Close enough," Sean said. "Are you ready?"

"Almost." I swallowed down a couple of vitamins just in case we got back late, then swished some mouthwash. "Alright, let's do this."

I tried to relax and stop taking my frustration out on Sean. I admitted he was right, and we made a plan on our car ride down to the marina. Gayla would have to know the full truth—possible mortality and all—if there was any hope of finding my mom. As a seer, there was a good chance she'd discover the truth anyway. But she'd be a lot more successful trying to elicit a vision if she had as much information beforehand as possible.

And as for Dom... "Can we trust her?" I asked as he pulled into the parking lot.

Sean shrugged. "I never really knew her. She didn't start coming around until we were older. But if she's a telepath, then she already saw everything you were thinking. So if the council is waiting on the dock to take you in for questioning, we'll have our answer. Otherwise, I guess we just have to wait and see if she can keep a secret."

"You don't actually think she'd do that, do you?"

"I don't know what to think when it comes to you. None of this is normal." He turned off the engine and hopped out of the vehicle. With a final deep breath, I followed him.

We walked across the parking lot to the docks. Luxurious boats lined up in rows, bobbing gently in the water. Several looked alive with twinkling lights and the sound of laughter rang out from behind us. The whole marina was buzzing with excitement.

I spotted a particularly large yacht ahead on the right. There was a crowd of ten or twelve gathered on the deck, and lights through the windows of the cabin told me there were more inside. But I didn't see Gayla. In fact, the passengers all looked to be in their fifties or sixties. I slowed as we reached the dock that led to the giant boat.

"What are you doing?" Sean asked.

I gestured to my side. "Is this not where we're going?"

He laughed. "Uh, no."

I looked around. This was the biggest personal boat on the water. We'd nearly reached the end of the marina, and all that lay in front of us were commercial ships. "Where is it?"

He pointed ahead. "It's that one."

My jaw dropped. "The cruise ship?"

"It's not a cruise ship." He laughed again. "That's Gayla's boat. They call it Scylla."

I paused. "As in Scylla and Charybdis?" A week ago the mention of monsters from Greek mythology wouldn't have bothered me at all. But I didn't know what was real anymore.

Sean grew serious. "You know about that?"

"I read about it once." I tapped on my temple. "Photographic memory. I don't forget things. Is that what they named the boat after?"

He frowned. "It's a *she*. And she has a lot of ears. You better hope Scylla doesn't hear you talking about her that way."

"Are you messing with me?"

He remained stoic.

"Sean, if there is a six-headed monster on that ship…"

He couldn't hold in his laughter anymore. He threw his head back and let out loud guffaws before bending over in half. I crossed my arms, waiting for him to finish. Finally, he stood tall again, red faced and still grinning. "Your expression was priceless!" He wiped his eye. "Oh man, I wish I had a picture."

I was not amused. "Okay. Now where is the boat? For real this time."

He was still chuckling a little as he responded. "That's really it. And it's really called Scylla. But don't worry, she doesn't exist anymore. Or- the sea monster doesn't. The boat does, obviously."

I took another look at the ship. I never would have guessed anyone could own a boat like that. It stood three stories tall on the water, emitting a blue glow across the gentle waves lapping up at its sides. White lights surrounded the entrance to the ship's private dock and lined the edges leading up to the massive boat. On board there must have been a couple hundred people spread across the various decks. A large pool faded from purple to blue to green and back again in waves of light. This was wealth like I'd never imagined. I felt wildly out of place.

"Come on." He grabbed my wrist and pulled me along. "Let's go find Gayla and see what we can get figured out."

I stumbled along after him. People stood in pairs along the dock, chatting in their beautiful attire like they didn't have a care in the world. We ducked around them making our way all the way to the entrance when I noticed the platinum blonde hair of the girl checking in each guest. *Please don't be…*

"Dom." I forced a smile as she looked up from the list in her hands. She tilted her head slightly before focusing on Sean.

"You can go in, Sean. Gayla is expecting you. But," she squared her shoulders as she turned to me, "I'm afraid we can't allow any mortals aboard tonight." She sucked air through her teeth, as though she was sorry she had to let me down.

"Gayla invited both of us," Sean protested. "Everly hasn't gotten her powers yet, but she's not mortal."

Dom narrowed her eyes at me. "That's not what she thinks."

Ugh! Apparently I was the one with the stupid traitorous brain. My eyes widened and I thought of my mother before I could stop myself. I didn't want her to get in trouble just because I had a passing thought of being mortal.

Dom tilted her head again, thoroughly examining me. "Where is she?"

"Who?"

"Your mother."

I cringed. But then the pain of reality hit me. "I don't know," I admitted.

She continued to study me with those dark brown eyes, and I couldn't bear to maintain eye contact. I looked over her shoulder to the deck of the boat just in time to see a flash of white hair disappear inside.

"Rossel!"

"What?" Dom asked.

"Where?" Sean stepped forward pushing Dom to the side. Her telepathy was nothing for his strength.

"There!" I pointed. "He just stepped inside."

"Well what are you waiting for? Go!"

CHAPTER 6

I RAN PAST A startled Dom with Sean hot on my heels. I reached the door and pushed through with too much force, tripping over my own feet and nearly knocking over Sean, who had been trailing way too closely, in the process.

But it didn't matter. I saw a snowy white head of hair, pulled back into an elegant low ponytail rather than his signature man bun. "Rossel! Stop!"

The man acted as though he couldn't hear me. He continued moving deeper into the crowd, his suit blending in with others just like it, and I pushed through the mass of strangers to reach him. Finally, I was close enough to reach out and wrap my hand around his arm. "Hey!" I shouted sternly.

He turned around, mouth agape.

"Oh, I'm so sorry, sir." I dropped my hand, and warmth climbed up into my cheeks. It wasn't Rossel.

The man turned away with a scowl, and I wished I was anywhere else. Thankfully, no one else seemed to notice or care much about what just happened. I glanced at Sean with a shrug. "I really thought it was him. What are the odds of running into two different men with long white hair like that on the same day?"

"They're Olympians, Everly."

"So?"

"Look around." Sean pulled me to his side and gestured throughout the room. "Blonds, everywhere."

About three quarters of the guests had some shade of blond hair. Many were platinum, and I noticed more than a handful were bordering on pure white hair, like Rossel and the man I'd just accosted. "Is that an Olympian thing, then? They all have blond or white hair?"

"Most of them, yeah. There are no hard and fast rules, but generally they'll have fair hair and skin with dark eyes."

That described Rossel, alright.

"So are there standard traits among Atlanteans, too? And Agarthians?"

Sean sighed. "I still can't get over how little you know about your heritage. Atlanteans have blue or green eyes, like the sea, but no specific hair color. We vary from gingers like me to yellow blond, all the way to deep brunettes."

"But your eyes are never brown?"

"Our eyes are never brown."

"Got it." The more I discovered about Atlanteans, the less convinced I became that I might be of pure Atlantean blood. At first glance I did have the signature blue eyes of my ancestors, but apparently some brown-eyed mortal tainted me with a slice of darkness in my left eye. It was just one more check in the *reasons Tate wants to kill me* column.

"And the Agarthians are a little trickier. They are typically darker in their natural form, with skin that ranges from a golden sunkissed bronze all the way to a deep dark umber. Their eyes are golden, like you saw with Tate. But here's the kicker—all Agarthians possess the power to change their appearance."

"All of them?"

Sean nodded.

"Is that the only power they possess?"

"No, it's just kind of a standard thing for their race. Like we can breathe underwater. And the Olympians don't require oxygen at all."

"*What?*"

He sucked air through his teeth. "You can't breathe underwater?"

"No."

"Don't worry." He tried to lighten his expression, but it was obvious that even Sean was beginning to lose faith that I was like him. "It'll come with your powers."

"Right. My powers..." I frowned. It was looking more and more like these mythical powers would never come. And at this point, I almost hoped they wouldn't. Tate wouldn't kill me if I had a pure mortal soul—only if I was fractured. Being mortal would mean bad news for my mom, though.

"Let's find Gayla," I straightened my shoulders, finding new determination. If I wasn't going to get my powers after all, then the least I could do was locate my mom and help her hide from the council. I couldn't hold my mortal blood against her, but the council would be much less forgiving.

"Alright," Sean agreed. "I bet she's upstairs."

I followed him through extravagantly decorated rooms, full of beautiful people. Leaning against the bar in a sleek game room beyond the area where we'd entered the interior of the boat, I spotted three familiar faces. They were the same faces plastered across every gossip magazine in every grocery store checkout line across the country. The Miles brothers—celebrity playboys known for the trail of A-List actresses they left crying in their wake. They were gorgeous—impossibly handsome. I wasn't the kind of girl to get star struck, but even I couldn't help but slow my pace as we passed the perfect male specimens.

"Keep it moving," Sean grumbled.

"Are they—"

"Agarthian. Half of the people you see on television and in the movies are. With their ever changing looks and their glamour, it's easy for Agarthians to become famous. You'll also find them in pro sports and politics. They're supposed to use their influence to help keep the humans' behavior in check, but I don't see the difference in what they're doing now versus what our people did in ancient Greece, personally. They think they're gods."

Sean was clearly harboring some hard feelings, but it explained a lot. I surveyed the room again with my new understanding, pausing on the classical pianist tickling the ivories in the corner. His music was absolutely enchanting. *Glamorous*, you might say. "So are there many Agarthians here?"

"Yes, several."

I inched my way closer and leaned in towards his ear. "Any hunters?"

"Unlikely. Only Keepers are invited to Mr. Swain's parties. Hunters wouldn't serve any purpose here. Also, once they are assigned a case, they stick with it until completion. Thaddeus has been assigned to you, which means no one else will come after you. So you can relax tonight."

Easy for him to say. I couldn't help but keep my eyes scanning every new room we entered. I even thought I felt a familiar buzzing sensation once, but it was a false alarm.

"So what about Atlanteans?" I asked. Sean had just pushed the three on the inside of an elevator in the middle of the yacht. Yes, really. An elevator. On a boat.

"What about them?"

"Based on your descriptions, I don't think I'm seeing many here."

"Yeah," he shoved his hands into the pockets of his khaki linen slacks. I never thought I could appreciate a guy in linen pants, but Sean made them look good somehow—like he was headed to a beach wedding. "Parties aren't really an Atlantean thing. Not anymore. We got burned pretty hard in the past for enjoying the finer things of this world. Now you'll find most of us avoid extreme opulence."

"Millie doesn't. She definitely enjoys her wealth."

"Yeah, that's why she and my mom get along so well. They're not afraid of the world. Most of our race doesn't even live on land, anymore."

"Where do they live?"

"Atlantis."

The elevator door opened with a ding.

"I thought Atlantis was destroyed—Millie said the city sank to the bottom of the ocean. Are you telling me it still exists? The myths are true?"

"Remember the whole breathing underwater thing?"

I wanted to quiz him further, but the music grew too loud. Apparently the third floor was where all the college-aged Keepers hung out. The bass was bumpin' so loud the doorknob across the hall vibrated to the beat. I pulled it open and saw a sea of bodies moving with the music inside. The lights were dim with neon flashes of color strobing out above us. Gayla danced clumsily on a platform in the center of the room. Even in her obviously intoxicated state, she was the center of attention. The life of the party.

"I think your friend is drunk," I murmured.

Sean inhaled deeply. "Ambrosia."

CHAPTER 7

"AMBROSIA? FOR REAL?"

Sean nodded grimly.

"Where is it? I want to try some!"

"No." He furrowed his brows as he shook his head. "First of all, mortal souls can't handle it. There's no way you could survive unless you knew for sure that you had an Atlantean soul. Secondly, that stuff is addictive. It's hard to stop once you get started."

"But don't you need it to stay immortal?"

"Nope. It just tastes good and feels good. It'll help our bodies recover from major injuries, but that's about it. And a little bit goes a long way." He shook his head again. "I didn't know Gayla had gotten into the stuff."

I looked back at the beautiful girl as her white skirt fluttered around her swirling frame. She looked so happy and free. I hated to interrupt her.

Sean wasn't bothered, though. He marched right through the crowd up to where Gayla grinned under the flashing lights. Blue and purple reflections glittered off of her platinum hair. Her face brightened when she noticed Sean, and she threw her arms around his neck, almost falling over in the process.

I grimaced as she slurred something into his ear. He raised his brows at her words, but quickly shook it off and whispered back into her ear. She nodded, and he pulled her through the crowds back to where I waited near the entrance of the room.

"Everlyyyyyy! I'm so glad you came!"

I smiled. "Hey, Gayla. Your boat is gorgeous."

She smiled, but she looked almost embarrassed. "I know, it's kind of ridiculous. But it makes Daddy happy, so..." she shrugged.

"Is there somewhere we can chat privately?" Sean asked.

Gayla grinned mischievously. "We can go back to my room."

"Perfect. Let's go, Ev."

Gayla's expression flickered ever-so-slightly at the mention of my name. She didn't seem jealous, exactly, but she was definitely a little disappointed that I would be accompanying them. It disappeared quickly enough, though. She even seemed to be walking a little straighter by the time we reached her room at the end of the hall.

Her bedroom on the boat was nicer than my entire house back in Oklahoma. A sparkling crystal chandelier hung over her four-poster bed. Air whooshed out from under me as I plopped down on her fluffy down bedding.

"Do you have the tablet?" Sean asked as the door clicked shut behind him.

I nodded and opened the small clutch I held under my arm. The tablet rested safely inside, still just as lifeless as it was when it broke back in the gallery. I hated to think about what kind of life was extinguished when it was dropped that night. But it definitely still held some sort of magic, as evidenced by the way it pieced itself back together.

I held the clay rectangle out toward Gayla. "Do you know what this is?"

Her eyes widened with excitement. "May I?" I nodded and she took it into her hands, turning it over and sliding her fingers reverently over its smooth surface. "I've never seen anything like this before, but it's definitely powerful. Where did you get it?"

Her mind seemed clearer now that we were away from the party. I glanced at Sean, who gave me an encouraging dip of his chin.

"Well, I found it about a week ago. My mother and I were exploring a gallery in the city. This is going to sound crazy, but it almost felt like it was... calling to me. Like we shared a heartbeat. It glowed blue that night, and its light pulsed along with mine. And that same day, my mother went missing. She just... disappeared, right from the gallery where I found the tablet. I can't help but think it's all tied together somehow, but I don't know what it says. Can you read it?"

"Incredible," she whispered. "Well it's obviously got some kind of connection to you. I don't recognize the language, though."

"Is there any way you can like, incite a vision or something and see what it means?" Sean shifted on his feet, just as anxious to get some answers as I was.

Gayla shook her head. "Visions don't work that way. They're more like dreams. I can't control when they come, and their meaning isn't always clear. I can try to get a sense of the object's history, but I doubt it'll tell me anything about what it says. And truth be told, I'm not a very skilled seer yet even without all this Ambrosia pulsing through my veins." She giggled nervously.

"That's okay. I'd love for you to try, if you don't mind."

"I'll try." She filled her lungs with air and closed her eyes, placing the tablet flat between her palms. She stayed that way for a minute—maybe longer before I noticed the muscles in her face twitching. It started slowly, a flick of her lip here, a twitch of her brow there. But after another minute her face was twisting into a painful looking grimace. Then, her eyes abruptly opened and everything was calm again.

Gayla laughed, the musical tinkle of her voice made even more endearing as it ended in a tiny snort. "Sorry guys, I tried, but all I can see is my trainer from the city."

"What does that mean?"

"Well, he was scowling, so it probably means my subconscious is feeling guilty about partying instead of focusing on my studies as he instructed me. But this is my last weekend of freedom, you know? Next week it'll be all training and studying, nonstop, all the time."

She set the tablet back on the bed, and we all stared down at it. But it remained lifeless, taunting me with its dull exterior and mysterious carvings. *What are you?*

"Where will you be starting school?" I asked, trying to change the subject and shake off my disappointment.

"Columbia." She said it as though it was obvious.

Sean pursed his lips from the other side of the room. I probably should have known that. Did all the Keepers attend Columbia?

"Right, of course. Guess the Ambrosia is getting to me, too." I giggled, trying to appear more relaxed, like Gayla. Sean cringed. "Is your trainer one of the professors, then?"

"No, he's not associated with the university. He only lives in the city so he can meet with the Olympian leaders. He's on the king's council, but he's not very well-known. I think the king likes to keep him a secret so he can have all of his visions for himself."

I laughed again, but Gayla tilted her head in confusion. Oh. She wasn't joking.

"So is that your lot as well? Will you go on to work for the king after you finish school?" I asked. If so, I could understand why she was trying to live up her last weekend of freedom. She was about to become a modern-day slave, in a sense.

"Oh, I don't know. Maybe. I'll definitely go into leadership because that's all we seers are good for. But I don't know if the king will want me directly. It's rare that a seer can become as skilled as Rossel, even if I do get to train directly under him."

CHAPTER 8

"DID YOU SAY ROSSEL?"

"Yeah, do you know him?"

"Like white man-bun, works in a gallery Rossel?"

Gayla giggled. "Rossel's not hot enough for you to call it a man-bun."

I locked my wide eyes onto Sean's and turned back to Gayla. "Is he here? At the party?"

"Probably." Her amusement was turning into more of a curiosity. "What about him?"

"I knew I saw him!" I grinned victoriously at Sean. "Come on." I stood abruptly and moved toward the door.

"Wait!" Gayla stood, only slightly unsteady on her feet now. Evidently the effects of Ambrosia wore off fairly quickly. "What do you want with Rossel?"

I hesitated. What would she say if I told her the tablet belonged to him? Would she report my theft? After all, I'd only just met her that afternoon. Surely she was more loyal to Rossel than me. I bit my lip as a plan formed loosely in my mind. I'd tell her the truth, even if it was only a partial truth.

"I saw Rossel there at the gallery. He was the last person who spoke to my mom before she disappeared—they might have even left together. He will know where she is."

Gayla's forehead wrinkled as she tried to make sense of my words. "What would Rossel want with your mom?"

I shrugged. "I think they might have known each other. He called her by her nickname, Tilly." I frowned, remembering that day and the fear I'd felt when my mom left. She just walked away with him. He had to be responsible somehow. "She was upset about his painting. She chewed him out pretty good, but she wasn't angry anymore when they disappeared."

"What was the painting of?"

I looked at Sean, unsure if I should answer her. He shifted uncomfortably on his feet, but nodded for me to go ahead. Her big brown eyes were full of curiosity as I turned back to answer her. "It was a portrait of me."

"You?" Gayla nodded silently. She opened her mouth, then shut it again with a slight shake of her head. Then she started pacing.

"What's wrong?" I asked. "What does that mean?"

"Tell me more about the painting."

Sean shrugged. He had just as little idea what she was thinking as I did. "Well, I say it was me, but it wasn't exactly. The girl in the painting was missing my scar." I pointed to my chin. "She was fierce, determined. She wore a gorgeous gown and sat on a throne in a room I've never seen before. The painting was titled Deliverance."

Gayla stopped, and rubbed her head. "Fascinating."

I wanted to ask more about what it might mean, but the door to her bedroom slammed open before I could form the words on my tongue.

Dom stepped inside, sneering in my direction. "Stop!" she shouted. "Whatever they're trying to get out of you, it's all under false pretenses." She looked pointedly at Gayla. "Sean's friend is not a Keeper. She's a human!"

Gayla glanced in my direction, but she didn't look shocked or even angry. Her dark eyes glittered with even more curiosity. "Are you sure?" she asked after a moment.

Dom put her hands on her hips, brows raised as she waited for me to admit the truth.

I shook my head. "Maybe. I don't know." I walked back to her bed and sat with another whoosh of air. A single feather shot out of the seam of her duvet and floated lazily to the ground. "I don't know what I am."

Sean finally spoke up, moving away from the wall to close the door again behind Dom, and the distant sound of music from the party faded into near silence again. "She was raised as a human. She only just learned of our world last week."

This information did surprise Gayla. Her mouth fell open, and she turned to Dom for confirmation. Dom narrowed her eyes at Sean, reading his mind no doubt, then nodded.

I dropped my face into my hands, embarrassed or ashamed, I wasn't sure. I just knew I didn't belong with them. This wasn't my world. And now that I had been identified as an imposter there was no way Gayla was going to help me out anymore.

The bed sank beside me and a thin arm wrapped around my back. "It's okay. Let's start at the beginning." I looked up to see Gayla's concerned eyes, then turned to the others. Sean looked apologetic, but this wasn't his fault. Dom was going to discover the truth either way, so there was no use trying to hide it anymore. They moved in, forming a half circle around me, each one watching with anticipation.

"Sean's right. Until my mom disappeared last week, I didn't know it was possible that I could be anything but human. But my aunt Millie has filled me in on a few things since then."

"Millie Gordon?" Gayla asked.

I nodded. "She explained that we are Atlantean. My mother was raised in this world, but she left when she became pregnant with me and hid for many years. The identity of my father is unknown."

"So you're not human. Your mother is a Keeper. But..."

"I could be fractured." I sighed. "There's a hunter already after me."

"But we don't know for sure," Sean added. "Her father may have been Atlantean, too. As of now, Everly has no powers, but that doesn't mean she never will."

We all sat silently for a moment. Surprisingly, it was Dom who spoke next. "You're worried that your mother bonded with a mortal and that she may be in trouble."

"Yes." It wasn't a question really, but I confirmed what she gathered from my mind. It felt good to admit the truth aloud, despite the weight it held.

"Well, you don't need to worry about that. You're not a mortal. Or, not a pure mortal, anyway." Gayla made the statement with so much confidence, it was difficult not to trust her implicitly.

"Did you have a vision?" Dom asked. "Have you seen her powers?"

"No," Gayla shook her head. "But Rossel did."

"What?" All three of us turned to Gayla with similar looks of confusion. Dom's features pulled together suddenly with concentration, but Gayla waved her off. She apparently didn't like her friend rooting around in her brain, either.

"When Rossel first began working for King Baerius in the 1400s, he had some difficulty describing his visions to the king in a meaningful way. The king didn't trust Rossel's interpretations—he wanted to see the visions for himself. So he asked Rossel to paint what he saw. The king would examine the paintings and draw his own conclusions. Eventually he learned to trust his seer, but the habit of painting his visions had become therapeutic for Rossel. It's something he still does today."

"So you're saying the painting of Everly is the image of a vision Rossel had?"

Gayla nodded.

"No," I rose to my feet again. "The girl in the painting wasn't me. Remember? No scar."

"That's just it, Everly. The fact that you had no scar in the painting is proof that you're immortal. Or at least... demi-immortal."

Demi-immortal. I liked that. It made me sound like Hercules instead of just some poor fractured soul. I appreciated Gayla's thoughts, but it still didn't make sense.

Dom, knowing my hesitation, explained further. "Keeper blood is different from human blood. We heal more quickly. More thoroughly. But it doesn't happen until your powers are activated. As kids, we all fell down and scraped our knees. Most of us had scars and broken bones, just like human children. But once we mature and receive our powers, the cleansing and healing power of Keeper blood restores us to perfect form."

"And your scars disappear?"

Gayla nodded. "So it had to have been you in the painting. But the Keeper version of you."

I shook my head again. "No, we still don't know for certain. I'm eighteen and still have no powers. Zero. Ziltch. Nothing. And the way my mom became so angry... I have another theory. I think perhaps I have a twin out there and the painting is of her. Maybe she got the full Keeper soul and I got left with the mortal leftovers."

Sean rolled his eyes. "Not the twin thing again."

Gayla shrugged. "Could be. But don't count yourself out."

"We don't have to theorize for long." I strode to the door and grabbed the handle. "Luckily for us, the answer is right here on this boat. We just have to find Rossel."

CHAPTER 9

WE SPILLED OUT INTO the hallway, and Gayla grabbed the door frame for balance before moving forward.

"You okay?" Dom asked. Her brows pinched together as she examined her friend.

"Yeah, I'll be fine. I just…" Gayla looked with longing back toward the main entertainment. The bass thumped through the hallway, reminding me that there were still hundreds of people on this boat who were completely oblivious to the stress pounding through my veins.

Sean reached out and touched her shoulder. "Don't, Gayla." Her cheeks flushed as she met his eyes, then she glanced down to the floor, hiding behind her long lashes.

"I'm good," she said, louder. "Let's get downstairs."

Dom locked an arm through Gayla's and the girls moved forward toward the elevator.

"What was that all about?" I whispered to Sean.

"The Ambrosia. It wears off just as fast as it kicks in, leaving your body thirsty for more. She's fighting through a strong craving right now."

We stepped into the elevator and Dom pushed the two button. Beside her, Gayla held her stomach, looking a little queasy as the elevator dropped and landed on the second floor. "This way." She was the first one out the door.

I followed her out into a small bar area, mostly empty, with doors propped wide open to a large deck. Dozens of adults stood out in the open air, sipping cocktails—or maybe it was Ambrosia given the company—and enjoying music coming through the speakers. It was less glitzy than the downstairs scene, but way more tame than the raucous college kids upstairs.

"Do you see him?" I asked no one in particular.

"Not yet," Gayla answered. "Let's go out on the deck."

We moved forward, each of us scanning the crowd as we went. The other three crossed straight over to the edge of the boat, grabbing a hold of the railing as they looked both directions down the sides. I stayed back. I wasn't eager to get any nearer the water than I had to.

I turned back to the crowd and almost plowed right into the best-smelling man I'd ever encountered. His cologne must have been made from concentrated pheromones with a hefty dash of aphrodisiac. And leather. Whatever it was, it was divine. I was all giggly before I even brought my line of sight up to his strong eyes, which were a deep mossy green with flecks of... *gold*.

"Clayton Miles," he grinned, flashing a broad smile of teeth that could have been carved from literal pearls. "I don't believe we've met."

"I, uh..." I giggled again, like an idiot. *Clayton freakin' Miles* was standing right in front of me, and he looked even better in person than he did on all those red carpet pre-shows I liked to watch. "I—I..."

"Everly!" I looked over in time to see Dom's platinum blond hair blowing over her shoulder as she stomped toward me.

"Yeah, that's it. I'm Everly," I said, turning back to the movie star standing in front of me.

"Well, Everly. Consider me charmed." He lifted my hand and kissed the back of my knuckles. *Clayton Miles kissed me!*

Dom's cold hand wrapped around my bicep and pulled me out of my reverie. "Snap out of it." We weaved in and out of small groups on the deck. "He had you hook, line, and sinker. You've gotta stay focused."

"How do you guys handle it?" I asked.

"Handle what?"

"Their charm. Or glamour or sway or whatever you want to call it. He's a siren, right?"

"He is. And I don't know. Maybe it comes with your powers?"

"You don't know?" I stopped and looked at the gorgeous girl across from me. "Do you mean to tell me you've never been swayed by one of those guys?"

She raised a shoulder. "I don't think they've ever tried."

"Or maybe they just know you'd see them coming. You probably know what they're going to try before they do."

Dom laughed, and for the first time, I wasn't intimidated by her. If there was any chance at all that Gayla was right and I did eventually grow into some powers, I might even like to call these girls my friends. And with my mom gone, I could definitely use a friend or two.

"There!" she said suddenly. I followed her gaze to a tall thin man. He wore an all black suit, which must have been incredibly hot on this sticky late summer evening, but somehow the sight of him still sent a cold shiver down my spine. His hair was pulled back into a ball high on the crown of his head, and his eyes were like pure darkness in the low light of the deck.

"Rossel." I practically growled his name as I made my way over to the shadowy corner where he stood. A shorter man with round pink cheeks stepped away when he saw us coming, but Rossel didn't move a muscle. He just stared with those dead-looking eyes of his.

"What a coincidence bumping into you here."

"I'm sorry. Do I know you?" Rossel responded flatly.

"Yes. I'm Tilly Gordon's daughter." *There. That should get his wheels turning.* Only, it didn't. He remained completely expressionless.

I swallowed down the panic notching its way up into my throat and glanced over at Dom. She was completely zeroed in on the man—her stare so intense that she didn't seem to notice me at all. And he ignored her completely.

Rossel glanced impatiently at his watch.

"You're Rossel, right? The seer?"

He blinked in my direction but said nothing. I continued anyway. I knew it was him. I'd recognize that vacant stare anywhere.

"Seems like it might be hard for you to forget a face like mine, seeing as how you painted it on a four foot canvas."

He blinked again, then looked over my shoulder. "Is there any security on this boat?" he muttered to himself.

"*Rossel and Jude.* Your little gallery in the city. My portrait is there. You painted it, and then you disappeared with my mother. And I will not leave you alone until I have some answers. Where is she?"

His face continued to show zero emotion. I wasn't sure if he was even capable of feeling anything at all. My panic was nearly choking me now as I looked desperately to Dom.

"Help me out here. Can you see it? In his mind?"

Dom shook her head, looking a little panicked herself. "No, I—"

"I think we're done here." Rossel rolled his eyes and pushed through us back toward the crowd. By the time I turned around he was completely out of sight again.

"What was that?" I asked Dom.

"I don't know. His mind was blank, or blocked off from me, anyway. I couldn't see a single thing."

"That was Rossel though, right?" I was beginning to doubt myself.

"It definitely was." Dom shook her head with disbelief. "That's never happened to me before."

"Well it seems he's pretty good at introducing new and completely bewildering events into people's lives."

Gayla and Sean approached us then. "Any luck?" Sean asked. But with one look at her friend, Gayla knew.

"You found him, didn't you? What happened?"

Dom looked at me to explain. "You can tell them," I said with a wave of my hand. "I think I need some air."

Sean eyed me but didn't follow, thank goodness. I just needed to think this through for a second. I darted through the people across the deck, keeping my eyes peeled for Rossel again, just in case. It was useless. He was long gone.

I paused in front of the doors, wondering if I should sneak back up to Gayla's room for some quiet, or try to search for somewhere to sit out here. I stepped toward the elevator when I felt a familiar tingle crawl its way up my spine. I looked around for the golden eyes that usually came with that feeling, and spotted two of the Miles brothers just inside near the bar area. Clayton looked up with a wink.

I hadn't noticed the tingle earlier with him, but there was no denying it now. It must have been a siren thing, and I wasn't about to get myself tangled up in one of those traps again. I turned instead, moving toward the edge of the boat. There was a clear area curving away from the cabin up ahead, but the walkway between the walls and the edge of the boat was narrow.

There's a rail. I tried to calm myself. *It'll be fine.*

I scampered over to open air, keeping my eyes on the wooden floor instead of peeking over the edge of the rails into the dark water below. Not only was I afraid of heights, but the water... *nope, not letting my mind go there right now.*

I crept along the walkway, keeping my body as close to the wall as possible, desperate to get the tingle off my skin. The Miles brothers were completely out of sight. Everyone was now, but the feeling just wouldn't go away.

Finally satisfied with my distance from the crowd, I slunk to the ground, careful to keep my dress in place. And I'd just barely gotten comfortable when I realized I wasn't alone.

CHAPTER 10

A SNOWY WHITE OWL sat perched on the rail across from me. It looked identical to the one I saw with my mother outside of the gallery in the city.

"Hey little fella, did you come here with Rossel?"

The owl blinked, but otherwise, didn't move a muscle.

"Yeah, that's how he responded to me, too." I groaned and pulled my clutch into my lap. The tablet still rested safely inside. I pulled it out and examined it again, tracing over the worn symbols etched into its smooth surface.

Did I dare to show it to Rossel? I could march right up to him and wave it proudly in his face—see how he liked that. There was no doubt it was valuable, and according to Gayla, a powerful piece. He wouldn't be able to brush me off so quickly then.

He could have me arrested for theft, though…

"What are you?" I whispered to it. Of course it didn't answer. It sat cold and still in my hands. Strange as it sounded, I almost wished it would come alive again. I wished its pulse would beat with my own. It was more than a clay tablet. It had to be. And I felt lonely knowing what it could be and seeing it without the life I knew it contained inside.

The owl shuffled on the railing, and the buzzy tingle across my skin became more prominent. I put the tablet back into my bag and ran my hands up and down my arms, trying to bring a normal feeling back into them. A quick look around at my surroundings confirmed I was still alone.

Well, alone except for the owl, anyway.

I inched toward it. "You're not the one making me feel like this, are you?"

The owl turned its head at an unnatural angle in response. The tingle spread further, up my shoulders and across the back of my neck. It was electric, very noticeable, but not uncomfortable. It was almost pleasant, actually.

"Well? Did it answer you?" The baritone voice caught me off guard. I might have jumped at the sound, but it was so soothing I couldn't move. I froze, looking into the owl's eyes for the reflection of the man I knew stood behind me.

Finally, I got my wits about me enough to turn around and face him. I knew what I would find, but seeing Tate in person again sent my heart bouncing wildly in my chest. My body was screaming at me to run, but my legs wouldn't cooperate. They couldn't. Because somehow Tate managed to send a feeling of exhilaration through me as well, and my limbs were too confused to do anything but stay right where they were.

He was the deadliest kind of predator. A man who made his prey feel excited about the hunt, even knowing how it all would end. But I wouldn't let it end tonight.

"No." I finally willed myself to take a step backwards. "Owls can't talk."

"Not even to you?" He raised one perfect, dark brow. The lights from the marina glittered off of his golden irises, creating an even more ethereal quality about him. I wondered how much of it he was generating through his glamour and how much of it was just naturally Tate. *My goodness, he was beautiful.*

"Especially not to me. Or did you forget how utterly powerless I am as a mortal?"

A smirk played at the corner of his perfect mouth as he considered that. "Mortal for now. But I expect that to change any day now. Perhaps you just need some kind of an emotional charge to get that fractured soul of yours ignited."

He stepped toward me, his movements lithe and effortless. He almost seemed to glide across the deck. His grace was made even more apparent by my stumbling awkwardly away from him. I wouldn't let him touch me again. I seemed to lose all control over myself when he touched me.

"Get back," I said. The shakiness in my voice revealed just how afraid I really was. But of course, he didn't listen. My back hit the cool metal bar of the railing, and my chest tightened. I was less than a foot away from the edge of the boat. "In case you didn't notice, I was hoping to be alone here."

"Oh, I noticed. I've been waiting to get you alone all night."

"Where did you come from, anyway?"

"Up there." He lifted his eyes to a deck on the floor above us. There was only one way he could've gotten down from that high, and I knew for certain a mortal wouldn't have survived the jump.

"How long were you watching me?"

"Long enough to get bored. That tablet obviously isn't doing anything for you. So like I said, I think it's time to take matters into my own hands and see if we can't get these powers started up for you."

He was practically touching me now, and my body buzzed all over. This glamour of his was unlike any other power I'd encountered among the Keepers so far—even greater than the Miles brothers. The way my body reacted to him was... unnerving at best.

I couldn't back up any farther, so I stepped sideways instead, moving along the edge of the boat. I kept one hand on the rail at all times. I knew what lay on the other side, and I wasn't feeling up to a cold bath in the bay tonight.

Tate stepped with me, never allowing more than a foot of space between us. With every step, my fear twisted closer to frustration. Tate admitted he couldn't do anything to me without proof of a fractured soul. And there was no proof. I might not even be fractured. This was getting ridiculous.

"That's kind of you to offer, but you can keep your hands off of me, thank you very much." My frustration won out.

To my complete surprise, he stopped. He lifted both hands in the air. "Okay."

"Okay?" There was something fishy about this. Predators didn't just stop mid-hunt without a good reason. He was up to something, and I wasn't going to let him get away with it.

"Yep. If you say you want me to leave you alone, I will. Even if that's not the impression I get from the way your heart races when I'm near."

"Maybe that's my body's way of telling me to run."

"And the flush in your cheeks?" He lifted a hand but left his fingers hovering in the air an inch from my face, never actually bringing them to touch me.

"Anger."

"Okay. But how do you explain the way your breath hitches when I lean in close?" He leaned down so near I could feel his breath fluttering the hair on top of my head as he whispered. *And dangit.* He was right. I released the breath caught in my throat as the realization dawned on me.

He laughed softly, but it sounded more like a purr. I stood another step back. "You think you're clever, huh?"

"I do." There was amusement in his voice. He was getting way too much enjoyment out of this ordeal.

"Well, unfortunately you've missed the main point. I have no powers. None. You're wasting your time. But I'm sure there are hundreds of fractured souls waiting for you back in the city."

"Ahh, but it's so noisy there. I much prefer the good company I have here on the water." He winked and my stomach did a little flip.

Shake it off. Dom's words from earlier echoed in my ears. I had to stay focused. "How'd you know I was here, anyway?"

"I have eyes everywhere."

"It was those Miles brothers, wasn't it?" I cursed under my breath. "I knew they were too pretty to be trusted."

"There are lots of Keepers who can't be trusted." He stepped forward again.

"Yeah, no kidding. I'm looking at the worst one of all."

"I don't think you understand." Tate smiled and I had to bite the inside of my lip to keep from returning it. This thrill he gave me was such an unfair advantage. "I won't let anything hurt you."

"Nothing except you?"

"Oh, darling. It's quite the opposite. My job is made easier when I make the process... enjoyable."

"You're sick, you know that?"

I stepped back again and my hand slipped off the railing. Tate thrust his arms out toward me and instinctively I moved away again. That was a mistake.

My heel rocked off the edge of the boat, and I saw the darkness of night dotted with stars like a life sized canvas of the sky as I fell backward. The air rushed past and all I could think about was how lucky I was to have such a glorious sight as my last.

The irony of it all wasn't lost on me. A descendant of Atlantis. Drowning. It looked like Tate was going to end up with my soul afterall.

Finally I hit the water with more force than was expected. The wind was knocked out of my lungs from the impact, and pain shot through my limbs as they slapped against the water. There was probably a splash, but I never saw it. I don't know which chilled me more—the coldness of the ocean or the complete void of light as I was engulfed on my way down.

As my final act in this world, I tucked my clutch with the tablet inside the top of my dress, under the front of a strap. At least it would be found with my body when they searched the bay the next morning. And maybe Sean and Millie could help save my mother. Maybe it would even be easier with me gone.

CHAPTER 11

DYING WAS NOTHING LIKE I'd expected it to be. I never saw my life flash before my eyes. I didn't watch myself drown through an out of body experience. There was no bright light. It was nothing like in the movies. It's not that I thought dying would be an enjoyable experience necessarily, I just didn't expect it to be so hard.

My arms and legs kicked and flailed wildly. But it was so dark, I didn't know which way was up. Even if I had been able to swim, I don't think I would have known which way to go. But I fought, nonetheless. My lungs began to burn, the need to inhale a gulp of fresh air all-consuming.

Something slippery fluttered against my bare leg, and then I felt the warmth. It started in my chest, replacing the fire under my sternum with a sense of calm. It spread through my torso and down into my legs. It danced across my shoulder blades and into my arms until even the tips of my fingers felt alive and sparking with energy. Then I was jerked upward.

I opened my eyes, ignoring the sting of salt and the murkiness clouding my vision. All I could see was the glow. He looked like an angel, strong and powerful. He swam through the water with ease, pulling me ever upward toward the sky. Was this the end? Was I finally crossing over to be with my Maker?

The air was warm when my head finally emerged from the dark depths of the bay. I gasped, spitting water as my lungs greedily gorged themselves on oxygen. My arms and legs hung limp by my sides, yet I didn't sink. Someone held me from behind, one strong arm wrapped around my waist, while his legs tread water as easily as he might hum a song. My angel.

I turned to look over my shoulder—to thank him. My nose brushed against a scruffy cheek and I pulled back enough to make out the shadowy silhouette of strong, high cheekbones and a well-defined jawline.

"Tate." My voice was gravelly from seawater still clinging to the edges of my throat.

"At your service."

I tried to get away, but he pulled me tighter, closer to the hard plane of his abs, and I hated how aware of his body I suddenly became.

"Calm down," he whispered, the air from his words tickling the air against my ear. "Are you trying to die?"

"No. I'm trying to survive. Which is exactly why I need to get away from you." I placed a foot on the front of his thigh and kicked off hard, trying to propel myself forward. It didn't work. Tate spun me around and scooped me into his arms like a toddler, wrapping my legs around his waist and holding onto to me with both arms wrapped securely behind my back. He kept us above water with his legs alone treading water, and the gentle movement was calming. Or was it the movement?

I was unnaturally at ease, given the circumstances. "Are you glamouring me?"

He laughed, the sound warm from deep in his chest. "I've got to keep you calm somehow. If you keep flailing around like that you'll drag us both under."

"Why did you jump in after me, anyway? I thought you wanted me dead so you could steal my soul."

"I don't want you dead. In fact, I need you alive to extract your soul. If you die it disappears."

"And after you extract it?"

"Well," he tilted his to the side, "*then* you die. But it won't hurt—I promise."

I placed both hands on his chest and shoved myself backward, but he only held on tighter.

"You seriously need to stop that. You're drawing attention."

I looked over his shoulder at the crowd gathering along the edge of the boat. They looked concerned and... perplexed. So much for pretending I was like them. My mortality was on full display, like a neon light with a bright flashing arrow pointing down that read *Not Atlantean*. The idea that a descendant of Atlantis would need to be rescued from *drowning* was preposterous. And by Tate of all people. Then again, this wasn't the first time Tate had appeared after a near-death experience.

"You know," I said, "it's funny how disaster always seems to strike when you're around. First the bomb at the gallery, then I almost drowned. How are you going to make an attempt on my life next time, golden eyes?"

He smirked. "I told you. I'm not trying to kill you."

"So you had nothing to do with the bomb?"

"I didn't say that."

"Well, you're going to have to explain how blowing up the gallery I was in and pushing me over the edge of a three-story yacht is your way of 'not trying to kill' me."

"First of all, I didn't push you. That was all you and your natural grace. I tried to grab you before you fell, but I'll be honest. I don't care much for your life. All I care about is getting your soul in one piece."

A growl started deep in my chest, and my mouth parted to yell at him. Tate held up a finger, and I felt compelled to remain silent, at least until he was finished.

"But," he said, continuing with a smirk, "I need to coax your powers out first, however fractured they may be. I just need proof. A few more shocking incidents, or 'attempts on your life' as you say, should do the trick."

"Well, why wait?" I struggled to keep my volume at a reasonable level. He knew exactly how to get under my skin, and whatever glamour he was using to keep me calm earlier had vanished now. "You've literally got me in the palm of your hands. You know I can't swim. Drop me. Let me sink. You'll see *once again* that I have no powers, and all those people standing at the rail will be happy to lock you up like the scum that you are."

"Such harsh words." He tsked. "Besides, I don't like an audience."

"Ha. You know, I'm starting to believe you can't actually do anything you say you will, anyway. I. Have. No. Powers. And as a mortal, I don't have to be afraid of you. You can't hurt me without ruining your own life. And both of your attempts to *coax* out my nonexistent powers so far have failed. I think you're just a lot of talk." I didn't know why I felt the urge to goad him. He just made me so angry! And I might have been physically powerless against him, but I wanted him to know he didn't have the upper hand. I really didn't have to be afraid of him. Not yet, anyway. Not until I knew for sure whether or not I was fractured.

"I'm just a lot of talk, huh?" He quirked a dark eyebrow.

I nodded. "You can't do anything to me." My voice was softer now, almost husky sounding from the saltwater.

He pulled me closer, a feat I didn't know was possible with how much we already touched under the water. He leaned in, his lips brushing against my ear as he whispered, "I can't make you do anything you don't want to do. You're right. But I don't think you know what you want."

My stomach flipped, and I felt my heart pulsing, its strong pounding rhythm betraying my cool exterior. Tate noticed. He had to have noticed.

My skin buzzed with anticipation. He released one arm from my waist and brought his hand to my face, using the soft pad of his thumb to wipe a spot under my left eye. "Your makeup is running."

"Oh." It was all I could manage. My words disappeared, stifled by the lump in my throat. What brought about this change? Why the shift in his demeanor?

His gaze lingered on my eye. It happened frequently. People often couldn't help but stare at the stark contrast of blue and the giant slice of brown in my iris. But most people didn't look like Tate. And the expression on his face almost seemed to have a hint of... longing.

He shook his head. "Sorry," he mumbled. "Your eyes are just so striking. I don't mean to stare, but you really are enchanting. I might be all talk, but I meant that at the gallery, and I mean it now. You're quite fun to admire."

We had just about reached the ladder that would take us back up to the deck of Gayla's boat. He leaned back with a thrust of his legs to propel us toward the ladder, then he took hold with his free hand, the other still holding me snugly against him.

"You're not so bad, yourself." I felt braver now that we were so close to safety again. Just another minute and my feet would be back on solid ground. Though strangely, I wasn't in a hurry to get out of Tate's arms.

He leaned down until our foreheads were touching, and everything else disappeared from my sight. I didn't care who might have been watching from the deck above. I didn't care about anything but hearing whatever it was Tate said next.

"I'm glad you're safe."

"Me, too. Thank you for rescuing me."

"Would it be alright if I—"

His eyes flashed down to my lips, and my breath caught in my throat. "Yes." I barely whispered my response as I tilted my head up to meet his lips. I paused for just a moment, exposed in the cool evening air, waiting to kiss my hero. My rescuer. My angel. But his lips never came.

I opened my eyes and found Tate grinning mischievously down at me.

"You might be careful next time you want to trash talk my powers. I *always* get what I want."

I scowled. I'd been glamoured. Again. I was such a fool. Reaching over his shoulder, I took hold of the bottom rung of the ladder and pulled myself up and out of his arms. Then, just for good measure, I turned back to face Tate.

"I hate you," I grumbled. With my left hand on top of his head, I shoved with all my weight, pushing his beautiful face under the water. Then I made my way up toward the deck, never turning to look back at him.

It might have been childish, but boy it felt good.

CHAPTER 12

SEAN, DOM, AND GAYLA all waited for me at the top of the ladder. Sean reached out to help me back onto the boat, casting a wary glance over my shoulder at Tate below.

"I'm so sorry," he mumbled. "I really had no idea he was here."

"I know. It's fine. I'm fine."

Dom shot me a knowing look, but thankfully she kept her mouth shut. I was already mortified by what had transpired with Tate. I didn't want to relive it now. Or ever.

"Do you still have the tablet?" Gayla whispered. "Dom told us everything that happened with Rossel. I can't believe he would do that to you. But don't worry. He can't play dumb with me."

"I do." I pulled my clutch from its spot, still tucked safely under the strap of my dress. A steady stream of water dripped from the corner as I extended my arm toward her. She didn't hesitate to take it and tuck it under her own arm, probably ruining the very expensive dress she wore.

"I'll keep it safe while you get dried off." She glanced nervously behind me as well, which meant Tate had finally made it aboard. I turned to see him grinning deviously as he passed me on his way towards the Miles brothers. He gave his head a little shake, sending water droplets flying towards me, and when he stopped his hair was perfectly tousled—like the model of a surfboard ad campaign.

"Ooh, he is hot." Gayla stared open mouthed as Tate passed us by.

"Yeah, it's too bad he only wants me for my soul."

Dom frowned. "Come on. Let's get you back upstairs. I'm sure Gayla has something you can change into."

Sean stepped by my side as we moved through the crowd. He turned his body in an attempt to shield me somewhat from the onlookers, but I knew they were staring. I was sure I'd made quite a spectacle of myself. Gayla's dad would probably never let me on his yacht again. And honestly, I was okay with that.

"First things first, when we get back to the city, we're getting you a YMCA membership," he said.

"Why?"

"Because you need swim lessons."

Gayla chimed in. "I've never known an Atlantean who couldn't swim. I thought it just came naturally to you all."

I shrugged. Maybe it did. Maybe Tate was right and I wasn't Atlantean. But I wouldn't let my mind go there now. "I'm beginning to think nothing comes naturally for me."

Gayla frowned. "I'm sorry. I didn't mean it like that."

"I know. It's just been a long day."

We reached the elevator inside the small bar area and waited patiently for the doors to open. All was silent except for the *drip, drip, drip* of salt water from the tattered hem of my dress.

"Well, I've decided I want to help. There are just too many weird things surrounding you and this tablet for me to ignore. My curiosity has gotten the best of me, I guess."

"Me, too," Dom said as we all stepped onto the elevator. "I understand better now where you were coming from. And what happened to your mom isn't right. We'll help you find her."

"Really?" The elevator closed behind me.

"Really," Gayla said. "First thing tomorrow I'm going to look for a bigger apartment in the city. I don't know where you were planning to stay before, but you can move in with Dom and me. We'll get a spot really close to campus."

"Oh, well I'm—"

"Nope." Gayla shook her head. "It's all on me. Really. You're going to need some extra friends to help keep you safe from that sexy golden-eyed devil, and I wouldn't dare trust anyone else."

I laughed as the reality hit me. Gayla wanted to get closer to Tate. I wouldn't argue with her tonight. She seemed pretty set on the idea. But unless she wanted to live near NYU and take a cab to Columbia each day, she was sadly mistaken on my roommate situation.

I felt Dom's dark eyes on me as the elevator opened again on the third floor. A party still raged on beyond the doors in front of us, and Gayla paused for a moment, still fighting her cravings most likely, before moving toward her room. I gave Dom a quiet shake of my head. It was going to take a while to get used to this whole mind reading thing.

Dom seemed to understand, and she didn't say anything about NYU or apartments or anything else. Sean agreed to keep guard outside the door as Gayla dragged me into her oversized closet in search of something dry to wear. Within minutes, I emerged in some of Gayla's workout gear. My makeup was a mess and my hair hung in straggly wet lines around me. I didn't want to get dressed up again. I'd had enough partying for the night. Some comfy running shorts and a baggy racerback were all I needed.

"I'll call you when we get to the city on Monday. We can all go apartment hunting together."

Dom winked at me as Gayla continued gabbing on about showing me her favorite coffee shops and boutiques near campus. Dom was much more fun as a co-conspirator than she had been as my enemy earlier in the day. We continued forward, me barefoot with Millie's wet heels tucked under my arm. It was a wonder they hadn't gotten lost in the bay.

"Ready?" I asked as we joined up with Sean again at the elevator. He waited patiently, holding my still damp clutch and the tablet inside.

"Yep, let's get out of here."

"Thank you again for coming tonight." Gayla wrapped her arms around me, then turned and did the same to Sean, adding a kiss on the cheek for him as well.

He shoved his hands into his pockets and looked at the ground when she pulled away, redness creeping obviously up into his fair skinned cheeks. Gayla just smiled.

"Things always did get more exciting when we were together," she said. He looked up and some unspoken understanding passed between the two of them. I looked to Dom who just raised her brows and shook her head in response.

Well, okay then.

"You really can stay if you want," I said to him as the elevator door shut and we began our descent to the bottom floor. "I'm sure Gayla would be pleased if you did."

He shot me a disapproving look. "Nah. The party scene isn't really my thing."

"Understood." I agreed. It wasn't my scene either. And selfishly, I was glad Sean offered to drive me home. I'd never had to call an Uber before, and the stories from the girls back home made me nervous. Just a little though. I knew now that there were worse monsters in New York than rogue Uber drivers.

All eyes were on me in my workout gear and bare feet as we made our way back through the glitzy ballroom on the first floor of the yacht. The pianist still poured his soul into the melodies coming from the corner, and I'd never stood out so much in my life. But I didn't care.

My eyes scanned the room for Tate. There was no tingle, no buzz, and no sign of those charming golden eyes anywhere. I didn't even see the Miles brothers anymore. Perhaps they'd all gone home or found some other celebrity party. Good. We were better off without them.

Sean paused before we left the cabin, gesturing toward the bathroom door. "Are you good here for just a sec?"

"Yeah, of course."

He handed me the clutch, and I smoothed out my hot pink shorts, trying my best to look inconspicuous as I swayed to the classical music. A hand on my arm startled me so much I almost dropped my bag and the tablet. I looked up to find Rossel's pitch black gaze glued to the clutch in my hand.

He knew.

He knew, but he didn't reach for it. After a moment, he moved his dark stare up to meet my own. "Are you leaving?" he asked. His voice was cold and flat.

"Yes." I tucked the clutch back under my arm, certain now that he wasn't after it. Maybe it was useless to him now that the life was gone from it.

"Good. Don't come back."

He certainly didn't have to worry about that. I'd had quite enough of this boat. "I won't."

"And stay away from Gayla."

That one I couldn't agree to. "Why?"

"I don't want her getting too attached to you." He frowned.

"What is that supposed to mean?"

"I think you know."

He was wrong. I had no clue what he was talking about, but I didn't like the tone of his voice. The bathroom door swung open again beside us.

"Everly?" Sean stepped out, patting his hands dry on his pants. "Was that Rossel?"

I turned back to find my white haired friend missing again. It was amazing how quickly that man could disappear.

"It was."

"Are you okay? What did he want?" Sean snapped his eyes to the clutch under my arm, relief apparent in his eyes once he saw it was safe.

"Nothing," I said. "Let's get home. We've got a mystery to solve."

THE APOTHECARY

CHAPTER 1

"HE'S CUTE. MAYBE YOU should look into that program."

Gayla pointed to a photo of a sharply dressed young man giving a PowerPoint presentation in a glossy brochure. I had several others just like it laying out across the countertop in the kitchen of her and Dom's new apartment. Each represented a different academic program at NYU. I was still stumped about which major I would declare, and the first day of school was just a week away. Unfortunately, none of those glossy photos was calling my name.

"He's a professor," I said, reading the caption below the image. "Of Chemical and Biomolecular Engineering. Hard pass."

"I could see you working as a chemical engineer," Dom piped in as she poured a glass of water. "I bet you'd ace that program."

"Of course I would. I have a photographic memory. I can ace any program, but that doesn't mean I *want* to."

"And you're so humble, too," Gayla said with a laugh.

I shrugged. "It's not bragging if it's true."

Dom slid a bowl full of grapes in my direction, and I popped one into my mouth. Watching my friends do the same, I suddenly understood how the ancient Greeks mistook the Olympians for gods and goddesses. They looked awfully magical even in a New York City apartment.

"That's exactly why you should *hard pass* on NYU altogether and come to Columbia with us, instead."

"I can't," I sighed. "I told you. I'm not Columbia material."

"You're exactly Columbia material. Probably half of the student population is made up of Keepers."

"It's nowhere near half—" Dom interrupted.

"Well, a lot, anyway," Gayla conceded. "Plus, you already got accepted."

"And I declined it."

"Bah—paperwork. It's a simple fix," Gayla said with a wave of her hand. "At least let us show you around before you decide for sure. I promise you will love it when you see it through our eyes."

"If it will get you to stop pestering me about it, then fine. I will let you show me around. But don't get your hopes up. I've been dreaming of attending NYU for forever. It's iconic."

"More iconic than Columbia?"

"They're both very iconic, girls." Dom gave us a matronly smile. Gayla and I weren't really fighting, of course, we both just had strong opinions. But Dom wasn't a fan of conflict—even in jest.

"You're right, Mama Dom." Gayla smiled warmly at her friend and turned back to me. "So when do we get to give you the grand tour?"

"Not today." I glanced at my watch. "I told Millie I'd head down to the shop and help her out. Maybe tomorrow afternoon?"

"Perfect." Gayla's face lit up. "I can't wait!"

I grabbed my purse, checked to make sure the clay tablet was tucked safely inside, and headed for the door. It was probably silly to carry the artifact around with me everywhere, but I couldn't bear to leave it behind. It was too valuable to me. And I still didn't know the extent of its powers, just that it had a lot. If it ended up in the wrong hands, it could mean bad news for me, and maybe for my mom, too. Wherever she was.

"By the way," Dom said on my way out the door. "Sean's coming over for pizza tonight. You should swing by too, after work."

"Sounds great. I'll see you guys later!"

Speaking of Sean, he leaned against the wall just outside of the entrance to their apartment building, waiting to escort me to Millie's shop.

"Morning!" I smiled. He grunted in return, slowly leaning forward off the side of the building. I grimaced. "Do you need some coffee?"

"No." He stormed off ahead of me down the sidewalk.

"Why the sour mood, then?"

"I'm not sour, I'm fine."

"Hmph." I scuttled ahead, trying to keep up with him. I didn't like having him as a bodyguard anymore than he liked tagging along with me everywhere, but he'd never been quite so grumpy about it before. "You know, you don't have to do this."

"Do what?"

"Follow me around everywhere. I won't say a word to Millie or your mom."

"They'd find out, anyway. If they want me to act as your guard, then that's my assignment. Official or not. But I don't mind it anyway."

"Could've fooled me," I mumbled under my breath.

"Look, I'm just not very excited about going into your aunt's shop this morning."

"Why not?"

"Abby's back in today."

Oooh, Abby. I remembered how he got all extra-concerned at the mention of her before we left town for the Hamptons. But before I could ask him any more about it we'd reached my aunt's shop. Technically, it was a pharmacy. And like many pharmacies, it had a little gift shop attached. But that was where it's normalcy ended.

The sign outside simply read *Apothecary*. That's it. No branding of any kind. It was painted in white letters on a black sign, looking like it may have come straight out of the early 1900s. Maybe it had.

Walking through the doors was like stepping into another world. Bundles of dried flowers and herbs hung sporadically from the ceiling. Giant antique wood tables sat in the middle of the room—one full of beauty products complete with an ornate round mirror in a sterling silver frame, and the other full of bath and body products surrounding an enormous copper wash basin built into the center of the old table. The walls were lined with ten-foot tall wooden cabinets, trimmed with great detail—arching frames, etched glass-fronted cabinet doors, and shelves on shelves on shelves. Glass bottles in various shapes and sizes held various pills and poultices and herbal concoctions. One shelf was designated for my aunt's natural tea blends.

Millie and a petite brunette girl stood in black aprons behind an old fashioned soda fountain style counter, though the actual soda fountain had been long removed. Behind them a set of thick, velvety, emerald green drapes hung from the ceiling to the floor, separating the front of the store from the private employees' area in the back of the shop.

It was a lot to take in, this strange mix of witchy wonders and hippy remedies and 1950s aesthetic all blended into one high-end Manhattan pharmacy. But it was quintessentially Millie.

"Good morning!" Millie beamed from the opposite side of the counter. "Come in, come in. I want you to meet Abby."

The girl bashfully smiled and extended her hand. I couldn't help but notice Sean's cheeks grow pink as he met her eyes. "Hi, Abby. I'm Everly."

"I've heard a lot about you. It's nice to put a face with the name." She shook my hand then looked behind me. "Hi, Sean. I haven't seen you around in a while." Abby's cheeks grew red as well, and she nervously began fidgeting with the hem of her apron.

"Yes, well..." Millie stacked up the papers she'd been examining and set them to the side. "Where should we begin?"

The door chimed as a customer entered behind us. I pulled Sean to the side so I could watch my aunt and Abby in action. I'd spent enough time down at the feed store back home to understand customer service, but I didn't know the slightest thing about the potions and salves and herbal remedies surrounding us now. I was content to sit back and see how they handled it.

"Good morning, sir. Is there something we can help you find today?"

The man was probably an inch or two shy of six feet, with walnut-colored hair and hazel eyes. He didn't fit any of the standard descriptions of Keepers, but then again, Agarthians could look however they wanted. I leaned into Sean. "What is he?"

Sean whispered back, "I don't sense any powers. He's just a human."

"Does Millie serve humans?"

"Of course," Sean chuckled.

Okay. Well, the stuff in these bottles must have been approved by mortal laws, then. I browsed the labels, wondering how she ever got away with selling things like "Dragon's Blood," and if the words beneath the label (dracaena draco) were code for the dragon's region or if it might actually be a nickname for some kind of herb. I hoped the latter, otherwise Millie had a lot more explaining to do.

She flitted around the edges of the shop, helping the man find all the items from his surprisingly long shopping list. And I don't think I'd ever seen anyone look as happy as he did by the end of it. He tossed in a stick of black licorice at the counter as he was checking out, and left with a smile as wide as the Brooklyn Bridge.

"Wow, Millie. You really made his day."

"Healing is a beautiful thing. Many of my customers have been burned by traditional medicine and doctors, so they turn to me for more natural solutions to their problems."

"That's so cool that you're able to help."

She sighed. "I wish I could help everyone. How's your father doing today, Abby?"

Abby raised a shoulder. "About the same, I guess. I just don't know what to do anymore. One minute he's totally high on life—full of energy and excited about the future. But when he crashes, he crashes hard. Lower each time. I honestly wasn't sure if he was going to make it through the weekend."

Millie frowned. "I'm sorry, sweetheart. And you're sure that he's not... using anything illicit?"

Abby's eyes grew wide. "No! No, of course not. My dad is a lot of things, but he's not a drug user. Especially not now. He's so wrapped up in this new business plan of his that he would die before he'd jeopardize things with drugs. He doesn't even drink wine with dinner anymore!"

"Hmm." Millie looked unconvinced. "Well, I keep meaning to swing by and check on him, we've just been so busy here."

"Go now," Sean said. "I can watch the shop while you're gone."

"Are you sure?"

"Yeah—I've done it loads of times before. I can handle it for an hour. Take Everly. I'm sure she'd love to meet Mr. Mason, and maybe you could teach her a thing or two about your business while you walk."

"Does that sound like something you'd like to do?" Millie asked me.

"Sure," I shrugged. Sean looked pretty eager to get us out of there. I suspected it had something to do with Abby. I looked at the girl. "Is that okay with you?"

"Yes—absolutely! Millie is like a miracle worker. I would love to bring you guys over to see my dad. He could really use your help."

CHAPTER 2

ABBY CONTINUED TO ELABORATE on her father's symptoms as we walked. Millie's electric blue heels gave us a steady cadence as we walked the six blocks to Abby's apartment.

"Do you remember when exactly all of this began?" Millie asked.

Abby thought for a moment. "I want to say it was right around the Fourth of July. We usually drive out to see my cousins and shoot fireworks, but he wasn't feeling well that day. It may have been before that, but that's the first instance I specifically remember."

"I see. And did anything else in his life change around that time? Maybe a new diet or a different gym? A new hobby?"

"No. Dad has been decidedly anti-social since my great aunt Linda passed away in the spring. I think her finances were a mess, so he's been working with her attorneys to get everything sorted out... when he's feeling up to it, that is."

"I see. Well, should we give him a call before we go up?"

"No. I'll go in first to make sure he's not asleep or anything. He'll be happy to see you." Abby stepped up to the door tucked under a green awning, and we followed her inside and across a quaint lobby toward the elevator. The building was clean and quiet, with an attendant ready to accept packages and greet guests.

Abby's apartment was on the fourth floor. After giving her a minute to ensure her father was awake, we followed her inside. The apartment was small but tidy, with charming herringbone wood floors and tall ceilings. The windows looked out to the building next door, but they let in enough light to offer a cheery vibe to the living area. To one side were doors to two bedrooms separated by a single bathroom. The other side held the kitchen and a small eat-in dining area. A middle aged woman with dark hair and deep set frown lines stood in the kitchen, unloading the dishwasher.

Abby's father laid under a blanket on the couch, and he set his copy of the Wall Street Journal on the coffee table as we entered.

"Millie Gordon." He smiled, but it didn't quite reach his eyes, which were bloodshot and framed inside dark circles.

"Mitch Mason," she smiled back. "It's been too long. Oh, no—don't stand. There's no need to be formal with me." She sat beside Abby's father on the couch. "You look like you're feeling better today."

"Spry as a kitten," he laughed. If this was good for him, I hated to think how he looked at his worst.

The woman in the kitchen hummed a song that sounded almost like a lullaby as she closed the dishwasher and dried her hands on a tea towel. I turned to Abby, who had been shooting me curious glances since we entered, and raised a brow, jerking my chin toward the kitchen. She responded by silently mouthing, "housekeeper."

It felt rude to stand around and listen in on Millie and Mitch's conversation. "Can I have a tour?" I asked Abby.

She looked embarrassed. "There's not much to see."

"Compared to where I'm from, everything in New York is worth seeing."

Abby nodded and gave me a quick walk through the place. Her room was narrow, with a twin sized bed pushed up against one wall, its pink comforter well-loved and probably used since she was a little girl. A full length mirror stood propped up in the corner, with pictures of Abby and her friends tucked in around the frame.

The bathroom held a pedestal sink and a small rolling cart with a hairdryer hanging out of the drawer. And her father's room wasn't much larger than hers. But the apartment had character and a homey feel that I couldn't help but find endearing.

Back in the living room we saw the housekeeper standing at the opposite end of the couch from Millie. "All finished Mr. Mason, and I left that information you requested on the counter. Is there anything else I can help you with today?"

"No, thank you, Nikki. I'll see you tomorrow."

The woman nodded and ducked out of the room, giving Millie a wide berth as she passed.

Abby and I moved toward the kitchen, grabbing seats at the two-person cafe table sitting just off to the side. "I figured we could let them talk in peace," she said.

"For a bit," I agreed. "But Millie could go on all day, so feel free to kick us out if you think your dad needs some more rest."

Abby grinned and looked down to the table, picking at some spot only she could see. It struck me that she already knew that about my aunt. She probably knew Millie better than I did.

"I'm sure he'll be okay," I said, not really certain at all. But if there was anyone who could get to the bottom of what was causing Mitch's illness, it was Millie. He was in good hands.

Abby's smile faded and she pressed her lips together. Her expression had changed when she looked back up to me. "So, I hear you're going to Columbia."

"Ha, you heard wrong. Did Millie tell you that?"

She nodded.

"She would like for me to go to Columbia, but I'm enrolled at NYU."

"Oh, nice. What are you studying?"

Good question. "I don't know yet. What about you? Where are you going?"

She looked back to the table. "I'm actually taking the year off to care for my dad. Millie was gracious enough to offer me full time employment at the shop."

"Oh…" I didn't know what else to say to that.

"Alright girls," Millie entered then, her usual cheerful demeanor snapping me out of the uncomfortable silence that had just passed between Abby and me. "I've got to get back to the shop. Abby, why don't you take the day off? With Everly and Sean both working today, I'll have all the help I need."

Abby started to protest, but Millie raised a hand and kept going. "I won't take no for an answer. Consider it a paid holiday."

Abby's cheeks flushed as she gave a reluctant nod. "Thank you."

"But you," Millie pointed to me, "are not so lucky. Come on now, you've got a lot to learn about the pharmaceutical sciences."

I stood, taking note of the bright blue and yellow folders on the kitchen counter as I left. A large amateurish looking logo was attached to front, reading *D&N Investments, The Opportunity of a Lifetime.* "Thank you for the tour, Abby. You've got a lovely apartment." I shot one more glance at the folders. Why would Mr. Mason be seeking investment advice from his housekeeper? *Eh, it wasn't any of my business.* "I'm sure I'll see you around at the shop again soon. And it was nice to meet you, Mr. Mason!"

"Come again," he called out as we exited.

Millie seemed on edge as soon as we got to the other side of the door. She moved quickly ahead, squeezing into the elevator next to an older woman with a giant handbag containing a gray-faced chihuahua. I waited until we were back on the sidewalk, safely inside a crowd of people surrounded by street noise before I finally asked, "So, were you able to figure out what's wrong?"

Millie frowned. "Dark magic. I've got to phone it in to the council immediately."

CHAPTER 3

"HOLD ON. *Dark magic?*"

Millie furrowed her brows. "Shhh. Keep your voice down. We'll talk back at the shop."

My mind was blown. I spent the rest of our walk back to the apothecary shrewdly examining every person we passed on the streets. I had to look at the entire world differently. A blond in leather pants caught my attention. Was she mortal or a Keeper? Agarthian or Olympian? Good or evil?

Dark magic. The words kept ringing in my mind. Was there dark magic at play in my mother's disappearance? Surely Millie would have mentioned it at the time if she'd suspected anything. It seemed like the kind of thing that should have been brought up sooner rather than later.

She brushed through the door of her shop and dashed straight past Sean, through the velvet curtain into the back of the building. Sean stopped what he was doing, looking from me to the curtain and back again.

"Did I miss something?" His features darkened and his muscles tensed. "Is it Abby? Did something happen? What's wrong?"

"Abby's fine." Or at least I thought she was fine. Was dark magic contagious? I shook the thought from my mind. "Millie's making a call to the council. She thinks she knows what's wrong with Mr. Mason."

"Well," Sean leaned against a bar stool in front of the old soda fountain counter. "Are you gonna tell me what it is?"

"Dark magic?" I sounded so unsure of myself. And by the look on Sean's face, he wasn't sure if he should believe it either.

He shook his head. "That doesn't make any sense. What kind of dark magic?"

"I have no idea. I was kind of hoping you might tell me what it is, I mean, aside from the obvious connotation. What does that look like among you all?"

Sean frowned. "Keepers don't practice dark magic."

"Then who—"

Millie shoved her way back through the curtain, wearing her black apron and smoothing the front of it nervously. She took a deep breath. "Okay, now where did we leave off? I suppose you should learn how to run a transaction, first. Then we can cover the basic sections of the store..."

"Uh-uh. Nope. She's talking about dark magic. What did you see, Millie?"

My aunt shot me a dirty look then turned to Sean. "You know I can't get into the details. It's against protocol. There may be some dark magic at play, but it has been reported and the council will take care of things from here."

"But how is he?" Sean pressed. "How's Abby? Do I need to go over there?"

Millie sighed. "Abby is fine. Mr. Mason will be fine, too. We just need to let the council do its job, and everything will work out." She dropped her chin and lowered her voice. "And I think you know it's best for you to stay away from there."

Sean groaned and began pacing, running a hand through his auburn hair. "I can't just sit here when I know they could be in danger."

"They're not in danger, Sean." She touched his arm, stilling him again as she continued. "You need to stay here. I spoke with your father and he agreed to give it high priority."

Sean was still scowling, but he didn't argue. Some quiet understanding passed between the two of them before Millie finally turned back to face me. "Come to the back with me. I'm sure you have some questions. Sean can manage the front a little longer while we chat." She shot a look in his direction that let him know the conversation was finished.

Well, that was one way to prevent him from leaving. He wouldn't make eye contact with me as I passed him on my way to the back with Millie. There was definitely more to this story. Hopefully I could get some details from my aunt.

At first glance, the area behind the curtain resembled any other employee storeroom. More glass bottles lined the walls here, and a table with two chairs sat in the middle of the room. Three lockers lined the back wall for purses and other personal items. But upon closer examination, it was clear that this was no ordinary break room.

A book shelf was packed to the brim with ancient looking tomes. Tattered spines boasted titles such as, "Bloodletting," "Materia Medica," and "Brewing with Belladonna." In the corner sat a four foot tall copper still that steadily dripped oil into a curved glass bottle.

Millie pulled out one of the chairs at the table and motioned for me to sit down while she scanned the bookshelf. "It is unlikely that you will take on powers like mine, but unfortunately, healing is all I know. Ah, there it is."

She pulled an especially thick textbook off of the shelf and blew dust from the top of its pages, then laid it on the table in front of me with a thud. "So while I can't teach you to diagnose illnesses at a glance or identify and erase certain sources of pain like I have the ability to do, I can give you some basics on herbal remedies."

"Wolfsbane, Mandrake, and Liverwort." I slid my fingers across the title as I read the words aloud. "*101 Effective Remedies from the Middle Ages.* I'm going to guess this wasn't one of your textbooks from college."

Millie laughed. "No, it wasn't. But the great thing about healing is that anyone can do it to some extent. You just need the right ingredients and a little know-how. So even if... even if healing is not your power, you'll at least have some understanding of our ancient knowledge as you enter the world as an adult."

What she'd wanted to say was that it would be helpful even if I never got any powers of my own, but neither of us wanted to discuss that now. Or ever. It wasn't exactly a favorite topic of mine.

"Thank you. I will definitely have a look."

"It's not very light reading, but I think you may find some parts interesting. And it's useful, nonetheless."

"I appreciate it. But what I'd really like to know is more about the dark magic you mentioned. I know you said you can't get into the details. I understand. But Sean said Keepers can't practice dark magic. So who, then, is making Mr. Mason ill?"

Millie steepled her fingers and her lips tensed, pursed and relaxed, opened and closed. But I wasn't in any hurry. I knew from one-too-many cop dramas on TV that I should let the quiet continue until it was uncomfortable. She'd talk eventually. And she did, after a minute or two of awkward silence.

"It's complicated."

"That's not a real answer. Who practices dark magic? Mortals? Or are there other supernaturals I haven't learned about yet?"

"Neither. It's... it's the fractured."

Oh. That's why she didn't want to say anything. She still thought I might be defective.

"Well, surely not all the fractured turn to dark magic, right? Is there like some secret coven or something?"

"They're not witches, Everly. Well, I take that back. They're not *all* witches. But by definition, any exertion of supernatural powers done outside of the council's knowledge is classified as dark magic. And the fractured are not governed by the council."

"Who are they governed by?"

Millie frowned. "No one. The fractured are supposed to be eradicated, and their souls preserved. That's what the hunters are for."

"But if one slips through the cracks, and they happen to '*exert a supernatural power*,' they're automatically assumed to be practicing dark magic? Even if said exertion is just, like, conjuring up some chocolate chip cookies or butterflies or something?"

"First of all, there is no power that allows for conjuring up cookies. And secondly, the power of a fractured soul is unpredictable at best, and often fatal. They can't control it, and with occasional surges that are beyond their natural abilities, it's not uncommon for a fractured soul to inadvertently kill themselves and every mortal around them."

"So you kill *them* instead?" I crossed my arms in front of me.

"I am a healer. I don't kill anyone. But the hunters—the Agarthians—they specialize in extracting fractured souls. They save them."

"Sounds like murder to me."

"I told you, it's complicated. But without the pureness of a Keeper's soul, the powers will usually... sour."

"Like spoiled milk?"

"It's not a great analogy, I know. But I'm not sure how else to explain it. I'll cut to the chase. Even if a fractured soul learns to wield their powers appropriately, the fact that their soul is incomplete is reason enough to remove them from the population. They turn, Everly. There is no goodness in a fractured soul, only greed and envy and joy from the pain of others. Fractured souls become evil."

She was pale, but she'd done it. She'd finally admitted the truth about me. It was why I was being guarded—she thought I might *sour*. It was why she was unconcerned about my mother. And it was exactly why I needed to get her back. My mother wouldn't do this to me. She just wouldn't. But without any powers to prove myself otherwise, I needed her to tell them the truth.

Millie might have thought my mother ran away from her problems when she became pregnant with me. And she probably thought my mother had done it again by disappearing again now. But I knew better. My mother didn't run away when things got hard. She was too careful, too caring, too full of love to risk having a fractured child. She wouldn't do that to the world, and she wouldn't do that to me.

My mother was still out there, somewhere. And I was going to find her.

CHAPTER 4

"MILLIE!" SEAN'S VOICE CALLED out from the other side of the curtain. "We've got a visitor."

She didn't get up right away, but instead stared at me for a long moment, as though she wanted to say more. But I was finished. I didn't care to hear Millie's theories on how I would soon turn evil and kill people with my broken powers and my fractured soul. I refused to believe it.

"Millie?" His voice was closer this time.

She stood abruptly. "Read the book," she said, tapping the dusty cover on the table. "When you're done, I have many more you can look through. And Everly..." The tension broke in her expression, and I saw the aunt I knew and loved, wrought with concern. "Hang in there. We don't know what the future holds."

She rushed out then, away from the unspoken words. The future we didn't want to face.

I followed her and felt the tingle across my skin before I made it to the other side of the curtain. And sure enough, as soon as the velvety green fabric brushed past my arms I saw him, grinning at the counter.

"Tate." I nodded and moved ahead, avoiding eye contact and pretending not to notice the way he made me lightheaded. I was uncertain if my reaction was one of fear or excitement.

"Everly." His voice was warm, and despite my best efforts, it drew my attention right back to his beautiful face. "Meet my friend, Osborne." And then I noticed his equally dangerous looking golden eyed friend.

I don't know if I was still recovering from the conversation I'd just had with Millie, or if the sight of Tate had me a little off-kilter, but something about the look of his friend Osborne took my breath away. Not in a love at first sight *"he's so dreamy,"* kind of way, but in an *"oh my stars I think he wants me dead,"* kind of way. I was terrified.

I grabbed the edge of the counter, trying not to panic as I scanned the shelves for a paper bag to breathe into. I was losing it and everyone was watching me spiral.

"Are you okay?" Sean whispered. He turned his body so that he was blocking my view of the others.

I nodded, but it still took me a few seconds before I could think clearly enough again to speak. I was vaguely aware of Millie's voice behind him, describing Mr. Mason's symptoms. They weren't here for me.

"Hunters," I whispered to Sean.

He nodded. "Yeah, they were sent by the council. They're here to investigate the dark magic Millie reported."

"She just called like twenty minutes ago."

"Keepers act quickly."

I peeked around the side of Sean's head and locked eyes with Osborne. It was brief, but it was enough to feel like I got the wind knocked out of me again. I felt like I was going to be sick. "I need some air."

Sean looked over his shoulder. "Hey Millie, you good here?"

A look of irritation flitted across her petite features. Sean had interrupted her. "Yeah, sure." She waved him off and got back to the conversation.

Sean untied his apron and tossed it on the counter. "Let's go."

I wouldn't argue with that. I grabbed the giant textbook Millie had given me and followed Sean out of the shop, careful to keep him between me and Osborne. I turned around to get one more quick glance as we slipped through the front door, but Osborne was engaged with Millie, listening intently to her recount of the afternoon. It was Tate who watched us leave, his expression indiscernible.

I smoothed the hairs on my arms and turned my back on them, anxious to get out into the open air.

"Are you sure you're okay?" Sean asked once we were out on the sidewalk.

"I think so, it's just... the hunters. Something in my subconscious knows they're after me I think. It's instant fight-or-flight syndrome when I see them, you know? And that buzzy-tingle they give me?" I shuddered. "I just don't like it."

"*Buzzy tingle?*" Sean looked perplexed.

"Yeah, that feeling of being hunted."

"Hmmm," Sean twisted his mouth to one side. "I'm not familiar. I've never felt any kind of 'buzzy-tingle.' Then again, I've never been hunted."

Interesting. So the feeling was definitely not associated with my powers coming in. I hadn't wanted to admit it out loud, but I sort of hoped it was the beginning of my transition—like maybe my body was saying, "*Nope, can't hunt me. See? Powers...*"

"So this hunter—Osborne, he was sent by the council to investigate the dark magic Millie reported?"

"Yep. This is one area where the different races work together. No matter who reports the dark magic, an Agarthian hunter is assigned to the case. Did Millie, uh, give you any specifics on how dark magic works?"

"Yes. She told me it's done by fractured souls."

"Right." Sean shrugged, uncomfortable and uncertain of what to say. I guess my tense shoulders were a dead giveaway that I didn't like this topic very much.

"And you're positive that Osborne is only here for the case Millie reported? He can't hunt anyone else?"

"I don't think so. That's not how it works. One hunter per soul—otherwise things get messy."

I didn't want to ask what messy looked like. "So why is Tate with him then? If only Osborne can hunt the suspect performing the magic on Mr. Mason, Tate shouldn't have anything to do with it."

"Thaddeus is assigned to you. Like I said, things can get messy when multiple hunters are involved. He'll have to accompany Osborne in this case to ensure lines aren't being crossed."

That wasn't all. I knew there had to be more to it. The pained expression on Sean's face was enough for me to know he wasn't telling me everything he knew.

Suddenly I understood. I stopped on the sidewalk and narrowed my eyes at Sean. "You know I have nothing to do with this, right?"

He grimaced. "Of course I know that. But the Agarthians— well they don't leave anything to chance. Thaddeus has to tag along with Osborne just in case they narrow the suspect down to you. In that case, the job will be handed back to Thaddeus."

No wonder Osborne was looking at me like that. I was a suspect in his case. I shivered again, recalling the feeling I got from Osborne's death stare and continued walking.

"There just aren't many fractured souls around here. They're usually caught early on," Sean muttered. He wasn't helping.

But there was another question bouncing around deep in the recesses of my mind, as well. A loophole of sorts, and one that would make me appear even more guilty if anyone found out. Millie mentioned that any powers or magic practiced outside of the council's knowledge were considered dark. But I also happened to remember that hunters could only hunt fractured souls. So what happened if a *mortal* soul practiced magic? Was it even possible?

The weight of Millie's book under my arm was suddenly much heavier. If I could learn to heal, would it be possible for me to learn other spells as well? Because if there were some sort of tracking spell or truth serum or anything I could use to find my mom, I wouldn't hesitate to do it. The question was whether these things were real or if my imagination was simply getting away from me. I'd read about too many other imaginary witches and wizards growing up.

But this wasn't fiction. This was real life. Real power. I could only hope that using it wouldn't be enough cause for Tate to pull the proverbial trigger.

CHAPTER 5

"THANKS FOR GETTING ME out of there." We paused in front of my aunt's doorstep. Her giant mastiffs whined on the other side, impatient for the attention they knew I'd give them when I came in.

"You got it," Sean replied. "Are you going to meet up at Gayla and Dom's place later? We're ordering pizza."

"Yeah, that's what they said. It sounds fun."

"Cool. I'll meet you here around six and we can walk over."

I said goodbye and pulled open Millie's front door, bracing myself for impact from the oversized canines inside. "Hey, Lemon Drop. Tiny, you enormous lovable goofball." I scratched their heads and pushed my way further into the foyer. "I'm home!" I called out toward the kitchen. I didn't know if Jeeves was home, but if so I knew he'd be in there chatting it up with Millie's chef.

"Hey Ev," he popped his head around the corner a moment later. "Pierre just made lunch. Want me to fix you a plate?"

"No, thanks." I held up the text book my aunt gave me. "I'm gonna go upstairs and get in some reading. Millie wants me to study up so I can help her at the shop."

"Alright," he said in his thick Alabaman drawl. "Holler if you get hungry!"

I bounced up two flights of stairs to Millie's study on the third floor. Gorgeous bay windows overlooked the street below, and Millie's desk sat in the center of the room on a plush, fuzzy cream colored rug. The shelves were full of eccentric tchotchkes, scattered among more ancient looking books like the one under my arm. I pulled out the desk chair and laid my textbook down, but I wanted to explore a bit before I sat to read it.

Once I'd wrapped my brain around the idea of looking for magic, I couldn't shake it. I had about four hours before Millie would return from the apothecary. Surely I'd be able to find something useful before then.

I ran my finger along the spines of the books lining the walls. There must have been hundreds, maybe thousands. And they didn't appear to be organized in any sort of recognizable fashion. If only she had some kind of digital card catalog. Or better yet—an encyclopedia of magic, where I could search by topic. First things first, I needed to know if it was possible for mortals to practice magic. Because as of now, I was still a mortal.

But there was nothing magical about any of the books in Millie's office. This was where she kept her actual textbooks from school. The older books were a mix of biographies and medieval history books. One shelf dedicated to Greek mythology looked promising, but upon closer inspection the titles all seemed to be mainstream books published in the last twenty years or so. Modern display copies Homer's Iliad and Odyssey were about the most interesting things on the shelves. She also seemed to have a slight addiction to dime store romances, but hunky Scotsman weren't going to help my current situation.

Of course she wouldn't keep books about magic hidden out in the open here. Jeeves, and Pierre, and her little housemaid had no idea what Millie really was. Even Abby didn't know, and she worked around all the strange objects at the apothecary every day. They probably all assumed my aunt was just into some quirky kind of witchcraft or something.

I considered calling it quits and heading back downstairs to eat lunch, but my stomach was still a little unsettled from the morning's events. So I plopped myself down into Millie's office chair and stared at the book. I swiveled the chair back and forth, looking at the title until my vision doubled.

I didn't want to read about herbs. I wanted my mom back! With my head thrown back, I spun the chair in a full circle, watching the light fixture twirl overhead. My foot pushed against the fluffy carpet, spinning me harder and faster until the room blurred around me.

A man cleared his voice from the doorway. "Ahem."

I stopped the chair, wobbling slightly as I waited for my dizziness to dissipate and my vision to clear. But Jeeves' massive form was hard to mistake for anyone else.

"Looks like you've really got your nose in the books in here." He laughed and brought a platter to the desk. It was a tiny charcuterie board, decked out with cured meats and fruits and cheeses with names I couldn't pronounce. "I thought I'd bring you a study snack."

"Aww, thanks, Jeeves."

"Don't thank me. It was all Pierre. I'd have brought you some Vienna Sausages and Kraft Singles, but he's got better taste than that. Whatcha reading? Or not reading?"

I slid the book in front of him.

"*101 Effective Remedies from the Middle Ages*. Sounds fascinating." He winked. "Anyhow. I'll let you get back to it. Come on down if you need a break. We're doing a self-clean cycle on the oven this afternoon." He waggled his brows and stole a small block of cheese from my plate.

"I think I'll stick to my reading here, thanks."

"Suit yourself!" He grinned and ducked back out of the office, leaving me alone with my thoughts and a very expensive snack board. Before long, the board was half empty and I still hadn't opened the book.

I rubbed my eyes with the heels of my hands and groaned. There was no use wasting time. If I wasn't going to read it, then I may as well make myself useful and head over to Gayla and Dom's apartment. Maybe I could help them set up for games and dinner.

With the textbook under one arm and the board balanced in my other hand, I snuck back down the stairs, put the half-eaten platter on a table in the foyer, and slipped out of the front door before the dogs could hear me tiptoeing around. If Jeeves and Pierre heard me leave without Sean there to guard me, I'd be in big trouble. But the girls' apartment was only a short walk away. And I was a grown woman. I didn't need a babysitter.

Life in Manhattan carried on as normal around me. People crowded the streets, talking on phones or blocking everyone out with earbuds. A mother ran past with a jogging stroller, headed for Central Park. *That was a good idea.* It would be safer to cut through the park toward my friends' apartment. That way if Millie happened to leave work early, she wouldn't see me.

I trotted along after her, inhaling the fresher air of the trees once I turned the corner into the park. Maybe one of the girls would know a thing or two about mortals performing magic. Could I trust them to keep it a secret, though? And did I dare risk them? If I didn't involve them, I could still plead ignorance if I got caught. After all, no one had given me any specific rules regarding magic—I'd only learned of it today. But if I got Gayla and Dom involved, we could all be punished.

The thought sent a shiver down my spine. I felt like I was in trouble already, and I hadn't even decided to do anything yet. I glanced around, worried suddenly that some passer-by may actually be telepathic like Dom. I felt... exposed.

Then I saw the eyes, gold and glowing like some nocturnal animal in the shadows, waiting for its prey, and I realized I *was* exposed. But these weren't animal eyes. They were human. No, not human either—Agarthian.

Osborne stepped out of the shadows of a large tree and crossed his arms. I didn't get my buzzy-tingle of a warning that I was being hunted, which made it all the more unsettling. I liked the warning.

After a quick scan of the horizon, I realized he was alone. Tate wasn't with him, but I didn't know if that left me feeling better or more concerned for my safety. At least Tate was a known enemy. I knew what to expect and I could handle him. Osborne was a wild card.

He watched me pass him by, staring blatantly. I gripped the book tighter under my arm and picked up my pace. I wasn't interested in hanging out alone in a park with a known hunter. He didn't follow me, thankfully. Instead he just stood in the center of the sidewalk, his eyes on my back until I finally disappeared around a curve. Out of his sight, I broke out into a dead sprint.

If he wanted to stop me, he would have. I had no doubt about that. But it didn't seem to be the case. He'd just wanted to intimidate me—let me know he was watching. Jerk.

I was gasping for air by the time I reached Gayla and Dom's place. My sweaty palms gripped the textbook under one arm, and my bag with the tablet on the other. I gave them two knocks before opening the door and quickly closing it again behind me. I didn't want to risk Osborne following me here. He wasn't welcome.

"Everly, hey. You look like a hot mess." Gayla jerked her head up from her cozy spot on the couch, a fashion magazine sprawled out across her tan legs.

"I am a hot mess." A quick scan of the living room showed no signs of Dom. It was a good thing, because I had no idea what kind of craziness she might pick up in my mind right now. My thoughts were spinning out of control.

"Hey—" I started to ask Gayla about magic, but seeing her happy, innocent dark eyes smiling back at me, I just couldn't do it. I didn't want to get my new friends in trouble. Switching gears, I continued. "Millie gave me some reading materials to study up on for my work at her shop. Do you mind if I hang out here and look through it? I can't focus back at her place."

"Of course!" Gayla sprang up from the couch. She wasn't the most observant person, which was ironic considering how she was supposedly a seer. But I was grateful in that moment. I didn't want to explain what just happened or why I was all out of breath. "You know we've already got a bedroom for you all set up."

It was true. They'd insisted on getting a three bedroom apartment, even knowing that I was going to NYU. Gayla seemed so sure that I'd change my mind and join them at Columbia. Like I said—not super observant. But her intentions were kind. She'd decked the room out with comfortable furnishings and a neat little white desk propped against the wall near the window.

I placed my book on the desk's glossy surface, and stared out onto the street below. My little white owl friend sat perched on a wrought iron railing of a second story balcony across the street. From here, it almost looked like he was watching me through the window with those wise old eyes of his. I gave him a nod, and immediately felt silly for it. But at this point, we were practically besties. He was always there.

And somehow, he helped to calm my nerves. At long last, I sank into the office chair and flipped open the book. It was time to learn a thing or two about natural herbal remedies.

CHAPTER 6

MILLIE'S BOOK WAS SURPRISINGLY full of fascinating facts. It might just come in useful one day after all. Like if I ever came across some Verbena I could fix gingivitis and anxiety... or I could make a man impotent for six days. And if I ever got a hold of Henbane, I could deprive a witch of her powers or mix it with menstrual blood to create a love potion.

Okay, so maybe the information was more entertaining than actually useful, but it had me captivated. Time flew by as I flipped through the pages, committing each page to memory. In any case, I'd be ready to help Millie at the shop, no matter what a customer may need.

About three quarters of the way through the book, I'd finished learning about the different herbs and their qualities, and stumbled into a section on elixirs. Millie's elegant penmanship looped its way across a tattered yellow piece of parchment, singed on one edge. The page was tucked into the fold of the book, and it looked like it may have been a hundred years old. It said:

Incantation for elixirs: De laqueo venantium, et os ad vitae ius et consumat te

My breath quickened. This was it. Magic. I'd found a spell. It had to be! But could it work for mortals? There was only one way to find out.

An introduction to the chapter described folklore and gave a strong disclaimer that most if not all of the following elixirs are unproven to work. *Ha! Yeah, right.* Millie wouldn't give me a book full of useless information. I bet they'd all work just fine with the addition of that incantation. I began flipping through the pages of elixirs that followed, looking for one that I could practice.

Knock, knock, knock. Someone pounded at my door. Suddenly feeling guilty, I slammed the book shut at exactly the same time Sean burst into the room.

"Everly Gordon, you are in big trouble!"

I raised my brows. I probably was in trouble, but I wasn't about to let Sean talk to me that way. "Excuse me?"

"You left! And you didn't tell anyone you were leaving. Millie was in a full panic when she got home from work. Jeeves never saw you leave, so she called me right away."

"And what did you tell her?"

"I told her we were here. Then I ran straight over and prayed I wasn't lying."

"Lucky for you I'm here, then."

"I don't think it's funny." His jaw clenched. "I know you don't like having me around, but if I fail at this simple job, there is no way my father is going to allow me to graduate to bigger missions. Please, Everly. Don't run off. For my sake, if not your own."

My smirk melted away. "I'm sorry. Really. I didn't think about it affecting you, I just wanted to get out. Tate's little hunter friend had me all shook up earlier."

"Tate's got a friend?"

I turned to see Gayla grinning from the doorway. "Trust me," I said. "It's no one you want to know." I shuddered.

Gayla shrugged. "You're probably right. Those hunters are usually too arrogant for my taste."

Isn't that the truth...

"Are you ready to take a break? Dom will be back any minute with the pizza."

I noticed the daylight fading through the window. I'd been cooped up in here reading for way longer than I'd realized. And yet, I was just getting to the good stuff. My gaze lingered on the book for another moment. I didn't want to stop now.

"Come on. School hasn't even started yet and you've already got your nose buried in books. Live a little." She tugged on my arm and I reluctantly fell into place behind her, following her into the living room. A couple of decks of cards were set out on the small dining table and music was playing from a speaker in the corner. Dom entered just moments later, carrying two of the biggest pizza boxes I'd ever seen.

The next couple of hours almost helped me forget the drama from the morning. Sean was way too competitive for his teammate, Gayla, during our game of Spades. Though I couldn't blame him for getting grumpy—I had a literal mind reader for my partner. We wiped the table with them. Otherwise, it was a normal, enjoyable evening. But I never could quite clear the thoughts nagging at the back of my brain.

Dom studied me once or twice, trying to figure out what was bothering me, but I don't think she was ever successful. I made it a point to keep those thoughts pushed down while I focused on cards and how the others all ate their pizza in a weird New York way, folded up like a taco. I tried to act normal. I was doing a good job of it too, until they started talking about school.

"Most of my classes are first thing in the morning. That way I have the whole day free to do anything I please." Dom grinned proudly. She was definitely the most responsible one in the room.

"Argh. I had to schedule early classes, too. Rossel wants me at his studio every day after lunch for my training sessions." Gayla groaned. "I don't know why they're making me go to school at all. We all know where I'm going to end up. Oh, sorry Ev."

She frowned in my direction. I really needed to work on not getting so upset at the mention of Rossel. I'd dragged Gayla and Dom back to the gallery as soon as we got back into the city the day after Gayla's big party on the yacht, but it had changed. The portrait of me that once hung on the wall inside was now replaced with an oil painted scene of a lavender field in France. The windows were all fixed, and the metal sign out front was replaced with a whitewashed wooden one that said *Roselina and Jude*.

"I swear it said Rossel!" I had exclaimed. "Tell them Sean! You saw it, too."

"I believe you," Dom had said.

But it didn't matter. Rossel denied everything when Gayla pressed him on it. I asked her not to push too hard, given his warning at our last encounter. *"Stay away from Gayla."* He sure wouldn't be happy to know that she had set up an entire bedroom for me in her apartment. Then again, I honestly couldn't care less about what Rossel thought of me. I knew he wouldn't hurt Gayla, and with Sean at my side and Tate in my shadow at all times, I didn't think he'd be able to do anything to me, either.

I guess that was one good thing about being stalked by a hunter.

"It's fine," I said to Gayla. "We'll get to the bottom of it whether Rossel decides to help us or not." Even if that meant I'd have to play with magic to find my mom.

Dom quirked a brow at me, and I quickly changed the subject back to their classes. "What about you, Sean? Are you going to be busy in the mornings, too?"

"Well, I was kind of hoping you'd get your schedule figured out soon so I could set mine. I'm supposed to stay with you on campus, remember?"

Right. I felt a pang of guilt again. Poor Sean. This couldn't be any easier on him than it was on me. He'd basically be attending both NYU and Columbia, between his schedule and mine.

"Since I haven't picked my classes yet, maybe you can help me decide." I smiled, trying to make him feel a little better about it. "Would you rather me take morning classes or afternoon?"

"I guess it doesn't matter much." He shrugged. "As long as the evenings are clear."

"Why do you need your evenings clear?" Gayla asked. "Are you getting a human job somewhere?"

"No, I just told Abby I'd be around if she needed anything."

Gayla's shoulders slumped, and Dom pressed her lips together. Things always got awkward around here when Abby entered the chat.

"Oh," was all Gayla could say.

Sean ran a hand through his hair, and his green eyes glistened as he spoke of her. "Things have just been really weird since her dad got sick. It's like they got this giant inheritance from his aunt and then he fell into his deathbed, almost like it was the wealth that made him sick. Every day I wonder if it'll be his last, and it's really hard on Abby."

"Well at least she'll be rich if he dies." Jealousy wasn't a good look for Gayla. Dom cringed, but Sean didn't seem to notice. His head was in the clouds.

"I normally am not a fan of the hunters, but in this case, I'm cheering them on. No one should be practicing magic. That kind of power belongs to Keepers and Keepers alone."

I gulped.

"Someone out there has enchanted the cash. That's what I think anyway. It's probably how his aunt Linda died, too. But I refuse to let it get to Abby." He banged his fist on the table, causing the rest of us to jump in our seats.

Sean was livid, understandably. And I was sick with guilt. Dark magic was taking the lives of people he really cared about. Was that something I should meddle with?

Dom glanced at me again, curiosity evident in her dark eyes. I stood, abruptly. "Well, it's getting late. I should probably get to bed."

"It's only 10:30," Gayla said.

"Yeah, I should have taken my vitamins half an hour ago. Sean, do you mind walking me home?"

"Sure," he muttered.

I retreated back to my room and grabbed the book before giving a hasty goodbye and bolting out the door as quickly as I could. My mind was racing with thoughts of magic and murder. I knew the risks, and yet, it was so tempting. If I could find the right elixir, maybe something to force the truth out of someone, I could get Rossel to talk and find my mom.

That kind of magic wasn't *really* dark, was it?

CHAPTER 7

ABBY RETURNED TO WORK the next day, slightly ragged and obviously exhausted. This situation with her dad really seemed to be taking a toll on her. She pulled her unwashed hair back into a messy bun on top of her head and slumped forward onto the countertop.

Sean hovered around her like a helicopter mom, fussing over every sigh and stumble she made. He was concerned the dark magic was getting to her, too. It wasn't though.

Abby was down, but she wasn't sick. She was dealing with grief. I knew the look well. It was the same look my mother used to get—a distant emptiness in her eyes, a hollow expression, an empty well of tears—whenever I asked about my father. Abby was slowly coming to grips with the fact that her father was probably going to die.

I didn't blame her for losing hope. I know that sounds harsh, but in a way, it seemed that if she could process some of her grief while he was still here, maybe it wouldn't be so bad when he finally did pass. My mother lost a piece of herself when my dad left, and that hole of despair haunted her throughout my entire childhood. Maybe if she'd seen it coming, like Abby could see the loss coming with her dad, it wouldn't have lingered. But no, my dad was a deadbeat who blindsided her by leaving when she needed him most.

"Sean, come here." I tossed him a rag and a bottle of furniture polish. Abby tended the counter while Millie rearranged supplies and over stock in the back room. I had been dusting shelves and straightening bottles, trying to learn where everything was in case I needed to fill in for Abby soon. But she needed a break from Sean. I would, if I were her, anyway.

With a pained expression, he finally pulled his eyes away from the poor girl and joined me near the front of the store.

"You've gotta let her breathe."

"I know." He shook his head. "I just don't want to miss anything, you know? If this fractured loser decides to go after Abby too, I want to spot the signs right away. Maybe if we catch it early, we can help her."

"She's going to be fine. She's just dealing with some stuff right now."

The door chimed, and a familiar face entered the shop. It was the same customer from the day before.

"Back so soon?" I asked.

Sean nudged me in the ribs and took over. "Welcome back to the apothecary, sir. Is there anything we can help you find?"

He smiled, the same wide grin I'd noticed the day before. This guy sure was cheerful. "I just need to grab a few more items. I think I know where they are."

"Great," Sean smiled back. "Let me know if you need any assistance."

His smile faded quickly as he turned back to me. I pointed to a dusty spot he missed and moved to the next section of shelves. Abby still leaned vacantly against the counter while the customer browsed some shelves on the other side of the store. He cast a glance over his shoulder, and upon meeting my eyes, flashed that broad smile again.

"Why are you so taken with Abby, anyway? You know you can't be with a mortal."

"Shh," Sean quieted me with a glare. "I know," he whispered. "But that doesn't mean I can't care for her wellbeing."

"I think you care for more than just her wellbeing." I raised my brows. "What about Gayla? Do you, uh, care for *her* wellbeing, too?"

Sean snorted. "I did, once. When we were younger. But time changes people." He shook his head. "It wouldn't matter anyway. I can't be with an Olympian any more than I can be with a mortal."

"What?" This was news to me. "Why not?"

"Our souls, Everly. It's like we explained that night at your aunt's house. We have soul mates, always within our own race. It's the only way our kind can survive. New souls are not simply created out of thin air. If we don't mate and have pure children, there aren't vessels for the old Atlantean souls to enter and return to the earth."

"But one Keeper is as good as another, right? It's not like the souls would be fractured."

Sean let out an exasperated sigh. "It can't happen. It's just a fact of life. There's a curse. If any two Keepers from different races seal a bond, *if you catch my drift*, they die."

"So you're telling me if you so much as hook up with Gayla, you'll both die? Like get struck down by lightning or what?"

He shrugged. "Possibly. The curse doesn't specify how you'll die, only that you will. Sometimes you just quit breathing, sometimes nature intervenes and does the job for you, or sometimes you're driven to insanity and take your own life. Like Romeo and Juliet."

"I hate it when people romanticize death."

"She was Atlantean, he was Agarthian."

I laughed. "You're kidding, right?"

"They knew better. Their families tried to warn them, but they didn't listen. So the fates did what had to be done."

"And Shakespeare just happened to be around, taking notes of everything?"

"I think he saw it in a vision, like all his other plays. He was Olympian, you know. Brilliant mind, that one."

Huh. If what Sean said was true, then the Keeper way of life was sounding less and less appealing. And I felt bad for poor Gayla. She was obviously smitten with Sean, but she could never have him. Just like how she had no say in her job, or where she went to school. She might be loaded to the gills with cash, but as they say, money can't buy happiness. In her case, it seemed like a fact.

Mr. Smiley cleared his throat at the counter, trying to get Abby's attention. She'd been staring off into nothing, but turned abruptly at the sound. He didn't seem upset at all, though. He simply grinned.

"Did you find everything you were looking for?" she asked.

"Just about. Is the shop owner here, today?"

Abby nodded. "I think she's still here, somewhere in the back. Want me to get her for you?"

The man shook his head. "Oh no, not if she's busy." He smiled again. It was getting old. No one was that happy. Something seemed off about this guy. I set down my rag and moved to join them at the counter.

"Oh!" the man put a finger in the air like he'd just had a brilliant idea. "I almost forgot. I do need a little Monkshood."

Monkshood. Why was that ringing alarm bells? My mind flashed back to the page I'd read in Millie's book. I remembered the big red letters that said TOXIC. Monkshood, also known as Aconite, was a well-known poison.

"Sure," Abby said, reaching for a key to the locked cabinet behind the counter. The man cut his eyes over to the curtain and back to Abby. He looked impatient.

"What are you using the Monkshood for?" I asked.

I tried to keep my tone light, but he clearly heard the accusation I implied. His smile faltered as he turned and raised his chin. "Lotion. My girlfriend has fibromyalgia, and the only thing we've been able to find to help with her nerve pain is this lotion we make from the powder."

Hmm. In small, controlled doses, I knew it could help with neuralgia. That's what I got from overloading on information. My mom used to joke that I would binge on one topic until I thought I was an expert. But with medicine, most everything was okay in moderation. His story checked out, and I needed to stop jumping to worst case scenarios...

Even if he did seem a little suspicious with his too-happy grins and anxious glances at the curtain.

Abby measured out the amount he requested and totaled up his purchase for the day. He tossed in another black licorice stick for good measure, and placed his messenger bag on the counter to retrieve his wallet. When he unclasped the bag, I noticed a bright blue and yellow folder sitting inside.

An amateurish logo flashed through my memories. *D&N Investments, The Opportunity of a Lifetime.*

"What did you say your name was?" I asked.

"David." He grinned and accepted the receipt from Abby. "Thanks again." With one more furtive glance toward the back room, he casually waved over his shoulder as he hurried out of the shop.

"Do you know that guy?" I set my gaze on Abby as the door swung shut behind him.

"Just from the shop. Why?"

"I think he may be friends with your housekeeper."

"I doubt it," she said. "Nikki just moved here last month and she's terrified of street crime. I don't think she gets out much."

Sean raised his brows at me, but I shook him off. Maybe I was jumping to conclusions again. I didn't know if it was the same folder in Mr. Smiley's bag or not. But I would definitely do some investment research later, just to ease my suspicions.

CHAPTER 8

GAYLA AND DOM WERE waiting for me near the Columbia gates on 116th after lunch. I approached them, warily eyeing the Greek-looking statue that stood to the right of the entrance.

"Hey girl," Gayla grinned as I approached, then followed my gaze to the statue.

The towering stone woman wore long robes and held a book open in front of her, showing the world pages that I couldn't quite make out. I shielded the sun from my eyes and squinted to get a better look.

"It's Latin," Dom said.

"What does it mean?"

Gayla shrugged. "Probably nothing. But who cares? I'd rather check out the hottie across the street."

I followed her to the statue on the opposite side of the gates. A similarly dressed man stood in robes that hung open to expose an attractively chiseled chest. "He does have rock hard abs," I said.

Gayla giggled. "Come on. There are way more interesting things to see inside."

I followed the girls through the gates and immediately felt like I was leaving New York city and stepping onto the set of a movie. It was the quintessential college experience, and as devoted to NYU as I was, I couldn't help the flutter of excitement I felt as we made our way down the tree covered path into campus.

I'd been reluctant to accept the girls' offer for a tour of Columbia, but since we were here, I figured I'd make the best of it. So I truly listened as Dom gabbed on about the history of the campus and its ties to the

Keepers. And Gayla was sure to point out all the best study spots, coffee shops, and where to find the hottest guys.

"Over there is where the lacrosse team hangs out," she said with a mischievous glint in her eyes.

"In other words, that's probably where you'll find Gayla most afternoons," Dom said with a laugh.

"I can't help it if the sun's rays are brighter on the Low steps. I've gotta get my vitamin D somehow," she winked.

"Speaking of the Low Library," Dom gestured ahead, "do you know the story behind Alma Mater?"

"She's the mother of knowledge, right?" We all turned to admire the giant statue standing guard at the front of a very Grecian looking library.

"Sort of. So Columbia was actually called King's College when it was founded by the Olympians shortly after coming to America."

"It was an Olympian college?"

"Yes and no. They never intended for it to be exclusive, but King Baerius thought it would be useful to educate the Keepers on our history. Mortals were admitted as well, though for different subjects, and eventually the name was changed to Columbia to be less auspicious. But he commissioned the statue of Alma Mater to sit here on the steps as a reminder to us all that the university is rooted in Keeper history."

I stepped closer to the intricate statue, admiring the details and taking in the woman's beautiful face.

"See the crown of laurels on her head? It represents fame, or notoriety. Influence. It's a nod to the Agarthians. The lamps on the arms of her chair represent wisdom and teaching, a nod to the Olympians. And the scepter is made of four heads of wheat—one for each Keeper race and one for the mortals, but it's topped by a crown. The crown is the symbol of all Keepers —a reminder that we are to work together to rule over the mortals and keep balance on the earth."

"What about the Atlanteans?" I asked. "Do they get a nod as well?"

Gayla laughed. "Alma Mater herself is Atlantean! The Keeper of the people. Do you see how she welcomes the human students in with open arms? Atlanteans have always been closest to the mortals. They lived and worked alongside them until Atlantis was sunk. But even now you'll find them walking the face of the earth more than the other Keepers."

"Hang on." I put my hands on my hips and turned to face the girls. "Where are the other Keepers, if not 'walking the face of the earth?'"

"Olympus is known as the city in the sky, and Agartha is at the core of the earth."

Now it was my turn to laugh. Gayla giggled, too, but I had a feeling she was laughing at me, not with me.

Dom frowned. "You don't believe me."

"I mean, I believe in science. And unless Tate lives in the molten rock core of the earth and 'city in the sky' is a poetic way of saying the Olympians live on mountains or something..." I shrugged. "It's not possible."

"You'd be surprised at what's really possible."

I looked at the statue again. This world, this history they spoke of was almost too much to take in at times. The bronze woman's expression seemed to echo my thoughts. She was graceful and strong, the epitome of truth and knowledge, and yet, it almost looked as though the weight of it all—the secrets behind her wise eyes— were burdensome.

Gayla turned back toward the lawn. "Let's go get some coffee. I heard they've got a back to school special at The Honey Pot— iced caramel lattes with an ambrosia flavored drizzle." She rubbed her hands together.

"Wait." Something else caught my eye, tucked away into the folds of the statue's robes. "Is... is that an owl?"

Dom smiled brightly. "It sure is. The mascot of Athena and messenger of the Keepers. Well done, young grasshopper. According to the mortals, the first freshman to find the owl will become the valedictorian of her class. Too bad you're going to NYU."

I put up my hand. "Rewind that back. Owls are messengers of the Keepers? Does that mean you all see them more often than mortals? Do you communicate with them?"

My mind flashed back to my many run-ins with little owl friends since I first arrived in New York. Each time, whoever I was with became very interested in whether or not I was communicating with the creatures. I'd shrugged it off before, but now... if it might be a sign that I actually was one of them...

"No." Dom shot my wishful thinking to bits. "Before modern technology, the owls were used to help the races communicate with each other. They would deliver messages to and from Olympus, since the other races weren't able to get up there. Atlantean messengers, those with extreme speed or the ability to teleport between locations would complete the delivery back on earth."

"Ah, so they were little mailmen. But no one could actually communicate with them?"

"Only Athena. It's said she could speak with the owls, that they were her eyes and ears where she could not go."

"Interesting."

"Why do you ask?" Gayla turned her attention back to us.

Dom stilled as well, appraising me. I tried to shake the thoughts free from my mind and shrugged. "Just wondering." I wasn't about to divulge my recent interactions with the creatures. It's not like they were communicating with me. It was probably all a coincidence. Just wishful thinking—hoping it might have more significant meaning.

"So about those lattes?" Gayla raised her brows.

"Let's get some." I fell into step behind her, thankful for the change in subject and Gayla's lighthearted willingness to move on and drop it. I wasn't sure if Dom dropped her curiosity quite as quickly, though. I swear I felt her eyes on me as we made our way through the lush green trees and down the path that would take us back out into Morningside Heights. How much had she heard in my thoughts? Would she be willing to drop it, too?

My question was answered a moment later as Dom persisted, continuing to talk up the wonders of Columbia. Her sales pitch grew stronger by the minute, and she watched my reactions closely. She was determined to get me there with them.

"You know," she said at last. "You seem to have lots of questions about Keeper history. There's truly no other school you can attend that will offer as much information about your background as Columbia. I know you're set on NYU, but our Ancient Histories program would probably help you understand a lot more about who we are and what our purpose is."

"Even I'll admit that our history is pretty interesting. There are scandals that would blow your mind!" Gayla grinned.

"And there's an Atlantean professor who specializes in ancient languages."

I paused, my hand subconsciously finding its way to my bag, where the tablet rested under my arm. "Do you think…"

I didn't have to finish my sentence. Dom knew exactly what I was thinking. She suppressed a grin and shrugged, shoving her hands into the pockets of her denim shorts. "Maybe you should enroll and find out." She winked and walked on ahead, following Gayla out onto the busy street ahead.

"You know what? I think I'm gonna head back to my aunt's house. You guys go ahead and get that coffee without me. I've got some things to think about."

CHAPTER 9

THOUGH SOME MIGHT CALL me stubborn, I liked to think I was sensible. In fact, I prided myself on a strong sense of individualism. I was never one to succumb to peer pressure, and I wasn't about to start now.

Even if Columbia did offer a warm feeling and a sense of home. Even if I was intrigued by the programs it offered— the ancient languages and opportunities of an environment steeped in history. The professors and Keeper classmates could be a real benefit if I eventually found some powers of my own. Or they could be a real detriment if it turned out I was just a mortal. Or worse—*fractured*.

But no, I wouldn't think about that now. I couldn't allow myself to think that I might be fractured or it would mean the textbook sitting at home was my gateway drug to dark magic. And I wouldn't go to the dark side, just like I wouldn't allow myself to be pressured into attending a university I never had any previous interest in.

I didn't have to go to Columbia to work with the professor on languages. Perhaps I could meet with him after hours to learn more about the symbols on my tablet. I would attend NYU. I'd find my mom, ensure her safety, and carry on with life as normal. It sounded like a fine plan to me.

Except, life could never be normal again.

As if the fates were really trying to drive that point home, I stopped to watch my snowy white owl friend flutter down to a street sign up ahead on the corner. I paused, looking to see if anyone else noticed the out of place creature, but my fellow New Yorkers were all too busy to care.

I tilted my head at the bird, it's sentient yellow eyes watching my every move. "I didn't tell them about you. They would have thought I was nuts."

It blinked, seemingly understanding my words.

"Are the legends true? Are you just an old mailman?"

The creature blinked again and I chuckled, enjoying what seemed like an inside joke we shared. "They don't know what they're talking about, do they?"

A woman walking down the sidewalk gripped her purse tighter and cast a wary glance in my direction as she picked up her pace and scurried away from me. "You know you're making me look like a weirdo talking to myself on a street corner." I swear the owl winked at me before turning its head down the street to my left and returning its wide eyes to mine. Then it flapped its wings, lifting two or three feet into the air and bobbing expectantly, never once moving its eyes away from mine.

I looked around again. Surely I was imagining this, right? Why wasn't anyone else staring in wonder at this beautiful, intelligent creature? In the back of my mind, somehow, I knew. It was here for me. The owl flapped ahead, flying twenty feet forward to another perch on a corner window in front of me.

With one more glance over my shoulder, I trotted after it. As I approached the creature, it lifted off again, hovering once more to ensure I was paying attention, then it flew another ten or fifteen yards ahead. We played this game of cat and mouse—or mortal and owl—for a bit, until the bird bobbed its head and turned to look down a shady alleyway.

We were several blocks from campus now, in an area I wasn't familiar with. But I'd seen enough TV shows to know I shouldn't go traipsing down alleyways. I'd either find singing cartoon cats banging on metal trash cans like drums, or more likely, find a man in a black ski mask ready to mug me.

The owl blinked expectantly. "Okay," I said. "If you're sure it's safe."

I took three hesitant steps, carefully dodging empty, wet fast food sacks and rat droppings. *Ew.* This place was gross. My owl friend flapped ahead to a filthy green dumpster. With a sigh, I continued after it, knowing with every step that I should probably be more cautious. Sean would be livid if he found out about this.

Just a few feet away from the dumpster, I heard voices, too muffled to make out. I looked at the owl, who blinked and turned to face the other side of the alley. Is this what he was trying to show me? I inched closer, trying my best to stay quiet, which was no easy feat—especially when a cockroach the size of my hand nearly ran over the top of my foot.

A makeshift shelter made from soggy cardboard boxes leaned against the side of the building the dumpster sat against. I tiptoed around it, peeked around the corner, and just barely made out two separate voices. A man and a woman joyfully giggled in hushed tones. There was something almost familiar about them, but not enough for me to sort it out on sound alone.

Just a few more steps to the next corner of the smelly bin, and I'd be able to see them. Of course, they'd be able to see me, too. But I was already in this far. Why not go for the gold?

They stopped talking as I poked the top of my head around the corner. Luckily for me, they were too busy sucking face to notice anyone at all. Who makes out by a dumpster? Another quick glance at the owl told me I had to stick around and find out. *Well, add peeping Tom to my list of accomplishments...*

The man leaned his back against the wall, rubbing his hands up and down the woman's slender frame as she lifted on her tiptoes to kiss him. Her hair was dark and stringy, hanging limply past her shoulders. Eventually, she dropped back down, revealing the man's face.

"We're gonna be so rich," Mr. Smiley grinned.

It was David, the customer from Millie's shop. The one who bought the poison for supposedly non-poison-making purposes. So was this his girlfriend with the nerve pain? She stepped back and I dashed around to the opposite side of the dumpster, diving into the cardboard lean-to.

I could just barely make them out as they rounded the edge of the bin, and a gasp escaped my lips when I saw the face of the woman. It was Nikki, Abby's housekeeper. The one who had given her father the investment information that Mr. Smiley had in his bag. I knew it!

But my excitement was premature... and overenthusiastic.

"Did you hear something?" The housekeeper paused, looking nervously around the alley.

"Probably just a rat." Mr. Smiley said.

I wished the housekeeper would have accepted that as an answer, but I was never so lucky. She continued searching, stepping closer and closer to the cardboard shack where I'd holed up. My legs burned with energy and adrenaline, my fight or flight kicking in hardcore. Through a hole in the tattered roof I could just barely see the outline of my owl friend hopping across the top of the dumpster. Then, he disappeared, dropping down inside.

The sound of scuffling claws immediately bounced through the walls of the alleyway.

"See?" Mr. Smiley said. He put on a tough face, but there was a flash of fear in his eyes. "Rats. And big ones from the sound of it."

But there were no rats. Just my owl, and whatever was chasing him through the trash. A moment later, a feral flash of gray fur jumped out of the dumpster with a hiss, and dashed across the alleyway, leaping up onto a fire escape on the opposite side and disappearing over the edge of a window sill.

"Ahh! I hate cats!" The housekeeper jumped backward with a sour expression. She took one final look at the dumpster, her eyes barely grazing over the box where I sat hidden, and then took Mr. Smiley by the hand. "Let's get out of here."

I waited a solid five minutes after I was sure they were gone. It took that long for my pulse to return to normal. Slowly standing, I gave my legs a kick to get the blood rushing back through them properly, then peered over the edge of the dumpster. The odor was so strong it brought tears to my eyes and stung at the back of my nose. No sign of the owl, anywhere.

It was just as well. He'd shown me what I needed to see. I wasted no time getting back to the coffee shop in Morningside Heights, only stopping once to pull up a Google map on my phone to find the way.

I couldn't confirm anything of course, but my suspicions were already running high when it came to Mr. Smiley and his purchase of Monkshood. Pair that with a shady new housekeeper and some sleazy looking investment paperwork, and the situation was ripe for conspiracy.

Maybe there was a chance I could save Mr. Mason after all.

CHAPTER 10

GOLDEN BELLS TINKLED OVERHEAD as I pulled open the door of The Honey Pot. Coeds sat huddled at tables and in worn armchairs throughout the small coffee shop. I scanned the room, trying to ignore the aromatic scent of espresso calling to me like a delightfully-caffeinated temptress.

There. Two platinum blonds leaned in close over steaming mugs at a table in the back corner. I rushed breathlessly across the shop. "Dom! Gayla!"

The girls looked up, faces twisted in confusion. Or perhaps those were sneers of disgust at the sweaty mortal who stood before them. I probably reeked of trash from the alley. With their ashy blond, almost silver hair and deep dark eyes, they had to be Olympian. They just weren't *my* Olympians.

In fact, after another good look around, it appeared that everyone in the shop was a Keeper of some kind. A gorgeous leggy brunette with sparkling amber eyes, leaned over the counter, grinning at me. "Can I help you?" she asked.

"Maybe." I wiped my sweaty palms across my thighs and approached her. I'd never interacted with a female Agarthian before. Was she going to try to make me fall in love with her, too? Surely not. They weren't all sirens, were they?

I swallowed down my nerves and steadied my voice. "I'm looking for a couple of... uh... blond girls. About yea high." I held my hand six inches above my head.

The girl unsuccessfully tried to hide a smirk. "I think you've got the wrong shop."

Uh huh. Because I'm a mortal. This was exactly why I'd never fit in at Columbia. "I'm sure they said they were coming here. One of them probably ordered your special with the Ambrosia drizzle. Real pretty girl, I'm sure you would remember her."

The barista wrinkled her nose. "Sorry. Our special today is the iced white chocolate mocha. You've definitely got the wrong shop."

I looked around again. There was no way I'd made a mistake. This place was crawling with Keepers. She was just trying to get me out of there—trying to keep their identities a secret.

"Look," I leaned in conspiratorially, dropping my voice to let her know I wasn't going to blow her cover. "I know what you think, but I'm not a mortal."

"You're not, huh?" A rough voice snagged my attention. I looked over in time to see Osborne slide onto a barstool to my right.

Crap. *Crapcrapcrap.* "That's not exactly what I meant." I looked back to the barista for a little help, but she'd already moved on to help a new customer.

Osborne did not look amused. His mouth pressed into a hard line, he dropped his chin toward the stool on the opposite side of his table.

"Oh, I can't." I backed up a step. "I've really got to get ba—"

"Sit." His golden eyes flickered, and I couldn't resist. I had to sit. Somewhere in the depths of my consciousness I knew he was glamouring me, but I was helpless to fight back.

"Okay," I murmured, sliding onto the stool across from him. The barista snickered, flicking a quick glance in our direction before sliding an iced mocha to-go across the counter to another unwitting mortal.

"First, I don't like liars. You're definitely a mortal—for now. Don't try to convince anyone otherwise."

I didn't dare object. My heart was thundering so loud I imagined the entire coffee shop could sense my fear. The two Atlantean guys at the table next to us could, anyway, judging by the wide eyes they had plastered to me. They probably had heightened senses, like Sean's friend Devon. I gave them an audible gulp for some comedic relief. They turned back to their own conversation and any humor was immediately sucked dry from the situation again as I looked at Osborne's golden eyes.

While Tate's were rich like honey, full of mystery and intrigue, Osborne's were harsh, cold and calculating. It was much more enjoyable to be glamoured by Tate. Osborne wasn't making this fun for me at all.

"Why are you here?"

"I'm looking for my friends." The words spilled from my lips before I could help myself.

"Where's your guardian?"

"Sean? I don't know." The AC blasted down on my clammy skin, sending chill bumps up my arms. Osborne glanced down, a wicked smirk playing at his lips.

"Are you afraid?"

"Yes." Stupid, traitorous mouth!

"You should be. It's dangerous to run around without your guardian. Why would you leave him behind? Attempting to poison his mortal girlfriend, perhaps?"

"No!" I shook my head emphatically. "I promise. It's not me."

He pursed his lips, staring at me long and hard before scooting off of his barstool. "I'm watching you. Everywhere. One slip up and you're mine."

"What about Tate?" It was strange how I felt defensive of the guy who admittedly wanted to kill me and take my soul. But Osborne wasn't playing by the rules. He wasn't supposed to come near another hunter's assignment without him. And I wanted him to know that I was aware of his mistake.

His eyes narrowed. "I don't care about Thaddeus. I care about getting the job done." He turned on his heels and disappeared through the door before I could get another word in.

At least he knew I wasn't responsible for Mr. Mason's illness now. There's no way I could have lied to him through the glamour. But I also didn't get a chance to tell him what I suspected about Mr. Smiley and the housekeeper. Not that he would have listened to me, anyway.

The Atlantean boys stared at me with raised brows. "Nothing to see here," I muttered as I stormed past them.

It took me just a moment to regain my bearings back on the sidewalk outside of the coffee shop. There was no sign of Osborne, but I knew he was near. I could practically feel his eyes burning into me. I grinned like a fool, trying to prove I wasn't afraid of him. *Take that, you pushy hunter.*

Gayla and Dom's apartment wasn't far from here. Ten minutes later I banged on their door, relief flooding through me when I saw Gayla's pretty face peek through the crack. "Everly! Come in." She stepped back, slurping a creamy iced coffee drink through her straw.

Dom glanced up from her spot at the kitchen island, immediately aware of the stress I was trying to keep under control. She stood and met us in the living room. "What's wrong, Ev?"

"I need to find Tate."

Gayla wiggled her brows at me. "I bet you do..."

"No, this is important."

Dom's eyes moved quickly back and forth over mine, trying to make out what was flashing through my mind. Bless her. It was probably a mess in there.

"You ran into Osborne? Alone?" Her mouth dropped open.

"Yes. And I think I have the information he needs to help Abby's dad. I know who is responsible for it, but he won't listen to me. I need to tell Tate."

Gayla tensed at my mention of Abby, but she nodded, agreeing that something needed to be done. "Osborne is kind of a creep. I understand why you'd rather talk to Tate, but I don't know if I'd recommend you running to him. Isn't that a bit like a rabbit seeking refuge in the fox's den?"

"I'd rather talk to the fox than the wolf."

She nodded grimly at that.

"Tell us what you know," Dom suggested. "Maybe we can talk to Tate and Osborne for you."

I shook my head. "No. He needs to hear it from me. I'm still working to prove my innocence here. But I also have first hand knowledge. If they glamour the truth out of me—or whatever it is they do—they'll have to believe me."

The girls exchanged a weary look. Gayla caved first. "Okay. I know where the Agarthians hang out in the evenings. I'm sure Tate will be there. Osborne might be there too, though."

I was sure he probably would be. But that was a risk I'd just have to take.

CHAPTER 11

THE CITY BUZZED WITH a new kind of energy after sundown. I stepped out of the cab behind Gayla, who stood tall on the sidewalk in the lower East Side, skin shimmery and perfectly bronzed as the streetlights reflected off of her exposed shoulders. She turned to Dom and me with a grin. "I love this place!"

"Have you been before?" Dom asked.

Gayla nodded. "Yep. Gabriella let me sneak down here with her and her friends one night a couple of years ago. It's where I got my first sip of absinthe. Daddy would've killed me if he knew. But it was worth it."

She was way more excited than I was. I struggled to keep up with their long confident strides through the streets, and tripped over my feet more than once for lack of paying attention. I was too busy scouting out my surroundings. If this was a popular Agarthian hangout, there was no telling how many hunters might be in the area.

Dom slowed and patted me on the shoulder as I caught up. "It's alright," she said. "We've got your back."

It was good to have them on my side, but I was beginning to regret not inviting Sean along. A weak seer and a telepath could only do so much. Sean's strength and speed would have been far more useful. But Sean wouldn't have been on board with me finding Tate. As a guardian, his job was to keep me away from the Agarthians, not lead me into one of their favorite hangouts.

"Here," Gayla said, pointing down a dark alleyway.

"Are you sure?" Memories of almost getting caught in a similar alleyway earlier that day surfaced, and I shuddered at the thought of rats and roaches and other nasties that lurked in places like this.

"Positive." She marched onward, and after a shared glance with Dom, we followed.

It was quiet, but not as gross as the place I hid earlier. It didn't smell like a rotten dumpster for one thing, but it also had almost a tidy feel to it. Or, as tidy as a dark alleyway in New York City could feel, anyway.

"Here we go. After you ladies." Gayla extended her arm to a dark stairwell that led down to an unmarked door below street level.

"Uhh, nope. You can go first. I insist."

Dom giggled as I halted at the top of the stairs, grabbing onto the railings like a cat refusing a bath. "You can still wait here if you want. We'll go see if we can find Tate and bring him up here to you."

"No, I'll be fine." The alley didn't seem so bad when I was with friends, but that certainly didn't mean I wanted to hang out here alone. Reluctantly, I released the rails and tiptoed after them down the stairs.

A small bell hung outside of the metal door at the bottom. I searched for signage or windows—anything to give me some kind of indication of what we could expect to find on the other side, but there was nothing. Just the bell. Gayla gave it a ring, its sound tinny in the cool night air.

A square peep hole cover slid open to reveal a dark beady eye on the other side of the door. "State your business." The voice was nasally and apathetic.

"We're here for The Vault." Gayla was practically glowing with excitement as she turned and gave us an enthusiastic thumbs up.

The peep hole closed and the sound of something scraping across the floor was followed by the door swinging open. I stepped inside after Gayla, noting the step stool just to our left. It was one of the few items in the small dank room we'd entered, and it sat lonely on the dirty linoleum floor.

A squatty woman with frizzy graying brown hair was waddling back to a warped cheap wooden table, stained with water rings. She climbed up into her chair and picked up the four inch thick book she was reading. I couldn't tell what it was, but there were definitely spaceships on the cover.

I raised my brows at Gayla. Her grin stretched even wider, and she gave a confident nod of her head toward a bookshelf built into the opposite wall. The woman, who just seemed to notice our delay, peered over the pages of her book. The fluorescent light flickering over her head highlighted the stray white hairs that had escaped her ponytail and now bobbed like unruly little dancers in the wind of her fan buzzing in the corner. "Was there something else you needed?" Her tone was laced with irritation. She probably wanted to get back to her book.

"No, thank you. We're going." Gayla moved toward the bookshelf and gave us a wink before pulling out a ratty old book with a burgundy spine. The title had faded to nothing but specks of gold, but it wasn't important. The book merely served as a trigger for the mechanism that was now swinging the bookshelf open and to the side to reveal the secret area behind it.

"The Vault is an old prohibition era bar hidden down here under the city. They used to store liquor here where it wouldn't be found and confiscated. Now it's just a hot spot for Keepers—primarily Agarthians—to kick back and enjoy themselves away from mortal eyes," Gayla explained.

"But the woman who let us in was a mortal, right?"

"Yeah. But she's glamoured. She'll forget everything about the strangeness of her job every night before she goes home. Then she'll return to do it again tomorrow. Don't worry about her though, she gets to read every book on the old shelves, and they pay her well."

We followed Gayla through the opening into a slightly larger warm space on the other side. Tufted Victorian couches and armchairs sat huddled together in small pairings through the room. An exposed brick wall held a glowing fireplace, adding to the ambiance as the reflection of its flames danced across the intricacies of the metal ceiling tiles overhead. A large mahogany bar sat at the far wall, next to a small stage where a jazz band was set up but not currently playing.

The room was nearly at capacity with just twenty or thirty patrons—all unnaturally beautiful and carefree. Well, carefree until their golden eyes all turned to me.

I immediately felt a surge of electricity jolt through my limbs. "This was a mistake," I whispered to Gayla. "I shouldn't be here."

"Too late now," she whispered back. Then she smiled and waved to a gorgeous dark skinned woman standing nearby. I moved to follow her over there, but a strange tug in my chest urged me to turn to my left, instead.

"We're right here if you need us," Dom said, squeezing my arm. Then she left me alone, staring like a fool at my future murderer.

Tate stalked across the room, long, feline-like strides that brought him to my side in a matter of seconds. "What are you doing here?"

The sound of his voice sent a tickle down my spine. He'd tried to sound intimidating, but it came off a little too caring. I almost sensed a touch of concern in his tone.

"I came to find you, actually."

The corner of his mouth twitched up into a shadow of a grin. "You're still mortal." His eyes trailed my figure, as though he could see my fragility radiating off of me. "So I know you're not here to offer your soul to me. What else could you possibly need?" His golden eyes glistened with amusement. I didn't fully understand Tate's game, but he obviously felt like he was winning. And the flutter in my belly led me to believe he was probably right about that.

Though, it wasn't unpleasant.

An ensemble of musicians resumed their spot on the stage, dressed as a jazz band might have dressed in the 1920s. A woman in a shimmery black knee-length cocktail dress stepped up to the microphone and began to sing. The song was like nothing I'd ever heard. In fact, I'm not even sure I was hearing it with my ears. It moved me within my soul.

Every fear I had immediately dissipated. My stress was gone. I swayed to the music, entranced by each exquisite note, feeling lighter and lighter with every word the woman sang.

"Everly."

The sound of Tate's voice, rich like honey, snapped my attention back to him. He was truly a magnificent creature, towering over me with his broad shoulders and slender waist, hands in his pockets. He cleared his throat, pulling my gaze away from his chest and back up to his glistening golden eyes. But I couldn't even be embarrassed. The song wouldn't allow it. All I felt was pure contentment.

"You like this song?" He asked with a grin.

"Very much." When had I reached out to him? I looked at my hand, sliding down his shoulder and the ridges of his bicep like it belonged to someone else. I would never be so bold as to reach out and feel a man's muscles. But I was.

"Everly!" Dom pulled me away. "We've got to get you out of here. You're not strong enough to resist the pull of the siren's song."

"I don't want to go." I looked back at the beautiful man beside me. Tate looked like he was suppressing a laugh.

Dom turned to him next. "Come on. We need to talk to you. It's important." She dragged me back to the bookshelf, which held celebrity memorabilia on this side of the wall.

"Go ahead," she said to Tate. "Pull the secret lever or whatever."

He twisted a signed portrait of Cary Grant and the shelf came to life again. I turned longingly back toward the warm room with the enchanting music we were leaving behind, but another tug from Dom pulled me into the blinking fluorescent lights of the room we'd first entered. The bored mortal with the space novel glanced in our direction.

"Do something with her," Dom commanded, waving her hand in the direction of the confused woman. To my surprise, Tate obeyed. He approached her as the shelf swung back into place behind us. With the sound of the music muffled out, I regained my ability to concentrate and think clearly. I was filled with great curiosity as Tate leaned across the old table and touched the small woman's arm.

"We're going to talk, and you can't hear anything we say for the next ten minutes. You're going to read your book, and you won't even know we're here. There is nothing unusual taking place tonight."

The woman pulled her book back in front of her and looked down at its pages without so much as acknowledging a word Tate said.

"Are you sure that worked?" I asked.

Tate nodded. Unbelieving, I clapped my hands together while simultaneously shouting, "HEY!" The woman didn't even flinch.

"Satisfied?" Tate smirked.

"I guess so." I shuffled, uncomfortable now that the glamour of the siren's song had worn off, and I realized how strangely I'd behaved moments earlier. But we only had ten minutes, so I had to cut to the chase.

"Look, I need to talk to you about something important. I know it's not technically your case to solve, but I think I have a lead on the dark magic incident with Mr. Mason."

Tate shook his head. "You need to talk to Osborne about that."

"I can't. When he tracked me down this afternoon he made it clear that he wouldn't hear a word I had to say. He doesn't trust me."

"Osborne tracked you down today?"

"Yes."

Tate's jaw tightened, just for the briefest of moments before he relaxed it again. But he couldn't hide the fists he still held clenched at his side. I knew Osborne had crossed a line. And thankfully, Tate seemed open to hearing me out now.

"I think I know who the fractured soul is. I think it's Mr. Mason's housekeeper. And she has an accomplice."

Gayla emerged from behind the bookshelf then, just in time for me to relay everything I'd seen between the housekeeper and Mr. Smiley. And within minutes we had a plan. Hopefully it would work. And hopefully Sean wouldn't be too angry with me when all was said and done.

CHAPTER 12

MY MIND WAS RACING a million miles an hour the next morning as I skipped down the stairs on my way to Millie's shop. Sean was waiting outside the door, oblivious to everything that had taken place the day before. Thank goodness he wasn't a mind reader, too. There was no way I'd be able to hide my anxiety.

I joined him on the sidewalk with an enthusiastic grin and patted him roughly on the shoulder. "Hey buddy, what's up? Having a good morning so far?" *Too much. Play it cool.*

Sean made a face. "How many cups of coffee have you had?"

"Just the right amount." I giggled, trying to act normal, and nearly choked on my spit.

He shook his head. "Whatever. I'm fine, I guess. But I really do need to get my schedule figured out. Have you nailed yours down yet?" He began walking toward the apothecary, but I stayed put.

"Oh shoot!" I put a hand to my forehead. "No, actually. I was meaning to talk to you about that. I accidentally left my pen at Abby's apartment the other day when Millie and I went to see her dad."

He stopped and looked over his shoulder at me. "So?"

"So, it's my lucky pen. I need it... to help me make a list of the classes I'm interested in."

He made that same face as before. Sean definitely thought I was some kind of special this morning.

"I know it sounds ridiculous, but I just don't think I'll be able to get my schedule sorted out until I can get that pen back. Is there any way we might be able to swing by her place before we head into the shop?" I clasped my hands together in front of my chest and batted my eyes like a cartoon. "Pretty please?"

Sean huffed and glanced down at his watch. "I don't think we have time. Maybe you can come back with Millie later."

"Nonsense! She won't mind if we're a little late. And I'm sure she doesn't want to walk all the way back over there after working all day. I'd go by myself, but they might not like it if I ditch my guardian again."

He grimaced. I knew he wasn't excited about going to see Abby. Which, I had to admit, was pretty confusing. He loved to be around her. Then again, maybe that was just it. He didn't trust himself not to fall more in love with her, and that was definitely forbidden.

"Fine, but we'll need to get in and out as quickly as possible."

I drew an x over my heart. "Promise. I'll be fast as lightning."

We picked up our speed in the opposite direction, back toward Abby's building. I tried to keep a straight face, but the truth was that I was giddy that my plan was working. And if the others were doing their parts, then we would see them any minute...

"Sean! Everly!" Gayla marched over and threw her arms around us in a three way hug while Dom smirked behind her on the sidewalk. We'd just rounded the corner of Abby's block, and they were waiting exactly where they said they'd be. The plan was still moving as smooth as silk.

Sean pulled away, flustered. He ran a hand through his hair and frowned. "Why are you two all the way over in this part of town?"

"We heard about this amazing new donut shop. They've invented something called a crenglish muffnut that is supposedly to die for. It's a cross between a croissant, an English muffin, and a donut, and it was featured in—"

Sean waved her off just in time. I was about to lose it. I bit the inside of my lip hard to keep from laughing out loud. The thrill of the chase had me jazzed, and Gayla's made-up breakfast treat was too bizarre to handle. Dom shook her head, dropping her face toward the ground to hide her smirk.

"Well, we'll let you get to your breakfast then. We're in kind of a hurry." Sean cut around Gayla to keep moving toward the apartment building. The green awning over the door was just a few yards ahead.

"We'll walk with you," Gayla replied, undeterred by Sean's attempt to shake her off. "I think the donut place is down the block somewhere over here. Where are you guys going, anyway?"

"Everly left a pen inside one of these apartments. We're gonna grab it before heading back to Millie's shop this morning." He cut his eyes over to me, not even attempting to hide his frustration over the matter.

"A pen?" Gayla raised her brows in my direction. We hadn't discussed exactly how I was going to lure Sean back to Abby's place. I had to think quickly this morning.

"It's my lucky pen." I shrugged. "I need it to help me narrow down which classes I'm going to enroll in. It's never let me down before!"

Gayla resumed her straight face as she launched into some long story about a lucky keychain she got when she turned sixteen. I appreciated her backing me up. That, and what I discovered was an incredible storytelling ability she possessed.

Dom winked in my direction as we slowed in front of the doorway. I knew what had to happen next.

"Well, here we are," said Sean. "Enjoy your pastries." But the girls didn't budge.

"Whose place did you say this was?" Gayla asked.

He didn't. And it was probably intentional.

"This is where Abby lives," I said. Sean shifted nervously on his feet.

"Abby? As in Sean's good friend, Abby? Oh, I'd love to meet her. I've heard so much about her. Mind if we go up with you?"

"*No.* I mean, yes. I do mind. You can't come up." The color drained from Sean's already pale face. I'd never seen him look quite as uncomfortable as he did at the prospect of Gayla and Abby meeting each other.

"Her father isn't feeling well." I shot Sean a sympathetic look. As far as I could tell he didn't suspect anything unusual about our chance meeting with the girls.

"Well, maybe he would like a muffnut. We should get one for Abby, too. You can bring it to her, Sean." Gayla smiled sweetly. She was a really great actress, too. If I didn't already know how difficult it was for her to think about Sean and Abby together, I wouldn't have noticed the pain behind her eyes at all.

Sean looked like he was going to be sick. Bringing Abby breakfast would definitely send her the wrong ideas.

"You know what, maybe Dom and I can go up together. You two can stay down here, and since neither of us are close enough to chit chat with Abby, we can make it quick. We'll be right back."

I pulled Dom by the elbow before Sean could object. It would only take a second for him to see through my weak reasoning, but I couldn't think of any other way to get Dom upstairs with me. And I needed Dom there.

Abby opened her door a few minutes later with wide eyes. "Oh," she said, startled. "Where's Sean?"

"He's catching up with a friend he ran into on the sidewalk outside. This is Dom."

Abby's forehead wrinkled as she glanced between us, but she stepped back and allowed us inside. Sean and I had sent a text before we left to let her know we were on our way.

"I looked everywhere, but I didn't see any pens," she said.

"Hmm... maybe your housekeeper saw it somewhere." I pushed past her toward the kitchen. The couch was empty, which probably meant Mr. Mason was in bed. *Stay strong, big guy,* I thought to myself. *We'll get you feeling better soon.*

Nikki, the stringy haired housekeeper, stood in the kitchen, wiping down the counters. She glanced up nervously as I approached, likely remembering that I was related to Millie.

"Hi." I leaned forward onto the freshly wiped granite, leaving elbow smudges on its glossy surface. "I'm Abby's friend, Everly. I think I left my pen here the other day when I stopped by with my aunt. You might know her—Millie? She's the pharmacist at the apothecary near Central Park. Anyway, have you seen it?"

The housekeeper's breathing quickened, her chest visibly rising and falling before us. She was nervous. Good. I glanced at Dom to see if she was getting anything from the woman's thoughts just yet, but I couldn't tell. *Time to turn it up a notch.*

"I think I set it down on the counter right here. I remember there was some kind of an investment folder by it. Yellow and blue? The logo looked kinda cheesy, like some con artist had designed it." I laughed, pretending I'd made an innocent joke. "I'm kidding, of course. I'm sure it was totally legit. But that pen... did you see it? It's kind of special to me."

"I haven't seen any pen." The kitchen light reflected off the sheen across the housekeeper's forehead as she stormed past us on her way to the other side of the apartment. Dom half smirked and gave a subtle nod to let me know she got what she needed.

"Well, maybe I was wrong. I must have left it somewhere else. Thanks anyway, Abby. Take care of yourself." I smiled and turned back to the door.

"Uh, you too." The girl looked completely bewildered as she led us back out into the hall. "Good luck finding it." She closed the door and I immediately turned to Dom.

"Get anything good?"

She grinned. "You were right about everything. Well, almost everything. But the housekeeper is the accomplice. Your Mr. Smiley is the fractured one. And I know just how we can get this sucker and make him pay."

CHAPTER 13

SEAN ABANDONED ALL EFFORTS to converse with me about midway through the day. I couldn't focus on a word he said. I was too busy obsessively checking my phone to see if a text had come through from the girls.

Dom said the housekeeper planned to meet up with Mr. Smiley after work. Gayla was grabbing Tate while Dom kept watch on the apartment building all day. As soon as she saw the housekeeper leave, she was going to text me to meet up with them. Then we'd confront her and her smiley lover-boy in the alley, where my hot hunter, Tate, could do his job.

Though I chose not to think too much about what that might entail. I wasn't particularly excited about the whole soul extraction part of the plan. I just wanted to ensure Mr. Mason's safety.

My pocket buzzed with a new message. "Eeep!"

Sean jerked his head in my direction at the squeak that slipped through my mouth. I quickly tried to regain my composure. Clearing my throat, I straightened my face the best that I could and said, "Hey, I've gotta go. Just got an SOS text from Dom."

"What kind of SOS? Is she in danger?" He was already pulling off his apron.

"No, no. No danger." I lifted both hands in front of me. "It's just... uh... girl problems."

Sean wrinkled his nose. "Enough said. But I still can't let you go alone."

"Go where?" Millie emerged from the back room with a cheerful grin.

"Dom's having some feminine issues. She asked me to swing by."

Millie's brows lifted. "Oh, well you should definitely go then. It's pretty slow here today. I'll be fine on my own. But here..." She rustled with something under the counter before emerging with a small white paper gift sack. "Take her some dark chocolate and this lavender-sage salve. It'll fix up 99% of those pesky lady cramps."

Sean grimaced. "Okay, okay. Let's go."

He could barely keep up with me as I trotted along the sidewalk.

"Is it really this big of an emergency?"

"Totally. Keep up."

We were about eight blocks away from the apothecary when he realized we weren't headed to Dom's apartment. "Hey, stop. Where are you taking me?"

"Hmm?" I played innocent and continued moving forward, pretending I didn't hear him.

"Everly, come on. You've been a little off all day. Tell me what's really going on here."

"Fine. We're catching the fractured soul that's been poisoning Mr. Mason." I grinned. He was going to find out soon enough, anyway.

"We're what?! *Uh-uh*. That's not our job. And you especially shouldn't go near any fractured souls."

"Why not? Are they contagious or something?" I picked up my pace, despite Sean's objections.

"No, but if the excitement or fear of the capture somehow sets off your powers, you're going to be surrounded by hunters. What do you think they're going to do then?"

I paused. The thought hadn't crossed my mind. "We won't be surrounded by hunters. There's only one—just Tate."

"Thaddeus is the only one you *need* to fear. Good grief, Everly! Did you honestly not think this through at all? Come on." He grabbed my arm. "We're heading back."

An owl fluttered down with an exaggerated flap of its wings and landed on a trash can beside us. It focused its deep yellow eyes on Sean, with a look that even he couldn't ignore.

"You need to let go of my arm." I glanced from him to my little owl friend, making my point clear.

The owl blinked once at Sean before he released me. "Fine," he muttered. "But let the record show that I do not support this plan. Not at all." He shot another uneasy glance at the bird.

"You'll still protect me though, right? If anything goes wrong?"

"Of course I will. But then I'm gonna chew you out about it real good when we get you back to safety."

I ruffled my hand through his auburn hair. "Thanks. I knew I could count on you."

The owl flew away and I checked my text once more. "We're almost there. Dom just sent an update that they are meeting in an alley not much farther from here."

"They who?"

"The fractured soul. Remember the smiley guy we helped a couple of times at the apothecary? The one who always bought black licorice?"

"Oh yeah, black licorice guy. You're not telling me he's the one poisoning Mr. Mason, are you?"

"Yep. He's the bad guy. And get this—Abby's housekeeper is helping him do it."

I explained everything as we walked, right up until I saw the tall young woman standing against the wall up ahead.

Gayla was the opposite of inconspicuous. She wore black leather leggings and a long sleeved black turtleneck—in August. Her oversized sunglasses covered half of her face, but her long blond hair fell across her shoulders in almost silvery waves.

"Stealth." I waggled my eyebrows and she flashed me a huge perfect Gayla grin.

"Thanks. I was going for a Mission Impossible vibe."

Sean rolled his eyes. "So where are they?"

"Dom and the guys are around the corner, watching Mr. Smiley and the housekeeper. Osborne refused to take our word for it, so he wants to listen in on their conversation before he makes any moves."

"Osborne is here?"

Gayla cringed. "I thought Dom told you."

"Dom didn't tell her, but I totally called it." Sean gave me a stern look.

"It's fine," I said. "I'll be fine." I wasn't sure if I was trying to reassure my friends or myself. But fine or not, there was no turning around now. We slunk around the corner and spotted our small group of Keepers up ahead.

Osborne turned as we rounded the corner and pierced me with his pale golden eyes. Dom, sensing my fear, turned and frowned apologetically. I couldn't let them get me worked up though. Not if the extreme stress might bring on any powers I could still potentially be harboring.

"How's it going?" I looked only at Dom. Osborne was a creep and Tate had me all tingly without even making eye contact.

"The housekeeper is panicking. You really scared her earlier. She's trying to get Smiley to act fast before you tell your aunt Millie."

"Act fast on what?" I swallowed, hoping her response was anything other than what I suspected.

"Killing Mr. Mason so they can steal his new inheritance." It was Osborne who answered, looking more lethal than ever.

Shoot.

"I guess it's now or never, then." I risked a quick glance at Tate. He nodded, the corner of his mouth quirking into a half-grin. But it quickly faded as Osborne began to speak. They may have been fellow hunters, but that did not mean they were on friendly terms. And part of me suspected I might have had something to do with this new animosity between the two of them. I would be flattered if they were fighting over anything other than who gets to kill me and take my soul first.

"You girls stay here while Tate and I go talk to them. We've got a station nearby—an abandoned loft over an old empty storefront. We can finish the job there."

"What about me?" Sean asked. Apparently now that he was here he wanted to join in on the mission, after all.

"Finesse, right?" Osborne looked Sean up and down.

"That's right."

"Then it's your job to catch them if they try to get away."

"They won't try to get away. Not with my glamour." Tate smirked.

"I wasn't referring to the suspects." Osborne glowered at me.

"So you really think you can just go out there and convince them to follow you back to your station to kill them? Won't they know you're hunters?" I asked.

"We can be very convincing." Tate winked at me. "Watch and learn."

The two Agarthians sauntered down the alleyway. Smiley jerked his head up fast at the sight of them. His body tensed, prepared to sprint, but Osborne raised his hands.

"Slow down there," Osborne said. His voice was smooth and calming. Smiley froze. "We're just here to talk."

The housekeeper was too busy ogling Tate to care much about what was happening between Osborne and her boyfriend. She looked like she'd just seen an angel, and she was welcoming him with open arms. Literally. The poor woman stepped forward trying to hug Tate. *Sheesh.* I hoped I didn't look quite so desperate when he glamoured me.

I couldn't hear the conversation after that. They were too far away.

"What's going on?" I asked Dom.

She shrugged. "They're too far for me to hear anything either."

A few minutes passed, then the whole group of four began walking back toward us. Smiley wasn't smiling anymore, but he obediently followed Osborne, never once pulling his gaze away from the back of the hunter's head. And the housekeeper, bless her heart, looked like she'd just received a puppy on Christmas morning. She had a death grip on Tate's hand. He winked at me as they approached.

He was having way too much fun messing with her emotions, and he wanted me to see how easy it was to manipulate her. Just like he could manipulate me. *Jerk.*

"Alright, thanks for the help," Osborne said to Dom and Gayla. He ignored me, and it was the best thing he could have done. I didn't need his gratitude or praise for my expert sleuthing. I just wanted him to forget I ever existed. "You all can go back now. We've got everything under control."

"Wait," I said. "What about the housekeeper?" She wasn't fractured. She wasn't very nice, but she certainly didn't deserve to die.

"Me and Tate are moving back to Jersey, aren't we babe?" She puckered her lips and glued herself to his arm. Gayla snorted, and Tate looked amused, but he was focused on me, not the housekeeper. Guess he still wasn't comfortable enough to let his real prey out of sight.

"Who cares about her?" Osborne said gruffly. "Let's go." They pushed past us, and I stepped right into line behind them. Osborne paused, turning to glare at me. "I said you're dismissed. Run along." He shooed me away with his hand.

"No." I straightened my shoulders. From the corner of my eye I saw Sean shake his head, embarrassed. "I want to see how this is done."

Tate frowned. "I don't think you do."

I put up a hand. "Don't try to glamour me out of this. I may be new to this world, but if you're planning on doing the same thing to me that you're going to do to Mr. Frowny here, I think I deserve to see how it works. Don't I?"

I really wanted to make sure they weren't going to hurt the housekeeper. But as much as I hated to admit it, there was a sick part of me that was curious about the process of soul extraction, too. First dark magic, now soul extraction. I was definitely playing in the darker part of the morally gray area I normally avoided.

"You don't deserve anything," Osborne spat. "But if you want to have nightmares, be my guest. It won't change your future either way."

Tate opened his mouth to speak, but thought better of it. Dom quirked an eyebrow.

"Was there something else you wanted to say?" I was probably mouthing off a little too harshly, given the current circumstances, but who could blame me for feeling a little moody? I was about to watch the hunters kill a man the same way they intended to kill me.

"No." Tate relaxed his features. "Follow us."

CHAPTER 14

THE LOFT CONTAINING THE hunters' "station" looked like every other abandoned warehouse where hostages were taken in every thriller movie ever. I half expected them to blindfold him and tie him to a chair in the middle of the empty space so they could kick him and fail to extract information. But that wasn't necessary. Frowny was glamoured. He'd do anything Osborne asked of him.

And the housekeeper would probably do anything Tate asked even if he removed the glamour. She was a smitten kitten.

Sean and the girls accompanied me to the loft with the Agarthians. It was slightly less terrifying with them by my side, but frightening, nonetheless. Osborne slid into a rolling chair in front of a folding table containing a closed laptop. Frowny stood right in front of him, straightfaced and apathetically awaiting his impending demise.

A pleasant buzz spread from my shoulder down through my left arm, and I turned to see Tate approaching from the side. He leaned in close to whisper in my ear, his hand blooming warmth from where it lightly rested on my shoulder blade. "It's not too late."

"Not too late for what? To leave? I told you I want to see how this works."

He left his hand on my back for a moment more without speaking. Then finally he muttered, "If you insist." I shivered from the cold left behind when he pulled away. Part of me wished he'd come back, and maybe even hold onto me a little more. Whether it was all an illusion or not, his presence was a welcome comfort.

But I had to learn to be brave. I'd find my own strength.

The housekeeper stood on the opposite side of Tate. "Are you doing alright?" I asked her. I wasn't sure how glamour worked, but it must have been strange for her on some level. At least, it seemed like it would be.

"Never better, sweetheart." She grinned widely and looked longingly at Tate. That glamour was some strong stuff. Maybe I'd underestimated just how powerful Tate really was. I'd have to give Sean some extra thanks later for keeping me safe. I understood better now why he insisted on following me everywhere I went.

Osborne leaned forward onto his knees, giving Mr. Frowny a hard once over. "Just to confirm, I want you to tell me what you've been doing to Mr. Mason."

"I've been creating a slow acting poison that Nikki has been putting into his coffee everyday."

"Why?" Osborne seemed bored, like discovering plans for premeditated murder was a daily occurrence for him.

"Because we want to take his money."

It was too easy to make him spill the truth with their glamour. Was there anything they couldn't do with the power of persuasion?

"How?"

Nikki answered this time. "Mr. Mason is growing anxious as his illness worsens. He wants to make sure his daughter is well taken care of when he passes away. So we introduced him to a new investment scheme. He is going to place his entire inheritance into our business so it can grow for his daughter. But once he wires the money, we'll finish him off and run."

"And who taught you to use your magic to create the poisons?"

"Rasputin," Frowny said. I liked him better when he was smiley. The glee over his evil plan made it easy for me to crave justice against him. But seeing him blank-faced with that slight frown and zero control over his own actions, I almost felt sorry for the man.

I glanced around to see what everyone else thought, and immediately felt afire when I locked eyes with Tate. How long had he been watching me? He was probably dreaming of the day he'd get to do this to me, too. *Sadistic creep.*

"Rasputin?!" The shock in Osborne's words immediately drew my attention back to the situation at hand. "Impossible." He looked to Sean. "*Right?*"

"As far as I know, yeah. Unless there's someone else with the same name."

Osborne, now slightly paler, sat tall and cleared his throat. "Tell me more about Rasputin."

"I don't know him well," Frowny began. "I followed my cousin to a big meeting in Philly last year. He knew I could do strange things with my body. Scars would fade. Wounds would heal overnight. Crazy powerful stuff. And he thought I might be able to meet some like minded people at this event. Rasputin was there. He drew a big crowd—a lively group of people dressed like witches and vampires from history. Rasputin's costume was good. Real beard, solid Russian accent. He gave a lecture on poisons. Taught a couple of spells to enact them in ways modern medicine can't. Undetectable, he said. He also taught us some spells to prevent the effects of poison on us. Real weird stuff, but it works. It worked for me, anyway. My cousin Larry couldn't do anything with it."

Sean and Osborne exchanged wary looks.

"Have you been in contact with him at all since the event?" Osborne asked.

Frowny shook his head.

"Do you have a card or anything with his contact information? Any way we could reach him?"

"No. I didn't get a good feeling from the guy, so I didn't ever plan to talk to him again."

"Okay." Osborne stood and pulled what looked like a small silver cigar box from his pocket. It couldn't have been more than six inches long, with intricate designs carved into all four sides. The bottom was smooth, but the top had otherworldly letters set into the lid. They weren't quite the same ancient letters from my tablet, but they definitely weren't anything I'd ever seen before.

Osborne covered the lid with his palm, closed his eyes, and began murmuring something under his breath. Then a clean metal click sounded through the air, and I noticed two sharp needles protruding from the top edge of the box. They were thicker than the needles on standard syringes, and nearly twice as long.

He approached Frowny, who stood tall and unafraid. With the box in one hand, he placed his other palm against Frowny's cheek. The man smiled again, his cheeks flushed. "It's time to go," Osborne said quietly.

I stepped forward, but Dom grabbed my arm. My heart was racing, my vision blurring around the edges. I was having a panic attack. They were about to kill him. He didn't even get to say goodbye to his cousin Larry! I clutched my chest and turned to my friend.

"It's okay," she whispered. "He's not in pain. It has to be this way."

Osborne raised the box, and before I could look away again, plunged both needles directly into the man's neck.

He didn't falter. Didn't sway. Didn't fight back. He looked at peace, in fact. Happy.

Osborne continued to whisper words I couldn't hear, and after about thirty seconds he removed the needles from his neck, and they withdrew back into the box.

Mr. Frowny, or maybe he was Mr. Smiley again, though he wasn't quite smiling either, dropped gently to his knees. He rested there, alone on the floor, expressionless and silent.

"What happened to him?" I asked, breathless.

"They took his soul," Dom replied.

"That's it?" It was so... *easy*. "What now? What about his body?"

"The life will fade from it over the next several minutes. But there's no soul. No intelligent life to feel any pain or fear," Tate's hand found its way to my back again and my muscles relaxed. He should probably have the opposite effect on me, but at this moment I didn't care. I appreciated the help he provided in calming my tense nerves.

I inspected the body more closely. He looked completely normal and alive, though more tired now. Aside from the two holes in his neck, there was no sign of any foul play at all.

"The Agarthian cleaning crew will be by to dispose of the body soon. He'll be a missing persons case here in the mortal world until the humans forget about him, and his fractured soul will rest in the Hall of Souls in Agartha until we can find a missing piece to complete it."

I pulled away from him. "You're killing these people so you can Frankenstein new souls back together again? And that works?"

"They don't know if it works or not," Sean grumbled. Tate shot him a dirty look.

I put up my hand. I couldn't think about that any more right now. Not when Smiley's girlfriend stood just six feet away with that sad puppy dog look in her eyes.

"Will you at least take care of her?" I nodded to the woman.

Tate sighed, pulling his glare away from Sean. He gingerly approached the housekeeper, then softly whispered. "I can't go to Jersey with you, but you're going to go there alone. Right now. You're going to forget everything you saw today. You're going to forget about your boyfriend, the Mason family, and the entire world of the Keepers. None of this ever happened. Go home and start a new life."

She nodded and immediately turned to leave.

"What about Mr. Mason?" Sean asked.

"He'll be fine," I said. "The poison may take some time to fully leave his system, but he'll be fully recovered in a couple of weeks."

Osborne cut his eyes accusingly in my direction. I shrugged. "I work in an apothecary and my aunt is a healer."

I'd been reading up on the poisons and how they are affected by the spells jotted down in Millie's book. Herbs that did nothing for common mortals could be completely transformed with a little healer magic and a few Latin phrases.

"I need to see Abby." Sean's eyes were glassy with unshed tears of joy.

"Of course," I said. "I'll stick with the girls. I promise. Swing by their place after you're finished. We'll talk more there."

"And remember to keep your mouth shut with Abby," Gayla said. Her tone wasn't unfriendly, but there was definitely a slightly bitter note to her words. "You don't want to reveal any secrets." She winked.

Sean dashed out the door and we moved to follow him, but Tate's warm hand on my shoulder stopped me.

"You okay?" he asked.

"What do you care?"

He grinned. "The process works best when the souls are at ease. I just wanted to make sure it didn't scare you. I need you to be nice and relaxed when your day comes."

I scoffed. "*If* my day comes. I'd sure hate to clog up your hall of horrors with a gross little mortal soul."

His golden eyes flashed slightly in the low light of the warehouse. "Oh I'm not worried about that at all. Your powers will show themselves eventually, broken as they may be. And I'll be ready."

"Come on, Everly." Gayla stepped up to my side, looping my arm through hers. Dom did the same on my opposite side. "Let's head back to the Honey Pot and grab some caffeine. Let the hunters clean up their carcass like the savages they are."

The girls spun me around and kept me upright until we were back on the street. "Thank you for getting me out of there."

"That's what we do, girl." Gayla smiled. "You know, we make a pretty good team. Just think of all the fun we could have if you were to enroll at Columbia with us."

"I've been thinking about that, actually. You said there's a professor of the ancient languages there, right?"

"Yep," Dom nodded.

"And I could learn more about our history. Will I also be able to learn more about the different races and their roles? Every time I think I have a grasp on your world someone throws something out of left field, like the Hall of Souls, and I'm totally lost again."

"Oh, definitely. You'll know as much as we do. Maybe more, since you'll have a degree in it!" Gayla was practically skipping down the sidewalk now.

"Okay." I sighed. "I think you're right. I've got to learn as much as possible, especially if I want any hope of finding my mom. If it's not too late, I think I'm going to switch my enrollment from NYU to Columbia."

Gayla squealed, and the girls wrapped me in a three way hug, spinning around on the sidewalk with zero regard for the pedestrian traffic jam we caused.

As soon as they released me, my eyes were drawn to a little white owl that fluttered down out of nowhere to land on the crosswalk sign up ahead. Taped to the pole was a flyer with a cheap black and white photo of Clayton Miles printed across the front.

I stared at his handsome Agarthian grin, wondering if somehow he was able to glamour through printed photographs as well. But no, I felt just fine. The words across the top were calling for extras in a movie that would soon be shooting in New York. And of course, the movie was going to be filmed on the Columbia campus.

"I just can't get away from these guys," I said with a sigh.

"I'm not sure why you *want* to. Wanna trade spots?" Gayla laughed and tugged me across the street. "Just kidding. Let's get you an iced coffee now so we can get your schedule figured out. With a major in locating lost mothers and a minor in kicking Agarthian butt, I'm sure you're going to have plenty of class options to choose from."

IN PURSUIT

PROLOGUE

THE STREETS WERE SLICK with light drizzle falling from the New York City sky. Lights reflecting from the wet pavement glittered in the darkness, undisturbed by pedestrians. The only people still out in the city were due to begin stumbling out of the bars at any moment, just in time to crawl into their beds before the warm glow of dawn could reach them.

A girl with fiery red curls giggled about twenty paces ahead. Her short pink dress did little to hide the dark liquid staining the front of it. Tate could smell the fruity alcoholic scent of the stain even from as far back as he stood.

Stupid mortals. So careless with their actions.

He moved ahead, noting the burly young man who prowled out of a nearby bar toward the girl. She giggled again, seemingly unafraid, but something about the man didn't sit well with Tate. His movement was too deliberate. His expression determined. His sobriety unusual for a man chasing after a girl as inebriated as the redhead he followed.

She giggled again, stumbled over her own feet, and landed against the wall, propping her sluggish body up against it for support. The man glued himself to her without a moment's hesitation. Only he wasn't helping her back to her friends or hailing a cab. Instead, he leaned in close, whispering something into the girl's ear.

Tate watched as her drunken grin faded to confusion, then slowly morphed into a scowl. She blinked, and it looked like a struggle for her to open her eyes again.

"Hey!" Tate shouted.

The man looked over his shoulder. "Can I help you with something?" His voice came out like a growl through his forced smile.

"Yeah, actually. You can get away from the girl." Tate picked up his pace, jogging over to what he knew was an already bad situation before it got any worse.

"She's fine. She's just had a little too much to drink. I'm gonna take her home and get her nice and taken care of." A street light glinted off of his menacing eyes.

"No, you're not."

"Oh yeah? What are you gonna do about it, chump?"

The man reared back his hairy fist, but Tate knew it was coming. He'd already drawn power from the well deep within his mind. "Stop."

The man froze.

"You will never step foot into another bar again. You will never drug or take advantage of another woman. In fact, you will never even *date* another woman. Prepare for a life of solitude. Now get out of here before I hit you and give you a life with a crooked nose, too."

The man ran down the sidewalk. Maybe Tate took it a little too far with the life of solitude bit, but he was tired of these mortal men feeling all high and mighty. That ought to knock him down a few notches.

Two other girls ran out of the bar a moment later. "Lacey! Oh my goodness, are you okay? We've been looking everywhere for you!" One of the girl's friends glared at Tate. "What did you do to her?"

"I saved her life. Now get her home so she can sleep this off."

He left, certain now that the girl was in good hands. Besides, he had more monsters to face tonight. If only this next meeting could go as smoothly...

Something scuttled across the road as he finally reached the warehouses at the edge of Hunts Point. Tate never liked this part of town, but especially not in the middle of the night. He could handle whatever the city might throw at him of course, he just didn't prefer to. But Rossel insisted this was where they meet.

He knocked on the door, eager to get off the streets just in case someone in the area recognized him. He didn't want to be seen associating with Olympians. If *she* found out somehow, the entire plan would be ruined.

"Come in," Rossel's creaky voice called out.

The interior of the warehouse wasn't much brighter than the streets outside. Rossel's hair appeared to glow in the silvery moonlight filtering in through the dingy windows overhead.

"You're late."

"I had something to take care of." Tate wouldn't apologize. Not to Rossel.

"Mm." Even his grunts sounded condescending. "Well, I'll keep this brief. I'm sure we both have other places we'd rather be. I brought you here tonight because it's time to see some action. He's growing impatient."

"There's not much else I can do. I'm not even convinced there are any powers to reveal. She might truly have a mortal soul."

"Impossible."

"How can you be sure?"

"Because I—" Rossel choked, grabbing at his throat as he fought for a lungful of air. He couldn't have been more than 700 years old, but he sounded like he was on his deathbed with all that wheezing.

"She does not have a mortal soul," he whispered at last. "I don't care how you force her powers to reveal themselves, I just need you to do it. Seduce her, or terrify her. Bring her to the edge of her life. It doesn't matter! Just get the proof you need to extract her soul."

"I've tried those things. She doesn't seem to be responding to me. I think we just need more time."

"There is no more time. I was assured you were the right man for the job. But if you can't do it, I'm happy to call—"

"*No.*" Tate clenched his fists. "I'll do it."

"Good. Find me when it's finished."

Tate didn't delay his exit. He leaned against the outside of the warehouse, allowing the cool night air to work against the weight on his chest. He couldn't fail this mission. Too much was on the line. He may not understand their infatuation with the girl, but he wouldn't let them down.

He would extract Everly's soul no matter what it took. Even if that meant calling on his friends for some help.

With a sigh, he pulled out his phone and dialed. The line rang four times before a groggy voice finally answered with a muffled curse. "What in the world do you want at this hour?"

"Sorry man, but I need to call in that favor you owe me."

CHAPTER 1

"I HAVE A CONFESSION." Gayla crinkled her nose and hid behind one of the throw pillows on her couch. Or, I suppose it was *our* couch now.

Ever since I'd agreed to attend Columbia, the girls had been moving at a hundred miles per hour to get me comfortable and settled into my bedroom in their apartment. *Our* apartment. It was going to take me some time to get used to saying that.

"What did you do?"

She scoffed, pretending to be insulted. "I didn't *do* anything. I'm basically the most angelic friend you have."

I snorted at that. Gayla was a sweet girl, but "innocent" wasn't at the top of the list of adjectives I'd use to describe her.

"It's more like I *saw* something..." She bit her lip, playing up the suspense.

"Well, are you going to tell me what it was?" I laughed. Gayla almost seemed nervous, and that wasn't like her at all.

"Okay." She took a deep breath. "I knew you weren't going to NYU."

"What do you mean?"

"I mean, I knew it before you decided. I saw you at Columbia with me and Dom."

"Like in a vision?!" I pulled my feet up underneath me and turned to face her, throwing the pillow away to get a better look at her.

Gayla nodded.

"That's incredible!"

"You're not mad at me for keeping it from you?"

"No, I'm not mad at all! In fact, I'm glad you didn't tell me before. If you had, I probably would've stayed at NYU just to prove you wrong. Then we'd all be grumpy."

She grinned. "Yeah, I figured as much. Plus, with as wonky as my visions are, I never can be too sure if it's real or a daydream, you know?"

I nodded. She hadn't had a single successful vision in the short time I'd known her, until now. "Maybe your lessons with Rossel are paying off."

"Ugh. I hope they pay off quickly. I'm sick of seeing that smug sonofa—"

"Helloooo!" Dom burst through the front door with more fervor than usual.

"Hey!" I glanced over my shoulder to greet her, and immediately jumped out of my seat when I caught a glimpse of her. "Dom! Your hair!"

Gayla jumped up too and followed me over to our smiling friend. Dom did a small circle in the entryway, then twisted her mouth nervously to one side. "Do you like it?"

"I love it!" Gayla squealed.

"I do too. It suits you." Dom's platinum blond hair, which once hung in waves a few inches past her shoulders—just like Gayla's, was now chopped short. Layers jutted out at fun angles, framing her high cheekbones like a rock star. She looked a little like Blondie from the 80s.

"Whew!" Dom exhaled. "I mean, I love it either way, but I'm relieved to hear you like it too. I finally feel like I'm ready to tackle the first day of classes on Monday."

We spent the next few minutes gushing over Dom's new 'do before I finally had to call it a night. In just three short days I would walk onto campus and finally get a little backstory on who I was and where I came from. The only problem was that I had about eighteen years of catching up to do just to even the playing field with my peers. They'd all grown up in this world. They knew what it meant to be a Keeper.

I didn't.

But with a few books from my aunt and the girls, I was absorbing as much information as possible. I wanted to be ready on Monday. Or at least come prepared with enough background information to not look like a total dunce if the professor called on me. Did professors call on students in college?

"Night girls!" I retreated into my room and pulled out my toiletries bag. The amber bottle that housed my vitamins clinked at the bottom.

There were only a handful left now, and I still wasn't sure where I could order more. I'd swing one by Millie's shop tomorrow to see if she knew what they were. Millie knew everything about medicine and supplements. Surely she could get me some more even if she didn't know where my mom originally ordered them from.

Wait a minute. My *mom* ordered them… "Gayla!" I darted back out of my bedroom door, an idea still stretching its way through my mind like taffy. "Gayla! I need your help!"

My roommates startled, with wide eyes and open mouths as I burst back into the living room, stumbling over the throw pillow I'd tossed haphazardly on the floor earlier.

"Here!" I shoved the amber bottle into her hand. "My vitamins. My mom was a freak about me taking these every day. She had them special ordered and everything. Do you think there's a strong enough connection to her that you might be able to use the bottle to induce another vision?"

"Everly, you know my visions are only mediocre at best. And that's *if* I can even get them to work."

"But you're getting better. You knew I was coming to Columbia, didn't you?"

Dom raised a knowing brow. That traitor. She knew it too, and neither one of them admitted it to me.

"I did," Gayla said. "But that was like one in a hundred. I'm still really bad at this."

"Will you try? Please?"

Gayla twirled the bottle around an inch from her nose, taking a closer look. "These look kinda sketchy."

"Nevermind the vitamins," I huffed. "Do you think they have a strong enough connection to my mom for you to see her? I'll take anything. Anything you can learn about where she might be."

She shrugged. "Only one way to find out."

Dom and I followed her back to the couch. Gayla sat cross-legged on the floor in front of us, holding the bottle between both hands. Eyes closed, she began mouthing something so quietly I only heard the softest ghost of a whisper drifting across the space between us.

One minute stretched to two. Three. Her mouth stopped moving but her eyes remained closed. I glanced at Dom who gave a small, reassuring nod. Maybe it was working.

After about five minutes, Gayla still hadn't moved. I was nearly ready to chalk it up as a failed attempt when at last her eyes popped open.

Her normally rich brown irises were stained black and enlarged until the whites of her eyes were just barely visible around the edges. She stared into the distance, beyond the room we sat within, seeing something I couldn't even begin to name.

And when she spoke, her voice wasn't hers. It was deeper. Raspier. Full of authority. And I knew... Gayla saw my mom.

"The bars," she began, "are firm and unrelenting. There's nowhere to go. It's impossible to run."

My breath hitched. Dom gripped my hand in hers as we both scooted to the edge of the couch, leaning in closer to Gayla so as not to miss a single word.

"The woman has great power. Her eyes glow with it—blue like the ocean. It's bursting at the seams, but it cannot be released. She must wait until he returns to set her free."

She dropped her chin and closed her eyes again. No one moved a muscle. I didn't even dare to take a breath.

After several more seconds of silence, Gayla's body was wracked with tremors. I jumped to her side, but they passed just as quickly as they had come on. She lifted her head and blinked her pretty brown eyes a few times before grinning. "I think it worked!"

"You saw her? My mom?"

"I think so." Gayla nodded emphatically. "She looked a little like you. But her eyes were so mesmerizing. Your mom's kinda hot."

I shook off her commentary and grabbed Gayla by the knees. We were all on the floor now, anxiously waiting to hear what else she might be able to reveal. "Okay, tell me everything."

"I did." Gayla looked confused. "I spoke out loud during the vision, right?"

"Yeah, but your language was vague. What did you see?"

"I saw your mom behind bars. She was in some kind of cell. And her eyes were glowing with power." She shrugged. "That's about it."

"You said she was waiting on someone to release her. Who?"

"I don't know. The visions aren't always clear, especially when they involve the thoughts of a subject rather than physical details."

"It's okay." Dom patted my back, picking up on my frustration. "She's got her powers, so she'll be able to bust out of that cell in no time. She was a messenger, right?"

"She had her powers bound after I was born." My shoulders slumped as I realized we were no closer to finding her now than we had been before.

"Not true," Gayla said. "If her eyes were glowing, she's got her powers back."

"How can that be? And if she has her powers, why is she still hanging out in the cell?"

"The binding only works on earth," Dom said. "If she's in Keeper territory, her powers would be fully restored. And if that's the case, there are different enchantments placed on Keeper prisons to prevent escape."

"But Millie reported her as missing to the council. They said she hadn't been located. Wouldn't they confer with the other Keepers?"

"I'm sure they did. But they may not get the truth if whoever took her as a prisoner doesn't want anyone else to know."

"But *why*? Why would someone want to take her at all?" I buried my face into my hands. None of this made any sense. I wanted to ask Gayla to try again, but the way she was sprawled out across the floor now told me that it had probably taken a lot out of her. She was awfully pale.

"Can we go to the Keeper territories ourselves and try to find her?"

Dom frowned. "Even if it were that easy, *which it's not*, you'd die if you tried to access the Keeper lands. You're still a mortal."

I cursed under my breath. The answer was so close, and yet there was still not a thing I could do about it. Not unless I somehow got my powers to shift into gear.

Assuming I had any, that is.

CHAPTER 2

SEAN KNOCKED ON OUR door the next morning, right on time. But my Atlantean guard dog was looking much less doberman and much more basset hound this morning.

"What's up?" I asked as we made our way out onto the street.

"Ah, nothing. I'm good. How's life with the Olympians?"

"It's great, actually. Gayla's visions are starting to work."

"Mmm." He shoved his hands into his pockets and stared straight ahead as we walked.

"Did you hear me? She had a vision last night, right in front of me and Dom. She saw my mom!"

"Mmhmm." He wasn't listening to a word I said.

"Sean?" I nudged him with my elbow.

"Yeah, I'm good."

Ugh. No use talking to a broken record. I left him alone and got lost in my own thoughts the rest of the way to Millie's shop. It was a long walk, but that was good. I had lots of thinking to do.

I would try to get Millie alone once we got there, and show her my vitamins to see if she could order me some more. And while we were on the subject, I might try to get a little more information about my mom's powers, as well. Dom had seemed really confident that being in Keeper territory would restore them. Surely Millie would know something about that.

Finally, we reached the door to the apothecary. Sean paused a few feet from the entrance.

"Aren't you coming in?" I asked.

"Nah, I'm gonna head back. I'll pick you up when you're done with your shift."

"Sean, that's crazy. You just walked for like half an hour. Come in and rest for a second. Get a drink before you head back."

He pursed his lips, but I grabbed him by the arm anyway and tugged him inside with me. I kind of wanted Millie to have a look at *him*, too. He was acting very strangely.

"Good morning," Abby called out from behind the counter. "Hi, Sean."

He yanked his arm loose and spun around, bolting out of the door in about half a second. Abby's lip trembled, and she cleared her throat. "Excuse me for a minute," she said, brushing past Millie on her way to the storage area in the back of the shop.

"Uh, good morning," I called out to no one in particular. "What was that all about?"

Millie shrugged, though I suspected she knew more than she was letting on. "Who knows? How are you doing this morning? All ready for school to start in a couple of days?"

"Just about. I've got one more textbook to pick up, then I think I'm set." I pulled the amber vitamin bottle from my purse and set it on the counter in front of my aunt. "Hey, do you know what kind of vitamins these are?"

She picked it up, examining the glass and the pills inside. "Nope, never seen these before. They don't have any markings." She squinted at the few pills rattling around in the bottom of the bottle.

"My mom always special ordered them for me, but I don't know from where. I was hoping to get some more."

"We can definitely get you some more vitamins. And maybe some that look a little more... *trustworthy*." Millie laughed.

That made two people in the last twenty-four hours who implied my vitamins were sketchy. But they were totally normal—I'd been taking them my entire life, and generally speaking, I wasn't *too* weird or messed up.

"No, I think it has to be these. Mom said she tried several different kinds when I was younger and I had bad reactions or something. I don't know. All I know is that she was kind of a dictator when it came to my vitamins. It had to be this kind and I had to take them *every* day, *right* on time."

Millie frowned. "Hmm," was all she said to that. "Well, I can send one off to the lab to see if they can break it down and figure out what it's made of, if it's really that important to you."

"Thanks. I know it sounds silly, but it really is important to me. It's like the last connection I still have to her, you know?"

Millie pulled me into a quick hug, kissing the top of my head as Abby reemerged from the back. "I know sweetheart. I'll do my best."

Unfortunately, with Abby back in the room I couldn't inquire further about my mom's powers. I'd have to save that discussion for later.

Millie stepped out to grab us some deli subs around lunchtime, and Abby cornered me the instant the door swung shut behind her.

"Hey, can I talk to you about something. It's... kind of personal."

"Yeah, sure." I scanned the shop looking for some excuse to get me out of this in case she started asking about Keeper stuff that I couldn't reveal. Had she overheard something? Maybe she saw Millie enchanting a draught for one of the Olympian men who swung by earlier. *Shoot.* I was not ready for this.

"Have you talked to Sean much lately?"

Oh. *That.* I might've rather dealt with the Keepers' secrets than talk to Abby about Sean. "Uh, not much. Why?"

"He seems a little standoffish lately. I was just wondering if he maybe confided anything to you about why he's behaving that way."

I paused to take a good look at the girl. Her puffy eyes and blotchy nose revealed that she was much more upset about this than she tried to let on. And if there was something truly wrong with Sean, I probably needed to suck it up and work with Abby to get it figured out.

"I'm sorry," I said. "I noticed he was really weird this morning with his head in the clouds, but he didn't say anything to me about why."

She sniffled. "Okay, thanks."

"Wait," I caught her elbow as she tried to turn away. "Is everything okay? Do you know something I don't? Does he need help?"

"I—" Her lip trembled again. "*I think I messed everything up!*" Her words were gobbled by sobs, and she buried her face on my shoulder.

"It's okay," I said, lightly patting her on the back. She sucked up a noseful of snot and released another wave of wails. Poor girl was ugly crying on me, and I was too uncomfortable to do anything but awkwardly pat her on the back. How on earth was anyone so worked up over *Sean*?

"Don't cry, Abby. I'm sure you didn't mess anything up. Tell me what happened." Last I knew he was rushing to comfort her after we eliminated the man poisoning her father. She was the first person on his mind. There was no way she could have messed up their friendship.

"I kissed him."

Okay, maybe there was *one* way.

She inhaled snotty mouthfuls of air. "He came over to check on me the other night. He was so concerned, and just really seemed like he cared. But I must have misinterpreted it, because I kissed him and he left right away. Now he's not talking to me at all!"

I pulled away to grab her a tissue, and she just kept right on spilling her secrets to me.

"Now I know he was only being nice to me because my dad was sick. And now my dad is feeling better, but I almost wish we could go back to how things were a week ago when Sean still cared. What kind of terrible person does that make me?"

Her words were drowned out again in a soft cry followed by a loud trumpet-like blow into her tissue.

"You're not a terrible person at all, Abby. Sean is just..." *a supernatural being who can never be with a mortal.* Ugh. How was I going to make her feel better about this? "He's just a guy. Guys this age don't know how to show their emotions. He probably really likes you, but he's scared, you know? I'm sure things will get back to normal between you two soon. But for now, maybe just give him a little bit of space."

"I just wish I could find a guy who wasn't afraid to show interest. Someone who puts me first and lets me know how he feels. Someone brave enough to let me know that he's only got eyes for me. There's got to be one out there somewhere, right?"

The front door chimed. I turned to greet our new customer, seeing as how Abby was in no kind of shape to talk to anyone, but my jaw dropped. Abby gasped behind me.

"Everly Gordon, I've been looking all over this city for you."

"Is that—" Abby whispered.

"Clayton Miles." The A-list actor gracing every tabloid in the country walked forward with his hand extended. Abby reached out, soggy tissue still clamped between her fingers, and shook his hand.

"Clayton Miles," she repeated, dumbstruck. She still had his hand gripped in hers, the snot rag the only thing separating them.

"Abby," I pulled her gently away from him. "Why don't you go get cleaned up. I need just a minute."

She nodded, mouth still agape, and retreated to the back of the shop. As soon as the green curtain swished shut behind her, I turned to face our handsome new visitor.

"Why would you be looking for *me*?" A quick glance over his shoulder revealed that he was alone.

"Well, I'm in town to film a movie, and I remembered you said you were in the city. You're going to Columbia, right?"

Did I mention where I lived to him? We only spoke for half a minute on Gayla's boat in the Hamptons. I definitely didn't say I was going to Columbia, because I didn't think I was at the time.

"There are eight million people in this city. I can't imagine why you would attempt to find me. And how did you wind up here at the apothecary?" Something about this seemed off.

"The Keepers are a tight-knit bunch." He winked, and I noticed his hazel eyes still contained the standard Agarthian golden flecks. I guess he couldn't completely hide his true identity.

I resisted the way my stomach still wanted to somersault at the sight of him, and focused on getting to the bottom of this. "I'm not a Keeper. Your *tight-knit bunch* doesn't even know who I am."

"They know your aunt. Come on, Ev." He reached out and allowed his hand to glide down my upper arm, the way a friend or a lover might do. "Lighten up. My movie is filming on your campus and I just thought it would be nice to have a friendly face around the set. Maybe you can show me some of your favorite spots around the area."

"It's Everly," I said, stepping away. "And I don't have any favorite spots on campus. I haven't even started school yet." I looked through the storefront windows again, searching for any reasonable evidence that might indicate why he was truly here. Was I being pranked? Did Gayla put him up to this?

If so, the prank was going sour. He might charm every girl in his path—he even charmed me the first night we met—but I was less than impressed by this encounter. In fact, it was a little unsettling.

Never in a million years would I have thought getting hit on by a gorgeous global celebrity would leave me feeling creeped out.

"Okay." He raised both hands in the air. "I can see that you're busy working right now. I shouldn't have interrupted you unannounced like this. But I happen to know there's a back to school party next week at St.

A's, and I'd love it if you came. I'm going so I can get into character for my role."

"St. A's?"

"Don't worry. I can get you in."

"I don't—no." I shook my head. "I don't know what that is or care to attend any parties. Look Clayton, I appreciate you stopping by, but I really just want to focus on my schoolwork. I'm not interested in—"

He laughed, cutting me off. This guy obviously wasn't used to rejection. But did I really just reject Clayton Miles? *Who was I?* I was a girl on a mission, that's who. And I didn't need any boys, celebrity heartthrob or otherwise, distracting me from my studies. I had to find my mom.

"Don't say no, just say you'll think about it." He winked again and turned toward the door. "I'll see you around, Ev."

"It's Everly," I called out, but the door had already swung shut behind him.

CHAPTER 3

I'D FORGOTTEN ALL ABOUT Clayton by the time Monday morning rolled around. I hadn't seen much of Sean, either. He'd laid low, content that Gayla and Dom were sufficient to keep me well-guarded in his absence. There were some definite perks to living with Keepers.

Dom and I shared our first class Monday morning. It was the one I'd been looking most forward to—*A Review of the Ancient Languages*—though it was more like an intro than a review for me. Still, apparently Professor Brossard was the go-to guy when it came to ancient texts and forgotten languages.

I guzzled down my latte from The Honey Pot and quickly wiped the foam from my upper lip.

"Easy there, killer." Dom laughed, but she looked just as excited as I felt. Her short hair bounced with each eager step she took, making her look more alive than I'd ever seen her. Maybe my enthusiasm was contagious.

"I can't help it. This feels like the first real step in finding my mom. I can't wait to meet Professor Brossard."

Dom paused on the sidewalk, pointing up ahead. "Hang on, what's going on up there?"

I followed her look with a groan. "Looks like a film set."

"Oh yeah, I remember seeing that flyer at The Honey Pot. I think it's a Clayton Miles movie."

"It is. Did I mention he stopped by the apothecary the other day?"

"Uhh, no." She turned and drilled her eyes into me. "And that's definitely something you should have mentioned."

I guess I'd been too concerned about Sean to mention Clayton. And I obviously didn't bring up either one to Gayla. There was no need to hurt her feelings by sharing stories of Sean and Abby. "I'll explain, but is there any other way to get to our class?"

"Not if you want to be on time."

"Alright, but let's try to hurry past the set. I don't want to get caught up in the crowd and be late."

I filled her in on my strange meeting with Clayton a few days earlier, pushing as quickly as we could through the thick crowd that had gathered around the set. They were mostly Freshmen, if I had to guess, wide-eyed and gushing over their luck at getting to attend such a famous school right alongside real celebrities. I rolled my eyes and continued telling Dom what happened, conveying to her with my mind what I couldn't say out loud in front of the mortals.

Ha. *The mortals.* As if I were any different.

I'd just gotten to the part about him inviting me to the party when the crowd parted. Dom's jaw dropped. "Don't look now, but—"

"Everly!"

I turned to find two muscular arms reaching out from a shirtless hunk of a man. No—not a hunk. Clayton. I couldn't let his good looks distract me. But there was no ignoring him even if I'd tried.

He swept me up against his chest and spun me in a circle. "I'm so glad you came out to watch us film!"

Wiping my face, I stepped away from him as soon as my feet reconnected with the ground. "Why are you all wet?"

"They had to spray me down with water to look like sweat. Do you like it? I look athletic, right?" He flexed, and a chorus of sighs and whistles from the student body surrounding us drew my attention back to the crowd. Cell phones were pointing at us from all directions. One girl even spoke into her camera—apparently live-streaming the event. Live-streaming *me.*

"Say cheese," Clayton whispered. He winked and blew a kiss to the camera.

"No. Clayton, I've gotta get to class."

"That's my girl. Go learn something good!" He called out as I stomped away.

Gross. I locked arms with Dom and scuttled away as quickly as I could without breaking into a full run.

"That was way worse than I was expecting," Dom muttered once we'd put some distance between us. A few cell phones still filmed me walking away, but most had turned their attention back to Clayton and the movie set.

"It's over the top, right? I'm not his girl!"

"Definitely over the top. And you're right. Something seems fishy about it."

A trio of girls up ahead stepped onto the sidewalk in front of us. In almost perfectly synchronized time, they crossed their arms over their chests and shot daggers at me through their eyes.

"Excuse us," I said, stepping around them. We were about to be late, and that was not the first impression I wanted to make with the Professor who was going to help me decipher the tablet and find my mom.

One girl scoffed, but they were the least of my worries.

"What is wrong with people today?" I asked Dom.

"Well, those three are Agarthians. And they're probably jealous."

"Jealous about what?"

"You and Clayton."

"Ha! They have no need to be jealous. That guy weirds me out. And even if I was into him, he can't be with a mortal. They know that."

"Well, he can't *bond* with a mortal. That doesn't mean he can't date one."

"But I thought Keepers all had soul mates, anyway. Why would they care?"

"They are probably hoping he *is* their soulmate. Even Keepers aren't immune to a good-looking guy and a little glamour. And they hate to see one of their kind fraternizing with a mortal. It's like a slap in the face."

"Are they really holding out hope that Clayton Miles might be their soulmate?" I cringed. "Seems a little desperate. Also, they would probably know it if he was, right?"

Dom shrugged. "They say you know your soulmate when you find them. But until you do, no one really knows what to expect. It's a little different for everyone, I imagine. But don't let those girls bother you. Let's just get on to class."

"Right." I risked one last look over my shoulder at the girls. They followed us, eyes hard set and trained on me. Thank goodness I had Dom here. After just three minutes on campus it seemed that I was already developing an army of enemies. This year was going to be just splendid.

Thanks a lot, *Clayton*.

CHAPTER 4

WE SLIPPED INTO THE classroom with two minutes to spare. I threw out my empty latte cup and settled into a desk next to Dom just a few rows from the back, extracting a notebook and pen from my bag. A quick glance around the room told me that I was likely the only mortal here.

A cluster of white and blond haired Olympians sat near the front, including a male who looked like he might grow up to be a weatherman. His hair was so perfectly placed that even an Oklahoma tornado wouldn't do much to move it. Behind them was a crowd of what I assumed were Atlanteans—all with gorgeous sparkling blue eyes and reddish-brown hair. A pang struck me at the thought that in another world I might have been sitting there alongside them.

The other students varied in appearance, some of the Agarthians maintaining their beautiful golden eyes, and some changing their appearance to better fit in around the mortals on campus. But they were all too beautiful to truly look human. Everyone except me. I was squarely in the mortal department when it came to looks.

And I wasn't the only one who noticed. A few beautiful faces turned to stare, leaning in close and whispering amongst their friends.

"Relax, guys. She's Atlantean, she just hasn't gotten her powers yet!" Dom huffed out an annoyed breath and turned to me. "It'll be fine. They'll get used to you."

"How do they know I'm a mortal?"

"It's hard to explain. But once a Keeper has received their powers, it becomes very obvious to all the others who and what they are. It's almost like an aura around them."

"How cool. What does my aura look like?"

"You have no aura." Dom frowned. "Or at least not the Keeper kind."

Well that explained all the dirty looks I'd gotten since entering the room. There was some shuffling in the seats behind us, followed by a grunt of disapproval. "The mortal is here." The newcomer didn't even attempt to lower her voice.

I turned to see the three Agarthian girls from outside earlier. *Great*. This day just couldn't get any worse. Thankfully a door at the front of the room opened then, and a tall older man entered. He was in no hurry to settle in, slowly removing a book and glasses case from his bag. He opened a laptop, furrowing his brows and clicking around with a stream of whispered curse words. Finally his brows lifted with a sigh.

"Ah, there we go." A large screen behind him lit up with a picture of the professor and a short bio. "I'm Professor Brossard. Welcome to A Review of the Ancient Languages." He smiled, moving his gaze across the faces in the classroom, faltering only slightly when he landed on me. Mercifully, he said nothing and continued with the lesson.

There wasn't much of a lecture—more just a review of the syllabus and what we could expect to come throughout the semester. The final slide showed a picture of the professor with another man standing in front of the Great Pyramid of Giza.

The men looked jovial. Professor Brossard wore a floppy canvas hat and a big grin under his sunburned nose. His companion wore a similar hat, but it wasn't enough to hide his curly orange hair. One section of curls stood out from the others—bright white, and it hung low over his forehead. His eyes sparkled a bright aqua blue—like my aunt Millie's. And something about him intrigued me, making it difficult to pull my eyes away. I imagined he had lots of good stories to tell.

We were dismissed a few minutes early, and the other students immediately shuffled through the aisles to get out. But I wasn't so eager to leave.

"Hey Dom, I think I'm gonna hang back for a few minutes. I need to talk to the professor."

She nodded, clearly seeing my true intentions. I had to find out if he could help me read the tablet. "That's fine, but I can't stay with you. I've got to get to the other side of campus. Sean is nearby, though. I'll text him to meet you on the Low steps after class."

"If you must." I grinned. Millie would be upset if I took off without my trusty bodyguard—or at least a friendly Keeper of some kind. But I wouldn't resist today. Not after seeing those cruel looks from the Agarthian girls.

I waved goodbye and made my way down to the front of the room. Most of the other students had already filtered out, but the professor was busy shutting down his computer. I cleared my throat as I approached, hesitant to interrupt him.

"Excuse me, Professor Brossard? Do you have a minute?"

"I think I can spare one." He bent over his desk, shuffling through papers and tidying up. He didn't seem particularly interested in chatting, but I figured I may as well continue since I was already here.

"Great, thank you. I'm Everly Gordon. I'm Atlantean," I added quickly. He would see that I had no *aura*, as Dom put it. "I just haven't received my powers yet."

"Yes, yes. I figured that was the case otherwise they wouldn't have allowed you into my room."

My mouth pulled itself into an embarrassed smile. "Right. Well, I'm honored to be in your class this semester. I look forward to learning from you. You see, I have this...artifact, that I can't decipher. I don't recognize the language, but I hear you are really knowledgeable with things like that, so I'm hoping after learning from you I'll be able to get it figured out."

"It is my specialty." He stopped shoving things into his bag and finally looked up at me, appraising me for just a moment before asking, "What kind of artifact?"

"It's a stone tablet. Or a piece of one, anyway. It may have been broken."

"I see." He zipped up his bag and slung it over his shoulder, squinting at me before continuing. "I would be happy to take a look at it if you'd like."

"Really? That would be amazing. When would be a good time?"

"Tonight? I have a dinner meeting this evening, but I can probably examine it before I go. How about 5:30?"

"That sounds great."

"Are you familiar with The Honey Pot?"

"I am."

"Let's meet there. Ancient tablets shouldn't be quite as shocking to our people as they would be to mortals, so it's a safe place to discuss our findings."

Our people. At least he considered me on the same level as the other Keeper students. "Very good, sir. And thank you again. I will see you later."

I practically skipped out of the room. Maybe this day would turn out alright after all.

CHAPTER 5

THE OTHER STUDENTS HAD completely cleared the hallway outside of our classroom. There wasn't a person in sight. There was, however, an adorably fluffy orange and white tabby cat sitting across the hall when I exited.

"Hey, little guy."

The cat stood and meandered over to me, winding itself lazily between my feet. I reached down to pet its head, but it ducked and moved off to the side.

"I don't think you're supposed to be in here. Come on, let's get you outside."

The cat moved in front of me and stopped, rolled onto its back, and shot me an expectant look.

"You want me to rub your belly?" It was an awfully canine move for a cat, and one that usually resulted in playful bites and claws to the arm from my experience with our barn kittens back in Oklahoma.

I reached down, and sure enough, the cat latched onto my arm with claws from all four feet. But it wasn't playing around. The animal instantly drew blood, and bit me with a feline ferocity I'd never experienced—more like a tiger than a barn cat.

"Ouch!" I tried to yank my arm away, but the cat held on tighter, kicking me with its back feet and shredding my skin with its front claws.

One of the Agarthian girls from earlier rushed around the corner. "You found my sweetiekins!"

Instantly the cat released me and sulkily trotted back over to the wall where I first found it.

"Your cat mauled me! Why would you bring a beast like that on campus?" The question burst from my mouth before I had time to think it through, and the cat hissed. But in that moment I didn't care if the girl could overpower me. It didn't matter that she'd tried to murder me with a glare earlier that day, or rudely pointed out my mortality in class. My arm was bleeding and I was ticked off.

But the Agarthian girl didn't react angrily. She appeared quite calm, in fact. A slow smile spread across her face, and her brown eyes flashed with a golden glow. "Please give me my cat."

"No! I told you it just attacked me."

"Give me my cat. Now."

The girl's eyes glowed brighter and something shifted within me. Back in the recesses of my mind, I knew I was being glamoured. I knew it, but there wasn't a darn thing I could do about it.

"Okay," I muttered, stepping toward the animal. It turned and quickly padded down the hall, opposite the girl.

"What are you waiting for?" She asked, her voice somehow made up of multiple harmonies. Even as she commanded me to do her bidding, I found myself enchanted by the sound of it. "Go get it."

The cat waited for me at the end of the hall. I moved for it, and just as I could almost reach out and pick it up, it moved again, turning to the left. It halted outside of a bathroom door.

"Stay, kitty." I lifted both hands and tiptoed forward, aware of the Agarthian girl on my heels. She made no attempt to get the cat herself, and I knew she was playing with me for her own entertainment.

I approached the animal again, and the bathroom door swung open. The cat darted inside. I turned back over my shoulder and the girl threw her hands in the air, her expression a clear and silent insult to my intelligence. She may as well have shouted, *get in there and grab it you idiot!*

Of course, she didn't have to say anything else. I was still under her spell from before. Bound by her command to get the cat. I knew I could do nothing else until my task was accomplished.

She followed me into the bathroom, where a second Agarthian from the mean girl squad stood waiting. Once inside, the second girl raised a hand and the door slammed shut behind us.

"Did you just—" My words were cut short by a huge gust of wind that slammed me back into the wall, pinning me there, unable to move.

The first girl laughed. "You weak little mortal." She turned toward the second girl. "You can drop her, Stella. She's not going anywhere, are you, mortal?"

The pressure of the wind released me, but the glow of the girl's eyes and melodic sound of her voice was just as strong a captor. I timidly shook my head, eliciting laughter from both girls now.

The cat circled in place on the floor, and in a move I never saw coming, grew and shifted, standing on its feet and rising up to our height. Its fur appeared to melt into smooth, tan skin, and its face morphed into the beautiful feline features of the third Agarthian girl. Her strawberry blond hair fell loosely to her shoulders and her large green eyes still sparkled with golden flecks.

She grimaced and marched over to the sink, scooping palmfuls of water into her mouth and swishing before spitting back into the basin. "Eww! You taste disgusting!"

"I can't believe you bit her!" The first girl laughed louder now. She was having way too much fun at my expense.

"Shut up, Camille. She was about to walk away. Maybe if you had shown up on time..."

"Enough, girls." Stella, the one who could apparently create gusts of wind with her bare hands, seemed to be in charge. The other two girls silenced at her command, and all eyes turned toward me.

"What are you doing here, mortal?" Stella made no attempt to change the color of her eyes. They were a beautiful amber color, like Tate's. Her hair was a rich espresso, and her skin a flawless deep golden brown tan. I imagined this was as close to a pure Agarthian appearance as they could get. She was strikingly beautiful, even with her face twisted into a mocking hatred.

"Being trapped against my will." I scowled.

Camille snorted. "No one is holding you here." She sneered, fully knowing that I couldn't resist her glamour.

"I mean, what are you doing in Keeper classes at Columbia? And don't tell me you belong here. No one has ever had to wait beyond their eighteenth birthday for their powers to come in. I'm not buying your story."

I gulped. At least none of these girls were telepaths like Dom.

"It doesn't matter if you buy my story or not. It's the truth." *Probably.*

She raised her hands and another gust of wind slammed me backward, causing me to knock my head against the wall.

"Watch your mouth, mortal. And watch your back, too. No one is going to sit quietly off to the side while you try to get cozy with one of our most sought-after males. If you can't keep your hands to yourself, we'll just have to show you your way out of New York."

The girl was fuming. I should have kept my big mouth shut if I knew what was good for me. But I couldn't resist just a little more trash talk. My words were the only power I had over them, after all. "Aww, what's wrong? Are you sad that he might be more attracted to a human than any of *you*? And what about your own soulmates? Nervous that maybe they don't exist? That maybe their souls have been fractured by all the other Agarthian men who've taken mortal lovers?"

I was going out on a limb with that one. But seeing as how the Agarthians seemed to hate fractured souls more than any of the other Keeper races, I thought it might be a bit of a sour spot for them. And I was right. My words definitely struck a chord.

The cat girl immediately shifted back into her feline form, jumping at me at the same time my hand turned the knob behind me. I'd caught them by surprise and knocked them off their guard. The door was unlocked, and I spun out into the hallway, pushing it closed behind me before I could suffer another claw attack or hurricane from Stella.

I'd been prepared to run, but the guy across the hall stopped me in my tracks.

"Tate! Thank goodness! I need your help!"

I swear he was bathed in golden light like a gift from above. A ridiculously attractive gift. He leaned propped against the wall, one ankle kicked over the other, expressionless with those gorgeous golden eyes trained on me. I gripped the doorknob hard, feeling the girls on the other side working to shove it open again.

"Little mortaaaal..." Camille's sing-songy voice was muffled, but I still felt its power fluttering through my mind.

"I can't hear you!" I shouted, drowning her out. "Lalalala!" Yep, I was resorting to the tactics of a ten year old. But it worked. Her already muffled voice was drowned out by my immature shouting.

A gust of wind blew out of the bottom edge of the door, nearly knocking me off my feet, but I leaned against it with all my weight and somehow managed to keep them inside. But I knew it wouldn't hold much longer.

"Please!" I cried out again to Tate. "Don't just stand there. They're trying to hurt me!"

He didn't say a word. His golden eyes looked straight into me, somehow making my body come alive. After what felt like several minutes, though it was probably just half a second or so, I was burning up.

"Come on, Tate! Do something!" The door gave way, and my body was thrown to the ground. I jumped up, barely risking a glance over my shoulder as I heard Stella say something to my hunter. I never made out what it was. I was too busy running.

Within seconds I was back at the front door of the building, relieved as the sunshine blasted down upon my cheeks. But I didn't dare stop. I wanted to put as much space between those Agarthians girls and me as possible.

And *Tate*. I didn't even know what to think about Tate. I knew he wasn't there to protect me. I knew he was just as big an enemy as anyone else on this campus. And yet, I felt betrayed. Why wouldn't he help me?

CHAPTER 6

I RAN AND RAN and ran. If I just kept moving, I wouldn't have to worry about the strange looks I got from other students or respond to the offers for help. Humans couldn't help me. Not with super powerful Agarthians on my tail. Though truth be told, I wasn't even sure if they'd followed me out of the classroom building.

And like all good things, eventually the adrenaline wore off. The burn in my legs brought me to a stop and the stitch in my side bent me in half. I'd somehow wound up in a parking lot. It was mostly empty, well-shaded by established trees, and it had no identifying features. I didn't even know which side of campus I was on anymore. I wished I'd paid better attention during my original tour with Dom and Gayla.

But the campus wasn't too large, so I had to be near one of the main roads by now. If I continued straight ahead, I'd run into one eventually.

After rubbing out a charley horse in my calf, I stood up to find my snowy white owl friend sitting on the asphalt a few feet in front of me.

Ugh, I groaned. "Please tell me you're not here to warn me of impending doom again." I stepped to the side and tried to get around the owl, but it bounced over right in front of me again.

I squatted down to look into its sentient yellow eyes. "I am trying to get away from some Agarthians who are trying to hurt me right now. I don't know if you can actually understand me or not, but if you can, I need you to move. Now."

I stood and tried to zag back to the left, but like before, the owl mimicked my movements and blocked my way again.

"Okay, really? Is this like back in the alley? Are you trying to guide me somewhere? You're better than a dog. Even a fluffy helpful one, like Lassie."

The owl blinked.

"Look bird, I honestly do not have time for this right now. You're cute and all, but I've got to get out of here."

We stared each other down for a few breaths, and then, without any warning, I lunged forward into a sprint. The plan was to catch the owl off guard and run right past it, but of course it saw me coming. Who knew owls had such great reflexes? Either that, or the bird read my mind like Dom and knew what was coming. But I refused to believe that. It was just an animal. Right?

The owl lifted off of the ground, flapping in place about as high as my shoulder. We collided, and out of instinct alone, I swatted the bird away. My hand made contact with the creature and it was tossed several feet over to the side. I should have used that opportunity to take off and run, but I couldn't just abandon the poor little guy. Even if it was an annoying distraction in my escape, I had to make sure it was okay.

I trotted over to where the owl sat on the ground. Its feathers were ruffled, but otherwise it looked to be in good shape. Good enough anyway. It didn't look happy though. "Are you alright?"

The bird hopped on its feet and flapped a few feet into the air before landing again.

"Good. Now please don't try to stop me again. I've really got to go."

The owl responded with a long blink.

I stood, walking backwards away from the animal. "We'll catch up again soon, I'm sure. You can show me whatever it was you wanted me to see next time."

I sighed, shaking my head at how crazy I probably looked. But at this point, I'd determined the owl was as big a part of my posse as Sean or Gayla. Or maybe even more than that. We were friends, in a weird *college student meets wild animal* sort of way.

I spun back to the front and froze in place, shocked to see a shiny black coupe barreling straight toward me. My fight or flight had been all used up, and I could not get my body to react in any sort of reasonable way. My scream matched the pitch of the brakes squealing across the asphalt almost perfectly, and time seemed to slow down as the details all clicked into place.

An astonishingly handsome young man sat in the driver's seat, his expression clear as the car sped toward me. Clayton Miles. He had what almost looked like a smirk on his face as our eyes locked onto each other.

Dark smoke billowed from behind the vehicle and a burnt rubber smell filled the air. My owl! He'd tried to warn me, and I didn't listen. I'd have to bring him a dead mouse or something later as a reward for trying to save my life. Again.

The car was only a couple of feet away from me now. It was still slowing, but not enough. And it struck me how odd it was that I was able to think through all of this in less than a second. My body wouldn't move, but my mind wouldn't stop.

And just like that, time was restored to its usual frantic pace, and the car slammed into me. Its bumper bit into my thighs, knocking me down at the same time it finally came to a stop, shadowing only my feet as I laid on the ground.

"Ouch!" I slid backward and stood, brushing the dirt from myself. That was going to leave a heck of an ugly bruise later. My black and blue thighs would go great with the still bloody scratches running down my forearms. I was quite the beauty queen.

The driver's side door swung open and Clayton dashed forward. "Everly, oh my goodness, I am so sorry!"

I took a step back. "It's fine. Really. You barely got me."

"I can't believe I actually hit you. Are you okay?" He knelt and reached for my legs, but I moved back again. "We need to get you to a doctor. Without your powers, you'll need medical attention to get healed up." He raised his eyes to mine, as though he were silently looking for confirmation that I still did not have my powers.

"Clayton." I put up both hands to stop him. "Seriously, I'm fine. I'll see you around."

I turned to walk away, but I only made it two steps before I was swooped up into his arms. "Nonsense," he said. "I'm not a hit and run kind of guy. If you won't let me take you to the hospital, then at least let me drive you home."

"I'll probably be safer walking," I mumbled, leaning away from his chest. He gripped me tighter, pulling me against him in a way that made it impossible for me to ignore the way he smelled—like bourbon and vanilla, and something woodsy that I couldn't quite put my finger on.

He pulled open the passenger side door of his car and gently deposited me onto the tan leather seat. I yanked on the handle as soon as the door closed behind me, but it wouldn't budge. Leaning across the console, I reached for the driver's side door next, but Clayton was already there, *tsk*ing at my feeble efforts to bust free.

I had managed to escape a siren, a shifter, and some girl who could control the wind, but here I was run over and trapped by child-locks in a movie star's car.

What a first day.

CHAPTER 7

SHIFTING MY WEIGHT TO one side, I tried to casually pull my phone from my back pocket, taking my time so as not to draw too much attention from Clayton. He was still babbling on about how I should really seek some medical attention, but I only half-listened.

Sean might still be waiting for me on the Low steps. If I could text him soon, he might be able to get over here and rescue me before Clayton got me too far away from campus. I really didn't relish the idea of Clayton bringing me all the way home. I was sure he could find our address just fine on his own if he really wanted to, but I wasn't going to offer it up to him. Dom was in class, and Gayla had probably left already too, which meant we'd be alone.

Nope. There was no way I was gonna let that happen.

Finally, I wrangled the device free and rested it by my leg, out of Clayton's direct line of sight.

"Which way do I need to turn?" He looked in my direction and I did my best to put on an innocent face.

"Uhh, let's see..." We were back on Broadway. I didn't want to lead him to my apartment, so I figured my aunt Millie's house was my next best bet. "Hang a right."

With his attention back on the road, I tapped my now-cracked phone screen. *Nothing.* After several more taps and a solid effort to restart the device, it was clear: my phone was dead—probably destroyed when I fell on it after I got hit with the car. *Freaking Clayton!*

The sound of his turn signal at the next intersection brought my attention back to him. "Actually, you need to keep going a few more blocks," I said, my heart rate increasing with each word. Where was he taking me now?

"You're sure you're not injured?"

I nodded, unsure how that was relevant to my question.

"Great. Because I want to make this up to you." He veered the car off in a direction I'd yet to explore. "I was checking out some of the locations where we'll be filming in Morningside Park, and I'd love to show you a really beautiful area over there. It can be like our own little secret getaway in the city."

"Oh, I am really fine with just going back home. You don't have to make it up to me at all." I tapped my phone desperately, praying that it might miraculously start working again.

"I refuse to take no for an answer. It'll be quick, I promise." He flashed a bright smile and winked at me. Okay, so I could definitely see why so many other girls were smitten with him. He was undeniably good looking. But he still gave me the creeps ever since he showed up unannounced, supposedly searching the city for me.

I needed to remember that when my heart began to flutter against my will.

A few minutes later he whipped his car into a spot just a couple of blocks away from a stunning old cathedral. The locks clicked up, and for a second I considered making a run for it. Clayton watched me closely, almost as if he suspected what I was thinking. But my legs were sore, and he was probably fast and strong. Realistically, he'd catch me without any difficulty. Maybe if I played nice, I could get through this quickly and get back home before anyone even noticed I was missing. That seemed like my only viable option at this point.

I followed him across the street, where he led me to an open platform overlooking a gorgeous park full of steep rock faces and flush with trees down below. "Wow, this is…"

"Pretty incredible, right?" Clayton grinned and reached for my hand, which I quickly shoved into my pocket. We weren't friends just because he showed me some trees. And we definitely weren't in hand holding territory.

He pretended not to notice my coldness, and gestured toward a staircase to the right. "Come on, the spot I want to show you is down this way."

My feet were heavy, reluctant to follow him down the winding staircase that would take us who knows where. Over my shoulder, way down the road, I could make out the gate that led onto campus. If I ran really hard...

"Clayton Miles! Oh my goodness!" A group of squealing Barnard students hurried across the street.

I turned in time to see his eyes narrow just a fraction for the briefest of seconds before he slapped on the smile he was famous for. The girls practically cooed as they skipped over to where he stood.

"Hello ladies."

"We're so sorry to bombard you like this, but would you mind taking a picture with us? Just one?"

He glanced in my direction, and I gave a small nod. "Here, hand me your phones and I'll take a few for you," I said.

The girls were practically bouncing with delight as they handed over their devices. I snapped a picture, then another. And when I picked up the third phone, an idea struck me.

"Whoops," I called out with a giggle. "I accidentally backed out of the camera. Hang on." I fumbled around with the phone, doing my best to look technologically inept, when in reality I was tapping out a text as quickly as I could to Sean. Photographic memories definitely came in handy when recalling phone numbers.

SOS. Everly. Morningside Park with Clayton Miles. Come quick! Do not respond to this number.

I gave it just a second to send, then quickly deleted the message and said a silent prayer. "There we go." I snapped the last picture and handed the phones back to the girls.

"Thanks," Clayton said as I rejoined him near the stairs. "Sorry about that. It's unavoidable sometimes."

"No need to apologize."

We began our way down the stairs, winding down to the park below. It was truly a lovely sight. If my legs weren't so sore and I was with anyone else, I might have even enjoyed it. Especially once we reached the bottom and wound our way over to a pond with a rocky waterfall.

"Here." Clayton grinned proudly. "I thought of you the moment I saw this the other day."

"It's lovely."

I inhaled and closed my eyes. With the sound of the rushing water and the scent of the greenery around me, I could almost imagine I wasn't standing in the middle of one of the most populous cities in the world.

Clayton's touch jerked me back to my senses. He gently took my arm in his hands. "What happened?" he asked, eyeing the scratches.

"I, uh, had a little run-in with a feral cat."

His jaw twitched, but if he suspected the Agarthian girls he didn't say anything. "Hopefully those powers will come in for you soon. Then you won't have to worry about cat scratches or bruises anymore."

With a frown, he ran his fingers gingerly over my skin. For a moment, I almost forgot who I was standing with. Here in the park, with birds chirping and children playing in the background, Clayton seemed more innocent. More genuine. More *human*.

Perhaps I was being too harsh. Maybe he really was just looking for a friend. I wouldn't allow myself to get too close, but maybe I could relax my defenses. *Just a little*. After all, if he wanted to hurt me he could have done it a hundred times over by now.

We walked through the park, commenting mostly on the things around us. We laughed as he nearly got hit in the head with a soccer ball. We admired a particularly colorful flower bed. And we grumbled together as we circled back around to the staircase that would lead us back up to Morningside Heights.

"Sooo many stairs," I complained.

Clayton's brows raised in the middle. "I forgot about your legs. You must be so sore. Here, let me help." He scooped me into his arms again, only this time, I didn't resist. I breathed in his smell and allowed myself to enjoy it. *Just a little*.

He began the ascent effortlessly. I wasn't exactly light as a feather, but I remembered the Keepers were stronger than your average Joe. This was nothing for him, so I wouldn't object.

We passed a woman carrying a tiny dog in her oversized bag. She grinned warmly at us, assuming we were a couple. Clayton hammed it up, of course. He pulled me closer and snuggled my cheek, much to the woman's delight. She laughed and did a little clap before moving past.

"Laying it on a little thick, aren't you?"

Clayton paused. "Oh, I don't know. I kind of like the way you feel in my arms. Maybe I was doing it just as much for me as I was for her." He pulled me close again with a crooked half grin.

This was what he was famous for. A charming smile and clever one-liners. He used them on many women before me. I shouldn't have been so gullible to fall for the same tricks. But in that moment, with sunlight falling across him like glittering confetti through the filtered canopy of trees, he just seemed so... likable.

So when he brought his face down toward mine, I lifted my chin to meet him halfway. My eyes closed and I prepared for our lips to touch. What I did not expect, was for him to drop me as an owl torpedoed him from out of nowhere.

"Argh!" He waved an arm around his head. The owl flapped off into the trees again, and he turned to where I sat, shocked with my jaw hanging nearly to the ground.

"Was that an owl?"

My mind raced. I almost kissed Clayton Miles. On the lips! But my owl stopped me. *Why?*

"I doubt it," I muttered, rising to my feet. "Seems unlikely that an owl would be right here in the middle of the afternoon in the city." For some reason I felt like I should keep my friendship with the little bird a secret, at least from Clayton.

"Everly!" I turned toward the familiar voice and caught sight of Sean flying down the stairs like his feet were wheels. *Finesse.* So that's what Sean's powers looked like. "Are you alright?"

He'd barely broken a sweat, but I could tell from his breathing that he'd run a really long way.

"I'm fine," I said. "Just ready to get home."

Sean turned and glared at Clayton—a clear warning that he better not have laid a hand on me.

Clayton's expression hardened, but he made no attempt to stop me from leaving. "Thanks for coming with me, Everly. I enjoyed it. We'll have to do it again sometime."

The warmth in his tone made me want to believe him. But the coldness of Sean's glare said it was best to keep going.

"And sorry again about earlier," he added as Sean and I turned toward home.

"Don't worry about it. See ya!" I called out.

"Sorry about what?" Sean asked under his breath, gaping at the scratches he just noticed adorning my arms.

"I'll explain when we get home. It's been a weird morning."

CHAPTER 8

SEAN REFUSED TO LEAVE the apartment after I detailed my eventful morning for him. He couldn't believe the Agarthian girls would be so bold as to attack me right there on campus. And over a boy who I didn't even like! *Probably.* I mean, I didn't think I liked him anyway.

He also thought the whole *Clayton accidentally hit me with his car* thing was a little suspect. And, it was. But he just seemed so genuine at the park. I didn't know what to believe, anymore.

"Are you sure he wasn't glamouring you?" Sean paced back and forth in our living room. We were just about to leave for my meeting at the Honey Pot with Professor Brossard, but he wanted to be sure he had the whole story straight in case we ran into any familiar faces while we were out.

"I'm pretty sure he wasn't. Camille definitely did." I pursed my lips at the memory of the Agarthian girl forcing me to retrieve her cat—or friend, or whatever. "But I didn't get that feeling of losing control with Clayton. I had my wits about me the entire time."

"Hmm." Sean ran a hand through his hair. "I just can't imagine what he wants with you."

"Uh..." I put my hands on my hips. "Maybe he actually *likes* me." My cheeks flushed at the thought. But would that really be so hard to imagine? And since when did I start arguing on behalf of Clayton Miles, anyway? "You know, some guys aren't afraid to show a girl that they like her." I shot him a knowing look, though I knew I was being unfair. He could never be with Abby, and it wasn't right for me to tease him about it.

Sean pretended not to notice and shrugged, quickly changing the subject. "It just seems weird. But we can worry about that later. We've got to get going or you'll be late for your meeting."

Thankfully our conversation shifted to the tablet as we walked over to the coffee shop where I would be meeting with Professor Brossard. Sean seemed almost as excited as I felt. We might finally be on the precipice of something huge. I knew Rossel had something to do with my mom going missing, and with the way his stone tablet called to me after her disappearance, I couldn't shake the thought that it was connected somehow, too.

And we were finally about to discover what it said.

The Honey Pot was crowded for a Monday night. Students filled the place to the brim, gathered in small groups throughout the warm and welcoming shop.

"I'll stay off to the side and catch up on my reading—classes just started and I'm already worried about falling behind. But I'm here if you need me for anything." Sean patted my back before going up to the counter to order a drink.

The espresso-filled aroma of the shop had me jonesing for a hot cup of my own, but I didn't want to waste any time in line. Not when I was this close to the truth. I scanned the room until my eyes settled on the oldest man in the place. Professor Brossard sat alone at a table near the back of the shop. His salt and pepper hair would lead me to believe he was probably in his late fifties, but as an Atlantean it probably meant he was actually in his 700s or 800s. *What a bizarre thought.*

Gripping the tablet inside my bag, I eagerly made a beeline back toward his table. A familiar chilly voice snagged my attention before I reached him, though. With a quick glance to my left, I found myself halted in place, as though the icy gold eyes staring back at me could actually freeze me in my tracks.

Osborne continued talking to the two shifty-looking students sitting opposite him, but his eyes were definitely locked onto me. Finally, after flashing a quick sneer in my direction, he turned back to the conversation at hand. I sucked in a deep breath, and finally got my feet to cooperate again.

"Everly!" Professor Brossard looked up and gave a small wave.

"Hi, Professor." I slid into the seat across from him, still a little breathless and on edge from seeing Osborne. What was he doing here? Was there another fractured soul on campus? Other than me, of course—

assuming that I was even fractured. Tate was already all over my case. Well, except when I actually needed him. *Jerk.*

"You okay?" Professor Brossard's fuzzy brows gathered in the middle like one long caterpillar.

"Yeah, sorry. I just thought I saw someone." I shook it off. *Time to focus.*

"Did you bring the artifact?"

"I did!" I fumbled around in my bag and carefully laid the stone tablet in front of him. It looked almost fake in this modern setting. It still hadn't shown any life since I dropped it that night in the gallery, but I knew it was special.

"Fascinating." The professor leaned in close. "May I?" He gestured toward the object.

"Of course." My blood rushed in loud waves through my ears as I waited with bated breath for his interpretation.

He picked up the tablet, cradling it in his hands with great care. I watched several different expressions transition across his face, awe and wonder followed by surprise and then frustration.

"What is it?" I asked, unable to wait any longer.

"Well," he rubbed his wrinkled forehead, "I'm not exactly sure."

My lungs deflated. "Do you have any guesses?"

He shook his head. "It looks a bit like cuneiform, but I don't recognize any of the symbols. And from the looks of it, it's much older than the cuneiform tablets I used to translate back in the middle east. Where did you get this?"

"Oh, uh..." *Shoot.* Why did I not think up an answer to this earlier? "It was passed on to me from an old family friend." *More like stolen from an old family enemy, but potato potahto.*

"Well it must be very special to your family, even if there is no way to know what it says." He laughed and handed the tablet back to me.

I forced a friendly giggle, but the situation was not funny to me at all. "Surely someone would be able to translate it, right?"

Professor Brossard frowned. "I used to know someone who might've been able to make something out of it, but he's long gone. I'm sorry I can't be of more help to you."

No. I refused to accept that as an answer. "What about overseas? Back in Egypt? There must be more people who learned alongside you. Perhaps one of your old classmates would know."

"There aren't many of my old classmates left, I'm afraid. And the ancient languages aren't exactly a hot topic for modern day studies. People just don't care anymore."

"I care!" *Whoops.* That was too loud. I noticed several faces from the surrounding tables turn to look in our direction.

The professor pulled back with raised brows. "Well, Ms. Gordon, I'm sorry. But I suggest you rethink your approach. Especially considering your mortal condition, you won't gain any favors with demands." He stood. "Now if you'll excuse me, I have a dinner meeting to attend."

He shuffled past me in a hurry, leaving me at the table to myself. I shoved the tablet back into my bag and rested my forehead on the cool tabletop. What was I supposed to do now?

"You have a habit of causing scenes, don't you?"

Crap. I lifted my gaze to find Osborne now sitting in the professor's chair across from me.

Where was Sean? Wasn't he supposed to be saving me from moments like this? I glanced over my shoulder to find him on a barstool near the front door, nose buried in a textbook while he sipped some frozen drink with a mountain of whipped cream on top.

"Care to tell me why you're shouting at professors?" Osborne grinned like he'd caught me with my hand in the cookie jar.

"No. Care to tell me why you care? Pretty sure we established you're not supposed to come around another hunter's case."

That wiped the smile from his face real fast. "I happen to be on another case here on campus. And I can't help but notice how all these fractured souls seem to be popping up in your vicinity." His eyes glowed and the energy shifted between us. The back of my brain seemed to hum with anticipation. *Glamour.* "So tell me, mortal. What do you know about Rasputin?"

"Ras who?" I wanted to please him. I didn't want to come up short for his request. But I had no idea who he was talking about.

"Rasputin," he repeated. "The mastermind who taught your fractured friend how to poison with dark magic."

"I know nothing about him," I replied honestly.

Osborne cursed loudly, once again drawing attention to my table. I wouldn't be surprised if they never let me into the Honey Pot again after this.

"Is something wrong over here?" Thankfully Osborne's filthy mouth drew Sean's attention as well. He stood at the edge of our table, a vein popping from his neck as he glared at the hunter.

"It's fine. Right Osborne?" I lifted my brows. The glamour was gone, snapped by Osborne's angry outburst. But I wanted to drive home the fact that I still was not the person he was looking for, and he knew it.

He grunted and waved his hand in a gesture that said *be gone*. He didn't have to tell me twice.

CHAPTER 9

"WHAT THE HECK, EV?" Sean walked backwards in front of me, his hands splayed to the sides. "I swear, I can't leave you alone for five seconds without something dramatic happening. Why were you talking to Osborne?"

"Not by choice, that's for sure!" I spat back. Now was not the time for a condescending lecture from Sean. "Maybe if my guardian had been paying better attention, he wouldn't have ever gotten to me!"

"Your *guardian* was under the assumption that you were meeting with your professor. Not a hunter."

"I did. And it was useless. Professor Brossard can't help. And according to him, nobody can."

"That's not possible," he muttered.

"Obviously. But I don't know what else to do."

"Well, you could start by staying away from Agarthians."

"*Really*? You want to keep going with this? I don't go around looking for trouble, okay? Trouble finds *me*. Just like it found my mom. But it's fine, if you don't want to stick around and help protect me, I am happy to find someone else who does. You need to fix your own problems, anyway."

"*My* problems? And what would those be?"

"Oh, I don't know, maybe being in love with a mortal? How was that *kiss*, Sean? Good enough to break Abby's heart? Because she sure thinks you hate her right now."

His face grew red and he turned around to stomp on ahead of me. Then he looked back over his shoulder with a scowl. "Abby is none of your business. And you know what? I don't think you need to talk to her anymore, either. I don't need you stirring the pot."

"Well, someone has to talk to her since you ditched her."

He stopped and threw his hands in the air. "You want me gone? Fine! I am happy to step down from my current assignment. And I wish the best of luck to anyone else who thinks they can possibly keep you under control." He gave a sarcastic salute and stomped off into the darkness.

I was left standing just outside my apartment building. I could feel the pressure of a hundred gallons building up behind my eyes, threatening to break down the dam. Choking down a sob, I pulled open the door and made my way up to our unit.

"Hey girl," Gayla called out lazily from her spot on the couch. She was binge-watching something on TV, barely noticing what kind of shape I was in. Thank goodness it was Gayla and not Dom. I didn't need some mind-reader watching the hot mess playing out in my brain right now.

I cut straight for my bedroom and closed the door behind me. Somehow, I managed to hold in all the tears until I crashed onto my bed, burying my face in my pillow to muffle the sound of my cries.

And even at eighteen years old, as a college student living in New York City, the only thing I wanted in that moment was my mom. Where was she, and how would I ever find her now? I didn't have Sean's help anymore, that was for sure. And I wouldn't request another guardian. I stood out enough as it was, being the only mortal in my Keeper classes. Some Atlantean guardian hovering over me at all times would only draw more attention and fan the Agarthian flame.

A new guardian would also prevent me from the only other option I had left. If interpreting the tablet was officially off the table, I had no choice but to take matters into my own hands. It was time to experiment with dark magic.

I kept my chin down for the next few days. Gayla and Dom traded off escorting me to class, and the only time I saw Sean on campus, he quickly looked the other way. The girls begged me to call him so we could make up and all hang out again, but I refused. Anyone who could bail on me so quickly just because I pointed out his own issues wasn't someone I wanted to beg to come back into my life. Sean was stubborn, but he had nothing on me.

Thankfully, with my Olympian friends by my side at all times, the mean girls on campus didn't make any more moves on me either. Life was almost... simple. Or it was on the outside anyway.

Inside, my mind was still a mess. Every waking moment that I wasn't in class or walking to or from campus, I was holed up in my room, poring over various old manuscripts I found at Millie's shop.

She didn't have much information about dark magic, unsurprisingly. I'd attempted a couple of the incantations I found tucked into old pharmaceutical books here and there, but nothing worked. Or maybe I just wasn't pronouncing them correctly. I certainly wasn't about to ask the girls for help with that.

By Thursday afternoon, I was about ready to throw in the towel. I'd even considered calling Osborne to see if I could get some info about that Rasputin guy, but I enjoyed staying alive too much to attempt that. Blowing the hair out of my face, I pulled out the last book in the pile I'd borrowed from Millie.

Calling it a book was being generous. It was more like a dirty old pamphlet. A cornflower blue cover was rolled at the corners and bore brown stains of various sizes. The yellowed pages smelled a bit like cigarette smoke and the spine was barely held together by two staples. The third staple had fallen out long ago.

Small, simple letters spelled, "Adverse Effects of Dream Waltzing and How to Remedy Them, a Personal Account, by Crisanna Vadim." *Dream Waltzing*. That didn't sound like it would be particularly useful in finding my mom, but it was an awfully romantic sounding power. I flipped open the worn cover to scan the table of contents and see if I might find anything useful inside.

There was an introduction, standard practices, adverse effects, the victim, the perpetrator, and the treatment. *Ooh, now we were getting somewhere good*. I read on, chewing off a loose hangnail as I committed every word to memory.

It seemed that dream waltzing was a fancy way of describing the act of entering another's mind. Not like a telepath, like Dom. But to actually interact with the other person within their mind, typically while they slept. Hence, the name *dream* waltzing. In this case, a fractured soul abused the ability and tortured a human victim in her sleep, trying to force her to later murder his enemy during her waking hours.

The perpetrator was a man by the name of Renard Soule, a fractured soul. Raised in Saint-Amand, it is believed he learned the dark arts with a clan in the forests of Felletin, though he refused to reveal the name of his teacher.

It is believed that he was born from an Olympian mother and a mortal father. As such, he was naturally capable of powers of the mind. A search of his home after his elimination revealed a book of spells, including the incantation used on the victim: almacansia, descansan, nitardariel.

I mouthed the words silently to myself. Could this be it? If I could somehow find a way to dream waltz into my mother's mind while she slept, maybe she could tell me where she was. It was definitely worth a shot. The worst case scenario would be that I might fail again. Well, either that or it would work and I'd be caught and killed by Tate for practicing dark magic with a fractured soul.

No risk, no reward though, right?

Two knocks sounded at the door, and it swung open before I could even ask who was there. Slamming the pamphlet closed, I pushed it under a school textbook and turned to see who my uninvited guest was.

Gayla. And right behind her was Dom. *Shoot!* I immediately thought back to our lecture earlier that day in my Politics of the Keepers class. If she tried to get into my brain, hopefully she'd be just as bored as I had been during that lecture and decide not to stick around long.

"Get up," Gayla said with her hands on her hips. "We're busting you outta here."

"Excuse me?"

"We know you've had a rough first week, sweetie." Dom made her way over to my desk, glancing only briefly at the stack of books before resting her focus back on me. "But we want to help you try to bounce back."

"Yep," Gayla slid into place beside her. "So get your nose out of the books, girl. It's time to have some fun. We're taking you to your first college party."

CHAPTER 10

"A PARTY? ON A Thursday? I don't think so." I risked a glance back to the pile of books on my desk. I was kind of in the middle of something way more interesting than a party.

Dom followed my gaze to the books and frowned. *Get out of my head!* She blinked hard, hearing me loud and clear. I thought she might object, but her shoulders loosened and she took a step back. I felt a tad guilty, but honestly it was a little invasive to have someone reading your thoughts all the time. I knew she was concerned, but it would be safer for her not to know what was going through my mind. I wasn't worried about getting myself into trouble—I wouldn't be able to avoid it if I was fractured, anyway. But I definitely didn't want to drag my friends down with me.

"Yep! A party on a Thursday. And any other day of the week. Welcome to college." Mischief glinted in Gayla's heavily made-up eyes. She marched over to my closet and began shifting through my clothes. "Maybe I'll let you borrow something of mine," she added, obviously unimpressed by my Oklahoman wardrobe.

Objecting would be futile. I could tell by the way Gayla moved that they weren't going to let me skip out on this. "Fine," I conceded. "But promise me we won't be out too late. I still have class in the morning."

Gayla crossed her heart. "Scout's honor." But her wink at the end did little to convince me she would stay true to her word.

An hour later we stood on Riverside Drive in front of a tall, Parisian-looking building adorned with windows and private latticed balconies. The building seemed alive, laughter trailing out through the windows, which glowed faintly in the twilight hour.

I glanced at my friends. "Are you sure we're not overdressed?" We stood on the sidewalk fully decked out in cocktail dresses and the highest of heels. Gayla looked like a model, her platinum blond hair falling in perfectly coiffed waves over her bare shoulders. She had more perfectly toned leg displayed than I knew was possible without being completely naked, and she left every girl within a three mile radius feeling completely inadequate. Dom, of course, looked just as good in a slightly more modest dress, more sassy than sexy. And I stood awkwardly between them in one of Gayla's less revealing numbers.

"Saint A's won't let you in if you're not dressed to the nines." Gayla dipped her chin toward the entrance. "Shall we?"

I followed them to the door, where a Freshman in a literal tuxedo stood as a doorman. He nodded at Gayla and Dom, but promptly extended his arm in front of me before I could step inside.

Gayla sighed and rolled her eyes. "Let her in. She's one of us."

The boy frowned, squinting at me like he was missing something. "I don't think so. I was given strict orders—"

"Move," a deep voice rumbled from over the boy's shoulder. I looked up to see Clayton grinning down at me. "You came." His voice was lighter now, and despite what was good for me, it sent a warm feeling through my belly.

Dom shot me a look of clear warning, but if they dragged me all the way here to get my mind off of school, then I might as well do it with the hottest young star in North America.

"She came with us, actor-boy." Gayla pushed Clayton out of the way, unimpressed by his fame and good looks. None of it was anything new or special to Gayla. She didn't care about Clayton; she was here for the party.

With a playful half-grin, I shrugged and followed the girls deeper into the building. This was nothing like the college parties they showed on TV. It looked more like an upscale fundraising gala, but instead of wealthy oil tycoons and their trophy wives, the elegantly designed interior was full of drunken rich twenty year olds.

"Be right back," Gayla said with a wink.

"I don't know if ambrosia is really a good idea tonight."

"Relax, Mama Dom. I'll only have one." Gayla dashed off through the crowd before Dom or anyone else could object.

"She'll be okay," I said, trying to reassure my friend. "We'll keep an eye on her."

Dom and I moved cautiously through the crowd of Keepers, many of whom had already succumbed to the blissful embrace of ambrosia. It was obvious who had consumed the sweet nectar and who had not. Those under the influence almost appeared to glow with a new kind of life. They were full of joy and free of care, practically floating through the room like the unearthly creatures they really were.

"Have you been to the Hall before?" Clayton's voice caught me off guard. I swung around to find him looking like a god, with his hands in the pockets of his snug fitting charcoal suit pants. His white button up was undone at the top, revealing just enough of his golden tan chest to leave me wishing I could see more. *Whew, was it getting hot in here?*

"Nope, never even heard of the place." I slapped a demure grin on my face and yanked my attention back up to his eyes and away from the muscles under his shirt.

"Saint A's is kind of like Columbia's version of a secret society. But it's less a secret than just an elitist group. Most people think you can only get in if you come from a really wealthy family. But the truth is you can only get in if you've got the right kind of soul."

"It's a Keeper society, then?"

Clayton nodded.

"Well, I guess it's good that Keepers and extreme wealth kind of go hand-in-hand then, huh?"

Clayton laughed, the golden flecks in his hazel eyes glittering in the light of the room. "Come on. I'll show you one of the coolest parts of the building."

Dom reached out to touch my arm, a gentle reminder to stay close. "I'll be fine," I whispered to her. "You just keep an eye on Gayla. Don't worry about me."

She looked nervously back and forth between Gayla and me.

"Seriously." I squeezed her shoulder. "There are a hundred people here. He'd have to be an idiot to try anything in front of all these witnesses. No one will mess with me."

Dom released a loud sigh. "I'll come find you just as soon as she's done." Then, turning toward the bar, she called out to Gayla.

"Let's go." Clayton laced his fingers with mine and pulled me down the hall. I didn't pull away this time. No, I was going to enjoy myself, even if just for one night. After all, it might be the last chance I had. Who knew what would happen after I tried the dream waltzing spell.

Watchful eyes of countless other Keepers followed us down the hall. We reached a wooden door near the back of the building, and Clayton gave my hand a quick squeeze before releasing my fingers. "Here we go," he said with a conspiratorial grin.

He had just reached for the knob when a loud voice called out from across the hall. "Hey! You're not allowed down there!"

A familiar thrill worked its way down the back of my neck and between my shoulder blades, until my whole body came alive with a slight buzzing sensation. *Tate?* I looked around as Clayton dealt with a bossy undergrad.

"Do you know who I am?" he asked the younger man. Yuck. That was kind of tacky. But maybe the other guy had made some kind of obvious mistake.

"Clayton Miles... I—I'm sorry. But the basement is for Saint A's members only."

The tingle grew stronger, through my arms and across my chest, pulling me... *where exactly?* Nothing seemed out of place around me. A frantic scan of the room revealed nothing unusual at all. No sign of Tate anywhere.

Clayton turned toward the young man, crossing his arms over his broad chest. "You're going to back away and allow me and my guest to have a look downstairs. Sound good?"

The guy nodded. "Yes, of course. There are suits and towels in the bathrooms."

Wait. *What?*—

Clayton pulled open the door and gestured for me to move down a narrow staircase. "After you."

CHAPTER 11

"DID YOU JUST GLAMOUR him?"

"I like to say I used my powers of persuasion, instead."

Oh, right. This was the real Clayton. The jerkwad who wasn't afraid to use other people to get what he really wanted. Now I remembered why I had been distrustful of him before. Why on earth did I allow myself to get so taken by his good looks that I forgot how to use common sense?

"Right, sooo, I think I've changed my mind. I need to go find Dom."

My shoulder pushed into his chest as I tried to squeeze my way past him, but he was like an unmovable slab of granite. "No," he said firmly.

He pulled the door closed behind him, and his eyes clearly glowed with a warm golden hue in the low light of the staircase. I brought my fingers to my ears as quickly as I could, but it was too late. I'd looked into his eyes. I'd heard the music in his tone. I was glamoured.

"Keep walking."

I obeyed without a word of protest. I had to. An internal battle with my own mind was raging strong. I knew I was glamoured. I could feel its power wriggling in the back of my head like a worm. But as long as it remained there, I was helpless to object to a word Clayton said. Even worse, I *wanted* to please him.

We reached the bottom of the stairs. In the center of the basement was an enormous inground swimming pool, complete with a hot tub and waterfall edge dripping over a stone grotto.

"I remembered how much you liked the waterfall at the park," Clayton said with a mischievous smile. "So I thought I would show you one we can play in."

My heart pounded against my ribs, desperately trying to break free and get away from him. But instead, I bobbed my head awaiting my next orders.

"Over there." He gestured toward the far wall. "Get a swimsuit from the bathroom and put it on. I want to see you out here again in less than five minutes."

The bathroom was pure white, with silver veined marble lining every surface. A small closet inside held a variety of swimsuits, each one smaller than the last. I squeezed my eyes tight, hoping with everything I had that when I opened them I would be somewhere else. Anywhere else. But alas, upon opening them I was still trapped in the basement of some frat house staring at a rack full of itty bitty bikinis. I settled on a little black number and rejoined Clayton back near the pool, leaving Gayla's dress and shoes in a neat pile on the vanity.

He sat on the edge of the pool, now stripped down to nothing but a pair of swim trunks he must have found in the mens bathroom. Blue and purple lights alternated beneath the surface of the water to create an ethereal glow throughout the room. It was lovely, as much as I hated to admit it.

Clayton tapped the spot next to him. "Join me."

I tiptoed to the water's edge, staring nervously into the depths below. One slip and I'd drown. Surely Clayton wouldn't let me die here, right? With a deep breath of chlorine scented air, I dropped to the ground beside him, allowing my legs to dangle into the pool. My purple toenails blurred in and out of the water's ripples, temporarily distracting me from the dangerous man controlling my mind.

"You look good in that bikini," he purred. "But those legs..." He ran a smooth hand across my thigh. "It's a shame they're so bruised."

I turned away. They were bruised because of him, and the irony of it all was not lost on me. We'd come full circle, and I was never more grateful for *not* kissing someone before. Now we sat while he ogled me in a bikini he forced me to wear. I did not appreciate being objectified, and as soon as this glamour wore off I would let him know about it.

"Come on." He dropped into the water, his head disappearing for just a moment beneath the surface before he reemerged, treading water like it was nothing for him. He turned and faced me with a grin. "The water's warm."

Why did my mom never enroll me in swim lessons...

"I can't swim." My chin dropped to my chest, shame flooding me. I wasn't ashamed that I couldn't swim though, I was ashamed that I had to let him down. I didn't want to let him down. I only wanted to please him.

"That's okay. Jump in. Now."

My fingertips dug into the concrete edge, even as my body betrayed me. I couldn't refuse a direct command while I was glamoured. It didn't matter if it would kill me.

Eyes closed, fingers now clamping the sides of my nose, I scooted toward the edge and removed myself from the safety of solid ground with a splash. The water *was* warm. At least I would die at a comfortable temperature. I felt myself sink, falling further and further until my feet hit concrete at the bottom of the pool. I kicked hard, flailing my legs in an effort to reach the air again. But it was no use. I was too deep.

I tried again and again, my lungs burning in my chest, crying out for sweet sweet oxygen. My legs were growing weak, my mind losing focus. I wouldn't last much longer. This was it. This was the end.

Two arms wrapped themselves under my arms, and a rush of water enveloped me as strong legs kicked us back to the surface. As soon as my face broke through the top of the pool, I coughed and gasped for air, water burning at the back of my throat and nose as it dripped back into the pool with a mixture of my own snot and tears.

"You really *can't* swim." Clayton chuckled to himself. There was no apology. No remorse in those still glowing eyes of his. I wanted nothing more than to break loose from his grip. I might even consider the bottom of the pool a more enjoyable place than being wrapped up in his arms, pressed against his hard wet chest.

"No. I told you I can't."

"That was fun, though. Wasn't it?" he asked, a grin creeping up one side of his jaw.

"No."

"Tell me it was fun."

"It was fun." Ugh. *Maybe it was fun for you, you sadistic jerk!* That's what I wanted to say, but of course I couldn't. That wouldn't please him.

"Wanna do it again?"

"No." My throat still burned from before. I was still breathing heavily in an effort to replace the oxygen I'd lost the first time I went under. I couldn't do it again.

"Tell me you do."

"I do." *Dangit.* I didn't!

"Tell me exactly what you want me to do to you."

I fought the urge to speak the words he wanted to hear. Biting down hard on my tongue, I tried to command it to stay still— to prevent myself from saying any more. I wanted to tell him to take me back to the edge of the pool. I wanted to tell him to let me go. That's what I *really* wanted. But that wouldn't please him.

The words caught in my throat, snagging like cotton on a rough wooden fence post. My mouth was clenched as tightly as it would go, and the taste of blood flooded the inside of my lips where my teeth tried to hold them in place. If I dared to open them, I knew what would happen. I'd ask him to throw me under the water again, and I couldn't let that happen.

"Too slow." He grinned, and with no additional warning, he released me. I leaned forward, frantically grasping for his legs as they propelled him away from me. The heat rose in my chest faster this time, practically lighting my lungs on fire with an electrical sensation.

My blood buzzed, begging me to give it the oxygen my body required. As my feet touched lightly to the bottom of the pool, I decided to reserve my energy. My limbs already felt tingly—I wouldn't exhaust them further. I knew I couldn't make it back to the surface anyway. I'd already tried that and failed. I'd just have to sit here and hold my breath until he hopefully decided to rescue me again.

It didn't take long this time, and as his arms wrapped around me I felt a jolt of electricity shoot through my veins. I coughed and coughed at the water's surface, rubbing the sting of chlorine from my eyes. Water wouldn't stop coming out of my mouth. How much had I swallowed? I coughed some more until I gagged, then finally inhaling a deep lungful of air, I opened my eyes.

Tate!

"Are you okay?" he asked. Concern tugged at his brows but his face was red hot.

"I will be," I whispered, my voice raw.

He swam over to the edge of the pool and gently set me back on solid ground. The worm in the back of my head was gone. The glamour was broken. I quickly stood and ran to where the towels sat on a chair outside of the bathrooms. Wrapping myself in a fluffy bath sheet, I turned to watch the fireworks show going off in the pool.

"What were you doing?!" Tate was swimming like Michael Phelps over to where Clayton waded in the shallow end of the pool.

"I was doing what you asked me to, man! Back off."

"You almost killed her!"

"I wasn't going to let her die."

Tate finally reached him and reared back a fist. I almost cheered as it moved to connect with Clayton's perfect nose, but his eyes began to glow again as he shouted, "stop it!"

It didn't stop Tate in his tracks like it would have done to me, but it did slow his momentum enough that his fist connected with Clayton's face with only a soft smack instead of the pounding I'd been hoping for.

"You took it too far." Tate was furious. The initial impact of Clayton's glamour wore off quickly, but Tate wasn't interested in hitting him again. He swam over to the edge of the pool and lifted out of the water, his collared shirt and suit pants drenched and clinging to his perfectly toned body like a wax mold.

My jaw slammed shut, and I pulled my eyes away as soon as I remembered what exactly I was looking at here: two beautiful dudes who had both attempted to drown me, glamour me, and now spoke like they were in on it together. They were gorgeous, but they were villains. I tiptoed toward the door, trying my best to not draw any attention.

"I didn't take it far enough," Clayton spat back at Tate. "Look at her! Still just a frail little mortal! She has no powers at all!" They both turned in my direction. *Crap.*

"Take my jacket!" Tate yelled at me. "You're dripping wet and it's chilly outside tonight."

His suit coat laid on the floor just a few feet from where I stood. I scurried over and nabbed it, throwing it over my shoulders as I dashed toward the stairs. No use sneaking now. They knew I was making a run for it.

I didn't wait to hear what they said next. I'd heard enough. Tate wasn't the only bad guy after my soul, apparently. He had help, and lots of it. I didn't know who I could trust anymore.

CHAPTER 12

I BURST THROUGH THE door at the top of the stairs and scanned the crowd, desperate for a friendly face. My eyes finally landed on Dom, and I rushed forward into her open arms. Her face was pale as she held me back at arm's length to examine me, then pulled me close again, patting my back. "Oh, Everly. I am so so sorry I let you go with him. I want to hear what happened, but first let's get you out of here and find you some clothes."

She released me and turned around. "Gayla!" Then, taking notice of the onlookers beginning to gather around, she put both hands on her hips, swiveling her head back and forth to make sure they were all paying attention to what she said next. "There is *nothing* to see here, people. Turn around and go about your business. This girl clearly does not need you all staring at her right now!"

Gayla stumbled into the circle, brown eyes bright and mouth in the shape of a perfect "o."

"We're leaving." Dom looped one arm through mine and one arm through Gayla's and tugged us toward the door. "Move it, people!"

The other college students scattered. No one messed with Mama Dom when she was angry.

With one last glance over my shoulder as we ducked out the front door, I saw the tall, toned figure of Tate, my rescuer and hunter. My enigma. Dripping wet at the end of the hall. And something stirred within me. I didn't know whether to feel grateful or angry. I probably should have been more afraid, really, but he had a knack for showing up and saving me just before things got really bad. Our eyes met briefly before Dom yanked me outside.

I pulled Tate's suit jacket tighter around my shoulders as the cool evening air cut through my wet towel. We turned back toward the apartment, and like a flash in the night, Sean appeared suddenly before us, panting as he bent forward to rest his hands on his knees.

"Sorry," Dom whispered. "I called him when I lost you back at the party."

"I... I came as fast—" He stood and looked me in the eye, his face contorted into a mask of regret. "I'm sorry, Everly."

"It's fine," I said, trying to choke down the emotion that was welling up in my throat.

"It's not fine. It was a stupid fight. And even if I wasn't assigned to you, I still wouldn't want you to get hurt."

"It *was* a stupid fight. I'm sorry I started it. I need to work on keeping my mouth shut. If anyone should apologize, it's me."

"No, really. I needed to hear it. And I need to talk to Abby. It's the truth, and it's no reason for me to stop protecting you. If I had been here tonight, doing my job, then... wait, what *did* happen here tonight?" He seemed to have just noticed me trembling in the wet bikini/towel/suit jacket combo.

Gayla nodded emphatically, eyes still a little glassy from the ambrosia. "Yeah, spill it, girl."

So I did. I told them everything that happened as we walked back to the apartment. Sean was like a raging bull by the time we reached our building, and Dom just kept shaking her head and apologizing.

"You can't blame yourselves like this." We stopped outside of the entrance to our building. "It's not your fault. I'm a big girl. I should've known better. Just know it won't happen again. I will never allow myself to be alone with Clayton Miles or any other Agarthian again."

"Never say never," Gayla mumbled as a shiny black coupe pulled to a stop beside us.

Clayton rolled down the passenger's window. "Can we talk?"

Sean rushed the vehicle before I could give an answer, and Clayton rolled the window back up until it was barely cracked open at the top. Sean's fist connected with the passenger's door, instead, leaving a sizable dent.

"Sean! Holy cow, that car didn't do anything to you!"

He shook out his hand. "No, but I needed to release that somehow. I feel better now." Then he turned to Clayton. "To answer your question, NO. You can't talk to her."

"Wait." Dom stepped forward, her head tilted slightly to the side. She touched the window, staring at Clayton for a long minute. Then with a small nod, she turned to me. "It's okay."

"What?!" Sean spun toward her. "There is no way in—"

"Really." She held up a hand. "I think you should talk to him. Just don't get in the car, mmkay?"

I took one hesitant step forward, pulled on the jacket again to cover myself and find some warmth, then turned to my friends for reassurance.

Sean scowled with his arms crossed, ready to pounce on Clayton at the first sign of foul play. Gayla stared dreamily at the lights glinting off the facets of her bracelet, seemingly unaware of the weight I was feeling. I knew she cared, she just had a funny way of showing it. Especially with ambrosia still coursing through her veins. But Dom... thank goodness for Mama Dom. She smiled, sensing my trepidation, and silently mouthed that it would be okay.

I moved forward to the vehicle as the window rolled down again. Over my shoulder I heard Dom telling the others to give us a little space.

"Hey," Clayton said, a sad smile playing across his handsome face.

I twisted my lips to the side, biting down on the sharp retort I wanted to send his way. He'd tried to kill me an hour ago, and I hadn't forgotten.

"Sorry about earlier. I'm not even sure I can give you a good excuse or explanation. But I'm sorry."

"Really? You tried to kill me, and you have no explanation for it? You just expect me to accept your apology?"

"I do have an explanation." He ran a hand through his hair. It had fully dried in all kinds of odd angles, and he looked more down to earth with the messy locks of a normal dude rather than the finely styled hair of a star. "I just can't share it with you."

"Because Tate told you not to?"

He gawked at me.

"Yeah, I heard you guys. Did he really ask you to try and kill me?" I swallowed the lump in my throat, unsure if I really wanted to know the answer. It was no secret that Tate was after my soul, but to think that he would ask his friends to help bring me down just... well, it kind of hurt my feelings. Which was ridiculous, I know.

"Not exactly. It's complicated. But no. I wasn't trying to kill you. And neither is he. We just... never mind."

"Nope. You can't *just never mind* the end of that thought. If you are genuinely asking for my forgiveness, you're gonna have to explain."

"I can't. But you know that sometimes a big emotional event can trigger your powers to kick into play, right?"

"I do now."

He smiled. "Well, I'll leave it at that. But I wanted to make sure you know that I'm done. I have nothing to do with whatever happens in the future. And I'm sorry for toying with you over the last week. But you did look good in that bikini." He winked. "Soo, truce?"

I shook my head. "I don't think so. Not yet. But I appreciate your apology."

"Well, I'm headed back to LA this weekend. The movie was canceled. If we run into each other again, I hope we can be on good terms, or at least start fresh. But if not... well, I appreciate you letting me get that off my chest, anyway. Take care of yourself, Everly."

"Thanks. You do the same."

He offered another genuine smile, then rolled the window back up and drove away. Once his red tail lights had rounded the corner ahead, I turned around to find myself alone on the sidewalk. Dom really knew nothing was going to happen to me. She must have coaxed Sean and Gayla back inside. I took a moment to breathe in the cool night air as Clayton's words swirled through my mind.

Tate couldn't take my soul until he had proof that it was fractured. And he wouldn't get that proof until my powers appeared. But what if I beat him to the punch? What if I could somehow induce my own emotional event that could bring them forth?

I thought through different scenarios as I made my way back up to the apartment. My friends were all gathered in the living room, anxiously awaiting my return. They'd probably been staring out the window at me, if I knew Sean.

"Everything okay?" Dom asked, though she already knew exactly what Clayton's intentions were.

"It will be." I sighed. "I'm gonna go get showered up and hit the hay. It's been a long week."

I disappeared into my room, draping Tate's jacket over my desk chair. My mom getting kidnapped was pretty traumatic, and that didn't trigger my powers. Tate caused an explosion in the gallery and almost drowned me on Gayla's boat, then Clayton almost ran me over and drowned me again for good measure. Nothing had caused my powers to appear.

Was there really anything I could do that would?

I picked up my vitamin bottle, shaking the very last pill into my palm. I looked at it, thinking of my mom. *Don't worry. I'll get my powers somehow and find you if it's the last thing I ever do.* I swallowed the vitamin and turned toward my bathroom, stopping for just a moment to eye the books still stacked on my desk.

If I couldn't trigger my own powers or practice dark magic on my own, I wondered if there was someone else who could lend a hand in that department. Osborne said there was another fractured soul on campus. What if I found them first? What if they could somehow lead me to this Rasputin guy and he could help me dream waltz to my mom?

Or better yet, what if he could help me trigger my own powers?

There was only one way to find out...

UNRAVELING

PROLOGUE

ROSSEL GLANCED AT THE clock hanging on his dingy white wall. The office space he rented in West Harlem left much to be desired, but it was only temporary. He'd had to find a new meeting location after his quick exit from the gallery, and his warehouse in Hunts Point wasn't suitable for polite conversation.

Then again, this meeting he was currently awaiting may not end in polite conversation, either. Rossel suspected he knew what the Professor would say. He'd suspected Everly took the tablet ever since he first discovered it missing the night after the explosion. But if the Professor dared to suggest any truth to the rumors surrounding the relic, things could get ugly. Rossel would have no choice but to take action against him.

A knock on the door sounded the man's arrival. "You may enter," Rossel called out.

Professor Brossard walked into the office and gave a timid bow. "Thank you for agreeing to meet with me. May I speak candidly here?" He scanned the corners of the room, likely searching for cameras or other recording devices. The Professor was naïve, but he wasn't a fool. Rossel appreciated that about him.

"You may." Rossel gestured toward the empty seat across the desk from him. "This is not the most luxurious building in New York, but it is quite secure. We will not be overheard."

"Very good, sir. You see, I've come to you about something rather important. It's... The Prophecy of Deliverance." He lowered his voice when he mentioned the tablet, despite Rossel's earlier reassurances. "A student approached me recently. She appears to have a piece of the original relic, and she was inquiring about its text. Have you noticed it missing from your collection?"

"Of course I have."

"Oh." The Professor's face went slack. He hadn't been expecting that. "Should I—uh... should I have retrieved it for you?"

"No, it's quite alright, Professor. You know the tablet has no true meaning. The prophecy isn't real, so this student—I'm sorry I didn't catch a name..."

"Everly Gordon, sir."

A frown tugged at Rossel's mouth. "Right. This Everly will find it useless. You know I only keep it tucked away to keep the rumors at bay. We don't want another incident with one becoming obsessed over it again, now do we?"

"No, sir." The Professor's Adam's apple bobbed with a large swallow.

"What did you tell her?"

"About the prophecy? Not a thing." Professor Brossard shook his head rapidly.

"Well, of course you told her nothing about the prophecy. As we discussed, it's all just folklore. But what did you tell her about the tablet?"

"I told her it was unreadable. I couldn't make out the symbols and I told her no one else would be able to either."

"Did you mention Driskell?"

"No. Of course not."

"Good." Rossel drummed his fingers on the desk. "Was there anything else?"

"No, sir." The Professor paused. "Well, actually... I *touched* the relic. As I was inspecting it. You don't think—" His face crinkled, a sheen of sweat reflecting the fluorescent lighting overhead.

"That you have been cursed?" Rossel raised a brow. "It's folklore, Brossard. What happened with Driskell is purely coincidental. He allowed his obsession with the object to get the best of him. Nothing more."

"Right. Thank you." The Professor stood, hesitating as though there was more he wanted to say. "Well, I guess I'll be on my way then."

"Goodbye, Professor."

As soon as the man disappeared through the doorway, Rossel extracted a notepad and pen from his desk drawer. He hastily scribbled a message and folded the paper, tucking it into an enchanted envelope that could only be opened by the intended recipient. On the outside, he wrote one word, "Baerius."

Two long strides had him at the window, which he struggled with momentarily before the glass finally lifted. He snapped his fingers, but he didn't have time to wait for the messenger. Instead, he clipped the note to a fastener placed just outside the sill and slammed the window closed.

He'd just gotten re-situated at his desk again when another knock sounded at the door. Gayla's voice called out. "Rossel? It's me. Sorry I'm late."

He wasn't sorry she was late. He'd been counting on it. "Enter." He pinned the girl was a disapproving glare as she dropped her designer bag on the floor beside her chair and plopped down with an annoyed huff of air. "Punctuality is a virtue."

She rolled her eyes. "I actually was on time today for once. But I ran into Professor Brossard at the elevator. Was he here to see you?"

Rossel's lip pulled up in disgust. "Why would I need to speak with a linguistics Professor?"

She shrugged. "I dunno. I was just surprised to see him here. Anyway, let's get this rolling. I have a date tonight and I don't want to be late."

A scuffling sound came from the window. Rossel glanced through the corner of his eye in time to see a large brown owl retrieve the note and take off into flight. Satisfied that he'd done all he could for the time being, he turned his attention back to the disrespectful seer before him.

"Have you managed any other visions since our last meeting?"

Gayla paused. "No."

She was lying, and she wasn't particularly good at it. But what was she afraid of revealing to him? He'd wager it was about Everly.

"Are you quite sure?"

Another pause. "Yes."

He'd have to speak with Baerius about putting a stop to her fledgling visions for the time being, at least until they were able to remove Everly from the equation. That girl was dangerous, and they couldn't risk Gayla seeing something incriminating.

"Very well, then. Let's begin with today's practice."

CHAPTER 1

MY MOTHER TAUGHT ME a trick to falling asleep when I was younger. She said to lay perfectly still and concentrate only on my toes. I would stop my wiggles and concentrate on holding them perfectly still. When the muscles had fully relaxed, I would move up my feet to my ankles, calves, knees, thighs, and so on, until every inch of my body had fully succumbed to peaceful rest. I made it to my elbows once. Otherwise, I would always doze off long before reaching my mind.

Not tonight though.

Tonight I'd gone from toes to head twenty times over. I counted sheep, whispered lullabies, and flipped my pillow over to the cold side countless times. My belly was a bundle of nerves, and there was just no use trying to sleep.

I checked my phone again. It was 2:22 A.M. With only eight minutes until my alarm would go off, I decided to quit pretending to rest and just get up. My socked feet hit the floor without a sound, and I tiptoed to my dresser where a bundle of rosemary, water hyssop, and pennywort awaited me. I slipped a robe over my shoulders, dropped my phone into my pocket, and eased open my door.

Gayla's room was on the opposite side of our apartment. I'd waited until I knew she would be tucked into bed, fast asleep before sneaking out of my room. I'd grown worried earlier in the evening. Gayla had a date with some Agarthian sophomore, and she didn't get in until well after midnight. But that was nearly two hours ago. I knew she would be sleeping by now. It was time to act.

I'd pored over the words in the dream waltzing pamphlet earlier that evening, though I already knew them by heart. And despite my best efforts, I hadn't located many other works on the topic, aside from a senior thesis written about twenty-five years ago. Evidently, the technique wasn't commonly practiced anymore. The modern telephone had eliminated the need to communicate through dreams in a sleeping state. Now it was only used for nefarious purposes, and therefore no longer encouraged or taught in the Keeper curriculum.

But my reason for attempting it was good. My mother was still locked away in some unknown Keeper prison, being held captive by some anonymous villain for who-knows-what. I couldn't just call her up, so I'd try to reach her by going directly to the source instead. I would visit her in her dreams.

The only problem was that I still didn't have any powers of my own. I relied instead on the hopes that something magical stirred deep down inside—even if it was just a fracture of a powerful soul. When combined with the herbs and the spell I'd memorized from my pamphlet, I hoped it would be enough to accomplish a successful dream waltz. And call it what they may, dream waltzing with my mother was in no way "dark magic," even if it was technically classified as such.

Practicing on Gayla without her expressed permission on the other hand... I would worry about that another day. Surely Gayla would understand. Between my two roommates, she was definitely my best option. Mama Dom would certainly disapprove, and I suspected her mind would be harder to crack. Plus, if she caught me, there would be no hiding my thoughts from my telepathic friend. Nope. It had to be Gayla.

I twisted the knob to her bedroom door and silently padded across her lush fuzzy area rug toward her bed. She lay there deep in what appeared to be a peaceful slumber. That was good. The deeper into sleep she was, the better my odds were of successfully entering her mind. I'd already planned how it would go. I would make it appear to her like a dream. I had the conversation already memorized—nothing special, just your standard *oh my goodness we're going to be late for our finals* kind of dream. Every student had them.

With the bundle of dried herbs in hand, I raised my arms over my friend and rubbed the leaves back and forth between my palms, grinding them together. Small flakes of the dried plants fell upon her sleeping form, gently dusting her over like a witchy confetti.

I silently mouthed the spell from the pamphlet, "almacansia, descansan, nitardariel." And I imagined myself entering her mind, searching through the darkness for some semblance of life. Nothing happened.

I repeated the spell, a little louder this time but still not more than a whisper, and I rested the herbs on her chest. With my eyes closed, I focused on the earthy green scent that had filled her room, matched my breathing to hers, and tried once again to find Gayla's thoughts swirling around somewhere within my own mind.

Silence. Either Gayla's brain was completely empty, or I was doing this wrong. But my pronunciation was accurate—I'd done the research. My herbs were of high quality, taken directly from Millie's storeroom at the apothecary. And Gayla was definitely deep in sleep, as evidenced by her soft snores.

I frowned and decided to try one more time. This time I leaned in close, rested my hands softly upon her shoulders, and spoke the words of the spell aloud, my voice a soft hum. "almacansia, descan—"

BEEP BEEP BEEP. My hand flew to the pocket of my robe to silence the alarm that obnoxiously rang out through the room. *Shoot.* I thought I turned that off!

Gayla snapped up into a sitting position, eyes as wide as saucers. I froze, then slowly backed up toward her dresser and squatted down, hoping to blend in with her furniture like a chameleon.

"Everly?" Her brows twisted. Then, glancing down at the pile of broken, crunchy leaves on her pajamas, her nose crinkled. "What is going on?"

"You're dreaming." I nodded and gestured around the room. "And it's a pretty bizarre dream. You should go back to sleep. I'm sure everything will be back to normal when you wake up."

She just stared at me for the longest time. I moved into a thinking position, resting my chin on my fist as though pretending to be a statue might help me convince her that this was all a dream. Gayla burst into a fit of giggles.

"I see what you're doing here." She brushed the debris off of her shirt and onto the floor. "You're paying me back for the Dylan thing, aren't you? Look—he was begging me to give him your number. He said you were the prettiest mortal he ever laid eyes on. How was I supposed to say no to that?" She shrugged, innocently.

"Dylan," I nodded. "Yep. This is payback." I had no idea what she was talking about. "Maybe you'll think twice before doing something like that again." I stood and wagged my finger at her, then moved to the door, my heart still racing from the adrenaline coursing through my veins.

Gayla laughed. "Touché." Then she shook her head and flicked a dried rosemary leaf off of her sheet. "But this was a strange prank. Every time I think I've got you figured out, you do something to keep me guessing again." She pulled the covers back up to her chin and rested on her pillow. "Goodnight, weirdo!"

"'Night, Gayla."

I closed her bedroom door behind me and leaned against the wall. Clearly, this dark magic business wasn't going to work for me until I manifested some semblance of Keeper powers on my own. My options were dwindling. I'd have to find some other fractured soul to help me, or possibly meet with this Rasputin guy myself. If anyone could help me discover my powers outside of the Keeper laws, it would be the man responsible for training all the other fractured souls in dark magic for the last hundred years.

It was time to locate Rasputin.

CHAPTER 2

SEAN MET ME OUTSIDE of my apartment the next morning. I focused entirely on my schoolwork during the week—well, that and reading up on dark magic—but I agreed to continue helping my aunt Millie at her apothecary on the weekends. And thankfully, my relationship with Sean had gotten back to normal since the whole Clayton catastrophe. It made the long walk to her shop much easier.

I'd accepted that I probably needed some kind of guardian to watch my back, and he'd accepted that I may be a little harder than average to keep track of. But I helped him with his girl problems and he helped me with my Agarthian problems, so we were both fine with it. It was a symbiotic relationship.

"You coming inside?" I asked as we reached the door. The last time we'd walked over to the apothecary together, Sean sprinted off into the sunset the moment he saw Abby.

He took a breath. "Yeah," he said through the air rushing out of his mouth. "I called Abby the other night, and I think we're good. I'm good."

"You're good, she's good, I'm good. Sound like it's all good then. Let's go." I patted my friend on the back and pulled open the glass door, gesturing for him to go first.

"How chivalrous of you," he teased.

"I try."

Abby and my aunt Millie both looked up from a catalog they'd been browsing together on the counter. "Hey, guys!" Millie called out.

Abby's cheeks flushed at the sight of Sean. He ducked his chin and gave her a stiff smile, which resulted in her withering in place. I nudged a covert elbow into his side, and he perked back up, joining them at the counter.

"I can't stay long," Sean said. "I'm meeting a friend for some basketball here in a bit, but I wanted to come and tell you ladies good morning." He held Abby's gaze for a few lingering moments and her smile returned.

"Good morning to you, too," Abby said.

Sean tapped the countertop and then turned back to me. "You still want me to swing back by around four?"

I glanced to my aunt for confirmation. "Yep, four should be great. Go slam some goals or whatever."

Sean laughed and headed for the exit. Abby's eyes remained glued to his back until he disappeared past the front windows.

"You look like you need a cold drink," Millie said to her.

"Or a cold shower." I wiggled my brows at her, but Abby just sighed.

"I'll get him one of these days. Just you wait and see."

Millie and I exchanged a brief glance but said nothing. Poor Abby. If only she knew the truth.

The door chimed and a tall man with russet-colored, casually mussed hair and faded, slim-fitting jeans swaggered into the shop. His face was scruffy with a five o'clock shadow that framed his strong jawline. He owned that rugged cowboy kind of look, and if he didn't appear to be twice my age, I might've even been into it. He reminded me of those laid-back ranchers from back home who loved to crack dry jokes with a straight face and slip in compliments when you least expected it. Only this rancher was kind of hot.

He pinned my aunt Millie with deep blue eyes that whispered of mischief, and his mouth pulled into a crooked half-grin as he slid onto a barstool in front of the old soda fountain.

"That's Wyatt," Abby told me quietly. "He comes in here at least once a week."

"Are he and Millie friends?" I asked, taking in their easy banter with one another as Abby and I whispered back and forth.

"He wishes," Abby said with a snort. "He's like a loyal little puppy. Totally adorable, but he has no idea when to back off and leave your poor aunt alone."

I turned back toward the pair, admiring their casual, playful conversation. Millie didn't look like she particularly minded the attention the cowboy gave her. In fact, she seemed to be enjoying herself almost as much as he was.

Abby disappeared through the curtain into the back room, drawing Millie's attention back to where I now stood alone. "Oh, Wyatt, I want to introduce you to my niece. This is Everly."

"Nice to meet you," I said, extending a hand.

We shook and Wyatt nodded. "That's quite the handshake you got there, girl. A firm handshake is the trademark of a strong woman. It must run in the family." He winked.

"Alright," Millie said with a smirk. "Knock it off. What can I get you today, Wyatt?"

"Besides a date?" He kept a completely straight face, but his twinkling eyes gave him away. "I dunno. You got any specials?"

"Not for you," Millie teased back.

I busied myself with organizing bags and rolls of receipt paper under the counter while they flirted back and forth. It was nice to see Millie with a man. She'd never been involved in a serious relationship that I was aware of.

Was Wyatt her soulmate? He was certainly good-looking enough to be a Keeper. Perhaps that was the reason he kept coming back into the shop. But if that were the case, wouldn't she know it? If I had a soulmate, I'd probably just run away with him—leave this messy world behind and live for a thousand years in blissful amour.

"Everly hasn't gotten her powers yet, but yes, she's Atlantean, too." Millie's tone had changed, her words clipped now. I hadn't been paying close enough attention to know how the conversation swung back around to me, and I was kicking myself for it. What did Wyatt care about me?

"Ah, I'm sure they'll kick in soon. And then we'll celebrate—the first glass of ambrosia is on me. Speaking of—you got any of them ambrosia berries around here?" He offered a smooth transition away from what was obviously a touchy subject, and I was grateful for it.

"You know that I don't." The sound of a smile had returned to Millie's voice.

"Nah, you're right. I know you like to play by the rules." Wyatt sounded a little dejected. "But that won't stop me from coming back next week."

"I know that it won't."

"See ya later, Mills."

"Bye, Wyatt."

I waited until the front door chimed to stand back up again. "Whew," I said, reaching for my head. "I think I stood up too fast." The room spun for a second and then a dull throb started at the base of my skull.

"Go on into the back and have a seat. I'm about to start counting inventory anyway, so I'll join you."

Abby stepped back through the curtain. "I'll take over out here," she said with a smile. It was no secret that Abby hated counting inventory.

Millie pushed open the curtain for me, and we stepped into the back room of her shop. I slid into a spot at the table, resting my forehead on my hand, and Millie lit some kind of herbal incense on a shelf in the corner.

"Is Wyatt a Keeper, too?"

"He is," she said, busying herself with a new shipment packaged up on the floor. "Atlantean."

"Are you guys... uh... close?"

She looked up with a raised brow. "We are friends, yes."

"Just friends?"

"He's not my soulmate if that's what you're asking."

"Oh." It was. But I felt it would be rude to pry. Millie's shoulders stiffened as she returned to her work, so I didn't think she was too interested in carrying the conversation any further.

It surprised me when she spoke again. "My soulmate died a hundred and fifty years ago. I was a young woman, and thinking we had eternity together, I didn't cherish the time as I should have. We'd only known each other a few short years. He was taken from this earth too early."

Her hands stopped moving and her chest rose and fell with a deep breath as she stared off into memories I couldn't see.

"How—" I stopped myself, realizing the question was probably insensitive. But Millie answered anyway.

"He was murdered."

"What? I thought you were immortal."

"Not exactly. We live for about a thousand years. We heal quickly and are difficult to kill. But it's not impossible with the right amount of power and malice in one's soul."

"But who would do such a thing?"

Millie sighed. "There are certain factions of Keepers who have different goals than the rest of us. They don't believe in protecting humans and keeping the earth safe. They're more interested in taking control of it themselves, even if that means eliminating other Keepers who stand in their way."

"I'm sorry, Millie."

"Me, too. But I can't lose hope. His soul may still return to this earth. We may be reunited, yet."

We sat quietly for a few minutes. She sorted through the package, and I rested my head until the throbbing in my skull dulled to a slight nuisance rather than a major distraction.

Then I remembered something Wyatt said, and it got my wheels turning. "Are ambrosia berries a real thing? I thought it was just a liquid?"

Millie laughed. "Yes. How do you think the drink is made?"

I supposed that made sense. I'd read stories from the ancient Greek myths that suggested Olympians ate the ambrosia rather than just drinking it. And I learned more and more how true many of those stories had been.

"Where does it grow?"

"Only in Olympus. And it's illegal to possess the berries on earth. They really don't even like us bringing the beverage down here, but they turn a blind eye in most cases. You know it's very dangerous if it falls into the hands of mortals. And you—" She looked pointedly in my direction. "You definitely need to stay away from the stuff."

"So Wyatt was joking then when he asked about them?"

"Yes." She smiled. "He loves to tease me about being a rule breaker because he knows how absurd the idea is to me. He's always playfully asking for black market herbs and berries."

Hmm… there was a black market for these kinds of things? I'd have to file that little tidbit away for later. "Why does he want you to break the rules?"

"Because then I'll go on a date with him. I swore to my soulmate that I would never betray him for another man. But Wyatt lost his soulmate as well, long before I did. She's never returned to this earth as far as he knows, and he says it would be better to bide our time together rather than pine for lost lovers alone. But I can't. I can't lose hope that he'll one day return."

I sighed. It turned out Millie was quite the romantic, but her story was so tragic. It broke my heart to hear the truth.

"I'm sure he will, Millie. I'm sure he will."

CHAPTER 3

OUR APARTMENT WAS QUIET when I returned after work. I thanked Sean for walking me home and quickly retreated into my room, closing the door behind me so I wouldn't be disturbed. The stack of books about Keeper history I'd accumulated loomed over my desk. One of these days, I would sit down and read each one cover to cover. But for now I would just continue to skim only the areas that interested me. Today, that meant looking for any mention of ambrosia berries.

It's not that I wanted to taste the illicit berries for myself, even if I was a little curious about them. I was more interested in how one might obtain such a thing. If there was truly a black market for Keepers, then I suspected there would be a good chance I might find a link to Rasputin through it. After all, how else would a discriminating fractured soul find the ingredients necessary to practice dark magic?

None of the information in my books was particularly relevant to today's modern society, though. There was an old Greek story about Tantalus, a man who decided to steal ambrosia berries from some unsuspecting Olympians and deliver them back to mortals on earth. Things... *didn't end well for him*. So it was no wonder the berries and other black market items would be carefully guarded these days. No one in his right mind would want to pay the consequences Tantalus had to pay.

I was still flipping through the musty pages of old books when a savory smell wafted by, pulling my attention back to the present. I perked up, glancing out the window at the empty sidewalk below before determining it must have been coming from our own kitchen. I'd been cooped up in my room for a couple of hours, so it was about time for me to take a break anyway.

I eased open my bedroom door to find Dom humming in the kitchen, rinsing what looked like dried brown rice under the faucet. Gayla sat curled up on the corner of the couch watching some reality TV show. "She's alive!" she said with a chuckle.

"I think I was brought back to life by this divine scent that crept under my door. What are you making out here, Dom? It smells amazing."

"Ah, just a simple sheet pan dinner. I've got some chopped broccoli, sweet potato, peppers, and chicken drizzled with olive oil and seasonings roasting in the oven."

My mouth was watering. "I had no idea you could cook."

"Mama Dom is good at everything!" Gayla said.

"I'll get this rice going, and we can eat shortly." Dom turned back to her work, and I sidled in next to Gayla on the couch. Dom really *was* good at everything it seemed. She was a star student, a caretaker, and above all else, a rule follower—like Millie. Gayla, on the other hand, liked to play in the gray areas.

"Hey Gayla," I whispered so Dom couldn't hear. "You know what would go great with dinner tonight? A glass of ambrosia."

She flashed a grin. "You little rebel. You know you can't have any of that."

"I know." I sighed. "But out of curiosity, where do you get it?"

"It's only made in Olympus. There's just one approved manufacturer of it, since it's so potent and dangerous in the wrong hands. They have it tightly monitored. Unfortunately, that means they can also charge whatever they want for it. And it's not cheap." She wrinkled her nose.

If it was expensive for Gayla, then it was definitely out of my league. "If it's so expensive, how are all these college kids getting a hold of it? There was a ton of it at that St. A's party."

"Rich parents?" She shrugged.

She wasn't biting. I would have to be a little more direct to get the information I was really after. "But *theoretically*, they could make their own, right? If they got their hands on some of the berries?"

She narrowed her eyes, and for a moment I thought I'd crossed a line. But thankfully she relaxed again and continued talking. "*Theoretically*, yeah. I guess you're right. But it's hard to come across those berries on earth. Smuggling them out of Olympus is no easy task."

"Where would they be, though? I mean, surely there's not just some ambrosia store sitting on a corner in Manhattan."

"No, you'd probably have to go through the black market."

"And how would one access that black market?"

She raised her brows. "You're asking lots of questions. If I didn't know any better, I might think you were trying to break some laws."

"I don't know of any mortal laws against ambrosia. And I *am* just a mortal, after all," I said with what I hoped looked like an innocent grin.

Her eyes twinkled. "That's true. You're crafty. I like it."

"So do you know how someone might *hypothetically* get some of those berries?"

"If I did, would I be able to get a couple as payment?"

"Sure, yeah. If that someone could actually find some."

Her lip twitched as she considered it. "Well if I knew, I wouldn't legally be able to tell you. But think about it. You said you saw lots of ambrosia at the St. A's party. That might lead you to believe they had access to that sort of thing. You know… if there were any dealers on campus, you might find them at St. A's. But obviously, I didn't tell you that."

"Right. Of course."

She grinned and turned back to the TV.

It wasn't long before Dom called us over to eat, and the food was as good as it smelled. We kept our conversation light, discussing school and Gayla's lame date with the Agarthian boy.

"I mean, I know they can't all be charming, but this guy seriously had zero personality. It was like talking to a wall." Gayla scraped up her remaining rice into a neat little pile that she scooped into her mouth.

"So I take it he wasn't a siren, then?" Unfortunately I'd had a few too many close interactions with the Agarthian sirens who could make you fall in love with them—or do anything else they commanded— just with a gleam in their eyes and a strange harmony in their words. This is how the hunters were so successful, like Tate and Osborne. But the mean girl, Camille, and the hot actor, Clayton, also had the ability to glamour.

"Ha! I wish he was."

"What was his power, then?" I knew of the other Agarthian mean girls… one with the power to shift into a cat, and one with some kind of weird wind power or something. But other than some of the Greek myths, which I couldn't be certain were even true, I wasn't entirely sure what other powers existed among the different Keeper races.

"Just a basic shifter. And not even a cool one. I think he said he's like a parakeet or something."

"You went out with Adam Polaski, right? I think he shifts into a peregrine falcon," Dom said. "Big difference."

Gayla shrugged. "A bird's a bird."

"You're a mess!" Dom laughed and stood to gather our dishes. I followed her into the kitchen to help her clean up. "Hey," she said quietly once we were alone. "Whatever you're considering... don't."

"Huh?" I set down the dish brush.

"You and Gayla were talking about something while I was cooking. Whatever it was, it's a bad idea."

"Were you eavesdropping on us?"

"No, but I can't help it when your thoughts are screaming from across the room. And I'm glad I couldn't hear exactly what you were saying. Because the little bit I picked up in your mind when you joined us at the table was enough for me to know that it's bad news."

"Well, maybe that's a sign that you shouldn't get involved, then."

"Believe me, I won't. And I hope you won't get involved with whatever scheme you're cooking up, either."

CHAPTER 4

I'VE ALWAYS BEEN A bad listener. And despite Dom's best attempts to keep me safe, I lived up to my reputation as I snuck out of our apartment a few days later. Gayla would sleep in, as she usually did, and Dom had an early class on Tuesdays and Thursdays, so it was my first real chance to get out of there unnoticed.

But even if I wasn't the world's greatest rule follower, I was no thief. That's why when I stepped out into the hall, I immediately turned back to retrieve the bikini I'd unintentionally taken from the St. A's house the night I ran from Clayton. One day I might return Tate's jacket, too. Or maybe not. It still smelled like him, and as much as I hated to admit it even to myself, I liked having it around. Besides, he knew I had it.

But not the bikini. Those tiny pieces of fabric had to go home.

Thankfully, Gayla slept like the dead, so I was back out in the hall in no time, dashing toward the stairs just in case someone I knew might be in the elevators. By the time I made it out onto the road, I was feeling really good. The plan was coming together beautifully.

I'd go to the St. A's house and see about getting some ambrosia berries. I wouldn't keep them for myself, of course. I didn't need them. But I wanted to establish a good relationship with whatever kind of black market dealer may reside there. Then, once we were on good enough terms, I'd ask him about Rasputin.

It should be easy enough. I'd seen enough crime dramas on TV to know that drug dealers were usually pretty friendly as long as you kept them paid and didn't snitch. And I'd been saving up cash from helping out at Millie's shop, so paying him wouldn't be an issue. Plus, I didn't expect rich Keepers to be quite as scary as the drug dealers on TV. It would be fine. *Just fine.*

But as I neared the house, memories of the party with Clayton came tumbling back into my mind. I remembered how he'd glamoured the other students out of the way so he could get me alone in the basement. The pool was entrancing with its blue and purple glow until I went under. I truly thought I would die that day. And maybe I would have if Tate hadn't arrived when he did.

It was pretty ironic, actually. Tate—the guy who asked Clayton to nearly kill me so that he could extract my soul and finish the job himself—*he* was the one who'd rescued me. Maybe he wasn't such a great hunter, after all... not that I was complaining.

I turned the corner onto Riverside and stopped dead in my tracks. My luck couldn't have been any worse. Standing on the sidewalk, looking directly at me, was Sean. He casually dribbled a basketball, chatting with a friend. Maybe, just maybe, I could still get out of there before he registered that I was walking alone without a Keeper guardian. I spun on my heel and took off in the opposite direction.

"Everly!"

Darn my bad luck.

"What are you doing out here?"

I stopped, filling my lungs with air before I turned to face him with a sweet smile. "Oh, hey Sean! Didn't see you there."

He narrowed his brows at me. I was so totally busted.

"Okay, I did. But I got nervous that you would be upset I was out here without you."

"So you were just gonna run away?"

"Yeah. Basically." I turned to his friend. "You look really familiar. Have we met?"

"This is Devon," Sean said. "I think you guys met briefly at the Keep."

"Oh yeah, in the Hamptons. Well it's good to see you again. Guess I'll catch you guys later." I tried to spin off and head back to the apartment again, but I didn't even make it one step.

"Uh-uh." Sean reached out and grabbed my arm. "Not so fast. You forgot to answer my question. What are you doing out here, Ev?"

His friend Devon looked away, trying his best to hide a grin. What exactly had Sean told him about me? The thought of getting chewed out by my babysitter in the middle of New York was not only embarrassing, it was infuriating.

I yanked my arm loose. "I was running an errand."

"Alone?"

"Yes. It's kind of a... personal matter."

"Personal or not, you shouldn't be running around out here alone. You know that can be dangerous."

"Trust me. No one remembers better than me." I pulled the stringy little black swimsuit from my purse and dangled it in front of the boys by one tiny strap.

Sean's eyes widened.

"Is that a swimsuit?" Devon asked.

"Yep. Wanna tell him how I got it, Sean? Go ahead." It was childish for me to bring up the night Sean let his guard down and I almost died as a result. But I was mad. And I needed to get myself out of this without Sean discovering the true nature of my visit to the St. A's house.

Sean shook his head. "I could have returned that for you if you'd asked. You didn't have to come back here alone."

"It's embarrassing enough as it is. I hate reliving that night, and I would especially hate for anyone else to have to remember me shivering on the city streets wearing nothing but an itty bitty wet bikini and a hunter's suit jacket."

Devon's brows raised. "I don't wanna know."

"Now if you'll excuse me, I'm just going to return this, like I had planned before you interrupted me."

I huffed and tried to move past the boys, but Sean stepped into my path. "I'll go with you."

Devon nodded. "Yep, I don't know what happened, but I'm getting the feeling you might need a little extra backup."

"I'm fine." Those words had been ringing on repeat through my brain all morning. It had become like a mantra, but even after saying it a million times, I wasn't so sure I believed it.

The boys didn't care if I thought I was fine, anyway. They moved to the sides of me like sentinels as I stepped up to the door and gave a quick knock.

No one answered. It was nine in the morning. Surely someone in that house was awake, right? I knocked again, and finally a messy haired guy in gray joggers answered the door. He was barefoot and shirtless, and it took me a minute to find my words.

"I, uh..." I held out the swimsuit, still dangling by a string. "I think this is yours."

He yawned and took the bathing suit without saying another word. He looked bored, and surprisingly unsurprised to be receiving a bikini delivery first thing in the morning. I suspected he'd seen much stranger things in that house. I tried to get a glimpse of the room behind him, though I don't know what I expected to see. A group of guys huddled around a coffee table, separating illicit berries with a razor blade? That was silly. These were just a bunch of sleepy college kids.

"Alright, well, bye." The door closed in my face. I turned to Sean with my hands on my hips. "See? Fine."

The boys escorted me back to our apartment, but I had no interest in entertaining them. Gayla was awake when we got there, and she poured them each a cup of coffee while I sulked in my room. Dom came home shortly after that, and I overheard her whispering with Sean after Gayla hopped in the shower.

And by *overheard*, I mean I had my ear pressed against the door, straining to make out any syllable I possibly could. It was obvious that they were talking about me.

"Yep," Sean said. "She was there, alright. But I don't think anything suspicious was going on. She was just returning that swimsuit."

"Hmm," Dom said. "I could've sworn there was more to it than that."

"What did you hear her say, exactly?"

"Nothing. But I got some seriously dark vibes from her the other night. I know she's up to something."

"Well it's not at the St. A's house."

"Alright." Dom sighed. "Well thanks for following up on it anyway."

"Any time. Let me know if you hear anything else. I happy to check it out."

"Will do. And thank you, too, Devon. It takes a village."

"No prob, Dom."

The front door opened and closed, and a few minutes later I heard Dom retreat to her room. Speaking of snitches, the drug dealers would hate Dom. I couldn't believe she tattled to Sean about some suspicion that I might be up to something bad. I mean yeah, she was right, but that was beside the point.

And then to say "it takes a village," like I was some toddler they all had to scramble around after? I was livid. And I wasn't going to give up so easily. I was going back to the St. A's house the first chance I had. And I would do it again and again until I found out where this Rasputin guy hung out.

Childish or not, I would do whatever it took to get to the bottom of this mess. If none of my so-called friends were willing to help me find my mom, I would have to find someone who would, even if that meant mingling with black market drug dealers or fractured souls.

I was going to find my mom or die trying.

CHAPTER 5

THE NEXT AFTERNOON, I found myself back on the streets, headed toward Riverside Dr. The girls thought I was studying with Sean, and Sean thought I was spending the afternoon at home. It wasn't exactly an airtight alibi, but it was enough to allot me some freedom for a couple of hours.

I knew morning visits wouldn't pay off with this crowd, so I had to go later in the day. And just to make sure I didn't run into Sean or anyone else who might rat me out, I took the long way to the St. A's house, going several blocks out of my way just to be safe.

I slowed as I neared the corner, peeking around the building like a child playing hide and seek. If Sean was sent to intercept me again, I was going to lose my mind. But the sidewalk was clear of anyone I recognized. Lucky for him.

With a deep breath, I mustered up all the courage I had and stepped up to the door, giving it two quick knocks. Once again there was no answer, but it was after lunchtime. Surely these guys weren't still asleep. I reached up to knock again, but before my knuckles made contact with the door, it swung open.

"Everly?"

Tingly chills immediately covered my body. It reminded me of the feeling I got when the hairdresser massaged my scalp during a wash and cut. It was delightful. But in this case, it came with a warning. "Tate! Oh my goodness, what are you doing here?"

"I live here. What are you doing here?"

"I, uh—" *Shoot.* Where was another bikini when I needed one?

It wasn't all that surprising that Tate was a member of the St. A's. He was ridiculously good-looking and had that carefree, *can't hold me down* attitude that came with extreme wealth. But I still felt foolish for not considering the fact that I might run into him here.

Now I just had to come up with a reasonable excuse for knocking on his door. "I was just wondering if you were recruiting."

"Seriously?"

I bit my lip. Why did he look so unconvinced? Was that a strange request? I really should have studied up more on how this not-so-secret society worked. "Yeah, I might be interested in joining."

He narrowed his eyes, drawing my attention back to the golden flecks that sparkled in the afternoon light. "You don't get to *ask* to be recruited. And we don't let fractured souls join."

A breath escaped me. I'd already come this far. Twice. There was no telling if I'd be able to escape my apartment without a guardian again anytime soon, and I didn't want to put off my secret little mission any longer. Tate wouldn't stop me. Not today.

"Okay, do you want the truth?" This was probably a huge mistake, but I was getting desperate.

"I always want the truth."

"I heard this was the place to go for... certain *remedies* that aren't available at the apothecary."

He crossed his arms over his chest and leaned against the doorframe. The movement stirred up a familiar smell—the comforting scent of Tate that I'd grown accustomed to on his jacket. It must have been some predatory advantage for the hunters. He could lure his victims in by his attractive features and a smell that destroyed our defenses and actually made us feel safe with the man who wanted our poor little fractured souls. I shook it off.

"Please tell me you're not another ambrosia junkie." He quirked an eyebrow. "I certainly wouldn't have pegged you for one."

"Ambrosia? No! I don't care about that stuff." It was true, but it was also my excuse for wanting to meet the dealer. I needed a Plan B, stat. "I actually need something else. It's kind of an unconventional remedy. Do you have access to, uh... that kind of stuff?"

"What kind of stuff?" A pretty little blond girl stepped into the doorway beside Tate, sliding in close to his side. She wiggled her way under his arm, so that it draped casually around her, with his hand settling on her waist. A jolt of jealousy shot through me, and I instantly rejected it. Why would I be jealous about some girl with Tate? He wanted me dead. I couldn't forget that.

She leaned her head gently against his side. Her hair was slightly darker than Gayla's and Dom's, with more golden yellow tones. But her eyes shared the same deep brown, and she was undoubtedly Olympian. She wore a flimsy white tank top and short, loose fitting pajama bottoms that exposed more of her toned legs than I cared to see. But as an Olympian I knew she wasn't Tate's soulmate. No bonding there. *Not that I would care.*

"Nothing, Viv. She's just a mortal."

The girl studied me closely, then stood on her tiptoes to whisper into Tate's ear. I ignored the way it made my stomach lurch to watch their casual exchange. Even my skin tingled harder, as if in protest. The sight literally stung.

Tate locked eyes with her and nodded, then he pulled his arm free and crossed it back over his chest again.

"What is it that you're after, sweetheart?" The girl put her hands on her hips.

Sweetheart? How does a girl like that get off calling me sweetheart? No. I needed to control myself. This was a real shot at getting to find the dealer. I needed to keep my very mortal reactions in check. I also needed to think of something to ask for.

"It's for my friend, actually. She's sick."

"Keepers don't get sick," Tate said.

"Sick of school, I mean. She knows what her future holds, and school is just a waste of time preventing her from her true calling."

"Her true calling, huh?" The girl smirked. "And what is that?"

"She's a seer." I held my breath, waiting to see what their reactions would be. Tate would undoubtedly know I was talking about Gayla. But did this other girl, Viv, know Gayla too? I really should have thought up a better story before spouting off lies that might get me and my friend into trouble.

When neither of them spoke, I continued. "The school work is becoming a grind, and it's distracting her from her visions. She's struggling. So I was hoping to find something to help her focus. Do you know anyone who has access to anything like that?"

Viv's mouth twisted to one side. I wished I had the power to read her mind, like Dom. Was she about to throw me back out on the street and call up the council to warn them of mortals creeping around in Keeper business?

"I can do you one better," she said. She closed her eyes and held out a hand. Tate let out a sigh of exasperation and focused on something across the street. I wasn't sure what was happening, so I waited, barely breathing. After a minute of silence, I lifted my hand, wondering if she was motioning for me to take hers and follow her somewhere. But before I touched her, a brown paper envelope—square shaped, and slightly larger than her palm—came flying out of nowhere from inside the house and landed softly upon her skin. She opened her eyes with a grin and extended the envelope toward me.

"Did you just—" I couldn't even find a word for what I'd just witnessed. "Did you just conjure that up out of thin air?"

She rolled her eyes. "*Mortals.* No, I didn't conjure it up. I'm not a witch. I'm telekinetic. I just pulled it out of my drawer upstairs and brought it down here."

With her mind. I tried to look less amazed, but that was really incredible. "Thanks," I said. "What should I tell my friend? Does she need to take it twice a day with meals or something like that?"

Viv groaned. "No. These will help induce the visions. She should only take them when she's ready for a major mind trip. They're powerful, and they might knock her off her feet for a couple of hours afterward, so tell her not to take one unless she's somewhere safe for a while."

"Got it." I fumbled around in my purse, looking for some cash. "Do you know how much I owe?" Then it dawned on me that this petite little blond girl was the one who'd given me the illicit substances. She was nothing like I'd expected. "Wait, are you—are *you* the dealer?"

She laughed, the sound like a thousand tinkling bells. "This one's on me. And never call me a dealer again." Then she turned to Tate. "Keep your mortal friends out of here." She smacked him on the rear end and turned back into the house, leaving us alone once again.

"She's right, Everly. You need to stay away from here. This isn't the crowd you want to get involved with." Concern tugged at his brows, but he didn't say anything more.

I looked down at the small envelope in my hand, feeling the pills tucked inside. "I will." Especially now that I knew Tate was involved with the St. A's, I'd have to keep my distance. One false move and I might just get my soul extracted.

He moved to close the door and I stepped back down onto the sidewalk before calling out to him one more time. "I still have your suit jacket, by the way."

The corner of his mouth pulled up. "I know."

He closed the door. The tingling sensation immediately vanished and somehow, I felt lonelier without it.

CHAPTER 6

THE BROWN ENVELOPE SAT propped up against the stack of books on my desk. I'd been staring at it for hours. Days, really. I wasn't sure what to do with it. There was a part of me that wondered what would happen if I took one. Would it be strong enough for a mortal to have a vision? Would it be possible to see my mom? Or would it be so powerful that it would knock me dead the moment it touched my tongue?

The concern Tate held in his eyes the day I got the pills told me it would likely be the latter. That, combined with the sudden reappearance of my little owl friend was enough to prevent me from trying... *so far, anyway*. I glanced to the window where the bird sat. There was no denying that he was here for me. He stared into my bedroom, not even pretending to act like a normal owl. He'd also been hanging around on campus any time I walked to class or the Honey Pot.

If I thought Sean was bad, this owl was relentless. I would never be able to go anywhere without some kind of guardian again. And it felt wrong to do something illegal like take a powerful vision-inducing drug while he watched.

Plus, I wasn't a drug kind of girl. I didn't even like taking Tylenol. But would my mom want me to do it if it meant locating her and bringing her safely home again? That was the burning question. I just had to do my research before making any decisions.

On Saturday morning, I found myself back at Millie's shop. Abby didn't argue when I offered to take the inventory duties for the day, and thankfully Millie was busy with customers most of the morning, which meant I had the back room to myself.

I worked a little. But mostly, I scoured Millie's old textbooks for information on what the pills might be. It was too bad I didn't know the name for them. That would have made my job much easier. After a couple of hours of flipping through the dusty old tomes, I was overcome by the same, throbbing headache I'd experienced the week before. It had appeared a few times since that first day, but never as strong. Today it came on hard and fast, like I'd been hit with a baseball bat.

I rubbed gingerly at the base of my skull, then stumbled out into the front of the apothecary to call for my aunt.

"What's the matter, Ev?"

"My head," I mumbled. "It's throbbing again."

Millie frowned. "Come on, let's see if we can get it fixed."

I slid back into my spot in her back room, resting my cheek on the cool tabletop while Millie once again lit the herbal incense that seemed to relieve my symptoms last time. She then set to work on mixing up some kind of medicinal draught.

I watched her work, trying to concentrate on her movements instead of the pain that refused to abate. She had her back to me, busying herself with measuring out a powder I couldn't identify, when suddenly another figure appeared in the store room. It was as if he materialized before my eyes. It happened in an instant, faster than a blink.

I sat up and rubbed my eyes with the heels of my hands, squeezing them shut hard before opening them again. The figure was still there. He turned, and I recognized him instantly. Devon, Sean's friend, grinned at me.

"Millie? I think I'm hallucinating."

My aunt turned around then and dropped the glass jar containing the powder. It hit the floor and shattered, sending up a cloud of white dust and spraying shards of glass across the floor into a broken mosaic around our feet.

Devon turned to the source of commotion and froze as they locked eyes. So it wasn't a hallucination, then. Millie could see him, too. Her eyes glistened with unshed tears, and a smile slowly found its way to her lips.

"Do... do you recognize me?" she asked.

Devon shook his head. "I don't think we've met, but... yeah. It's weird. I feel like I do recognize you." He stepped forward and lifted a hand toward my aunt, then dropped it again. In his other hand, he held a red envelope.

"This is Sean's friend, Devon. Devon, this is my aunt Millie. How on earth did you just appear here?"

Neither of them paid me or my words any attention. They continued to stare at one another like a child might watch the flames flicker on her birthday candles. There was awe and wonder and longing. And it creeped me out.

"Guys?"

Millie finally pulled her gaze away from the boy and focused on me as a single tear broke free from her lid and rolled slowly down her cheek. "I think I should be the one doing the introductions, here. Everly, this is my soulmate."

My jaw dropped. I turned to Devon. "What? Is that true?"

He still had his eyes glued to my aunt. "I—I don't know. Maybe? I'm only eighteen. I've never met my soulmate before. But… I—yeah. Yeah, I think it's true. It feels like your name is written on my bones. I know that sounds crazy, but I don't know how else to say it. I can't describe this feeling. I just—I just want to hold you in my arms."

Another tear fell from Millie's eye. She nodded and extended her arms. Devon rushed forward and they wrapped each other in an intimate embrace, the way lovers would do. I had to look away.

"She's like four hundred years older than you. Maybe you shouldn't rush into things," I said, staring into the opposite corner.

They ignored me. After a moment, I laid my head back on the table and closed my eyes, tuning them out and breathing in the smell of the incense that finally began to fill the room. I wasn't sure how much time had passed before Millie finally spoke again.

"Everly's right. You're so young. We don't have to rush back into a relationship. But when you're ready, I'm here. I've been waiting for you to return, just like I promised."

"I'm sorry, I don't remember."

"I know." Millie wiped her eyes. "The mind is weak, but the soul knows. I'll catch you up on everything when you're ready. But your past life shouldn't diminish your current life. We'll be together, but only when you're ready."

"I'm ready now," Devon said. "Now that I've met you, I can't imagine not being with you."

It was the craziest thing I'd ever seen, and I'd seen plenty of crazy things over the last several weeks. As if he just remembered I was in the room,

Devon turned to me then with a goofy grin. "Mind if I marry your aunt?"

"You just met! Maybe you should date her first." His eighteen year old body had just begun to fill out into that of a man. His muscles were lean, and his curly brown hair was a mess. Next to my aunt's perfectly put-together figure, he looked like a joke. She was hundreds of years old, and even to the average mortal eye, she appeared to be about forty. They would certainly draw negative attention. And yet, I suspected neither of them could care any less.

"Oh!" Devon held out the red envelope. "I almost forgot why I came. This is for you."

Millie took the envelope with a frown. "Urgent? What could it be?" She slid a thumb under the seal and pulled out a small note.

While she read silently to herself, I turned back to Devon. "So, are you a messenger?"

He nodded. "Yeah, normally I'd be busy with school, but since the Order of the Keepers convention is coming up, they've called upon all of us to help with the increase in correspondence."

"So you just squeeze in teleporting between classes?"

Devon laughed. "Yeah, pretty much."

It was amazing to see it happen. I knew it was possible—after all, my own mother was supposedly a messenger just like this—but to actually witness it in person was beyond incredible.

Millie clutched the note she'd received and looked up to the ceiling. With a heavy sigh, she refocused her attention back to me, and took the chair across from me at the small table. "Everly, dear. I've just found the source of your headaches."

"Great! What is it?" I was ready for some relief.

She slid the note across the table for me to examine. The paper was just a lab report. I picked it up and scanned the words, my pulse picking up in speed with each line of text. This wasn't an ordinary lab report. This was a Keeper lab, specializing in elements outside of human comprehension. And my last vitamin—the one I'd given to Millie to research—brought up some very interesting results.

"How sure are you that this is accurate?"

Her face split into a full smile. "One hundred percent."

"But... *why?*"

"She wanted to keep you safe." Millie's smile vanished and she grew serious again. "Everly, darling. This changes everything. Those vitamins were designed to bind your powers. *Keeper* powers. There's no way your mother would have utilized something with such a high strength if you were fractured."

"So I'm a Keeper?"

She nodded and reached for my hand, giving it a gentle squeeze. "Welcome to life as an Atlantean."

CHAPTER 7

"WHEN WILL THEY KICK in?" My heart was thundering against my chest. I was Atlantean. Full blooded. A Keeper. With powers. Holy cow!

"How long has it been since your last dose?"

"About a week," I said. "Maybe eight days?"

"I expect it will be soon, but it's hard to say. Most binding substances are designed to be stored in the body long term, so that if you were to miss a dose, you would never know it. But with these specific pills coming from an unaccredited supplier…"

"Is that the nice way of saying black market?"

Millie frowned and ignored my question. "It's hard to say. It could be any minute. Or it could be a few more weeks. For many young Keepers, their powers aren't ignited until some kind of outer stimulus forces them into action."

"Right, I've heard about that." That's why Tate and Clayton had brought me to the edge of my life so many times. They were trying to terrify the powers out of me. Which gave me an idea… "Thank you, Millie!" I wrapped her in a hug, nearly squeezing the life out of her. When I released her, I noticed Devon still standing awkwardly off to the side. "I'll uh… let you two get back to catching up."

I dashed through the curtain back into the front of the shop. *Atlantean.* I still couldn't wrap my mind around it. I had to test it out, and I knew just the thing. I would just have to get alone, first.

"Hey Abby, I'm gonna go grab some lunch. If Millie asks where I am, let her know I'm with Sean." The lie slipped out too easily. I would probably get caught, but hopefully it wouldn't matter by then. I planned to have my powers kicked into high gear in no time. I wouldn't need a guardian anymore.

I practically skipped down the sidewalk back to my apartment. Nothing could keep me down today. I was a powerful immortal being.

About three blocks away from our building, just on the outskirts of campus, I spotted Viv, the Olympian dealer from the St. A's, chatting with some scrawny human-looking boy. A smug smile pulled at my lips. *Sorry, Tate. Your girl is cheating on you with a mortal.*

Except, she wasn't. She pulled an envelope from her pocket and covertly handed it off to the boy. I took another look, just to be sure I knew what I was seeing. That kid was definitely mortal. There was no way such a sickly looking boy could be a Keeper. But his smile wasn't sickly at all. No—it was strong, and menacing.

Viv gave the boy a stern look and then disappeared around a corner. His grin widened, and then he looked up and locked eyes with me from across the street. The smile faded into a scowl and he scurried off in the opposite direction.

That was strange. I should have probably just let it be, but a nagging curiosity urged me to follow him. I couldn't resist a good mystery. Why would a black market dealer be conspiring with a mortal? Unless he wasn't a mortal.

Not a Keeper. Not a mortal. That only left one other option. This kid was a fractured soul.

I picked up my pace, fully convinced now that I was going to catch him doing some dark magic in an alleyway somewhere. I shouldn't have cared. I knew now that I didn't need the fractured souls or Rasputin anymore. All I had to do was take one of the vision-inducing pills to locate my mother, and with Keeper powers, I could search their territories until I rescued her myself.

But then again, the visions might not work—not for an Atlantean. Wouldn't it still be easier to dream waltz right into her mind and ask where she was being held? There weren't any Atlantean powers that would give me such an advantage. Even when mine did emerge, it didn't mean I'd be able to locate her.

So maybe meeting up with Rasputin wouldn't be such a bad idea after all. I would just have to do it before my powers emerged, or he would refuse to see me. I was certain he wouldn't agree to meeting with a full Keeper, but if I could convince him that I was fractured…

I'd been so wrapped up in my thoughts that I lost track of the fractured boy. *Shoot.* I stopped on the sidewalk, looking down the road to my left and right, before deciding to stick to my original plan. All this fractured soul and black market dealer nonsense was going to get me in trouble if I wasn't careful. I turned back in the direction of my apartment and nearly ran right into the last person I wanted to see.

Osborne sneered at me. "Looking for someone?"

"No." I shrugged him off and tried to pass him.

"Oh, I think you were. I saw you spying."

"Spying on who?"

"The fractured boy. Is he one of your friends?"

"I don't know what you're talking about." I tried to push past him again, but he reached out and grabbed my arm. "Ow! Get off of me!"

"I know you're involved. And I'll put the pieces together soon. Mark my words."

I yanked my arm again, hard, but Osborne's dirty fingers gripped me even tighter. I would probably be bruised.

"She said get off."

A wave of electricity danced across my skin. Tate. My dark knight was saving me yet again.

Osborne's grip loosened, but he didn't let go. "You need to do a better job of keeping your pet on her leash. She's stepping dangerously close to my territory, and I won't hesitate to do your job for you if the occasion presents itself. I'll gladly take the credit, too. Especially if it gets me into that shiny seat they supposedly have reserved for you."

"Enough!" I'd never seen Tate so angry, except for maybe when Clayton tried to drown me. "Get your hands off of her. Now."

Osborne's lip curled into a seriously frightening snarl. He did as Tate asked, but not before giving my arm one final squeeze as hard as he could. I bit down on a whimper. He wouldn't get the satisfaction of knowing he'd hurt me.

I waited until he turned away before trying to rub the feeling back into my bicep. Tate reached out to see the damage, and a soothing warmth spread from his fingers the moment his hand made contact with my arm.

"Oh, wow." I closed my eyes briefly and inhaled, appreciating the comfort of his touch. "Is that some kind of healing power?"

"What?" Tate's head tilted to one side, but he left his hand lingering gently on my arm. The feeling of his touch spread through me like hot cocoa on a cold day, warming me from the inside out and completely distracting me from the pain.

"That warm feeling."

"You can feel that?" He yanked his hand quickly away. I wished he would put it back, but at least the soreness had disappeared before he removed it. "No. I can't share any healing powers."

"So what is it, then?"

He shrugged. "Probably your imagination."

That wasn't true. He'd admitted to feeling it, too. I wondered if he also got the tingling sensation when we were near each other. Maybe that's how the hunters knew when they were close to their prey.

Tate turned back toward Riverside Dr., but I wasn't going to let him get away so easily. This wasn't a frequently traversed area outside of the campus, so he better have had a good explanation for how he suddenly appeared when I was in danger again.

"It's strange how we keep running into each other in a city this big." I pursed my lips and shot him an accusing look, scurrying to keep up with his long strides.

"Nah, it's not strange. I've been following you."

"What?"

"You knew that. I told you as much the first time we met in Central Park."

"But I haven't seen you around much, lately. It kind of seems like you only show up when I'm in danger."

"Well, that's when your powers are most likely to appear. I need to be there to catch you when it happens."

"So you can lure me back to your lair and extract my soul?"

Half of his mouth pulled into a crooked grin, somehow looking more charming than calculating. I was such a fool for being attracted to a guy who just admitted to stalking me so he could eventually kill me.

"I like the word *lair*. It makes me sound like a mastermind."

It struck me that Tate and I actually had similar goals now. He wanted my powers to appear just as badly as I did. And I didn't have any reason to fear him anymore. Now that I knew I was a full-blooded Atlantean, he wouldn't be able to extract my soul. I wasn't fractured, but I didn't have to tell him that.

"You know, if you're going to follow me around the city, you may as well walk beside me instead of lurking in the shadows."

He stopped and looked me dead in the eye. Side by side, it was much more evident how tall he was. He stood a good foot higher than my five-foot-six frame. I had to lift my chin to maintain eye contact.

"You're not afraid of me anymore," he said. "Why?"

"You don't look very scary to me. Besides, if you were truly evil, you would have let me die when I fell off the yacht. Or when the gallery exploded."

"That's an over exaggeration—the gallery didn't explode."

"Or when Clayton tried to drown me. Or when Osborne tried to break my arm. Should I go on?"

"You do have a habit of getting yourself into trouble."

"If you're so determined to take my soul—*assuming I'm even fractured*—why don't you try to get my powers jump-started yourself?"

Tate paused, and I could practically see the wheels turning in his mind. "Do you know something I don't?"

"Guess you'll have to wait and see..." I touched my fingertip to his chest on the last word and turned to walk ahead without him, ignoring the jolt of electricity that still had my hand tingling from where we touched.

I risked a quick glance over my shoulder and spotted Tate standing motionless on the sidewalk, his hand over the spot where I'd touched him.

CHAPTER 8

I CHICKENED OUT. I couldn't bring myself to take the vision-inducing pills. Maybe it was my conscience… or intuition. Or maybe it was the glowing yellow glare of my owl's eyes through the window. But every time I picked up the envelope, I heard a voice in my brain that told me to set it back down again.

Technically, I was still a mortal until my powers kicked in, and taking an unknown substance like that now could be deadly. I would reconsider taking the pills once I was officially Atlantean. Until then, I would just dream of what having powers might feel like.

I tried to play it cool the next day. I didn't want to reveal the news about my powers to my friends until I had proof. It almost seemed too good to be true, even to me. But it must have been written all over my face.

"I don't mean any offense by this, but are you feeling okay?" Sean studied me a little too closely on our walk to campus the next morning.

"I feel great. Why?" My voice came out in an overly enthusiastic high pitch, destroying any plausibility that I was telling the truth.

His eyes narrowed further. "Something's up."

"Nope. You're wrong." We stopped outside of my classroom building. Normally Sean would have waved goodbye here and continued toward his own class, but he seemed dead-set on getting to the bottom of my mood. He crossed his arms over his chest and opened his mouth to speak, but I cut him off. I knew just the thing to keep him moving. "How's Abby doing? She mentioned you guys might hang out this weekend."

His jaw snapped shut and he shook his head. "See ya after class, Ev."

Ha. Sucker. I was about to turn for the building when I spotted a familiar face across the lawn. He was too far away for me to be certain, but he looked a lot like the sick little mortal boy I saw the day before. He checked his watch and glanced around, like he was waiting for someone. Was he doing another deal with Viv, maybe? This seemed like a bad place to go unnoticed.

I knew I should have ignored him and gone to class. It was the right thing to do. It's what Dom would have done. But who knew how long it would be before my powers came in? Millie mentioned it could be weeks.

And here was this fractured soul, right in front of me. I could talk to him now, and possibly find my mom *today* if he was willing to lead me to Rasputin. Why would I wait for my powers to come in when I could get my mom back today?

Ignoring the faulty logic behind my scheme, I moved for the boy. He glanced up and locked eyes with me again. As soon as he realized I was heading for him, he turned and jogged off toward the opposite side of campus.

I picked up my pace as well. That same voice in my head that urged me to set down the pills at home was screaming at me now to stop and turn back for class. But there was adrenaline pumping through my veins now. I was high on the thrill of a good mystery, and common sense went right out the window.

He disappeared between some cars in a parking lot up ahead. I ran harder to see where he went, when my owl flapped down and landed on a curb. I frowned at the creature. "I already know this guy is probably bad news. You don't have to tell me. But I need to talk to him."

The owl tilted its head at me, and I swore I could hear my conscience yelling at me to go to class again. But I was so close. I just needed to see where the boy went.

I took just a second to catch my breath and rub at the spot on the back of my head. A headache was ramping up again, throbbing with my heavy breathing. Ignoring it the best I could, I stepped over the curb and looked both ways in the parking lot. An engine started in the next aisle over, so I hurried toward the noise. A blue sedan backed out of a narrow spot, and the mousy brown hair of the mortal boy was visible through the back window.

"Hey!" I called out, though I knew he wouldn't be able to hear me. Even if he did hear me, he had no reason to stop. I certainly wouldn't have stopped for some panting girl who'd chased me across campus and yelled at me in a parking lot.

I knew what I was doing didn't make any sense. And yet, I couldn't stop.

I moved forward with the intention of tapping on his trunk, but a pair of sturdy arms caught me before I could get near the car. I froze, knowing who it was before he even spoke. A buzz shot through my limbs, and my heartbeat quickened.

"What in the world are you doing?"

I turned to face Tate and the sensation strengthened. He quickly released me, and I suspected he'd felt it, too. "I'm trying to catch that guy." I turned to follow the car, which was headed toward the exit of the parking lot.

"Why?" Tate jogged up to my side.

"Because he... he has some information that I need. It's important."

"You're not making any sense. That guy doesn't know anything. He's a mortal."

"I don't think so. I think he's fractured."

Tate's eyes widened just a fraction. "Are you sure?"

"Yes... I mean no. I strongly suspect it."

"Then we've got to follow him."

"Yes. Wait—"

Tate was already gone. He ran ahead to a young woman who'd just set her water bottle on top of a car as she loaded the backseat with her books. He leaned in and spoke quietly to her. Next thing I knew, she grinned widely and handed him the keys. Tate glanced over his shoulder and hollered at me to get in.

This wasn't how I pictured my morning going. Not at all. But I wouldn't object to Tate chasing after the fractured boy, as long as I could tag along. I would just have to find some way to speak to the boy privately before Tate stole his soul.

Okay, so maybe it wasn't such a great idea after all.

I pulled the car door closed behind me as the vehicle was already rolling forward after the fractured boy. "Do you steal cars from unsuspecting mortals often?"

He cut me a sideways glance. "About as often as you chase people across campus."

"Well played," I mumbled with a grin.

"So why do you think this guy is fractured?"

I chewed on the inside of my lip. Should I tell him the truth? On one hand, I wouldn't mind throwing that pretty little Olympian girl under the bus, but I didn't want to upset him.

Nevermind... he was a hunter. I didn't care about his feelings. "Your girlfriend gave him some drugs."

"Who?"

"Viv. I saw them doing a deal yesterday. He's definitely not a Keeper, so I assume he must be fractured."

Tate made a choking sound. "First of all, Viv is not my girlfriend." He shuddered. "Second of all, if you're sure you spotted her giving him something, then he's most definitely up to no good." He cut his eyes over to me again. "I'm glad you didn't take the stuff she gave you, by the way."

"Would it have killed me?"

"Definitely, and your fractured soul would have been permanently lost."

We'd caught up to the blue sedan, and we drove quietly for several minutes. My head was really pounding now, and I could see my pulse inching in around the edges of my eyesight with every heartbeat. Thankfully Tate was driving—not me. He did a good job of trailing the car without drawing the driver's attention. I wondered if he'd trailed many fractured souls like this before.

After a bit, I dug a little deeper into the pills, asking the question that had been dancing on the tip of my tongue. "Would those pills kill a Keeper, too?"

"No. We're immortal. Nothing short of a century can kill a Keeper."

"That's not true."

Tate's brows wrinkled and he shot me a quick glance again. "Who told you that?"

"Does it matter?"

He sighed and continued driving, ignoring my question. His face remained tense though, like there was more he wanted to say. But he didn't.

We drove on for quite some time until we reached an industrial part of the city. Worn buildings lined the road with broken glass windows and boarded up doors. The car turned down an empty road of warehouses toward the Long Island Sound, and stopped at an abandoned looking building at the end of the road. Tate moved past the street and parked around the corner. "You stay here."

"Okay." There was no use arguing. If I refused, he'd glamour me and force me to stay put. But if I played along, there was still a chance I could act on my own accord.

Tate climbed out of the car, but he paused before closing the door. Leaning back in to face me, his expression grew serious. "I mean it, mortal. Don't leave this car. If there are other hunters here, they'll assume the worst about you. They won't wait for proof."

"Got it." I swallowed, waiting for his eyes to glow or his voice to change. But after a long pause, he closed the door and jogged around the corner toward the fractured boy.

I released a pent up breath the moment he disappeared from my view. If Tate thought there would be other hunters here, this was a much bigger deal than I thought. Could that sick mortal boy be meeting with Rasputin himself?

I wouldn't wait to find out.

CHAPTER 9

I COUNTED TO THIRTY before slowly easing open my car door. The sun shone brightly, and two slow clouds lazily crawled across the blue sky. The calm, quiet, atmosphere definitely did not match the excitement surging through my bones.

In fact, it seemed a little *too* quiet. There were millions of people in this city. Why wasn't anyone around mid-morning on a Monday? We were in an industrial zone. It should have been bustling with trucks and deliveries and hard-working men and women carrying out their daily tasks.

Shaking off the uneasy feeling trying to settle into my gut, I snuck up to the corner and peeked around, staring at the empty road where Tate and the fractured boy had disappeared. There was just... *nothing*. Where had they gone? Aside from a few other cars parked at the very end of the road, there was no evidence of life anywhere.

I crept forward, trying my best to stick to the shadows cast by the dilapidated building to my left. There was a doorway about halfway down the block. My guess was that they'd gone inside. A moment later I reached the door—large and rusty where the old blue paint had chipped off. There was no handle. No knob. No knocker and no peephole. It must have been an exit only. Even so, I wedged my fingers into the edge and tried to pry it open.

It wouldn't budge. I exhaled and looked around again. Nothing had changed. The street was empty, and the area was quiet aside from the waves and a cool breeze I could just barely make out coming from the Long Island Sound at the end of the road. I took just a moment to enjoy the quiet, grateful that my already pounding head didn't have to endure honking horns and sirens and shouts.

My eyes settled on the boy's blue sedan. Unsure of what else to do, I dashed over to the vehicle and crouched down low. The passenger's door was locked. Keeping myself near the ground, I inched around to the other side. The driver's door was locked, too. What now?

I rose just enough to peek inside the windows. I don't know what I expected to find—ambrosia? Keeper paraphernalia? A book of spells?

This was silly. With no other clear options, there was nothing else to do but go back to the car and wait for Tate. I stood to move in that direction when a flapping sound drew my attention overhead. A flash of white feathers flew low and landed on the chain link fence at the end of the road.

"What are you doing here?" I asked my owl.

The bird swiveled its head on its small fluffy body, turning to look at rows of giant metal shipping containers stacked up on the other side of the fence. The water of the sound glimmered in the sunlight just beyond them.

"It's locked," I said, noting the heavy metal chain wrapped around the gate. The owl tilted its head hard to the right and blinked at me. I shrugged. "I don't know what you want me to."

The bird turned its head again, taking its time to deliberately look toward the shipping containers and then back at me.

"I can't just climb over."

Its sentient yellow eyes narrowed.

"You seriously want me to jump a fence? In broad daylight? As if that won't draw any negative attention…"

The owl looked back and forth down the empty road before settling back on me. He had a point. There was no one around.

"Fine." I marched up to the fence, cast one final glance warily over my shoulder to be sure no one was around, then scrambled up as quickly as I could. Swinging one leg over the top, I became instantly grateful for two things. One: there was no barbed wire. And two: I wore jeans today. I wasn't a child anymore, and climbing fences was a lot rougher than I remembered it being when I was a girl.

Finally, my feet touched concrete on the other side. I glared at the bird. "Now what?"

It launched into flight and landed in between a couple of the shipping containers a few yards away. Hesitantly, I followed it. There was no kind of rail or anything around the edge of the cargo dock the containers were stacked upon, and the water made me nervous. It shouldn't have been too deep, but I didn't like being so close to it anyway. I'd just stick to the center of the slab.

As I neared the first row of containers, I heard the soft hum of voices, but I had no idea where they were coming from. The stacks of metal boxes made a labyrinth of dirt and grime, and the noise bounced off the sides of the containers in strange ways, leaving me thoroughly confused. All I knew was that I didn't want to get close to the water. I didn't want to accidentally stumble upon those voices, either.

And to make matters worse, my owl had essentially disappeared. I could have sworn I saw him land right where I stood, but he was nowhere to be seen. I didn't dare call out to him. Perhaps he'd landed in the next aisle over.

Carefully, and oh-so-slowly, I eased around the corner of a container, keeping my back flush against the metal, and tried to get a glimpse of the other side. I needed to make sure the coast was clear. But I never expected to find the pair of golden eyes waiting on the other side.

Osborne was inches from my face, waiting for me. And before I could even think about moving, he spoke in the entrancing tone of a hundred different melodies. "Freeze."

I had no choice but to obey.

"I knew it," he said, moving around the edge to get a better look at me. I was still motionless, held in the same awkward position I'd been in when he commanded me to freeze. My back was flat against the shipping container, and my head was crooked in an unnatural position around the corner. The pose combined with a racing pulse did little to help my headache. It had grown into an all-encompassing pain now, my vision blinking in and out with every beat of my heart like a strobe light.

"Knew what?" I asked, swallowing down my panic. Tate said other hunters wouldn't wait for proof. And no other hunter wanted me dead as much as Osborne did.

"Knew I'd find you here, with the rest of your kind."

"You're wrong. I'm not fractured. And you can't hurt me."

"I beg to differ." Osborne sneered and began pacing before me. "All I have to do is prove that I put forth my best effort. Mortals don't stumble around fractured meeting sites. And I'm sorry to tell you this, but the meeting is a farce, anyway. Rasputin isn't even here. I put out the lie myself, to draw out the other evil souls like yours. That's how a *real* hunter gets the job done. I never expected such a large turnout, though."

"I told you. I'm not fractured."

"Prove it."

"I have no powers. Isn't that proof enough? Fractured souls, by definition, have partial powers. I have none."

"I'll coax them out of you." He grinned and pulled something metal out of his pocket, then slipped it onto his hand. Brass knuckles. "They say all it takes is a little trauma. Too bad your prince isn't here to save you now." He reared back his fist and I squeezed my eyes shut, preparing for impact.

CHAPTER 10

THE HIT NEVER CAME. My eyes opened again to find the world as utterly frozen as I was. Osborne's hateful face was frozen in a perpetual sneer, just a foot from mine, his fist pulled back above his shoulder.

This couldn't be real. There was no way something like this was possible. But there he was—unblinking. Unbreathing. It was as if the whole world had stopped.

No. Not the *whole* world. I gasped as I watched my owl flutter down and land on the shipping container behind Osborne. It blinked at me, and suddenly I knew the freeze was about to break. It was like I heard that voice in my head again, giving me a *ready, set, go*... and we were back to normal.

The sunlight glinted off of the metal knuckles adorning Osborne's hand as his fist reached prime position. But just as he prepared to swing it forward, a flash of white appeared from the sky, flying a hundred miles an hour and dive bombing straight into Osborne's head. The owl connected with Osborne before he could hit me, and a flutter of white feathers went flying as he cursed loudly.

The glamour broke along with Osborne's concentration, and I ran. Hard. His footsteps were hot on my heels as I rounded the corner, no longer fearing who else I might run into. No one would be as terrifying as Osborne.

I ran the length of two more shipping containers and turned the corner again, finding myself in a small open area with a crowd of about ten or twelve men and women—mortals by the look of them—squished together in the center. They were silent, frozen just as I had been moments earlier, and their clothes flapped in a wind that only seemed to affect their small group.

"Stop!" Tate's voice yelled out from somewhere overhead. I looked up to find him standing on a stack of containers beside a tall, dark skinned man who appeared to be carved from stone. The man was inhumanly handsome, and the lines of his muscles were sharp as the sun cast shadows over his shirtless torso.

Agarthian. Another hunter? This was bad.

Electricity danced over my skin as I drew nearer to Tate, but he wasn't watching me. His eyes were on Osborne as he called his command again, this time with a thousand layers of intricate harmonies. "Stop right there," he said, his words laced with glamour.

But it didn't work. I could still move. I risked a quick glance over my shoulder as I reached the shipping container Tate and the other Agarthian stood upon, and saw Osborne, motionless before the group of terrified humans.

"Give me your hand." Tate was flat on his stomach, reaching down to me over the edge of the container. I didn't hesitate. My skin came alive where his hand wrapped around mine, and the ground fell away beneath my feet as he pulled me effortlessly to the top of the stack.

"What did you do to Daniel?" Osborne's wicked voice drew my attention back to the ground. He was struggling to move, fighting against Tate's glamour and looking like his feet were stuck in wet cement.

I turned to the other Agarthian man beside us, Daniel, and noticed that he, too, was frozen. A small sweat glistened off of Tate's forehead as he worked to maintain his concentration and rescue me at the same time.

"I told you to stay in the car," he said.

"I'm not a very good listener."

"Understatement of the year…"

"Daniel…" Osborne's voice took on a tone of glamour now, too; magic rolled off of his tongue. The man beside us turned slowly to face him. "You are released from Thaddeus' control. Do not let the girl escape."

"No!" Tate cried out, but he was too late. He and the Agarthian man shrank away as I was swept up high into the air, arms pinned to my sides by an invisible and powerful wind. Below me I could see the small group of humans, staring up with mouths agape. Daniel stood on the roof of the shipping container, arms extended above his head, holding me in the air with wind that came from his fingertips.

Tate could do nothing to Daniel without also injuring me in the process. One major hit would drop me from the sky, and there was no way my frail mortal body could sustain that kind of impact. I would splat like a bug on the front of an eighteen-wheeler.

Rather than risk the danger associated with Daniel, Tate focused his efforts on Osborne, who was freely moving again now that Tate was too distracted to hold the glamour. He leapt down from the roof and dove for Osborne. There were shouts, but nothing I could make out from as high as I was in the air. There was absolutely nothing I could do. I was trapped.

Glancing over my shoulder, I remembered that I was also surrounded by water on three sides, and I didn't know which would be a worse way to die. Hitting the ground would be messy, but there was a chance it would be over before I realized it even hurt. But the *water*... I wouldn't die from impact if I dropped into the sound. No—I'd sink slowly to the filthy bottom, holding my breath until my lungs burned and cried out for oxygen.

Choking and drowning would be the worse option. No question.

The world spun around me, my head throbbing forcefully. Millie had said the headaches were a symptom of my powers coming in. This was a traumatic event, right? Surely being flung up into the air by an invisible wind held by your arch-enemy's equally powerful crony qualified. But was it enough to bring my true nature to light?

I closed my eyes, tuning out everything except the way the wind whipped strands of hair across my cheeks. My mother was a messenger, like Devon. Maybe I inherited her powers. I thought about how Devon appeared in the storeroom at Millie's apothecary. He'd arrived out of nowhere, as though he cut right through the fabric of this world and stepped into it from another. I could do that, too. I had to.

My pulse quickened, along with the throbbing in my head. And right as it seemed to reach a fever pitch, I did it. Well, I *thought* about doing it. Technically my hands were still pinned to my sides, but mentally, I cut right through that invisible wind that bound me. I imagined stepping straight through it. Right out of this world and into...

Nothing. I stepped nowhere. My eyes opened to see the same terrifying sight as before. All I got from my efforts was a worsened headache.

Tate and Osborne rolled over one another in a good old fashioned fist fight down below. I supposed when two sirens squared off against each other, their glamour became ineffective. And Daniel couldn't help his friend. Not without dropping me.

After a particularly solid hit to Osborne's jaw, Tate broke away. He reached for the top of the shipping containers and gracefully pulled himself up, like a panther leaping into a tree. He landed with ease and turned his focus back to Daniel. Osborne wasn't far behind, reaching for the container right behind Tate.

Hurry, I thought. *If Osborne gets to Daniel before you, I'm toast.* Tate looked up to me, and even from my height I could see the gold of his eyes glittering with determination in the sunshine. He moved away from the edge, dashing around to the other side of Daniel right as Osborne reached the rooftop. Daniel turned, and I went flying with him. His hands barely moved, but I probably flew thirty feet across the sky.

Hurry up, Tate. Do something.

He and Osborne circled around Daniel, who must've been getting shaky. My steady, invisible wind prison in the sky grew more turbulent with every passing second. I heard shouting again, but still couldn't make out what the guys were saying over the whipping of the wind and the distance between us.

Then I saw it—a flash of white from the corner of my eye. I turned in time to see my friend—my true hero—the owl, right as he swooped down from across the way. A grin spread across my face. I was going to be saved.

I watched with bated breath as the owl dove straight for Daniel. "Wait," I whispered to myself as I understood what was happening. "Wait, no!"

The owl collided with Daniel's outstretched arms, and all three men turned to me with similar looks of shock as Daniel's control over me was severed. The owl's impact sent me flying fast, moving almost horizontally through the air before I began my descent.

And as I began my fall, I swore I heard a familiar voice in my mind. It said everything was going to be okay. I looked at the rapidly approaching water and prayed that the voice was right.

CHAPTER 11

THE WATER CAME AT me like a wall, the murkiness of its depths contrasted by the light reflecting off of its choppy surface. Other details came to me as well, like a water bug paddling lazily across the top of a wave, and the bubbles that popped up to the surface near the cement wall of the cargo dock.

And then it dawned on me—I wasn't falling anymore. Or rather, I wasn't speeding toward the water. I reached out and touched the surface, the tips of my fingers barely breaking through to the wetness below. Had Daniel stopped me?

No. The wind was gone. I scanned back over the water's surface to confirm my suspicions. The bug was still. The bubbles ceased. Time had stopped. Again.

Maybe it was the owl—he was the only piece of the world still alive the last time this happened. "What am I supposed to do?!" I yelled. But the owl didn't respond. Of course it didn't respond. It was an animal, and it was still up on the dock with the Agarthians.

I reached out to slap the water out of frustration. A small splash was followed by concentric rings of waves. I watched them in awe as they moved unnaturally through the otherwise motionless, dark surface. I could still interact with the world, the world just couldn't interact with me. How very interesting.

Everything is going to be okay. It wasn't a voice I heard. Not exactly. There weren't physical words or sounds in my brain, but there was a reassurance. Maybe it was just me talking to myself, but at this point, anything was possible. I believed the words, no matter where they came from.

And just as quickly as everything had stopped, time snapped back into motion and I plunged headfirst into the cold and dirty water of the Long Island Sound.

Air escaping my lungs bubbled up from my mouth as I dropped through the water. I wasn't ready for this. I wasn't prepared. I hadn't even gotten a final lungful of air to last me a couple of short, final minutes.

I opened my eyes, looking for something I could possibly grab a hold of to stop me from sinking to the bottom. If I had any breath left, the sight before me would have taken it all away. I could see everything—every particle of dust, every piece of trash lining the bottom of the sound, every bug and fish that surrounded me. It was like I watched the water through a lens.

I paused for a moment, staring in wonder at the way the sun's rays bent through the waves to glitter off the silvery scales of a tiny school of fish wiggling their bodies past me. I reached for one, momentarily distracted by their beauty.

The fish swam away too fast for me to touch. But me? I wasn't moving much at all. My feet swayed back and forth, casually treading water like I'd seen so many people do before. It was a skill I'd never mastered. And now I didn't even have to think about it. The skill had become ingrained within me. It was a part of me now. I kicked harder, propelling myself up to the water's surface as easily as I might kick a playground ball.

My cheeks broke free, feeling the breeze and the sunshine kiss my face. But I wasn't done yet. I wanted more. With a grin, I dove back under the water, faster and freer than I'd ever felt on land. I sped through the water, delighting in the feel of its ripples across my skin. My lungs didn't burn. I didn't feel the need to come up for air at all. It was like I didn't have to breathe. Or maybe I *was* breathing. All I knew was that this was what life was supposed to feel like.

With a kick and a twirl, I circled back through the waves to the area where I'd first fallen in. As much as I would have loved to swim and play in the water all day, there were some major issues taking place on the cargo dock. Tate was fighting against two of his own kind, and he needed help. An hour before I was a worthless companion for him. Just dead weight he had to fight to keep alive. But now—now I felt power surging through my muscles. My blood pumped energy and vitality to every stretch of my body. I was strong. I was Atlantean. And there was nothing Osborne could do to stop me.

I reached the edge of the concrete and came up to the air just in time to see my hunter dive into the sound above me. His entire body seemed to glow with a warm, earthy golden hue, almost tangerine in color—like a sunset, or the light of dawn. I stilled, entranced by the sight of him. He'd had a running start and flew out across the water's surface, breaking through like a swan, elegant but strong. I waited a moment longer to see if Osborne or Daniel would follow, but no one came. Tate was alone.

With a grin, I dove back in and spotted the back of his head as he scanned the water below, looking for me. I reached him in half a second, and he spun around to face me at the exact moment I reached him. Something went taut in my chest as his eyes met mine, and I felt drawn to reach out and touch him, like there was an invisible thread tying us together. I reached for his hand, the electric sensation that bloomed between us feeling stronger than ever beneath the water, and motioned upward. His eyes grew to half dollars, and with one kick, I propelled us both back up to the surface.

We emerged through the surface of the sound, and Tate shook water free from his hair and his eyes, then pulled his hand from mine. His jaw dropped and his breathing was heavy. "You're swimming."

I grinned. "I'm pretty good at it, too."

He reached slowly toward my face and paused, pulling his hand back again and examining it. I still felt it, too. A humming sensation, pleasant and warm where we'd touched.

"You're not fractured." His voice was barely a whisper, and confusion contorted his handsome features.

"Nope. I'm Atlantean."

His face remained twisted as his eyes darted back and forth over me. He shook his head. "No. You're not Atlantean."

"What are you talking about?" I looked around, my senses sharper than humanly possible. I could hear birds chirping a few blocks over in the small park near a pier. I smelled the exhaust of a delivery vehicle somewhere in the distance, and noted the logo of a passenger plane soaring through the clouds overhead. I was strong. I was full of life. I was definitely a Keeper now.

"Your aura... it's not like anything I've ever seen."

"I don't understand."

The sound of footsteps over my shoulder clattered loudly through my ears. Osborne and Daniel were on their way. Tate put a hand on my shoulder and shoved me back below the water, pushing hard until I floated beneath his feet. And there I stayed, certain that he must have had a good reason to keep me hidden from them.

What had he meant about my aura? I'd seen his—a gorgeous golden color like the sunlight of an autumn morning. But looking down at my own arms and legs, I saw nothing. What did Tate see? And what was it *supposed* to look like?

Whatever it was, he didn't trust it to keep me safe from Osborne. Though the water was plenty murky enough to conceal me at my current depth, I swam lower, nearing the bottom of the sound just to be safe.

I didn't know how much time had passed, and I realized it didn't matter. I could stay under the water forever if I wanted to. Being an Atlantean was amazing. When Tate's face reappeared below the water's surface, searching for me, I was almost reluctant to leave.

Almost. But the feeling in my chest drew me upward, closer to him. He took my hand, and together we swam back up to the water's surface. Back up top, Tate scanned me again. His beautiful eyes moved quickly over every inch of me, as though he couldn't believe what he was seeing.

"I can't take your soul," he said.

"Because it's whole?" I asked hopefully. "I'm not fractured."

"No. You're not fractured. I don't know what you are."

CHAPTER 12

"I FEEL AWFUL ABOUT soaking this poor girl's upholstery in salt water." I looked at Tate in the driver's seat to see if my efforts to lighten the mood had any effect on him at all, but he remained lost in thought. I sighed. "Are you going to explain to me what is going on, or not? You said my aura wasn't Atlantean. What is it, then?"

He glanced warily at me from the corners of his eyes, then turned back to the road without answering. I groaned and leaned my head against the window.

"I'll leave her some money," he said.

"Huh?"

"To have the car detailed. That water is rancid."

The water didn't seem all that bad to me, but maybe it was due to my new affinity for it. The car rolled to a stop in front of my apartment building. "Thanks for bringing me home," I said.

Tate killed the engine and pushed his door open. "Oh, I'm not dropping you off. I'm not going anywhere until we figure this out."

Ignoring the thrill of excitement I felt at the thought of hanging out with Tate a little while longer, I simply nodded. "No one wants to understand what you're talking about more than I do."

He pulled open the door to my building and allowed me to step in before him. He was such a gentlemanly assassin. We walked to the elevator, and I couldn't help but notice how Tate shifted nervously on his feet as the doors closed us in together. The elevator had never felt so small. The feeling in my chest emerged again, and I resisted the pull to him. We were like opposite ends of a magnet, fighting to prevent ourselves from snapping right together.

I looked away, determining the buzzy tingle that washed over me was still a warning. If I wasn't a true Atlantean, as Tate indicated, could he still hunt me? Was my soul still in danger? It was the only explanation I had for this strange sensation I continued to feel when I was near him.

The doors opened on my floor and we raced each other to exit the elevator, each of us eager to put some space between ourselves. But the plan backfired. We ran into each other and stumbled clumsily out into the hallway.

His hands settled on my hips to steady me when I tripped, and he didn't immediately pull them away. His heart raced as fast as mine. I could hear it now with my heightened senses. His eyes dropped down to my lips, and I lifted my chin without even thinking.

But he didn't kiss me. He lifted a hand and brushed his thumb across my chin and up onto my lower lip. "Your scar is gone." His thumb lingered there, warm and soft, and I didn't want him to pull it away. His touch was everything. It was like I was under his spell, but there was no glamour there. And based on the look in eyes, he was just as enchanted.

The sound of a door slamming open down the hall startled us quickly apart. I turned to find Dom's wide eyes staring back at me.

"Everly! You—*nevermind*. I'm glad you're here. I need your help!" Her face was pale, and twisted into a terror I couldn't imagine.

Tate and I rushed over to the apartment and followed Dom inside. Gayla lay prone in the middle of our living room floor, convulsing. I immediately dropped by her side, Dom taking position across from me.

Reaching for her hand, I pleaded with her, softly. "Gayla, can you hear me? Please. *Please...* you've got to be alright." I looked up at Dom, noting the panic flashing in her eyes. "What happened?"

"I don't know. I just got back from class and found her like this. I walked in just before you did... I—*I don't know*," she said again, her voice cracking.

Tate crossed the room and picked up a small brown envelope from the arm of our couch, cursing under his breath. He crushed the empty paper in his fist. "It's the pills from Viv."

"Pills?" Dom asked.

"What's going to happen to her? Is she dying?" I gently moved a piece of white-blond hair from her face.

He knelt beside us and felt her forehead. Then, with careful fingers, he lifted her lids. Dom and I gasped in unison. Her beautiful brown eyes were deep black pools, swirling in a way that reminded me of an ominous thunderhead before a storm. Foam leaked from the corners of her mouth as her body continued to be wracked with violent tremors.

"I don't think so," Tate said. "Just stay here with her until this passes."

We held her hands and I whispered silent prayers until all of a sudden, it stopped. Her body went rigid as a board, then her eyes popped open and she sat up tall, ramrod straight.

"Scoot back," Tate said.

We did as we were told. Gayla said nothing at first. She didn't move. She barely looked to be breathing. When her lips finally parted, it wasn't her voice we heard at all. It was the sound of another creature—a thousand otherworldly voices speaking as one.

"He sees you coming, Deliverer.
He knows your story.
They've hidden him in the cleft of the rock, but the beacon still stands.
He watches the waves.
He waits for you.
It won't be long now.
It won't be long.
He sees you coming.
Go.
Go now.
You must GO!"

Gayla stilled again. Her lids grew heavy and closed over the storms in her eyes. She swayed, and Dom dove forward with a pillow to catch her fall just before she hit the floor. I reached out and released a breath of relief as I felt her pulse, strong and regular.

"I think she's going to be alright," I said. "But what was that?"

"A vision," Tate said.

"It's never happened like that before." Dom shook her head. "Where did the drugs come from?" she glared first at Tate, then turned her hard eyes on me. "Oh, Everly."

"I'm sorry," I whispered. "I didn't know. She's going to be alright though, right Tate?"

He nodded. "Yeah, I think she just needs to rest. But those words..." He turned to Dom. "What do you know about the Deliverer?"

"Nothing. I've never heard anything like that in my life."

Tate frowned.

"What do *you* know about it, Tate?" I asked. "Is this something we should be concerned about?"

"I don't know. I remember a story about it. I only heard it once, as a child." He scratched the back of his head. "Technically, I overhead it during one of my *brother's* lessons."

Dom made an O shape with her mouth, and I suspected there were a few more layers to that simple statement. But I'd have to save my questions for another time.

"There were rumors once of a prophecy. It spoke of a Deliverer, who would one day come to the earth and reunite the people—every race, every creed, every color. But the change would destroy the Keepers. It's folklore, of course... just a story parents used to tell their children when they fought with their siblings. They'd warn the children to settle down or they might bring on the Deliverer." He laughed, humorlessly.

"But several years ago a man became obsessed with the so-called prophecy. He lost his mind while trying to piece it together. The lesson I heard given to my brother was more of a reminder. We are to erase evidence of this story from our history. It's damaging when taken seriously, and my brother was instructed to report any indication that the rumors may be spreading through Agartha."

Chill bumps dotted my arms. "So what does that vision mean, then?"

"I don't know. There are lots of things I can't explain today."

"Like Everly's new aura?" Dom shot a knowing look in Tate's direction.

"That's one thing."

It was then that I noticed a faint lavender glow emanating from Dom and Gayla. *Their auras.* They were subtle, easily overlooked unless one was searching for them. It was almost like I had to shift my eyes into a different line of sight to see them. Agarthians were gold, and Olympians were purple...

"What color are Atlantean auras?"

Dom and Tate exchanged worried looks. "A deep blue-green," Dom said.

"Like the ocean," Tate added.

"And what color is mine?" I looked back down at my arms, seeing nothing.

"White."

Old Man on the Sea

CHAPTER 1

THE OVEN BEEPED, A signal for my mouth to begin to water. I could practically taste the fudge-nutty goodness of Dom's brownies through the air. It was a refreshing distraction from the conversation at hand.

Dom and Tate had been grilling me since Gayla quieted down after her vision. They acted like I should maybe have some clue as to what she was talking about, but I couldn't even stop to dwell on it. My mind was still reeling from the afternoon's events. I had powers now, which meant I would be able to survive a trip into Keeper territories.

I could find my mom.

Dom slid a paper plate in front of me, the brownie looking more like a pile of mud than a neat little square. But I didn't dare criticize her for pulling them out of the oven early or cutting into them too soon. Melty, gooey piles of fudge were exactly how I preferred to eat my brownies. I scooped the pile into my mouth, then opened wide and breathed in and out quickly while fanning with my hand to cool my scalded tongue.

"Hot?" Tate asked with a smirk.

I stole his glass of milk and chugged it down with my brownie in three swallows. "Better now."

Dom smirked and slid into her seat at the table. "Okay, so back to what we were discussing..."

"About the Deliverer?" Tate asked.

"No. About Everly's aura. I think that's where we need to begin. We can worry about finding this so-called *Deliverer* later."

A groan echoed from the living room. "Do I smell brownies?" Gayla croaked.

Dom winked. "Told you it would work."

Three chairs scooted across the tile in unison as we all went to check on our friend.

Gayla still lay on the floor, mouth half open and eyes squinting in the light from overhead. She looked like she was going to be sick.

"How are you feeling?" I asked.

"I'm feeling like I will never swallow another pill in my life."

"That's probably a good thing." Dom extended a hand, and Gayla's arm still shook as she accepted the help back onto her feet. "Do you want a brownie?"

"Not yet." Gayla's nose scrunched. "Maybe some water?"

They were already seated around our small breakfast table when I set the glass of water down in front of Gayla.

"So you mentioned a Deliverer." Tate steepled his fingers, as though he were the CEO of an important meeting in some sky rise downtown.

"Who let the hunter in?"

"Everly did." Dom shot me a knowing look. "We've got a lot to catch you up on."

"Like Everly's new white aura?" Gayla tilted her head in my direction.

"See?" Dom said to Tate. "The aura takes priority."

"I really think there's something important in that vision, though," he argued.

"Guys!" I shouted through a mouthful of half-chewed brownie number two. "Yes, I am a freak with a white aura. But I've always been a misfit. There's nothing new there. And Gayla's vision was... *strange*. But I don't know that it necessarily matters right now." I swallowed my food, hoping Dom wouldn't be able to read the lie I just told. "I think you're all forgetting the most important thing of all. I'm a Keeper now. That means we can get outta town and go find where they've got my mom locked up in the territories."

All three of my friends began shooting that idea down at once, and I couldn't make out what any of them said as they all spoke over one another. The truth was, I suspected all of this was important and interconnected somehow. I hadn't forgotten my first full day in New York —the day my mom went missing. We were in Rossel's gallery, looking at a four-foot tall picture of *me*. Not the old scarred up me. The new me. The Keeper me. And the plaque under the portrait clearly showed the title: *Deliverance.*

It couldn't have been a coincidence. But trying to piece that mystery all together felt overwhelming. We needed to start with the most basic piece. We had to find my mom. It didn't matter what color my aura was or what Gayla thought she saw. Rescuing my mother was all I could think about.

"No," I repeated. "I've got to find my mom. She could be in danger."

Tate looked like he wanted to say something, but he stood instead, moving to refill his milk glass. Dom must have noticed, too. She stared hard in his direction, eyes slightly narrowed. I wondered what she was discovering in that mind of his.

Finally, Dom turned back to Gayla and me. "Maybe Tate's right. We should focus on the vision. If there truly is some prophecy that the royalty is trying to erase from history, it might be connected."

I clenched my teeth, but Dom continued before I could object. "Your aura is different. What if it relates to the prophecy somehow? Maybe that's why your mother was kidnapped. Maybe she knew. There's just too much revolving around you for this to all be a coincidence."

She had a point. My mother obviously knew something was different about me. Otherwise, she wouldn't have needed to hide my powers. I wasn't fractured. I was just... *not like anyone else.*

Gayla nodded. "Yeah, I definitely think the vision was for you, Ev."

"Why would you think that?"

She shrugged. "Just a strong hunch. This wasn't like the others. This was more visceral. I felt things. I knew things that I couldn't see. It's hard to explain."

"Try," Tate said, sliding back into his seat.

"So bossy," Gayla grumbled, but she tried anyway. With her eyes closed, she began rubbing her temples, wrinkling her forehead as she lost herself in the memory of the vision. "So there was this old man with white hair. Or—part of it was white, anyway."

"Olympian, then," Dom said.

"No. I don't think he was. He was definitely crazy though."

"How so?" I asked.

She paused, and her eyelids twitched with movement from underneath. "He just sits by the window, mumbling to himself and watching the water."

"Ocean water or river water or what?"

"Definitely the ocean. And I'm certain he's waiting for you."

"I thought you said he was waiting for the Deliverer."

Her eyes flicked open and settled on me. She swallowed and nodded slowly. The others were staring at me as well.

"Seriously? You think *I'm* the Deliverer?"

She cocked her head to the side. "Yeah, I think maybe you are."

Dom's eyes darted back and forth across my face, attempting to gauge my reaction.

"What does that even mean? I can't change the world. I barely understand how Keepers relate to the mortal world at all. And when it comes to powers, I don't even know what exactly I can do!"

"That's why we need to get to the bottom of this prophecy." Tate reached across the table and rested his hand on my arm, effectively lighting me up from wrist to shoulder. I pulled away, risking just a quick glance in his direction to see if he felt it too, but he gave no indication one way or the other.

"I agree," Dom said. "We should definitely look more into the prophecy if we want to have any idea of what you're supposed to do."

"Assuming it's more than folklore and that I'm the Deliverer it speaks of." I shook my head, still unbelieving anything like that could be true.

"Right. But I think you've got a point, too. You just got your powers like an hour or two ago, right? Let's allow things to settle and see what you can do. You won't be able to change the world until you at least have a grasp of your own powers. What have you noticed so far?"

"Well, my senses are definitely sharper. I can see further and hear better. And I can see your auras now. I can't see mine, though."

"I can't see mine, either." Gayla shrugged.

"Yeah, I don't think anyone can see their own, so nothing strange there," Dom said. "What else?"

"I can swim now. And maybe breathe underwater? Or maybe I don't have to breathe underwater anymore. Either way, I'm definitely comfortable staying down there for however long I need to."

"Yeah, that's Atlantean alright. But those are just the basics. All descendants of Atlantis can do that. What about teleporting? Your mom was a messenger, right?"

"Right, but I'm not. I tried and it didn't work."

"Can you heal, like Millie?" Dom stood and walked to the kitchen.

"I don't know. I haven't tried to—DOM! What are you doing?!"

She'd sliced open her palm with the brownie knife, and cupped it to prevent blood from dripping to the floor.

I leapt to my feet, but Tate and Gayla looked as relaxed as ever, propped lazily on the table. Gayla swirled the water with her glass, and Tate just watched me expectantly.

Dom extended her hand toward me. "See if you can heal me."

"How?"

"I don't know. Just take my hand and think about the wound closing up."

I did, trying my best to keep my own hands steady. Her skin was cold except for the sticky warmth of her blood leaking between her fingers as she settled her hand between my palms. I took a good look at the wound, then closed my eyes and inhaled deeply, thinking of nothing but the sides of her cut coming back together and stitching her wound closed.

When I opened them, everyone was staring at me. I slowly lifted my hand from where it covered Dom's, and with a shaky breath, I peered down to find that nothing had changed.

"It didn't work."

"That's okay." Dom raised her shoulder. "It'll heal in a couple of hours anyway—that's another perk of being a Keeper. Healers just make it happen a little faster."

"So you're not a messenger, and you're not a healer. Can you run fast like Sean?" Gayla asked.

"I don't know. I haven't tried."

"There's energy manipulation, too," Tate said. "It's not as common as the others, but it's pretty cool in action. That's an Atlantean thing, too."

"I don't even know what that would look like." I plopped back down into my chair with a huff and rested my forehead on my arms atop the table.

"Okay," Dom said. "We will definitely get this all figured out, but it doesn't have to be right now. Gayla looks like she's going to pass out at any second, and Everly looks like she could use a nap, too."

"She smells like she could use a shower first," Gayla added with a laugh.

I shot her a sarcastic look, but then glanced down at my damp, dirty clothes. I probably smelled just like the Long Island Sound and all of its filthy glory. She was right. I needed to get cleaned up.

"Let's put a pin in this for now. I think I've got an idea brewing so we can discover what Everly is capable of really soon. But in the meantime, nothing that happened here today can leave this room. Got it?" Dom looked pointedly at Tate.

"Got it."

Dom nodded, satisfied that he was telling the truth. "And Ev, unfortunately, I think we need to keep you hidden until we know what exactly this white aura is all about. Can you promise me not to sneak out or anything until we figure some things out?"

"I promise," I said. And at the time, I meant it.

CHAPTER 2

MY HEART THUMPED HARDER as we stepped through the double glass doors that led into the gym. The air stung with the scent of chlorine, and my thoughts immediately raced back to Clayton nearly drowning me in the St. A's basement. Logically, I knew that wasn't possible anymore. As an Atlantean, I was an amazing swimmer now. But evidently, my adrenaline hadn't gotten the memo.

"Can I help you?" A man with deep brown skin and muscles that could have easily graced the cover of any men's fitness magazine looked up at us with a grin.

Gayla noticed him as well. She sauntered over to the front desk, tucking a thumb under one of her bikini straps that peeked out of the loose neckline of her tank top. "Actually, you can." The man's grin widened and Dom rolled her eyes as Gayla cranked up the charm. "We're looking for the pool."

"I'm sorry, the pool is booked for the next hour and a half, but you're welcome to hang out here until it's available. There's a juice bar around the corner."

Dom pushed her way past Gayla and set a box of cupcakes on the counter. Muscle man's eyes widened at the sight of them. "We're the ones who booked the pool."

"You're the birthday party?" he asked.

"Yup." Dom did not look amused.

"Oh, my apologies. Right this way." He led us down a hall and into a large room with walls of glass windows. The real star of the room, however, was an Olympic-sized swimming pool, glittering in the middle.

"Would it be possible to close these blinds?" Gayla asked, sweetly.

"Afraid not. Corporate doesn't allow that for parties. It's a liability."

"Close the blinds," Tate said. I felt the harmonies of his words in my bones, and it gave me a little shiver.

"Yes, of course," the glamoured muscle man responded with a nod and scurried over to the windows, closing the blinds window by window.

Dom utilized the time he spent working to set up the cupcakes on a small table off to the side. Three colorful helium-filled balloons rose from each corner of the table, wishing some imaginary child a happy birthday. It was genius for her to book this pool for us. There wasn't anywhere else that I'd be able to swim and experiment in the water so freely without the burden of watchful eyes. And there were cupcakes in the deal, which was always a bonus.

Muscle man finished up with the blinds and turned back to Dom, sensing that she was the one in charge. "I'll direct the rest of your guests this way as they arrive."

"There are no more guests. Just us."

The man glanced nervously between me, Tate, Dom, and Gayla. But he knew better than to object. Instead, he nodded and dashed over to the doors, pulling them quickly closed behind him as he exited.

"You guys didn't have to run him off so quickly," Gayla pouted.

"We don't need him." Dom placed her hands on her hips. "Alright, Everly. Let's see what you can do."

With a deep breath, I shimmied out of the shorts and t-shirt that covered my modest one-piece. It covered so much more than the bikini from the St. A's house had, but I still felt exposed. My cheeks heated, and I couldn't bring myself to make eye contact with Tate. The tightening of my chest was enough for me to know he was still there.

But as soon as I broke through the surface of the water, all my insecurities just disappeared. The water in the pool was so much clearer than the water of the sound, and my muscles came alive with the freedom to speed and swirl and spin through the water. I raced back and forth down the length of the pool, then decided to skirt around the outer perimeter. Everything about the water felt natural, like this was where I was meant to be.

After some time, another body splashed down into the water across the pool. I was by Dom's side in three seconds, emerging from the water with a grin.

"Holy cow! You weren't kidding."

"It feels so good, Dom. I can't even begin to describe this feeling." Something drew my attention to Tate, who sat in a chair on the outside the pool. He watched me closely, amusement glimmering in his golden eyes.

"Well you're definitely Atlantean," Gayla said with a laugh. She had stripped down to her swimsuit as well, and sat on the edge of the pool with her long legs dangling in the water, kicking softly back and forth.

"Okay," Dom said as she hoisted herself back out of the water on the edge of the pool. "Let's see what else you can do."

I climbed out as well, no longer embarrassed about my lack of clothing. I felt strong and powerful, and frankly, I didn't care who noticed. Though I still didn't look at Tate for too long. He was distracting enough as it was.

Dom called me over to the corner of the room and pulled out a stopwatch. "Alright, I want to see if you've got finesse. I want you to run around the edge of the room as fast as you can. I'll time you to see how your speed compares to the other Atlanteans with finesse. On your mark, get set, go!"

I jolted into action, my bare feet slapping against the wet concrete as I sprinted around the perimeter of the room, ignoring all the signs that said "Please Walk" in giant red letters. I took the first corner, definitely moving more quickly than I'd ever run before. And I wasn't feeling very winded, either. This was incredible.

If I had finesse, I would likely end up as a guardian, like Sean. Though I suppose I could still be a messenger under the right circumstances. What else could these powerful muscles do? I remembered Sean mentioning once that he could run faster and jump higher. I decided to try that as well, just as I was coming around the third corner of the room.

With one final surge of power through my legs, I leaped into the air, jumping as high and far as I could. I landed gracefully on my feet, feeling especially feline as I came to a stop inches away from the hard chest that stood like a wall in front of me.

"Time!" Dom yelled.

I refilled my lungs with air and gave Tate a quick smirk before turning my attention back to Dom. "So, how did I do?" I swaggered over to where she and Gayla stood, feeling exhilarated and ready to bite into my gold medal.

"Well, you're definitely faster than you used to be. You'd blow mortals out of the water."

I gave Tate a quick wink over my shoulder.

"But for an Atlantean, you were exceptionally..."

"Slow." Tate winked back, and I felt my ego go tumbling down.

"Okay, then. So I can't teleport, I'm not a healer, and I clearly have no finesse. What does that leave?"

"Energy manipulation," Tate said, rubbing his hands together. "Definitely the coolest Atlantean power."

"But also the rarest." Dom didn't sound convinced.

"Well, tell me what to do. How does one *manipulate energy*?"

"I knew a guy once who could make the lights turn on and off with his mind. Try that," Tate suggested.

"Oooh—and I had a friend back in Connecticut whose mom could alter kinetic energy. Any moving object was under her control. It was amazing. Except for when we tried to sneak out to go to Dionne Miller's house party and she stopped our car at the bottom of the driveway." Gayla chuckled.

"Okay, you're right. It sounds awesome, but I still have no idea how to make any of that happen. Do I just blink my eyes or wiggle my nose and *poof*?"

Dom frowned. "I think you probably would have noticed something like that happening before now. It's kind of beyond your control. We don't learn how to create our powers. We learn to *control* them. The powers manifest on their own."

"So you're saying I probably can't do anything like that?"

"Yeah, unfortunately."

"So what Atlantean powers are left, then?"

Our small group shifted gazes back and forth, each of us waiting for someone else to answer. Finally, it was Gayla who spoke. "I think we need to call Sean."

"No." Tate and I spoke in unison.

"Wait," I said. "Why don't you want Sean getting involved?"

"I just think we need to keep everything surrounding you and your powers under wraps until we know more about that aura."

"He's right," Dom said. "But why are *you* against calling Sean?"

"He's assigned to be my guardian right now. The only way I've kept him out of our apartment for the last couple of days is by telling him I had the flu. Once he knows I've got my powers, he'll need to report back to the council. Plus..." I looked down at my feet. "I'm afraid he'll try to talk me out of searching for my mom."

"He's not the only one," Tate said. "Cutting you loose in Keeper territories is about the worst idea I can think of."

"Well, standing around here isn't getting us anywhere!" I marched over to the table and snatched a chocolate cupcake from the box.

Gayla joined me a moment later. "It's going to be alright, Ev. I promise we haven't forgotten about your mom. We'll find her."

"You say that, but so far we haven't done a single thing to get her back. It's like everyone else has just moved on."

"That's not true. If it's important to you, it's important to me. I will—" Her voice trailed off and her hands froze in place, the cupcake wrapper in her fingers only half-pulled away from the cake.

"Gayla?" I waved my hand in front of her face. "Guys!" Dom and Tate jerked their faces to me, pulling themselves out of whatever kind of private discussion they'd been engaged in. "Something's going on with Gayla."

Her eyes darkened, the whites disappearing as she stared off into a distant nothing. She was having a vision. Dom rushed over to my side, and together we lowered her to the ground. We'd seen enough now to know that Gayla's visions typically ended in tremors. Tate slid a folded-up towel under her head and we waited.

Then we waited some more. About five minutes passed with none of us making a sound when finally Gayla's features softened and her eyes returned to their normal warm brown.

She sat up, rubbing her head. "That was weird."

"Was it a vision? You didn't say anything."

"Yeah, sort of." She turned toward me. "Your crazy old man is getting impatient."

"Well, did he tell you where I could find him? Because I'm still pretty clueless about the whole thing."

"He's in a lighthouse."

"A lighthouse where?" Tate asked.

Gayla raised a shoulder. "In the cleft of a rock?"

"Not helpful," Dom said.

"It's more than we knew before!" Gayla said. "And Everly—this mess is definitely tied in with your mom, somehow. I don't know how I know, but I do. I can feel it."

I squeezed my friend's hand. "Thank you." I mouthed the words but no noise came out.

"Now where did my cupcake go?" Gayla stood and eyed me suspiciously before grinning and grabbing the half-opened dessert from where we'd laid it on the table. "I need to hurry and eat it before my training."

"You're supposed to meet with Rossel today?" Dom asked her.

"Yeah, I was anyway. But if there's some reason I shouldn't, I'm all ears. I hate these meetings."

"Given your last couple of visions, I'm thinking maybe it would be a good time to catch Everly's imaginary flu," Tate said. "You don't want him hearing anything you might mutter in a vision right now."

"My flu is very contagious," I added.

"You know, I am feeling a little under the weather..." Gayla fake coughed into the crook of her elbow and then shoved half the cupcake into her mouth. "I'll send him a text."

"And I guess I'll go back to Millie's and see if I can learn anything additional about my mom's powers. Maybe there was more to them than most people knew."

"I don't think that's a good idea," Dom said. "Millie likes to play by the books. If she realizes your powers have come in, she'll report you to the council even faster than Sean would."

"Not if my aura might put me in danger. Millie wouldn't want me to get hurt."

Dom frowned. "I wouldn't risk it."

"Well, I don't have any other options unless you know where some old man is hiding in a lighthouse in the cleft of a rock. Look, I'll be careful to avoid her. I just need to find some old journals or something. There's got to be information about my heritage somewhere in that library of hers."

"Just be careful."

CHAPTER 3

TATE VOLUNTEERED TO DRIVE me over to Millie's place, but we didn't talk much. I was unable to think of anything other than the way the air seemed to sizzle along that invisible string between us, and he—well, I don't know for sure what he was thinking. But he was definitely lost in thought.

He slowed the car to a stop in front of Millie's townhouse and finally turned to me. "I might know a way to keep your aura disguised, but I'm going to have to practice it first. It's not a technique I've had to use before. Until then, please try to stay out of sight of any Keepers, especially your aunt."

"I'll do my best."

"I'm gonna stay close by, so send me a text as soon as you're ready to go. We definitely don't want you walking around on the streets."

"I will."

"And Everly—" My heart fluttered at the sound of my name coming from his lips. I hoped he didn't notice. "Be careful." His mouth twitched like he wanted to say more, but nothing else came out.

I nodded and tugged on the door handle, quickly rushing from his car to my aunt Millie's front door. I didn't notice any other Keepers out on the street, but there was no telling who might be lurking in the shadows or watching from windows. You'd think that being practically immortal would give me courage, but instead it only made me more paranoid.

Once inside, I leaned my head back against the door and took a moment to just breathe. The past couple of days had been a whirlwind. And somehow, my guardian had become a guy I was now trying to avoid, and my hunter had become my new guardian.

The thought of it almost made me laugh. Tate had once wanted my soul so badly that he enlisted the help of friends from across the country to help bring me near the brink of death. But now I truly believed he only wanted to help me get to the bottom of my mysteries. There was no way Dom would have allowed him to hang around if he still wanted me dead. Not that he could kill me now, anyway. In fact, if the feeling that buzzed between the two of us was mutual at all, I would guess he wanted quite the opposite of getting me dead.

"Ohhh, I know that face." Jeeves appeared from around the corner with a grin. His Alabama twang came out even stronger when he was teasing me. "Where have you been lately?"

I shrugged, trying to play it cool. "Eh, you know. School, work, my new apartment. Nothing too interesting." Other than discovering I'm an immortal with strange and unidentifiable powers. Oh, and also maybe the subject of a prophecy that could irrevocably change the world as we know it.

"Uh-huh… and does 'nothing interesting' include tall, dark, and handsome out there who still hasn't pulled away from the curb?"

I peeked through the foyer window and sure enough, Tate still sat in the car, tapping his thumb on the steering wheel and staring off into space.

A flush crept its way up my neck and Jeeves looked pleased as punch. He laughed. "Come on, heartbreaker. Let's see if Pierre has anything good to eat in there." He gestured for me to follow him into the kitchen.

"Oh, thanks. But I'm not staying here long. I just need to run upstairs and grab something from Millie's library."

Jeeves pouted. "Okay. But try to stop by more often. We never get to see you anymore."

"I will. I promise. Just as soon as things settle down."

The sound of claws clicking across the hard floor announced the arrival of my other two giant hairy friends who resided at Millie's place. Tiny Tim and Lemondrop, her bull mastiffs, gave me slobbery greetings of their own. I patted their heads, scratching Tiny Tim for a moment in the spot behind his ear that he loved so much. "And I will see more of you guys, too," I said in a high tone with my lips pushed out. Then I dashed up the stairs toward Millie's library.

The room was quiet, and the sunshine filtering in through the window gave me a sense of calm. I stood in the center of the room, amazed by how well I could make out the titles of the books that lined her shelves without having to step any nearer. There were some real perks to these Atlantean senses. But I didn't expect to find any old personal journals on her bookshelves. No, those would likely be hidden away in a more secure location. But where?

Millie's desk was the most likely location. I made for it, but stopped halfway across the room when I heard a fluttering noise from outside the window. My owl! I hadn't seen him since he stopped time for me back at the cargo dock, right before my powers emerged. I needed to thank him for that. And yes, I knew how crazy the thought was, but something told me he'd understand.

The window was sealed shut, and there was no way I'd be able to get it open. Coming to the same conclusion, I watched my feathery friend fly down and around to the small courtyard on the back side of Millie's townhouse. He would no doubt wait for me there.

The dogs were sitting with their chins on their paws outside of the library door, not satisfied with the small number of snuggles they'd received from me. They joined me on the stairs, stepping in front me on my way down—trying to block my movement so I would stop and pay them more attention. "Hang on, guys. I'll be right back."

But of course they didn't listen. They lacked the intelligence of my owl.

I snuck past the kitchen, where Jeeves was reading something at the counter, and made my way to the french doors leading out to the courtyard. Just as my fingers wrapped around the handle, I heard the front door of the townhouse open as well.

I slipped out the doors as quickly and quietly as I could, gluing myself to the outer wall of the building and straining with all my might to hear who'd just entered the house. But it didn't take much straining to make out the sing-songy cadence of Millie's chipper words.

"Hey Jeeves! We just thought we'd grab some lunch and take the afternoon off. You guys have enough to feed a couple more?"

Shoot! I prayed Jeeves wouldn't say anything about me being here.

"You bet we do! Everly is here, too."

Well that was just perfect. *Thanks a lot, Jeeves.*

"She's upstairs in the library," he added.

"Wonderful! I'll go change clothes and see if she wants to join us."

"I'll wait here with Jeeves," a third voice said. I knew that voice... but I couldn't place it right away.

What are you doing?

The voice sounded as clear as the horns blaring on the road in front of the townhouse. I startled and spun back around to face the courtyard. My owl perched calmly on the fence between the patio and the small green area beyond it. No one else was around.

"Did you—" No. That was impossible.

Did I ask you a question? Yes. Now don't be rude. Answer me. I know you can hear me now. And it's about time, too.

"You've gotta be kidding me."

The owl blinked. Twice.

"You're not kidding?"

Nope. And I've been waiting 2700 years to be heard again. Do you know how hard it is to shout into a void for multiple millennia?

I glanced around the courtyard, searching for a camera and half expecting Gayla to jump out and laugh about another successful prank. But it was just me and the owl.

"I think I'm losing my mind."

You and me both, honey. Now are you going to tell me who you're hiding from?

"My aunt Millie. I'm not ready to reveal my new... uh... situation to her just yet. Am I really talking to an owl right now?"

It's so frustrating that you don't remember.

"Remember what?"

Nevermind. More importantly, if you're wanting to hide, I suggest you do something about those monsters.

Tiny Tim and Lemondrop let out loud whines on the other side of the glass doors. The bird was right. They were going to draw attention. I released a sigh and pulled open the doors, hoping they might quiet down out here with us.

Nope. That was a bad idea.

Ew, call these smelly beasts down! The owl flapped a few feet into the air as the pair of canines rushed over and lifted their front paws onto the fence. Tiny started barking when the owl moved, which worked Lemondrop up into a tizzy as well.

"Shh! It's okay. Come here, sweet pups."

Sweet? Those mangy creatures are about as sweet as—

The door opened again behind me, cutting the owl's words—or thoughts, maybe?—short.

"There you are."

I turned to face the familiar voice I'd heard earlier and found Devon grinning at me. A quick look over my shoulder revealed that my owl had flown away upon Devon's arrival.

"Millie went upstairs to look for you. We're about to eat lunch if you want to join us." He paused and his eyes narrowed a fraction of an inch. "Hey... Something seems different about you." He tilted his head to examine me further.

"Nope everything is fine. Can't stay for lunch, though. Gotta run!" I tried to squeeze past him and back into the house, but he stepped in front of me before I could make it very far.

"Wait. Your aura! Did you get your powers? No—that's not right. It's —"

I slapped my hand over his mouth before he could finish. "Shh!" I yanked him out of the clear glass doorway and pushed him up against the wall. "Devon, I need you to promise me you will keep your mouth shut if I drop my hand. Do you understand?"

He nodded, eyes wide.

"Good." I slowly dropped my hand, but he began to speak as soon as his lips were free. I quickly covered him up again.

"Get off," he mumbled against the inside of his hand.

"You promised you wouldn't speak!"

"Okay, okay," he mumbled again. But when I dropped my hand a second time, he let out a quiet "sheesh."

"Listen, this is really important. I know you're in love with my aunt or whatever, but I need you to keep this aura thing a secret for now. From her and everyone else, too, including Sean."

"Why?"

"It's a lot to explain, but... wait, you can teleport, right?"

"Yeah, so?"

"So how far are you able to go?"

"As far as I want, as long as I'm familiar with the location."

"Would a picture and a map be enough?"

"Maybe."

"Excellent." I nodded, a grin slowly working its way across my face. "Alright, as your future niece, I have an enormous request. I will tell you all about the aura, but first, I need you to help me find a lighthouse."

CHAPTER 4

"ARE YOU SURE WE can trust him?" Dom crossed her arms over her chest and leaned back against the kitchen counter. Tate had been scowling since he picked me up from Millie's house. Gayla was the only person who wasn't furious with me for getting caught by Devon.

"No, I'm not sure. I barely know the guy. But my aunt sure seems to think highly of him, and despite being her soulmate, he didn't reveal my secret to her—at least not before I left the house."

"I hope you're right. Millie is best friends with Claudia, and if Claudia finds out about some new white aura, you're screwed. She won't hesitate to report it to the council. Her husband has been on thin ice with them lately, and she'll do anything to get him back into their good graces."

"Sean's dad is on thin ice? Why?" I hadn't seen Claudia in a few weeks—not since Sean and I first met Gayla and Dom in the Hamptons. But the little I knew of her seemed right in line with what Dom described. She didn't seem too happy to have Sean involved with a potentially fractured soul even before I started getting myself into trouble. If it weren't for Millie, Claudia would have reported me long ago.

"I'm not sure. I just heard they were keeping a closer eye on him," Dom said.

"You heard as in someone *told* you that? Or did you read it in someone's mind?"

"The means by which I acquire my information are unimportant." Dom waved her hand in the air as if shooing the question away.

"Dom gets all the juicy gossip straight from the source," Gayla said, tapping her temple with one finger.

A knock sounded from the door. "I bet that's him." I jumped up from my seat to let Devon in. He'd agreed to meet us here after lunch, and I told him we'd fill him in on the details if he would help us out.

Another impatient knock pounded on the door just before I pulled it open, and the moment I turned the knob, Sean came barreling through. "Looks like your *flu* is gone, Everly." It was difficult not to wither under his stern glare.

Devon slinked in behind him, casting me an apologetic look.

Apology not accepted. "You had one job," I growled at Devon. "Come to my apartment without telling anyone. Why was that so difficult?"

"A better question," Sean pointed at me, "is why you've been lying to me for the past several days. Why didn't you just tell me you got your pow—" He paused, only just noticing my aura. "Your powers," He finished, softly.

"I'm sorry," Devon said. "But I knew Sean would kill me if he found out I was getting involved with you guys behind his back. Plus, if this is as important as you seem to think it is, having a little finesse on our side will be helpful."

"But you didn't tell Millie?" I chewed the inside of my lip, hoping with everything I had that he at least kept our bargain there.

"No." Devon's mouth pulled into a frown. "I wanted to. And I probably will at some point. But I can't bear to see her hurting or stressed over this until we know for sure what's going on. Now, tell me about this aura and why you're searching for a lighthouse."

The guys followed me into the living room, and Sean stopped in front of the couch where Tate sat, not even attempting to hide his glare. "What is he doing here?"

"Tate was with me when my powers emerged. He saved me from Osborne and rushed me back to the apartment. Plus—he's the only one who seems to know anything about the prophecy."

"Prophecy?" Devon settled cross-legged on the floor in front of our coffee table. "Ooh, this is getting good."

Dom filled them in on Gayla's vision and how we thought it could be related to the prophecy Tate overheard when he was younger. Then Gayla let them know she thought it might all tie back in with my mother's disappearance somehow, as well. I allowed them to answer the questions and fill in all the blanks. I'd gone over all the details enough, and I was already busy with the next step of our puzzle, anyway.

As soon as Sean and Devon seemed to have a good grasp on the whole situation, I spun my laptop around and pointed at a list I'd made in a spreadsheet.

"What is that?" Sean asked.

"This is a list of lighthouses near here," I said with a triumphant grin. "I've linked to maps and images, so Devon can pop in and out easily. It's not a comprehensive list by any means, but I figured it would be enough to get us started."

"You want me to just *pop in and out* of lighthouses all along the coast?"

"Yeah." I shrugged. "You can do that right?"

"Well, I can do a few at a time. But teleporting takes a lot out of a person. I only have so much energy to use. Besides, I don't even know what I'm looking for. How will I know if I've found the right one?"

"There will be an old man there, hiding in the cleft of a rock," Gayla said.

"Right." Devon rubbed at the back of his neck. "I heard. But I'm not sure that's enough to go on."

"It's gonna have to be. For now anyway." I gave my best attempt at big round puppy-dog eyes to soften him up.

"Okay, but can we start tomorrow? Millie is probably already wondering where I am."

"I don't think—"

"Yes." Dom interrupted, shooting me a sideways glance. "Tomorrow will be great. Can everyone meet here after lunch?"

Mumbles of agreement echoed out through the living room, and all the guys stood to leave. Tate hung back for another second though, pulling me off to the side.

"I think I figured out the whole disguising your aura trick. I'm gonna head down to the library tomorrow morning to see if I can find out anything else about the prophecy. Do you wanna come? I can practice hiding you."

"Yes," I said too quickly. "I mean, if you're sure you'll be able to keep me hidden."

"Great. I'll do a practice run before we leave, just to be sure. Meet you here at nine?"

"It's a date." My cheeks warmed. "I mean, not a date, but—"

Tate grinned. "See you in the morning."

I watched him leave, my stomach rolling with an anxious excitement. By this time tomorrow there was a good chance we might be visiting with some supposedly crazy old man in a lighthouse, learning about my true destiny as the Deliverer or whatever. More importantly, I might finally be able to see my mom again soon.

Dom nudged me, shaking me out of my stupor. "I'd keep my distance from him if I were you."

"From who? Tate? He's harmless now that he can't kill me and extract my soul."

"I certainly wouldn't call him harmless."

"Why? Do you know something I don't?"

Dom pursed her lips, and I suspected she knew *plenty* that she wasn't telling me. "I can't be certain, but I think he knows something about your mom."

"What?" I grabbed her arm. "Tell me everything you heard."

She pulled her arm away, gently. "That's just it. I didn't exactly *hear* anything. But Tate is good. He knows how to hide his thoughts, or at least beguile to the point where I can't perceive them clearly. But I can't shake the sense that he isn't telling you everything he knows."

"And are you telling me everything *you* know?" I paused, realizing the question came out a lot like an accusation. But it seemed like everyone was better informed than me, and once again, they weren't exactly racing in to lift me out of my ignorance. Not even Dom.

"I would tell you if I knew more about your mom. I promise. I don't know any more about where she might be than you do."

That wasn't exactly what I asked, but it was all the answer I needed. Dom wasn't giving me the whole story. But why? And who was she protecting?

CHAPTER 5

GAYLA STUMBLED OUT OF her room the next morning with a messy topknot balancing high on her head and a sleepy grin. "Do you prefer Taterly or Evate? I'm having a hard time settling on your new couple name."

"You are ridiculous." I pulled a light jacket off the hook near our door. The mornings were already beginning to cool off here in New York, though it would probably still hit a hundred degrees back in Oklahoma. That was one thing I didn't miss about home. "And those are both awful. Lucky for you, we're not in a relationship, so you don't have to come up with anything better."

"Uh-huh. Keep telling yourself that, but I don't think Tate's done hunting you at all." She winked and leaned against her bedroom door frame. "You better get downstairs, or you're gonna be Everlate."

I snorted out a laugh. "Alright, that one's pretty good."

"I thought so, too." She grinned. "You two kids have fun. Don't do anything I would do."

"Ha! Trust me, I won't. I'll see you guys after lunch!"

I pushed open the door and let out a little squeak of surprise to find Tate standing there in the hallway. My face warmed, realizing he'd probably heard us talking about him.

"Perfect timing." His crooked grin warmed me even more. He was almost unbearably good looking. "I just walked up."

Gayla's soft giggle trickled out as I shut the door behind me.

"Alright," I said, turning back to Tate. "So let's hear this plan you have to disguise my aura."

"We will definitely talk about that. But first—coffee." He extended his arm and handed me a hot drink from the Honey Pot. Our fingers brushed as I accepted the cup, sending a familiar tingle down my arm. I inhaled the aroma of warm vanilla and espresso with just a touch of something that reminded me of home.

"What is this?"

"It's a cinnamon vanilla latte. I heard it was your favorite."

"It is. Thank you." I closed my eyes and breathed it in again, and when I opened them I caught Tate smiling down at me. Maybe Gayla was right. Could this be the beginning of something?

Or was I being manipulated, like Dom suggested?

Wiping the grin from my face, I decided to push away any tender feelings that may be brewing between us and get down to business. "Alright, so how are we gonna hide me?"

"Well, we're not going to hide *you*, exactly. We're just going to hide your aura. I've been looking into it, and I should be able to cover you in a glamour that would hide the aura from everyone else." He pushed the elevator button and we stepped inside, each of us gluing ourselves to opposite walls. Yep, he definitely felt that same strange connection I did.

"But you still need to be careful. You'll have to stay close to me, because the glamour will weaken with too much distance. And if another skilled siren comes along, they may be able to see through it."

"Got it." I extended my arms to the sides. "Well, cover me up. Let's see if it works."

Tate mumbled some incoherent whisper of words and his eyes flared into a warm golden light. I felt nothing, aside from the usual buzz of energy I got from him. But there was no glamour worm in my head or any strange compulsion pushing me forward. Everything felt normal.

I released a breath. "Did it work?"

He inclined his head toward me and a muscle twitched at the corner of his mouth. "Of course it worked."

The elevator dinged open and I hesitantly followed him into the lobby. It was mostly empty, with a couple of mortals standing off to one side. But there was no way for me to verify if my aura was actually hidden from other Keepers. I couldn't see it myself.

"Just to confirm, no one is going to notice anything strange, right?"

Tate held the front door open for me. "Right. Just act normal."

That was easier said than done. I found myself scanning the streets like a guilty criminal, just waiting to be caught by the first Keeper who passed us by. It didn't take long before we strolled past a group of Columbia students—a mix of Atlanteans and an Olympian. Two of them cast casual glances in our direction, but there was no indication that they noticed anything off.

"You can relax." Tate gently touched the small of my back, and his whisper sent a thrill down my spine. I shivered a bit, and he pulled his hand away. "I've got you covered."

I would just have to trust him. Finally, we reached the Butler library and quietly made our way through the gorgeous stacks of books. The library was one of my favorite places on campus. It held an old world charm, with towering windows and columns, and giant ringed chandeliers hanging from the ceiling. And there were more books than I could ever dream of reading.

We took the stairs, hoping to avoid any other Agarthian sirens who may be studying in the building. Once we were alone in the stairwell, I finally felt comfortable enough to probe a bit into Tate's motives.

"Why are you so interested in this prophecy, anyway?"

He didn't seem bothered by the question at all as he spun around the fourth floor landing and continued upward through the building. "Because I never believed it could be real. I've been told it's just folklore my entire life. If it's real, the whole world could change."

It seemed like an honest answer. "Is that why you're being so nice to me lately, buying me my favorite coffee and whatnot? You think I'm the Deliverer?"

He paused and I nearly ran into the back of him. Slowly looking over his shoulder, he set his jaw before finally speaking. "I was only hunting you before because it was my job. There's no need for me to distance myself now that I can't have your soul."

"And are you disappointed that you can't have my soul?"

He quirked a brow and started to say something, but stopped. Then he was moving up the stairs again. "I'm interested to see what it means for my position moving forward. I wouldn't say I'm disappointed. Just curious."

I wasn't sure how not retrieving my soul could possibly affect his position, but the thought was secondary to what I really wanted to know. "You were there the day my mom went missing at the gallery."

"Yeah." He pulled open a door to the sixth floor, and I followed him through, dropping my voice now that we were in the midst of other Keepers again.

"Do you know anything more about where she might be?"

"Hello." An Atlantean girl with a pretty, almost-turquoise aura unknowingly interrupted me as she glanced up from a desk outside of the rare book and manuscript library. She nodded at Tate, then pinned me with a hard stare. "I'm afraid the reading room is open by appointment only."

"She's with me," Tate said.

The girl shook her head. "Appointment only," she repeated.

Tate dropped his voice to a whisper, though no one else was around. "She's Atlantean. She just hasn't gotten her powers yet."

The girl's eyes narrowed, and my heart thudded against my chest under her scrutinous gaze. "I don't—"

"It's fine," Tate said, the melodies of his voice dancing together in a song I didn't want to end. The girl nodded and allowed us to enter the reading room.

"Did you glamour her?"

"I had to. You Atlanteans can be really uptight with the rules, sometimes. She's not supposed to allow mortals into the room, and I didn't think she would budge without a little encouragement."

"Why aren't mortals allowed in here?" The room wasn't terribly impressive, though it was obvious we were surrounded by some incredibly valuable pieces of history.

"Because of this." Tate stepped between two stacks of books and placed his hands on either side of a glass case holding an old oil painting. No one outside of the reading room could see us between the stacks, and we were the only people within the room. He slid his hands down the edges of the case until he found whatever it was he was looking for. With a small creak, the entire wall panel lurched forward like a hidden doorway, and Tate gestured for me to go ahead.

Stepping through to the other side was like entering a whole new world. The dusty-smelling reading room behind us couldn't compare to the life that buzzed on the other side of the wall. It was an enormous room hidden in the center of the building, with massively high arched ceilings and exquisite details carved into the rich woodwork of the mouldings. Two-story shelves created short aisles down the sides of the large room, and cozy nooks with armchairs, desks, or tables occupied the spaces between the rows. The whole room felt alive, and there wasn't another mortal in sight.

Clusters of Keeper students gathered in many of the nooks, working together on projects and quietly quizzing one another in their studies. None of them looked up at us as we made our way through the room. The only person who seemed to notice us at all was an Olympian girl sitting behind the massive desk in the center of the space. She appeared to be a point of contact for anyone who had questions, and she stumbled over her response to an Agarthian boy as her eyes settled on me and Tate. He quickly shoved me into an empty nook, out of the girl's sight.

"Sit here," he said, pointing to an empty table. "Pretend you're studying. Don't speak to anyone or look up from this book until I get back. I'm going to explain ourselves to Lydia. She definitely saw you come in."

"Did she see my aura?"

"No. That's the problem. I could get into major trouble if she reports me for bringing a mortal into the Keepers' library. I'll let her know you're Atlantean. You just stay here."

I slid into my seat, eyeing the book Tate had randomly pulled off of one of the shelves for me to pretend to study. *Arbitration: Settling Disputes Across Keeper Races*. My eyes crossed before I even got to the end of the title. Surely there had to be something a little more interesting for me to read until Tate got back. Since no one else was around my little hiding nook, I decided to take just a quick moment to scan the shelves for a different book. I wouldn't go far—just the shelves immediately bordering my table.

That was my plan, anyway, until I heard Osborne on the other side of the stacks.

CHAPTER 6

I FROZE, UNSURE IF I should stay put or run.

"She wasn't in the sound. We searched the bottom for hours. And there's only one other way she could have gotten out. Where'd you put her?" Osborne's harsh tone sent a chill down my spine.

"I didn't put her anywhere," Tate said. His voice was closer to a whisper, and I had to lean in to hear him.

"Well, I know her soul wasn't taken back to the hall. I let the others know about it, too. I told them you had the chance to take it, and you let her get away."

"If I'd had the chance to take it, I would have. I don't want her alive anymore than you do."

A nearly silent gasp slipped through my lips. I couldn't be sure if Tate was telling him the truth or just trying to get Osborne off of his back, but the words stung. And though I tried not to make a sound, Tate must have heard me, or at least sensed my presence.

"I've got to *go*." The last word was laced with that ethereal sound that only a siren could make.

"Are you trying to glamour me, you fool?" Osborne growled.

No, he glamoured *me*. I had no choice but to walk away from the stacks. Tate's voice still sang out in the back of my mind. I knew I was under his control, and I couldn't resist.

I left their quiet exchange behind and strolled to the end of the aisle, unsure of where to go next. Keepers flitted to and fro across my vision. This part of the library was busy, full of these beautiful god-like creatures immersed in their own individual studies. Lydia, the girl at the desk, looked briefly in my direction. Her mouth was a hard set line, but she said nothing.

I could feel the tingle of Tate's presence dancing across my skin, so I knew he was still near. I also knew better than to be seen by Osborne, which left me in quite a predicament. I couldn't stay close to Tate, but I couldn't drift too far from him, either, or everyone else would notice my aura.

What did that leave?

I figured my safest bet would be to stay hidden back between the shelves of the aisles. As long as I kept note of where Osborne stood, I could avoid him with rows of books between us, and still hopefully maintain the glamour over my aura. Pulling the hood of my jacket over my head, I dipped back and around the corner, nearest the wall.

The first aisle was full of law books—something I should probably study up on at some point now that I was officially a Keeper. But the next aisle was far more interesting. It was a history section, the largest I'd ever seen. There were books covering every time period throughout every nation.

Titles before me read of Agarthian families of Australia in the 1400s, hundreds of years before it would be established as a country by mortals. My fingers twitched, eager to discover the secrets kept within those pages, but now was not the time for history lessons.

I continued down the aisle, moving until I felt the tingle in my blood begin to fade. Tate had commanded me to go away from where he and Osborne spoke, but this was as far as I could go without losing the disguising glamour for my aura.

There was no one else around. I leaned in, straining my ears, but I could no longer hear Tate or Osborne. I appeared to be alone, and yet, I couldn't shake the sense that I wasn't. Almost beyond any perception I had the words to describe, I knew someone was close. And it felt as though they were watching me.

No. You're being paranoid. Tate's glamour held strong. As long as he was near, no one would be able to discern that I was different.

Physically shaking the feeling off, I browsed the books lining the shelves before me. Most on this shelf bore titles from the colonial period of United States history. One stood out more than the others, however. It was called, *The Fractured Souls of Salem*. Without a second thought, I yanked the book from the shelf, quickly flipping it open to discover my suspicion was true. According to this book, the Salem Witch Trials were held against real fractured souls.

Excitement fluttered in my chest. I wasn't fractured. I knew that now. But the thought of these individuals roaming the earth still fascinated me. After all, Tate's entire life revolved around locating them and extracting their souls. I wanted to know more.

With the book held tightly to my chest, I spun around to find some dark corner where I could read until Tate reappeared or broke the glamour keeping me away from him. I couldn't drop my guard completely, but I may as well take the time to learn more about Keeper history while I waited, right? It sounded like a good plan, anyway.

But as I stepped toward the nook at the back of the aisle, I noticed something move in the shadows. I halted, straining my ears and eyes, extending every improved sense I had to see who or what may have been lurking in the back of my aisle. But there was nothing there. Nothing but the sense of danger that tickled at my nerve endings.

It was probably wise to go with that unnamed sense. I moved away from the shadows, back toward the center of the library. I could barely feel Tate at all when I stepped out from between the shelves, and I quickly dashed back into the first aisle I'd hidden in, surrounded by the law books. The tingle was weak, but it was definitely stronger here than it was in the middle.

"Everly Gordon?" A soft, female voice called out from behind me. I turned to see Lydia standing at the edge of her desk in the center of the room. She held an old textbook, and watched me expectantly.

"Yes?" I didn't want to meet her in the center. It was too far from Tate, and standing in the middle of an enormous room packed full of Keepers was the last place I wanted to reveal my new aura. I glanced nervously over my shoulder, hoping to see him coming around the corner to help me out. But I was still alone.

"I have your book ready here."

The textbook she held was turned away from me, obscuring its title. "I'm sorry, I'm not sure what you mean. I didn't reserve any books."

She extended her arms. "I was told this was for you. That's all I know."

We stared one another down for a moment. I didn't want to go to her, away from the protection of Tate's glamour. But she was clearly not going to bring the book to me. Swallowing down my fear, I dashed forward, nabbed the book from her outstretched hands, and dashed back into my little nook, barely grunting a thanks as I left her standing alone near her desk. Hopefully the movement was too fast for anyone to notice my aura.

Pulling the hood of my jacket securely back up over my head, I settled into my seat at the table where Tate had first left me and examined my new book, pushing the one about Salem to the side. The textbook was old, and I rubbed a thin layer of grime from the cover with the heel of my hand. It's title read, *The Rise and Fall of the Manticorians.* I'd never heard of them.

Glancing up to ensure that I was still alone, I felt the tingle of Tate grow stronger. He was coming back. That was good. I flipped open the textbook, content to learn more until Tate was back.

Scanning quickly through the introduction, I learned that the Manticorians were a group established in the middle ages with one goal: to relieve the Keepers of their power.

What? Why would the librarian girl give me this? I flipped through the pages, allowing them to quickly fall until a natural break opened the book wider about halfway through. A note was tucked into the pages with my name written on it.

The handwriting was small and otherworldly, slanted with odd shaped but smooth lettering. I unfolded the note and read the brief message inside:

I have the answers you seek. Meet me at St. John the Divine tonight at midnight to learn more. -R

I flipped the note over, looking to see if there was something I may have missed, but there was nothing else. My skin was alive now. Tate would be coming around the corner any second, so this little mystery would have to wait until later.

Slipping the note back into the crack of the book, I noticed which chapter it had bookmarked. *Rasputin: the Fallen Keeper's Attempted Revival.* My chest ached with the intense pounding of my heart. Was this from him?

"Everly, thank goodness you're still here."

I slammed the book closed and tucked it into my bag at the sound of Tate's voice.

"We've got to get you out of here. Now. We'll have to look into the prophecy another day, when Osborne's not sniffing around for you."

CHAPTER 7

DEVON VISITED EXACTLY SIX lighthouses before his body was trembling with weakness.

"Are you sure you can't try one more?" I asked, scrolling through the list in my spreadsheet. "I've got a good feeling about this next one."

"Everly!" Dom scolded. "Give him a break." She turned to Devon. "Thank you again for searching for us. You have no idea how much we appreciate it."

"No problem. It's definitely flexing my teleportation muscles." He cracked his knuckles. "I'm sorry I can't do more, but it seems to drain my energy faster when I'm going to a place I've never actually been to in person before."

"We understand." She smiled warmly.

"When do you think you'll be up for another round?" Tate asked. He was almost as anxious about finding the old man from Gayla's vision as I was, though for different reasons. Tate was becoming slightly obsessed about the prophecy. I just wanted to find my mom.

"I can try again tonight, maybe?" Devon looked doubtful.

"Tomorrow will be fine." Dom stood, bringing the discussion to a quick end. "No need to force too much on the first day."

"But there are seven hundred lighthouses on this list." I turned my screen back to face the others.

"And you won't be able to discover what is in any of them if you deplete our messenger of every ounce of energy in his body." Dom put her hands on her hips and then turned back to Devon. "Get some rest tonight, and we'll meet back here tomorrow afternoon."

Tate's eyes found mine, his expression thoughtful as though he was checking to see if I was okay with Dom's call. The process was painstakingly slow for me, but I would be alright. There was another secret burning a hole in the bag on my bedroom desk. I would occupy myself with the Rasputin mystery until Devon could try for the lighthouses again.

"Do you guys want to go to the Honey Pot with us?" Sean asked, trying to smooth over the tension in the air. "They've got half priced baklava until four o'clock."

"No thanks." I was already halfway to my bedroom door. "But you guys have fun. I'll see ya tomorrow."

I shut the door behind me and dashed over to my desk, carefully pulling out the book I'd been given at the library and re-examining the note inside. I hadn't mentioned it to Tate. He had been so wound up after his encounter with Osborne that he was mostly silent on our way back to the apartment. And my pulse didn't slow down until we'd gotten safely back inside—I'd practically sprinted away from the library once I knew the coast was clear. I still couldn't believe Tate's glamour had held and Osborne never found me. It almost seemed too good to be true.

At first I thought maybe Osborne had given Lydia the book for me. It seemed just like him to set up a trap like that and lure me away from my friends. But if he'd known I was in the library, I don't think he would have had the willpower to keep himself from taking me captive right then and there. So it couldn't have been him.

But if it wasn't Osborne, that meant it had to have been Rasputin himself, which left me with so many questions my head was spinning. How would he know who I was, and why would he care? I wasn't fractured. I wasn't anyone of importance. It should have been easy to dismiss the whole thing as a prank, but the note said he had the answers I sought. And if there was any chance that he knew something about where my mom was held, I had to give it a shot.

I pored over the pages of the old textbook for the next several hours, stopping only to grab a sandwich from the kitchen for dinner. I told the girls I was busy studying, which wasn't exactly a lie. It was close enough to the truth to get past Dom's radar, anyway.

And in my reading I learned that the Manticorians were established thousands of years ago in the middle east. They were comprised of humans, Keepers who had betrayed their races, and fractured souls who all shared a single goal: removing the Keepers from power.

According to the book, back in the days when magical creatures still roamed the earth's surface, the Manticorians had used dark magic to cobble together a beast whose sole purpose was to kill any Keeper who crossed its path. The beast, a manticore, thrived on the magic of the Keepers it consumed. It was named a man-eater, though it didn't eat mortals—only the most powerful Olympians, Atlanteans, and Agarthians it encountered. Each Keeper it consumed strengthened it just enough to obliterate its next meal.

The beast lived for hundreds of years, but it never even made a dent in the power structure of the Keepers. They fought back. At one point, there were armies on both sides. All of the Keeper races fought against the Manticorians, and even with a few fallen Keepers in their ranks, they were never a strong enough match.

Eventually, the beast was killed and the Manticorians dissolved. That's where Rasputin came into play. Rasputin was an Agarthian who left the Keepers to live in the mortal world. He never hid his powers from the mortals, instead using them to rise in the ranks of the Russian empire. And all the while, he used his notoriety to re-establish a secret branch of new Manticorians.

After several attempts on his life, Rasputin finally allowed the mortals to believe they'd successfully murdered him, and he disappeared along with any knowledge of the Manticorians. Some believed he really did pass, but others suspected he still roamed the earth to this day through the shadows, building an army of fractured souls and rebels, just waiting for his opportunity to destroy the Keeper empires once and for all.

But did this information deter me from meeting with him? Not a chance. With any luck, I'd be able to meet with the man, discover what he knew about my mother, and politely decline any recruitment speeches he tried to give before returning home. It sounded simple enough.

I repeated positive thoughts to myself the whole walk down Amsterdam Ave. to the enormous and elaborate Cathedral of St. John the Divine. The church was massive, taking up an entire city block, and I had no idea where exactly I was supposed to meet this mysterious "R."

This is a bad idea.

The voice of the owl broke through my concentration. Of course, only I could hear it. I paused on the sidewalk, searching the fence lines and sign posts for my feathery friend. "Where are you?"

Your eyesight is even worse than I remember. I'm in the tree.

I squinted toward the branches on the opposite side of the street. Empty.

Other tree. A groan echoed through my brain.

"Oh!" I startled at the sight of him high in a branch just off to my right, on the other side of the cathedral gates. "There you are. How long have you been following me?"

For weeks. He chuckled. *But this might be your dumbest move yet. Walking around out here at night without any protection is gonna get you killed. You're glowing like a Christmas tree.*

I looked down at my arm, though I knew I wouldn't be able to see my aura. It was strange that the owl could, though. "You can see my aura?"

Of course I can. I'm not blind.

"Do you know what it means?"

Not a clue. But it's different, and that's enough to get you killed.

"That's a pessimistic way to look at it."

I am not a pessimist. I'm a realist.

"Well either way, you'll be glad to know I'm getting off the streets as soon as I can find the person I'm meeting."

And who is that?

The note felt like it was burning a hole in my pocket. For reasons I couldn't explain, I felt like I needed to keep my theories a secret. Even though this was just an owl, I suspected he may try to stop me if he knew who I thought I was meeting. "I'm not entirely sure. Who are you, anyway? And why are you following me?"

Could my owl be the mysterious "R?" It hadn't crossed my mind that the bird might have a name. But if it could talk, and it had been following me for weeks, the possibility of it bringing me a book didn't sound so delusional anymore.

The name is Alphaeus Chenzira. And I've sworn an oath to protect you.

"Sworn it to who?"

You.

A door creaked open somewhere within the gates. "Sounds like that might be my person. I want to know more about this sworn oath business, but right now I have to go. It was nice to meet you, Al. Can I assume I will see you again soon?"

It's Alphaeus. And you'll only see me again if you can manage to stay alive.

I turned away from the owl and made my way to the entrance of the cathedral grounds. The bird hopped along the branches of the tree, moving deeper into the grounds with me to get a better look. A hooded figure stood in the shadows of the building, a cloak hanging to the ground. Chill bumps instantly covered me from head to toe. Perhaps I should have given this more thought...

"Everly Gordon?" The man's voice was like ice on the back of my neck. My feet froze to the spot where I stood. "Come on inside, darling. I won't bite."

I took three shaky steps forward before turning over my shoulder for one last look at Al.

I told you this was a bad idea.

The man stepped forward as well, crossing the lawn and slowly lowering his hood. Streetlights cast eerie shadows on the sharp features of his face, and his long beard seemed to collect darkness from all across the grounds.

The owl cursed loudly in my mind. *Everly, run! That's—*

"Rasputin," the man said, extending his arm to shake my hand. "I am so pleased to finally make your acquaintance."

CHAPTER 8

RASPUTIN'S HAND WAS COLD as ice, and it chilled me to my core. His eyes cut briefly to the flutter of wings erupting overhead as Al flew away, but they quickly returned to me, hungrily drinking in my appearance.

"Your aura is... magnificent." His accent was foreign to me. It wasn't quite Russian, but more like it was from another world. He lifted a hand as though he wanted to stroke my cheek, but quickly regained control of his features and gestured for me to follow him inside.

"What do you know about it?" I paused in the doorway. "My aura, that is." I would have much rather held the conversation outside than follow him to who-knows-where in the giant building before me.

"I know that it's the sign we've all been waiting for." He paused to examine me once more before turning back toward the dark hallway ahead. "Come, child. Follow me and I will tell you everything I know."

I didn't get the greatest of vibes from him, but I didn't get the sense that he wanted to harm me, either. In fact, he seemed quite delighted to see me.

With one more wary glance over my shoulder, I decided to follow him. The halls of the cathedral were mostly dark. The only illumination was moonlight that trickled in through stained glass windows, creating a blurred mosaic of eerie colors across the hard floor.

"What part of the cathedral are we in right now?"

"The part that leads to my office." Rasputin pulled open a door and gestured for me to go ahead of him.

"You first." I tried to keep my voice steady.

He gave a soft smile and a nod, then disappeared through the doorway. It was a stairwell leading down through a musty darkness. A faint yellow glow emanated from the bottom of the stairs.

"Do you work here? In the cathedral?"

"I work wherever I'm needed," he responded cryptically.

I examined his aura as we crept lower into the building. It had a warmer glow than Tate's or Osborne's. It was almost reddish in hue, like a molten lava. I wondered briefly what the variations in color might mean. Were they indicative of the Keeper's individual abilities? Or maybe their intentions? Surely they wouldn't allow evil to be on display like that. And if that was the case, Osborne's aura wouldn't be an icy golden glow compared to Rasputin's red hot hue.

Finally, we reached what I assumed was a basement, only it didn't open up wide. It was yet another drab hallway, more sinister than those above ground because it lacked windows.

As though he heard my thoughts, Rasputin explained where we were while leading me through the nondescript maze of dimly lit walls. "These are escape tunnels. They are rarely used anymore, but they haven't been closed off in case of an emergency that could require the clergy to leave the cathedral unnoticed. My office is just around the corner here." He stopped and pulled a tarnished golden key from the pocket of his cloak.

The click of the lock seemed to ignite my common sense, and my stomach twisted with the urge to run. We were so far below ground, so deep in the winding halls of unmonitored tunnels, that I wasn't even sure if I could get away before Rasputin used whatever powers he possessed to stop me in my tracks. What was I thinking following him down here? No one would even be able to hear me scream.

Al was right. This was a really, *really* bad idea.

Just before my panic could fully drag me under, Rasputin's door swung open wide to reveal the cave-like room on the other side. Calling it an office was generous. The only thing that gave any indication that it was used was a piece of artwork hanging on the stone wall opposite the door. The room was dark, but the yellow light from the hall revealed just enough of an outline to get my heart pounding.

"Is that…"

"Yes, Deliverer. That is a painting of you."

Against my better judgment, I entered the small space to get a better look. It was the painting from the gallery. The one of me on a throne.

Scarless and fierce. My fingers brushed the area below my lip, where my scar used to protrude from my skin. It was smooth now, gone once my powers were activated. And the title below the painting still bore the words I'd seen upon my arrival in the city. *Deliverance.*

"Where did you get this? Are you working with Rossel?" I could barely hear my own whispered words against the thunderous pounding of my heart.

Rasputin scoffed. "Never. But I do appreciate his artistic abilities. He captured you perfectly."

"What does it mean?"

"It means the prophecy is true. Rossel must have seen it in a vision. And now, seeing you here with that luminous aura... it's simply divine."

"But why? Why would he have it on display?"

"It reeked of a luring enchantment. He displayed it to attract you. And it worked. But he failed to kill you."

"Rossel wants me dead?"

"Indeed." He tilted his head, looking almost reptilian in the process. "That's why I created the explosion. I gave you a chance to escape."

"No." I took a step back and shook my head. That couldn't be true.

"Yes."

"I thought Tate created the explosion."

Rasputin laughed, a raspy choking sound, like he was gargling mothballs. "You thought wrong. The prince was only there to destroy you. To capture your beautiful soul. But he couldn't. Your powers didn't emerge as Rossel hoped they would. And by the time you turned, the prince had already realized you were more than another fractured soul. He couldn't do it."

"You keep saying *prince*. I don't know a prince."

"Ah, but you do. Thaddeus is Agarthian royalty." Rasputin stroked his wiry beard. "Interesting that he hasn't revealed that to you. All the more reason you should leave him behind and stick with me, I suppose."

Tate was a prince? How could that be? And why had no one told me?

"I'm sorry." I shook my head again, and moved back to the door. "I can't work with you." Even if what he said was true, Rasputin's goals didn't align with mine. He'd spent the last century trying to destroy the Keepers. Keepers like my friends, my aunt Millie, my mom... I couldn't allow that to happen.

"Whether or not you choose to work with me, it will not change your fate. You are the Deliverer. You are destined to change this world. I only offer my services to help you do it sooner."

"I don't need your help." I turned to leave, but something in his tone when he spoke again stopped me on the spot.

"I don't expect you to trust me, but I've never tried to hide who I am. In fact, I offered full information about my history to you on a silver platter. The same cannot be said for those who call themselves your friends." I turned to face him again, and a slow grin pulled his scraggly beard wide.

"Just be careful with what you say in front of Thaddeus. He does not care about you. He only cares about power, and he's using you to get it. Once he inherits the throne, he'll do what all the royalty before him has done. He'll squash any rumors of the prophecy flat and use his forces to destroy you. You see, your life means the end of the Keepers' power forever."

Pressure stung at the back of my eyes. I wanted to deny it—to call Rasputin a liar. But he almost seemed to echo what Dom had implied the day before. "If Tate wants me dead, why hasn't he done it already? He's had no shortage of opportunities to kill me."

"He can't kill you until he gets the throne, or his bargaining chip will be gone."

"I don't believe that." I didn't want to believe it, anyway. I moved back to the door.

"Oh, it's true. The royalty has great interest in ending you. In fact, I'd be willing to bet your mother is hidden away inside one of the royal prisons as we speak."

He was toying with me. I knew it, but I couldn't just walk away if he really knew something about my mother. "You know where she is?"

"If I knew, I would have found a way to release her, myself. We're on the same side. I know you find that hard to believe, but I want you to succeed."

"And what's in it for you?"

He grinned again. The expression looked unnatural on his face. "It's not about what's in it for me. It's about the betterment of all humanity."

I snorted. "I doubt that."

He shrugged. "You saw the other hunter, Osborne, take the lives of my people at the cargo dock."

A gasp caught in my throat. "I didn't. I escaped before it happened." But I should have known they wouldn't have been as lucky as I was that day.

"Well, he did. And hundreds of other lives as well. They say they're doing it to save the souls. Collecting the 'fractured pieces' in the hopes that they will one day piece them back into whole souls again. But ask Thaddeus how successful the operation has been so far. They've been extracting souls for thousands of years, and do you know how many they've actually pieced back together?"

The dry lump in my throat grew larger. I couldn't swallow it down, so my voice was gravelly as I answered. "Zero?"

"Zero." Rasputin's smile morphed into a scowl.

"So how do we stop them?"

"I don't have the details. All I know is that *you* are the one who will bring about the change we seek. You will deliver us from the overreaching power of greedy Keepers, who use the world and mortals for their own wicked gain."

"How?"

"Find Driskell."

"Who is Driskell?"

"He's the only one who can help you. He knows about the prophecy."

I believed him. He was a liar and a criminal and a murderer. But on this, I believed he was sincere. "Where can I find him?"

"They've banished him." Rasputin's eyes flashed faintly gold for just a moment, but his powers weren't directed at me. "He's trapped forevermore on Eilean Mor."

"On... *what*?"

"The Flannan Isles."

I repeated the location silently to myself. "Will he know who I am?"

"He's been waiting for you for over a century."

"Then I guess I should get going."

Rasputin nodded. "You know where to find me if you need my assistance." His eyes flared once more as he whispered a string of words I couldn't understand. Then I left him in the shadows.

CHAPTER 9

THERE WAS NO SLEEPING that night. I tossed and turned, tangling myself in the covers until the sky lightened into a pale gray through my window. Resigned to the fact that I would go without rest, I tucked my laptop under my arm and slid into position on the living room couch.

Three minutes later, I flipped back and forth between my fourteen open tabs, learning as much as I could about the Flannen Isles Rasputin had mentioned. There was a lighthouse on one of the islands there—Eilean Mor. And unsurprisingly, the lighthouse was shrouded in mystery after an unexplained disappearance of its Keepers over a hundred years ago. If I had to guess, that would have been right about the time this Driskell fellow was banished there.

Was Driskell the old man from Gayla's vision?

A quick glance at my phone revealed that it was 6:57 AM. That was close enough to lunchtime for me. I sent out a quick group text telling the guys to get here as soon as possible, then went and banged on Dom's and Gayla's bedroom doors. Gayla slept through the racket. Dom peeked out just long enough to let me know she was headed to an early morning class.

"But this is really important." I busted into her room to chat as she finished getting ready for the day. "I know where the old man is! I found the right lighthouse. I'm sure of it!"

"He'll still be there at lunchtime, when we agreed to meet."

"No—Dom, you don't understand!"

She flashed me a sympathetic smile. "Even if you're right, and this is the one, waiting a few more hours won't change a thing. The guys said they'd meet us here after lunch today. We'll all be ready to check out your lighthouse then."

By the time she left for class, Tate was standing in the hall, holding two cups of coffee. "Sorry," he said. "I would have been here a few minutes earlier, but there was some kind of issue with the espresso machine at the Honey Pot, and—hey Dom. Where are you going?"

She glanced at me with a look of warning, then told Tate she was going to class. "But you can meet us here after lunch. Like we all *agreed*."

"It's fine. Come on, Tate. Maybe we can get this started a little earlier. We just need Devon." I waved goodbye to Dom and gestured for Tate to come inside, gladly accepting the cinnamon vanilla latte he brought for me.

But Devon wasn't coming. Both he and Sean sent messages through in the next few minutes saying they wouldn't be able to make it until the afternoon. That meant Tate and I were all alone, at least until Gayla crawled out of bed.

"I went back to the library last night." He pulled a dining chair into the living room, and I was grateful to not be thigh-to-thigh with him on the couch. Tate had always made my stomach flip, and I didn't need his gorgeous face and the flutter in my chest distracting me. Not when he could very well still be an enemy. "Of course I couldn't find anything about the prophecy, so I searched for information about different auras instead."

"Did you find anything about mine?" I sipped the drink and recoiled as it scalded my tongue. Still too hot.

"No, unfortunately we're not any closer to figuring this out than when we started. Unless you found something? Why'd you text us all to come over here so early?"

"About that..." I bit the inside of my lip, wondering how much I should tell him. Neither Dom nor Rasputin seemed to fully trust Tate. But I wanted to. Even through all of their suspicions, I just didn't get the feeling that he was here to cause me harm. "Actually, I have a question for you."

He lifted his brows and took a sip of his own steaming beverage.

"Are you a prince?"

His eyes bulged as he fought to keep the drink in his mouth. Swallowing it down, he wiped his lips. "Where did you hear that?"

"Just answer me."

Tate's brows pulled together. "My father is the king, yes. But I can hardly be considered a prince."

"Uhh, I'm pretty sure that's the definition of a prince."

"It's not that simple." Tate set his drink on the coffee table. "My older brother, Cassius, is the crown prince. I have nothing to do with them. *That much has been made very clear.*" He mumbled the last part, his irritation evident.

"Why haven't you ever told me?"

"It hasn't been relevant."

"Okay, I have another question."

Tate inhaled deeply. "Hit me with it."

"Tell me about your work. You extract fractured souls, and then what?"

"We take them to the Hall of Souls in Agartha."

"Why?"

"Aside from their evil tendencies?" He shot me a suspicious look. "We want to piece them back together. We figure if a soul is split, then the other half or pieces of it must exist somewhere, within someone else. The fractured pieces can reunite in the hall, and whole Keepers can be born again in future generations with the repaired souls. It's the only way to save our kind from extinction."

"How many fractured souls have you extracted?"

"Personally? Six. But there have been thousands over the ages." He looked pleased.

"And how many have been successfully pieced back together?"

Tate's jaw clenched. "It's difficult to know for sure."

"How many are you certain of?"

He didn't respond, and that was answer enough for me. They'd killed thousands of people by pulling their souls straight out of their bodies, and there was no proof that they were helping anyone. They were just murdering them. Rasputin was right.

I stood and slammed my laptop shut with a bit too much force. "Well since no one else is coming until lunchtime, maybe you should go, too."

"But what was it you discovered? Maybe I can help you figure it out while we wait on the others."

"Maybe not. We'll talk later." It would have to wait, because I certainly wasn't going to reveal what I'd learned to Tate alone. If Rasputin was right about the fractured souls, he could have been right about Tate using me for power, too, as much as I hated to think about it.

"Everly, is there something wrong?"

"Nope." I ignored the way I felt drawn to him when he said my name. The invisible thread pulling us together seemed to tighten, and it took much effort to move away from him. Tate was a manipulator, and I wouldn't allow these false feelings to deceive me.

I stepped to the door and motioned for him to go out. "Just no use hanging out until the others arrive. Go home. Take a nap. I'll see you later."

He slowly stepped to the door and paused, a strange expression twisting the corner of his mouth as he examined me once more. He looked as though there was more he wanted to say, but after a few moments he turned into the hall. I immediately shut the door and turned both locks into place. Then I dumped the steaming contents of my coffee down the drain and retreated into my room.

An emotional storm was trying to work itself up inside me, and I was having a hard time shaking it off. I shouldn't be so upset about Tate. He'd never really been on my side. But I couldn't help but feel betrayed, anyway. Why oh why couldn't he just be good?

CHAPTER 10

MY LIMBS BURNED WITH adrenaline by the time Sean and Devon finally arrived that afternoon. I'd been thinking about it all morning, and I'd decided that I was going to ask Devon to take me with him to the lighthouse. I'd learned through my studies that Atlantean messengers could teleport others with enough energy, and I wasn't going to let Devon use it all up before taking me. I was going to meet Driskell.

I nearly tackled him with excitement when he entered our apartment.

"Whoa!" He took a step back.

"I know where he is."

"Who?" Sean asked. We joined Dom, Gayla, and Tate, who were already seated in the living room.

"The old man from Gayla's vision."

"What?" Tate asked. "Why didn't you say something earlier?"

"Because she doesn't know for sure." Dom interjected. "She *thinks* she knows where he is."

"I do know. Without a doubt. And I want to go with you," I said to Devon.

"Hang on. Where did all this confidence come from?" Gayla asked.

I turned back to the girls to find Dom watching me closely, her head tilted to one side. She was looking for the answer in my mind, and try as I might, there was no hiding it. In fact, I was surprised she hadn't already asked me about Rasputin. It was all I could think about all morning.

After a bit, Dom shook her head, keeping her eyes on me as she spoke. "She's not really confident. And Devon, I think you should go alone at first. We don't want to use up all your energy on the first lighthouse in case it's wrong."

"It's not wrong!" Why was Dom denying this? I knew she could see into my mind. I couldn't understand why she was hiding my meeting with Rasputin from the others. I figured she'd rat me out right away, being the rule follower she was. Unless she was trying to keep me out of trouble…

Dom's eyes narrowed. "What is going on in there, Ev?"

"Come on, Dom. I know you know." Everyone else remained silent as they took in the tense interaction between us.

She stood and reached her hands out toward my cheeks. "May I?"

I nodded. There was no use trying to hide anything from her now, anyway. Her cool palms cupped my cheeks, and her brown eyes darkened slightly as she stared deeply into mine. Then she gasped and dropped her hands. "Everly, I think you've been cursed."

"What?"

She nodded. "Tell the others how you know about the lighthouse."

I took a deep breath, steadying myself for the influx of objections I was probably about to receive. "I met—" My throat closed in on itself, restricting my airflow and leaving me choking on Rasputin's name. My hand clenched around my neck, willing it to open and provide me the oxygen I needed. Very slowly, after lots of coughing, the sudden choke hold eased up.

A whole minute had passed before I was able to breathe properly again. Wiping the wetness from my eyes and shrugging off Dom's concerned arm over my shoulder, I tried again. "I—"

"No!" Dom clamped her hand over my mouth. "You'll choke and die if you try too hard to reveal your source. You've been cursed to secrecy."

A curse. Suddenly, memories of my mother choking until she vomited in the basement of the gallery flooded my mind. She'd been cursed as well. It's why she couldn't reveal my heritage. It's why she couldn't tell me where she was going. If only I could have read her thoughts like Dom could read mine. "You can see it in my mind though, right?"

"No." Her eyes were sad. "It's like a dark blanket has swallowed up anything that might reveal what you saw."

"But what about the lighthouse? I can mention *it* without dying." Or I thought I could, anyway. I had to try. The Flannan Isles were on the opposite side of the world. I would never be able to reach them without help from the others.

"You can try," she said.

I closed my eyes and inhaled deeply, listening to the thunderous beat of my heart. *Here goes nothing...* "The old man is in the lighthouse on Eilean Mor." I blurted the words as fast as I could, before I would keel over. But they came out in a jumbled mess of syllables.

"What?" Devon scrunched his eyebrows.

I grinned, happy to still be breathing normally. Apparently information about the lighthouse wasn't cursed—only Rasputin's name. "Eilean Mor. It's an island in Scotland." I opened up my laptop and showed them pictures and the maps I'd saved during my research that morning.

"And you're certain this is where he is?" Devon asked.

"Yes. Can you take me with you?"

"Wait wait wait..." Sean stood with both hands in the air before him. "If you're sure this is where the old man is, then we all need to go. You're going to need some backup."

"I can't take everyone at once," Devon said. "I'm not strong enough."

"How many can you take at a time?" Tate asked.

"I've never gotten more than two."

"Alright," Tate said. "I'll go with her on this first run."

"No." I spoke a little too loudly, and Tate turned to me like he'd been burned by the word. "If we meet the man, I'll need to know if I can trust him."

"I'll glamour him."

I shook my head. "I want Dom with me. She'll be able to hear the truth in what he tells us and see what he doesn't tell us."

She stepped forward and grabbed my hand. "Of course I'll go with you."

"And no offense Tate, but I think Sean and Gayla should be next. We'll need Sean's finesse in case things go sour, and only Gayla will be able to verify if the scene matches her vision."

He looked offended, but he didn't object. "Fine, but don't do anything until we're all together again. Just stay put."

"Devon, are you ready?" I turned away without agreeing to Tate's request.

"I am if you are. The first time is a little jolting, but I promise you'll be fine."

"Will it hurt?"

"Nah, it's just a little chilly."

I picked up a bag I'd prepared for the trip. Inside sat the stone tablet I'd taken from Rossel, the note from Rasputin, a flashlight, two water bottles, and a granola bar. I added my phone to a zip-up pocket and secured it over my shoulders. Then Devon, Dom, and I took each other's hands and made a small circle.

"On the count of three. One, two..."

It felt like I was yanked out of New York and dragged across the icy arctic tundra, but only for a fraction of a second. Then I stood wide eyed and trembling in a green field surrounded by choppy ocean waters.

"You okay?" Devon asked with a chuckle.

"Uh, that was more than a little chilly." I rubbed the goosebumps across my arms. "But yeah, I'm fine. This is incredible."

The rocky island we stood upon was high above the sea. It wasn't overly large, but very steep, and it was sparse of any signs of life other than the lighthouse standing tall at the center of a hill and the ancient looking ruins of an old stone chapel. An abandoned railway and stairs led up to the white lighthouse. All around the island were steep, rocky cliffs and inlets. There were plenty of areas that could qualify as a "cleft in the rock." So where would we find old man Driskell?

"Wow," Dom murmured. I followed her gaze to the overcast sky, where just a trickle of golden light from the setting sun was breaking through beneath thick gray storm clouds. It was much later in Scotland than it had been back at the apartment.

"Well, it looks like your best bet will be up there in the lighthouse. You wanna go now, or should I bring the others here, first?"

"Go ahead and bring Sean and Gayla," I said. "But Devon... I don't want Tate to come."

"What? Why?" Devon looked shocked, but Dom physically relaxed, the hint of a grin pulling at her lips.

"I just think we should keep this a small group for now. We shouldn't be quick to forget that he was tasked with killing me just last week. Let's see what the old man has to say, then we can pull him back into the mix if we need to."

"If you say so." Devon shrugged. "You guys okay here while I go back?"

"We're fine," Dom said. Devon nodded and disappeared into the air before us. Once he was gone, Dom turned back to me with a sad smile. "I think that was the right call."

"I hope so." I was less certain. I wanted to trust Tate, but if Dom and Rasputin's suspicions were true, it was definitely best to leave him out of this.

The sunlight disappeared entirely while Devon was gone, dipping below the horizon for the night. Giant raindrops began to fall in scattered splashes on our arms and the rocky earth. "I hope they hurry. This reminds me of storms back on the ranch at home. Any minute now this sky is gonna open up and dump buckets on us."

Dom squinted up into the clouds and a roar of thunder cracked across the sky. "I think you're right."

Devon reappeared then, right on cue, with Sean and Gayla's hands clasped in his and Tate's half-bent form wrapped around his waist, like they'd been mid-tackle when Devon left. *What was he thinking?* Tate had latched onto Devon like an uninvited hitchhiker, and it was a wonder Devon was able to make it here at all! Weak from the extra exertion of teleporting a third person, Devon fell to his knees and held his head in his hands.

"Tate! What did you do?" I scowled at him and knelt to check on Devon. "Are you okay?"

Devon groaned with a gentle nod. A flash of lightning illuminated the world around us, almost immediately followed by a thunderous boom—the opening act of an ominous storm rolling across the sky. A few more heavy drops fell from the clouds. Then, as though someone turned on a faucet, the heavens opened the floodgates and drenched us to the bones almost instantly.

Sean helped me get Devon back to his feet, but he was still too weak to move. Without another thought, Sean scooped his friend up in his arms and pointed to the lighthouse, now glowly brightly atop the hill. "Let's go!"

We took off after him, pushing through the heavy rain like curtains of water blocking our way. A gust of wind blew across the open air atop the island, and I nearly lost my footing. The ground was slick, and it was difficult to gain much speed through the mud and rocks that jutted up from the grassy earth.

Another bolt of lightning flashed through the sky, striking the island itself not far from where we ran. No—it didn't strike the island. "Taaaate!"

I veered off to my right to where Tate was laying on the ground. He appeared to be unconscious. The others were by my side a moment later, and the sky lit up once more with a bright flash of electricity. Then everything went dark.

CHAPTER 11

MY WRISTS ACHED. AND it was cold. Too cold. Why did the girls turn the air conditioner on? A groan escaped my lips and I tried to brush away whatever was tickling my nose, but my hand was stuck.

"Everly?" a voice whispered. I wanted to open my eyes and see who was there, see what my hand was caught on, but my eyelids were too heavy. And it was so, so cold. I just wanted to curl up and drift back to sleep.

"Everly," the voice whispered again.

I slowly fought the gravity holding my lids closed. Low flickering light reached my half-open eyes, and the brightness was too much to handle. Though it wasn't more than a candle in a jar, the light felt as though it seared my brain.

I groaned again, then heard a rough cough from across the room. Fighting against the pain from the candlelight, I forced my eyes open wide enough to see the hunched over outline of a strange man pacing back and forth in front of a window. No light shone through aside from occasional flashes of lightning in the distance.

It all came back to me. The island. The storm. Was that Driskell? Where was I now?

I moved to sit up, but quickly realized my wrists were tied to bedposts above my head. My ankles were tied together as well.

"Everly!" The whisper from before was more like a growl now, but the old man pacing in front of the window didn't seem to notice. I arched my back enough to twist and steal a glance over my shoulder. Gayla's platinum colored locks fell through slats of what appeared to be a prison cell built into the wall behind the bed I was tied to. Her dark eyes were wide with fear. Behind her lay the lifeless bodies of the rest of our crew. Dom, Sean, Devon... they were all there except one.

"Where's Tate?" I whispered. Gayla's dark eyes shifted to the other side of the room where Tate was strapped to a chair and gagged. He was still unconscious, and his head lolled limply to one side. "Is he alive? And the others? Is everyone okay?"

"I think so. I just woke up before you. But that's him. That's the old man from my vision. I told you he was crazy."

I glanced back at the man mumbling incoherently in front of the window. The low light made it difficult to make out his features, but I could see a long scraggly beard and fiery orange untamed hair hanging down well-past his shoulders like a matted mane of a lion.

"Wake up Devon so he can zap us out of here," I suggested.

"I tried. He's out cold."

I turned back toward the old man. It was going to have to be me, then. I'd have to be the one to get us out of here. I searched the space immediately around me, looking for anything sharp that I might be able to use to cut through the ropes that bound me, but there was nothing. There was nothing in the room at all, save for two chairs, a small table near the window, and the bed.

Well, there was the prison cell, too. The floor and walls were solid stone, as though the room was carved right out of a mountainside. And perhaps it was. We certainly weren't in the lighthouse. Perhaps we were in the cleft of the rock from Gayla's vision. That meant the old man was definitely who I was looking for.

"Driskell." My voice was raspy, my throat raw from yelling in the storm. I cleared it and tried again, louder this time. "Driskell!"

The old man stopped mumbling his gibberish and turned to face me. He froze there for a long time—much longer than was comfortable, and it was too dark for me to make out his expression. A clap of thunder boomed from outside, and it seemed to restart his motor. He immediately set into motion, marching straight toward me.

I braced myself, pulling my chin in and turning away slightly as he raised his arms in the air. I couldn't make out what he held, but it looked like it would hurt if he used it as a weapon. Thankfully, that wasn't his intention.

With one swift motion, he brought his arms down from over his head and released the object, throwing it down on the stone floor with all his might. It shattered into a hundred tiny pieces, and as the object burst into bits, my chest felt as though it was cracked open as well.

"The tablet!" Gayla gasped behind me. He must have retrieved it from my bag, which I noticed hanging limply off the edge of his table.

Driskell met my eyes again. His glowed a beautiful shade of blue, almost a turquoise, and they were wild with an energy I couldn't decipher. Did he want to kill me? Because shattering the tablet definitely made me feel like I was one step closer to death. It wasn't just the emotional loss of the piece, but physically I felt broken as well.

"Everly. You're glowing," Gayla said.

I glanced down at my arms and saw nothing. Driskell must have seen it though. A strange grin spread its way slowly across his scruffy face. The candlelight glinted off of his teeth, casting eerie yellow flashes from his mouth. It added to the madness he already projected.

Another crack of thunder drew my attention briefly to the window. It was loud enough to cause Tate to stir, and with his movement returned the strange tingle across my skin. Only it was different this time. It wasn't the invisible thread that drew me into Tate that I felt buzzing through my body, it was more like a new sense of life. An energy I'd never felt before.

It pulsed along with my heart, increasing in speed and force with every thump in my chest. Driskell threw his head back and laughed maniacally. Then he looked down at the floor where the pieces of my tablet still lay scattered like leaves in the fall.

It was easy to see where the pieces had fallen, because they now emitted that same strange glow I'd seen back in the gallery. Driskell, Gayla and I all watched in silent wonder as the pieces moved back together, dragging themselves roughly across the floor until they snapped back into place, like a magnetic puzzle. It was the same thing they'd done when I dropped it in the gallery.

But this time I felt each piece as it reconnected with the whole. As the tablet came back together, so did I. I could feel its power surging through my veins, again and again until at long last the tablet had been fully restored.

With one quick tug, I broke through the ropes binding me to the bed. I jerked my feet apart, snapping the rope that had been wrapped around my ankles as well. I sat up, stronger than I'd ever been, rubbing the tender area where my wrists had gone slightly raw, then stood.

Driskell took one step back as I approached him. There wasn't fear in his eyes—it was something else. Respect? Reverence, maybe. Whatever it was, it was undeserved. I bent down and picked up the tablet, examining the carvings in the stone and confirming it was the same as it had been before it was broken. Then I pulled it to my chest, and a bright white light filled the small stone room.

Driskell fell to his knees, bowing his head clear down to the floor. The wind howled through the rain that pelted the small window on the outside wall, but even through the racket I heard his shaky voice croak out a single word that would change my life forever.

"Deliverer."

CHAPTER 12

THE BRIGHT LIGHT FADED as quickly as it had come on. Dom, Sean, Devon, and Tate all stirred, awakened by the flash and groaning in pain. Gayla rushed to help the others in the cell, and I shot Tate a wary glance from where he sat tied to his chair.

Turning away again, I extended a hand to the old man who was still bowing with his face to the ground. "Driskell, stand up. We need to talk." He slowly raised his face, but did not meet my eyes. I wiggled my hand, urging him to take it, then helped him to his feet.

"Will you please release my friends?"

"The friends, yes. The prince?" He cut a sharp look to where Tate sat. "I think not." Driskell's words were thick with a German accent, and though he looked like a hermit driven to solitary insanity, he spoke with a high level of intelligence and carried himself like a man who had plenty of experience in the highest echelons of society.

Tate caught my eyes, and I held his gaze for a long minute while Driskell fumbled with some keys to open the prison cell behind me. His expression was pleading, almost desperate. He turned to Driskell and his irises flashed gold, but nothing happened. A siren needed his voice for glamour, and Driskell had Tate gagged. He was as helpless in that chair as a mortal.

I felt no joy seeing him in that state, but I wasn't ready to set him free, either. Not yet. With clenched teeth I turned away in time to see my friends stumble out of the prison cell. Gayla and Dom rushed forward and wrapped me in their arms. Devon, still too weak to move much, slinked out and plopped himself down on the bed I'd been tied to.

Sean was a whole different story, however. His guardian training kicked in, and he bowed up—chest out, hands clenched into fists, chin held high—giving Driskell the most intimidating look he could muster. "You've got some explaining to do, old man." His voice came out like a growl.

Driskell was unfazed. Once his keys were secured back in his pocket, he approached me and placed his hands on my shoulders. I clutched the tablet even tighter, feeling its power become one with my own. I didn't fear Driskell. It was hard to explain, but there was a new confidence ignited within me. I feared nothing.

With a gentle squeeze on my shoulders, Driskell spoke. "Deliverer. I've been waiting for this day. I knew you would come."

"Why do you believe that I am the Deliverer?"

"Because you are alive. The curse did not strike you dead. The earth wants you to know of the prophecy, and you will know."

"And my friends?"

"The Deliverer's power does not answer to the laws of the Keepers' world. You wanted your friends to live, and they did." He cut his eyes back over to Tate. "Even the prince," he mumbled, bitterly.

"Please, Driskell. Tell me everything you know."

"Follow me. My notes are stored in the lighthouse."

We turned toward a primitive doorway carved into the stone beyond the prison cell. It was opposite the window wall, and I suspected it led deeper into the center of the island. This was how he'd stayed hidden from mortals for so many years. He lived within the island rather than on top of it.

Tate fought against his restraints, grunting through the gag to get my attention. We couldn't just leave him there, but the list of people who didn't trust him was growing longer by the minute. "If I let you free, will you promise not to use your powers on anyone here on the island?"

Tate nodded, and I turned to Dom. She stared thoughtfully at him, head slightly inclined as she studied his inner thoughts. Finally, with a small frown, she turned to me. "He's telling the truth. He will not use his powers here, as much as he hates to hold them back."

His brows furrowed, annoyed and probably feeling a little violated at having Dom root around in his mind. I could relate. I stepped toward him, and my skin responded immediately to the proximity. Energy buzzed along my arms, urging me to reach out and touch him.

Tate's eyes met mine, his breathing faster. He felt it too. Ignoring the urge, I settled on the ropes binding his legs, and easily snapped them apart with some superhuman strength I'd never before possessed. I could get used to this. I broke the bind tying his torso to the chair next, but I left the gag and his wrists secured behind his back.

"I want to trust you," I whispered so that only he could hear it. "But I just—" The explanation caught in my throat. I wasn't sure how to finish. A clap of thunder rattled the windows, taking the pressure off of me.

"Come," Driskell said. "The curse is growing angry."

We followed him into a narrow stone passageway illuminated only by the flickering candle in the lantern he carried. Devon had one arm thrown over Sean's shoulder, and Sean half-carried, half-dragged his friend's weak body along.

Driskell mumbled more as we followed him through the winding tunnel. It was a constant incline drawing us ever upward—up to the top of the island, where the white lighthouse stood like a beacon in the night. Though I couldn't quite make out his words—they may have been German or Bavarian—there was a strong undertone of courage. He was nervous for sure, but Driskell fought through his fear to do what he felt was right.

"We won't let anything happen to you." I tried to sound braver than I felt.

"What do you mean?" he asked over his shoulder.

"You mentioned a curse surrounding the prophecy. I assume it affects you as well. But if it's true that my powers somehow counteract those of the Keepers and their curse, I want you to know that you are safe. I won't let them hurt you."

Driskell laughed the same maniacal chortle from before. "It is my destiny." He pushed a large flat rock up over his head and shifted it to one side. Light immediately filled the dingy stone tunnel we huddled in, flooding down from the artificially illuminated lighthouse above us.

We climbed out, one by one. I stood behind Tate, steadying him as he ascended the ladder without any hands. My hands felt hot on his lower back, and that invisible force pushiing us together didn't want me to pull away when he reached the room above. But this was no time to fantasize about embracing Tate. We were on the precipice of something great, and everyone knew it. Finally, I emerged from the tunnel and gathered together with the others in a small room lined with shelves.

"Would you care for tea?"

"No thank you," Dom said at the same time Gayla exclaimed, "yes!"

"Me too." Driskell smiled at Gayla, then set off to the small kitchen to fill a kettle and bring the water to a boil. The storm raged on outside as he went about his work, with lightning flashes and booms of thunder filling the room every few minutes.

I examined the books and files on the shelves as he worked, but most were written in languages I was unfamiliar with. After a short time, Driskell returned with hot cups of tea for everyone but Tate. Maybe it was a slight against him, but Tate wouldn't be able to enjoy it with the gag in his mouth anyway. Still, I couldn't bring myself to make eye contact with him or else I'd probably crack from the guilt and set him free.

"So," Driskell said, settling into a seat at a small table near the kitchen area. "What do you know about the prophecy?"

"Nothing," I admitted. "Tate is the only one of us who had even heard of it before. Would you like him to share what he knows?"

"No." Driskell scoffed. "He is Agarthian royalty, yes?"

Tate hung his head as we confirmed it.

"Then he should not be here at all! The royalty is to blame for this curse on our world! They destroyed the prophecy. They do not want it to come to fruition. But it must. You must Deliver us from their evil." The old man trembled, revealing his desperation.

Tate lifted his gaze back to mine, his eyes wide and glistening. They weren't filled with guilt or hatred. He looked very much like a victim rather than a villain. I couldn't believe that Tate had anything to do with the evil Driskell spoke of—royalty or not.

"He will kill you now that he knows what you are," Driskell continued. "That is *his* destiny."

"No," Dom said. "He may not be entirely forthcoming, but he doesn't want Everly dead. I can see that clearly."

Tate's eyes glimmered in the light, the golden flecks calling out to me on some deeper level. And I couldn't resist any longer. With a new swiftness, I broke the binding on his wrists and removed his gag, praying that I wouldn't soon come to regret it.

"I will never kill you." The words spilled from his mouth in a hurry, as though he expected me to gag him again at any moment. "Never. You have my word. I will do whatever it takes to protect you for as long as I live.

This is my oath, through the sky, the sea, and the earth on which we stand."

A collective gasp filled the room. "Well there you have it," Gayla said, calmly sipping her tea. "The hunter has sworn himself to you. If he kills you now, he'll die on the spot." She put a hand on her chest and looked up to the sky.

"Is that true?" My voice was shakier than I would have preferred.

Tate nodded. "But Dom is right. There's something I haven't mentioned."

Driskell snorted and took a long drink from his own mug.

"My mission to hunt you did not come from my own Agarthian superiors—not directly anyway. It was an order from a higher power. You see, there is a group of elite Keepers across the races, the highest ranks within the royal courts. And they work together for the betterment of the earth. The order to extract your soul came directly from them. From Rossel and the Olympian king, specifically."

"Why?"

"I don't know. They didn't say. But it was important. Important enough that I was promised the crown if I could pull it off."

My chest cracked. It was true then, what Rasputin said. Tate only wanted power. He only wanted the Agarthian throne. And after he got it, what would become of me?

"So what now? Are you still after the crown?"

"No." Tate shook his head emphatically. "Now there is something bigger to work toward. I don't have to save my kingdom by sacrificing myself for the Agarthian throne. I can save it by helping you destroy it."

CHAPTER 13

TATE'S WORDS HUNG HEAVILY in the air for some time. I couldn't be certain that what he said was true. How could someone—a prince no less—be so enthusiastic about destroying his own kingdom? It didn't make sense. But at least I didn't have to worry about him trying to kill me now that he'd given the oath.

"Well," I said after a minute. "Then I suppose we need to learn as much as we can about this prophecy."

Driskell grunted his approval and downed the rest of his tea. He set his cup on the table, steepled his fingers, and inhaled a deep breath. I knew then there was much more to this prophecy than I could have imagined.

"There have always been rumors," he began. "Ever since I was a child. Stories of our kind—how we began, our purpose on the earth, and how we would end. Over time, it became more like a fairytale than actual history. But I could never forget those stories from my youth. They struck a chord in me, and I dedicated my life to discovering more about the secrets of our ancestry.

"At university, I specialized in lost and forgotten languages. My partner and I traveled across the globe, reviewing ancient artifacts and deciphering their meanings for museums and private collections. But a little over a century ago, we found something truly incredible. A stone tablet."

His eyes cut briefly to the object I clutched in my arms, and I found myself squeezing it tighter. He watched me with wonder, his aqua blue eyes twinkling with respect, framed by his wild mane of orange hair. But there was one tuft of curls that didn't blend in with the rest of his fiery head of hair. One white swirl of curls hung low over his brow. Though he was older now, and certainly aged by the stress of his situation, there was no denying who this man was. I'd seen him before, in a slideshow on my first day at Columbia.

"You worked with Professor Brossard, didn't you?"

Driskell nodded sadly. "Indeed."

The professor had lied to me. How many people were in on this? How many people knew my true identity?

"The tablet we found was but a fraction of the whole. We knew what it said, but it made no sense. Not without the other pieces. I paused all of my other projects, devoting everything I had to this one stone tablet."

"Why?" I asked. "Why this one?"

"Because I knew it was special. I did not understand the greater context, but there was one word that revealed enough for me to know that the world would never be the same."

I looked down at the object in my arms, and I could practically feel it pulsing along with my heart—faster as the power of the object became more and more tangible. "What is it?" My voice was a whisper. "What does it say?"

Driskell held out his hand, and I gently laid my treasure on his palm. He grinned, as though he were seeing the face of a long lost friend. "It says: The daughter of... together with... ignites her... centennial... shall form a... the powers... The Deliverer." He pointed to the different symbols as he read their meanings aloud.

My stomach sank. "That means nothing to me."

Driskell chuckled. "It means nothing to anyone. But it mentions The Deliverer, and that was enough for me to give it further exploration. I was so close to cracking the code. Too close. The elites took notice of my efforts. You see, they've known about the prophecy since the dawn of time. It was carved into stone by the prophets of the first century. The royalty did not like what they saw. They did not want to hear of their demise, and they believed that in destroying the prophecy, they could destroy the truth behind it, as well.

"But the prophecy could not be destroyed, as you have noticed. The greatest damage they could achieve was breaking the tablet into four pieces. Each kingdom took one quarter of the stone to hide within their territories, and the fourth was cast deep into the depths of the earth—buried beneath the arctic where neither man nor Keeper would ever dare to locate it.

"But by some miracle, it washed upon the shores of Greenland a little over one hundred years ago. It was found by a mortal, who called upon my partner and I to inspect it. I discovered what it was through ancient writings. Diaries and fictional accounts provided more information, and I made it my personal mission to learn whatever I could about this Deliverer. As the world grew more evil each year, I saw the need for you to destroy the status quo and give us the reset we all so desperately need.

"When the elites realized what I was trying to achieve, they tried again to destroy the object you hold now, but it was not possible. It could not be destroyed, and it could not be cursed. So they cursed me instead, and banished me here to this island, which is also cursed. They created a fictional narrative—convincing Keepers across the world that any mention of the tablet or the prophecy would curse them as well.

"They believe I lost my mind." He chuckled. "And perhaps I have. But I know that you are real, and I know that you have the power to change the world."

The storm roared outside, and a particularly loud crack of thunder made me jump in my seat. Driskell looked nervously toward the lighthouse windows. "I've said too much. The island will kill me now. It is my destiny."

"It's not," I argued. "I won't let anything happen to you. Tell me, Driskell. What do I do now? How do I change the world?"

He took my hand in his and gave it a firm squeeze. "You must find the other pieces of the tablet. You must travel to each of the three kingdoms to restore it and use its power to accomplish the task before you."

"I can help," Tate said. "I can get us into the Agarthian palace."

I wanted to trust him, but common sense won out again. "Maybe we should start with Atlantis. That's the one place I should be welcomed."

Driskell took another deep breath and looked up to the sky. "It is time." He squeezed my hand again. "I wish you well."

The entire lighthouse reverberated with a jolt of electricity, followed by a crack of thunder so loud it made my bones ache. A moment later I became aware of smoke and Tate pulling on my hand. "The lighthouse is burning! We've got to get out."

He pulled me through the doors and out onto the island. Darkness covered the earth like a blanket—a heavy, wet blanket that threatened to snuff out any life that dared to stand up against it. The storm raged harder than ever, wind whipping the raindrops against my cheeks like stones.

We'd made it about twenty paces away from the building before we turned to stare in awe. The lighthouse tower burned, blazing brightly even through the torrential downpour.

Waves rose from the ocean surrounding us, like angry giants waking from a slumber. They grew taller and taller—an army of great walls moving toward the island.

"The curse is here for me," Driskell said. "I pray it won't get us all."

"It won't. I will keep you safe. All of you." I turned to look at my friends one at a time, allowing my eyes to linger on each of theirs long enough for them to understand just how serious I was. "I swear it as the Deliverer—as my oath—through the sky, the sea, and the earth on which we stand." I repeated the words Tate had uttered just minutes earlier, and felt a lock snap taut in my chest as some greater power made my words a reality.

The largest of the waves was nearing the island, growing larger with every passing second and I knew my words wouldn't be enough. It wasn't stopping. The curse was going to wipe us all away into the depths of the ocean. I'd survive, and the other Atlanteans, perhaps, but I would not allow it to kill my friends. We'd come too far to be swept away by some water.

Anger boiled red hot inside me, and I lifted my arms as though I might block the water from reaching us. A guttural yell escaped my throat, originating from deep in my belly and sounding like something from another creature in another world. I couldn't explain where it came from if I tried, but it did the trick. The wave split into two, avoiding my outstretched arms and my deathlike war cry. It crashed to the earth extinguishing the flames of the lighthouse and falling back into the ocean.

"Enough!" I yelled again. Spinning around with my arms still outstretched above my head. I stared down the storm, scolding it like a naughty child, and to my amazement, it cowered at my voice. The rain slowed, the wind stilled, and after another minute, all was quiet.

I turned to find my friends' open mouthed stares. They were shocked— all of them except Driskell. He fell to his knees once more, bowing to me. "What are you doing? Get up, the storm is over."

Devon was next.

"Guys, please don't do this."

Then went Dom, Sean, and Gayla.

"Tate. Thank you. Please talk some sense into them. Tell them to get up. This is not necessary."

He shook his head. The corner of his mouth curled up ever so slightly—not with derision, but more like a proud parent might regard a child on stage, accepting a medal. Then he dropped, his knees splashing into the mud, and lowered his face to the ground.

I dropped as well, placing myself squarely on their level and wiping the tears stinging at my eyes. The weight of everything I'd learned squeezed my chest, and I felt so alone and ill-prepared for whatever lay ahead. "Please," I said softly. "Raise your heads. I need you all beside me, not below me. If we're going to change the world, it's going to take all of us."

FINDING ATLANTIS

CHAPTER 1

MY CHEEK WAS WET and smashed up against the moist fabric of my too-hard pillow. I reached up to wipe the drool from my face, licking my dry lips and choking on my own morning breath. My neck ached, my back was sore, and—

I gasped as everything from the night before came crashing back into my memory. I didn't want to open my eyes, because it would only confirm what I feared was true.

My pillow moved, and Tate's chuckle warmed me as he pushed a strand of hair off of my forehead. I lifted one lid and saw his golden eyes glistening with amusement as he stared back down at me. "It's about time you woke up. It would be a shame to survive the storm only to drown in your drool."

I punched him in the wet spot on his arm and sat up to find that everyone was right as I'd left them the night before, huddled together in the stone hallway that adjoined Driskell's cliffside shelter and the lighthouse at the top of the hill. It had seemed the safest place to hide and try to catch some sleep—between the fire damage above ground and the towering waves that crashed into the windows of Driskell's shelter in the side of the cliff.

After a quick headcount to ensure each of my friends was still with us, I stood and stretched my aching muscles. The hall was still dark, but a faint gray light shone through from the shelter windows overlooking the ocean below. It was morning here in Scotland. How late did that make it back in New York?

"Devon." I extended a hand to the boy beside Tate. "How are you feeling?"

"Much better this morning."

"Strong enough to get us all back home?"

He cast a quick glance to Sean, who returned a subtle nod. "Uh, yeah. Probably. But maybe I should start with just one person to make sure. I'd hate to get us all stranded in New Jersey or something because I can't make it back with a group. You wanna go first?"

I nodded. "Sure. Do you need to eat or anything before we go?" I fished around for the granola bar buried in the bottom of my bag, and my fingers tingled as they made contact with the piece of stone tablet tucked away inside.

"No, I'm good." Devon held out a hand, and I grabbed onto it, bracing myself for the cold I would feel as he transported me through reality and back into our apartment in New York. But there was nothing that could prepare me for the intensity of it. It was even colder than I remembered—so chilling I thought my bones might freeze and crack if I were there any longer than the millisecond it took to teleport.

My eyes squinted in the darkness of our new location, and still shivering, I turned to Devon. "Thanks."

"Yep, you got it. Bye." The words fell quickly out of his mouth.

"Wait—" He was gone, already through the fabric of reality. As my eyes slowly adjusted to the lack of light, I realized I was not in my apartment, but in a different familiar room. *That scoundrel!*

"Everly?" My aunt Millie sat up in her king-sized bed, pushing an eye mask up onto her forehead. I could barely see her over the mountain of pillows surrounding her small frame, but she definitely saw me. "You're glowing! What time is it? Is everything okay?"

A couple of pillows tumbled to the plush carpet as she swung her legs around to get a glimpse at the clock on her nightstand. It was two in the morning.

"What is going on?"

"Uhh..." I looked around, expecting Devon and some of the others to zap back in here and help me out, but they didn't come. It was just me and my very sleepy, very concerned aunt. Had he teleported here by accident? The thought that he might know my aunt Millie's bedroom so well made me shudder—soulmates or not. Or had he dropped me off here on purpose?

I suspected the latter, seeing as how he bolted the second my feet touched the ground.

"Everly." Millie's voice had turned stern, drawing my attention back to her.

How was I going to get out of this? "Maybe we should go downstairs and brew some tea," I suggested. This could take a while.

She nodded, sliding her feet into some fluffy slippers and pulling on a silky robe. "Was that Devon who dropped you off?"

"Yes."

She padded toward the stairs behind me. A million thoughts raced through my mind. I hadn't intended to tell Millie about my powers just yet, and I definitely hadn't planned to mention the prophecy until I understood more about it. But now that I was here, I wasn't sure how I would get out without spilling everything.

"How long have you had your powers?" Her eyes brushed over me, examining the white aura that emanated from my skin.

"A few days." *Ugh!* Devon could have at least warned me he was throwing me into this!

"Care to elaborate?"

I paused on the stairs, turning to face her. "I think you should be sitting for this. Let's get that tea going, and I will explain everything."

Thirty minutes later, Millie looked even more exhausted than before. She rested with her elbows on the countertop, forehead in the palms of her hands. I half wondered if she'd heard a word I'd said, because she'd hadn't made a sound the entire time I spoke. I'd explained how my powers emerged while Osborne chased me, Tate's suspicions about the prophecy, our trip to Scotland, the storm's reaction to my powers, and Driskell. She didn't say a word. The only thing I didn't mention was Rasputin. Not that I could have, even if I'd wanted to.

Finally, she lifted her weary eyes and sighed. "Oh, Tilly."

I set my cup down hard on the counter. "What does any of this have to do with my mom?"

Millie just shook her head. "I knew her secrets were going to get the best of her. But I never would have guessed about any of this."

"Do you have any idea where she might be?"

Millie pursed her lips. "No. Well, probably not."

"Probably?"

A noise in the kitchen doorway stopped the conversation from moving any further. Devon's nervously grinning face peeked around the corner. "Hi."

I scowled, but Millie smiled widely. "I was hoping you'd be back," she said. Waving him into the kitchen, she chuckled. "You may as well bring the others in, too. I know you've got them with you."

With a sheepish shrug, Devon entered the room, followed by Sean, Dom, Gayla, and Tate.

"How long have you guys been here?" I demanded. "And why didn't you tell me you were abandoning me to explain everything to my aunt alone?"

"I did tell you I would have to inform her about all of this eventually. I just thought it would be better coming from you." Devon looked sincerely apologetic. "Besides, this is getting too big for us to handle on our own. I thought we could use her help."

He was right of course, but I didn't want to admit it.

Driskell came around the corner next, eyes wide with astonishment. He probably hadn't been off the island in a century. Part of me was surprised to see that he'd survived the trip with Devon. The curse should have killed him. But then, another part of me knew it was all somehow related to my new aura and the tablet. Just because I didn't yet know how to wield the power it provided me didn't negate the fact that it was some seriously strong stuff. Having more power than the Keeper curse that had kept Driskell imprisoned for so long was both exhilarating and terrifying. I just hoped I'd be able to use it for good.

"Hallo," Driskell said in his rough German accent.

Millie let out a startled squeak. "I'll boil some more tea," she mumbled. "We've got some figuring out to do."

CHAPTER 2

ONCE EVERYONE WAS FULLY caffeinated, we headed upstairs into Millie's study. Watching Driskell take in his surroundings was like watching a child explore a new classroom on their first day of school. This was a foreign and strange world to him, but there was enough familiarity to drum up excitement that radiated from him with every step he took.

"How long have you been trapped on that island?" I asked as we filed into the study.

"Since December of 1900."

"I suppose a lot has changed since then."

He walked over to the window and stared out at the quiet Manhattan street below. It was scattered with parked cars and tall glowing street lights, but there really wasn't much activity on Millie's street at 3:30 in the morning. "You could say that."

Millie cleared her desk while Sean and Tate pushed a couple of chairs closer to the small sofa that sat in the room. Dom and Gayla pulled me off to one side while the others worked.

"You okay?" Dom asked.

"I think so. Millie took the news as well as she could, I think."

Dom glanced over to where my aunt was now whispering with Devon and a frown tugged at her lips. "She's not handling it as well as she's letting on. She's pretty concerned about you and what this might mean."

"We all are," Gayla said. "I wish I could jump right into another vision and tell you what to expect next. I'd do it if I could!"

"I know you would." I surveyed the room, and my gaze snagged on Tate. He watched me with those gorgeous golden eyes, sending a flutter through my chest against my will. Everything had happened so fast. I still didn't have a good grasp of what it all meant.

All I knew for certain, was that despite everyone telling me to keep my distance, the one thing I wanted was to wrap myself in Tate's arms and have him tell me everything would be okay. I shook the thought from my mind, and we joined everyone else in the center of the room.

Driskell plopped himself down to the couch, and his mouth made a small "o" shape. He raised up and fell back again, grinning as the plush cushions bounced him back into place once more. Then he pulled a soft gray blanket from the back on the sofa and began to unfold it.

"So," Millie said, immediately taking command of the room. "First things first. We need to unravel everything you know about this prophecy."

We all turned back to Driskell, who was still fumbling with the blanket. "How big is this thing?"

"It's ten feet by ten feet." Millie grinned. "It's my giant blanket, special ordered. Isn't it delightful?"

Driskell's bushy brows furrowed. "Are all blankets this large now?"

"No." I stood and snapped the blanket wide in the air so that it fell over both him and Gayla, who sat beside him on the sofa. He turned and lifted his brows at her playfully, eliciting a loud groan from my friend. "Can we please get back to the prophecy?"

"Yes, sorry." Driskell cleared his throat and launched into the same information he'd told us at the lighthouse.

Millie nodded along as he spoke, and when he finished, she asked, "And what about you?"

"Me?" Driskell shook his head. "What about me? I am not the Deliverer. It has nothing to do with me."

"But the curse was for you. It's either been broken or breached. Either way, the royalty will know, and they will come looking for you. You can't stay here. It's too dangerous. You'll have to get out of New York."

Driskell scratched his head as though the thought hadn't occurred to him.

"Where do you suggest he goes?" Sean asked. Something had shifted in him since we landed on the island in Scotland. He sat taller, more focused, eyes clear. Sean was in guardian mode, and it was clear that this was what he was made for.

"Porta Maris," Millie said.

"That's a terrible idea!" Driskell stood, and his enormous blanket pooled at his feet. "You might as well serve me up on a silver platter!"

Millie sighed. "Hear me out. Porta Maris is not a part of any sovereign nation, which is good. You can't exactly go seeking asylum in another territory—they *all* want your head. But I know some guys."

I laughed. "You know some guys? That's how every bad crime drama starts."

"No really. They'll keep him safe." She looked at Devon as though she expected him to chime in, but he was silent. Devon looked as clueless as I felt.

"Okay, so where is this Porta Maris?" I asked.

"It's in the Caribbean," Millie said.

"In the Bermuda Triangle." Driskell scoffed and waved a hand in the air before plopping back down on the couch with a bounce.

"The gateway to Atlantis," Sean said softly. There was no denying the reverence in his tone.

"I'm out!" Gayla raised both hands in the air. "That's a little too risky for me. I kinda feel like staying alive for a little while longer."

"What are you talking about?" I turned from Gayla back to Millie. "Is it dangerous?"

"The gateways are designed to keep anyone out of the territories who doesn't belong there. So yes, technically for non-Atlanteans, it could be dangerous. But Driskell is Atlantean."

"That doesn't make it safe." He crossed his arms over his chest.

"Well, I'm Atlantean. I'll take you, Driskell. You already know that I will do everything in my power to keep you safe." My chest tightened as I recalled the oath I'd made on the island.

"Right," Millie said. "That brings us to the next issue we need to get figured out. Your aura."

I'd almost forgotten about that. It was difficult to remember when I couldn't even see it myself. But the looks on all the other faces in the room reminded me that they could definitely see it—and it was not as easy for them to forget.

"I found a way to hide it," Tate said. "It worked when we went to the library."

Millie smiled, but I knew her well enough to see that it wasn't sincere. Was she skeptical of Tate's intentions as well? "That's great, but Everly needs to do more than hide it. She needs it to be blue. We want to let everyone know she's Atlantean without revealing too much else. Also, she needs to be able to move about freely, without you by her side."

I mean, I wouldn't necessarily mind having Tate by my side twenty-four-seven, but I understood her point.

"I do think I can use your help, though. Meet me down at the apothecary and—"

A knock sounded at the door. "Millie?" Jeeves' voice was laced with concern. "Are you okay? I thought I heard a man's voice."

The color drained from my aunt's face. "I'm fine. Just getting started with work a little early." Her response was strained, but I wondered if Jeeves would pick up on it. Hopefully he'd take her word and be on his way. There wouldn't be any easy way to explain why she was holed up in her study with a random group of college students and an old hairy German man in the middle of the night. Make that dawn, I noted as I took in the gray light shining through the window.

"Okay." Jeeves hesitated. "Then I'll be right up with some coffee. Pierre has breakfast started already, too."

He hurried down the hall and Millie faced us with big round eyes. "You guys have to go. Devon, can you get them back to their apartment?"

Devon grimaced. "Usually, yes. But I used up everything I had teleporting them all here. It'll be a bit before I have my strength back."

"It's fine." I stood. "I'll just let Jeeves know I stayed the night. He'll assume you were talking to me." I cleared my throat and dropped my tone a few octaves. "I have a manly voice."

Gayla snorted, and I rushed over to the door. I'd meet Jeeves in the hallway and stop him before he entered the room. Hopefully seeing me would ease any of his suspicions. He wasn't exactly a bodyguard, but he was a previous college linebacker, and that was as close to personal security as a butler could be. If he suspected any foul play going on in the study, he wouldn't hesitate before busting in and coming to Millie's rescue. I had to play it cool and make him believe everything was fine.

I twisted the knob and found Jeeves already standing in the hallway again with a tray holding a coffee carafe and a yogurt parfait. "Everly." He took a startled step back. "I didn't know you were here."

"Yeah, I uh—" I coughed and dropped my voice lower again. "I had some studying to do and it got too late for me to go back to my apartment. I'll take that."

He glanced at my outstretched hands with a frown and pulled the tray in closer. "I've got it." Jeeves looked more concerned than ever as he scanned me in the hall. I followed his eyes down to my clothing and found myself looking like I'd just completed a mud run. *Shoot.* I'd been struck by lightning, tied up with ropes, laid down on the soggy ground, and then slept in a stone hallway. This was not the effect I was going for.

"Are you sure everything is okay in there?" He pushed past me and froze after stepping through the doorway into the study. I swallowed and peeked around his large frame, already thinking through what kind of story I could tell him to make this seem normal.

But all we saw in the room was Millie and Devon cuddled up on the couch with that enormous blanket sprawled out all around them. I stifled a laugh picturing all of my friends hidden underneath in that cramped space with old man Driskell.

"Uh, sorry." Jeeves stammered and quickly set the tray on Millie's desk, avoiding eye contact with her the best he could. "I didn't realize you had company." He turned his back on them and gave me a look that said he clearly did not approve of my aunt's relationship with Devon.

Oh Jeeves, if only you knew the truth.

I bit my lip and nodded thanks to him. "We won't need any more coffee, Jeeves. Thanks, though. We'll be out of here soon."

He just shook his head as he hurried out of the room. I locked the door behind him and turned back toward a very grumpy group of people emerging from under the blanket on the floor. Gayla's hair was alive with static, and Driskell tried to calm it with his hairy hands.

I couldn't keep it in anymore. A laugh bubbled up out of my chest and escaped through the room. I was the Deliverer. I was going to save the world. It was the craziest thing I'd ever heard of, but at least I would get to do it with this ragtag crew of mine.

CHAPTER 3

IT TURNED OUT TELEPORTATION could leave me feeling just as jetlagged as an airplane could. I found myself dragging through Millie's house, ready to let my head hit the pillow by supper time. But Jeeves and Pierre didn't know that I'd traveled halfway across the world. They wouldn't understand that I had somehow stopped a deadly storm with nothing but my bare hands and some kind of savage yell. All they knew was that something strange was going on.

"I don't like it." Pierre's French accent grew even thicker when he was worked up about something. And judging by the speed of his chopping, he was pretty worked up.

He and Jeeves had been giving Millie the side-eye all day, ever since Jeeves caught her snuggling up with Devon on the couch that morning. And to make matters worse, Devon didn't leave with the others. He stayed behind instead, to help Millie get Driskell secretly set up in a spare bedroom. Thankfully, the butler and chef didn't know about Driskell, thanks to an enchantment Tate had put into place that kept them oblivious to his presence. Devon was bad enough. There was no telling what they'd say if they caught a glimpse of my favorite cursed old man.

"It's weird, right?" Jeeves grabbed a piece of the green bell pepper on Pierre's cutting board and popped it into his mouth. "I mean, technically, it's legal. But he's like nineteen. And how old is Millie? Forty?"

Actually she was four-hundred, twenty-six years old. But who was counting?

"Maybe it's true love." I shrugged. They didn't know the half of it.

"People are going to talk." Pierre gave one final chop with enough force to rattle the counter top. He met my eyes and lowered his voice. "And if he thinks he is going to move into our home and order me around, he can walk right back out the door." His knife waved through the air, enunciating his words with sharp jabs, forcing me to lean out of his way until he was done talking.

"Oh, give him a chance. He's not moving in." I reached for a veggie. "Maybe he'll grow on you. It's been so long since Millie has fallen for someone."

Pierre scoffed and swatted my hand away. "He is a child. And as for Millie, *mieux vaut être seule que mal accompagnée.*"

"Do I even want to know what that means?" I whispered to Jeeves.

He shrugged. "All I know is that I saw a movie like this on TV once with mama." Jeeves' Alabama twang was almost comical after Pierre's rant. Over his shoulder, through the kitchen window, I saw a quick flash of white. "There was this rich widow—real pretty lady—who fell for her pool boy, and..."

"I'll be right back, guys." I interrupted Jeeves to get a closer look at what I hoped had flown by the window. Pierre shot me a dirty look, but Jeeves kept right on with his story as I casually made my way back out into the foyer. Tiny Tim and Lemon Drop, Millie's giant English Mastiffs rose from their beds under the stairs and trotted after me toward the back door.

"You two have to stay inside," I whispered. Things didn't go so great the last time they'd seen my owl. "Sorry guys." Their droopy eyes made them look like they were pouting. "I'll be quick."

I slid through the glass doors into Millie's small courtyard off the back of her house, and sure enough, my feathery friend was perched up on the railing. "Al!"

It's Alpheus. He somehow sounded irritated without even making any actual noise.

"Right, *Alpheus.*" I was just happy to see him. He hadn't been around since the night I met with Rasputin at the cathedral. Then again, maybe I was the one who hadn't been around much. Al probably had no idea what was going on.

I'm glad to see you survived the deadly grip of the Manticorian lord.

I laughed. "Wow. You make that sound intense."

Well, he's tried to kill you before.

"When?"

I heard a groan in my head and Al shifted his little owl feet across the wrought iron. He was so cute it was difficult to take him seriously. *It always surprises me that you never remember your previous lives.*

"Yeah, you've mentioned something like that before. But you're going to have to be a little more direct. I don't know what you're talking about. Does this have anything to do with that oath you mentioned the last time I saw you? Because I do understand Keeper oaths a little more now. I've even made one of my own!"

If owls could shake their heads to make a person feel like an idiot, that is exactly what Al would have been doing in that moment.

Yes. I made an oath to you in your first life, and I've been forced to carry it out in this ridiculous bird body ever since.

"You haven't always been an owl?"

Of course not! His head twisted to one side.

"What happened?"

It's not important. Not anymore. The point is, I am sworn to protect you, through all of your days, no matter how many times your soul returns to the earth. Even when you return looking like... that.

I glanced down at my running tights and oversized t-shirt. "What's wrong with—you know what? Nevermind. Back to the topic. You're telling me that you knew me before? Same soul, different body?"

Bodies. Plural. And yes.

"Al, that's great!"

Alpheus.

"So how do I normally handle this whole white aura situation? Like, what did I do in previous lives?"

There's never been a white aura situation to handle before.

"You mean this is new? Please, tell me everything you know. Anything that could help me."

I'm obviously not going to review the last few millennia with you. But I'll give you the basics. You were Berenice when we first met. You were a stunning woman, but cold hearted. Not many people cared for you in those days.

"But you did."

I never said that. Regardless of your pleasantness, or lack thereof, you were powerful. Something happened in those days—you never told me what—but it was serious enough that you believed your life to be in danger. I owed you a favor, so you asked for my oath of protection. I've been by your side ever since, stuck for an eternity in this frail body. Destined to serve you despite your natural strength. I never understood why.

"Wow. I don't know what to say. Thank you." I shuffled my feet trying to make sense of it all. "So do you still have powers of your own?"

His large yellow eyes closed for a long moment. *No, but you don't need me for that anyway. You've always been very powerful. It's how you earned your nickname by the mortals in a later life.*

"What was my nickname?"

They called you the goddess of wisdom and war.

"Like Athena?"

He cocked his fluffy head at a ninety degree angle and blinked. *I swear it's like speaking to a toddler sometimes. Yes. Like Athena...* he mumbled to himself, the words muffled in my brain. *You* were *Athena.*

"I was a goddess?"

You've got to be kidding me. No, you weren't a goddess. There are no such things as gods and goddesses. There is only one God. But the humans back then were just as stupid as they are today, and they believed you were a goddess.

"Hey now. Let's knock it off with the name calling."

Fine. He shifted his taloned toes again. *I'll be nice. Yes, you were Athena. You have always had a sharp mind and a fierceness in battle. That has remained true in every incarnation.*

"So what does that mean for me today? Battle skills aren't exactly useful in today's society."

You might be surprised. Look, I don't know what you're supposed to do. I've never really known. I just know that you're destined for greatness—you told me as much thousands of years ago. But you always figure it out. Just lean into your natural instincts, and find what is right. Fight for it. You've got the strength, you just need to believe it.

"And you'll help me?"

However I can.

"Great. Then I have a favor to ask. I need you to locate someone for me—someone who may have the answers I need."

Who?

I chuckled.

What's so funny?

"Al the owl just said *who*..."

I can't do this anymore. He lifted his wings.

"Wait, wait, wait... I'm sorry. I really do need your help though. You see, there's this prophecy. I'll explain the details later, but it's kind of a big deal. And I'm pretty sure we're not the only ones who know about it. There's a very powerful Keeper who may be able to fill in some blanks and possibly even lead me to my mom. If it's true that I have the courage and fight of Athena, then it's time for me to put on my big girl pants and face my fears." I took a deep breath and looked Al in the eyes. "I need to find Rossel."

CHAPTER 4

DEVON LEFT LATER THAT evening, and Tate swung by the next morning. It was embarrassing how excited I was to see his face. The only thing that might have made it better would have been another one of those cinnamon lattes he'd gotten into the habit of bringing me from the Honey Pot.

But there was no coffee today, Tate was on a mission, focused on one thing and one thing only: turning my aura blue. Oddly enough, my presence wasn't required for it.

He'd barely given me a wave before trotting up the stairs to meet Millie in her study. Abby was at the apothecary today, so they wouldn't be able to speak freely there. They'd decided to experiment with some different ideas here in Millie's study, instead.

"Maybe you should go be a chaperone," Jeeves whispered as he joined me in the foyer. "Millie's first teenage boyfriend might be upset to find out she's spending time with another teenage boyfriend."

"Tate's twenty." I couldn't even make eye contact with Jeeves. My gaze was still glued to the outside of the door to Millie's study. I felt surprisingly lonely, even surrounded by everyone in the house. It was strange to know that everyone was working on this grand plan that centered around me, and yet I felt completely useless.

"That's hardly any better," Jeeves muttered. After a pause, he elbowed me in the arm. "Hey, are you alright?"

"Yeah, of course. Why?" I plastered a smile on my face. Judging by Jeeves' reaction, I overdid it.

The corners of his mouth dropped and he rested a heavy hand on my shoulder. "Oh, no. You like this one, don't you?"

"No... I—"

His expression hardened. "Look, your aunt is a pretty lady. But this is too far. She should not be going after young men at all, especially not those who have already caught the eyes of another Gordon woman. I'll go have a talk with her."

He pushed toward the stairs and I grabbed his arm, slowing him down. Stopping a former college linebacker should have been difficult, but I brought his two hundred thirty pound body to a halt with ease. Even previous 'bama players were no match for my new Keeper strength.

Jeeves quirked a brow at me.

"It's fine." I sighed. "I'll go be a chaperone."

I took my time going up the stairs and paused for a long minute outside of the study. A quick glance over my shoulder back to the foyer below revealed a determined Jeeves, nodding his encouragement for me to go in. I rolled my shoulders back and gave a soft knock on the door.

"Yes?" Millie's voice called out. She sounded distracted. Of course I knew there was nothing going on between her and Tate, but I was still admittedly a little jealous that everyone was getting to hang out without me.

"It's me. Can I come in?"

"Yes, of course."

Tate and Millie were hunched over her desk, a pile of books off to one side and a couple of jars of dried herbs stacked beside them. "How's it going so far?"

Tate moved to the side, making a spot for me to join them. I felt the tug toward him with every step I took, and he looked up with surprise as my elbow brushed against his. He must've felt the same jolt of electricity that I did when we touched.

"It's good... I think," he amended as he glanced up at the worry lines etching Millie's face. "We're getting close. Maybe."

"I just don't think the power amplification draught is exactly what we're looking for. Too much of that will be taxing on her body, and she doesn't need amplification right now." Millie frowned.

"We don't know that more Atlantean power will make the aura turn blue, anyway," Tate said. "It could make it glow a brighter white."

They continued to work as though I wasn't in the room. I nodded along, waiting for my chance to add something of value.

"But you can't just follow her around with a curtain of glamour forever. There's got to be a way to keep it intact without your presence. Maybe if you enchanted a charm or some kind of jewelry she could keep on herself?"

Tate shook his head. "I can't glamour inanimate objects. There has to be some life." He expanded on it, going deep into some kind of Agarthian science I couldn't even begin to understand. I tried to keep up for a while, but there wasn't anything I could add to the conversation without first taking some kind of Keeper Physics 101 class.

I was useless. Once again. "Alright, well I'm gonna get back to... something."

Millie nodded and waved, never pulling her eyes away from the textbook laid open before her. Tate didn't look up either. They were fully engrossed in their work, which was a good thing, I supposed. I just wished I could do something to help.

I left them to their business and slipped out into the hallway in search of Driskell. There probably wasn't any more information he could provide—we'd gone over all the details a million times already—but at least we could keep each other company while we were essentially prisoners in Millie's house. Though, if I had to be a prisoner, a multi-million dollar townhouse in Manhattan complete with a butler and private chef was a pretty good place to serve my sentence.

Driskell's room was down the hall. As I neared it, I could just make out the sound of him singing. I knocked on the door, but it wasn't latched all the way. It swung open as my knuckles met the wood, and the room was empty. To the right, I noticed light shining from under his bathroom door. His singing was louder now—some kind of upbeat German folk song layered with the sound of a draining bathtub. I had no idea what his lyrics meant, but it sounded like he was enjoying himself.

Feeling mopey and alone once again, I let him be and peeked out the open window at the end of the hall. It was warm for an autumn day, and the breeze blowing in from outside reminded me that I hadn't even seen Al since I'd sent him on to find Rossel. Hopefully Rossel hadn't hurt him. Then again, Al had been alive for thousands of years. I wasn't so sure anything could hurt him.

A pounding came from the front door downstairs. "Millie! Your shop girl said you were working from home today. Are you in there?" Claudia's voice rang out through the door, followed by more pounding. I hadn't seen her in ages—not since Sean and I first left to meet Gayla. And I wasn't about to let her see me now with a white glow.

"Millie!" she called out again. She sounded flustered.

I ran down the hall to tell my aunt, nearly colliding with Tate as he stepped out of the study with a panicked look on his face. "We've got to hide you," he said.

I glanced downstairs again to find Jeeves making his way through the foyer to greet our guest.

"Hurry!" Millie whisper-yelled from over Tate's shoulder. "And hide Driskell, too. Claudia can't know about any of this."

Tate gently took hold of my wrist and guided me back down the hall to Driskell's room, but the door was now closed and Driskell's voice was louder as he hummed on the other side. Tate didn't hesitate to twist the knob, but it was locked. "Driskell, let us in!"

"One minute, please. I have just bathed and I am moisturizing."

Jeeves opened the door and greeted Claudia downstairs. "Is Millie home?" she asked impatiently.

"Yes, she's upstairs in the study."

I looked back down the hall to see a wide-eyed Millie shooing me away silently with two hands. I shrugged and mouthed *it's locked*.

Tate whispered through the door. "Alright Driskell, just be quiet. We have company."

Thank goodness Claudia was complaining loudly as she made her way up the stairs, otherwise she would have heard him for sure. But Tate and I were still trapped in plain sight at the end of the hall, and Claudia's footsteps were growing closer.

"Millie, darling. I hope you don't mind me barging in, but I have to vent about the council to someone. They are on my last nerve." Claudia's whiny voice carried from halfway up the stairs. I glanced back at the window, wondering if we could survive a jump outside, down into Millie's courtyard. But Tate yanked me across the hall into a linen closet before I could make my move. The door closed silently behind us right as we overheard Claudia reach the top of the stairs.

"There you are!" she exclaimed. "Whatever is the matter, Millie? You look like you've seen a ghost."

For a moment, all of my awareness was focused on my breathing, trying to bring it down into a slow and steady rhythm that couldn't be heard out in the hall. But then my body reminded me of how close I was to Tate.

We were practically wrapped around each other, a tangle of limbs as he held himself upright with arms extended over my shoulders against the wall behind me. My nose couldn't have been a full inch away from his Adam's apple, and I became acutely aware of his breathing and racing pulse. The air seemed to sizzle around us, the skin on my left knee prickling where it rested against Tate's leg. I couldn't move it away because of how the shelves pressed hard into the outside of my thigh.

"Yes, of course I'm fine," Millie's voice rang out from the hall, followed by a nervous laugh. "You're having problems with the council again? Come, let's talk about it in the study."

I reached for the door handle, anxious to put some space between me and Tate. If I didn't get away from him soon, I might wrap my arms around him and never let go. And that didn't seem like a wise decision.

"Wait." Tate's whisper was barely audible. I might have missed it if not for my better Keeper hearing and the rustle of his breath in my hair.

"I just don't know what to do anymore!" Claudia despaired. She strode down the hall, and I watched with dread as her shadow passed under the crack of the door, pausing just outside of where we stood, likely stopping to look out the same window I'd been eyeballing moments earlier. When she spoke again, her voice was louder. "They're asking too much of him. There is just no way—"

"Claudia." Millie's voice was stern. "I must insist that we take this conversation back into the study." She dropped into a whisper. "The help may overhear you."

A Charley horse was developing in my thigh where it was still shoved against the shelf. I shifted slightly to ease the cramp, and inadvertently bumped my toe against a basket of cleaning supplies tucked under the shelves on the floor. The movement was small, but it was just enough to knock one bottle of cleaner over into another, causing a soft tap where the plastic bottles met.

Tate's arms instinctively dropped and he pulled me toward him, pressing our bodies together. My cheek smushed against his chest, where his heart was beating as fast and hard as mine. And in this position, with our bodies placed perfectly together as though we were formed from the same mold—two pieces of the same puzzle—the burning, tingling, prickling sensation stopped. It just felt... right.

"Did you hear something?" Claudia asked.

Tate's hands pulled me against him even tighter to keep me quiet. Or maybe it was because he felt the same undeniably pull toward me that I felt toward him.

"It was probably just Jeeves downstairs," Millie said quickly. "I told you, we need to get back into the study so we can speak freely."

"Right." Claudia hesitated for just a moment longer before following my aunt down the hall.

Neither Tate nor I moved even a millimeter until we heard the click of the study door. Then, he couldn't get our door open fast enough. "See ya," he whispered.

I peeked out of the closet just in time to see him slip out of the window. He jumped down to the courtyard with ease, and disappeared over the side of the fence.

Driskell's door opened then, and his bushy brows lifted at the sight of me. "Why are you all red?"

"I don't know," I whispered. My heart still pounded in my chest—a mixture of nerves over my close call with Claudia and... something else. I peered out the window again, hoping to catch one more glimpse of my Agarthian prince.

No, not my Agarthian prince. He was just Tate. Just a guy I needed to look out for. A master manipulator and potentially a man who could destroy the prophecy before we even got started.

"Well, come in." Driskell interrupted my thoughts. "You can wait with me until the woman is gone."

CHAPTER 5

TATE WAS BACK THE next morning, but I made no attempt to talk to him this time. I'd tossed and turned all night, thinking over the effect his nearness had on me. I'd even gathered a few books from Millie's secret stash of Keeper text to try to understand my reaction to him a little better.

Though it wasn't common, there had been a few reports throughout history of Agarthian sirens whose mere proximity could move their victims to submission. Most of the stories were from back before they'd developed the technology currently used to extract souls, so they still relied on archaic means of removing life back then. It was where rumors of vampires began.

Apparently these insanely attractive men and women would identify fractured souls and lure them alone, where they would extract the victims' souls through a fatal puncture wound—via their teeth—in the neck. Typically, they used the same glamour that was still so effective today, but occasionally no glamour was needed at all. The closer the "vampires" got, the more willing their victims became.

I refused to let Tate suck the life out of me like a vampire—even if it was only figuratively. I needed to maintain strict control over my actions and remain clear headed. It was time to put some distance between us.

That was a lot easier said than done when he spent so many hours hanging out at Millie's house. And though I had protested and made what I thought was a really compelling argument to go back to my apartment with Gayla and Dom, the majority ruled against me. They wanted me to stay here with Driskell, off the streets and away from anyone who might catch a glimpse of my white aura.

That meant hours and hours in the same house as Tate.

After another pouty lunch with Jeeves and Pierre, I was startled to hear Millie's voice call out from the stairs. "Everly! Come here!"

Her excitement was palpable. Had they figured something out?

I tried to put some energy into my steps, but I wasn't eager to see Tate again. I couldn't be trusted to control myself around him. Millie took my hand as I reached the top of the stairs and anxiously pulled me into her study.

"We did it!" She closed the door behind her and clapped her hands together.

"You found a way to conceal my aura?"

"Not conceal it." Tate's voice called out from the opposite wall. He'd placed himself as far from the doorway as possible. "But change it to blue."

"No way." My shoulders relaxed as the impact of the news overshadowed my earlier concerns about Tate. If they could turn my aura blue, I would be free to leave the house again. I could even use my powers around other Keepers and no one would be any wiser.

Millie nodded, her grin stretching from ear to ear. "It's true! We think, anyway. Everything adds up on paper, but obviously we need to test it on you to be sure."

A jar sat atop Millie's desk containing a muddy brown paste-like substance in the bottom. I eyed the goop suspiciously. "Are you sure it's safe?"

"Of course!" Millie's smile stayed strong, but there was a definite twitch in her eye. "But even if it's not, you happen to be in the presence of a very skilled healer." She took a bow. "And I promise not to let anything hurt you."

Tate moved forward just a few steps, carefully keeping Millie's couch between us. "We found a way to infuse one of Millie's concoctions here with some of my glamour."

"I thought you couldn't glamour inanimate objects."

Tate held up a finger and smirked. "I can't glamour *unliving* objects. But technically, plants are living."

"He enchanted my kava." Millie gestured toward a bowl full of heart-shaped green leaves. "It acts as a booster for some of the other herbs I've muddled together here in the jar. We hypothesize that the enchantment will stay with the leaves, even after they are pulled from the plant and dried. It only has to be living when the spell is initially cast. When used with an Atlantean amplifier, and a hefty dose of borage for the blue color inducer, we think we should be able to make your aura appear blue."

"And taking a constant amplifier won't be damaging?" I remembered her warning from the day before.

Millie shifted on her feet. "I've done my best to counteract those effects as well. But I would caution you to only consume this when you absolutely need to go out in public."

I frowned, turning the jar around in my hand. I would still be a prisoner most of the time, sentenced to remain locked up in this house as much as possible. But at least it wouldn't be forever.

"Go on." Millie handed me a soup spoon. "If it works, I will put it into capsules to make it easier to transport and consume. But for the test, just take a small amount in the spoon here."

My gaze drifted momentarily to Tate, but he wouldn't meet my eyes. That wasn't reassuring. But my aunt wouldn't do anything to harm me. I believed that with my whole heart. I mentally counted to three, then shoved half a spoonful of the disgusting brown mash into my mouth and swallowed before my tongue could register just how bitter and nasty the stuff was.

"Blech! Is there any way to make it taste better?"

"Once it's in the capsules it—" Millie's words cut off and her hand flew to her mouth with a gasp.

"What?" I looked down, but saw nothing. I felt nothing, either. "What is it?"

"It worked." Tate smirked. "I knew it would."

"Am I blue?" I raised the back of my hand closer to my eyes for better inspection.

"A gorgeous cerulean." Millie clapped her hands together. "Well done, Thaddeus!"

"It wasn't just me." Tate dropped his chin and ran a hand through his dark tousled hair. Then he turned those glistening golden eyes on me. "How are you feeling, Ev?"

I wiggled my fingers. "I feel... exactly the same. What does an amplifier do, exactly?"

"It enhances your natural powers," Millie said. "Which in your case, well, is still undetermined."

"Undetermined." I could stop storms and breathe underwater. But both of those could still be related to standard Atlantean abilities to control and manipulate water. I couldn't heal or teleport or run faster or jump higher like the others. My powers were *undetermined*.

"Well, I obviously didn't inherit my mom's abilities. Perhaps I got my dad's powers."

Millie frowned. "Since our souls are reincarnated, we don't exactly inherit powers from our parents. And even if we did, I've told you, I truly do not know who your father is. Your mother has always been a fierce secret-keeper. It's one reason she was so valued as a messenger."

"Right. Then I guess I'll just have to add 'search for long-lost-father' to my ever growing to-do list. Who knows... maybe he'll stumble across my path when I go to Atlantis to find another part of the prophecy."

"Oh!" Millie turned back to the desk and shuffled around through some papers. "That reminds me, there was something positive that came out of Claudia's impromptu visit yesterday. I got some good intel on where the royal prisons are located."

"What? The secret ones in Atlantis? Did she know if my mom was there?"

Millie grimaced. "I couldn't ask her that. And this is vague at best. But Sean's dad works with the Atlantean council. He's a guardian, like Sean, but his work is confidential. I know he doesn't work in the common prison, but I definitely heard her mention prisoners in her frustrated rant session yesterday. I also happen to know that he works beneath the palace."

"There's a real palace? Under the sea?"

"Yes."

I sighed and looked up at the ceiling. "I wish I could be part of your world."

Millie shot me a disapproving look. She obviously didn't appreciate my cartoon mermaid humor. "I can only assume it's the royal prison."

"So how do we get there?"

"Well, I refuse to let you go anywhere until we've had more time to test this aura-changing amplifier. But it certainly won't be easy when you do go. You can't access it from outside of the palace."

"And if the queen is anything like my father, she won't let you into the palace without a really good reason." I'd almost forgotten Tate was still in the room. If anyone knew about breaking into royal Keeper palaces and prisons, it would be him. He was an Agarthian prince, after all.

"So what do we do then?"

"First, we keep an eye on the effects of this medicine. We'll worry about devising a plan into Atlantis once we know you can safely leave the house."

Little did she know I was already devising my plan. But there were a few things I had to take care of first. My gaze drifted to the window, wondering if Al had made it back yet. Now that my aura was blue, I definitely needed to find Rossel.

CHAPTER 6

THE MEDICINE, OR *potion* as I liked to call it (Millie hated that word), stayed effective for just over thirty hours, which seemed pretty remarkable to me. But Millie thought we could do better. She and Tate continued to experiment over the next week until they reached a product both were satisfied with. I had a potion pill that would keep my aura blue for two solid days.

It was supposedly an amplifier, but since I had no discernible power to amplify, I didn't see any effects on that front. Maybe I could swim faster, but I hadn't tried. Without the amplification in use, it also meant that the pills didn't seem to have any draining effects on me when they wore off. They did their job—my aura was blue, and that was all that was necessary for me to get out of the house. And get out I did.

It felt good to walk back onto campus with Gayla and Dom. "Is it still blue?" I muttered out of the side of my mouth.

"Yep." Gayla grinned. "You look just like one of us, just like a Keeper."

I *looked* like one of them, but I wasn't really. They still considered me different. The image of my friends all bowing before me on the island where we found Driskell was a memory I'd tried hard to burn from my brain. I didn't want to be different.

The girls did a good job of making me feel normal for the most part, but every once in a while I would see a strange expression dance across Gayla's face, or Dom's eyebrows would turn up in a way that reminded me of how they truly saw me. I wasn't one of them. I would never be one of them. But I certainly didn't feel like anyone special.

Thankfully, the other Keepers on campus didn't see me as anything special, either. I was just an average Atlantean girl in their eyes. And yet, it still wasn't enough to ease the glares I got from the group of Agarthian girls we shared our Review of the Ancient Languages class with.

Camille, the siren who'd lured me into a trap after the girls saw me with Clayton, feigned a look of smug indifference as I passed her group on my way to class, but it still sent a chill down my spine. I wouldn't let her know it though. I smiled sweetly, and gave a little wave. She rolled her eyes and turned back to her cat shifter friend and the wind-wielder to her left.

"They're brats." Gayla shrugged. "Don't let them get to you. You look great." She nodded toward the library. "This is where I've gotta split. We still meeting for lunch?"

"Yep. We'll meet back at the apartment at noon," Dom said. Then turning to me she asked, "You ready to go talk to Brossard?"

"Let's do it." It was convenient that my first class this morning happened to be with the same professor who had lied to me about the tablet just a few weeks earlier. Since he was Driskell's former colleague and partner in the archaeological sites, I had some insider tips now for how to handle the man. According to Driskell, Brossard was a bit of a coward. Driskell wasn't surprised at all that he had pretended not to recognize the tablet. Brossard was afraid of the curse.

Dom and I took the steps up to our classroom building, and as I reached for the door, the hairs on the back of my neck stood at attention.

"What is it?" Dom asked, sensing the tension that had just come over me.

"I don't know." I looked over my shoulder, scanning the sidewalks and trees around us. Groups of students—both Keepers and mortals alike—moved in pairs and small groups, chattering and laughing as they went about their mornings. Nothing seemed out of place. "I just got the sense that somebody might be watching us."

"I don't see anyone." Dom surveyed the area as well. "But let them look if they want. I promise, nothing seems off at all."

"Okay." I cast one more wary glance across the campus, then followed Dom inside and down the hall toward our class.

Brossard was late, as usual. He wouldn't make eye contact with me at all through class, though he had to have noticed my new blue aura. He could ignore me during the lecture all he wanted, but I'd missed a week of school, and he had no choice but to talk to me after class. It was his job to help me get caught up with my assignments.

"Ready?" I asked Dom as he finished up the day's lecture. She'd agreed to accompany me after class. I wanted to toy with the professor a little bit. There wasn't any new information he could provide that Driskell hadn't already told us, but I hated to let him get away with a lie. He had no idea that I was the Deliverer mentioned in the prophecy, so it didn't seem like it would hurt to let him know I'd discovered the meaning of the tablet. I didn't appreciate being lied to, and I wanted to let him know it... and maybe watch him squirm just a little.

But our path down to the front of the room was blocked as soon as all the students stood to leave. The trio of Agarthian mean girls created a wall in front of me and Dom.

"Looks like you had a little fun on your vacation, didn't you, Atlantis?" Camille crossed her arms with a sneer. She thought I'd been on a family trip. That was the rumor Gayla and Dom had spread in my absence. "Went and got yourself some powers, huh? Well, it's about time. Let's see what you can do."

I glanced over her shoulder to where Professor Brossard was hurrying to pack his things and get out of the room. I didn't want to let him get away so easily, and I had zero interest in playing the mean girls' head games.

"I need to talk to the professor," I said, ignoring her prodding. "Excuse me." The girls crowded in tighter, blocking my passage.

"She said move, Camille. We've got stuff to do." Dom tried to push past the girls, but they were being especially obstinate this morning.

"I wanna see what the water girl can do," Camille said again.

"She can certainly *drown you* if you don't get out of the way."

The girls continued to bicker as I watched Professor Brossard pack the last of his things into his computer bag and cast a nervous glance in our direction.

"Professor! I need to talk to you about my assignments!" I called out over the girls' shoulders, but he acted as if he couldn't hear me. Driskell was right. He was a coward.

"I'm gonna tell you one more time," Dom gritted through her teeth. Get out of the way or—"

I spread my arms and the girls went crashing into the tables on either side of our row. I hadn't intended to throw them out of the way so violently, but it was as though the power came from a different part of my brain—some subconscious area that didn't think through consequences, but acted merely out of emotions and a loss of self control. I didn't even realize what was happening until it was done.

Camille's mouth dropped open, and Dom turned to me with wide eyes. But I scurried past them toward Brossard as he reached for the door handle at the front of the classroom.

"Professor!" He didn't spare me even the briefest consideration before bolting out of the room. "*Argh!*" A frustrated yell escaped me, and the Agarthian girls almost seemed to cower at the sound.

Camille quickly regained her composure, however, and the other two girls followed suit. She *tsked* as I made my way up to the back exit, Dom hot on my heels. "You really need to learn to control that better," she teased. "It would be a shame for the administration to find out you've been using your powers on campus. And with all these witnesses around…" She gestured to her friends with a wicked grin.

I ignored her, tugging hard on the door handle and causing it to swing open with a hard slam into the opposite wall.

"What was that?" Dom asked as we scurried out into the hall. Her voice was a whisper.

"I don't know." My words were shaky. "I just got so… mad."

"Well, you better get back to the apartment before you get *mad* again. They're right. You need to figure out how to control this. I'll help you get to the bottom of this after my next class. I'll call Sean and Devon, too."

"Okay." I nodded. "But Dom, before you go, do you have any idea why Professor Brossard was in such a hurry to get away from me?"

She grimaced. "I'm not sure exactly, but there was one person on his mind as he hurried out of there."

"Who?"

"Rossel."

CHAPTER 7

DOM WAS PROBABLY RIGHT. I needed to get home and get a grip on myself. But first I had to calm my nerves enough to walk in public without blowing people over with an indescribable power I couldn't control.

A splash of cool water on my face in the bathroom helped only slightly. I studied myself in the mirror, squinting at the girl staring back at me. My eyes were still mostly blue, with the exception of that one slice of brown in my left iris. Other than my missing scar, nothing looked different at all. I didn't feel much different, either. And yet I knew, everything had changed. *Who are you?*

With a deep breath, I steadied myself and tossed my bag back over my shoulder. Everything would be fine. I just needed to get home until we could figure out what happened back there.

But each step took me further from that sense of calm I tried to maintain. I couldn't quit thinking about what Dom had told me. Why would Professor Brossard be thinking of Rossel? Surely they weren't working together. Rossel wanted me dead, and Brossard had plenty of opportunities to hurt me. But he wasn't trying to get me alone or cause harm. He was *avoiding* me. Why?

An unnaturally high-pitched giggle shook me from my thoughts on the sidewalk outside of the classroom building. I looked up to find the Agarthian girl with the wind power walking with an exaggerated sway of her hips, arm slung through the crook of Tate's elbow. Camille and the cat girl walked behind them. Four sets of golden eyes glanced up as they approached me on the sidewalk.

"Everly!" Tate dropped the girl's arm like a hot potato and stepped toward me. Her smile disappeared, replaced with a glare. But Camille stepped up to her side, her grin growing ever wider.

"Ahh, it's the water girl with the temper again." Camille placed her hands on her hips. "You better look out for that one, Tate."

I ignored them, focusing my attention instead on the tall, handsome prince that stood before me. "You're outside," he said quietly. He stopped just beyond arm's reach.

"I needed some sunshine." I shrugged. "I was feeling a little *blue* after being cooped up for a week."

The corner of his mouth perked up, and his eyes briefly grazed over me. "You still look a little blue. Need some company?"

"*Ahem.*" The wind wielder cleared her throat loudly over Tate's shoulder. His jaw tensed slightly before he turned to look back at the girls. "I thought we were gonna grab some coffee at the Honey Pot." She pushed her lower lip out playfully, but Tate wasn't amused.

"Sorry, Stella. We'll have to reschedule," he said. *Stella*. I'd have to remember that was the wind girl's name.

"The paper is due tomorrow. We can't reschedule." Her glare hardened, but it was definitely focused on me, not Tate.

"I'm not—" He stopped himself and took a deep breath. "I'm not going to be able to go right this second. You all go ahead, and I'll meet you there in a bit."

Camille narrowed her eyes, and cat girl literally bared her teeth at me. Their little hissy fits weren't doing much to improve my own bad attitude, either. They'd taken the brunt of my power once already today. There was no telling what might happen if I got angry again.

"It's fine, Tate. We can talk later." I forced a smile and tried to walk away before my emotions got the best of me. But Tate jogged back up to my side.

"No, that's just it. I—" He paused as the Agarthian girls moved down the sidewalk toward the coffee shop. Stella flicked her wrist as they passed us, and a gust of wind blew my hair into my face. "Not cool, Stella," Tate called out.

Their snickering carried on as they rounded a curve in the sidewalk. I was definitely frustrated, but I'd somehow managed to keep my reaction under control this time. They didn't get to me quite as much when I had Tate by my side. That was good. I was making progress.

"Sorry about them," Tate grumbled when we were alone. We walked at a casual pace behind them, allowing the gap between us and the Agarthian girls to widen with every step they took.

"It's fine. It's not your fault. Besides, Dom says they only act that way because they don't like seeing Agarthian guys talking to girls outside of their race. I'm sure it's ten times worse when it's their *prince* who is doing it." I raised my brows at him.

"That's probably true. Though I'm sure you're used to other girls being jealous of you."

"Me?" My cheeks warmed. He'd obviously forgotten who my beautiful roommates were. "I wouldn't say that's true."

Tate paused and locked his eyes on mine. "Well, you should probably get used to it, then." He grinned, and it took all my strength not to melt into a puddle on the sidewalk. He was just a guy, but I could not deny my attraction to him. Especially when I remembered our bodies pushed close together in that linen closet...

He jerked his gaze away and started walking again, breaking the spell he had on me. And maybe it was just a spell. He was a talented siren, after all. But that wouldn't explain why he seemed just as rattled as I did.

"I'm glad I ran into you. I was planning on swinging by your place later to talk to you, anyway. There's been a request for me back home."

"In Agartha?"

He nodded. His kingdom of Agartha was a mythical place, somewhere deep under the ground, inside a massive chasm within the earth's core. It sounded fake, like a story someone had made up long ago. But then again, my entire life seemed pretty unreal these days. Still, it was hard for me to imagine him living there.

"What for? Will you be gone long?"

"I don't know. They're never very forthcoming with these things." He pinched the bridge of his nose. "I don't want to go, but the drama that'll get stirred up if I disobey the order isn't worth it. They want me there as soon as possible."

"When are you leaving?"

"First thing in the morning."

My stomach sank. He had done his part in turning my aura blue. We had plenty of the pills left, and we really didn't need Tate for the next part of my journey. But that didn't mean I wanted him to go away. I was more disappointed to see him go than I would have expected to be.

"Oh." It was all I managed to say in response.

"Anyway, I just wanted to let you know so you wouldn't think I'd disappeared on you. But make sure you stay out of trouble while I'm gone."

"I never get into trouble."

He laughed. "Seriously. Promise me you'll stay home—either at your place or Millie's until I get back?"

"When will that be?"

"I can't say."

"Then I can't promise." The truth was that I wasn't planning on staying inside long at all. As soon as Al came back with a location, I had every intention of marching down to talk to Rossel. Especially now that I knew he was involved with Brossard, somehow. This situation with him just kept getting weirder, and enough was enough.

"You could at least pretend you'll be safe."

"I'm not big into pretending." I winked and patted him on the back. "Now go get to your Agarthian girls before they come and hunt me down to find you."

He hesitated, unsatisfied with ending the conversation there. But thankfully, he didn't push it any further. I was glad he didn't, because my emotions were all kinds of mixed up and I couldn't be sure how or if my powers might reveal themselves again.

"Alright," Tate said. "Will you tell the others where I'm going?"

"I will. And Tate?"

"Yeah?"

"You be safe, too."

CHAPTER 8

I PEELED AWAY FROM Tate, lost in my thoughts as I made the short walk back to our apartment. Rossel was up to no good. Rasputin claimed Rossel wanted me dead, and even Tate had admitted that his orders to extract my soul came from the Olympian seer. But the only reason I could come up with for why Rossel would care so much about me, was that he knew something about the prophecy.

If Rossel knew about the prophecy and the meaning of the tablet, it made sense for Professor Brossard to think of him. After all, the tablet was originally in Rossel's care. But how did he know *I* was involved? He knew I was the Deliverer before *I did*...

A vision. It must have been a vision. Gayla had once mentioned that Rossel's visions came to life on canvas—he painted what he saw. It was why he'd owned the art gallery. And it was why the Olympian king kept him close by. He liked to literally see the future in painting form.

And Rossel had seen me as the Deliverer. He should have killed me on the spot that day in his gallery, but he didn't. He could have offed me that night on Gayla's yacht when he'd warned me to stay away from her. But again, he didn't. He sent Tate after me, instead. And though it was probably a false sense of security, I walked a little taller knowing that Rossel couldn't—or maybe just wouldn't—physically kill me himself.

I picked up my pace, chin held high, anxious to get home so I could plan out exactly what I would say to him when I got him alone. But as I rounded a corner, I got the same sensation I had before class—that someone was watching me. I slowed to a stop, looking over my shoulder, up and down the street. Nothing seemed unusual.

What are you doing? Al's voice called out in my mind.

I startled and turned my gaze upward. He was perched on a metal flag pole extending outward from a building.

"Al, It's just you. Thank goodness!"

Quiet. If people see you talking to an owl on the street, they'll call the authorities.

He had a point. Maybe I could talk to him in my mind. I focused my thoughts, trying to direct them at the owl. I asked him if he'd found Rossel.

Why are you making that face? You look like you have gas. Stop it.

I rolled my eyes. *That* didn't work. Obviously I wasn't telepathic. "I'm going to the park." It wasn't far from campus, and I figured I'd have better luck finding a spot to speak privately with my owl there. Not to mention, he would look a lot less suspicious in a tree than he looked perched on a window sill in Manhattan.

Al flew ahead, and I joined him by the waterfall in Morningside Park just a few minutes later. "Alright," I said, parking myself on a large rock. "Tell me everything. Did you find him?"

Not exactly. But I have to believe he's still in town somewhere.

"Why's that?"

The place is crawling with Olympians. And they seem angry.

"What? Why? Ohhh, wait. Claudia mentioned the annual convention coming up. Are they here for that?"

No, it's still a few weeks out.

"What do they need, then?"

He flapped down to a lower branch a little closer to me. *I think they're looking for Driskell. I wasn't sure at first, but after you left Millie's place, the activity really picked up in that area. I think it has to do with your aura.*

"What do you mean?"

I mean when you were at Millie's house, Driskell was basically invisible. I think your aura must have shielded him from the effects of the curse somehow. But now that you're gone, the Olympians have discovered him. There have been some bad looking dudes sitting outside of Millie's place around the clock since you left.

"Oh my goodness. You think they're just waiting to catch him?"

Possibly. Either that, or they're waiting to catch you.

My heart raced at the thought. "I've got to find Rossel."

I'm sorry. I tried to find him. Really, I did.

"I know you did. And I appreciate it."

I'll keep looking. Until then, you might want to stay away from your aunt. He bobbed his feathery head and took flight. I stayed on the rock, watching until his white form disappeared behind the trees and back into the city.

As my gaze shifted back to the waterfall, I felt a chill across the back of my neck again. But if Al was gone, that meant someone else's eyes were watching me from the shadows. I turned over my shoulder and struggled to keep my expression calm as I saw Osborne approaching.

He cracked his knuckles, sneering like a bully from some eighties movie. "I always knew you were crazy. But talking to yourself in a city park takes it to a whole new level."

"What do you want, Osborne?" He couldn't legally hurt me anymore. I wasn't fractured, which meant I was no longer a target for the hunters.

"I want to help you. You're looking for Rossel, huh? Well wouldn't you know, he's looking for you, too." He'd overheard me talking to Al. Thank goodness he couldn't hear what Al said, as well.

"I'm sure that he is. But you and he should both know that there's nothing you can do to me now. I've got my full powers, or hadn't you noticed?" I gestured to my sides, showing off what I hoped he could see as a blue aura. I kept my spine straight, shoulders back, and prayed I looked more brave and confident than I felt.

"Even full powers won't exonerate you from the law."

"And what law have I broken?" Did he know about my meeting with Rasputin?

Osborne stopped just a foot in front of me. We were both standing now, the water at my back and the rest of the park laid out before me. There weren't many people out in the middle of a work day, but there were enough to notice if he tried to harm me here. I hoped they would notice, anyway.

"I don't know." Osborne shrugged. "And honestly, I don't care. The price on your head is good enough for me. Never seeing your face again is just an added perk."

"So you expect me to just turn myself in for some unknown crime I never committed?"

"That would be easiest, yeah. But I can use force if necessary."

The logical part of my mind knew I should be afraid. My brain was sending out the red alert with lights flashing and sirens blaring—*Osborne bad! Everly run!*—but there was a disconnect somewhere. My body didn't get the memo.

No, my body was mad. The power that resided somewhere deep in my core wanted to fight back. How dare he follow me to the park? Who did he think he was, trying to take me captive? I was innocent! My fingers felt twitchy as the water at my back called to me, beckoning for me to wield it against anyone who might oppose me.

Before I could think or reason with myself, my hands rushed forward, pulling the water from the pond with them. A small tidal wave rushed forward, focused on a single spot—one person. Osborne was knocked off of his feet as the water engulfed him.

That's when I should have run, but my inner Athena wasn't done with him yet. The water splashed back into the pond and Osborne growled from the ground, shaking dirty droplets from his hair.

"That was a mistake."

"You're right. It was." I placed my foot on his chest, kicking him back onto his rear as he attempted to stand up again. "It was a mistake for you to think you could take me so easily. Tell Rossel he can come and talk to me face to face like a man."

"Tell him yourself." Osborne thrust his legs forward like a ninja, jumping back to his feet in one graceful move. Then he was on me like a flash of light, snagging my hair into his fist, and yanking my head back. "Sleep."

The sound of a thousand harmonies in his single word was the last thing I heard before my body went limp.

CHAPTER 9

IT SMELLED LIKE MAMA Mae's basement. That was the first thing I noticed as my awareness returned. But I wasn't back in Oklahoma, and this wasn't the storage room of my small town's favorite old widow.

Keeping my eyes closed so that my captor wouldn't know I was awake, I tried to gather as many additional details about my location as I could. It was chilly—drafty, which meant a window was open. Or perhaps we were just in a really old building. Street noise confirmed that we were definitely still in the city, though.

My shoulders ached, pulled at an unnatural angle. My wrists were bound together behind my back with what I guessed were zip ties. Another rope stretched across my stomach, tying me to what felt like a metal folding chair. My feet were on hard ground. Little light made it through my closed lids, so I lifted them just enough to sneak a peek of my surroundings through my lashes.

I was in some kind of warehouse, dimly lit by dingy windows placed high on the filthy walls. The space was vast and empty. I was all alone.

"You can stop pretending to be asleep."

Scratch that. I wasn't alone. Unfortunately Osborne was still here, too.

"And you can stop pretending to be righteous," I spat back. "We both know how much you enjoy seeing me tied up like this."

"I don't have to pretend."

I scoffed, then gave a hard tug on the ties binding my wrists. The plastic cut sharply into my skin, but they didn't break. I tried again, yanking harder, and stifled a little yelp as the skin on my wrist broke open on the sharp edges. It shouldn't have been so difficult with my new powers. The ties back at Driskell's lighthouse had broken apart like threads.

"What did you do to me?"

Osborne finally made his way into my view, sighing as he strolled past like he was enjoying a casual walk through the park. "I made you sleep. I trust you got plenty of rest?" He grinned, taunting me. I lunged forward, but the rope held the chair tightly to my backside.

"Sit down," Osborne said. His voice was laced with glamour and I had no choice but to obey.

"I mean, what did you do to my powers?" My voice was like a growl through clenched teeth. Osborne wasn't playing fairly. If he got to use his powers, I should have access to mine as well.

I thought I saw a brief flash of confusion in his features before he squared his jaw again. Perhaps I was imagining it though, because he quickly shifted back into bully-mode. "I didn't do a thing to your powers. You're just weak."

I wanted to lunge again, but his glamour still wormed through my mind, forcing me to remain still. But one thing was clear: when it came to my powers, Osborne had no idea what I could do. And while a part of me wanted to rip off the binding on my hands and bring him down just like I'd done with the thunderstorm and the Agarthian girls, a bigger part of me knew my power would be more useful if it was kept a secret for now. So I would let Osborne think I was weak until it really counted.

I didn't think he'd hurt me anyway, or else he would have already done it by now. "So what are you gonna do with me, then? Just leave me tied up here in this warehouse?"

"Yep." He pulled a phone out of his back pocket and checked a message on the screen. "That's all I was hired to do. Looks like my work here is done, so I'll just be on my way. Good luck." He snorted. "You're gonna need it."

My pulse quickened as he turned toward the rusted metal door to my right. My lips parted, and I stopped myself before calling out for him to wait. It wasn't like Osborne would help me even if I asked him to. And I certainly didn't plan on asking him to.

Light from the alleyway beyond flooded in briefly as Osborne stepped out of the warehouse, but it was quickly blotted out by a tall, wiry shadowed figure who took his place. The door slammed shut again behind the new man, and I instantly recognized the white knot of hair balanced atop his head.

Rossel glided toward me—his unique gait identifiable anywhere. He wore all black, from head to toe, and I wondered briefly if he owned anything in any other color. Probably not. Nothing else would look quite as intimidating as the darkness against his pale skin and the shock of white hair on his head. Plus—it brought out the soul-sucking blackness of his hollow eyes.

He was like a phantom. But this ghost couldn't hurt me. His only power was the ability to see the future. My new Keeper strength would certainly give me the upper hand if push came to shove.

That's what I told myself anyway. Everyone needed a little internal pep talk now and again.

"Ms. Gordon." His thin lips pulled into a pout as he assessed me. He didn't look quite as excited to see me bound to this chair as Osborne had, but I suspected he was simply more skilled at hiding his reactions. I tried once more to break free of the ties around my wrists, but whatever strength my powers had once provided seemed to have disappeared.

"Rossel, what a pleasant surprise. If I'd known you were coming I would have fixed the place up." I couldn't hide the sarcasm in my tone. It was a defense mechanism, and I hated it. My snark never packed the punch I hoped it would—it just made me sound immature.

Rossel wasn't amused, either. "I thought we had an agreement. I asked you to stay away from Gayla."

"And I asked you to tell me where my mother is."

He pursed his lips, neither confirming nor denying that he knew where she was. After a beat, he laced his fingers loosely together behind his back and began pacing before me.

"Will you tell me where she is?" I prodded again.

"No."

"Will you at least confirm that she is still alive?"

"No."

"She's dead?"

He paused, turning his hollow black eyes on me. "I will say no more about your mother."

"What about my father?" I didn't know where the thought came from, but I had a hunch that if anyone knew about my father, it might be Rossel.

Rossel stiffened, but continued pacing the dirty floor as though he didn't hear me. But I knew he had. And based on his reaction, I suspected my hunch might have been correct. Now I just needed to get the upper hand on him, somehow. I gave another feeble tug on the restraints around my wrists, but it was no use. My powers had abandoned me.

"I need you to leave," he said finally. His face had twisted into a strange mix of uncertainty and regret.

"Gladly," I said. "Just untie me from this chair first, please."

"I need you to go *far* away. You must tell no one. And you must never return."

"Oh, like you tried to do with Driskell?"

He turned a hard gaze on me.

"I know you cursed him to remain on an island in the middle of the sea. But don't worry, I rescued him. I delivered him to safety. You can't hurt him anymore. You can't hurt me either, can you?" I was going out on a limb, but it was all starting to come together in my mind. The pieces fit, but the puzzle looked a lot different than I would have guessed before.

Rossel began pacing again, so I continued with my hypothesis, trying to see what kind of reactions I might elicit from the old man. He was reluctant to tell me anything, but maybe if I guessed correctly, I would be able to see the truth in his response.

"He knew about the tablet, so you hid him away. But now that I have it, you can't control him anymore. You can't control me either. My power is too strong. Is this why you tried to kill me before my power emerged?"

He gave me no response. He didn't so much as glance in my direction. So I kept going.

"It's why you wanted me to stay away from Gayla, too. Isn't it? If she got too close, you knew she could have a vision that would lead me to the truth. Well you were right, Rossel. I know the truth. And you can't stop me from what is going to happen now."

"You know *nothing*!" He snapped, and the fierceness in his dark eyes made my heart stop. In three long strides he was standing inches from my face, and I fought to keep my breathing steady. I was terrified, but I wouldn't let him know it.

"You are a child, and a fool!" He spat the words like they were on fire, then turned on his heels and walked away from me again. "You don't understand the finer balance of our world, and you will destroy it."

"Maybe it needs to be destroyed."

Rossel whirled around, and a flash of silver glinted off of a blade in his hand. In the same breath, he flicked his wrist and sent the blade flying end over end straight for my chest.

CHAPTER 10

A SCREAM BUILT UP in my throat. I felt it rise from my chest in slow motion, like a teapot about to boil over. And just before it erupted from my lips, everything stopped.

The knife hovered before me in mid-air, an inch away from my chest wall. The hilt was a tarnished gold, ornate in design with otherworldly creatures breathing swirls of fire from the pommel to to the blade. Years of grime—probably centuries—had darkened the crevices between the glittering swirls. It looked ancient, but the blade was no more dull than it had been when it was first forged.

And instead of a scream, a laugh bubbled out of me. Why was I focused on the design of the dagger that was about to kill me? My hyper-awareness and observation of detail almost overshadowed the fact that *time* had stopped, once again.

"Al?" I scanned all the windows of the warehouse, looking for my feathery friend and protector. I repeated his name, but there was still no answer. He wasn't here... which meant the power to stop time could only have come from *me*. But how? Was it something I could command at will, or just some built-in safeguard to protect me from certain death?

I refocused on Rossel, his body frozen mid-throw. His lip was curled in rage, but his eyes told another story. Again, I got the impression that he regretted something. Killing me? Or maybe not doing it before now?

It didn't matter. He'd failed, for now. Though I wasn't sure how long the time would hold for me. I leaned carefully forward, close enough for the rope around my midsection to meet the blade. If I touched it, would it fall from the air and stab me in the leg? Or would contact simply renew its original momentum, propelling it through my gut?

I hoped neither of those options were the case. I really just needed it to stay in the air so I could use it to my advantage. "Please don't move," I whispered. Then I gently brought the rope down along the edge of the blade.

Miraculously, the knife remained motionless in the air. I breathed a sigh of relief, and did it again, moving my body up and down like some uncoordinated version of the chicken dance as I attempted to fray the rope. My thighs burned, held in a perpetual squat with the chair still stuck to my backside, but after just a couple of minutes the rope broke. The chair clattered to the hard ground, the rope still attached to it.

But my hands were still bound behind my back with the hard plastic zip ties. With a quick glance to ensure Rossel was still frozen, I righted the chair with a foot, bumped it closer to the knife with my hip, then stepped onto it and turned around.

The knife hadn't moved when I needed it to stay still, but now I needed it to move. "Will you please let me take you?" I felt like a fool speaking to the inanimate blade that was still frozen in time. But it did what I'd asked it to before. Maybe it would fulfill my wish again.

I stretched my arms backward until I made contact with the cool metal side of the blade. Taking it between my thumb and fingers, I gave a little tug. Somehow again, the knife submitted to my will. The handle fell, and the edge of the blade cut into me slightly as I gripped harder to keep from dropping it. But a small cut on my hand was worlds better than an open chest wound, so I wouldn't complain.

Rossel was unmoving, still snarling like a statue across from me. I had to get these ties off as quickly as possible. My clock had to have been running out. This was the longest I'd ever kept time stopped before.

I readjusted the knife awkwardly in my hand until I was able to twist the blade against the plastic around my wrists. It took about a minute of pushing and pulling the blade, but finally, it cut through the ties.

I immediately rolled my shoulders back to stretch my achy muscles, cracked my neck, then inspected the bloody cuts around my wrist from where the ties had dug into my skin. Thankfully these new Keeper powers would help me to heal more quickly. I'd always been kind of a wimp when it came to cuts, and this was like a papercut on steroids.

Knife in hand, free from all the ropes and ties that bound me moments before, I stalked over to Rossel's frozen body. This was my chance. I could end him without a fight. Without a struggle of any kind. And I probably should have, considering he'd just launched a dagger at my heart.

But I couldn't bring myself to do it. It felt wrong. Cowardly. And I couldn't forget that hint of regret in his eyes. Perhaps there was still some good left in his soul. And if not some good, there was definitely some information I needed to get out of him.

Rossel knew where my mom was hidden. That much I was certain of. And now, I wondered if he might know something about who my father was, also. No, I definitely couldn't kill Rossel today. Not until I found out exactly what he was hiding from me.

A faint pressure was building in my chest, like a string attached to my sternum was being gently tugged away from me. And somehow I knew this was my body losing control of the time stopping trick. "No." My voice was firm, but inside I was pleading. *No, please, not yet. I just need a few more minutes.*

The pressure stopped, and Rossel remained still. I knew I was pushing my luck, so without another moment of delay I rushed back over to the chair and untied the rope from it. It was now in two pieces. I used one to secure Rossel's hands behind his back the way mine had been tied, and I used the second piece to tie his ankles together. It wasn't a permanent solution, but hopefully it would hold until I could figure out what to do next.

I sat his lanky body into the chair and whispered to his lifeless face. "I'll be back for you."

Osborne was next.

CHAPTER 11

THE PRESSURE WAS ALREADY building in my chest again when I slipped out of the warehouse. The sun was bright, even in the shaded alleyway. It called to me, tempting me to seize this moment and just run. Run as far as I could—far away from Rossel and Osborne and some ancient prophecy that I could never escape.

But I was in too deep for that. And it wouldn't only affect me. There were other people's lives at stake now, too. Millie and my friends. Tate. And the man in the most imminent danger—Driskell.

I turned the dagger over in my hand, watching the sun play off of its gilded surface. The string tugging my sternum was at full force. I felt as though it would crack at any moment.

With a deep breath, I raised the blade toward Osborne, determined to keep him still once time began moving again. I lifted my hand, and from the corner of my eye I noticed another person who had frozen in place while casually walking past the alleyway on the street beyond. I couldn't risk him looking our way when the spell broke.

I lowered my weapon and sprinted over to the young man. He stared at his phone screen, one foot lifted slightly off the ground. I took his shoulders in my hands and pushed him forward slightly. "Move along," I said. I'd expected him to remain stationary, waiting for me to drag his body forward past the alleyway. But surprisingly, his feet moved with my encouragement. It was like pushing a bicycle and watching the pedals move as the wheels spun. His feet walked, holding him upright even as the top half of his body remained still.

"This is so cool," I whispered to myself.

Once he was fully past the alleyway, I ran back to Osborne and grabbed hold of the blade again. Raising it to his throat, I finally relaxed and planned out my words. My chest ached with the pressure of my power, but time was still stuck in place.

How could I make it move again? What was I missing? I glanced back at Osborne, whose blank expression was fixed on the wall across the street. I couldn't just leave him here. Rossel would sic him after me just as soon as he came to. But I didn't have anything to tie him up with either.

I looked back and forth, up and down the alley. There was nothing but an old dirty sock laying crumpled against the wall across from me. Then again, maybe the sock could be of some use. I risked another six seconds to go fetch the dirty thing, and I was shoving it into Osborne's mouth when the string in my chest finally snapped.

The breeze blew through my hair, rushing down the alley like a wind tunnel, and the sound of the city filled the air once more. Osborne's eyes grew into full circles, and his hands shot up to grab a hold of my wrists. I pushed the flat side of the blade against his neck and shook my head, a clear warning not to try anything stupid.

"Hey, Osborne. Surprised to see me?" I couldn't keep my smile at bay. The look on his face was just too stunned. He must have believed I appeared out of thin air. *Good.* Maybe he'd think I had the powers of a messenger, teleporting through space the way Devon and my mom could.

"Look here, I will take that disgusting used sock out of your mouth on one condition: you will *not* use your glamour on me. The second I hear the sound of the siren's call out of you, I will flick my wrist and use Rossel's pretty little dagger here to carve that voice box right out of your throat. Am I making myself clear?"

A look of pure shock flashed across his face, and he gave a little nod—barely moving against the knife I had on his skin.

"Good. Don't make me regret this act of mercy." I gagged a little as the crusty sock crunched under my fingers. But I made good on my word and yanked it from Osborne's mouth.

He snarled as a thanks.

"Where are your manners?" I pushed the knife a little harder into his skin. "I can get the sock again if you'd like."

Osborne didn't say a word, but his eyes could have torched me.

"Easy there, killer. You don't want to push me. Now listen up. You are going to stop chasing me. You will not hunt me down anymore, or I can promise you, the hunter will become the hunted. I've got Rossel tied up inside. He got testy with me, and I guarantee you *he* won't do it again, either.

"I will not tolerate you two—and whoever you work for—inconveniencing me anymore. So run back to whoever is in charge of this mess, and let him know I'm done playing his game. Tell Rossel, too. It's over."

"You know..." Osborne's eye twitched as he spoke. "I didn't actually care about what happened to you before. I was just doing my job. But now? Now I hope they rip you apart."

"I'd like to see them try." I pulled the knife back from his neck and twirled the blade in my hand. It was showy—not really my style. But something powerful had come over me. I felt invincible. And somehow, Osborne felt it too. He knew not to mess with me. My inner Athena was showing.

"What happened to you?" he asked.

"I learned the truth."

"Yeah? And what's that?" he sneered.

"Ask Rossel. He can tell you all about what he saw me do in his vision."

A muscle ticked in Osborne's jaw. I could tell he wasn't sure whether or not to believe me, but he knew there would be repercussions if what I said was true. Rossel was one of the greatest seers of all time. His visions were highly regarded as the truth in the Keeper world. Whether or not Rossel told him about me being the Deliverer, the seed of doubt had been planted in Osborne's mind. He looked to the side, trying to appear unimpressed.

"You'll find out soon enough." I shrugged. "And sorry, by the way, if you lose out on your reward for letting me get away." I dropped my voice to a whisper and grinned. "And I *will* be getting away."

I tucked Rossel's blade into my waistband, no longer concerned about Osborne attacking me. I could practically see his fear radiating off of him now—he wouldn't dare make a move on me again until he talked to Rossel.

"The whole system is changing soon. I'm turning the world on its head. In fact, I highly suggest you work on getting on my good side."

Osborne scoffed and I quirked a brow at him. "Or don't. Makes no difference to me." I took two steps away from him before turning back over my shoulder. "Oh, and Osborne? Don't let me see your face again unless you're coming to grovel at my feet. I won't be so gracious next time."

I didn't look back again. My pace was steady and confident through the alley and back out onto the street. But as soon as I rounded the corner, a sweat broke out across my brow and hands shook.

That was not Everly Gordon speaking back there. I would never have the guts to talk to Osborne that way. Something had come over me. It was terrifying, and yet, I wanted more. I remembered the fierceness of the girl in Rossel's painting, and for the first time since I laid eyes on it, I believed it could actually be me.

I ran, fueled by adrenaline, until I found a crowded cafe several blocks away from the warehouse. Only after I was inside, safely hidden by the other bodies in the room, did I pull out my phone. I dialed the first person who came to my mind—the only person I wanted to see.

"Tate. It's me. Are you still in town?"

CHAPTER 12

TATE BOMBARDED ME WITH questions the entire drive back to my apartment. His expressions had run the gamut from initial disbelief, to rage, to respect. And as we pulled up in front of my building, he held a half-smirk that wouldn't fade.

"What's so funny?" I asked as we climbed out of his car.

"Nothing." He chuckled. "You're just full of surprises."

I'd sent messages to Sean and the girls during our drive, asking them to meet us back at the apartment. Devon was there as well, everyone waiting in our small living room when Tate and I walked in.

"Everly—are you okay?" Dom scanned me the moment I crossed through the door, searching for any injuries. She frowned when she saw my wrists, but they were already healing. I would be fine. Then her frown morphed into an open-mouthed gape as she met my eyes and saw a flash of what I was thinking.

Tate laughed again. "She's fine, but I'm not so sure about the other guys. Buckle up, you guys are in for a crazy story."

I told them about how I'd run into Osborne at the park, but I didn't mention Al. For some reason, it still felt as though our relationship needed to remain a secret. Which meant I didn't mention my previous life as Athena, either. It all sounded a little too grandiose to be entirely believable, and it really didn't matter. What mattered was that Rossel was looking to get rid of me. And he knew about the tablet—though how much he understood of the prophecy itself was still a mystery.

I told them about how I'd somehow stopped time, too. I described Rossel's attempt to stab me, and then my threat to stab Osborne. It was all too much for Sean, who paced the floor as I spoke, running both hands through his hair. He looked like he might yell—or possibly jump right out of the window and hunt Osborne down himself. But I assured them that Osborne wouldn't be a threat to me anymore. I truly believed that. Rossel, on the other hand, I imagined I would see again soon.

In fact, I counted on it.

"How much of this did you already know?" Sean rounded suddenly on Tate, the accusation clear in his tone.

"None of it. Rossel asked me to hunt Everly. He warned me that she was fractured, and she was dangerous. He said he needed a skilled hunter to counter her, and to take her soul the moment her powers emerged—before she could do any real damage. The orders came from higher up, and that's all I know."

Dom kept a scrupulous eye on Tate as he spoke, and I wondered what else she was gathering from his mind. But she didn't push him any further.

"Hang on," Gayla said. "I'm not surprised that Rossel knew about the tablet and the prophecy. After all, he painted a giant portrait of you, Ev. We really should have put that together a long time ago. What I am more interested in is this time-stopping ability you have. That's not typical."

They all turned to face me, as though waiting for me to explain myself. I just shrugged. "I don't have much control over it. In fact, I didn't even think I was responsible for it the first couple of times it happened."

"It's happened before?" Dom leaned forward on her knees.

"Yes." I told them about how everything seemed to slow down before Clayton ran me over in the parking lot. And how I froze mid-air just before my real powers emerged at the loading docks when I was running from Osborne. Tate frowned, disappointed that this was the first he'd heard of it even though he was there that day.

"But I can't make it stop on my own. It only seems to happen when my life is in danger."

"Fascinating." Dom leaned back again, nodding slowly.

"Do you think I can learn to control it?" I asked. "I mean, surely there are others like me? Could they teach me, maybe when we go to Atlantis?"

Sean shook his head. "I've never heard of an Atlantean being able to stop time before."

"I've never heard of *anyone* being able to stop time before," Gayla added.

Surely that couldn't be true. I looked at the other faces in the room. Gayla was grinning and Devon looked a little confused. The rest were all examining me like I was something from another planet.

"There is a folktale." Dom frowned. "You've heard of the god Chronos? He wasn't real, as far as the Keeper history books go. But there are plenty of stories of him that have floated down through the years. Many refer to him as Father Time."

"But he was an Olympian in the stories," Gayla said.

"I know. But they're only stories. If it was true, I suppose he could've been Atlantean just as easily. The mortals who passed the stories along wouldn't have known the difference."

Huh. So I might've been both Athena *and* Father Time in my past lives? I'd have to ask Al about that the next time I saw him. This was all getting too weird.

The others were still staring at me, and I was growing more uncomfortable by the minute, so I stood and changed the subject. "Who knows about the time thing... I'm still not entirely convinced it's anything more than a fluke. But what *I'm* really concerned about is Driskell. I definitely said too much to Rossel. I got caught up in the moment, and basically confirmed that we had him. I'm worried that Rossel will try to retaliate. I can't let him hurt Driskell, and I don't want him creeping around Millie's place, either. I vowed to keep Driskell safe, so I think it's time we move him."

"You're probably right," Sean said. "But where can we take him to keep him safe?"

"Millie suggested Porta Maris. Unless you think of a better idea, I'd say we should go with that. I can take him there." Devon looked like he'd already made up his mind.

I nodded. "I'll go, too."

"But we can't follow you there," Dom said.

"I can." Sean stood. "We've got to head into Atlantis, anyway. Right?" He grinned at me.

"Indeed. That tablet isn't going to piece *itself* back together."

"Are you sure you're ready for that?" Tate asked. His eyes had darkened slightly into a deep warm hue of gold. "I don't want you to put yourself into danger. I hate that I can't go with you."

"I'll have Sean. And I think I accidentally moved the game forward, whether I'm ready for it or not. Our jig is up with Rossel. He knows that we know about the prophecy. Now it's just a race to who can find the missing pieces first."

"I'll see if I can slow Rossel down here," Gayla said. "I'm supposed to meet him for another training session tonight."

"I doubt you'll be training with him anymore," Dom said. "Not now that he knows you're on Team Everly."

"I'm sorry if I messed up your apprenticeship." I put a hand on Gayla's shoulder.

She grinned wider. "I can only pray that you did. I've never wanted to be a seer for the king. And I'll be happy if I never see Rossel again. But first, of course, I'm going to at least try to discover what he's up to. And like I said, I'll do whatever I can to throw a wrench into his plans."

"And I'll look for another piece of the tablet while I'm in Agartha," Tate added. I'd forgotten that he was preparing to leave us. Dom shifted uncomfortably, and I wondered again what she knew that she wasn't telling me. Could Tate be trusted to handle a piece of the prophecy? Or would he try to destroy it, the way his ancestors had tried to do for centuries before?

I supposed there wasn't anything I could do about it at this point. He knew it existed. He'd either find it or he wouldn't. I just had to believe that he would do the right thing.

He stepped toward me, and it was only then that I realized I had been staring at him. It was like he knew just what I was thinking. He reached out and moved a piece of hair from my face, his fingers making my skin come alive where they brushed against my cheek. "You can trust me."

I nodded, unsure of what else to say.

"*Ahem*." Sean cleared his throat loudly, shaking me from my stupor. Darn Tate and his perfect face.

"Right," I said, shoving my hands into my pockets. "Gayla and Dom can stop Rossel if possible. Tate can look for a missing piece of the tablet in Agartha, and Sean and I can look in Atlantis. But first, we need to get Driskell to safety."

Everyone nodded, all on the same page. It was go time.

CHAPTER 13

I SAID GOODBYE TO Tate and the girls, then headed back to Millie's house with my Atlantean friends. It still sounded strange in my ears to admit that I was a descendant of Atlantis. But seeing as how I could breathe underwater and stop time with my mind, it had to be true.

I scanned the streets carefully as we pulled up in front of Millie's place. Al had mentioned "bad looking dudes" hanging around, and I wasn't sure how much fight I had left in me after the encounter with Rossel and Osborne earlier. But I didn't see anyone. Perhaps my message to Osborne had gotten through to Rossel and his crew after all. Though I wouldn't hold my breath.

"Millie?" No one greeted us at the door. Jeeves and Pierre must have gone to the market or something. It was unusual for both to be gone at the same time. I called my aunt's name one more time.

"Something isn't right," Devon whispered.

Sean marched past us through the foyer and up the stairs. "Let's go see." Something shifted in him, and he appeared bigger, stronger before my very eyes. This was *guardian* Sean, and he wasn't happy.

Devon and I followed him up the stairs. My heart raced faster with every step we took, dread pumping through my veins. Devon was correct. Something felt really wrong.

The door to Millie's study was closed. I gave a soft knock. "Millie? Are you in there?" No response.

Sean was at the end of the hall, peering into Driskell's room. He glanced back to us with a frown and shook his head. Then he held up his hands for us to step back and prowled over to the door. He moved Devon and me to the sides of the doorway, placing us flat against the wall.

Then he twisted the knob and immediately dropped to the floor as the door swung open. It was a good thing he did, because Millie's heavy iron bookend came flying straight to where Sean's head should have been. It sank into the drywall across the hall, marring the wall.

The color drained from Devon's face, leaving his dark skin an ashy gray as his suspicions were confirmed. Millie was in danger. He disappeared in the next instant, teleporting inside the office to his soulmate's side.

I peeked around the corner to find several books hovering in the air off of Millie's bookcase, and one by one they went flying toward Devon.

"Telekinetics," Sean said. "Stay out here, I'll take care of them."

He ran into the room—a flash of speed before my eyes, and batted down the books in mid air. He lifted the sofa in the center of the room and tossed it back into the corner like it was made of Styrofoam. It flew through the air toward two Olympians, who I'd just noticed off in the shadows. One was a short man who let out an angry roar at the furniture. The other was a tall, wispy looking woman with sharp cheekbones and a ferocious glare. She raised a hand and the couch stopped in the air, then reversed its path back toward Sean.

"Look out!" I shouted, and my feet were moving before I could think better of it. I dove to protect Sean, but he swept me behind him with one arm and took the brunt of the impact of the couch for the both of us. It simply bounced off of his hard body, and it struck me how valuable having a guardian like this really was. I'd taken Sean for granted.

Trusting that he could handle the Olympians on his own, I turned to examine the others. Devon was working furiously to untie the ropes binding Millie and Driskell to her heavy oak desk. Millie's eyes were wide, but Driskell didn't look afraid. He'd been expecting this, I realized. He believed his time was short. But I'd made him a promise and I wasn't going to back out on it now.

I rushed over to help Devon. "We've gotta get out of here. Do you think you can take us all at once?" I asked.

"Probably." He scowled over his shoulder. "But we need to do something about these guys first."

I followed his gaze to where Sean was still putting up a really impressive fight. The Olympians both appeared to be telekinetic—they could lift and throw objects in the room with their minds. But their brain power was no match for Sean's strength. He swatted their efforts down like bugs, stalking closer to them with every attack they sent his way.

I thought Sean would take them out for sure until his feet lifted off the ground. The Olympians were working together, their hands lifting in tandem as Sean rose higher and higher from the ground. "Put me down!" he shouted.

It wasn't easy—I could tell by the quiver of the woman's hands and the strain in the man's face. They were struggling to keep him in the air, but it was effective.

Devon cursed under his breath. "Hang on," he whispered. Then he stepped through the fabric of our reality and re-emerged beside the Olympians. He swung a fist, making contact with the man's nose with a sickening *whack*. Sean dropped a few feet in the air, his body falling sideways, but he didn't hit the ground. The woman was visibly shaking as she worked to keep him in the air on her own.

The man swung back at Devon, but he'd reappeared by my side before the man could make contact. His fist whiffed through empty air.

"Get the window," the woman said through gritted teeth. Her squatty little sidekick did as he was told, slamming the window open with a quick flick of his hand and so much force I was surprised the glass didn't break. Then his arms were extended back toward Sean, assisting his partner by lifting the other half of my friend's body. They were moving Sean toward the open air outside the window.

"I don't think so." I growled and lunged for the Olympians. As I leapt over the fallen couch, I felt a gathering in my chest. The sound of the city street stopped coming in from outside. Sean's heavy breathing went silent. And best of all, the Olympians were no longer moving my friend toward the window. Time had stopped again. But this time, I could feel the pressure in my chest immediately. I didn't have long before that delicate string of power would snap again. I'd used too much already today.

Instead of attacking the Olympians, I decided to use what remaining strength I had to rescue Sean. I wrapped my arms around his calves and pulled him closer to the ground. "Sean, can you hear me? Snap out of it—I need you to move."

Sean didn't respond. It wasn't a surprise, but it was a little disappointing to find the limits of my ability. This sure would have been a lot easier if I got to choose *who* was affected by time stopping.

I pulled him again and again, until his feet were on the ground. Then, as I did with the stranger on the street near the warehouse, I attempted to push him forward toward Devon. Thankfully, the foot-pedaling walking trick still worked.

The pressure continued to mount in my chest as I truly stretched the limits of my power. A groan escaped me as I fought to keep time stilled, just for a little longer. Rossel's blade was still in my waistband, and I used it to cut through the ropes binding Millie and Driskell to her desk. Then I gathered us all into a circle, clasping everyone's hands together as I went. I was almost finished when the string snapped and time moved forward again.

"What—" Millie started, but I interrupted her.

"Get us out of here. Now!"

It only took Devon half a second to register what was going on, and next thing I knew I was submerged into the most frigid stinging cold sensation imaginable. I didn't think I'd ever get used to the feeling of teleporting. It took my breath away, freezing my lungs. And then it was gone.

CHAPTER 14

I SURVEYED MY PEOPLE first, counting faces to make sure everyone had arrived safely. We were all here. Then I leaned back to examine where exactly *here* was.

We stood on white sand near a rocky outcrop of an island. The water was an impossible turquoise, stretching out to reach the hazy blue sky above.

"Porta Maris," Millie whispered.

"It's beautiful." I turned to find tropical trees dotting the island at my back. There were no other people around—no roads or buildings. Just paradise.

"This way." She marched toward the rocks, which towered about two stories overhead. "Are you alright, Sean?"

"I'm great." He gave one nod. His shoulders remained tense, his expression flat. But he was in one piece. We all were.

The only person who seemed unwilling to follow Millie toward the rocks was Driskell. In fact, he was downright stubborn about it. When we all started walking, he sat in the sand like a toddler preparing for a tantrum.

I turned back for the old man and extended my hand. "Come on."

"No." He scrunched his nose, and his white mustache wiggled in the sunlight.

"Driskell, please. I want to keep you safe."

His brows furrowed. "Just because the Olympians can't get me here, it doesn't mean I'm safe. There are other dangers out there. More than curses and royalty."

"I promise, nothing will happen to you here."

"You shouldn't make promises you can't keep." Driskell huffed and rose back to his feet, brushing the sand from his backside. He didn't say another word as he fell into step beside me. A moment later we were back with the others.

"I love you, but there's something you need to know," Millie said, turning to Devon. "I'm going to ignore you when we get inside. I will essentially pretend you don't exist. You can't let them know about our connection here."

"Why not?" he asked. The poor guy's feelings were hurt and it was written all over his face.

"There isn't time to explain everything right now. Just trust me on this." My aunt took a deep breath, straightened her shoulders, then pushed her hands into a crevice of the rock. The stones moved apart, revealing a narrow stairwell. We followed her down just a little ways before the space opened up again into a seaside tavern built into the cliffs.

Atlantean men and women sat at a long bar top overlooking the water. An older man with muddy brown hair looked up as we entered, settling on Millie with a cruel smile.

"Mildred. I never would have expected to see *you* here again."

"What exactly is this place?" I whispered to Sean, as others in the room turned to see the exchange taking place between Millie and the Atlantean man.

"Porta Maris. The island isn't governed by any organized body, and it offers asylum to all Atlanteans. As long as they remain here on this land, they are safe from the laws of the Keepers."

"Right. That's why Driskell will be safe here."

Sean's gaze hardened. "Driskell will be surrounded by all the other Atlantean criminals and misfits who also seek asylum."

Ohh. Suddenly it seemed a little less appealing.

"I'm not here for a fight, Tano. I'm just dropping someone off," Millie said. She stood tall, putting on a brave face.

The man—Tano's eyes grazed over our crew, skipping right over Sean, Devon, and me. He squinted at Driskell. "The old man?"

Driskell made a *hrmmph* and crossed his arms over his chest.

"Yes. See to it that he isn't harmed."

"Why would I care what happens to him?" Tano smirked.

"Because you owe me one, and you know it." Millie's voice was hard. It didn't sound like the gentleness of the aunt I knew and loved.

"Oh come on, Millie. It's been over a hundred years. When are you gonna forgive me?"

"I don't forgive murderers." She turned her head slightly but didn't make eye contact with Devon. "Especially not those who kill my *soulmate*."

Devon tensed beside me, but I had to give him credit for remaining calm. He was doing much better than I would have done in his situation.

Tano paused for a moment, then let out a loud barking laugh. "You need to relax, Millie. Let bygones be bygones. Your soulmate will be back one day, and hopefully in a smarter body. And as for the old man…" Tano waved Driskell off. "I don't see why anyone would care a lick about him. Look at him. He's harmless."

A pent up breath escaped my lips. They didn't know who Driskell was, then. I could only hope he would be able to stay anonymous.

"Good," Millie remained remarkably in control of herself. "Then there's one more thing—we need a couple of rooms. Probably just for one night. They'll be going under to Atlantis tomorrow," she dipped her chin toward us, "and I'll be heading home. But tonight we'll need somewhere to sleep."

"That's gonna cost you." Tano licked his chapped lips.

Sean had to grab Devon's arm to keep him from hitting the man. Tano looked over to see what the movement was all about, but Millie reached out for his shoulder, drawing his attention back to her.

"Just show me to the kitchen," she said. "I'll get right to work."

Devon relaxed, and we followed Tano through the crowd to an archway behind the bar. A short hall led us back to the kitchen, where Millie seemed to make herself right at home. She went straight for a pantry and emerged with a couple of aprons.

Tano seemed satisfied with that, and after another minute or two of mouthing off to my aunt, he left us alone. After a few more minutes of Millie rummaging through cabinets and drawers, she had a stack of ingredients on the counter. She put her hands on her hips and turned to me.

"Driskell will be safe, and you'll be off to Atlantis by morning. But right now, I need your help."

I didn't know what lay ahead, but I trusted that Millie had it under control. And finally, after a very long day, I leaned into the hope flickering inside. With a guardian by my side and a warrior-goddess somewhere deep within me, I knew we were going to be successful. We would reach Atlantis, find a missing piece of the tablet, and eventually carry out the prophecy.

But first, we had some work to do.

THE WATER PRINCESS

CHAPTER 1

THE SITUATION WASN'T FUNNY at all, but I couldn't help but laugh. Sean, a broad-shouldered muscular hulk of a man, hunched over at the counter, whining over a mixing bowl. Giant flour handprints were smeared across his apron, and he pouted to my aunt Millie. "I don't know what I'm doing wrong. They keep breaking!"

"They're eggs, Sean. They're supposed to break."

I peered into his bowl at the puddle of broken yolks and pulverized shells. "Maybe you should try a more delicate touch."

We tried to keep our conversation light and fluffy in the hopes it would make Driskell and Devon a little less sour. Devon still had his undies in a wad about losing his previous life to these people, and old man Driskell wanted to be anywhere else.

But at least we were all alive now. Rossel couldn't get us here. And as soon as we helped Millie with her chore, we would have clean beds to sleep in before our trip to Atlantis tomorrow.

"Done." I stepped back from my own mixing bowl, proudly examining the batter within. "Do you want me to pour it into the baking dish?"

"Not yet." Millie's shoulders sagged. "We're missing the final ingredient."

She dragged her feet over to a narrow cabinet with steel bars running across the front of it. With a click of the lock, the door swung open to reveal a pharmaceutical smorgasbord.

"Ohhh!" I put the heel of my hand against my forehead. "Of course! This is all making much better sense now. You're making some kind of healing products, aren't you? I was wondering why they would put *you* in charge of restocking their baked goods." I licked some raw brownie batter off of my thumb and gave an approving nod. "No offense, of course. This is actually really good. You're just not exactly known for your baking skills."

"I am around here." Millie sighed and walked over to me with a medicine bottle in her hand. She twisted off the lid, and I sneaked a quick peek inside. A silvery-greenish substance swirled at the bottom like liquid metal.

"What is that?"

"It's concentrated soma, and it's incredibly illegal."

"And you're putting it in the brownies?"

Millie frowned. "It takes a special touch to... uh... enhance these baked goods without going overboard. They need a healer to do it. This is how we pay for our accommodations."

"They want to feel good without losing their minds." Driskell waved an angry hand from the corner of the room and began grumbling something about how the whole lot of them were a bunch of druggies. Millie didn't disagree.

"So you're making special brownies?" I laughed. My little rule-following aunt had a rebellious streak in her after all. "Seems fitting for an island of supernatural misfits."

"They're criminals!" Driskell bellowed.

"Soma is like ten times stronger than ambrosia," Sean said. "It was too strong to remain on earth. It's only grown in Olympus now, which makes me wonder how they have a store of it here." He shot a disapproving look in Millie's direction.

"There are always outside groups looking to hire Keepers for their less than admirable jobs. But money has little value here, so they find other methods of keeping everyone happy." Millie cut sad eyes over to Devon, who sat stone faced beside Driskell. When he didn't respond, she set the bottle of soma on the counter and joined him on the bench.

"When you were here before, in your past life, we worked together on some of these missions." Millie took Devon's hand in hers. Though she looked at him while she spoke, I suspected this explanation was just as much for the rest of us as it was for him. "There was an active group of evil, powerful beings whose only goal was to destroy the Keepers and everything we stood for."

"The Manticorians," I whispered.

"Yes." Millie's expression hardened as her eyes rested on me for a moment. Thankfully she didn't ask how I knew about the Manticorians. It would be difficult to explain that I gathered all of my information from a textbook given to me by the leader of that group—Rastputin, himself.

"Some of the jobs we were tasked with required tactics that weren't exactly above board." Millie dropped her chin, lost in a memory. "So we took sanctuary here, where we could be safe in between missions. We made friends with like-minded soldiers—others who were dedicated to the cause. Tano was one of our best and brightest men. You two were like brothers," she said to Devon. He visibly stiffened, but still made no response.

"But someone got to him. Tano turned on us in Saint Petersburg. He struck a deal with someone up high in the Atlantean council—someone within our very own ranks who was working for the Manticorians. He knew we were close to eliminating them, and the councilman offered to exonerate Tano for all of his previous crimes if he killed us."

"So he did?"

Millie nodded. "We trusted Tano. We never saw it coming. I escaped," she touched Devon's cheek, "but you weren't so lucky. To Tano's credit, he knew he'd made a mistake. He took out four of our own men, which was enough to erase his criminal history per the deal he'd struck with the council, but then he turned on Rasputin as well. Tano became a free agent."

"So how did he end up back here again?" I asked.

"Tano needs boundaries. Freedom doesn't work out too well for him. When left to his own devices, he makes poor decisions. One list of crimes was replaced by another, and here he is again."

"What happened to you?" Devon asked. His eyes were glossy, focused intently on my aunt.

"I served my sentence for a hundred years, and I've been playing by the law ever since." With one final squeeze of Devon's hand, Millie stood and returned to work. "But that's enough talk about the past. We have more important things to focus on, like the future." She measured out the soma, pouring exactly six drops into the batter and mixing it in before transferring it to the baking dish. She turned the conversation toward me as she worked.

"When you go to Atlantis tomorrow, you'll need to act as though you are a guardian. It's the most common power among Atlanteans, and they will not ask you to prove anything. If they do, run as fast as you can and we'll just say you're not particularly adept."

I nodded. "Got it."

"But as for your real powers..." She put the brownies in the oven and turned to me. The whole room drew a collective breath, everyone wondering the same thing. "Did you really stop time back in my study?"

"I did." I busied myself with cleaning up the mess I'd made on the countertop, trying to avoid making eye contact with anyone.

"Is it something you can replicate?"

"Nope."

"Are you sure? Have you tried it again? Maybe under different circumstances? I could help. We could try to—"

"Millie. I can't." I threw a hand towel onto the counter, sending a cloud of cocoa powder into the air. "I've tried. It's actually really frustrating. And apparently no one has ever heard of a power like this. I'm tired of being the weird one. I'd rather just drop it if that's okay? There's nothing you can do."

"I'm sorry, Everly. I didn't mean to upset you."

"You didn't. It's just—I'm just tired. It's been a long day."

"Of course. And I'm sure that must've taken a lot out of you. Why don't you go get some rest? We're almost finished here, and I can wrap things up on my own. Let's find you a room and some supper. You've got an even bigger day ahead of you tomorrow."

She was right. And that big day ahead of me was exactly what had me so tense. Though, I didn't know what scared me more—the thought of going into Atlantis, or the fear of what might happen if we really did find the missing piece of the prophecy.

There was no backing out now.

CHAPTER 2

TANO DIDN'T COME AROUND again. Some other man showed us to comfortable rooms within the rock of Porta Maris. As we ventured through the hallways, I realized the secret hideout was not only hidden within the stony cliffs of the island, but it extended well below the shore, down under the water as well. Small windows punctuating the hall revealed sea life in the clear water outside of the building.

We all shared one room. Sean and I split a bunk bed, Driskell slept on the couch, and Millie and Devon shared the queen sized bed in the corner. I tried really hard not to let myself think too much about my aunt and Devon. It still weirded me out if I let it.

We were all exhausted and slept like the dead right up until the sound of someone knocking at our door brought us back to life the next morning. "Coming!" Millie called out as her feet swung down to the floor.

I sat up and rubbed my eyes, only to find Millie gaping at me when I dropped my hands. "What is it?"

"Your aura. It's white again," she whispered.

The knock sounded once more, louder this time. "One minute!" Millie's sweet voice was like a song to the stranger on the opposite side of the door, but she practically growled at me as she flew across the room and tossed my covers over my head. "Get under there. Don't move. Don't even breathe. We can't let them see you."

I held my breath as the door eased open and Millie said hello. A man's voice responded—Tano. *Shoot.* If only it could have been anyone else. Was it even possible to hide an aura through a blanket, or would it radiate out, unconstrained by fabric and pillows?

"Breakfast is ready. Georgette took one look at that tray full of goodies you left in the kitchen and insisted we feed you before we kick you out. There's a stack of pancakes three feet tall in there." His laugh was deep and hollow.

"Great, thank you. We'll be right down."

I heard a hand smack against the door, and Tano's voice grew louder and closer. "Wait. Did everyone sleep okay last night?"

"Just fine." Millie's voice was higher, on the verge of panic.

Tano's wheezy breathing came even closer, audible through the blanket. He had to have been right over me. "Aren't you missing someone?"

"She's in the bathroom!" Driskell shouted. "And she better hurry up or I might wet myself!" He banged on the wall as he yelled.

Tano grunted a sound of disgust, and I loosed a silent breath as his heavy footfalls left my side. "Alright. We'll see you in the dining room."

It was a full thirty seconds after the door closed before Sean yanked the blanket off of me. "That was too close. We've got to get you more of your pills."

"You didn't happen to bring them with you, did ya?" I looked hopefully at Millie.

"I didn't. And I don't think I can make any more without Thaddeus or another Agarthian with strong glamour. Do you think you might be able to take Sean and Everly back to retrieve them real quick?" she asked Devon.

"Sounds like we probably better. But can I grab some pancakes first?"

"No." Sean and Millie answered in unison.

"Fine," Devon grumbled. "Come on." He extended two hands to his sides. Sean and I approached, and Devon frowned at our attire. Sean was barefoot in athletic shorts and a holey, stained t-shirt with the sleeves cut off. I was wearing a faded old night shirt with a cartoon bird on the front that hung down to my knees. It wasn't unusual for guests to arrive at Porta Maris with nothing but the clothes on their backs, but unfortunately the selection of extra clothing they had to change into was pretty limited.

"Don't look at me like that," I muttered. "We'll get some other clothes at Millie's house before we come back."

"That's a good idea, for all of our sakes." He wrinkled his nose.

I moved to elbow him in the ribs, but we were gone before I could. I was dipped into the frigid sensation of teleporting across the fabric of reality, but only for a moment before I found myself standing on a pile of papers on the floor of Millie's study.

The room had been ravaged from our magical fight the day before, but the Olympians were gone. I dropped the boys' hands and spun in a circle, surveying the damage.

"This place is a wreck," Sean said.

"No kidding. I can't believe Jeeves hasn't... oh my goodness! I forgot about Jeeves! And Pierre!" I turned from the room, taking the stairs two at a time and calling out to my aunt's butler and private chef.

"Everly, wait!" Sean's voice called out from the study, but he was by my side in a flash—one of the benefits of his powers. "If they're still here, you're gonna have a lot of explaining to do."

"I don't care. We'll figure that out later. I need to know that the Olympians didn't get to them. We've got to make sure they're okay."

I continued calling out their names until we reached the foyer at the bottom of the stairs. The house was silent. Millie's place had never been so quiet. I had to strain my ears to hear the faintest whine and a scratch at the back door. I whipped around to find two enormous, drooling faces looking through the glass door from the patio in Millie's courtyard.

"Lemon Drop! Tiny Tim!"

Sean got to the door before I did, of course, and he let Millie's giant Mastiffs inside. They greeted us with slobbery noses mushed into our legs.

"Hey pups. Can you help us find Jeeves and Pierre?" They tilted their huge faces to the side, tails wagging as they looked up at us. "They're not exactly bloodhounds," I said with a shrug to Sean.

But we didn't need the dogs to help us find the others. Devon had already stumbled across them in the most obvious of places—their usual hangout, the kitchen. We went running at his call, and I gasped as I took in Jeeves' massive body tied down to a chair with his back facing Pierre.

Both men were restrained at the wrists, waists, and ankles, with giant gags in their mouths. They must've been this way overnight. We hurried to pull the gags and remove their bindings as fast as we could.

"Everly! What is going on?" Jeeves' voice was hoarse, and it broke my heart to think of them screaming or calling out for help for so many hours.

Sean gave me the side eye. He'd warned me about this, and I didn't have an explanation ready. So I would turn the question back around to them, instead. At least until I thought up a plan.

"You tell me! Who did this to you? And are you hurt?" I turned Jeeves' wrists over in my hands, searching for any injuries before doing the same to Pierre. Pierre wasn't as outwardly appreciative, however. He wrinkled his brow as he examined my bird nightgown.

"Yes, we are fine. But the woman and the short man—they were searching for something. She wanted to kill us but the man said no. I am so thankful for the small little man." Pierre wiped his brow.

"I know this is gonna sound crazy," Jeeves ran a hand through his hair and took a deep breath, "but these weren't ordinary people. They—"

"Zip it!" Pierre warned sternly.

Sean and I exchanged looks. They saw the Olympians' powers. We were going to have to do something about that. But at least they weren't interested in talking about it for now.

Devon backed toward the door. He was never a fan of confrontation. "I'm gonna head back upstairs to get... uh... *you know*."

"Thanks." I nodded to him. "I'll get myself a glass of water ready." I had to hurry and take the pills before we teleported back to Porta Maris. We didn't have much time before they expected us for breakfast there. "Sean, can you run and see if the tablet is still here? It was in Driskell's room. I think Tate put some kind of glamour on it, so I'm hoping it's still there."

"I'm on it." He took off after Devon, leaving me alone with Millie's help.

"Should I call the cops?" Jeeves glanced back and forth between Pierre and me.

"No, Jeeves. It's fine. We'll get everything taken care of. But I need you to sit down so I can explain." I pulled out my phone to dial Tate. He needed to get over here as fast as possible to remove their memories of the Keepers. But after four rings, I remembered: Tate was gone. He'd gone back down to Agartha. "Shoot!" I slammed my phone down on the counter.

"Are you sure everything is okay, Everly? I really think I should call the cops."

"No." My voice came out louder than I'd intended. "Do not call the cops. I promise, I've got everything under control." Jeeves startled, and settled onto a barstool next to Pierre while I typed out a rapid-fire group text to Gayla and Dom asking them to get an Agarthian siren over here, stat.

Sean popped back through the door. "It's here." He patted his back pocket. "But I don't think it would be wise to take it to our final destination." He lifted his brows, hoping I'd understand. I had to agree with his assessment. Taking the tablet into Atlantis didn't sound like a great plan. But we couldn't leave it *here*, either—not with Olympians searching town for it.

"What about Porta Maris?" I asked.

Sean shrugged. "I guess that might be the safest option for now. Millie will know what to do with it."

"You know where Millie is?" Pierre asked.

I shushed him and looked back to the doorway in time to see Devon join us again. He tossed me my small bottle of pills, and I quickly swallowed one down, gulping the glass of water I'd prepared.

"Oh no, Ev. Please tell me you're not turning to drugs." Jeeves frowned.

"They're not drugs. I just..." I rubbed my temples. "I just need to think for a second."

My phone rang. Dom. I tossed it to Sean. "Here. You talk. I'm gonna go change clothes. I think we need to head straight for Atlantis. I don't want to waste anymore time eating pancakes by the sea or making special brownies. I've got a bad feeling. We need to hurry this along."

"Hang on." Jeeves held out a hand. "Did you just say—"

"Don't worry, Jeeves. You won't remember any of this." I turned back to Devon. "Keep an eye on them for a sec, please. I'll be right back."

Then I turned my back on my friends, leaving them to manage the chaos we'd created. It only took twenty-four hours for our whole world to get flipped on its head. Dom could get someone to help Jeeves and Pierre forget, but what about the rest of us? I wouldn't forget the insanity gleaming in that Olympian woman's eyes as she tried to throw Sean from the window, or the red face of the man who threw books and furniture at me and my friends. No, they were after something, and they were willing to go to drastic measures to get it.

If it was the tablet, that meant the stakes had been raised. Rossel let me keep it for a while, but he obviously wanted it back. I'd started something back at the warehouse, and I was afraid it might be something bigger than I was prepared to handle.

We had to get to Atlantis. We had to figure out what the prophecy said before Rossel and his Olympians got their hands on it again.

CHAPTER 3

WE WAITED AT MILLIE'S until Dom arrived with some Agarthian girl she'd gone to high school with. I gave them a quick rundown of what had happened the day before, and the girl promised she'd be able to clear Jeeves' and Pierre's memories without any difficulty.

I was more than a little nervous watching her work, but she stayed true to her word. Jeeves and Pierre remembered nothing when she finished. She even added a great little story about how I'd brought a kitten into Millie's house, which sent the dogs into a frenzy in her study, tearing up half of Millie's things in an effort to catch the cuddly little thing. After her work was done, the Agarthian girl left, leaving me alone with Dom, Jeeves, and Pierre.

I apologized for the mess, assured them the kitten was gone, then asked them to go to the store to get Millie more of that fancy cheese she liked so much as my apology gift. I bid them a silent goodbye as they left.

You'll see them again, I thought to myself. *Just don't die in Atlantis*.

"Be safe." Dom squeezed me tight, picking up on my nerves, no doubt. Devon and Sean reappeared as we were mid-hug, each wearing fresh clothes and carrying a small bag. Sean handed me his—a messenger bag holding my pills, the dagger I'd taken from Rossel, and a couple of snacks. Devon's bag was from Millie's closet, and I suspected it was packed especially for her. He was such a thoughtful little soulmate.

"I will," I promised. "Am I all blue?" I spun so they could examine my aura from all angles.

"You're blue," she assured me.

"Great. And who knows, with any luck the amplifying action of these pills might just come in handy when we're in Atlantis."

"Maybe so." Dom smiled and gave my hand a little squeeze before turning to Sean. "Don't let anything happen to her down there."

"I won't."

"About that..." Devon said. "How would you feel about going straight to Atlantis from here?"

"Right now?" I asked.

He nodded. "It took a little more out of me than I expected to get us here and then to Sean's apartment for fresh clothes. I'm not sure if we go back to Porta Maris that I'll have the strength to get you into Atlantis this morning, too. That's a lot of traveling on low energy."

Sean shrugged. "It's up to you, Ev. We can take the long way there down the Bimini Road if you're feeling brave. Or we can just go in with Devon later tonight."

"I don't want to wait until later." I turned to Devon. "Would you be able to look after the tablet for us? Just bring it to Millie. She'll know how to keep it safe. And look out for Driskell, too, please. He doesn't like staying in Porta Maris, but we need to make sure he doesn't leave. I'm worried about him, even though I know it's the safest place for him right now."

"Of course I will." Devon nodded. "Even if Millie and I decide to come back to New York, I'll make it a point to check on Driskell everyday until you're back."

"Thank you."

"Anything else?" Devon asked.

I thought for a minute. There was one other thing, but I wasn't sure if Devon had enough self-control to handle it on his own. "Yes," I said, turning to Dom. "There's this guy named Tano in Porta Maris." Devon stiffened again beside me. "Make sure Devon doesn't kill him."

"You have my word," she said, pinning Devon with a hard gaze.

"Alright then. Let's do this."

Devon stretched out his hands, and Sean and I took hold of them. I cast one final glance in Dom's direction before I plunged into the frigid split of our world.

When I opened my eyes again I was submerged in what felt like hundreds of miles of water. I hadn't been prepared for this and choked, holding my breath and trying to cough out the water that remained in my throat without actually opening my mouth.

Sean grabbed me by the shoulders and smiled. "Breathe."

His voice was loud and clear, not garbled by the water or strangled by his lack of oxygen. Sean was breathing freely in the water. Devon, too. And something inside of me felt at ease—at peace with the whole situation, even though my mind was shouting at me to seek dry land.

"I can't," I said. The water filled my mouth, but the choking sensation abated. My body welcomed the salty water. Craved it, even. I was one with the sea, and the sea with me.

Sean grinned. "There you go. You don't have to worry about breathing here. Your body handles it for you. Just like it allows you to see through the darkness and resist the pressure of the water above you."

"How far down are we?"

"About seven miles below the ocean's surface. There's no light here, and mortals would be crushed by the pressure. They haven't even gotten subs this deep, though they've gotten close," Devon said.

"Yes they have," Sean argued. "They just don't remember it. Our council does a good job of helping the mortals forget anything they shouldn't see."

"Speaking of not seeing things," I interrupted, "where is Atlantis? I thought it was supposed to be the size of a giant city or a small country."

"It's here." Sean turned and gestured toward a small cave to my right. "You just can't see it. It's been enchanted to remain hidden forever to all who are not welcome here. But the fact that you're able to talk and breathe and... you know... *not be crushed* means you'll be fine. They'll let you right in."

We treaded water above what looked to be random stones on the ocean floor, but upon closer inspection I realized it was actually a broken path of some sort. "Is this the road you mentioned earlier?" I asked Sean.

"Yep. The Bimini Road. It'll take you right past Porta Maris if you follow it long enough."

"But don't worry. You won't have to," Devon said. "There are plenty of messengers in there who should be able to get you back home. Just have them send the bill to Millie."

"Is this goodbye then?"

"For now. But like I promised, I'll check on Driskell everyday and make sure nothing crazy is going on while you're gone." Devon grinned. "Now do us proud in there. Get that missing piece so we can get ready for our next adventure."

"You make it sound so easy." I gave Devon a quick hug and whispered in his ear. "Take care of Millie, too, okay?"

He nodded. "Will do. Good luck guys!" And in a flash, he was gone.

Sean and I turned toward the cave a few yards away. "After you." He gestured for me to go ahead. Though it should have been pitch black, my eyes somehow allowed me to see through the murky waters of the cave. It was empty save for a small school of fish that dashed away as we approached. We'd only been swimming for a minute or so when I saw two faint blue glows up ahead.

"Those are the guards," Sean whispered. "We're almost there."

"Name?" A woman's voice called out as we neared. Her aura was a lighter blue than the man's across from her. But the way the light played off the walls of the cave was mesmerizing.

"Sean Bratton."

"Everly Gordon."

"And what's the purpose of your visit?" The woman's eyes scanned us and I prayed my aura still appeared blue under the water.

"Everly has just recently gotten her powers, so I wanted to show her Atlantis for the first time."

"I see," said the woman. Her gaze was sharp and lingering, and I struggled to stay calm. I felt like I'd been caught with my hand in the cookie jar when she looked at me like that.

"Well, make sure you take her by Café de la Mer in the second ring. Cherise's croissants are to die for!" The male guard's voice startled me. I'd almost forgotten he was there.

"Are you really going to bring up the croissants again?" The woman finally turned away from me, putting her hands on her hips as she frowned at the other soldier. "It was an accident, okay?"

I glanced at Sean who shrugged with a grin. "So can we proceed?" he asked the guards.

"Go ahead." The woman waved us through and immediately began jesting with the other guard again. We swam past them and around a corner, where I stopped dead in my wake.

"What is that?" We stared into what looked like a shimmering wall, fully illuminated by something unseen on the other side.

"*That* is Altantis." And without another word, Sean disappeared through the wall.

CHAPTER 4

IT TOOK ALL OF two heartbeats for me to panic. No, panic wasn't the right word. I was mad. Sean brought me all the way down here, seven miles under the sea and past some goofy guards just to leave me stranded here in this cave? *I don't think so.*

I took one deep breath and dove toward the wall after him, not giving myself a chance to consider what might be on the other side, and I landed with a hard thud in the open air.

"Graceful as always," Sean said with a chuckle.

"You could have waited—" I stopped mid-tirade as I realized where we were. Sean and I stood at the top of a craggy cliffside overlooking a world like I could have never imagined. Our feet were planted firmly on solid ground, we were somehow completely dry, and we breathed oxygen from the clear air, but I could still see the ripples of the Atlantic ocean rolling around us. We were in a massive bubble of sorts, so large that I couldn't see the other side. The distant border was trimmed with jagged mountains higher than the Rockies and more treacherous than the Himalayas. But between here and there sat a modern city designed in concentric rings circling out from a white palace in the very center.

The earth was green and lush with plants and flowers intricately placed throughout well-designed gardens, and though daylight seemed to fill the air, it wasn't quite like the light I knew from the earth above. There was no sun—no discernible source of energy that emitted the light. Instead, it was like the territory had an aura of its own.

"Welcome to Atlantis," Sean said. "Come on, I'll show you around, and then we can try to find a way into the palace."

He led me over to a steep stone stairwell that took us down the cliffside. "So the palace sits on the central island, as I'm sure you've noticed. It's the home of Maxwell and Gloriana, our leaders, and their daughter, Anasasha."

"I thought they had two children." I remembered Sean mentioning something about the royal family, who they didn't actually call "royal," once before.

"Their son is the youngest, so he's moved on to stay with cousins somewhere in Europe. Second children of the monarchs don't exactly have a purpose in the territories. They're kind of useless, really. Just supposed to sit tight somewhere safe in case something ever happens to the next-in-line for the throne."

"Tate doesn't sit off to the side, playing it safe."

"Tate's situation is a little different. But let's focus on Atlantis. The central island houses all of the courtiers and official buildings. That's where we'll find my father and hopefully our ticket into the palace. He stays in an apartment building for the council men and women while he's on business here in the main territory."

"Wait. How is Tate's situation different?" I paused on the steps, partly to catch my breath because there were like a million stairs, and partly because Sean had piqued my curiosity about Tate's background even more.

"Tate's older brother is... *well...* let's just say that a lot of people don't believe he's fit to lead. So certain members of the Agarthian council have made it their duty to show Tate's worth to the King, in the hopes that he will be chosen to lead instead. But the king is very stuck in his ways. He's a firm believer in tradition. So there's a rift in their ranks and Tate is caught in the middle of it."

"Hmm." It still seemed like I was missing a big part of the story, but that was more than anyone had ever told me before. I'd start watching for other clues regarding the Agarthian power structure when we got back home, but for now I needed to remain focused on the task before me.

"Okay. So tell me about the rest of Atlantis. What am I looking at with all these circles?" A ring of water circled the inner island. Around that was another ring of land, and the pattern repeated twice more. There was the island with the palace and a total of four rings of land circling out from it, all connected by bridges.

"Ah, that's just the rest of the city. You'll see a mix of residential areas and businesses. There are different neighborhoods on the various rings, for example the finance district is on ring one with some of the fancier restaurants and shopping. And the agricultural areas are primarily on the outer ring, just because it's the largest and least convenient for traveling. But really it's kind of a mixed bag. See the boats floating through all the canals? That's the main mode of transportation here. Well, that and the messenger service. It would take half a day to walk from the outer ring to the palace on foot, even with the bridge system. That's where the messengers make their money."

"That's fascinating." I admired the architecture as we finally reached the bottom of the stone stairwell—sleek and solid, but somehow completely cohesive with the more delicate gardens surrounding the structures. It was truly like nothing I'd ever seen before. And there were people, or *Atlanteans* I supposed, everywhere. The stairs took us straight into an open air marketplace, which made sense with Sean's description of this outer ring being mostly agricultural.

The marketplace was bustling, and the stairs we'd come down turned into a sidewalk that led right alongside one of the canals that cut through this ring. A large boat was being loaded with produce down in the water below.

"How far in are you going?" Sean asked one of the men loading up a box of greens.

"All the way to the center," the man replied. "But I've only got one seat left." His bushy brows gathered in the middle as he glanced my way.

"That's okay," I said, sidling up close to Sean and taking his hand. "I'll just sit in his lap." I nuzzled my nose along his jawline, trying not to pull back at the scratch of his two-day baby beard.

The man set down his box and grinned at us. "Newly found soulmates?"

"Are we that obvious?" I asked, pushing out my lips into a little pout.

The man laughed. "Go ahead," he said, waving us on.

Sean yanked his hand away from mine the second we were out of sight on the stairs taking us below deck. "Gross," he gritted through his teeth. "Your breath smells awful."

"I didn't have a toothbrush at Millie's place this morning. Be nice. At least I got us on the boat." We entered the passenger area below and I grabbed his hand again as we searched for the open seat. But unfortunately for us, we never got that far.

"Sean! Everly!"

This time *I* was the one who dropped *his* hand like a hot coal. "Is that..."

"Hi mom." Sean's face reddened. "What are you doing here?"

"I could ask you the same." Claudia's voice carried like she was speaking into a microphone. She only had one volume, and it was loud. The woman next to her looked up from the book she held with a frown.

"When did you get your powers?" Claudia's gaze zeroed in on me.

"Uh, just last week."

"That's why we're here," Sean said. "Everly's having a hard time in her history class at school, so I thought I'd bring her here to give her better context and show her some of the artifacts and things in person."

"Huh." Claudia's mouth didn't fully close as her eyes still grazed over me, like she was looking for a chink in my armor. Then, as if shaking herself out of a daze, she turned back to Sean. "Well I'm so glad you're here. I have been busting myself trying to help your father prepare for the convention coming up, and I just don't think there's any way we'll be able to get everything ready in time on our own. Any chance you two might be willing to help while you're here?"

"Actually, we—"

"Would love to." Sean nudged me in the side as he interrupted my objection. Following his lead, I flashed my prettiest smile to Claudia.

"Just let us know how we can help."

The woman next to Claudia closed her book with a huff. "Would you like to trade seats?"

"Sure," Sean said. "We're uh..." He scanned the small passenger area until he landed on a single seat across the aisle. "There."

"Just one seat?" Claudia raised a brow.

"It was all they had," Sean grumbled as he slid in next to his mother.

What was already going to be an uncomfortable ride on Sean's knee just grew ten times worse. But at least we were on the right track. Sean knew what he was doing. By agreeing to help his dad with the report, we were one step closer to accessing the palace and any hidden artifacts within. That missing piece of the tablet would be mine in no time.

CHAPTER 5

CLAUDIA TALKED THROUGH THE entire ride. Everyone within a ten foot radius knew that her husband was preparing a presentation for the Annual Order of the Keepers conference. She mentioned it to anyone with ears. But just underneath her outward display of hubris, she was actually a bundle of nerves.

"I just don't know how they expect him to be able to gather all the information he needs with the hours they have him working," she explained as we stepped off the boat. I only half-heard the rest of her complaints. It was difficult to stay focused with the towering white palace shimmering before me.

It was almost iridescent, like the whole palace was inlaid with mother of pearl. From where we stood, we could see people within the building, moving to and fro through open air passageways and across some of its numerous balconies.

"This is amazing," I whispered.

"Ah, yes," Claudia said with a careless wave of her hand. "Welcome to the Atlantean Palace, home of our dearest leader, Maxwell." There was more than a hint of sarcasm in her tone.

"Do they just let anyone in?" I asked as I followed her up a stone pathway toward the two story double doors at the front entrance.

The palace was maybe a quarter of a mile back from the canal, but it was so huge that I felt like we were standing on its doorstep. Other Atlanteans scattered as they exited the boat, taking sidewalks around the palace and into the rest of the central island. But I couldn't be concerned with what lay behind it. The structure was too breathtaking for me to pull my eyes away.

"The first floor is open to the public," Sean explained. "There are a couple of offices and a small museum inside, and a large garden out back. The leader's residence makes up the top two floors, and the second and third floors are reserved for members of the council to do their business."

"But as the family of a *councilman*, we are granted access to the middle floors as well. Which is great, because we need to use the library to access the records required for Desmond's presentation." With a haughty toss of her hair over her shoulder, Claudia marched ahead, straight for the palace doors, like she owned the place.

"But I'm not family," I said, scurrying up the steps after her. Sean offered an apologetic shrug, but Claudia gave no response.

"Hey mom, Everly's right. I'm not sure it's right to ask her to help out with dad's presentation. I mean, we weren't really planning on coming all this way to hang out in the library."

"Trust me." Claudia stopped dead in her tracks and spun around to face us. "If you help us with this, I will make sure you get to see far more history than any of the museums can offer. Don't forget, Sean. With a good presentation, we can expect a good *promotion*, which will lead to additional benefits a standard councilman couldn't dream of. Please. You have no idea how important this is to your father and me. We have been waiting a long time for an opportunity like this. This is our chance to get in tight with Maxwell."

I sent a pleading look in Sean's direction. If what Claudia said was true, then maybe it would be in our best interest to help them out. We had no idea where the missing piece of the tablet could be right now. But if Sean's family got closer to the leaders, maybe we'd have a better shot at finding it.

"Alright. Show us what to do." Sean's shoulders drooped, but he fell quietly into place behind his mother.

I worked to keep my jaw shut as we strode through the palace. There was too much to see and not enough time to take it all in. It was such an interesting mix of natural materials like abalone and coral combined with all of the conveniences of modern technology. Screens filled one wall, showing a twenty-hour news cycle from countries all over the world. The palace was illuminated by the same unseen light source as the rest of the city, and I couldn't tell if it was magic or just some advanced technology that they had yet to share with the mortals.

Without warning, Claudia stopped again maybe ten yards away from a set of crystal-looking doors and the two guards who stood in front of them. She pulled Sean and I close and dropped her voice. "I probably should get this approved before telling you, but the information we need is not actually in the second floor library. There's another." She glanced quickly over her shoulder at the guards. "In the basement."

"We don't have approval to go down there," Sean said.

"I took a test when your father was last promoted. I'm not sure if the privilege extends to you by default or not, but I know one of these guards personally. I'll see what I can do."

I admired a grand staircase along the wall as they spoke. The steps were inlaid with the same mother of pearl as the exterior of the palace, and crystals dotted the banister, glittering in the mysterious light of the massive space and sending a mosaic of colors across the walls. Two more guards who stood sentry at the bottom watched our quiet discussion with cautious eyes.

"Whatever we do, we should keep things moving. These whispers are drawing unwanted attention." I tilted my head back toward the guards in what I hoped was a totally natural and not-at-all suspicious looking move.

Claudia frowned. "Follow my lead."

With a big fake smile plastered on her pretty face, she approached the first guards by the crystal doors. "Morning, fellas." She pushed her thumb onto a keypad outside the doors. A small light flashed green, and the guards pulled the doors open for her. "Thank you!"

Claudia gestured for Sean and me to go ahead, but one of the guards held out the staff in his hands, blocking our way. "Sorry Mrs. Bratton, we'll have to scan you in one at a time."

Claudia huffed. "We're in a bit of a hurry. They're with me, Marcus." She tried once again to shoo us on through the doors ahead of her, but the guards wouldn't relent.

A shuffling of feet drew my attention back toward the stairs while she argued with her guard friend. The two of them went back and forth about the rules and Claudia's precious time, but I lost track of what they were saying as I watched a new crowd of guards descending the stairs. They were dressed a bit more formally than those on the first floor, and it only took a moment for me to realize why. In the center of their small circle, wearing a shimmering floor length gown that I only thought existed in fairy tales, was a young, auburn-haired woman.

"They call her the water princess," Sean whispered behind me. "But rumor is she hates the nickname."

"So that's Maxwell's daughter? Anasasha?"

As though she heard my softly spoken words, her head turned in our direction at the sound of her name. Her eyes were as blue as her gown, and her lips as red as her hair. I guessed she was approximately our age, if not slightly younger.

A look of innocent curiosity flitted across her delicate features as she took me in, but then her eyes landed on Sean and her body language changed completely. She pointed toward us, whispering in the ear of one of her guards, who looked our way as she spoke. Then they were headed this way.

"Hey mom..." Sean placed a hand on Claudia's shoulder, but she was too busy arguing with the guards to pay him any mind. "Mom."

The footsteps were nearing us, and Claudia still had no idea. It wasn't until her friend Marcus shifted his gaze over her shoulder and stood at attention that she finally shut up.

"What is going on here?" Anasasha's voice was surprisingly deep and raspy for such a delicate looking thing.

"My apologies." Marcus dropped into a deep bow. "We had a small misunderstanding, but there are no issues. Our people here were just leaving. I assure you they will not cause any additional interruptions to your morning."

"On the contrary." Ansasha grinned, pinning her eyes on Sean again. "I haven't been bothered at all. I'm quite intrigued to see some new faces in the palace."

Sean's cheeks reddened, and I had to bite the inside of my lip to keep from laughing. But Claudia recognized what was going through the princess's head immediately. She straightened her shoulders, pulling back into the overconfident stance she held so well.

"What an honor it is to be graced by your presence," Claudia cooed.

Anasasha turned an appraising gaze in her direction. "What is it that you seek in my palace today?"

"We simply wanted to access the basement library. My husband needs some records for a presentation your father has asked him to give at the convention."

Anasasha turned to the guards. "Well, let them go," she said simply.

"Only one of the three has clearance."

"I see." She drank in the sight of Sean once again before turning back to the guard. "And do you have reason to doubt the integrity of these people?"

"We don't. It's just protocol. Your father has systems in place to ensure the—"

Anasasha waved him off. "I don't care about the protocol. If this is an issue of a security clearance, then perhaps we should find another way to gain my father's confidence in their loyalty. I'll arrange a meeting with him."

Claudia perked up, her lips pulling into a pleased little smirk.

"Tonight," Anasasha added. She turned and smiled at Sean. "Would you like to join me for dinner this evening?"

"I—I think, uh..." Sweat glistened on his forehead as he stammered.

"Of course we would." Claudia dipped into an awkward curtsy. "Thank you so much for the generous invitation."

"It will be my pleasure. Seven o'clock. Marcus will meet you here at the bottom of the steps and take you up to the dining hall. I am looking forward to it very much." Her gaze lingered on Sean for longer than was comfortable, even for me. But eventually, she and her entourage disappeared through the hall, greeting other Atlanteans who explored the vignettes of the first floor of the palace.

"Holy cow, Sean." I nudged him once I was certain she was out of earshot. "I don't know how you get all these gorgeous ladies fawning all over you, but I'm sure glad that you do."

Claudia ruffled his hair. "Bratton men have always had a way with the ladies. Your father is going to be thrilled when he hears about this. I'll go tell him now. You two can go find a museum or whatever it was you were planning to do, but make sure you're back here in time for dinner. And here." She reached into her purse and pulled out a card. "Buy yourselves something decent to wear tonight." She gave a soft squeal. "There's no way they'll overlook our promotion after this!"

CHAPTER 6

"ARE YOU SURE I'M not under dressed?" I fussed with my hair, ducking so I could see my reflection in the compact mirror I had stacked on a pile of books.

"You're fine. Gloriana insists on their family dressing like royalty, but no one else does. I think she's a little bitter that they're the only Keeper leaders who don't call themselves kings and queens. You definitely don't have to dress like them. In fact, the wider the gap between our social status and theirs, the better her mood will probably be."

"She sounds like a peach." I closed my compact and took a look at Sean, whose nose was buried in a book. He'd rushed me through what I hoped would be a fun-filled day of exploring Atlantean shops and fashions, just to hurry me back into the second floor library for a quick cram session before dinner.

I tucked the compact back into the messenger bag I'd brought with me from Millie's house, right next to my aura-changing pills and the dagger, then hid the entire bag behind some giant reference books in a little used area of the library. I would have to hope it would be safe there until after our meal.

We didn't have time to book a hotel room before the dinner. Apparently hotels for lowly "guardians" like us were on the second ring of Atlantis, and it would have taken too long to get there and back before we needed to be ready. Which reminded me... "It's almost time to go."

"I know," Sean said, crinkling his brow. "I just want to make sure I get this right."

He'd spent the last half hour studying up on everything that had ever been written about Maxwell and his family. He was treating this dinner like it was the most important test of his life. And I supposed it was, if you stopped to consider that the future of our people hung in the balance of the prophecy. Getting on Maxwell's good side would take us one step closer to finding the missing piece so we could get out of here and move on with saving the world or whatever I was supposed to do as the Deliverer.

But while we were here, I planned to live it up. "So what does Atlantean royalty eat for dinner? Selkie pie? Nessie stew?"

Sean closed his book and shot me a disapproving look.

"Ooh! Maybe some Kraken cake for dessert?"

"Please don't embarrass me tonight." He placed the books back on the shelves where he got them and led me out into the hall.

Sean put some effort into his appearance for the dinner with his hair combed to the side in a classic but sophisticated style that suited him. He wore new navy slacks and a crisp white shirt that was buttoned one hole too high. I had to admit, he didn't look half bad for getting himself ready in a public bathroom. Which was good, because our likelihood of getting in good with the royal family was probably more dependent on Anasasha and how much she enjoyed admiring Sean's physique than any real qualifications.

With that in mind, I decided to make some adjustments. I stopped him before we reached the door and undid another button at the top of his shirt, exposing a small hint of his chest, then gently tousled his hair. "Whether I say something embarrassing or not, I don't think it's possible to make you look bad in the eyes of the water princess. I thought I might have to wipe her drool away earlier."

Sean rolled his eyes and kept walking. I hurried to keep up, my silver heels clicking on the hard floors behind him. My dress was simple—a pale muted blue sheath with just a hint of shimmer when I moved. It would have been great for a night out at a restaurant back home, but I still wasn't convinced that it would be up to snuff at a royal dinner. Or, *almost royal*, anyway.

Claudia met us downstairs, wearing something between my casual cocktail attire and Anasasha's royal gown from earlier. It was a floor length emerald green number with a high collar and a mermaid style flare at the bottom. Fitting for an Atlantean.

"You look wonderful!" Claudia gushed over Sean as though I wasn't even there. And that was just fine with me. I was perfectly content staying under the radar here. "I know how you hate being the center of attention, but I need you to lean into it tonight, mmkay? Play nice with the princess, and maybe she'll play nice with us."

"I wouldn't call her princess." The guard Claudia argued with earlier stood tall at the bottom of the stairs that led up to the leader's private family residence. "Not if you want her to *play nice*." He cut a harsh look in Claudia's direction.

"Oh, you know what I mean, Marcus. We just want everyone to enjoy themselves."

He led us up the glossy stairs, into a wide hall with polished white stone floors that glittered with sterling silver veins running through them. Another set of double stairs lay ahead, which I assumed led up to the bedrooms and personal suites of the family. From where we stood, the grand hall opened into several other large rooms. The dining room was on the left.

It held an expansive bleached wood table, adorned with crystal goblets and fine linens. Two large chandeliers hung overhead, a dazzling combination of shells and crystals, with an occasional piece of blue sea glass for dramatic flair. Marcus gestured for us to go in, and we found seats in the middle of the table, leaving those at the head open for the "not royal" family.

We'd just pulled out our chairs when the doors at the opposite end of the room opened. In strode two guards, followed by a curvy woman in a pewter colored ball gown with fiery red curls piled high atop her head. Her eyes were a green that rivaled Sean's, but icy as she took us in. Anasasha came in after her mother, with more guards behind her. There was no sign of Maxwell.

Marcus fell into a deep bow and made formal introductions. "Mrs. Gloriana Ligon, wife of Maxwell Ligon, leader of Atlantis, and their daughter Anasasha."

The latter swept her gaze across the dining room until she landed on Sean, and her pretty rouge lips curled into a feline grin.

Poor Sean. I wondered if he knew he was just man-candy to her.

"Claudia Bratton, wife of councilman and level two security guard Peter Bratton, and her son, Sean. And Ms. Everly Gordon, niece of healer Mildred Gordon of Manhattan."

My chest tightened at my introduction. Marcus hadn't asked for my name or any personal information, so this must have all come straight from Claudia. And of course she didn't mention my mother—I'd always gotten the sense that Claudia looked down on me and my background.

I watched Gloriana's reaction as well. But if the name rang any bells, she gave no indication of it. There was a small chance my mother was concealed in some secret enchanted prison here, but Gloriana didn't seem to know about it if she was.

"You can sit here, Sean." Anasasha gestured toward the chair beside her and a guard immediately stepped forward to pull it out for Sean. Gloriana took a seat at the head of the table, with Anasasha and Sean to her right. Claudia immediately moved to the chair to Gloriana's left, which put me across from Sean.

Gloriana's lips pursed as we took our seats, and I swore I saw the hint of an eye roll as she noticed her daughter's attention pinned to Sean. "Sit up straight, Anasasha. You look like a commoner all hunched over that way."

"Yes, mother." The girl's jaw hardened as she obeyed. Another young woman appeared from the kitchen, carrying a silver platter full of salad plates. I lifted my brows at Sean, excited to see what kind of strange creatures might adorn my bed of lettuce, but it was a typical dinner salad. Delicious—but not especially unique in any way.

Anasasha peppered Sean with questions as we ate. Where did he go to school? What was he studying? What was New York really like? Did he have any siblings? How often does he come to Atlantis?

Sean kept his answers short and to the point, but Claudia elaborated on his behalf any chance she got. That woman just loved to hear herself talk. She was trying a little too hard to make their family seem important, and Gloriana noticed.

Midway through the main course, Gloriana set down her fork and turned to Claudia, who positively beamed under the direct attention until she realized she was about to be grilled.

"Tell me about your family, Claudia."

She straightened in her chair. "My husband, Peter, has been a valued member of the council for a little over a century, now. He has done so well, in fact, that they've asked him to—"

Gloriana shook her head and waved her hand for Claudia to stop talking. "No. I mean your parents. Your background. Where did *you* grow up?"

"Oh," Claudia giggled with a quiver in her voice. "There's not much to tell there, really. Just a normal childhood. Everly has a much more exciting history than I do."

I could've kicked her under the table had I been better situated in my seat. It seemed Gloriana had touched on a hot topic with Claudia's family history. I'd have to file that away for later.

The calculating green eyes of the matriarch of Atlantis focused on me, her thin auburn brows flicking up in feigned interest. "Really? You're so young. Tell me, what makes your history so exciting?"

Sean tensed across the table from me. I couldn't tell if it was from Gloriana's questioning or the way her daughter's hand had found its way to the back of his chair, where she now lightly ran her fingers back and forth across the tops of his shoulders.

"I don't know that I'd call it exciting. I was raised by my mother in a small town in Oklahoma, and I just recently came into my powers when I moved to New York with my aunt for college."

"Oklahoma? Interesting." Gloriana dabbed at her mouth with a cloth napkin. "I can't recall any official business in that part of the country. Tell me what it is your mother does for us."

"She was a messenger." I debated whether or not to say more, but ultimately decided to see how this played out. If Gloriana knew something about her whereabouts, I should be able to pick up on it from her expressions or tone. Otherwise, I could scratch Atlantis off the list of potential Keeper prisons holding my mother captive.

I didn't really expect her to be here, anyway. Rossel was the last person I saw with my mother. If she was locked away, it was almost certainly in Olympus, which was unfortunate. As an Atlantean, I'd never be able to access the Olympian territory. I'd have to find another way to break her out.

"*Was* a messenger?" Gloriana sat a little taller in her chair. "Has she passed?"

"No, actually. She's—"

"Traveling." Claudia leaned forward to block my line of sight with Gloriana. "She's traveling. Being an empty nester now... she thought it would be good to get out of Oklahoma. And who can blame her really?" She laughed, an insidious sound that instantly left me suspicious.

I had no reason to suspect Claudia had anything to do with my mother's disappearance, but her behavior tonight was odd. First she drew

Gloriana's attention to me and my family, then instantly turned her away from the truth. What was Claudia hiding? And more importantly, did my aunt Millie know?

The rest of the dinner was a blur. My mind was too busy working through the many new questions I had to focus on Claudia's obnoxious story telling or Gloriana's glazed over eyes. I couldn't even delight in Anasasha's over-the-top flirting with Sean, or the way their hands were entwined as we finally stood from the dining table.

"So you see, Mrs. Ligon, it would be very beneficial for everyone in the council if you would be so kind as to grant my son and our dear family friend access to the basement library. The information we compile will be of great use to everyone in attendance at the annual conference." Claudia mustered up as much poise as she had to win Gloriana's blessing and grant us the security clearance we required. She'd dropped hints about it all through the supper, but this was the first time she'd asked for Gloriana's blessing outright.

"It may be." Gloriana pursed her full lips. "But it would be especially beneficial to your husband who you believe to be *incapable* of doing the work on his own. What did you say his name was again? Peter Bratton?"

The color blanched from Claudia's face. "Yes."

"Very well. You may all have the clearance you need to access the basement library and prevent your husband from falling behind in his duties. I'll make note of our discussion with Maxwell, so that he is aware of where our level two guards are lacking. Is there anything else?"

"No ma'am." Claudia looked like she might cry. Her plan had backfired.

"Actually, mother..." Anasasha looped her arm through Sean's. "Sean mentioned that he and his friend were going to stay in a hotel while they were here. Could we possibly put them up in some guest rooms here in the palace, instead?" The fire in her eyes fooled no one, and especially not her mother. Anasasha curved her body closer to Sean so that they were touching, and I'd never seen him look so uncomfortable.

But Gloriana was so eager to end the evening that she simply waved her hand in the air as she exited the room. "Let it be done," she called out over her shoulder.

Anasasha squealed with delight and Sean looked sicker than his mother, who was already sulking back to the stairs.

"Wait, mom. Didn't you say you needed us to help you with something tonight? We don't have to stay here." Sean's question sounded more like a plea for help.

"No." She turned around, her expression hard and a new ferocity in her eyes. "You will help me more by staying here." Her gaze flicked over to Anasasha and back to her son. "I'll meet you downstairs at eight o'clock tomorrow morning. We'll go to the library then."

Sean was frozen to the spot as his mother disappeared. This was a side of her I'd never seen, and I was appalled at the insinuation in her silent command. I wouldn't stand for it. I wouldn't let her walk all over my friend like that.

No longer caring how Anasasha felt, I waltzed right up to Sean and took his hand in mine, pulling him away from her and toward the staircase. "We'll only need one room." I smiled sweetly at the girl, ignoring the burning glare I earned in return. But the soft squeeze of Sean's hand in mine was all the thanks I needed.

I didn't believe in using other people for personal gain, and I refused to let Claudia hang Sean out like a piece of bait. Who cared if it angered Anasasha? Claudia had ruined her husband's chance at a promotion all on her own, and pleasing Maxwell's daughter wouldn't do anything to erase her mistake.

Anasasha stomped up the stairs, and one of the palace maids showed Sean and me to our room. Thankfully the bed was king-sized, so we never had to touch. And I had a full night to try and come up with a new plan for trying to locate the missing piece of the tablet.

CHAPTER 7

"I THINK WE SHOULD stick to the original plan, at least until we see how this plays out." Sean pulled on a dirty sock from the day before. All we had were the clothes we came to Atlantis wearing, shoved inside shopping bags from our trip to the boutiques for formal wear the day before.

The messenger bag I'd brought from Millie's house was untouched, and I breathed a sigh of relief to find everything still tucked safely inside after retrieving it from the library first thing this morning. My aura would only remain blue for one more day before I'd need another dose of the pills Millie made for me. I certainly didn't want anyone in the palace to see my white aura.

"We have access to some high security areas now. Even if it's just a room full of boring legal documents, there may be something useful in the basement library. After all, it wouldn't be on the high security floor if there wasn't *something* juicy in there right?"

"Right, but I don't know how much exploring we'll get to do while we're pretending to help your dad with his report. And after last night..." *What was a nice way to tell Sean I didn't trust his mom?* I chewed the inside of my lip, trying to think of something polite before finally just coming out with it. "I don't trust your mom."

He laughed. "I'm not sure I do after last night either. She was pushing me at the water princess pretty hard." I didn't find it nearly as funny as Sean did. "But why are *you* feeling that way?"

I pulled my feet up onto the bed, sitting cross-legged atop the duvet while Sean got his shoes on. "I've just been going over some of the things she said last night, and it has me wondering... do you think it's possible she might have something to do with my mother's disappearance?"

"No. I really don't. But you obviously have some suspicions. What did she say to you?"

"It was the way she butted in so fast to tell Gloriana my mother was traveling. It just seemed weird, especially since she had just directed the conversation to me and my family."

Sean joined me on the bed. "She drew attention to you to avoid talking about her past. I love my mom, but she is a ridiculously selfish woman. She spends every minute of every day trying to get ahead in life. Her dad, my grandpa, was pretty shady. He got involved in the wrong crowd and wound up getting himself killed before I was born. My mom will do anything to avoid telling anyone that story. She likes to pretend she's always been from the upper class."

"But why would she lie about my mother's disappearance?"

"Because if Gloriana knew she was missing it might have made her wonder if *your* family was wrapped up in some kind of criminal circle, too. You're with me, and I bet my mom just wanted you to look just as rosy as the make-believe world she pretends she came from. She's sensitive to that kind of stuff."

"If you say so." I wasn't so sure I believed it, but then I also couldn't see any motive for Claudia to abduct my mom. "Alright, back to the plan... are you thinking we should just search the library for any hint of the prophecy while we're supposed to be helping your dad?"

"I guess. I've never been down there before. I'm not even sure what he does in the basement."

"He's a guard, right? So he must be protecting something *important*." I lifted my brows, but Sean shook his head.

"There's no way it'll be that easy."

"But what if it is? What if we walk down those stairs and find your dad standing in front of the broken tablet piece, up on a pedestal under the lights, just waiting for us to take it?"

Sean snorted. "Keep dreaming."

Obviously, I was wrong. There was no pedestal. No tablet. Not even any overhead lights—just the same mysterious brightness that filled the rest of

Atlantis.

I had to bite my tongue as Claudia inquired about Sean's evening with the princess on our walk down the basement stairs. Part of me wanted to kick out a leg and trip her. There was no way my mother would have ever put me in the situation Claudia put Sean in. He was right. She operated purely out of selfish gain. And yet it was *my mom* who had been kidnapped and locked away. The world really wasn't fair.

Marcus let us down into the basement now that we had Gloriana's blessing, and with all the hoops we had to jump through to get it, I guess I'd expected something more interesting. Instead, what we found at the bottom of the stairs was a small lobby leading into a sterile looking hall lined with doors. It resembled an old Oklahoma high school more than a high security floor of a supernatural palace under the sea. I was a little disappointed.

A plain desk was situated off to the side of the lobby, and behind it sat another guard, only this one wasn't Atlantean. "Is that an Olympian?" I asked Sean quietly as his mother approached the blond-haired man.

"Yep. There aren't many other races here, but occasionally someone will formally withdraw from their own territory. The wards on Atlantis keep out anyone with ill intent, so we know they are loyal to us here, or else they'd be killed. We employ them, but once they pledge themselves to Atlantis, they can never leave—not even to visit the mortal lands."

"Is it the same in the other territories? You can't enter unless your intentions are good?"

Sean nodded. "You've got to be the territory's primary race or willing to dedicate the rest of your life to serve them. That's why it's so rare."

"But why would anyone choose to leave their own people behind?" I turned my gaze back to the Olympian guard, who was now speaking into an intercom.

Sean shrugged. "People have their reasons."

Dom wasn't kidding when she'd told me before that it would be very difficult to access other Keeper territories. But I didn't realize I'd have to dedicate my life to them just to enter. That would certainly complicate things.

Claudia turned away from the guard with a roll of her eyes. "They insist that we can't enter the library without your father, even though I told him that Gloriana herself gave us clearance to be here."

"That's alright," Sean said, stepping forward to calm his mother. "I'm sure dad won't mind letting us in."

Sean was wrong. His dad did mind. Very much. We heard his footsteps pounding down the hall before we ever saw him. And when he finally rounded the corner I realized where Sean had inherited his guardian physique. Peter Bratton was a hulk of a man, and at the moment he looked like he might want to smash something.

"Claudia." His tone was venomous. "What are you doing down here? I told you I didn't need your help, and yet you came anyway." His eyes cut over sharply to where Sean and I stood. "With our son. And who are you?"

"Everly Gordon, sir. Nice to meet you." I extended a hand which he ignored.

"You *do* need our help," Claudia interjected. "Especially now. We've got to make this the best presentation any guard has ever given. Let us get started so you can get back to work."

From the look on Peter's face, I knew she'd already confessed her blunder from the night before. He was seething as he cut his eyes over to me again. "I can understand why *they'd* want to help, seeing as how my paycheck puts those expensive clothes on their backs. But what's in it for you?"

"Nothing." I shrugged. "I was here with Sean, exploring Atlantis when your wife asked us to help. We've got the extra time, so I thought I'd contribute however I can."

His gaze narrowed and I tried my best to keep an innocent smile on my face. I wanted to look friendly and helpful and naive, like a normal girl who wasn't secretly going to search for ancient artifacts as soon as he turned his back.

"Fine. But only because they've got me scheduled to stand guard for sixty hours over the next week."

"What do you guard?" I asked a bit too casually.

"That," Peter snapped, "is none of your business."

And that's the moment I knew I would have to abandon the research for his report and focus my attention on Peter, instead. I trusted Sean with my whole heart, but his family was up to no good. I could feel it.

CHAPTER 8

PETER'S FACE WAS ETCHED into a permanent grimace as he showed us to the library. Once again, I was let down by what we found. "Library," it turned out, was just a fancy word for *filing room*. While shelves lined the walls, the center—and majority—of the room was comprised of rows of gray filing cabinets, standing still like a small army of lifeless robots.

"Nothing you see in this room can leave. The information you'll find here is strictly confidential, and the files are cursed to prevent anyone from taking them and living to tell about it. Claudia can explain the details of my presentation, but I need information gathered from the census reports of a certain segment of our population."

"Oh, for crying out loud, Peter. Just say it. They're going to discover it soon enough, anyway." Claudia turned to Sean and me. "Peter stands guard for a high security prison here under the palace. These aren't your average criminals—they're intelligent, and the only reason they're being kept alive is for collateral with the other territories or because we believe they have information that we need."

"How did they survive?" I asked. "How are they living here with the wards?"

Claudia looked at me like I was an idiot. "Maxwell can allow anyone to enter who he wishes. That's one of the perks of being a leader." She shook her head. "Anyhow, extra security is needed for these criminals, despite the enchantments on the cells themselves. So Peter has been working long hours lately while they're short staffed. But if he presents the information required at the annual convention coming up, and does a good job, he could very well be in line for the next warden position, which is a fast track to *palace guard*." She clasped her hands excitedly in front of her chest.

"Let's not get ahead of ourselves." Peter frowned. "Just gather all the census reports from the last century for the high security prisoners and create a spreadsheet for me. I'll handle it from there."

And so we did. Or, two of us did, anyway. While Sean and Claudia worked to gather and input information into Claudia's laptop, I explored the cabinets under the ruse that I was searching for the 1954 files, which I had conveniently hidden from the first drawer I opened.

At first I was surprised at how antiquated the filing system was for such a high tech territory, but then I figured it was actually pretty standard for official government files to be way behind the times—even for supernaturals. And I was grateful for it. The lack of organization gave me plenty of opportunity to snoop around.

We worked that way the entire morning, and I was losing hope by the time lunch came around. After quickly scarfing down some tuna sandwiches, we were back at it. I avoided Claudia as much as possible because I didn't trust myself not to mouth off to her. What little respect I had for the woman had gone down the drain. It was a wonder Sean turned out as good as he did with parents like that.

Near the end of the day, I was prepared to throw in the towel. I'd searched probably thirty different filing cabinets, each one full of more boring documents than the last. There was nothing but papers and court records and more papers. With a frustrated huff, I shoved the bottom drawer of my last cabinet closed, and heard a rattle.

"Did you break it?" Sean chuckled from over my shoulder.

"I hope not." I opened the drawer again and pulled all the files forward to see if the tracks were still sturdy. At the very back of the drawer, tucked behind all the folders, lay a single key. It had to have been at least a hundred years old. "Hey, check this out."

Sean looked over my shoulder at the dusty object. "What does it go to?"

"I don't know," I said, blowing off the dust. "But I'm gonna find out." I tucked the key into my pocket, checking first to make sure Claudia wasn't watching. Maybe it was nothing. But maybe it would grant me access to some of the other secrets hiding here under the palace.

We'd have to wait to find out, though. The library hours matched a standard Atlantean workday. It was closing, and Claudia expected us to join her for dinner.

Later that night, after we'd eaten an awkward meal with Claudia, Sean and I excused ourselves early to retreat back to our guest room in the palace. Locking the door behind us, I finally pulled the key back out of my pocket and laid it on the bed. I'd been waiting very impatiently for the opportunity to make a plan with it since we'd found it earlier that day.

"It looks too old to be of any use," Sean said. "All the doors downstairs are too modern for it to work."

"I wouldn't be so sure about that." I ran my finger across the key's smooth surface. "There aren't any serrations on it. It's a skeleton key. Besides, we've only seen a small number of those doors downstairs. Perhaps the *older* mysteries are hidden behind *older* doors."

"Always the optimist," Sean said. "How do you propose we get back down there?"

"Well, I've been thinking about that, too. And I have a hypothesis. You know how every once in a while I'm able to stop time? I think it might be connected to the prophecy somehow. It seems like every time I'm getting closer to learning something about it, my powers kick into gear. So maybe, if exploring the rest of the basement gets us closer to the missing piece of the tablet, my powers will activate and I'll be able to stop time to slip past the guards."

"That's a lot of maybes," Sean said with a frown.

"That's the best I've got." I reached into my bag and pulled out the bottle of pills. "But I also have some amplifiers here in my little bag of tricks. Maybe an extra dose will help. I'm due for another one in the morning, anyway."

"Another *maybe*." Sean shook his head. "Alright, but if something happens to you from taking it again too soon, I can't help you. I have zero healing abilities."

"I'll be fine," I said. And I hoped it was true as I dropped the pill on my tongue and swallowed before I could think better of it. "When we were testing the pills out, Millie and Tate had me taking them everyday at first and I was perfectly fine. At this point, I'm not even sure if the amplifier works anymore. But I figured it's worth a try." I sat on the edge of the bed, waiting for something to happen.

"How do you feel?" Sean asked after a few minutes.

"Exactly the same. How do I look? Is my aura any different?"

"Just as blue as before. How long should we wait for something to happen?"

"It was almost instant back at Millie's house. I'd say we're good to go."

"Right now?" Sean's eyes widened.

"There's no better time than the present." I pulled Rossel's dagger from my bag and tucked it into my waistband, hoping we wouldn't need it.

Then we slipped out of our room and into the hall. The lights were dimmed with the late hour, and no one was around, not even the maids. Even so, I kept my voice at a whisper as I laid out my plan for Sean on our way down.

"I haven't found a way to keep anyone else awake with me while I stop time. But I can move you like a statue. So once we reach the bottom of the stairs, I'll push pause on reality and just peddle you through the halls with me. The first place I want to check is the prison. Just in case."

Sean nodded, understanding my motive.

"Then I figured we could just try out all the other doors—see if any of them will open with the key."

"How long are you able to keep time stopped?" Sean asked.

"I got probably ten minutes or so when I was at the warehouse with Rossel. It'll be long enough to get out of sight of any guards on the night shift. But your mom said they were short staffed right now, so I'm hoping we don't run into too many."

A faint whimper from the landing below stopped our conversation short. Sean and I both looked through the darkness of the entry hall to see where the noise was coming from. All I could make out was a pile of lavender silk in the corner of a small sitting area off to the side.

"Sean?" Anasasha rose from a heap on the floor, quickly wiping the tears from her eyes.

"Is everything okay?" Sean rushed forward, always the protector. Being a guardian was innate in him. He couldn't help but come to her rescue, no matter how she'd viewed him before.

"Yeah, of course," Anasasha lied. "I was just looking for a ring I dropped. But I found it. See you later." She quickly moved away from him, trying to hide her sniffle under a fake cough.

Sean held out his hand and placed it gently on Anasasha's forearm to stop her. She halted immediately, lifting her glossy, bloodshot shot eyes to his. "Are you sure? Because I'll help you if something is wrong."

Her floodgates opened then, and she buried her face into his shoulder, letting the tears pour freely. "It's just my parents again. Nothing I do is ever enough, and they act like having me as the heir is a burden for them.

They wish I'd been a boy. But I don't even want to be the leader of Atlantis! If they want a boy so bad, they should train up my brother instead of just enabling his bad decisions." She sobbed loudly. "I'm sorry, I don't know why I just told you all of that. Please forget I said anything." She pulled back and wiped the snot from her nose.

"I get it," Sean said, gently patting her back. "Believe me. I know what it's like to have parents with impossible standards."

"You do?" Anasasha rested her cheek on his shoulder again. Sean glanced at me over the top of her head and silently mouthed for me to *go ahead*.

I hated to leave him behind with the water-works princess, but she seemed pretty harmless in her current state. And Sean knew how to take care of himself, anyway. I needed to get the tablet. That was my priority.

After waiting another minute to make sure he was okay, I bid Sean a silent farewell and continued downstairs on my own.

The first floor of the palace was empty. The front doors were closed to the public at this hour, and the guards had gone home for the evening. But I knew that wouldn't be the case downstairs in the basement.

I slipped through the doors without being seen, and my confidence was rising as I reached the bottom floor unscathed. A quick peek around the corner revealed the Olympian guard's desk to be empty, and I released the breath I'd been holding on my descent.

I entered the lobby and paused for a beat, allowing the adrenaline to filter through my system before trying any of the doors. With the key in hand, I made for the hallway a moment later, only to stop dead in my tracks at the sound of a toilet flushing.

I squeezed my eyes shut, imagining everything around me coming to a stop. This was it—my chance to put my powers to use and see what those amplifiers could really do. Pressure built in my chest, and I opened my eyes to find the world exactly as I'd left it. It was still and quiet, but had time actually stopped?

My question was answered by the sound of someone whistling and pushing open the bathroom door. There wasn't time for another try. I spun on my heels and made a mad dash for the stairs, taking them two at a time until I was safely out of sight.

The pressure in my chest was gone, and a new pressure was building behind my eyes. I blinked away the tears of frustration before they could fall. What good were my powers if I couldn't even use them when I *needed* them? What kind of Atlantean was I?

With a deep breath, I headed back for the stairs, trying to convince myself that everything would be okay. I still had the key. I'd just have to find a different way to use it.

CHAPTER 9

SEAN GOT UP EARLY the next morning to meet Anasasha for breakfast. "She's really not so bad when you get to know her. And she apologized for how she treated me the other night. Her parents are pushing her to marry early because they don't trust her to lead Atlantis on her own."

"Because she's a woman?"

Sean grimaced. "Not all Atlanteans are horrible. I know you've seen an ugly side to our people since you've been down here, but I promise—some of us are good."

"I know. My mom was good. *Is* good." I corrected myself as I ran a brush through my hair. Anasasha had sent some new clothes and toiletries to our room as a thank you for Sean cheering her up. I felt like a new woman in some clean underwear and freshly washed hair. "I'm gonna go look for her today."

"Your mom? How? I thought you said your time-stopping didn't work last night."

"People have been sneaking around without the ability to stop time for centuries. I'm sure I'll find a way." The truth was I didn't have a clue what I was going to do. I just knew I had to act soon. Our work in the library for Mr. Bratton was nearly finished, and our excuse to be in the palace would expire once it was complete. I had to do something today.

Sliding Rossel's dagger into the back of my waistband and under my shirt, I made my way down to the library with Sean after breakfast and waited for my opportunity to get out. I'd considered my different options all morning, and after about half an hour of pulling files, I finally landed on a classic move from all the old eighties high school movies I'd seen about kids getting out of class. "Hey Claudia, do you know where the restroom is?"

"It's a couple of doors down the hall on your right," she said, never pulling her eyes from her laptop screen. We were in the final push for the report, and she had buried herself in spreadsheets, trying to get everything perfect for her husband.

Of course, I already knew where the bathroom was after my close encounter with the guard the night before. And I knew it was in the direction I wanted to go. Sean and I locked eyes briefly as I made my way to the door, a silent understanding passing through us that this was it. I was making my move.

I nodded a greeting to the Olympian guard in the lobby outside of the library and turned deeper into the hallway. *Play it cool, Everly.* I made a pit stop in the bathroom, confirming my alibi and checking my reflection in the mirror while giving myself a mental pep talk. And I noticed a supply closet against the wall near the mirrors that gave me an idea.

I tried the knob and found the closet locked, just as I expected. This was the perfect opportunity to test out my new key. I pulled it from my pocket and pushed it into the lock, but it wouldn't fit. I couldn't even get the stupid key inside.

That's okay, I thought to myself, taking a deep breath. I didn't care about bathroom supply closets. I cared about finding the Atlantean piece of the prophecy. I wouldn't give up on the key yet.

Poking my head back out into the hall to make sure it was clear, I eased through the door and spun around the corner into a deeper part of the basement. I hadn't been back this far before, and I knew my time was short before Claudia grew suspicious of my absence. I'd have to act quickly.

With my key at the ready, I tested a couple of locked doors as I went, none of them working. The problem was that nothing was marked. I had no idea if I was breaking into someone's office or a janitorial closet. The only markings on the walls were small numbers above the rooms: 037... 039... 041. But still I continued ahead toward a set of white double doors at the end of the hall.

They were locked as well, and solid metal with no room for a key. Instead, there was a fingerprint scanner on the wall outside. A high security zone on a high security floor. *I must be getting close.* But I didn't dare try my own fingerprints. Perhaps there was another way in.

I twisted the knob to my right, fully expecting it to be locked like all the others, so I nearly fell in as the door swung open with ease. And I almost laughed as I stumbled into a broom. At least I got one open.

Feeling a little more confident, I tried for the room across the hall as well. Locked. Then I heard a whir and a click from the double doors beside me.

I dove back for the janitorial closet, but I wasn't fast enough. The doors swung open, and I slid my body behind one, hoping the door itself would shield me from the sight of whoever was coming through.

Please don't be Peter. Please don't be Peter. Please don't be Peter.

It wasn't. It was a guard I didn't recognize. And by some miracle of the sea, he didn't see me as I swung around to the backside of the door and slipped to the other side. He was too distracted, running in the opposite direction and yelling into some kind of walkie talkie. "Unmanned. I'm searching now!"

I didn't stop to consider what he meant as the doors closed behind me, sealing me off in the high security area. Everything on this side of the doors was different.

Gone were the white walls and sterile feel of the basement library. This was more in line with what I would have expected to see in the basement of an ancient palace. Unrenovated. Unrestored. Buzzing with magic.

The light was dimmer, bluer on this part of the floor. Or maybe it was just the way it played off of the rough stone floors of a hall that looked like it had been carved through a mountain. There was a chair, empty, to my left. And ahead of me, lining both sides of the hall, were prison cells.

I inched forward slowly at first, afraid to let the prisoners see my face. The hilt of Rossel's dagger dug into my back as I walked, reminding me of how dangerous this could be if I wasn't careful. But I had to know if my mom was here.

The first cell was empty, but a cough drew my eyes to another one across the hall. Inside sat a small woman with pale skin and golden eyes. Her hair hung in limp strands around her gaunt face. She may have once been beautiful, but now the Agarthian woman looked too sick and frail to even stand. "Please, Miss. There's been a mistake. I need to go to the infirmary. *Please.*" She lifted one shaky hand into the air.

I stepped closer, eyeing the woman carefully. She didn't look cruel, but I was no fool. Claudia had mentioned the intelligence of these criminals, and I knew I was being manipulated. But still, curiosity tugged me closer to her. She stared back at me, those golden eyes hollow and tired, but also full of cunning and experience. After a long look, I shook my head. I didn't know what the woman had possibly done to end up here, but I didn't have time to ask. I needed to keep searching.

"I'm sorry," I said, stepping back.

The woman leapt to her feet and jabbed a bony arm through the bars of her cell, reaching out for me with a wicked sneer, but she was just shy of making contact. I'd moved in the knick of time. I made a mental note not to get too close to any of the other cells, and ignored her loud and crude insults as I moved on to the other cells.

A few other prisoners sat quietly, watching me make my way down the hall. One old Olympian man sang a sad song in a language I'd never heard. And at the very end of the hall sat a young red-haired Atlantean man, not any older than myself. I drew nearer, studying his features as he slept on the hard floor of his cell. Why would an Atlantean be locked up in the palace prison under extra protection? And why did he seem familiar to me?

It didn't matter, I supposed, as I reached the end of the row. My mother wasn't here, though I couldn't say whether that was a relief or not. It would have been nice to have her with me again, helping me navigate the strange waters I now found myself in. Did she know? Did she know that I was the Deliverer?

A clatter from behind whipped my attention back to where I started as the double doors slammed open with enough force to shake the walls. My feet were frozen to the spot, paralized with fear as Peter Bratton stormed into the prison hall. He was nearly twice the size I'd last seen him, his guardian powers fully activated.

Then came Sean, sprinting in behind him, breathless and equal parts angry and afraid. "Everly—run!"

CHAPTER 10

IT SOUNDED LIKE A good idea in theory, but I couldn't run. There was only one way out of this hall, and Peter Bratton blocked the exit like a wall. A raging bull of a wall.

"You." He pointed at me with a finger the size of a sausage. "Who are you really?"

The prisoners were all on their feet now, fingers wrapped around the bars of their cells, grinning widely as they anxiously awaited whatever show was about to take place.

"I told you... I'm just a friend of the family." I raised both hands in the air, showing Peter I meant no harm while simultaneously trying to stir up any kind of power that might still be inside me. The well was empty. I still had no power.

"Liar." He threw something. It moved so fast I couldn't make out what it was. It slammed into my gut like a sucker punch, knocking the air out of me and landing on the ground in front of me with a thud.

"Dad, stop!" Sean yelled, but Peter just pushed him aside.

I looked down to see what hit me, and yelped as I noted all of the pills Millie made me lying broken on the floor. He must have gotten them from our room... unless Sean passed them over to him. Did Sean betray me?

Glancing up again, I tried to stay brave and stand tall, even as Peter Bratton stalked his way over to me. Sean grabbed at his arms, trying to slow him down, but it was no use. The man was a machine. He stopped about three feet in front of me and stomped on what was left of the pills, crushing them into dust.

"Try drugging the prince now, you little traitor."

"What?" My confusion was spoken in unison with a voice behind me. Sean and Peter both turned their attention over my shoulder, so I followed their gaze to the red-haired Atlantean boy in the last cell.

"Where are the drugs?" the boy asked.

"I don't have any drugs," I said. "I don't know what you're talking about. I don't even know who you are!"

"I don't believe you for a second," Peter snapped. "Who are you working for?"

"I'm not working for anyone!"

"Where are the drugs?" the boy repeated, a frantic glaze over his hazel eyes.

"I told you, there are no drugs!" I was losing patience. Someone had seriously gotten their wires crossed, and I didn't want to be caught in the middle. If Peter wanted to be angry about me sneaking in here without permission, that was one thing. But to accuse me of drugging prisoners? It was absurd.

"Are you Baldric?" Sean stepped toward the boy, whose frenzied expression turned to surprise.

The boy looked to Peter before answering. "I am."

"Not another word," Peter growled.

"Why not?" a raspy voice called out from the other end of the hall. "Afraid the truth might get out about my brother being an addict?" All eyes turned toward Anasasha, who stood with two of her guards in the doorway. The frail female Agarthian prisoner near the front of the hall loosed a laugh like a hyena.

Peter gritted his teeth and dropped into a bow. "Forgive us, Ms. Ligon, for disturbing you. I've just caught this girl feeding your brother's habit. I believe she may be working with the enemy."

"Nonsense." Anasasha picked up her skirts and marched forward, completely unafraid of the man. "You two may go," she said to her other guards. "Wait upstairs until I'm finished here. It looks like we may need to have a personal conversation."

She waited to speak again until we were alone. "What evidence do you have?"

Peter gestured to the powder on the floor. "She's a stranger. A face I've never seen from parents no one knows. She shows up, weasels her way in with my family, and enters the palace with a bottle full of pills. She doesn't have access to this area, yet here she is. What else would bring her here?"

"Perhaps she was trying to locate the man who broke into her private room and rummaged through her personal things? Perhaps she was prepared to confront the thief who stole her medication."

Peter's face reddened. "I was gathering evidence."

"You were setting a trap and embarrassing a guest of this palace. And you've caused undue stress on Baldric that you know he cannot sustain." Anasasha was fuming. Over her shoulder, I saw a frown tugging at Sean's mouth. "I won't let it happen again. Charberon!" she called out.

"No, please. Don't involve Charberon. I can make it up to you." Peter dropped to his knees.

The Olympian guard entered the prison hall. "Yes, Ms. Ligon?"

"Peter Bratton is no longer a guard of Atlantis. He will be removed from his position immediately. He shall never step foot inside this palace again, and he shall be struck dead on the spot if he ever speaks of the confidential information he has gleaned in his work here, including personal matters surrounding my family." Her eyes cut briefly to the boy behind bars, who had settled back onto the floor in a daze.

"Yes, Ms. Ligon. Follow me, sir." There was pity in the Olympian guard's eyes as he gestured for Peter to get on his feet and follow him.

We waited in silence as Peter's sobs drifted down the hall and out through the double doors. Anasasha pierced me with a glare the moment they swung shut again. "Now," she said. "You better have a very compelling reason for being here with my brother."

CHAPTER 11

"I DO HAVE A good reason. And I promise I did not know your brother was here. I was told that he lived in Europe." I glanced from Anasasha to Sean and back again. "I'm here to look for someone else—a missing person who I thought could have been locked away here in the palace prison. But she's not. I'm sorry we caused such a scene. How did you know we were down here?"

"Sean tipped me off this morning at breakfast. He said he was worried his father was up to something, so I sent a guard and some palace staff on a mission to watch for anything suspicious. Peter abandoned his post this morning, leaving the prisoners completely alone, and one of my maids reported him in your room. Knowing how he can get at times..." She looked briefly at Sean, "I figured it would be best to handle the situation myself, though I'm surprised to find *you* here. What are the pills?"

I tried to swallow the lump in my throat. Thankfully I took an extra dose the night before, otherwise I would have been in serious trouble. We couldn't stay in Atlantis much longer either way, though. Without the pills, I had a hard deadline before my aura returned to white.

"They're kind of like supplements. Specially made for me by my aunt. She's a healer."

Anasasha's eyes narrowed. "I'll say this only once. I have a knack for feeling out lies. You lie to me, and you're done. But these half truths you're speaking? They're not gonna work either. I suggest you tell me the *whole* truth. Now."

Tate had once said he knew about the Deliverer prophecy because he'd overheard it during some of his brother's lessons. And through my conversations with Driskell and Rasputin, I had surmised that all royalty, and hopefully *non-royal* leaders too, in this case, learned of it in order to keep rumors and rogue explorers under control in the Keeper territories.

Assuming all of that was true, Anasasha would have heard of the prophecy as well. Whether or not she believed it was another story. And then there was the question of whether or not she'd let me live if she discovered who I really was.

"Sometimes the truth is less believable than a lie," I said.

"Try me."

"Okay." I steeled myself, preparing for whatever reaction I might get from her. "The pills keep my aura blue."

Sean's jaw dropped and Anasasha's hardened. "You're not Atlantean?"

"I am. But my aura is different."

"How is it different?" She crossed her arms over her chest, not fully buying what I had to say, but staying remarkably open minded to my explanation.

"It's... white."

The Agarthian prisoner at the front of the hall gasped and covered her mouth with a frail hand. At first I thought she was ridiculing me, but then she dropped to her knees and bowed her face down low to the ground. Anasasha turned to look at the prisoner, and her expression was completely different when she met my eyes again.

"What does that mean?" she asked. Her demeanor had changed from defensive to inquisitive, curiosity written plainly across her face.

"Have you heard of the Deliverer?"

I gave her a condensed version of my story. I told her my mother went missing the same day I found the first piece of the tablet, and that the stone responded to me. Sean confirmed that my aura was white, and that I'd stopped a storm to save his life. We left out anything about Driskell—there was no need to add any danger to *his* life—and I didn't tell her about my ability to stop time. I wasn't even sure if it was an ability anymore or just a strange coincidence that occurred any time my friends or I were about to die.

"I know this sounds crazy," I said. "And maybe you've even been raised to believe that I am somehow your enemy. But I can assure you, I don't want to hurt anyone. I just want to find my mom and figure out what this prophecy really means."

Anasasha's eyes grew misty as she looked back at her brother, who was now sleeping on the floor of his prison cell. "Do you really think you can do it?"

"Do what?"

"Change the world." She set her tear-filled eyes back on me. "Remove the Keepers from power. Get us out of this eternal loop of tragedy and greed. Deliver us from the shackles of this responsibility that turns man against man…"

Sean reached out for her hand and gave it a gentle squeeze, but he remained silent. And while Sean worked to calm Anasasha, something awakened in me. Her words reminded me of the magnitude of this prophecy and the task that lay before me. It was about so much more than finding my mom. It was about setting people free and exterminating evil from the face of the earth and the depths of the sea.

My inner Athena raised a sword at the thought. "Yes," I said with confidence. "I know that I can."

"Then follow me."

All of the prisoners watched us carefully as we made our way back through the hall. There was a different feeling in the air. Respect maybe. Or fear. Or the thrill of knowing something big was about to happen.

I felt it too.

Sean and I followed Anasasha through the double doors and back into the sterile basement toward the library. But she stopped at another door on her way: 045. There was a fingerprint scanner there on the wall, and it opened at her touch with a whir and a click. She ushered us through, and I was surprised to find that we were in another hallway rather than a room.

The halls here more closely resembled the prison than the library, with stone floors and that odd blue tinted light. And they quickly turned into more of a maze than I could keep up with.

"I'm sorry about your dad," I said quietly to Sean after a few minutes of walking.

"He had it coming." Sean's face remained hard. I'm sure it wasn't easy to see his father fall so egregiously from grace, but I didn't know much about their relationship. Maybe Sean was right and this wasn't Peter's first infraction against him or the people of Atlantis. Maybe he did have it coming.

"Is Charberon…"

"A cursemaker." Sean said flatly.

But the conversation stopped there along with Anasasha. She placed a hand on the doorknob before her and turned back to face us.

"I haven't been in this room in ages. It contains a collection of artifacts and secrets from our history. Few have access to the room, and it is important that you never speak of it to another living soul. Can I have your word on that?"

"Absolutely," I said. Sean agreed as well.

"Thank you." Anasasha closed her eyes and inhaled deeply before twisting the knob. "I think you may find what you're looking for here."

The moment the door swung open, I felt it, beating along with my own heart. Chill bumps dotted my skin as something invisible pulled me into the room. The broken piece of the tablet was waiting for me somewhere here.

The interior of the room, once again, was drastically different from the halls outside. This room, though it had the same stone floors and walls of the hallway maze we'd left, also had been updated with ten foot tall cases made of wood and reinforced glass. Inside each case lay a wide array of objects from another time and place, similar to the collection I'd seen in the basement of Rossel's gallery. There were goblets and books and sculptures, and other objects I couldn't identify.

But I wasn't interested in any of that. The invisible thread pulled me ever deeper into the room, with Sean and Anasasha now trailing behind me. My heart thumped harder and harder as we neared the back, and we all saw it at once.

A blue glow emanated from a cabinet on the very farthest wall, brighter and a more alluring color than the rest of the territory's mysterious light.

Anasasha gasped. "It's true."

I ran forward and placed my hands on the glass, wanting so badly to rip it apart and take hold of what was mine. The prophecy was begging to go with me. We wouldn't be complete until we were together.

"How do we get it out?" I asked.

"They're permanently sealed. We'll have to take the cabinet apart. There is no door or other way to access it that I'm aware of."

I searched the room for something heavy enough to break it open, but there were only more cabinets. Pulling the dagger from my waistband, I turned the hilt toward the glass and prepared to strike.

"Wait!" Ansasha grabbed my arm. "The moment you make impact with the cabinet, sirens are going to blare through the basement. We'll have guards on us in thirty seconds or less. And they can't know that I've helped you. It would be best if they didn't know who took the tablet at all."

"So you'll let us take it then?" I hadn't even stopped to consider that I was stealing a valuable piece of history right in front of the water princess.

"If you promise to do what needs to be done. Fulfill the prophecy and it's yours."

"Thank you. I promise." I met her eyes and tried to convey that I would do anything within my power to stay true to my word. I think she understood.

"There's a hidden passage behind these walls. I just have to remember how to access it. Give me just a minute." Anasasha ran her hand along the walls of the room, feeling along each of the rough edges of the stone. Sean joined her, and I tried to remain patient as they felt their way across the room.

"Is this it?" Sean asked, sliding his fingers down a thick line in the rock.

Anasasha rushed to his side to take a look. "Yes! Help me pull it." Together they dug in with their nails. I stepped to help them out when suddenly a portion of the wall moved forward with a sleepy groan. The hallway behind it was dark and dank. It would be perfect for our escape.

"You won't be able to leave Atlantis through the main gate," Anasasha warned. "These tunnels will lead you to a back exit near the end of the Bimini Road. But I have to warn you that it's dangerous and full of monsters trained to keep our territory safe. You'll need to be careful."

"We will," Sean said, meeting her eyes. There was some kind of unspoken agreement that passed between them in that moment, and I felt like I should look away.

I turned back to the stone tablet, still pulsing with energy, faster now along with my own racing heart. This was it. It almost seemed too easy. "Ready?" I asked.

"Whenever you are."

I lifted the dagger again and felt the warrior awakening inside me. My muscles ached, as though they were stirring after a long nap, stretching and preparing for battle. The dagger felt cool in my palm, its reflection catching my eye in the glass of the case just before I struck.

And with all the power of Athena, strike it I did.

The glass shattered into a million fragments, almost in slow motion. I became acutely aware of every piece as it fell. And the tablet... taking it into my hands was like finding a lost path that led me home.

"Let's go, Everly."

I wrapped the piece under one arm, hugging it tightly to my side, and ran for the passageway. Together, the three of us pulled the door shut again behind us.

"You'll need to go left. The hall will take you straight to the exit. I can't go with you, but please let me know if there is anything I can do in the future to help with the prophecy."

"We will. Thank you, Anasasha. Truly." I dug into my pocket and pulled out the useless skeleton key. "This is yours, by the way. I don't know what it goes to, but you can keep it."

The girl smiled. "That's just the key to my diary. And I'm glad you didn't find it. Now go! Be safe on your travels!" She placed a quick kiss on Sean's cheek, and then we parted ways.

Though we could barely hear the sirens through the thick stone walls, we knew the guardians were coming for us. Sean and I ran like our lives depended on it.

CHAPTER 12

THE HALL WOUND AROUND the palace, down to a narrow set of stairs. And we knew the moment we stumbled across the exit. It shimmered before us, a wall of liquid that we couldn't see through.

"Hold your breath," Sean called out, and he dove straight into the moving surface of the wall. I didn't hesitate to follow him this time.

We were back in the ocean, treading water in unfamiliar territory. Sean whirled around in a circle, searching for something. "There!" He pointed to a pile of rocks on the seafloor not far from where we swam. I followed him over to see what they were.

"The Bimini Road. This will lead us past Porta Maris. We'll need to swim fast though. I can pull you along if you want."

Even as he said it, I could feel the power pulsing through my limbs, stronger now than it had ever been before. "I think I'll be able to keep up." I dove forward, leaving Sean in my wake.

"Holy cow!" He caught up to my side. "You're almost as fast as me. Is it the tablet?"

"I don't know," I confessed. I had a hard time deciphering between the tablet's power and my own. The only thing I could be certain of was that I was a lot stronger when I had warrior-mode engaged. That inner Athena could really come in handy.

The tablet pulsed warm and steady under my arm, the dagger cold and hard in the waistband of my pants. I wasn't exactly prepared for battle, but I definitely felt strong enough to face the task ahead, whatever it might be. The look on Anasasha's face when she understood that I was the

Deliverer would be forever etched in my brain. Such hope. She needed me to set her free.

I couldn't even begin to guess how quickly we were moving now. We blasted through the water like dual torpedos, the ocean a blur except for the broken stone trail on the bottom of the sea that guided us home.

"Thank you, by the way, for looking out for me back at the palace. I hate to admit that I actually wondered if you had sold me out to your dad for a second there."

"You're welcome." Sean glanced at me with a crooked grin. "I would never—"

He was gone. Mid-sentence. Just... *gone*.

I stopped and spun around just in time to duck under the enormous black tentacle that swung my way.

"What in Atlantis is *that*?"

Anasasha said the road was guarded by monsters, but I never guessed she meant it literally.

I darted around a large piece of coral searching for Sean. From this angle I was able to see the entire creature. It was like a shadow under the water, and it was difficult to see exactly how large it was with its mass of undulating tentacles, but it looked about the size of a full basketball court. And wrapped up in one of those disgusting appendages was Sean, waving through the air, delivering punch after punch to the beast that held him, to no avail.

Another of the tentacles came shooting at me, but I was faster. I threw myself down to the floor of the sea, grabbing at the first rock I could get my hands around. It was slightly bigger than a bowling ball and maybe four times as heavy. I chucked it at the tentacle with all my might, causing the squirming appendage to pull back just enough for me to get away.

Sean called out for me to get away, but there wasn't a chance I was going to leave him for dead with this beast. I blasted through the water, pulling out Rossel's dagger as I swam, and prepared to fight until he was free.

But there were so many tentacles. So many writhing, twisting, stretching limbs of solid muscle. I couldn't keep track of them all, and I couldn't outrun them, especially as I got closer to the monster's body. I was only a few yards away from Sean when the life was squeezed out of me. My vision darkened around the edges and something cracked in my chest.

I gasped for one more lungful of air before my ribs were crushed, and then everything stopped. A piece of seaweed was suspended before me, frozen in time within an unmoving ocean. My power had activated again, all on its own. I didn't understand how this kept happening, but I was definitely grateful for it. And there was no time to question it now.

Dagger still in hand, I cut through the beast, sawing back and forth through the thick muscles that wrapped around me and trying not to gag at the black blood that leaked from it. Then it was time to release Sean.

I propelled myself through the water, unsure of how long I had before time started moving again. I plunged the dagger down into the tentacle that wrapped around him, cutting through its flesh and severing a small piece at the end of the long appendage, about the length of my hand. Taking a hold of the small piece, I tucked it into my pocket like a trophy and continued sawing until Sean was free.

The pressure was already building in my chest again. I had a minute at most to get us as far away from the beast as possible. Tucking the dagger back into my waistband and tightening my grip on the stone tablet in one arm, I wrapped the other around Sean and swam as hard and fast as I could.

I didn't know how long I swam, or how far we'd gone, or even the exact moment time clicked back into place as it should be. But at some point, Sean broke free from my grasp and stopped me.

"Everly." His eyes were wide. "It happened again, didn't it?"

I nodded.

"You saved my life."

I nodded again.

"Are you okay?"

My heart was racing and my chest ached. But yes, I realized, I was fine. Power of unknown origin pulsed through my veins. I couldn't wield it, but it was there. We'd escaped Atlantis, gotten another piece of the prophecy, and were halfway back to Porta Maris by now.

"Yeah," I said with a grin. "I'm okay." I pulled the small piece of tentacle from my pocket and held it out to Sean. "I got you a souvenir."

He gaped. "You've got a piece of the Kraken."

"You bet I do." A laugh bubbled up from my chest, a small giggle at first. And before I knew it, Sean and I were both laughing until tears streamed from our eyes. After the morning we'd had, it was a wonder we were still alive. The laugh did us good.

The swim back to Porta Maris didn't take long with my newfound speed through the water. And I shouldn't have been as surprised as I was to find Driskell sitting on a rock on the sand as we emerged above the water's surface near the island. After all, Gayla said in her vision that he watched and waited, and he knew when I was coming.

We staggered onto the land, our wet clothes dragging and weighing us down. It was too bad the magical properties of Atlantis didn't extend themselves here. I sure wouldn't have minded being instantly dry again.

Driskell met us at the water's edge, eyes glued to the glowing piece of stone under my arm. "You found it." His hands were shaky as they reached forward, but he thought better of it before trying to take the piece from me. He must have seen the look in my eyes that said I wasn't handing it over to anyone. For any purpose.

Because even though I wanted Driskell to tell me what it said, the tablet made me ache with the need to reconnect it to the other piece. Some part of my brain became innately aware of where the other piece rested, below the sand we stood upon, hidden inside the room the people here had offered for Driskell.

And I was moving before I could give it another thought.

"Hide it!" Driskell shouted after me, running to catch up. "Put it under your shirt or something!"

We entered the hidden compound of Porta Maris, moving quickly through the restaurant and down the halls back into the sleeping quarters below. I was a woman on a mission, never stopping to give anyone a chance to ask who I was or where I was going.

I vaguely heard Driskell and Sean giving explanations behind me as I moved toward my destination. And the closer I got to the other piece of the tablet, the stronger my need was to reconnect them.

I didn't have to ask where it was when we entered Driskell's room at last. It called to me. And with a deep breath I took the other piece into my hands and pushed the broken edges of the two together.

A blinding light filled the room as a jolt of energy knocked me to the floor. Driskell and Sean were still shielding their eyes as I got back to my feet and inspected the prophecy. The two pieces had fused themselves seamlessly together to create one perfect half of the full prophecy. Driskell released a breath of wonder as he approached.

"May I?" he asked.

"Of course." Now that the pieces had been restored, the tension that had propelled me earlier finally eased. The tablet no longer glowed blue, but I could still feel its heartbeat in tandem with my own. I passed it to Driskell, confident that it would be safe for him to hold.

His bushy brows furrowed together as he took it in.

"Well," Sean stepped closer, "what does it say?"

"The daughter of sea and sky,
together with the one who
ignites her heart, in her
centennial incarnation,
shall form a white braid of
the powers that bind.
The Deliverer alone can wield..."

"Can wield what?" I asked, desperate for more.

"That..." Driskell said. "Is yet to be determined. You must find the other two pieces of the prophecy."

"I will," I said, a new ferocity sparking inside me. And no one would stop me. Not Rossel, or Osborne, or Peter Bratton. I couldn't even be stopped by the Kraken.

I would find the prophecy, and I would unite our people. It was my destiny.

IGNITED

CHAPTER 1

"GILGAMESH!" DOM CAME BARRELING out of her room and hurdled over the back of the couch like a track star, landing with a neat little bounce on the cushion beside me.

"Huh?" Gayla wrinkled her nose from across the room, looking just as confused as I felt.

"The Epic of Gilgamesh. It's an ancient poem, and I think it might have a clue for us."

Dom had gone full blown Velma ever since I got back with the second piece of the tablet. I half expected her to pick me up from class in a modern-day Mystery Machine any day now. Between the two of us, we probably had someone poring over various ancient texts twenty-six hours a day, desperately searching for anything that could relate to the prophecy somehow.

And so far, we'd come up short.

"I'll bite," I said. "What's your clue?"

"Okay, so Gilgamesh was on this journey to find immortality. But he didn't, or at least, not in the physical sense. Of course his story lives on..."

"Get to it, Dom!" Gayla called out.

"Right. So as he's dying and sad and stuff, the narrator says something about how eternal life wasn't his destiny. His destiny involved the '*power to bind*.'" She lifted her brows pointedly in my direction before continuing, "and something about darkness and light for all mankind. Sounds serious, right? But there's more. There's also mention of a three stranded rope that cannot be broken... you know, like a *braid*."

"This is good." I nodded, thoughtfully. "I can see a connection... I think."

"The prophecy mentioned a white braid of the powers that bind. And we know this is your destiny." Dom pulled a folded up piece of paper from her back pocket and spread it out on the coffee table. She pointed at the words she'd scrawled out as she read the prophecy aloud, even though we all had it memorized at this point.

*"The daughter of sea and sky,
together with the one who
ignites her heart, in her
centennial incarnation
shall form a white braid of
the powers that bind.
The Deliverer alone can wield..."*

"But how does the rest of Gilgamesh come into play?" I asked. "Was he real? Maybe an old Atlantean?"

Dom furrowed her brows. "Well, I haven't gotten that far yet."

My phone chirped with a new message, and I took a peek while Dom folded her paper up again. "Hey guys, I've gotta run. Sean says Millie is freaking out at the apothecary and he needs some help."

"Can we come?" Gayla stood and straightened her shirt. "I've been stuck in this apartment for weeks."

"It's been two days," Dom corrected. "But I wouldn't mind getting out, either. That cold front is supposed to roll in this weekend, so we should enjoy the sunshine while we still have it."

The girls accompanied me down to Millie's shop. It was a beautiful fall day, but I couldn't relax as we walked the city streets. I'd managed to keep my aura covered in blue for a couple of weeks now, thanks to Tate and Millie's magic pills, but it still felt like I was just waiting for the other shoe to drop.

There were always plenty of Keepers near the Columbia campus, and I found myself eyeing every one of them as we passed, preparing to bolt if they somehow discovered I wasn't a normal Atlantean. None of them paid me any attention, though, which was a good thing. I wasn't very fast on my feet.

Meanwhile, Gayla and Dom chatted about the upcoming convention and all the big names who would be attending—including Gayla's dad. She wasn't exactly thrilled about seeing him again. Rossel had disappeared after my little run-in with him at his warehouse, and Gayla's dad was furious about it. As horrible as Rossel was, he was known as the greatest seer in the modern-day world, and Gayla's dad paid good money to have Gayla apprentice under him.

"I'm sure he's up in Olympus with King Baerius," Gayla said, twisting a lock of platinum blond hair around her finger. "He'll be back when it's convenient for him. But I guarantee he's not gonna be giving me any more lessons—not after what Everly did to him."

"I think he got off pretty easy, all things considered," I said as we walked up to the front door of the apothecary. "He did throw a dagger at my face, after all." Some smug little part of me smiled inside, knowing that I was still in possession of his weapon. It had served me well so far, and I had no plans to give it back any time soon.

A faint hint of lavender and tea tree oil hung in the air outside the entrance of Millie's shop. Abby was probably making bath bombs again. The bells on the door chimed when we walked through, and at first I wasn't sure if anyone was around. "Hello?"

"Oh, goodness. I love lavender but that's so strong it's making my eyes water." Gayla gently rubbed moisture from her lower lids, careful not to smudge her eyeliner.

"Hey." Sean popped up from behind the counter, followed by a red faced Abby.

I grinned. "What were *you* guys—"

Millie cut me off, busting through the curtain from the back room with an armful of towels. "Here, let me help!"

"No." Sean held out his arms to take the towels and stop my aunt from stepping behind the counter. "You've done enough." He shot a glare in my direction before dropping back behind the counter.

Millie let out an exasperated sigh as she noted me and my roommates at the front of her shop. "Hi girls. Sorry about the smell. I just knocked over an entire shelf full of essential oils. The *big* jars." She grimaced.

"We hardly noticed," I lied with a smile. "But you look pretty frazzled. Do you need some help here today?"

"Help?" Millie giggled, a slight craze gleaming from her blue eyes.

"Yes," Sean said shooing my aunt toward the door. "She could definitely use your help. Millie's been put in charge of the welcome dinner for Maximus and Gloriana this year. They'll be coming up for the convention next week, and normally my mother would host a fancy dinner for them the night they arrive, but this year..." He trailed off.

Claudia had basically been ousted from Keeper society after what happened to her husband in Atlantis. She'd been curled up in her bed, lights off, barely even eating unless Sean was there bringing her food. And his dad, Peter, had disappeared entirely. Not a soul knew where he was, except maybe Claudia, but she wasn't speaking. Not coherently, anyway.

"Gotcha. Well, put me to work. What can I do?"

"Abby and I can manage the shop," Sean said, dropping his chin. "Since I'm not taking part in the convention this year. But I'm sure Millie could use your help with planning the dinner."

"Ooh, that happens to be my specialty." Gayla stepped forward and looped my aunt's arm through her own. "Let's get you home and see what you've got figured out so far. We'll make this dinner so good they'll want to stay on dry land forever." She gently guided my aunt back to the door as she spoke.

Dom scowled in Gayla's direction for speaking so carelessly in front of a human, but Abby didn't seem bothered or confused by her words at all. She must have been too distracted with cleaning up the oily mess on the floor to notice.

"Okay." Millie nodded. "Thank you. But are you sure you guys can handle things on your own here?"

"We've got it under control," Sean said. "Between me and Abby and the rest of the staff, I don't think you'll need to come in all week. Take your time, try to relax, and come back after the convention. I'll call you if anything comes up."

Millie hesitated by the front door before finally nodding again. "Alright. I appreciate you girls offering to help. There is a lot to get done in a very short amount of time. Let's go."

CHAPTER 2

DOM AND GAYLA TOOK turns helping me at Millie's house over the next week. She was uncharacteristically frazzled. My normally calm, cool, and collected aunt had turned into a tornado, bouncing from one idea to the next and leaving a trail of destruction in her path. But my roommates handled it with grace.

And Gayla wasn't joking when she'd said party planning was her forte. She knew all the best caterers, florists, decorators and event planners in New York City. But in the end, Pierre won out. He was one stubborn Frenchman, and he refused to allow some unknown catering crew into *his kitchen*. So on the big night, it was me who wound up in the kitchen with him instead.

Dom and Gayla each had other plans that night, so I found myself stuffing goat cheese into green olives by myself, while Jeeves organized a bar cart and Pierre sauteed something that smelled delicious on the stove.

"This has got to be the weirdest thing I've ever done," I said to no one in particular. So maybe it wasn't the *weirdest* thing. I mean... I'd sliced off a part of the Kraken. But it definitely ranked up there as one of the weirdest *human* things I'd ever done. I shoved the last bit of cheese into a greasy olive and licked the remainder off my fingers.

"Ew!" I shuddered. "I will never understand people who eat goat cheese. Goats are like the total opposite of fancy. My friend Hattie used to have goats. Her favorite was named Jack Sparrow. He used to jump on the trampoline with us and eat Froot Loops right out of our hands."

"Stories like this are exactly why you are not invited to the dinner." Pierre swiped his hand through the air at me.

He was only halfway right about that. I wasn't invited to the dinner—but it wasn't my stories that would embarrass my aunt. It was more about my association with Sean and his family. Being involved with that lot down in Atlantis had marked me as a pariah just as much as them, at least in Gloriana's eyes.

It left me wondering how Millie got tapped to host the dinner, being my aunt and all. Sean explained that she was one of the most well-respected Atlanteans in New York. Her wealth and propensity to do the right thing were enough to outshine my youthful indiscretions. But the pressure of getting everything perfect enough to erase my connections to the Bratton family was almost too much for my poor aunt to bear.

I peeked out of the kitchen when Jeeves greeted the non-royal family a short while later. The glamour placed on Jeeves and Pierre after the Olympian attack still held strong, and they were under the impression that Millie was hosting some big-wig's family from the pharmaceutical association—the same pharmaceutical association that she'd told Abby and the rest of her staff was hosting the upcoming convention.

Gloriana stepped through the door first, overdressed as usual. Jeeves, always the gentleman, said nothing about the woman's strange attire. Anasasha was next, wearing a similar full length gown as her mother, but in a pretty pale mauve, as opposed to her mother's deep navy blue. I held my breath as Jeeves greeted the patriarch of the family next.

Maxwell's voice was deep and silky, like a late night radio DJ. Jeeves stepped to the side, welcoming the man into Millie's home, and as he entered I was shocked to see that his head barely reached the butler's outstretched arm. Now Jeeves was a big guy, literally college-linebacker-huge. But Maxwell was... not. I couldn't explain why, but I'd expected the leader of Atlantis to have a bit more of a commanding presence. Especially with that voice.

"Maxwell, Gloriana! How wonderful to see you!" Millie strutted down from the top of the stairs, looking elegant as always. "And Anasasha, you've grown into such a beautiful young woman."

"Thank you." Anasasha dipped her chin in thanks, and when she looked up her gaze snagged on my doorway. I tensed, ready to pull back into the kitchen, but there was a kind curiosity in her eyes. I smiled at the girl, instead.

Jeeves turned back in my direction after showing them into the dining room, so I quickly jumped out of the way.

"Welp... looks like you guys have it all under control here," I said, snatching a lobster crostini off the hors d'oeuvre plate before Jeeves picked it up. "I'll be outside if you need me!" I dashed off toward the back courtyard before they could object. The prep work was all done, and I knew they would be fine without me. Besides, I needed to get a better view of the dinner.

I settled onto the cold cement of the patio and wrapped a blanket over my shoulders to keep out the evening's chill. Lemon Drop and Tiny Tim, Millie's mastiffs, quickly found their way to my sides.

"You guys weren't invited either, huh?" I held the blanket out for Lemon Drop. She looked like she needed a cuddle buddy. But Tiny Tim was too distraught over being locked outside to care about the blanket. He let out a whimper and pawed at the back door.

"Shhh! You're gonna get me caught, Tiny."

Are we really resorting to lying with the dogs now? A flutter of wings announced Al's arrival behind me.

"They're better company than birds."

He scoffed—a sound I could only hear in my mind. *How's the dinner going so far?*

"They're just sitting down. But Millie did a fabulous job preparing everything. I'm sure it'll be great."

Then why do you feel the need to sit out here in the shadows and watch them?

"I just want to."

Al had been particularly thorny since I returned from Atlantis. He did not approve of my tactics for acquiring the tablet, and I did not approve of his lecture about Kraken safety. I also found it hard to believe that this feathery friend of mine had no further information about the prophecy.

He'd supposedly been my sidekick in every incarnation over the last 12,000 years, yet he couldn't so much as take a guess at what the prophecy meant. According to him, there were long spans of time where we were apart. He was only able to find me in each life after my powers began to manifest.

You're still mad at me, aren't you?

I shrugged.

So be it. But you sitting out here in the cold watching them eat dinner is absurd. Either march inside, tell them you're the Deliverer, and get this show on the road... or leave them be. You've got better things to do than watch through a window like a sad little puppy.*

Tiny Tim whimpered again as if that was his cue. His giant paw hit the door a little louder this time, and everyone inside looked up at the noise. I pressed myself up against the courtyard wall, trying to stay out of sight as Millie stood, apologizing profusely. Then Anasasha stood as well, with one hand raised. There was some brief discourse between her and Millie, but I couldn't see their lips well enough from where I sat to know what was said. Then Anasasha walked this way.

Be careful, Al's voice called out in my mind, followed by the sound of him flying up to a higher perch.

Anasasha paused on the other side of the door, her eyes quietly scanning the darkened courtyard until they landed on me. Her mouth twitched into a smile, and she grabbed two leashes from their hooks on the wall inside.

"Hey pups!" Her raspy voice was light and carefree as she stepped onto the patio and greeted Millie's dogs. "Need to go for a walk?" She cast a quick wink in my direction before attaching the leashes and tugging the dogs toward the gate.

I followed, keeping the blanket held over my body in a dramatic sweep low across the courtyard until we stepped out onto the chilled Manhattan street that led us to Central Park. We must have been a sight to behold: one girl who smelled like goat cheese and olives wearing a fuzzy blanket around her shoulders like a cape, and the other dressed like a princess, armed with two massive beasts on leashes. People in Oklahoma would have gawked at us. But in New York? No one batted an eye.

"Hey," I said once I was sure we were out of earshot. "Did you know I was outside?"

"I suspected." Anasasha grinned. "It's what I would have done in your shoes. But I was glad to see you. I haven't heard any big news since you left. How are... things?"

She wanted to know why we hadn't taken action with the tablet yet. I did make her a promise, after all, and it had been a few weeks with no major strides.

"Slow going," I admitted. "We only have half of the story right now. I'm not sure what steps to take next."

Anasasha nodded. "Well, all of the Keeper leaders will be here for the convention. Perhaps you will find a way to get the rest of the story soon.

How's Sean?"

"He's good." He was better than good. Almost running into a death trap in Atlantis had given Sean a new lease on life, and he was living it to its fullest. For the first time ever, he allowed himself to flirt with Abby, relaxing his guard and finally enjoying her company. He didn't even care about his dad missing. In fact, I suspect his father's absence actually removed some of the weight from Sean's shoulders.

But obviously I wasn't going to tell Anasasha all of that. "Were you okay after we left? It was kind of chaotic."

"Oh yeah, I was fine. The guards suspected it was Peter who set off the alarm, and they never even noticed I was missing. There's been a search for him since the day you left. They think he stole the tablet."

"What will they do to him if they find him?"

"Kill him." Anasasha shrugged. "But don't worry—there is no reason for them to suspect you and Sean. I made sure to clear our tracks thoroughly."

Peter was a jerk, but he didn't deserve to die. I made a mental note to try and locate him before the Atlantean guards did. Maybe I could get him to Porta Maris with Driskell.

"Thank you," I said after a beat, "for helping us out of there."

"You're the one who deserves the thanks. Just don't let me down."

We crossed over into the park and waited as a small group of teenagers passed on the sidewalk, giving us a wide berth to avoid the enormous dogs we had with us. I waited until I was sure we were alone again before dropping my voice to a near whisper and continuing the conversation.

"So you said *all* the royal families would be in attendance at the convention, right? Including the Agarthian family?" My heart picked up at the thought of Tate. I hadn't seen him since before we left for Porta Maris. He'd been tied up in some family affairs in Agartha.

"Yeah, everyone got into town yesterday."

"*Yesterday*?" Why hadn't he called me yet? Rasputin's warning about Tate working against me flashed through my mind, but I shoved the thought away. If Tate was working against me, he never would have helped Millie turn my aura blue. But why hadn't he reached out?

"Is something wrong?" Anasasha lifted her delicate brows.

"No, I just think I realized what my next step should be. But I need to get into the convention. Is there any way you can get me on the list?"

"I don't think so. My mother would definitely not approve of me adding you to our group—no offense. But maybe Millie can find a way to get you in."

It was last minute, but it was worth a try. Tate had promised before he left to keep an eye out for the missing piece of the tablet in Agartha. I had to see him.

CHAPTER 3

"MY HANDS ARE TIED Everly, I'm sorry." Millie frowned and squeezed my shoulder. "But I will be sure to keep an eye out for anything suspicious. I'll try to find out where Rossel ran off to, and I will definitely let you know if I hear anything about your mother. I miss her, too."

"I understand." I picked out a necklace from Millie's jewelry box and passed it to her as a finishing touch for her outfit. She was sitting on some kind panel at the convention today, so I wanted her to look her best, even if they wouldn't allow me in.

She'd explained that due to high security concerns, they limited the attendees to those who were absolutely required to attend. Though, I didn't see how Gayla and Dom would have made the list if it weren't for Gayla's father. Unfortunately, he couldn't do anything for me as an Atlantean.

A soft knock sounded at Millie's bedroom door. "You ready?" Devon called out through the crack.

Millie rubbed a fresh coat of bright pink lipstick onto her mouth and smiled. "Now I am." He cracked open the door and entered with a wide grin as he took in his much-older soulmate.

"Are you sure I can't just get Devon to teleport me in there?" I asked.

"They cast wards over the entire convention center," Devon said. "I can't even teleport *us* in there. All powers are rendered useless inside those walls."

Millie rolled her eyes. "It's Baerius's favorite trick. That man loves to make others powerless at any chance he gets."

"Baerius as in *King* Baerius of Olympus? Rossel's boss?"

Millie nodded. "Yes. And like I told you, I'll find out where Rossel is if I can. But there's no way he will show up at the convention after that report we filed on his cronies who ransacked my study."

"Right. Well be careful, just in case. Oh, and Millie? Will you please ask Tate to call me if you see him there?" I added as an afterthought.

"I will. We'll see you tonight at supper, okay? I'll bring you all my notes." She crossed a finger over her heart.

"Thanks, Millie. I'll see you then."

I waited a full five minutes before pulling out the bag I'd stashed under my aunt's guest room bed, and I changed into black pants and a long sleeved white button up-shirt. I didn't actually know who would be catering the event, but I'd watched enough TV shows in my life to guess that this was probably the caterer's uniform. Now I just had to get over to the convention center before the rest of the crew started without me. I was going to be the newest addition to their staff—they just didn't know it yet.

I was about two blocks away when a familiar voice called out in my mind. *You're a little overdressed for a casual morning stroll, don't you think?*

Without slowing, I turned my gaze upward to scan the window sills and balconies of the buildings that surrounded me. I wasn't sure how much distance could be between us for Al's mind to mind communication to work. And I really wished I could communicate back without speaking out loud.

I'm on the streetlight up ahead, just waiting for you to turn around and go back home.

I found him, perched casually on the light as if owls commonly hung out in Manhattan. Meeting his yellow eyes, I shook my head softly.

You're not seriously going to try to break into the convention, are you? That's a horrible idea. They will know immediately that you're not on the list, and if you're not careful, you'll get yourself put on a different *list instead.*

I ignored him, picking up my pace as I passed his little perch. He fluttered up ahead, talking silently into my mind again.

By different, I mean bad. Like hit-list kind of bad.

I shrugged and picked up into a jog.

Everly, seriously. Stop. You're obviously not a human, and no one is going to let you in when they see your aura—even if it is blue. How do you expect this to go down?

I didn't care how it went down. I just had to get closer to the action. If I couldn't actually get into the building without getting caught, then I'd hang out outside until they all left. They couldn't arrest me for hanging out on the street.

Of course, I still wasn't sure what exactly I was looking for. All I knew was that every Keeper leader was going to be in attendance, and they held any chance at getting the rest of the missing pieces of the tablet. And if I happened to run into Tate while I was there… Well, that would be okay, too.

Are you really just going to ignore me?

"Yup!" I said aloud, not caring who might overhear. I'd just spotted the catering van pull down the alley behind the convention center, and I wasn't interested in listening to the dire warnings of an owl anymore. It was show time.

I jogged across the street and waited for people to begin unloading from the vehicle before trotting around the corner. "Whew!" I wiped fake sweat from my forehead. "Looks like I made it just in time. I would hate to be late for my first day of work!"

Two guys and a girl stood outside the van wearing similar clothes to my own, though theirs had a company logo embroidered on the shirts. One of the guys furrowed his brow. "Who are you?"

I stepped up and extended my hand. "I'm Everly. The boss thought you might need some back up with the big event today, so I was asked to start right away. I hope you guys don't mind showing me the ropes?"

"Where's your apron?" the girl asked, noting my empty hands.

"Shoot! I knew I forgot something. Is there an extra I can borrow, just for today?"

"I'll look," the first guy said. "Follow me."

I turned briefly to flash a smug smile at Al, but he was gone. The others got back to work while the boy walked around to the back of a second van already parked in the alley. He opened the doors and made no effort at small talk and he rummaged through a couple of boxes sitting in the back. The rest of the staff was already carrying chafing dishes into a back door of the building, and I was itching to catch up to them.

The door was wide open. It would be so easy for me to just slip inside. Unless, of course, some of the wards Devon mentioned were designed to stop those of us who weren't on the list. Maybe Al was right. I shifted on my feet at the realization. What would I do if some kind of magical alarm was set off by my mere entrance into the building?

Some shuffling near the door drew my attention away from the van. "Sorry," a familiar voice said. "Pardon me... excuse me... oh, hellllooo."

The catering girl gawked at the tall handsome man who had just clumsily bumped into her. Tate winked and then slinked out of the door, trotting a little deeper into the alley away from where everyone was working.

"I'll be right back," I said to the boy who still hadn't found me an apron. "Tate!" I whisper-yelled his name as I neared the spot where he'd stopped, sleepily resting his head back against the wall. He opened one eye. "Hey. Why haven't you returned my calls?"

Never changing his casual stance, he grinned. "Sorry babe. I've been busy with work."

Babe? I took a step back. "Are you okay?"

"I am now that you're here." He winked at me.

I glanced over my shoulder, half-expecting to see Gayla with a camera, ready to laugh at another successful prank. But we were all alone other than the catering crew who seemed to have forgotten about me.

"What happened down there?"

"In Agartha?" He lifted his brows, seemingly a lot more interested in the conversation now.

"Yeah."

He thought for a minute before the corner of his mouth pulled up into a half grin. "I'll tell you, but it's gonna cost you."

I had no idea what had gotten into him. A million thoughts rushed through my brain. Had they drugged him? Was he under someone's glamour? Did Agartha simply bring out a different side of him?

"What's it gonna cost?"

His smile widened. "A kiss."

I knew he wasn't acting like himself, and yet the word still made my heart leap in my chest. "You're joking right?" A nervous giggle escaped me.

"Nope. Not joking." He stepped forward and reached for my hand, rubbing his thumb gently across the back of it before pulling me a little closer. We were nearly touching when he looked down at me with half-lidded eyes. "What do you say? A kiss for my secrets?"

He dropped his chin toward me, and common sense said to push him away. But common sense couldn't put up much of a fight with a face that pretty. It was only then that I began to feel that familiar faint buzz that simmered between us. It was different somehow, though.

Tate slid one hand behind my head, his fingers gently weaving into my hair as he lifted my face to his. My heart raced as he closed the gap. Something wasn't right.

"Titus!"

Tate dropped his hands, and we both spun toward the voice. The electricity dancing across my skin intensified, and I realized the figure sprinting across the alley toward us was... *Tate*.

I looked back and forth between the two Tates. "What in the world is going on?"

"That's what I was about to ask," the new Tate said. The tingly buzz was out of control as he approached, pulling me into him. This Tate—the new one—was the *real* Tate. No doubt about it.

"Who are you?" I turned back to the man I almost kissed.

"That's Titus. My brother."

CHAPTER 4

TITUS PUT TWO HANDS in the air with a laugh. "Sorry man. I haven't gotten to play Thaddeus in years. I couldn't resist. Especially with such a willing member of your fan club."

My cheeks heated. I couldn't believe I actually almost kissed this guy. What a jerk.

Tate frowned, avoiding eye contact with me. "You need to get back inside before they lose their minds."

"You always ruin my fun." Titus pouted.

"Go. I'll meet you in there in a second."

He hesitated with a look that told me he wanted to challenge his brother's command, but eventually Titus turned back toward the building. I waited until he was all the way back through the doors before spinning toward Tate. "How have you never mentioned you have a twin?"

"Nice to see you, too." Amusement flashed across Tate's eyes, and even that had my heart swooning in a way his imposter brother never came close to triggering. Maybe Titus was right. I'd forgotten how big of a fan I was of Tate.

I punched him playfully on the arm, causing a pleasant zing where my skin contacted his. He looked down as though he felt it too, but neither of us mentioned it.

"I'm serious," I said, suddenly feeling more emotional than the situation called for.

"I'm sorry. I can see why that might have been a shock to you. I never thought to mention it because I never expected the two of you to meet.

You knew I had a brother and I guess his appearance wouldn't have made any difference to you before now."

"I thought you had an *older* brother..."

"He is older—by eight minutes. And since I was born after midnight, technically we have two different birthdays, too."

I shook my head. "That's wild."

"I know. Who would have thought that a mere eight minutes would change the future of Agartha..." Tate grew serious again as he focused on me. "What are you doing here with the caterers?"

"Uh... definitely *not* trying to sneak into the convention."

"Right." Laughter shone in his eyes again. "And definitely not against the advice of all your friends."

"Not all my friends have been answering their phones to give me advice."

Tate ran a hand through his hair. "I feel like that was a jab against me."

"You're very perceptive."

"I didn't know you'd called. They took my phone."

"What? Why?"

He looked over his shoulder. "Things are a little shaky in Agartha right now. There's a certain part of our population who isn't very happy with some of the decisions my father is making in regards to his heir."

"Titus?"

Tate nodded. "He doesn't always make the best, uh... life decisions. In fact he's high as a kite right now on soma. So understandably, many Agarthians don't think he's fit for the job of king. And I guess my father's personal council has advised him to keep me close and cut off from anyone who may try to convince me to stake my claim on the throne. So they took my phone."

"Do you even *want* the throne?"

Tate shrugged. "I don't want to be king. But I don't want to watch Agartha implode because my brother is too busy looking for his next hit to lead the territory, either."

"That's rough. I'm sorry."

Tate forced a smile. "I didn't mean to unload all that on you. It's nothing you should have to worry about."

"Actually I do. I'm the Deliverer, remember?" I took a showy bow. "At your service."

Tate touched his fingertip to my lips and I thought I might melt into a puddle on the concrete. "Shh. You never know who's listening around here." He dropped his finger again and my lips were cold without it.

I wanted to touch him again, but I couldn't find any reasonable excuse for it. So I resorted to awkward humor instead. "You're right. That catering crew might be staging a coup as we speak."

He laughed, glancing down at my attire. "You know the Olympian guards inside would have had you pinned against the wall the moment you stepped foot into that building."

"Not once they tasted my goat cheese stuffed olives."

"I'm not sure how to respond to that."

"Maybe it's best if you don't." I wrinkled my nose, clamping my mouth shut before I started rambling about Jack Sparrow and trampolines again.

"You know there's nothing interesting that ever happens at these events, right? It's just the three races pretending we're all friends by sharing surface level data about what's going on in our territories. There's nothing useful. They keep their real secrets to themselves."

"I know," I admitted. "I'm just tired of sitting around and waiting on the sidelines. I'm ready to take action. And if I can get any kind of clue in here about where to go next, it'll be worth it."

"Are you sure?"

I nodded.

"Alright. Everly Gordon of Atlantis, I am officially requesting your assistance as a member of the royal Agarthian staff. Will you accompany me at the Annual Convention of the Keepers?"

"Agarthian staff?"

"We're not permitted to bring guests. But being royal has its perks. I can assign you a role on my staff."

"Is it permanent?" I remembered the Olympian guard I'd seen down in the prison of Atlantis. He could never leave.

"No. Not unless you request asylum in Agartha. This is just a one time thing."

"If you're sure... then yes. It's gotta be better than this alley. Besides, there's a lot that has happened since the last time I saw you. Is there a safe place we can talk inside?"

"I'll see what I can find. But first I have to attend a couple of meetings. You're welcome to join me, if you want. You'll need to look a little less like a caterer, though." He pulled my hair from my ponytail and ruffled his fingers through it, shaking out the waves as it fell to my shoulders. His fingertips on my scalp gave me ten times the goosebumps I got from a shampoo at my hairdresser. The touch was somehow both warm and tingly cool, and I never wanted it to stop. I was a bit breathless when he pulled his hands away.

We locked eyes, the gold flaring slightly in his amber colored irises, and I could feel that invisible thread pulling me ever nearer. Tate was gonna be trouble for me if I wasn't careful. I looked away, snapping the connection. "Let's get inside."

We walked slowly back toward the convention center, and I was acutely aware of how closely our hands swung with each step. It was like a magnetic pendulum, and I had to stay focused to prevent my fingers from reaching out to his as we moved together.

"This isn't the first time I've heard of soma. With that and ambrosia and the other myriad of substances I've heard mentioned on campus, I've gotta ask: do Keepers have a problem with addiction?"

"We're just like humans in many ways, only our substances are stronger. So yeah, a lot of Keepers do get addicted, unfortunately. But it's especially common in royal families. The pressure of leading a territory gets to be too much. There's a whole world to explore, but royal children are generally confined to a palace in a hidden territory, away from it all. It's hard."

I remembered Anasasha's brother tucked away in the prison in Atlantis, detoxing from some addiction of his own, and a chill ran down my spine. "How did you get out?"

Tate frowned. "I proved I could be useful in other ways."

Like hunting souls. It was all coming together now. And he must have been particularly skilled if Rossel sought him out specifically for me.

Tate paused outside the door. "I don't know if the agreement we had in the alley is enough for you to get past the wards. Is it alright if I take your hand until we can make sure you're safely added to the list? I'll try to shield you, just in case."

"Yeah, that's fine." I tried not to smile as his hand slid into mine. Every muscle in my body relaxed a little at the contact. It was like every cell had been yearning for his touch, and now that Tate and I were hand in hand, some of the tension could finally be relieved.

I couldn't even care about the confused faces of the catering staff as we hurried through the kitchen—right past the boy who had finally found me an apron. It wasn't until we were out in the main hall of the enormous building that the foolishness of my plan finally hit me.

There were thousands of Keepers around us. Auras of blue-green and purple and gold filled the space like a glowing Mardi Gras party, only much stiffer, with attendees wearing business attire instead of plastic beads. There were no white auras. Not one.

I squeezed Tate's hand and whispered softly. "Am I still... blue?"

"The bluest," he said with a grin.

He led me to a large concierge desk near the front entrance where a stunningly beautiful Olympian woman sat before a stack of glowing parchment. "Excuse me," Tate said to her. "I need to verify that Everly Gordon of Atlantis has been added to the list."

The woman placed her hand atop the stack and closed her eyes. "Everly Gordon. Personal attendant for Thaddeus Castellanos of the royal Agarthian family. She's here."

The ten year old version of myself immediately thought, *Everly Castellanos*. It was a bit long but not too bad. But I shook myself back to the present when Tate dropped my hand. Once again, I felt cold and alone. I wasn't ready to let go of him yet.

"You're official," he said with a nod.

We turned back to the main hall and I spotted Anasasha surrounded by a wall of guards just up ahead. She saw me as well, and a knowing smile spread across her pretty face. She looked from Tate to me and gave a not-so-subtle wink before getting moved along by her entourage.

"Was Anasasha winking at you?"

"Oh *that*? I dunno." I tried to play it off.

"How do you know her?"

I glanced around, unwilling to share too much where all these super-sensitive Keeper ears could hear me. "She was at Millie's house last night for a welcome dinner."

"Ah." Tate stepped over to the wall outside of some double doors leading into a large room set up for one of the morning's sessions. "One more question before we go in here."

"Sure." I leaned against the wall, happy to catch my breath before entering the room full of Agarthians. I had no idea what to say if any of them challenged me on my new role or tried to ask any questions.

Tate stepped in front of me, mischief gleaming in his eyes. He leaned in close enough that I felt his breath as he whispered the question in my ear.

"Were you really about to kiss my brother outside when you thought he was me?"

He pulled back enough to make eye contact again, a soft grin pulling at one side of his perfect lips. I pulled my gaze away from his mouth, desperately trying to calm my racing heart as I pretended to be stronger than I was. My whole body felt like it was on fire in the best of ways.

"He said he would tell me his secrets in exchange for a kiss. It sounded like a winning business transaction for me." I smirked and pushed Tate back away from me, knowing I didn't have the strength to stay there under his gorgeous gaze any longer.

And as we entered the room, I spotted Titus at a front table, surrounded by a small group of guards, but I only recognized one.

Osborne.

CHAPTER 5

"WHAT IS SHE DOING here?" Osborne rose from his feet, shouting across the room and drawing the attention of every golden-eyed Agarthian in the place.

Tate stepped closer to me, angling his body like a shield between me and Osborne. "She's my attendant for the day."

"Don't be a fool, Thaddeus. You're flirting with the enemy, here. I refuse to stand by while she gathers intel on our private matters, just to spoon-feed the information back to Rasputin!"

A collective gasp from the other Agarthians filled the air.

"You really think I wouldn't know if a member of my own staff was working with the enemy? You forget how powerful I am." Even with the wards cast over the building, Tate's power was evident. It radiated from him in a way that left the other Agarthians silent. He normally kept that card tucked away, but I was glad to see him playing it now with Osborne. Because secretly, it was taking a lot of self-control not to play my own power card.

"You better watch how you speak to a member of the royal family, Ozzie." Titus grinned. It was obvious now how glazed over his eyes were—half-lidded and slow moving. I didn't know how I'd missed it before. "Besides, I kind of like this girl." He gave me an exaggerated wink.

"I respect your opinion, your Highness." Osborne lied with a dip of his chin. "But I really have to insist that she leaves this room. It's a matter of security."

"Despite your blatant disrespect for the future leader of our territory, I would have to agree that my attendant should go. Not because she is a security threat," Tate chuckled, making eye contact with several of the other Agarthians around the room to ensure they recognized his condescension toward Osborne. "But rather because I would hate to subject her to such foolishness. Of course, I'll have to accompany her. As my attendant, she is not permitted to roam the convention without me. Come on, Everly. Let's get out of here."

"Bring her back for lunch!" Titus called out as we made our way back out to the main hall.

The building suddenly seemed much more crowded than before. Seeing Osborne had stirred something within me—something sinister that I didn't want to acknowledge right now. I needed to get somewhere quiet where I could calm myself.

We hadn't made it more than ten steps away from the room before Osborne said my name again behind us. I paused, and Tate put his hand lightly on the small of my back, somehow filling me with strength and confidence as I spun around to face the angry hunter on my heels.

"I know what you are," he said, and every muscle in my body tensed. "I know you're with the Manticorians, and if you're here it means Rasputin isn't far behind. But you can tell him that I'm ready for him. And I'm ready to finally take you down, once and for all. I'm waiting for any reason... Any reason at all. So go ahead—do what you came to do. Just know that I'm watching." Osborne sneered and then turned his glare on Tate. "And as for you, we're all just waiting for Titus to screw up so we can lock him away. Once I prove your association with this trash," he jerked his chin in my direction, "we'll lock you up alongside him. I'll finish the job you couldn't, and I will gladly take your place on the throne. It deserves someone who wants it. You were never cut out to be king anyway."

I lunged, but Tate's arm stopped me before I could get to Osborne. I wanted so badly to hurt him—to bash in that crooked nose of his, but of course that wouldn't do us any good.

"Nice monologue, Osborne. Very dramatic. But you can save it for the meeting you're about to be late for." Tate gestured back toward the room. "Now leave me. That's an order."

Osborne's jaw tightened so hard I expected it to crack, but he managed to hold in whatever insult was on the tip of his tongue. Eventually, he turned back toward the meeting room.

But even with Osborne gone, we were surrounded by hundreds or maybe thousands of other Keepers bustling around the convention center.

And seeing Osborne reminded me of my original task. I had to find the other pieces of the tablet. Now that I had Tate—and maybe even Titus on my side—I wondered if it would be possible for me to search Agartha for the next piece.

"I need to talk to you." I looked at Tate and dropped my voice to a whisper. "Privately."

He nodded. "There's only one place I trust in this building. But we'll have to get around my father first."

CHAPTER 6

TATE LED ME OVER to a glass elevator at the center of the main hall and hit a button on the wall beside it.

"A glass cage in the middle of all the most powerful Keepers in the world? Obviously the top choice for privacy. Good idea."

He tried to hide his amusement. "Just get on."

I followed him into the small space, actually grateful that we were on full display in the middle of the convention hall. Last time we'd been in an elevator together it took everything I had to keep myself away from him. Knowing there were thousands of powerful eyes watching now seemed to help numb that sensation. Just a little, though.

The doors closed silently behind me, and I noted that Tate had put as much distance between us as he could. That was a good thing. I could ignore the invisible electric thread tugging me toward him if he stayed far enough away.

"Each of the royal families gets a designated conference suite here at the hall. There are extra protections over the rooms so sensitive information can be freely discussed. When we were kids, Titus and I used to play around with the wards, looking for any way to tear them down and spy on the other families, but it was impossible. So anything you have to say will be safe within the suite."

"I think I'm less afraid of being overheard than I am of meeting your dad. If he's been trying to keep you cut off from everyone, he probably won't be too thrilled to see that you've picked up a new *attendant*."

"You don't need to worry about him." It looked like there was more Tate wanted to say, but he bit down on the words. It was probably wise as we had just reached the top floor. The elevator doors opened to reveal a sky bridge leading over the road outside and into an attached hotel next to the convention center.

Neither of us spoke as we meandered down a hall over plush, colorful carpet. We passed a couple of other small groups of Keepers—none of the races mixing together much—and I only got a couple of raised brows from the Atlanteans when they saw me trailing Tate.

We'd been walking maybe five minutes and gone up another elevator when a door slammed open at the end of the hotel hallway.

"Shoot," Tate said under his breath. "I think that's our suite."

Sure enough, three tall Agarthians marched out into the hallway, looking like they didn't have time for anyone or anything that may cross their path. They were on a mission. Next came a silver fox of a man—strikingly handsome. His salt and pepper hair was the only thing that aged him at all, and I noted the similarities between him and his sons immediately.

"Well, we found your dad," I whispered.

Three more Agarthian guards followed in back, effectively surrounding the king. Two of them landed their scrutinizing eyes on me, but the king seemed indifferent. He hardly even greeted his own son.

"Everything alright?" Tate asked as his father rushed by us.

"Fine," the king replied gruffly. He definitely didn't look fine, though. A couple more of the guards were eyeing me now, as well. "Keep it moving," he barked at his people.

Tate didn't press any further. He scooted me back toward the wall, keeping one arm spread before me like a bodyguard, even though I was supposed to be the one attending to *him*. I didn't mind it though. The warmth radiating off his skin brought me a sense of comfort.

The crowd rushed by us and turned a corner at the end of the hall without once looking back. "What was that all about?" I asked once they were gone.

"I have no idea. But judging by the look on his face it was much more urgent than he wanted me to believe it was." Tate stared after them down the empty hall for just another moment before shaking his head and gesturing toward the suite they'd exited. "At least we have the room to ourselves now."

My stomach flipped a little bit at the thought. It was fine. Everything would be fine. There was no good reason for me to freak out at the thought of being alone with him. It's not like I would lose all self-control without a chaperone...

I took a deep breath as he scanned a card and unlocked the door. No one was inside, but it looked like the king and his guards had been engaged in a meeting before hurrying out into the hall. Several half-finished glasses of a golden beverage sat throughout the room, condensation leaving glistening trails down the sides of the glasses and pooling onto the coffee table in the center of the room.

The suite was huge—more like an apartment than a hotel room. There was the living area that we'd entered into, a small kitchenette, and two separate wings of what I assumed were individual bedrooms.

"This place is fancy," I said, taking it all in. "Are you sure there's no one else here? Where are *your* guards?"

"I don't get any guards." Tate plopped down onto the middle cushion of the couch. "Those are reserved for the king and the heir. I forfeited my right to royal coddling when I joined the hunters."

I sat next to him and immediately felt that invisible thread tighten. It was a jolt, warm and electric in my chest, pulling me hard toward Tate. I refused it, leaning back to the arm of the couch instead. And Tate scooted down to the other arm, leaving a full cushion open between us.

"You feel it too, don't you?"

His golden gaze jerked up to mine, and his hand moved toward his chest. "Huh?"

"That tingly buzz. The... nevermind." One look at his blank expression stopped me in my tracks. I felt like a fool. There was no way I was about to explain how I felt some invisible connection pulling me toward him. That was a one way ticket to crazy ex-girlfriend territory. Not that I was his girlfriend. Just a friend. And a girl... who was mildly attracted to him.

It could never work between us even if I *was* attracted to him. He was Agarthian. I was Atlantean. It was forbidden. I didn't want him bad enough to be cursed and die for it.

"Okay... so... you're sure we're alone?" I asked, getting back to what really mattered.

"Positive. What did you want to tell me?"

"I went to Atlantis."

"How was it?" He turned his body toward me, folding one leg under as he pulled it up onto the couch.

"It was nothing like I imagined." I explained our heated run-in with Peter, and Anasasha's crush on Sean. He stared wide eyed as I told him about the tablet and our speedy escape through the ocean. Then I mentioned the Kraken.

"You did not cut off a piece of the Kraken," he said with a laugh.

"Oh, I totally did. You can ask Sean. I think he's still got the slimy little tentacle." I shuddered. "Nasty monster."

"You're amazing," he said, shaking his head with a smile.

I dipped my chin, trying to hide the blush I felt creeping into my cheeks. "I'm just doing my job. Fulfilling my destiny and all that." When I looked up again I realized we'd both somehow drifted closer to the center during my tale, but I didn't want to scoot back again. "Anyway, we got the tablet back to Driskell."

"Was he able to interpret it?"

I nodded and recited it to him from memory.

"The daughter of sea and sky?" Tate rubbed his forehead. "And you don't know who your dad is, right?"

"Nope. That might make this whole thing a little easier."

He repeated the words again under his breath. "Sea makes sense, being from Atlantis and all. But sky? I can't think of any Atlantean powers that involve the sky."

"My mom was a messenger."

"Yeah, but that's more about bending reality than flying through the air. Olympus is known as the city in the sky. And there are Agarthians who can control the wind and move clouds and stuff. But for Atlanteans?" He shook his head again. "I've got nothing."

"What about talking to owls?"

Tate's brows pulled together. "That seems like a very specific question."

"Athena could talk to owls. And she was Atlantean, right?"

"Oh." He nodded. "Yeah. That seems like a stretch though."

I'd have to ask Al about it the next time I saw him. I hadn't ever really considered it from that angle before.

Tate leaned toward me with that crooked grin that only meant mischief again. "Maybe we should focus on the next line of the prophecy instead. The part about the one who ignites your heart."

"Dom thinks it's referring to my soulmate."

"That makes sense." Tate's grin widened. "Although you looked pretty ignited by my brother earlier."

I punched him again, intensifying the electric tug between us. "I told you it was just a business transaction."

He looked down at his arm, his grin fading slightly. "I do feel it."

"Feel what?" My heart jumped in my chest.

"The *tingly buzz*, I think you called it?"

He reached for my hand, igniting the skin where we touched. His thumb rubbed gently over my knuckles, creating a fizzy sensation. It almost tickled, but in a much more serious, personal way.

"Oh," was all I could say.

"It's strange, isn't it? At first I thought it had to do with black magic. You know, Rossel told me you were deep in the stuff. I thought it was some ancient hunter instinct coming through, warning me that you were bad news. But now I know I'm the only one who feels it, other than you. Do you feel it around anyone else?"

I shook my head, unable to speak. My heart was pounding so loud I thought the neighbors in the suite next door might complain.

"It keeps drawing me back to you. I can't seem to get enough. I thought about you the whole time I was in Agartha. I searched the entire palace for that tablet, just so I could see you smile when I brought it back."

"My smiles aren't cheap, but I bet you could have found an easier way to get one." I grinned, just to prove my point. I wasn't sure how else to respond. I'd never seen Tate behave so sincerely.

"I wonder," he said, meeting my eyes. The gold flared, creating a subtle glow that I couldn't look away from.

"Wonder what?" My voice was barely a whisper.

"What would happen if I kissed you?"

I didn't even realize how much closer we'd gotten until he rested his hand on my cheek. Every cell in my body was alive, dancing and whirling in the electric sensation humming between us.

"There's only one way to find out." It was more than a dare. It was a request. I needed to know—needed to feel his lips on mine.

And Tate did not disappoint.

CHAPTER 7

TATE CASTELLANOS WAS NOT my first kiss.

I got a swollen lip from Chad Rankin's braces one year at church camp. Owen Griggs smooched me on the hay in his daddy's barn, and Zach Bajek made me feel like the prettiest girl in Oklahoma when he kissed me under the stars at Homecoming.

But every one of those moments was laughable compared to what I felt when Tate's lips found mine. I'm not even exaggerating when I say it felt like the world shifted. Everything changed in an instant.

The thread that seemed to tie us together was now an unbreakable rope holding us close, never letting us go. It was stronger than the grip of the Kraken. It was stronger than I cared to admit, honestly. It was something ancient. Something bigger than life itself.

We leaned into the kiss more—neither of us able to contain ourselves nor willing to try. And the sound of blood rushing through my ears from my pounding heart was almost enough to drown out the incessant tapping noise at the window.

Almost.

Tate pulled away an inch or so, smiling down at me. But his smile quickly faded. "Everly!" his hands slid from my shoulders down to my wrists, extending my arms. "You're glowing."

I looked down, but saw only skin.

Tap tap. Tap tap tap.

A quick glance over to the window confirmed what I somehow knew I'd see. A little white owl sat perched on the window sill, yellow eyes wide as his little feet moved nervously from side to side. Al tapped again.

Tate followed my gaze. "It's an owl." Then back to me, "daughter of sea and sky... Do you have the soul of Athena?"

"Apparently." I shrugged. "Do you mind if I let him in?"

"Go ahead." Tate ran a hand through his hair, looking as confused as I felt. The connection between us was still palpable, but it seemed less urgent and more confident somehow as I strolled away from Tate and toward the window. It was like the buzzing had been satisfied, and it was replaced with a bond of some kind.

I lifted the window, and Al hopped inside. *The Manticorians are here*, he said silently in my mind.

"Here?! At the convention? That's not good."

"Did the owl tell you something?" Tate stood and met us by the window. "Is everything okay? Your glow is..."

Bright. Al blinked and tilted his head at a strange angle. *It's more than an aura, Everly. You're actually glowing white.*

I looked down again as Tate gently ran his hand back and forth over my skin. I saw nothing but chill bumps in response to Tate's touch.

"It's beautiful," he whispered, "but we can't let anyone see you like this. When's the last time you took your aura pills?"

"This morning. I didn't want to risk it fading while I was here."

"I wonder if it's a reaction to that kiss." Tate's eyes were round, the gold a deeper, richer hue than normal. A butterfly flipped over in my belly, and despite Al's bad news, I wanted to kiss Tate again and see just how bright my glow could get.

I glanced nervously at Al.

Oh don't worry. I already saw everything. There was judgment in those sentient eyes. *But I don't care right now. Like I said... Manticorians. Here. Now. You've got to get out before they destroy the place.*

"We've got to go, Tate. Al said the Manticorians are here."

"Al?" He looked at the creature. "Al the owl?"

Alpheus, he called out in my mind, but of course Tate couldn't hear him.

"Yeah."

"Okay, but I don't know how we're going to get you out of here with you glowing like that."

I walked over the window and quickly marked it off our list of options. We were at least ten stories in the air. Even with my new Keeper strength and power, I didn't think I'd survive a fall like that.

"I'll go check the hall," Tate said, pacing nervously. "Stay here. You'll be safe as long as you're in my suite. I promise."

He ducked out into the hall a moment later, leaving me alone with Al. "Are the Manticorians here for *me*?"

I don't know for sure, but it's likely.

I rubbed my hands over my face. They wouldn't kill me. Rasputin had made it clear that he wanted me on their side. But based on the stories I'd heard from Millie, they wouldn't hesitate to kill anyone else who got in their way. That meant Tate was in danger.

"Hey Al, what do you know about my soulmate?"

What soulmate?

"Like from past lives. Who was he?"

Al flew over to the back of the couch. *You've never found your soulmate.*

"Never?"

He blinked. *You've taken lovers over the centuries, but it's never been anything more than casual. You've never had children. Never bonded with another soul.*

"What would it feel like if I had?"

Al turned toward the door. *They say it's different for everyone; and you just know. But Everly, it's impossible for you to have a non-Atlantean soulmate. The races can't mix. You'd be cursed and killed.*

"I know." I ran a hand across my arm where Tate had touched me moments earlier, my skin still singing from his contact. "But what if I'm not Atlantean? What if I'm something different altogether?"

Uttering the words aloud felt good. I was emboldened by the thought. My inner Athena rose up and cheered, and I began to see the situation at hand in a whole new light.

I'm starting to wonder if that might just be true, Al said.

"In that case, bring on the Manticorians."

CHAPTER 8

AL EXPLAINED SOME OF my favorite fighting moves from previous lives, which would have been great had I been armed with a spear or a longbow. Unfortunately, I had nothing but my fists. I'd even left Rossel's dagger at home, not thinking I'd be going into battle today.

Obviously Al's wings weren't teaching me much in the way of hand to hand combat. But still, I wasn't afraid. I was more eager than anything. Deep down, I was confident that my inner Athena would pull through for me somehow.

The sound of a key card in the door sent Al into the air. He flew to the window sill and turned back to me. *Stay close to Tate. I'll wait for you downstairs.* Then he was off.

I turned back just in time to watch Tate stumble through the front door, gag in his mouth and arms held tightly behind his back. My blood turned to lava and I immediately stepped forward, ready to destroy whoever had him bound. But the look in Tate's eyes cautioned me to stay back.

The next person through the door was the last man I expected to see. Peter Bratton entered, shoving Tate further into the room and sneering in my direction. "We meet again," he said with an evil grin.

"Let go of him." I wasn't afraid of Peter. I'd already won one fight against him. There was no way I'd let him walk away again—not after seeing what he'd done to Tate. I moved forward once more, only to see another slow moving body enter the room.

She was ancient. Older than old. Her hair was so white it looked translucent, and she probably had cobwebs in her ears. Her eyes were blacker than a starless sky, her skin pale and wrinkled like a raisin. She was Olympian, but not like any other I'd ever seen.

And she wasn't the last. Standing a full two feet taller than the hunched old woman was Rasputin, looking absolutely delighted to see me.

"Don't be rude," he said to Peter in his thick Russian accent. "We are the guests here. We do not want to wear out our welcome."

"No one said you were welcome here. Especially not when you've got a royal son of Agartha bound up like a criminal."

"He tried to hit me," Peter said.

"You probably deserved it," I spat back.

"Now, now." Rasputin raised his arms like he was calming a pair of fighting siblings. Meanwhile, the old woman glided deeper into the suite, almost floating across the ground the way Rossel did, and plopped down on the couch. Peter grabbed Tate's arms and shoved him forward as well.

"That's not necessary! Untie him."

"Not until we know he won't strike against us," Rasputin said before turning to me with a pout. "You never came back to see me. And there is much left for us to discuss. Have you given any more thought to my offer?"

"What offer? Going to work with you?" I scoffed. "Never. I've heard about the things you've done."

"No one can help you like I can. Do you see anyone else able to blow down these simple wards? Anyone else with enough power and resources to know where you are at all times? Your prince here could not have saved you if we'd meant harm. What would you have done?"

"I would have fought. And if I died, then so be it. It would be more honorable than joining you."

"You say that now, but you know so little." Rasputin stepped toward me, and I felt Tate tense from across the room. He was seated on the couch beside the old Olympian woman, who downed one of the half-finished Agarthian beverages leftover from before we arrived.

"Take Peter here." Rasputin stopped a foot before me and gestured toward the sitting area. "He was so underappreciated by his people that they chased him out, even when he put his career on the line to warn them of you. But don't worry my darling, he knows you are what we need now. He has joined the right side now, and look how much good it has done him. He is more powerful than ever."

Peter lifted the entire couch with Tate and the old woman still on it. He didn't even break a sweat. He set them back on the ground and grinned at me, cracking his knuckles.

I maintained an even expression... or tried to, anyway. "I see you got rid of the wards to block your powers. Have they been destroyed across the entire convention?"

"Only for those with the right connections." He winked and stepped uncomfortably close to me. "I am more powerful than they are. Join me and I can help you maximize *your* power, as well. It is the only way you will be able to accomplish what the prophecy asks of you." He paused, reaching an old hand out to my face. "The glow is quite lovely. It is different from the powers of the other Keepers. Lucky for you, I know about the lost arts. I know the magic that the rest of the world has forgotten. The time is growing near for you to put your powers to use. You can feel it too, can't you darling?" His wrinkled fingers grazed my cheek and Tate leapt up from his spot on the couch, only to be quickly brought to his knees by Peter.

"Get your hands off of him!" My voice was like a growl—something foreign I'd never heard before. My heart beat in my chest like a war song, building me up. I could feel the power flooding my veins, ready to break free at a moment's notice. It was stronger now than I'd ever felt it before, like a tidal wave sweeping me off my feet. I wasn't fully in control of it.

Peter must have heard the power in my voice. He raised his hands in the air but remained close enough to knock Tate back down if he had to. I was seconds away from putting Peter in his place when I saw a flash of white near the window. Rasputin glanced that way as well.

There are more, Al said in my mind. *They're everywhere out here. We're going to have to fight back.*

I nodded to show that I understood. Rasputin looked from the window to me and back again, a small smile curling at the corner of his mouth, pulling up his long mustache. It faltered when the door slammed open into the wall at the front of the suite.

I whipped around to see who had joined us, only to be more disheartened than ever.

"I knew it!" Osborne shouted. "As soon as I saw you here I knew Rasputin would be close behind. Your game is up."

He raised his arm and I braced myself for impact, but it wasn't me he aimed for. A strong fist struck Rasputin squarely in the jaw. It should have knocked the old man down, but he somehow vanished and reappeared on the opposite side of the room. Osborne let out a roar and lunged for him. With a flicker of a smile, Rasputin played his trick again.

Now is our chance, Al's voice said in my mind. I'd forgotten he was there. *We'll attack while they're distracted. We need to get Tate free so he can help us. Aim for Peter on the count of three. Ready?*

I nodded.

One… two…

On three we converged. I went for Peter's legs while Al dive bombed his face. Secretly, I hoped he pecked the man's eyes out.

I had a surprising amount of momentum—definitely more than Peter was expecting. Not only did I knock him off his feet, but I sent him flying over the coffee table and into the opposite wall. A yell came from somewhere out in the hall and I wondered how many other Manticorians we would soon be facing.

At least I wouldn't have to do it alone. I dropped to Tate's side, yanking the gag from his mouth and ripping the restraints from his wrists. "That was amazing," he said breathlessly.

"Less complimenting and more action!" I pulled him up to his feet. "Also, thanks," I added with a grin. "Are your powers working at all?"

His face tightened into a look of concentration, but nothing happened. "Stay down, Peter."

His voice contained the many layers I'd heard before when he went into siren mode, but it felt weak. And it was completely ineffective. Peter stood, lip curled as he turned back to face me.

More yelling poured in from the hall, and Al's voice rang out in my mind again. *They're coming.*

I turned back to the door, ready to take on whoever Rasputin had behind him, but all I saw was a crowd of other Keepers, pale faced and slack jawed as they took in the fight in our room.

Not there, Al said. *At the window.*

Peter barked out a laugh as I discovered the real threat rising up outside the building. Through the window, levitating in the air ten stories off the ground, was a small army of strange looking humans. They had no auras as far as I could tell, but there was something off about them.

"Witches," Tate whispered.

Rasputin appeared from thin air just feet away from me with a wide grin. "Are you sure you don't want to reconsider my offer, darling?"

CHAPTER 9

THIS TIME IT WAS Tate's fist that swung for Rasputin's face, but the man was quick. He didn't fight fairly, but he could certainly get out of the way in a jiffy when he needed to. Rasputin appeared near the window, mouth moving silently as the army of floating witches shifted to almost a single file line coming toward the building.

Al flew across the room like a bolt of lightning, headed straight for the Manticorians before they could reach us.

Tate was already moving back toward Rasputin. I ran over and grabbed his arm. "You go help Al. I'll handle him."

"Are you sure?"

I nodded. I was positive that I wanted to be the one to put a stop to Rasputin and his army of evil. But more than that, I didn't want Tate to get hurt. I knew Rasputin wouldn't hurt me because I had what he wanted: power. "Just keep the witches out of here if you can."

Tate listened without putting up a fight, and his confidence in me boosted my own. I marched over to Rasputin without any real clue as to what I was going to do. I just knew I wanted to stop him.

From my periphery, I saw Osborne run out into the hall. I heard him yelling, but I couldn't quite make out his words. My only focus was on the evil old bearded man before me.

"Don't you touch him!" Peter's voice boomed behind me. Some sense I didn't know I possessed felt him coming, and without even pausing to look over my shoulder, I instinctively thrust my hands out to the sides and heard Peter's body hit the floor.

Power surged white hot through my limbs. Wards or no wards, nothing was holding me back. But Rasputin didn't look afraid. If anything, he looked almost proud. "Well done, darling."

I flicked my wrist at him next, feeling the heat of power gather into my hands and fly out toward the man. Rasputin met the surge with a hand in the air, calmly lifting his palm toward me and effectively halting the magic I'd thrown his way.

"I don't want to hurt you. I wish you would not try to hurt me, either. Come. Let me show you how to use that power you harbor. I have much to teach you."

I tried again to throw something his way, and again it was blocked.

Tate stood by the window, knocking out any witches who Al hadn't already thrown off course. There was some scuffling out in the hall and the sound of Peter groaning on the floor behind me. I was aware of every movement, every action taking place around me. And as I continued to move toward Rasputin, the warrior part of my brain kicked into high gear, evaluating every object in the room along with its ease of use and potential for massive damage if used as a weapon.

I'd become a machine, and I loved it.

The noise from the hall grew louder, and I heard gasps along with the shout of a man in power. "Move over!"

Tate turned from the window, an unreadable expression on his handsome face. I couldn't even fathom what he might have been thinking as his father entered the room, along with Osborne and the small group of guards who'd accompanied him out earlier.

"There!" Osborne pointed to me. "That's the girl I warned you about. She led Rasputin right to us. If there's anyone to blame for Titus' disappearance, it's her."

We were standing in a room with the leader of the Manticorians and a gang of witches flying outside the window, and all Osborne could think about was throwing me under the bus.

What a vengeful idiot.

I snorted. Al took the words right out of my mouth. But no one else found the situation funny at all. Tate's father looked at me for a moment, but he was much more interested in Rasputin.

"Hello again, your majesty." Rasputin's voice dripped with condescension.

"Where's my heir?"

Rasputin grinned. "How should I know?"

"I'll ask you one more time. Where is my heir?" The king's voice boomed, shaking my bones. Even the witches took pause at the authority he commanded.

"Titus is missing?" Tate stepped forward but his father held out a hand to silence him. The gesture made me angrier than it probably should have.

"Listen to me you crazy old man. I am backed by some of the greatest guardians of Agartha. Hand me my son and I will let you leave, never to return. Don't, and I will allow my team of fire-wielders, shapeshifters, and sirens to do with you as they please."

"We both know that cannot happen," Rasputin replied, calmly. "They have no power here. And I do."

"So do I." I sent a blast of magic toward the old man, finally catching the king's attention. Rasputin stumbled, losing his balance, but he didn't fall like Peter. I wasn't sure if my powers had already been somewhat used up or if Rasputin was simply powerful enough to withstand them. It didn't matter, though. He was off-balance enough to provide an opening for attack.

"Go!" the king shouted, and his guards seized the opportunity to lunge for Rasputin. Some tried their powers and confirmed that they did not work under the wards. Others went straight for the man with fists and knives.

Rasputin played the same party trick he'd done with Osborne earlier, disappearing and reappearing at random across the room. It was infuriating, and the Agarthians grew angrier with every dodge.

I joined Tate and Al near the window, helping to fight off any other witches that tried to join in on the fun while Osborne grappled with Peter in the living room. All the while, the old Olympian woman stared blankly into dead space, her eyes black and unmoving, completely indifferent to the chaos taking place around her.

One large swipe of my power through the air took out an entire wave of the witches, buying us a moment of time to survey the damage in the room. Tate's father paced, barking out orders as the guards tried again and again to take Rasputin down.

I expected the Maticorian to destroy them all within minutes, but he surprisingly made no moves to injure anyone. He simply dodged their attacks, grinning with every move.

Peter was a different story, however. With his powers strengthened and Osborne's powers dead, he easily overcame the younger man and made straight for the king at his first opportunity.

"Don't even think about it," Osborne said, running to save his leader from harm. Peter swatted him away easily.

The king tried to fight back as well, but it was no use. Peter wrapped the king in a stranglehold, red faced and gasping for air. No one stood a chance next to Peter's strength and finesse under these circumstances. No one except me.

"Let him go, Peter. He's just looking for his son. You know what it's like to care about your son."

Peter sneered. "My son turned on me."

"That's not true," I said, stepping closer. I saw the crazed look in his eyes and knew we were treading on delicate ground here. "It's not too late for you to come back to us, Peter. Come back to Atlantis. Back to our people. Show them you can do the right thing. Just let the king go and you'll be recognized as a hero—the man who saved the annual convention."

He yanked harder on the king's neck. Tate's muscles were coiled, and he was ready to pounce on the man at any moment. But he saw the look in Peter's eyes just as well as I did. One wrong move could mean disaster.

"Atlantis doesn't care about me. They won't care about you, either. Rasputin was right. Your only option now is to join us. They'll slaughter you for that aura. Once they know who you really are, you're dead."

"That's enough." Rasputin appeared inches away from Peter and placed a hand on the man's arm. "Not another word. Let me speak with the king."

He'd no more than finished his sentence when Osborne came sprinting at him out of nowhere. He'd intended to strike the king, but his target vanished, as he'd done so many times before. And Peter, misinterpreting Osborne's move as an attack against him, struck as well.

The crack of Tate's father's neck under Peter's massive arm was sickening. His body went limp instantly, and Peter dropped him to the floor.

"No!" Tate yelled.

Something clicked within me. Time stopped. The room went silent. Motionless. I walked slowly over to where the king lay dead on the floor and shook my head. Surely there was something I could do. If I could stop time, perhaps I could reverse it, too.

I tried. I tried again and again to find a rewind button until the tears streamed down my face. Nothing worked. I looked up to where Tate still stood with his face twisted into shock and grief, and I felt broken. Useless. What good were my powers if I couldn't use them when it mattered?

I looked back at Rasputin then. He was still like the others, but there was something about the expression on his face that left me feeling uncomfortable. I got the sense that I was being watched. That he knew exactly what was happening.

The feeling threw me off, and I willed time to kick back into gear again. Rasputin fixed his gaze on me and winked. Then, in a flash he was gone.

He'd left the premises entirely this time, along with Peter and every one of his witches. They were all just... *gone.*

All that remained was the damage they'd done. Broken glass lay on the floor beside a dead king of Agartha. The guards nursed light wounds, and Osborne dropped in despair down to the king's side.

My heart ached for Tate and his loss. But more than that, it ached for the loss of this world as we knew it. Rasputin was on the loose, the king was dead, and strange power pulsed through my veins. I was pretty sure I'd created an impossible bond with Tate that would one day kill me. And despite myself, I stood in that messy suite silently wondering just what exactly my connection to Rasputin really was.

What if he wasn't lying? What if he really could help me?

CHAPTER 10

"WHAT HAVE YOU DONE?" Osborne stood and wiped his forearm across his wet nose. "All of this for *her*? Your father is dead, Thaddeus. Dead! Your brother is missing. And it's all because you were too weak to carry out a simple task. You should have killed her the first time."

Tate was still too shocked to respond, staring down at his father's lifeless body. A couple of the guards gathered around to console him while the rest went to do crowd control on the Keepers that curiously gathered around the entrance to the suite.

"You've got it all wrong, Osborne," I said, trying to calm the warrior soul rising up again in my chest. "*You* got the king killed. *You* frightened the man who had the king's life in his hands. *You* attacked when you should have paused. War is about more than taking every life in sight. It's about knowing when to strike and when to hold back."

"It's also about having the spine to do what needs to be done. Tate is too weak."

I was on him like a flash of light, my arm pressed against his throat, holding him to the wall. "Do not disrespect him. He is stronger than you know. And from where I stand, it looks like he may be your new ruler."

Tate glanced in my direction. "What?"

Osborne cursed loudly. I released him from my hold and turned to Tate. "If it's true that your brother is missing, I assume that leaves you in line as the next heir to the throne, right?"

"We'll bring it to the council," one of the guards said, resting a hand on Tate's back. "They'll tell us how to proceed."

"What happened in here?" Gayla's voice exclaimed from the door. A moment later she pushed through the crowd of nosy onlookers, followed by Dom. "Oh, Everly!" She rushed forward and threw her arms around my neck. "You're glowing."

"We heard Rasputin was here," Dom added. Then, noticing the king, she gasped and threw a hand up over her mouth.

"You need to get out of here," Tate said softly. "Osborne will try to blame this on you and you'll be locked up without a trial. Let me explain what happened and maybe get a telepath to confirm it. The guards will have my back. Find Sean to protect you until I finish up here—not that you *need* any protection." He tried to smile, but the pain of losing his father was still fresh.

"Was there a seer here?" Gayla stood stone-still in front of the couch. Her eyes had gone dark and her expression was unclear. "I can smell the magic in the air." She spun slowly, as though searching for something, then knelt before the coffee table. "Look."

We gathered around to see what she'd found. Drawn out by an ancient finger dipped in the water of the condensation on the table were three words: *The Firelake Blade*.

"What does it mean?" I whispered. I couldn't smell the magic as Gayla could, but I felt it. Something old and powerful hung heavily in the air. It called to me in the way the tablet's pieces did.

"I'll explain later. Get to Sean. I'll meet you at the apothecary as soon as I can." Tate ushered me to the door, but I made sure to give Osborne one last steely look before leaving. It was a warning. *Chase after me, and you're done.* Judging by the clenching of his jaw, I think my message was received.

"Move, people." Dom led the way, pushing a clear path through the crowd full of gaping Keepers. Whispers filled the hall as we made our way through. Word about the fight had spread fast, and it seemed like everyone from the convention had made their way over into the hotel. So much for keeping my glowing white aura a secret.

Millie and Devon spilled out of an elevator down the hall just before we disappeared into the stairwell. "There you are!" she rushed forward with tears in her eyes. "Hurry, let's get out of the building so Devon can get you back to safety."

We hurried down the stairs and Devon wasted no time teleporting Millie and I into the back room of her shop the moment we stepped foot on the sidewalk. He left again, and a moment later returned with Gayla and Dom.

"Millie? Is that you?" Abby peeked through the curtains, startled to see such a large group of us suddenly sitting around the table in the back of the apothecary.

Millie did a poor job of playing it cool. She tried to smile, but her hands were still visibly shaking. "We had a break between sessions and decided to come back here for a pit stop. We came through the back door. Sorry I didn't say anything when we arrived."

Abby looked skeptical but didn't have time to respond before Sean popped his head through the curtain as well. "Do you mind taking over up front, Abby? There's a woman looking for natural arthritis relief and I'm not sure what to suggest."

She frowned. "Alright."

The second she was gone, Sean fixed his gaze on me. "Holy cow, Everly. You're glowing like a light bulb. What on earth happened?"

Millie fixed us all some kind of calming herbal tea while I explained everything that took place with Rasputin and his Manticorians. I told them how the Agarthian king died, and Titus apparently went missing. But I left out the part about Tate and I, and our possible new... bond? I wasn't even sure what to say about it. I just knew that something was different.

"How many people saw you?" Sean asked, waving his finger up and down. "Looking like that..."

"A lot," I admitted. "They're already talking. Osborne will probably tell them I'm working with Rasputin, but Tate thinks the other guards will defend me. I just don't know."

I watched Millie's expression as we discussed Rasputin. There was still a nagging suspicion in the back of my mind that he may be more connected to me than I'd ever guessed. But I was afraid to voice my question aloud. Millie gave no indication that she knew anything more than I did.

"Everly!" Abby called out from the front of the apothecary. "You have a visitor."

I ran through the front door, feeling the warmth in my chest before I ever saw him there. Tate stood just inside the door, looking only slightly disheveled despite all the action that had taken place earlier. Through the window I spotted Al as well, watching through the glass with those sharp yellow eyes.

"Hey." My feet moved of their own accord. Tate walked forward as well, that invisible rope yanking us together. The only difference was that neither of us fought against it now. We met in the middle of the shop, and Tate slid his fingers into my hair, pulling my face up to his. He kissed me, and again I felt like the world shifted around us. His touch fed the power within me, physically strengthening me as our mouths moved together as one.

"Ahem." Millie cleared her throat. We pulled away to find our friends all gawking along the side of the wall.

I didn't care. I stared into his golden eyes, which reflected the same relief I felt. I needed that... needed him on some deeper level I didn't yet understand.

"You're safe," he whispered.

"I am. But it's time to figure out where we go from here."

CHAPTER 11

"I ALWAYS KNEW YOU two were gonna get together eventually." Gayla grinned, then clarified. "Not like through a vision or anything. You've just got *chemistry*." She did a little shimmy.

Dom was less enthused. She stood off to the side with a frown, slightly shaking her head. She knew I thought there was something more to my connection with Tate, but she didn't believe it. It was understandable, considering everyone else in the history of the world who tried to bond with a member of a different Keeper race met certain death. But this was... different.

"What happened after we left?" I asked.

Dom cleared her throat and gestured toward Abby—the human who was supposed to be oblivious to all things *Keeper*.

"It's fine," Tate said with a shrug. "My powers are working fine again. I'll erase all of this from her mind when we're done."

Abby furrowed her brows, but made no comment. Sean looked wistfully in her direction, stepping a little closer in case she became afraid by what was about to be revealed.

"We went straight to the council. They'd already heard about what happened, of course. I think all of New York knows by now. And it's true. Titus is gone. Apparently Osborne made some calls after we ran into him earlier. He raised the alarm about you being in the building. He was still convinced that you were connected to Rasputin, so he had my father send out all the available guards to search the perimeter for him or any of the other Manticorians. They wanted to stop him before he tried to enter the convention."

"So that's where they were going when we went up to your room?"

Tate nodded. "But Titus went missing somewhere between the time we spoke with Osborne and when my father arrived. They suspected he'd gone out in search of another hit, but all of his usual spots were empty. He's a master at sneaking away, so it's not terribly unusual. There's a chance he'll still turn up…" He frowned.

"But you don't think so?"

Tate shook his head. "No. I saw the way Rasputin grinned when my father accused him of taking Titus. I think it's all connected, somehow."

"Why?"

"Maybe Rasputin knows about *this*." Dom stepped forward, motioning between Tate and me with her hand. "If he really does want you on his side, and he knows that you've got some kind of bond with Tate, maybe he was deliberately trying to put Tate into power. It makes sense, if he thinks it will get him closer to his goals. And I'm sorry about your dad," she added to Tate.

"Well, it worked. The council moved to make me the interim ruler, until Titus can be located."

"How do you feel about that?" I asked quietly.

He shrugged. "It doesn't matter how I feel. It's done. But there is some good news to come of it. That message on the table back in the suite about the Firelake Blade? I can get you there now."

"What do you mean?"

"The Firelake is in Agartha."

"No." Millie stood. "There is no way you're getting her involved with that."

"Why? What is it?"

"There's said to be a blade at the very center of the lake, but the entire thing is engulfed in blue flames. Thousands of lives have been lost in an attempt to retrieve the blade. I won't allow you to be next."

"Why would so many risk their lives for a blade?" I didn't understand the appeal.

"Because whoever wields the blade is invincible. Or so the legend says."

"But we don't even know if it's real!" Millie threw her hands into the air. "No one has ever seen it."

"It's real," I said. "And I'll get it."

"Woo!" Abby clapped from the corner. "If anyone can do it, it's you!"

We all turned to stare at the mortal girl.

"What? You really think I haven't picked up on things in my time here? I don't understand all of it, but I can tell by the way people look at Everly that she's special. I might not be some powerful being like you all are, but even I can sense that something big is going on."

We exchanged looks, none of us knowing how to respond to that. Dom rested her gaze on the girl for a long while, presumably reading her mind. "She knows a lot. Like... *a lot* a lot."

"Why haven't you ever said anything?" Sean asked her.

Abby shrugged. "It seemed like the kind of thing I shouldn't speak of."

Sean released a breath and pulled Abby in for a hug. "It feels good in a way. I like that you know. But I'm sorry we're going to have to erase your knowledge again."

"I don't know," Dom said, tilting her head slightly in Abby's direction. "I really think our secret might be safe with her."

I grinned. "Welcome to the club, Abby. You reacted a lot better to it than I did."

"But my answer is still no to the blade," Millie said firmly. Devon tried to take her hand to calm her down, but she shrugged him off.

"With all due respect, Millie, I love you, but you're not in charge of me. I'm an adult."

"You can't even get into Agartha!"

"She can." Tate took my hand. "As the interim ruler, I can allow anyone in who I deem acceptable."

"You think I'm acceptable?" I asked, grinning up at him.

He smirked. "Most of the time." A small squeeze of his hand sent another wave of power coursing through my veins. "But Osborne is livid. He'll do whatever he can to get the decision reversed. He doesn't think I've had enough training to rule, so we'll need to move quickly, just in case they remove me from power."

"None of that explains how you expect to keep her alive in a lake of literal flames," Millie said.

"Water." I looked at my aunt. "I'm Atlantean. I'll just make water."

"You can't just *make* water," Sean said.

"Keepers may not be able to do it, but I bet the Deliverer can. Besides, I think we're one step closer to figuring out this whole prophecy, now that I've found the one who ignites my heart." My cheeks warmed as I spoke the words aloud, but another squeeze from Tate's hand left me feeling a little more sure of it.

"Everly." Dom stepped forward, her brows pulled together with concern. "It doesn't work like that. The prophecy is referring to your soulmate, and it's not possible for Tate to fill that role, no matter how much chemistry you think you have."

"Soulmate or not, he ignited something. And I don't mean that in the way you think," I added, noting Gayla's smirk. "Nothing about me is normal. My aura is white. My powers are unheard of. I can talk to owls for crying out loud!" I threw my hands back toward the window where Al blinked from his perch on Millie's shop sign. "Is it so hard to think that maybe my soulmate breaks conventions, too? And on that note, is it possible that I come from a lineage of rule breakers?"

"What do you mean by that?" Millie put her hands on her hips.

"The prophecy refers to me as the daughter of sea and sky. My mother is of the sea, but my father... what if he's not what we thought? Tate mentioned that some Agarthians can manipulate the wind and clouds in the sky. And Rasputin was Agarthian, right?"

"*Rasputin?!*"

"Yes." I put up my hands to calm my aunt. "He has done nothing to hurt me. Nothing at all. He kept calling me darling, and he legitimately looked proud when he saw my powers back at the hotel. Is there any chance my mother may have run into him at some point, and... uh... *bonded*?" The question sent a chill down my spine. I hated to even ask, but I had to know.

"No," she said, vehemently shaking her head. "Tilly wouldn't dream of getting close to that disgusting man!"

"Besides," Dom added. "Rasputin already had a soulmate. He can't sire any more offspring."

I hoped she was right. I would never want to call Rasputin my father, but I wasn't fully convinced. "Anyway, I think we need to open our minds to the fact that the impossible is actually quite possible when it comes to me and this prophecy. So I'd like to go with Tate. I'd like to at least take a look at this flaming lake and see what I can do. And maybe we'll be able to find another piece of the tablet while we're in Agartha as well."

Devon stepped forward and put his hand on Millie's back. "Look at them, Mills. It's real. As real as you and me. You know he won't let anything happen to her."

Tears filled her eyes as she finally relented, giving us the smallest of nods. "Okay. But please, Everly. Please be safe."

"I will." I leaned into her embrace, staying still for as long as she needed. This wasn't goodbye. It was just the next step in our journey.

I bid adieu to Gayla and Dom next, telling them to behave while I was away. Then came Sean.

"Look out for your dad," I whispered as I hugged his neck. "Give him some grace. He's done bad things, and he's definitely in with the wrong crowd right now, but I think he's broken. Let's try to piece him back together before we write him off entirely."

Sean pulled back, looking a little glassy-eyed, himself. "Thanks, Ev. Be careful."

Finally, I came to Abby. I grinned at the girl. "I can't believe you knew something was up this entire time."

She smiled back at me. "I can be surprisingly crafty when necessary. Now go get that blade, girl. Show 'em what you've got!"

"Alright," I said, joining Tate's side again. "I guess we're doing this."

"I'm glad." he pulled me in close before turning to Devon. "Can you get us to Kentucky, by any chance?"

"Kentucky?" I whirled around to face him. "Agartha is in *Kentucky*?"

Tate grinned. "Only the entrance. Let's go—I can't wait to show you my world."

I didn't know what we would find, but I knew I would be safe with Tate. I had never been more sure of anything in my life. I took his hand and a deep breath. Devon stepped up beside us, and in a wink, we were gone.

THE CENTER OF THE EARTH

CHAPTER 1

THE GRASS WASN'T REALLY blue in Kentucky.

I mean, logically, I knew it wouldn't be. But it was always referred to as The Bluegrass State, and I guess a small part of me thought the grass might be a slightly different shade. A blue-green maybe?

"What are you thinking about?" Tate asked, coming up to a stop.

"Oh...uh... nothing. Nothing at all."

He grinned. "You don't have to be nervous. I promise, I'll keep you safe."

I began to tell him that I wasn't nervous at all, but figured I'd keep my ego intact better if I didn't reveal my ponderings on blue grass. Besides, we were about to leave the grass behind altogether.

Devon had brought us to an empty, wooded part of western Kentucky, just outside of Mammoth Cave National Park. He didn't stay long because he had to get back to Millie, so it had just been Tate and I walking through the forest for the last ten minutes or so. He'd explained that the Mammoth cave system was over four hundred miles long, and apparently there was an entrance to Agartha at its depths.

"Seems kind of strange to put the entrance to an ancient hidden territory right in the middle of a tourist destination," I said.

"It's protected. But there are only a couple of humans brave enough to approach the entrance each year, anyway. It's not exactly convenient."

"And you have to do this every time you want to go back to Agartha?"

Tate laughed. "No way. Hardly anyone messes with the cave entrances anymore. We usually enter and exit through the poles."

"As in the *north* pole? Like... where Santa lives?"

"You're cute," he said, brushing a thumb across my cheek. "But Santa stays far away from the poles. We've got a private air strip up there, and a facility that allows us entrance into the openings."

"Hang on." I stopped and put my hands on my hips. "Do you really mean to tell me that there are giant holes at the poles of the earth that lead down into the middle—complete with an airport—and humans haven't discovered them yet?"

"No." Tate shook his head. "The humans definitely know they're there. We've got a working arrangement with the leaders of some of the largest governments on the surface. They've agreed to help us keep it a secret. Why do you think you've never seen maps or satellite images of the poles? And no airlines fly over? We let them give very expensive tours a couple of times per year to keep suspicions down, but only to a handful of people. And we always clear their memories of our presence before they leave."

"That's nuts. I never would have guessed."

"That's the point," he said, pushing some small branches out of the way to reveal a large crevice in the stone wall we'd just reached. "After you."

I hesitated for just a moment before stepping into the shadows. Tate was right behind me, and the golden glow of his aura seemed to intensify and light the way before us. It was a narrow passage that immediately wound away from the opening. It would have been pitch-black in short time if not for Tate's warm illumination.

"This is one of the secret openings to the cave system. There are many, but the bigger ones have all been taken over by mortals giving tours."

"They're all connected though, right?"

"Right. So technically someone could find Agartha from any of the entrances if they hiked long enough. But our guardians would never let them in."

The passage opened up around a second bend into a cavernous chamber. Tate's aura was no match for the blackness that consumed the large space. We could see only a few feet in front of us now. His hand found mine, and any hint of fear I might have felt disappeared.

"It's not much farther," he said.

We walked across the hard earth, and I did my best to ignore the sounds of scuttering I heard across the floor and the flapping of wings overhead. All-powerful leaders of sinister groups like the Manticorians barely registered on my radar, but bats? Bats were a different story. I bit down on a soft squeal and ducked as one of the nasty critters flew a little too close for comfort.

Tate chuckled and pulled me along. The air changed as we walked farther into the cavern. It grew cool and damp, and it almost felt as though the cave was breathing. "I thought you said we were almost—"

"Shh." Tate stopped abruptly and froze himself to the spot. I stilled as well, straining my eyes to locate whatever it was that had given him pause. "Listen." His whispered words tickled my ear.

I held my breath, listening past the sounds of the cave critters and the distant drips of water falling from somewhere within its depths. I could barely make out the sound of rushing water, like a river. And secondary to that was a murmur of voices.

"Who is it?" I asked.

"I don't know. But we should prepare for the worst just in case."

We moved ahead, more quietly now. Every so often we would pause and listen again. The voices grew louder as we went on, and as the chamber curved off to the right, the walls began to narrow. Up ahead, the sound of the rushing water now filled the damp air, and the soft white glow of two large flashlights shone on a cave wall at the opposite end.

Our Keeper hearing was much more sensitive than the humans'—*and it was clear now that we were dealing with humans*—but we still didn't want to get careless with our approach. We moved to the edge of the chamber, still careful with soft steps and slow breathing to remain unnoticed by the people ahead.

There were two of them. Both men. One looked to be just slightly older than us, and the other could have been his father. They stood at the edge of an underground river, talking quietly back and forth. Their words became clear as we neared them.

"I can't see anything on the other side, Dad. Just a wall. Please don't do this."

"It's just murky. There's an opening there. I know it. I've spent the last ten years preparing for this moment."

I squeezed Tate's hand, and he lowered his head so I could whisper in his ear. "Do you know what they're trying to do?"

"They're trying to get into Agartha."

"Is that the way?"

Tate looked ahead toward the flashlight's beam disappearing into the water of the river. "Yep."

A thrill of excitement danced through my chest. Agartha was underwater? Maybe this whole breaking into other territories business would be easier than I'd thought.

A loud splash drew my attention back to the men—or *man*, rather—as the younger dropped his flashlight and yelled after his father who had disappeared beneath the dark river's surface. A second later he leapt into the rushing water as well.

I didn't have a chance to think before my feet were moving. I flew across the hard earth faster than I knew I was capable of running, and the sound of Tate calling my name barely registered as I dove headfirst into the river.

I instantly saw more clearly below the water's surface. My muscles came alive along with my senses, and it only took half a second to spot the younger man flailing in the murky water. He whipped his head back and forth searching for the older man, but it was too dark for him to see his father.

It wasn't too dark for *me*, though.

Above ground, there was only a wall on the opposite side of the river. But here I could see a flat opening about four feet below the surface. The older man's kicking feet disappeared under the wall, while his son still waved his arms around blindly. I wrapped an arm around the younger man's waist and propelled us forward after his dad.

The water looked much the same on the other side of the wall, and miraculously, the older man was still kicking. I watched as he confidently swam back up to the surface. His son thrashed and fought against my grip, but the water gave me strength I didn't have on land. Securing my grip around his torso, I swam up toward his father.

The older man was pulling himself back onto dry ground when our heads broke through the surface.

"Get off me!" The younger man squeezed a boot between us and shoved me hard in the stomach. It was enough to break my hold on him, but I wasn't injured. It would take much more than that to hurt me in the water. "Who are you?!"

The father turned back with a grin. "It's one of them. One of the Nephilim."

The younger man looked like he'd been burned. He backed away from me, looking horrified, and quickly swam to the bank to rejoin his father.

"I'm not a Nephilim," I said. The older man simply nodded once in my direction, then helped his son onto the land. The cave on this side of the wall was still very dark, but there was light coming from somewhere—just enough to prevent us from feeling completely blind. I was about to climb out and ask the men what exactly they expected to find here when Tate came up from the water at my side.

"There's another one," the older man said. "It's a wonder they haven't killed us yet."

"I told you, we're not—"

Tate put a hand on my back, stopping me from finishing my sentence. "We won't kill you," he said simply. "In fact, we'll even escort you to the entrance."

"What are you doing?" I whispered as we waded through the water toward the underground river bank.

"I don't want to drain anymore power today. I may need it when we get to Agartha. Besides, the guys at the entrance never get much action. I'll let them handle the mortals."

"They're not going to kill them, are they?" I risked a glance up at the men. The younger watched me, pale faced and walking backward like I might infect him with some invisible disease.

"Probably not."

The older man was smiling wide as we joined them. "I knew it! I've been saying for years that your kind still existed. Tell me, is there really another sun at the center of the earth?"

"Something like that." Tate tried to suppress a smile. We turned another corner and immediately saw the source of the light. Two guards stood against a flat stone wall about twenty yards away. They both glowed with the same golden hue as Tate. And as soon as we were all in their sights they shot what looked like bolts of lighting from their palms.

CHAPTER 2

THE AIR SIZZLED WITH electricity. I should have been dead. We all should have died from a shock that large. But there was some kind of invisible barrier surrounding us and offering us protection.

One of the Agarthian guards paled. "Thaddeus. I'm so sorry. We were told to be on high alert in case of an attack."

The second guard kept his palms extended forward until his partner elbowed him in the side. He squinted ahead, as though he didn't quite believe what he saw.

Tate dropped his hands to his sides. He'd been the one controlling the shield. "I'm glad to see it. But there are no enemies here."

"What about her?" The second guard gestured toward me. Suspicion tugged his brows together. "What *is* she?"

"I'm Atlantean... ish."

The old human man gasped, and the noise seemed to remind the Agarthians that there were mortals in our presence.

"Atlantis is real, too?" The old man laughed. "Even if you kill me right here, I feel like my life is complete."

"Don't give them any ideas," the younger man said.

"Are the mortals with you, too?" The second guard lifted his hands again, ready to fire that strange lightning once more at Tate's command.

"No. They just want to see the Nephilim." He winked.

"Got it." The guard frowned. "Come on over boys."

The older man stepped forward and his son grabbed at the back of his shirt. "It's a trap."

"It's not a trap." The guard turned to face the stone wall, placing both hands on it. The wall seemed to shimmer before fading away to reveal a city bustling with life down below. It looked more like a screen playing a live video feed than a window, but there was no doubt that this place—whatever it was—was not from the world we knew.

The older man's eyes grew wide with wonder. Entranced, he moved toward the wall. Even the son couldn't deny the magnificence playing out before them.

"A city within a hollow earth." The older man shook his head in disbelief. "It's incredible. But why?" He turned to face the guard. "Why are you so willing to show us your home?"

"You won't remember it." The guard's voice had taken on a songlike quality—a hundred voices, high and low, all blended together into one strange and enchanting melody of words. "You will watch for a moment longer before turning back to the river. You will swim to the other side, return to your lives on the surface, and forget you ever found the entrance to Agartha. You will tell your friends the *Nephilim* are not real. You will laugh at anyone who claims the earth is hollow. And you will give up your search for other intelligent life forms."

The old man nodded. "Yes, I will. But it sure is beautiful right now, while I'm aware of it."

"That it is," Tate said, stepping forward. "That it is."

The mortal men turned away a moment later, just as the guards had instructed them to do through their glamour. With one final longing glance at the entrance to Agartha, they rounded the corner back to the river that would lead them away. That was the last we saw of them.

"Now," Tate said, turning back toward the guards. "If you don't mind, I need to get to the palace."

The first guard immediately obliged, scooting out of our way while the second kept a sharp eye on me. We stepped forward, but just before I reached the wall, the second guard—*good ol' lightning hands*—moved to block my access.

"I was hired for this position because of my natural ability to sense danger." He frowned. "Call it intuition. Call it a sixth sense. But it's telling me that this is a bad idea."

"Well as your interim ruler, I can tell you that your sense is wrong this time. She's with me."

The guard swallowed and gave a slight shake of his head. "I just—"

The first guard elbowed him again. "Watch yourself, Jasper. This is our king."

"*Interim* king," lightning hands corrected. "And like I said, this is a bad idea. I'll have to report it back to Osborne."

I tensed at Osborne's name. Why would his opinion matter at all? And why did the thought frighten me as much as it did? I knew I could take him. I'd already proven that twice over.

"Give Osborne my regards," Tate grinned, but the gleam in his eye was anything but friendly. Jasper recognized it, too. He stepped silently to the side, allowing me to follow Tate toward the wall.

Tate reached out, and the stone shimmered into a new image as his hand made contact with it. It was less shocking now than it had been in Atlantis. I suppose I was becoming used to the magical aspects of Keeper life now. When he stepped through to the other side, I didn't hesitate to follow him into the new territory.

There was no city. I didn't know what kind of image the guards had played for the mortal men earlier, but this wasn't it. We were still in a cave, not much different from the system of tunnels and caverns we'd just left. The only difference was that this one sloped down at an incline so steep I had to physically concentrate on keeping myself upright.

A small, childlike part of my brain wanted to lay down and roll to the bottom the way I did down grassy hills back in Oklahoma when I was a kid. Only I couldn't see the bottom of this hill. Knowing the Agarthians, I'd probably roll right into the mouth of a dragon or something equally terrifying.

Tate reached for my hand again, and I immediately felt a sense of calm. We were in this together. With him by my side, I could do anything—even slay whatever dragon may wait at the bottom of this hill.

But of course, there was no dragon. In fact, after just a few minutes of walking down through the steep sloping tunnel, an opening jutted off to our left. Tate led me into the darkness, back to level ground. The space was small enough again that his glow easily illuminated the path before us, and it was a hundred times easier to walk on the flat ground here.

"You're not really Nephilim, right?"

Tate laughed. "No. Not any more than you are. But we don't mind the mortals believing that. If that's what they need to call us to make sense of it all in their minds, then it's fine by us."

"And what they said about a hollow earth?"

"Yeah, that part's true. We don't have another sun, of course. We'd all fry. But we do have a source of light down there at the core. Mostly it's still a lot of tunnels and caves, but there is a surface in the middle where gravity shifts, and the city they showed the mortals is our capital— Shamballa."

"The center of the earth, accessible only by the poles and a cave in Kentucky..." I shook my head in disbelief.

"Oh, it's accessible in many different areas. You can enter through Brazil, the Himalayas... even under the Great Pyramid of Giza. Kentucky was just the most convenient to us."

This time it was my turn to laugh. I'd call him crazy if I wasn't seeing it first hand for myself. "So this palace of yours... I'm guessing it's in Shamballa?"

"Yep. It's about a seven day hike from here. Lucky for you, we have portals built into the cave systems." He slid his hand across the dusty wall. "And we're juuuust about... *here*." He glanced over his shoulder with a mischievous grin, then stepped through the stone wall.

I took a deep breath, then walked through the wall behind him.

CHAPTER 3

THE OTHER SIDE OF the wall couldn't have been more opposite from the cave in appearance. I'd pictured the middle of the earth as looking very dark, maybe with a red glow. I'd expected damp, dank halls and bats. Lots of bats.

Instead I stepped upon the glistening white marble floors of a great hall of a palace. Tate's hands were in the air, calming the guards who surrounded us. Their eyes were all wide golden circles, glued to me.

"Hi," I squeaked.

"That's her!" Movement from the left side of the room drew my attention to a guard who was quickly making his way toward me. The other guards glanced around uncertainly, but Tate immediately jumped into action. He rounded on the guard, and I swore it looked like he grew a half a foot taller as he funneled his anger at the older man.

"Back down!" Tate bellowed.

The guard stopped in place, shooting daggers in my direction but silently obeying his interim king's command.

"No one is to lay a hand on her. Everly Gordon is my guest, and she is to be treated with the utmost respect for as long as she chooses to remain in Agartha. Am I clear?"

"Yes, your *Majesty*. But Osborne—"

"I don't care what Osborne said." Tate narrowed his eyes, daring another guard to speak against him. "She is welcome here."

We waited for several seconds more before Tate turned toward an attendant I hadn't previously noticed standing in the doorway. "Please prepare the Noble Suite for Ms. Gordon. I'd like Hattie to attend to her. Will you please let the others know as well?"

"Yes, your Majesty." The young attendant scurried away.

He took my hand then. "Would you like to wait in my rooms until yours are ready?"

"Uh, sure." I hadn't quite gotten my wits about me again just yet, so I followed him without question. He led me out into a foyer with a winding staircase up to what I assumed were the guest suites. One floor past that was the royal residence.

The whole palace was bright, with glossy white marble and glistening gold accents. Warm light filtered in through giant leaded windows, and I craned my neck to see its source. There was no sun here, but that definitely looked like sunlight illuminating an airy world outside, with lush greenery surrounding the bustling city of Shamballa.

"Are you sure we're in the middle of the earth?"

"Positive," Tate said with a laugh. "It's beautiful, isn't it?"

"Gorgeous." We stopped to gaze out of a floor-to-ceiling window on the landing just in front of the royal residence. There were mountains and rivers and forests just beyond a city that was somehow futuristic in appearance while simultaneously looking like it was pulled from the pages of a fairytale picture book.

"It's too bad we'll have to destroy it."

"*What*?" I whipped around to face him, certain I'd misheard what he said.

"According to legend surrounding the prophecy, it's your job to destroy the Keepers. I assume that means our territories and all other aspects of our lives will fall as well." He frowned, lost in thought as he looked over his city below. "And it's probably for the best, if I'm being honest. Our people are too far gone."

The main door to his residence swung open, and an older man dressed in a suit stepped out into the hall before I had a chance to ask anything more about what Tate said.

"Your Majesty." The man bowed unbelievably low. I thought his nose might've kissed the ground. "I heard you were on your way. I've put in a request to have dinner sent up for you and your guest shortly."

"Thank you, Jacoby. We'll get cleaned up." Tate popped his elbow out for me to lace my arm through, then led me into the most luxurious living accommodations I'd ever seen.

Tate's family residence put Millie's multi-million dollar Manhattan townhouse to shame. Every surface was marble or gold, and it looked like someone took a giant bedazzler and added real gemstones the size of my fists throughout the rooms like confetti. Yet somehow, even though it was totally over the top, it didn't feel ostentatious. Or maybe I was just too blinded by my love for this man to realize how tacky it really was.

No... not *love*. Right? Or maybe it was... Maybe the universe was playing the cruelest kind of trick on me, making me fall in love with a man who could never be my soulmate. Igniting my heart with a man who would quite literally be the death of me if I gave in to these emotions.

"You okay?" Tate asked. He snapped his fingers and a candle in the center of a small table for two sprung to life.

"Yeah, I'm fine." I wasn't about to share those thoughts with him. Not right now, anyway. Besides, I was pretty sure I'd just witnessed a miracle. "Did you just make fire?"

He crinkled his nose and scratched the back of his head. "Kind of. It's an enchantment they put on the palace here. It's supposed to bend to the whims of the ruler."

"And you're the ruler." I shook my head. "That's still kind of hard for me to believe."

"You and me both." He moved over to a window beside the table, overlooking his kingdom again.

I joined him there, rubbing gentle circles on his back. "You keep asking if I'm doing alright, but how about you? How are you handling everything?" So much had happened, I'd almost forgotten that his father was killed right in front of him just a few hours earlier. And his twin was missing, too.

He gave a small shrug. "I thought I'd be more upset. He was a terrible ruler and a worse father. But still, he was the only dad I had."

"You're probably still a little numb from the shock of it all," I suggested.

"No, I don't think that's it. It's like somewhere, deep inside, I know this is right. This is how things are supposed to play out." He turned to me and took my hands in his. "This is your destiny, and I think it might be mine, too."

We stood there looking into one another's eyes for a moment. It was definitely not the most appropriate time, but I couldn't resist the urge to lean in and kiss him again. I craved that feeling of unity our kiss had provided back in the hotel, and I wanted to see if we could replicate it. Our faces were merely an inch apart when he turned away.

I ignored the flush that crept its way up my neck. Of course he turned away. That was the responsible thing to do. He was supposed to be mourning, not making out.

The butler returned a few minutes later with a mouth watering dinner prepared by the palace chefs. We enjoyed the meal alone, while Tate told me a little more about Agartha and its wonders. "Would you like to explore it tomorrow?" he asked once his plate was cleaned.

I pushed my own empty plate to the side. "I would definitely like to see the *Firelake*." Subtlety was never my strong suit. As amazing as Agartha sounded, I was here on a mission. I had a blade to retrieve and a prophecy to fulfill. We could tour the place afterward.

But seeing Tate's features deflate gave me a change of heart. If it was true that the territory would be destroyed by my Deliverance, then perhaps I should make some time to see it with him first. It seemed important to him, and that was good enough of a reason for me.

"But of course I would love to see the rest of Shamballa first. If you're sure you have time for that."

"I have all the time in the world for you." His golden eyes glistened, and my heart flipped in response. He escorted me to my rooms after dinner, and I fought to give him the space he needed. I couldn't get enough of this man, the ruler of Agartha. He was a bit rough on the outside, but now that he'd let me into his heart, I never wanted to leave.

We lingered for just a moment before saying goodnight, but I didn't try to kiss him again. No, not tonight. Instead I would try to find a way for us to enjoy each other's company—and kisses—for the rest of eternity. Just as soon as I fulfilled this prophecy...

CHAPTER 4

A FIT OF GIGGLES erupted from a small group of Agarthian children peering over the rail of the bridge we walked across. I paused for a moment, glancing at Tate to signal for him to stop. We'd escaped the palace without much fuss and walked the streets of Shamballa in the warm mid-morning sunlight, and getting out had ignited my curiosity for this city.

There had been other children playing as well, all bright-eyed and happy as they ran and rolled in the grass between tents in the marketplace. But this group on the bridge was distracted by something in the water below.

"What are you guys looking at?" I asked, stepping up to the rail a little ways down from them.

"Watch this." A golden eyed boy flashed me a mischievous grin as he pinched off a piece of bread from the loaf in his hand. "Throw this is the water." He dropped the fluffy lump into my palm.

"Just anywhere down there?"

The girl next to him giggled again with anticipation, nodding. I tossed the bread down into the water, watching it send ripples outward. It only lasted for a moment though before an enormous iridescent hot-pink fish rose from the depths of the river and took the bite in a single gulp. The creature was unlike anything I'd ever seen. It was the size of a seal, but more closely resembled a goldfish covered in neon cotton candy.

The children laughed uncontrollably. Tate did too, as he reached over and tapped the underside of my chin to close my gaping mouth.

"What was that?"

"That was a rosy bubble bass."

"That was not a bass like any I've ever seen."

"Then I'd say you've got a lot more to see in your life." Tate winked and pulled me along.

"Bye, Prince Tate!" One of the little girls batted her lashes and waved goodbye until a boy I guessed was her brother stepped on her toes.

"It's *King Thaddeus*," he whispered angrily. The rest of the children all laughed some more.

I had to admit, the Agarthian people were growing on me. We might have gotten off to a rough start, what with Tate hunting my soul and the girls on campus pinning me to walls—oh, and Clayton Miles stalking me, of course—but it turned out most of the people here were delightful.

And Tate was eager to show me all of the wonders Shamballa offered. There were shops and restaurants, musicians in the street and artists painting on the corners. The Agarthians all seemed so happy and at ease. It left me wondering why Tate believed them to be too far gone. I couldn't imagine bringing any harm to this city.

Many of the citizens stopped to greet Tate as we passed them. They dipped their chins with respect, referring to him as the rightful ruler of Agartha. Their King. But as we walked deeper into the city, further from the palace, I began to see others who would avert their eyes, or even scowl as they saw us coming down the street. Tate didn't seem bothered by them, though I was certain he must have noticed.

We approached a large park in the middle of the city, walking along an outer sidewalk for a moment before crossing the street toward more shops on the other side. Tate gestured toward a lovely blue cottage with a perfectly manicured lawn and a sign overhead that read, *Moonflower*.

He tugged my hand to follow him across the street, and though he may have been trying to shield me from seeing what lay ahead in the park, his plan failed. A quaint little park bench—one that would have looked warm and welcoming on any other day—was vandalized in fresh red paint, bright as the flowers planted beside it. Someone had hastily written: *Bow to Titus, or bow to no one.*

Judging by the hard set of his jaw, Tate had seen it. But by the time we reached the little cottage, his muscles had relaxed and his frown was replaced with that boyishly charming half grin of his. "Let me introduce you to Hattie."

A small old woman threw her arms around Tate's waist when we stepped inside. She looked about eighty in human years, which meant she was probably pushing nine hundred in reality. "Thaddeus! I was beginning to wonder if you'd forgotten how to get here."

He knelt down to give the tiny old woman a hug. "Impossible! A man can't forget chocolate like yours." He winked. "Hattie, I'd like to introduce you to someone. This is Everly."

The woman turned her gaze to me. Her eyes were a little milky, but the golden glow behind the glassy surface seemed to intensify for a moment as she took in my features. After a long minute, realization seemed to strike and she clutched her hand to her chest, attempting to bow at the same time.

"Woah, Hattie. That's not necessary." Tate put up a hand beside his mouth and whispered loudly so I could hear. "She doesn't like it when people point out how special she is."

"I'm not—" I couldn't even finish the sentence before Hattie was standing before me, tears in her eyes.

"The Deliverer." Her shaky voice was barely more than a whisper.

"You know about that?" Tate asked with an incredulous grin.

"I know everything." Hattie whacked him gently on the arm and pulled him farther into her little shop. "Now come. Let's get this beautiful creature some chocolate."

Tate waggled his brows at me as we followed Hattie to a counter in the back. The cottage was full of exotic Agarthian flowers I couldn't name, all wonderfully arranged into exquisite pieces. It was a rainbow of colors, all impossibly vivid, and the entire place smelled incredible. Other gifts lined the walls, but it wasn't until we reached the enclosed glass counter that I saw the chocolates.

They were works of art. Some were glossy, some glittered. Others were shaped into mythical creatures. There were truffles and nuts and bars all mixed in with the delicate sculptures as well. My mouth was watering before she even opened the door, but once the smell hit me, it took all my power not to gasp at the aroma.

"Did you really make all of these?"

Hattie nodded proudly. "Pick anything you like. It's on the house today for my king and my Deliverer." She gave a small bow again before gesturing toward the open shelves.

"Thank you." I looked nervously toward a very excited Tate before examining the delicious treats more closely. It only took a second for my eyes to settle on the chocolate of my choice. It was an owl, sculpted from white chocolate and brushed with a glittering gold dust. He was perched on a dark chocolate branch, complete with knots and twists like that of an ancient tree. It was completely enchanting, and it reminded me of Al.

"Wise choice." Hattie winked. "Go on. Take a bite!"

It was so pretty I hated to ruin it. But it smelled so good I couldn't resist. I snapped off a small piece of the branch and moaned. "Oh my goodness, this is the best thing that has ever touched my lips."

"I take offense to that." Tate quirked a brow and Hattie cackled in the background.

"I think I have some flowers that need watering out back. I'm going to step out for a minute," she said with a knowing look.

Tate glanced back at me with a twinkle in his eye once the door closed behind her. "Some people say that Hattie's chocolates are magic. I've even heard some of the young girls bragging about how they used them to make poor unsuspecting Agarthian boys fall in love with them."

I took another bite of the heavenly treat. "I can see why."

He stepped toward me and wrapped his hand around the back of my neck, lifting my face to his. Slowly he leaned down, and the butterflies in my belly went wild at the realization of what was about to happen. Our last kiss had been magical, and it was only an experiment. Now that our feelings were out in the open, what kind of an effect would we get this time?

"Everly, I—"

I batted my lashes waiting for him to hurry up and finish his thought or else I might just cut him off with my lips.

"I... think you've got a little chocolate on your mouth." He swiped my bottom lip with his thumb and popped it into his mouth. Then he kissed my forehead and walked away.

I was too stunned to speak for a second, sorting through the rush of adrenaline I had from his proximity and the hurt I felt from him choosing not to kiss me again. Was I mistaken? Was I the only one who felt the bond?

There wasn't time to ask him. Hattie came running back through the doors, panting. "You need to get out there, Thaddeus. There's a commotion across the street, and I think you are the only one who can stop it."

CHAPTER 5

"YOU SHOULD WAIT HERE." Any mirth from our exchange just moments before completely vanished from Tate's face. His golden eyes darkened, a storm brewing within them.

"Should? Maybe. But there's not a chance I'm leaving you to face whatever is out there alone." I strode confidently ahead, moving past him to grab the front door. "Thank you, Hattie," I called out over my shoulder. "It was a pleasure to meet you."

Tate touched my arm before I could step out. "Are you sure you don't want to stay and finish your chocolate? Things could get ugly out there. Agarthians can be a bit... unpredictable."

"I'm sure." I remembered the red paint dripping down the bench out front, and I suspected whatever commotion Hattie referred to had something to do with Tate's new position. It seemed not everyone was happy to have him in charge. "After you." I pulled open the wooden door and gestured for him to go out.

The light outside was bright, though I still couldn't place where it was coming from since there was no sun. I heard the shouting across the street before my eyes adjusted enough to make out the angry mob. Standing on the park bench was the guard who had reluctantly allowed my entrance into this underground world the day before. *Lightning hands.* Beside him stood Osborne.

"As Agarthians, it is our duty to our territory, and to the greater earth above, to lead with the highest nobility. We need a king who understands the complicated inner workings of Agartha. We need a leader who has studied the political history of the Keepers—one who can rule with the knowledge of our ancestors. And most importantly, we need a king who *wants* to lead. Aside from the true heir to the throne, there is no man who loves Agartha and its people more than this man." The guard gestured to Osborne. "Until we can locate King Titus, we should insist that Osborne takes the role as interim leader. It should be up to the people of Agartha to choose who takes the reins of our territory, not some stuffy old council members behind closed doors at a conference we weren't even invited to attend."

Tate clenched his teeth and made his way to the growing crowd in the park. I hurried to keep in step beside him. They didn't look dangerous, but they weren't exactly a cheerful group of kids at a carnival, either. Tate was crashing their meeting, and he was the last person they wanted to see.

Tate fixed his face into a cocky sneer—the kind of look he used to give me when he was still hunting my soul. He clapped slowly, loud enough to draw the attention of the bystanders back to him. "Such a moving speech from this *previous* member of the royal guard. Did you have anything to add, Osborne?"

Murmurs filled the crowd as realization dawned on them that the guard had just lost his job. They shifted uncomfortably on their feet, suddenly worried about what other punishments Tate might bring upon them for being involved. But Tate's eyes were glued to one man only.

Osborne sneered right back at him with an arrogance only an Agarthian hunter could be capable of. "Ah, Thaddeus. We were just talking about you."

"I heard."

"Well since you're here, I suppose you should know our people have a slightly different idea for the future of Agartha than the members of the council did. I hate that Titus is still missing, and I can't just sit around any more while he's still out there somewhere. So I've agreed to lead the charge in finding him. But it seems the people may wish for me to lead more than just the manhunt. Given my track record of loyalty and dedication to the royal family, they've nominated *me* as the interim ruler."

My blood boiled as Osborne spoke. But to Tate's credit, he didn't so much as flinch at Osborne's words. The men never broke eye contact. It was a mental game of chicken, and my money was on Tate.

"How very noble of you. Unfortunately, the laws don't work that way. I am the second-born son, and next in line for the throne."

"You abdicated the throne," Osborne shot back.

"I never had a throne to abdicate. Titus was primed to fulfill the role of king. I went on to carry out other work for the nation. Now that it's my turn to serve, I'm here. At least until we find my brother."

Osborne looked like he bit into the sourest lemon, his features twisted with disgust. "I fear that may be a conflict of interest, seeing as how you're the reason your brother is missing."

"He is not!" The words flew from my mouth before I had time to think them through. Osborne had that effect on me. I was raging. Darkness crept in around the edges of my vision, and my inner Athena urged me to strike against him. Goodness knows he deserved it, but thankfully I had enough reason to know better than to attack him here in Agartha.

"You were there when Rasputin struck," I continued. "You watched his men kill the king. Tate had nothing to do with it, and you know it! It was Rasputin and his Manticorians who took Titus."

"Rasputin and *your* Manticorians. Don't play dumb, girl. We all know you're working together. You're not like the rest of us, and you can't hide it any more."

My fingers felt for Rossel's small dagger I had hidden in the waistband of my pants as Osborne took two long strides toward me. His accusation thickened the air, making it difficult to breathe as every Agarthian eye turned toward me. The murmurs started again. They'd just noticed how different I was. Not Agarthian, but not quite Atlantean either. My white aura suddenly felt like a spotlight.

Power heated up in my chest, pumping out from my heart through my limbs. I was filled with a charge, and I wouldn't be able to hold it in much longer. The moment Osborne laid a finger on me the power would unleash, and I wasn't sure exactly what that would mean for everyone else standing nearby. I wasn't even sure if I'd be able to protect Tate.

"Touch her and you die." Tate's warning was a low, feral growl. And it wasn't an empty threat. Anyone who saw the look on his face knew that he'd snap the life out of Osborne or anyone else who dared to put a hand on me.

I didn't need his protection, but seeing his fierce loyalty for me was a welcome change. And it was further confirmation that we were connected on a different level now. Soulmates or not, Tate was more than a friend. We were two pieces of the same puzzle.

The men silently circled around one another for what seemed like forever. Eventually, the other Agarthians in the crowd began shuffling their feet, moving away from the rally turned staring contest.

"Come on," I said after another moment. Tate's bicep was tight under my hand as I gently pulled him away from Osborne. My inner warrior had decided Osborne wasn't a threat... for now, anyway. And we had more important things to do than play Osborne's games. There was a blade waiting for me to retrieve it in a fiery lake somewhere around here.

Tate turned toward me, his jaw instantly relaxing as he laid eyes on me. "You're right. We should go. This guy isn't worth our time."

He took my hand and we walked slowly back through the park toward the palace. I felt Osborne's eyes on our backs until we turned a corner out of sight. It was only then that I felt comfortable asking about the blade.

"I don't want to wait another day, Tate. We've got to get it as soon as possible. I'm sure that's not the last you'll hear from Osborne and his cronies. I want to be ready in case he makes another scene... or worse."

Tate ran a hand through his hair. "It's more than just a handful of cronies. Half the nation wants Osborne on the throne. That was their goal all along. Even if Titus became king, it would be Osborne calling the shots. He's been trained right alongside my brother since the three of us could walk."

"So what? It's not his throne to take. And if only half of your people want him to lead them, then that leaves another half who want *you*. Besides, you've got the power of the Deliverer on your side." I winked. "And after we get the blade he really won't stand a chance against you. So what do you say? Should we go get it?"

"I wish it was that easy." His throat bobbed. "Let's wait until tomorrow at least. Please? I really just want one perfect day with you."

He didn't finish his thought, but he didn't have to. I knew what he was thinking. He wanted one perfect day together because he thought it might be our last. No one had ever survived an attempt to get the Firelake Blade before.

Maybe I was a fool for thinking I could be the first.

CHAPTER 6

I STABBED THE STEAK on my plate and dunked it in the yolk of an egg. Any other day I would have been thrilled to eat steak and eggs for breakfast. It was the kind of thing I'd always heard about but never actually been able to afford for myself. But today, even the most delectable breakfast turned my stomach.

I was a bundle of nerves. Tate and I had shared a lovely afternoon and evening touring Shamballa, but he retreated to his room early last night without so much as a kiss goodnight. I tossed and turned in my own suite for hours, thinking about the mission that lay ahead of me.

Today was the day I was going to retrieve the Firelake Blade. As far as anyone else was concerned, this was the last day of my life. Maybe that's why they prepared steak and eggs for me. It would've been a good last meal if I'd have been able to eat it without getting nauseous.

Tate didn't eat much either. We spoke a little about the blade over breakfast, but there wasn't much to discuss. It was a bit of a mystery. No one knew what it looked like or where exactly in the lake it was hidden. Other than some folklore passed down through the ages, we didn't have any solid evidence that it existed at all.

Our plates had long been cleared, and I swirled my spoon through my lukewarm coffee as I built up the courage to stand and move forward with my mission. When I looked up from my cup, Tate's golden eyes were trained on me, his emotion unreadable.

"We better get going," I said more to myself than to him.

He gave a solemn nod. Standing, he led me silently back through the palace toward the great hall we'd entered into on my first day in Agartha.

After commanding a couple of guards to clear the room, Tate grabbed two water bottles resting for us on a small table beside a giant portrait of a knight. "You can go first." He waved a hand toward the painting.

"I take it this is another portal?"

A small smile tugged at the corner of his mouth. "I forget you're new to this." He took my hand into his. "We can go together."

I hadn't realized how badly I'd been craving his touch. This was the first time we'd made contact since the chaos in the park yesterday. My heart still pounded every time he was near, but I'd been so focused on giving him the space he needed to grieve for his father and overcome the challenges with Osborne that I'd forgotten how complete I felt when we were together. I hoped he still felt it too.

The portrait shimmered as we touched it and together we moved through the cool plane inside the frame and into a dank cave system on the other side. He immediately dropped my hand again, but I tried to shake it off, focusing on our surroundings, instead. "Are we back in Kentucky?"

"No. Though Kentucky doesn't sound half bad right now. This is still within Agartha. We're about halfway between our world and the surface. Entering through this portal covers us in a shield that will protect us from the heat at these depths. Otherwise it would get pretty steamy."

"But it's not enough to shield me from the Firelake?"

"Not even close." He frowned. "Come on, I'll take you to it."

The only sound in the dark cave tunnels was the crunch of our shoes on the gravelly floor. We walked silently for ten minutes or so before the cave began to brighten. Tate's golden glow was overpowered by a deep blue light. It was so faint at first I thought I might've been imagining it, but it grew brighter and brighter as we moved ahead.

The ground began to drop downhill as we neared the light, and though I knew it was coming, I still wasn't prepared for the sight that lay ahead once we finally cleared the hill. The Firelake was stunning. A small stone staircase led down to the expansive lake, and from where we stood it looked like the most incredible crystal blue water. But it wasn't a real lake. It was an expanse of rolling blue flames.

"Take a sip of your water," Tate instructed as he did the same. "You can't feel much of the heat because of the protective shield, but it will still burn you up. You need to stay hydrated."

I *was* burning, but it wasn't from the gorgeous blue flames licking across the surface of the lake. It was something internal—a fire in my chest, white-hot, urging me closer to the lake.

"It's here," I whispered. "I can feel it."

Tate wore a brave face, but it didn't conceal the worry in his eyes. He looked like he might ask me to turn around and go back home at any moment. But now that I was here, and I could feel the power of the blade calling to me, there was no turning back. Tate must have known, because he didn't say a word.

I moved down the stone steps, following an invisible string tugging me along. As I neared the shore of the lake, the heat began to break through my shield. I could feel the skin across my cheeks growing tight under the dry warmth.

"Everly, back up! You're on fire!"

I glanced down to find a flame dancing across the hem of my jeans. I brushed it off and took two steps back, turning in time to see warring emotions across Tate's face.

"The blade is in there. I'm gonna have to go in."

He shook his head silently but didn't object. He thought I was going to die. And really, how could I survive it? I turned back to the lake, mesmerized by the motion of the fiery surface. It was almost choreographed. The way the flames moved reminded me of a ballet. I could even hear the music—ancient and full of emotion. It was a song of sorrow and a song of promise. The lyrics were enchanting, sung in a language I'd never before heard.

I pulled my gaze away, back to Tate. He couldn't hear it. No, this song was for me. An idea occurred to me then. Twisting off the plastic lid of my water bottle, I channeled all of my energy into the liquid, willing it to rise out of the bottle.

The water responded, rising and growing as I urged it forward with my mind. If I could somehow overpower the flames with water, I could forge a pathway to the blade. It was my only reasonable option—the only way I could survive this insane mission.

As I worked, I realized I was humming a tune of my own. It was different from the song of the blade, but complementary somehow. Words formed on my tongue that I'd never before heard. It was the song of Atlantis, and it was something I knew in my soul but not in my mind.

Perhaps it was time for me to step out of my soul's way and let my ancient untapped knowledge get to work.

The water continued to pour out of the bottle growing into a large flowing liquid wall. Once I was certain it was enough, I lowered my hands in a calming motion before me, laying the watery wall over the flames like a blanket to create a narrow pathway. I wasn't sure if I could extinguish them or if I would have to use the water as a vehicle to enter the lake like a highway over the scorching surface.

Unfortunately for me, neither was true. The water met the flaming surface with a sizzle and steam. Then it was gone. No one knew how deep the Firelake was. There could have been miles of flames to cut through for all I knew. But my little water blanket wasn't even close to being strong enough to overcome the vast waves of heat emanating from the lake.

I tried again to pull more water from the bottle, but the spot where power burned in my chest before was nearly empty now. I'd used it all up. Cursing, I threw the bottle into the lake and watched it instantly melt to nothing.

"It's okay, Ev. We'll do some more research and try a different approach another day." Tate's cheeks were flushed from the heat, but noticeably more relaxed. His whole stance had changed as relief flooded him.

I wish I had felt some relief as well, but all I could focus on was my failure. There had to be a way to get in there. I could hear the song of the blade even now as I regretfully left it behind.

With tensions running high in Agartha, Rossel unleashing terror on the Keepers, and Rasputin's Manticorians threatening the entire surface of the earth, there wasn't time to delay. If I couldn't get the blade, I at least had to find the next piece of the tablet while I was here. I wouldn't let my time in Agartha go to waste.

And just maybe the tablet would have the information I needed to retrieve the blade. All I knew was that there was definitely a connection between the blade and the prophecy. I could feel it as clearly as I felt my connection with Tate.

"I'll agree to try for the blade another day under one condition."

"What's that?" Amusement flickered in Tate's golden eyes. I suspected the interim king of Agartha wasn't so used to little Atlantean girls calling the shots.

"I'd like to spend the rest of today searching for the Agarthian piece of the tablet. Know of any highly classified locations we might be able to explore?"

"There might be a couple, but they're all back near the palace."

"There's nothing else here in the caves?"

"Just the Hall of Souls."

My heart skipped a beat. I knew I wasn't at risk anymore, but the thought of entering the place where fractured souls were left to die was chilling. I doubted the tablet would be there, but I couldn't deny my curiosity.

"Will you take me there?"

CHAPTER 7

THE HALL OF SOULS wasn't close to the Firelake at all. It was about halfway between the portal and the palace in Shamballa, but it turned out there were miles between the two. The cave system was never-ending, and my feet were aching by the time we arrived.

While the Firelake was an intense blue, the Hall of Souls emanated a redder hue. It wasn't warm like a sunset, but haunting and almost cruel. This was how I'd always pictured Agartha before I arrived. And really, this was at the heart of what they did. It was the Agarthians' duty to extract all the fractured souls from the surface. And this is where the souls were kept.

The hall was too large to be called a room. It reminded me more of the size of the convention center where my high school prom was held. Only instead of blue and green brocade carpet and gaudy chandeliers, we were surrounded by stone. It wasn't any less beautiful, though. The red-gold glow held an enchanting quality. Enchanting and *terrifying*.

The air was cool and damp; chill bumps dotted my arms. There was one main aisle down the center of the space, with rows and rows of wading pool sized openings in the floor on either side. I paused near the entrance to peek inside one of the pools. These were the source of the glow, but instead of being filled with water, they were filled with a heavy mist, like a low-laying fog swirling at an indiscernible depth.

"We don't have to stay here." Tate's voice cut through the silence. "There is nothing to search in here. It's just the pools."

He said it so casually, like we were at a water park. But there was an inescapable weight in the air. These were souls. Brothers, sisters, husbands, wives. Real people whose lives were taken from them. They weren't just pools.

I swallowed the lump in my throat and moved deeper into the hall. "The tablet can wait. I need to..." What did I need to do? Pay my respects?

I was dead center in the large room, turning in a small circle to examine the space from every angle. Tate stepped closer to me, presumably to move me along, but I wasn't finished yet. Kneeling down, I examined one of the pools more closely as I vaguely registered him stopping behind me.

I don't know what I expected to see. Souls weren't visible. At least, I didn't think they were. Thinking back to the incident with the fractured attack on Abby's dad, I remembered Osborne extracting the con-artist's soul through a silver box, but I never saw inside. Was it full of this same swirling fog? Were these the souls?

I tilted my head, examining the mist. How many fractured souls were in here now? The hall was massive, and each pool was large enough to hold hundreds of those little silver boxes. Certainly some of them were evil, like Rasputin's Manticorians. But how many of them were mistakenly taken? I could have been in one of these pools if my luck had played out differently.

Warmth spread across the left side of my body as Tate dropped to his knees beside me. I looked up to see his eyes reflecting the emotion I fought inside. Perhaps he'd had the same thought.

"I'm glad to be on the outside of these pools right now instead of swirling around inside with the others."

A flicker of hurt pinched Tate's features. No, not hurt. Regret. "I'm glad, too. If I had carried out those orders—" He grimaced, unable to finish the thought. "I'm so sorry, Ev. I didn't know."

I turned back to the mist. "How many others do you think were wrongfully taken? And do they know where they are right now? Do they know what happened?"

Tate stared thoughtfully into the mist for a long time. I was wondering if he planned to answer me at all when he finally spoke again. "A few months ago, I would have said none of them were wrongfully taken. I honestly believed that every fractured soul belonged here. But I'm not so sure about *anything* anymore."

"It just doesn't seem right. They could be here for an eternity, just... waiting. Waiting for another piece of themselves that might not even exist anymore. Maybe they aren't fractured at all. Maybe they're just different."

I thought of Sean and Abby, and how they could never be together or else they'd risk having fractured children. It wasn't fair. The Keepers were amazing in many ways, but they really got it wrong when it came to managing relationships.

"What if it's all a lie, Tate? What if the fractured aren't inherently evil? They just don't know how to manage their powers because they've never had the opportunity to learn. All these lives..." I swallowed and bit back the tears that had come unbidden to my eyes. This was making me much more emotional than I expected. "All these lives could have been saved. Things could have turned out differently for them."

I turned to find him staring at me. The air between us practically sizzled with the electricity of our bond, as though it grew more powerful with the weight our emotion. "What if things could turn out differently for us, too?"

If the laws around the fractured were a lie, how could we be sure the curse between lovers of different Keeper races wasn't a lie as well? This bond between us couldn't be imagined. It was as real as the air we breathed. And I couldn't believe that the universe would be so cruel as to make us soulmates only to kill us with some Keeper curse because we fell in love.

Love. There was that word again. And as I stared into those warm glowing golden eyes, I knew it was true. I knew it in the marrow of my bones.

Tate's gaze dipped down to my lips, and before I knew it I was leaning into him, welcoming his kiss. My eyes closed, and I held my breath in anticipation. But when his lips came, they met me with a chaste peck on the forehead before I immediately grew cold.

Opening my eyes, I found him standing in the next row over. He must've run away from me as fast as he could.

"Have I done something?" I asked, incredulous. It wasn't like me to be so bold, but I knew I wasn't imagining this connection. He'd admitted as much. "Because I thought there was something special between us. When we kissed at the convention..." I shook my head, unable to put that feeling into words. "But now... now it's like you're afraid to come close to me at all. What is it? What happened?"

Tate squeezed his eyes shut, hands balled into fists at his sides. I'd upset him somehow.

My cheeks warmed with embarrassment. I was such a fool. This wasn't love. Not for him, anyway. I remembered back to the conversation I had with Rasputin about how Tate was using me for my power. I couldn't have believed it was true at the time. I still couldn't believe it. But why else would he be so hot and cold? Why would he pretend to be crazy about me one minute and then refuse to show me any kind of affection the next?

With a deep breath, I steadied my chaotic emotions and made for the exit. This hall was full enough. I didn't need to add a fractured heart to the mix as well. Tate stood between me and the cave beyond, but I put as much space between us as possible as I stormed ahead. His grasp on my arm caught me off guard.

I spun in place, but before I could speak, Tate's mouth covered mine. I leaned into him, not of my own control, but under the orders of some ancient need that had been awoken. My fingers twisted into his hair as he pulled me even closer with a hand curving around my waist. I was his. He was mine. There would be no separating us now.

The kiss lit a fire in me, white-hot. It started in my chest and worked its way through each of my limbs until my entire body was aflame. But it still wasn't enough. It could never be enough.

I don't know how long it lasted, but all too soon, Tate pulled away, leaving me breathless and panting in my place. "That," he said on shaky legs, "is why I've tried to keep some distance between us. This thing between us, whatever it is, is too much for me. I'm not strong enough to resist it. And I know once I start, I won't be able to stop."

I nodded, understanding and agreeing with every sentiment.

"You're too important, Everly." His grin and the way his gaze raked over me left my belly in a knot. "As badly as I want you, I can't get you killed. Save the world, first. Deliver us. Then we can really ignite this bond. Screw the consequences. Even if the curse kills us, I can't think of a better way to go."

CHAPTER 8

I WAS SO COLD. I tossed and turned, rubbing my arms to bring some warmth back into my flesh, but it was no use. Wrenching open my eyes, I realized I wasn't in my bed anymore. I was floating, rolling in the waves.

But this wasn't water. It was too cold to be water, and I was drowning—impossible for an Atlantean. Shivers wracked my body as I searched for the surface. I needed oxygen. I couldn't breathe. My legs thrashed and kicked, but I couldn't move. I couldn't swim.

It was only then that I realized I wasn't alone. I was surrounded by hundreds of other beings, non-corporeal, all fighting to find a surface that didn't exist. All drowning in our own sorrows. They couldn't speak, but I knew who they were.

The fractured.

Together we clung to the faintest wisp of life in the Hall of Souls.

I wasn't fractured! What was I doing here?

What were any of us doing here?

I fought against the cold some more, refusing to let it drag me down. If I allowed it to take me to the dregs of the bottom, I was certain there would be no coming back.

The others fought alongside me, each of us engaged in our own private war. We would not succumb.

Something sparked in my chest at thought of a battle. Athena. I had the strength of a warrior goddess brewing inside me. I leaned into the spark, fanning it into that now familiar white-hot flame. It melted through the cold, providing me strength as it extended from my chest to my shoulders, down through my arms and legs. I was stronger than the cold.

I would not succumb.

The white heat fully engulfed me now in the protective shield of its flames. I was invincible.

A yell escaped my raw throat, burning as it erupted and shaking the hall to its core. With one final surge of strength, I thrust myself up up up until my face broke through the surface of the pool.

I gasped for air, sweaty and tangled in my sheets. A dream. It was only a dream. I repeated the words out loud, rubbing my temples and willing my heart to stop racing. But a hint of heat remained in my chest, tugging me from my bed.

I stood, sliding my feet into slippers, and my hand found its way to the doorknob before I had a chance to consider what I was doing.

My body gave me no choice in the matter. I had to find Tate.

I knew the way to his rooms. In fact, after an afternoon of searching for the missing piece of the tablet, I knew my way around the palace and the inner part of Shamballa far better than I'd ever expected.

But there had to be more to it. After all, we still hadn't gotten any closer to the tablet. What other secrets did Agartha hold?

There were no guards outside of Tate's suite. They were either remarkably trusting of everyone in the palace—including me—or they didn't actually care much about Tate's welfare. My money was on the latter, especially after seeing the crowds following Osborne in the park. In fact, I wouldn't be surprised if Osborne had somehow paid them to leave Tate unattended.

My blood was beginning to boil again as I silently pulled open the door. His sitting room was dark and quiet. No one in sight. My teeth ground together as I realized how alone he was in here. These people should be ashamed of themselves for leaving their interim king unprotected.

Finally I reached his room, and I was fully prepared to take up the position of guard outside of his door just as soon as I could confirm he was safe. But the moment I saw his still, sleeping face, all traces of anger completely dissipated.

He looked like an angel. I wanted nothing more than to curl up beside him and snuggle his peaceful sleeping form. But I didn't want to disturb him. In fact, I wasn't entirely sure why I was standing in his room at all. It had seemed like the right thing to do when I awoke from my nightmare, but now it just seemed childish.

And yet, I couldn't pull myself away from him. I told myself I would just adjust the blanket to cover his bare shoulder, then be on my way. That was it.

But it wasn't. I knelt down at his bedside, admiring the way his dark lashes fell across his cheek. I was fully aware of just how stalker-like my behavior was in that moment, but I didn't care. I loved this man, and I cherished every moment I was with him.

The feeling was so strong, I couldn't hold it in any longer. My voice was barely audible as I said the words aloud. "Maybe we're soulmates. Maybe we're not. But one thing is for sure: I love you, Thaddeus Castellanos."

His eyes didn't so much as flutter. He was still passed out cold. But that didn't stop the world from shifting. First I noticed the light—pure, unfiltered, without a source. It filled the room, gently illuminating the space like the first rays of morning sunshine.

Then I felt the warmth in my chest. Or maybe it was there all along. But it grew hot—hotter still, until I was reunited with that white-hot flame from my dream. And suddenly, I knew exactly what I had to do.

With one final look at my love, I turned and silently left his rooms behind. I tiptoed down the stairs, finding my way back to the great hall on the first floor of the palace. Amazingly, there were still no guards. No attendants. It was as though we were the only two souls in the entire city.

That was a good thing, because I couldn't imagine the guards would have been too thrilled with what I had planned next. With a final lungful of air, I stepped through the portrait of the knight, ready to retrieve a blade of my own.

CHAPTER 9

MY FRIENDS WERE ALWAYS jealous of my photographic memory. It was understandable. It definitely gave me a leg up when taking tests in high school. But it was never as useful then as it was in this moment—navigating the cool caves of Agartha alone.

Again, I swore I could feel the cave breathing. It inhaled and exhaled as I carefully plodded my way through its winding halls, reminding me that I was merely a visitor here. I tried to be respectful. I needed the cave on my side, just in case something grew angry with my next move.

I was going to steal the Firelake blade.

I didn't think of it as *stealing*, though. It was more like returning the blade to its rightful owner. The sword didn't belong to Everly Gordon, necessarily, but somewhere in my history I knew that it was mine. One of my incarnations, at some point in the distant past, owned that sword. And my soul was ready to take it back.

I fought against the warmth in my chest as I neared the lake. My inner warrior was desperate to be freed, but it wasn't time. I needed her to stay put with my powers tamped down until the time was right. There wasn't an infinite supply, after all.

I'd never felt as much strength in real life as I did in my dream when I set the warrior free in the Hall of Souls. I knew that if I did it again, she would protect me from the flames. I was betting my life on it.

The blade's song reached me before I saw the lake. I recognized the sad tune immediately, but it was more urgent now. The blade knew I meant business this time. I was coming to rescue it from its fiery prison.

My steps picked up speed as I neared the flaming expanse of the Firelake. As I reached its shore, I began to peel back the restraints on my power. The warmth under my sternum exploded the instant I gave it space to do so. A heat that couldn't be explained spread through my shoulders and belly, down my arms and my legs, until the tip of each toe was bursting with enough power to bring the whole cave down.

I looked down at my skin, and for the first time, I saw the white glow of my aura. I was lit from within, and instinct told me I was fully protected by the shield the white-hot flames provided only to me. Looking out over the lake, I uttered a single word. "Stop." The flames obeyed as time jerked still.

One step. Then another. I kicked off my slippers before dipping a toe slowly into the blue flame, and pulling it out for a quick examination. There was no pain. No redness. The heat had no effect on me.

With the confidence of a general stepping into battle, I strode all the way into the lake.

The bottom dropped quickly, and the flames consumed my body after only a few steps. Frozen in time, they more closely resembled a blue version of the northern lights, and I imagined myself the subject of a painting rather than a girl in a nightgown at the bottom of a flaming pit.

The song was louder now, pleading for me to come. I stopped thinking, pushing all logic and reason from my mind as I allowed the natural instinct of my soul to lead me to the blade. I walked for some time, never wavering as my power stayed strong. There was no guessing when I finally reached my destination.

A large boulder sat at the bottom at what I guessed was the center of the large lake. The top of the stone reached my shoulder, and it was as wide as a small car. The flames kept their distance from the stone, offering up clearing, frozen in time around the boulder like a kaleidoscope of color.

But the most striking detail was the gilded handle of a sword, plunged deep into the rock, all the way down to its hilt.

The Firelake blade.

I paused only for a moment before reaching for the handle. It was surprisingly cool in my palm, and new tendrils of power from the blade danced their way up my arm, meeting my own white-hot power at its source beneath my sternum.

Mine.

One gentle tug was all it took to slide sword from the rock. It slipped out as easily as the stick of a half-melted grape Popsicle in the middle of an Oklahoma summer. But power of this blade was far more delicious.

The blade extended as long as my arm. There was a considerable weight to it, but holding it felt natural. And the power of the blade buzzed through my entire body now, entangling with my ancient untapped powers and leaving Athena quite pleased with her new possession.

Blade in hand, there was one more thing I needed to do. I practically ran back up the steep slope of the lake bed, stopping short only when I noticed the dark figure of another person standing on the shore up top.

"Everly!" Tate's tear-streaked face kicked time back into gear. Blue flames danced around me as I closed the distance between us, feeling much like a fiery siren emerging from her lair.

"Are you okay?" Tate's eyes widened when he took in the giant sword in my hand, but his focus was entirely on me and my wellbeing. "I had a dream. You were in my room, and…" He ran a shaky hand through his hair.

"And I told you I love you." Power surged in my chest again at the words.

Tate's throat bobbed, and he nodded. "I knew you were coming here. I came to stop you. But I was too late. I reached the lake just in time to watch you freeze the flames and step inside. Then you were gone."

"You watched me walk in?"

"Yeah. I couldn't move after you stopped time. I wasn't even breathing, but somehow I still saw what happened. It's like my physical body was frozen, but my soul was with you."

His face blurred as tears sprang to my eyes. With the blade held at my side, I wrapped my left hand behind Tate's neck and met his glistening gaze. "I hope your soul will stay with me always. I love you, Tate."

"I love you, too." We kissed, a gentle thing full of relief and comfort. And as we stood in one another's arms, the invisible rope seemed to wrap itself around us, binding us permanently together. "My soul is all yours," he whispered as he pulled away.

And I knew it was true. My heart was ignited. More than that, it was engulfed in flames that fed into my power. We were stronger together with our souls entwined. And I knew without a doubt that everything the Keepers had been taught about soulmates and fractured souls was wrong. I would Deliver them the freedom they deserved.

Stepping back into my fuzzy slippers, I took Tate's hand in mine. "Come on. We need to go back to the Hall of Souls."

CHAPTER 10

THE WALK SEEMED MUCH shorter this time. Perhaps I was high on the rush of adrenaline after securing the blade. Or maybe the blade's power combined with my own made me that much faster. I couldn't explain it, but as we reached the Hall of Souls I knew without a doubt that we were doing the right thing.

A soft white light still emanated from my skin, and Tate's golden glow seemed more prominent now as well. Whether it was the power of the sword or the power of our bond didn't matter. We were a force to be reckoned with.

Thankfully, we didn't have to concern ourselves with any danger from these poor fractured souls. They swirled in the pools just as I'd remembered. It was just as I'd dreamed, and my heart cracked at the unspoken fear and turmoil they experienced. I wanted to save them. I wanted to set them free. But how?

My pulse thumped hard in the hand that gripped my sword. I closed my eyes, tuning out everything in the world aside from that steady pulse. There was another, beating in time with my own heartbeat. It wasn't Tate. It wasn't even the blade. There was something else in the hall, and it called to me.

Never opening my eyes, I followed the beat, entranced by its rhythm. Led by instinct, protected by my blade and backed by my soulmate, I feared nothing. I simply allowed my feet to do the walking.

The beat of the pulse worked itself up into a crescendo, taking my heart right along with it. The anticipation was nearly killing me when suddenly the pounding stopped. My eyes snapped open, and I found myself standing before an especially golden tinted pool along the back wall of the hall.

The souls here had worked themselves into a tizzy, swirling into a furious chaos. It was like they knew I was here. They knew what I was planning to do before even I knew it. Lifting the sword over my head with both hands, I plunged the blade deep into the depths of the pool.

The mist parted, the souls splitting to opposite sides. And there on the stone bottom, about three feet from the top of the pool, lay a rough-edged corner of an ancient stone tablet.

The tablet glowed with a blue light, its pulse keeping time with my own, inaudible but visual with flashes of light. I held out a hand, and the tablet lifted from the ground, flying into my grasp.

"The prophecy," Tate whispered from over my shoulder. "It was here all along."

"There could be no better place in Agartha to hide it than a pool of souls that would never be emptied." I sighed. "Never emptied before now, anyway."

The souls quivered at my words, but I knew it wasn't time. There wasn't anything I could do for them just yet, but I vowed in my heart to come back and make things right as soon as I was able to. The answer was just out of my grasp, but something told me the prophecy would piece everything together. We just had to decipher what it said.

"We need to find Driskell."

We turned toward the palace rather than backtracking to the portal. The tunnels were thick with the air of anticipation, and occasionally the ancient cave system seemed to groan and creak like a beast awakening.

Still, we ran. Tate felt the sudden urgency as well. The tablet pushed us ahead, faster and faster. It needed to be reunited with the other pieces, and nothing would stand in its way.

We were nearly back to the underground entrance to the palace when the hairs on the back of my neck stood on end. "Tate, wait. Something is wrong."

The blade warmed itself in my hand, preparing for battle. Tate and I backed up against each other, circling around to locate the potential threat we both could now feel. But as far as we could see, we were alone.

"What do you suggest?" he asked in a low voice.

"We've got to keep moving."

We'd only gone another twenty yards or so before the first wave of power rushed toward us. It ricocheted off of a bend in the wall, crackling over my skin as I threw out my arms to protect Tate. An invisible shield blocked the attack from reaching him, and the effects of the lightning power couldn't reach me, either. The sword in my hand glowed bright—its steel full of the same white-hot power I felt coursing through my veins. It protected me.

Footsteps crunched on the gravel around the corner as what sounded like three or four men came running toward us. The shock of seeing Tate and me still standing drew them up short once they cleared the corner. But it only took a moment for their surprise to morph into rage.

"It didn't work. Get him!" A small team of Agarthian guards rushed us, some holding weapons and others blasting electric power toward us with a flick of their wrists.

I slashed my sword in an arc through air, and a gust of white-hot power sprayed out from its tip. The guards were thrown back against the cave walls, their breath forcefully expunged from their lungs as my hit made impact. They were alive, but they wouldn't move for a while. I'd made sure of that.

"Keep going, we've got to get out of here!"

I didn't know how many other guards would be sent after Tate, and I didn't want to find out. We needed to get back to the surface to find Driskell. As soon as we knew what the prophecy said, these measly little Agarthian guards would mean nothing. Osborne's claim to the throne would be laughable—if there was a throne left to to claim at all.

We ran through the tunnels, stepping over the fallen guards until we finally reached the palace entrance. More men stood on the other side. The palace had been empty in the night because apparently all the guards were preparing to stage a coup. Too bad they didn't see me coming.

My sword sliced through the arm of a man who had just nocked an arrow directed at Tate. His bow fell to the floor with a clatter, and I ignored his cries of pain as he gripped the sticky sleeve where my deep cut had made its mark.

"Try that again and I'll take off the whole arm," I growled.

The other guards stepped back then, some still ready to fight but others recognizing me as a threat. None of them made another move to attack, though one emboldened by the group of men surrounding him raised a fist with a shout.

"We will not bow to you, Thaddeus!"

"No one is asking you to. I'm simply stepping in until the time comes for you to bow to *her*." Tate gestured toward me, dipping his chin in reverence. The move might have embarrassed me before, but now I was starting to believe he may be right. Like it or not, these men would be mine to deal with soon enough. All the Keepers would be under me, if they were able to survive whatever I dealt them through the prophecy.

The tablet buzzed in my hand at the thought, reminding me that we were on a mission that couldn't be sidetracked by some angry Agarthians.

"I'll die before I bow to that fractured trash." The loudmouthed guard sneered in my direction.

"As you wish," Tate said, raising his hands.

"No." I held out an arm. "Don't hurt him. We don't have time for this. We've got to keep moving."

The guard snorted, feeling like he'd won. Poor little guard. He had no idea what was coming. Tate and I moved forward, but I paused just long enough to press my blade into the soft spot of the guard's neck. "You're welcome for allowing you to live. Tell the others Deliverance is coming. Oh, and give your buddy Osborne my regards. I'm sure I'll be seeing him again soon."

A single drop of blood slid down the guard's neck from the small cut left by my sword. He pretended to scoff, but I felt him tremble before I turned away. A renewed sense of purpose rushed through me as we ascended the stairs to the first floor of the palace. The tapestry portal leading back to the mortal world was just steps away.

Soon we would find Driskell, decipher another part of the prophecy, and change the world as we knew it. It was only a matter of time now.

Deliverance was coming.

CHAPTER 11

"IT WILL BE A long hike in the mortal world," Tate said as we stood in the great hall of the palace. The world was still dark through the windows, though I suspected the first light of morning would announce its arrival at any moment. "Devon won't be waiting for us this time, so we'll have to walk until we find a lodge and can arrange transportation back to the city."

"We better get started, then."

"Did you want to change, or grab a bag or anything first?"

I held up the tablet and the sword. "I have everything I need. As long as you're by my side, I think we'll be fine."

Tate grinned. "I wouldn't have it any other way."

The woven tapestry that took us back into the mortal world hung on the large wall to our left. An image of an old English garden was displayed in muted colors across the large wall hanging. Talk about false advertising... I remembered the cool cave where we'd left the caves in Kentucky with a shiver. They weren't half as welcoming as that garden would be. But at least I'd get to be back in the water of the underground river.

"Remember, there will probably be guards positioned on the other side of the portal. I honestly don't know how many have been charmed by Osborne. I couldn't tell you if they will be friends or foes, but it would be best to expect the worst just in case."

I nodded, already having reached that conclusion myself. "I'm good to go when you are."

With my sword at the ready, I joined Tate's side. On a whispered count of three, we stepped through the invisible portal. The moment we reached the other side, we were immediately thrust against the wall.

There was a carnival ride I used to love as a little girl. It resembled a spaceship, and we would all file in one by one, taking a spot around the inner perimeter. The ride would spin so fast that the centrifugal force would plaster our bodies to the wall against sliding cushions. We could turn ourselves upside down so that our feet were above our heads, but we wouldn't fall. That's exactly how I felt on the inside of the cave wall. But instead of laughing with joy and the thrill of the ride, I was fuming with rage and concern over my soulmate.

"Finally," a familiar voice droned. "I was beginning to think you would never show up."

I craned my neck enough to see Rossel and a small army of Olympians. The same short man who broke into Millie's house had his arms extended, holding me in place on the wall beside Tate and the two Agarthian guards who must have been on patrol when the Olympians arrived. The guards were asleep. At least, I hoped they were just sleeping.

"Put us down, Rossel." There was fire in my command, and fire in my palm as I maintained my grip on the sword.

"I plan to. But first I need you to agree to play nice with my men." He didn't look afraid, but the fact that he made any requests at all told me he knew what kind of power I now yielded. Otherwise he would have simply taken whatever he was after without any regard for me. Perhaps my attack at the warehouse made an impact on him, after all.

I considered freezing time, but in doing so I would trap myself here against the wall. I needed the Olympian to release his hold on me. Then I could make my move.

"I'll play just as nicely as you do." I looked pointedly at Rossel, and he seemed to catch my drift.

A flicker of fear dashed across his face before he steeled his features into a look of apathetic confidence. "You don't look like you're in a position to be bargaining, I'm afraid. So I'll make the offer again—and it will be the last time. You can agree to keep your hands off my men and I will have them set you down."

"What if I don't?"

"You don't have to." Tate's voice took on an unnatural song-like quality. "Because these Olympians are going to set us gently back on the ground, and they will not use their powers on you again. Not today. Not ever."

I knew the effects of the sirens were weaker on other Keepers than they were on the mortals, but Tate's boost in power from our bond made his glamour surprisingly effective. I had to actively hide my look of surprise as the Olympians wordlessly obeyed, lowering our feet to the ground.

Wrapping my fingers around the handle of the sword, I had every intention of taking Rossel out right here, once and for all. But my traitorous arm wouldn't do as I wanted. Something inside held me back, and meeting Rossel's eyes, I knew there was more to the story. Much more.

"May I see the blade?" There was a childlike wonder to his words. Maybe I was a fool, but I didn't think he would pose a risk. Not with the blade anyway.

The handle of the sword pulsed in my hand in response, letting me know I was correct in my assumptions. The human part of my brain still didn't want him to have it though. "I don't think that's gonna happen."

He tilted his head, studying it more closely. "It's remarkable. I never thought I'd see the Firelake blade in my lifetime."

My heart raced as my chest began to heat up again. I looked at Tate to see if he felt it too, but I couldn't get a read on his expression. Rossel leaned forward to inspect the finer details engraved into the handle of the sword, and the strangest idea took hold in my brain.

"You know what? On second thought, go ahead."

Rossel lifted his black eyes to me with surprise. "Really?"

I raised the sword toward him, laid across both of my palms like a peace offering. "Be my guest."

"Everly, what are you doing?" Tate asked, not even trying to hide his disapproval. The other Olympians all looked tense as well, none of us trusting the others.

But the blade knew its owner. It wouldn't betray me. And if this was what I needed to get the information I still required out of Rossel, then so be it. I still believed he might be the only person who knew where my mom was. I couldn't kill him until I discovered what he knew, at least.

We stood silently for a long minute as Rossel visibly warred with himself. Ultimately, his greed—or curiosity, perhaps—won out. He lifted his hands and hesitantly reached out for the sword.

I knew the second he made contact with the metal. I heard the sizzle in his fingers as his flesh began to melt from the incendiary blade. He cried out in pain, and the mob of Olympians who had followed him into the caves immediately rushed me. Everything happened so fast, I didn't even see who struck me, or what they used to knock me out.

All I knew was the fear on Tate's face one minute, and darkness the next.

CHAPTER 12

A COOL HAND AND soft-spoken words stirred me awake. An icy compress was mashed against the back of my skull, but I was otherwise quite comfortable, propped up by a mountain of pillows and covered in a fuzzy never-ending blanket.

"Millie?" I squinted at the hazy outline of my aunt, willing the world to come back into focus. I moved to wrap my arms around her neck, thankful that I was still alive. But my right hand was weighed down with a death grip still holding fast to the handle of the Firelake blade.

I felt Tate next—a welcome tingle caressing my skin, just before he came into view. His lips pressed against my forehead, leaching the pain right out of me and leaving a tender warmth in its place. "Are you okay?" His fingers gently brushed a stray piece of hair from my face, distracting me from the pain and everything else other than his glittering gold irises.

"She's awake! Dom!" Tate was shoved out of my view with a hard bump of Gayla's hip. Her perky platinum bun wobbled atop her head as she clapped her hands. "Dom! Get in here!"

Dom appeared next, looking happy to see me. But there was definitely more trepidation in her gaze than there had been in the others. I'd learned long ago to trust Dom's instincts.

"What's going on?" I croaked. I sat up and surveyed the room. We were in Millie's study, which had been pieced back together after the Olympian attack. I had no recollection of how we got here, or how long I had been out. The last thing I remembered was...

"Rossel." His name escaped in a breathless growl. He stood nervously against a shelf in the far corner of the room.

What were they thinking letting him in here? His people had nearly killed me!

I lifted my sword. It was a struggle at first, but the warmth in my chest came easily now. I summoned it, gathering it up in my fist as I prepared to launch it from the sword and sizzle Rossel on the spot.

"Everly, wait!" It was Tate who called out. It was a good thing, too. I don't know that anyone else's voice could have cut through to me.

I paused, keeping the sword ready.

"It's okay." Tate joined me on the couch, resting a hand delicately on my shoulder. "Rossel's on our side."

"Yeah right." I lifted my weapon again, bringing it down only after a few seconds of Tate's hand relaxing the tension in my shoulder.

"It's true," Millie said. "He was with Tate when Devon found you in that motel in Kentucky. He helped carry your body there."

"The Olympians weren't supposed to strike you," Tate added. His face reddened slightly, and his jaw clenched. "It's my fault. I prevented them from using their powers against you. So when they thought you were attacking Rossel they resorted to physical force, instead."

"As did you after she fell," Rossel said, his words dripping with derision.

Tate's chin dropped, and I wondered just how many of Rossel's Olympian guards fell at his hands. Maybe I should have felt some guilt, but all I knew was pride. My soulmate had stepped up to defend me the best way he knew how. I couldn't feel bad about him harming the very same people who almost threw Sean out of the window. They got what was coming to them.

But as for Rossel... "Just because you found him with Tate, it doesn't mean he's gone good. His men nearly killed me. Twice. Rossel has tried before, too! But I get my hands on the Firelake blade and he's suddenly reformed? Fat chance."

Rossel moved forward then, a storm rolling in his black eyes. My chest heated in response, my muscles flexing under his attention. "I won't try to defend my actions. I've made some grave errors. But time is running out and I need you to come with me now."

"*Pfft.*" I glanced around the room to see solemn looks on the faces of my friends and loved ones. They were buying his crap.

"I'm not going anywhere until I find Driskell." I looked around again, hoping maybe I'd missed him in my first survey of the space. But he wasn't there. The tablet was, though. I saw its familiar blue glow pulsing from atop Millie's desk.

"Everly, honey. We have some bad news." My aunt lowered herself to a knee before me. "Driskell is missing."

"What?!" I stood, dropping the enormous blanket to the floor. "What do you mean he's missing?"

"Devon went to retrieve him from Porta Maris after he brought you three back here. But he's gone. No one knows what happened to him. Devon is still searching even now, investigating every possibility. Sean is doing the same here in the city. We'll find him."

"If he's still alive," Rossel added.

I spun around to face him, sword extended again. "What did you do to him? I know it was you. Is he banished to some island again? Bound by one of your wicked curses?"

Rossel's shoulders fell. "No. Driskell is not the cursed one you should be concerned for right now."

"Who else have you cursed?" My gaze swept the room again. Everyone looked slightly uncomfortable.

Dom spoke next. "I believe Rossel is cursed. I can't glean any information from his mind, and he becomes violently ill when he tries to speak about certain subjects."

"Certain subjects like what?"

"The prophecy," Dom said. Then, more quietly she added, "and your mom."

The source of my power squeezed tightly in my chest, burning up the sob that tried to escape. I knew it. I knew he was responsible for my mother's disappearance. And now he held the rest of the prophecy in his power as well. It looked like I only had one choice.

"Will you come with me to Olympus?" he asked again, softly.

"I'll need the king's permission, right? Is Baerius okay with it?"

Rossel's lips pinched together.

"We don't think you will require anyone's permission." Dom stepped forward and rested her hand on my shoulder. "I've been doing some more thinking, and the braid of power mentioned in the prophecy may just be your ticket into any of the territories."

"You mean I'm part Olympian?"

Rossel turned away.

Gayla shrugged. "We can't know for sure. But you do have some unique powers. You've got a crazy glow. An Agarthian soulmate. And that sliver of brown in your eye makes me wonder if there might be a little Olympian magic in you somewhere, too."

"That seems like a stretch."

"Yeah, it does. But then there was that vision I had of you walking through the Olympian gates."

My eyes narrowed. "You had another vision? Maybe you should have led with that."

Everyone's attention was glued to me as they awaited my response. Even Rossel turned back to face me. I closed my eyes and inhaled deeply, deferring the decision to the ancient, wiser part of me deep inside. And the answer was clear.

"Should I pack a bag?" I asked. "Or will the Olympians accept me as I am?"

LIES IN OLYMPUS

CHAPTER 1

THE ASSISTANT FOOTBALL COACH also happened to be my Biology teacher in my senior year of high school. That meant we watched a lot more videos and nature documentaries than was probably good for us—especially during the playoffs. One video in particular sprang to mind as I prepared for my trip to Olympus.

The video was about a very rare leucistic snake. It was white as snow and albino in appearance, but its eyes were black instead of pink. I remembered being grossly fascinated by this writhing creature, both horrified and hypnotized by its calculated movements and restrained power.

Rossel gave me a similar feeling.

I watched him work on making notes for Millie and jotting down a message to be carried by owl to someone already in Olympus. And I got the same crawly skin sensation as I did from the snake. Were they really going to send me away with this man? The same man who I believed to be responsible for my mother's disappearance? The same man who kidnapped me, tied me up, and tried to kill me not long ago in a warehouse?

It was hard to believe that he was our best option, but I knew there was no other way we'd get our hands on the final piece of the tablet. I got the sense that Rossel knew where it was, even if he couldn't say as much. And if he still wanted me dead, he could have easily made it happen when I was still unconscious back in Kentucky.

That logic didn't do much to ease my nerves, though. The only reason I'd agreed to this at all was because Gayla offered to tag along. As an

Olympian, she would have access to the territory without issue. And since she had the vision about me entering into Olympus as well, we thought it might be good for her to come. You know, just in case the vision changed or something. I'd sure hate to be struck dead before I ever passed through the gates.

Stupid Keeper curses.

There was still one condition before we left though. "Any word on Driskell?"

Millie checked her phone. "Nothing yet."

I glanced cautiously at Rossel, knowing how he'd react even before I said my next words. "Hopefully we'll find him soon. I'd like to stay here in the city until we can locate him. I don't want to go to Olympus until I know what the Agarthian piece of the tablet says."

Rossel whirled around to face me, looking all too graceful like the creepy snake man that he was. "We cannot wait. We must go now."

"Go ahead." I raised a shoulder. "I'm not holding you back. But I intend to stay right here until we find Driskell. If you have a guess as to where he might be, now would be a good time to mention it." I plopped down on Millie's sofa for emphasis.

"Everly." My aunt slid into the spot beside me, trying and failing to not sound patronizing. "Rossel is not responsible for Driskell's disappearance. He was in Agartha, like you."

"Well someone took him. Driskell wouldn't have tried to leave Porta Maris on his own. He knows the risks."

"We couldn't access Porta Maris even if we tried!" Rossel furrowed his brows. "It's visible to Atlanteans, only."

"You're right." I chewed on my lips for a moment, thinking it over. "Then it had to have been someone already on the island." And there was definitely one man there who had a history of betrayal against us. "It must have been Tano."

"It wasn't." Millie seemed completely convinced.

"How can you be so sure? He's turned against you before, or have you forgotten about the time he killed your soulmate in cold blood?" My words came out with more of a bite than intended, and they struck my aunt where it hurt.

"Of course I haven't forgotten! How could I? He was the first suspect that sprang to my mind when we learned Driskell was missing. Don't you think we considered that option? We've been up and down that path already, Everly. It wasn't Tano."

"It's true," Dom added. "I was here when they brought him back for questioning. He truly doesn't have anything to do with the disappearance."

Millie was still tense when I placed my hand on her shoulder. "I'm sorry. I shouldn't have said that. I'm pretty tightly wound right now, but I shouldn't have taken it out on you. You didn't deserve that."

Her eyes softened. "It's okay. We're all on edge." Her eyes cut accusingly over to Rossel, further confirming my own suspicions.

"So if it wasn't Tano, who could it have been? What other Atlantean could have some vendetta against poor old Driskell?"

Tate stood suddenly, a growl rumbling from his chest. "This isn't about Driskell at all. It's about you. I would bet my life on it." He began pacing, his golden eyes flaming. " Driskell was kidnapped to bring *you* in. I can't believe I didn't see it before. They took Titus, not suspecting the Agarthians would take over the case. They expected you to follow. But when you didn't, they went after Driskell instead."

"Who?" Millie asked, shaking her head.

"Rasputin." Every eye in the room turned to me. "I think Tate's right."

"But Rasputin isn't Atlantean," Millie argued. "He can't access Porta Maris, either."

"He can't. But Peter Bratton can." It felt like the air was sucked out of the room. Everyone sat quietly for a moment, considering the possibility. But I'd already made up my mind on how to proceed. "I'm gonna get him back."

"That's exactly what they want you to do. Even if you knew where they held him, they would be ready to strike the moment you showed up." Tate's jaw hardened at the thought.

"I do know where they're holding him. And they can't strike me if I strike first." I blew a piece of hair out of my face, casually regarding a glint of light off of the Firelake blade before turning back to the others. "How long does it take to get to the Cathedral of St. John the Divine from here?"

CHAPTER 2

I WASN'T A FAN of Tate using his glamour on mortals, but in this case, it was necessary. Jeeves sat stoically in the driver's seat of Millie's limousine, never once questioning the strange group of us crowded into the back. He didn't even ask about the sword I carried. It was a good thing too, because I found myself unable to set it down. It was like something inside me refused to let it go.

But there was no way Tate would be able to use his powers on everyone walking the city streets. That's where the hood came into play. It was actually Gayla's idea—maybe her best one yet. "You ready?" she asked, hand on the door handle.

The limousine was parked right alongside the cathedral where I suspected we'd find Rasputin—and hopefully Driskell. "Let's do this." I pulled the red hood of the cape I wore up over my head.

Gayla stepped out of the vehicle first, lifting her phone camera at arm's length in front of her face and barking out orders like the director of a movie set. I snickered at Tate. "You're next."

He groaned and pulled a fuzzy werewolf mask over his face. The effect was even more believable with those glowing golden irises peeking through the eye holes.

"That's a good boy," I said as he climbed out. Perhaps this wasn't the best time for cutting up, but if I didn't laugh I feared I might crumble from the weight of the task laid before me.

"Are you sure you don't want any of us to come with you?" Millie's brows were pinched with concern from the opposite side of the limo.

"I'm positive. Rasputin won't hurt me. He's made that very clear. I'm invincible with this anyway," I added, lifting my sword into the air. There was also the thought that I suspected Rasputin could be my father, but Millie got upset the last time I'd mentioned the idea, so I held my tongue.

"Okay. But please let us know if you find yourself in any trouble. If you're not back in fifteen minutes, we're going in after you."

There was no use arguing with her about that. We Gordon women knew how to stand our ground on matters we found important.

"Understood."

"I said, *action!*" Gayla shouted from outside the vehicle.

"Gotta go." I turned and hopped out of the vehicle, immediately raising my sword in the air toward Tate. He released a very unconvincing growl and made half-hearted claws with his hands in the air.

"You killed my grandmother, you mangy mutt! Prepare to die!" My acting skills weren't much better than his, but they served our purpose. Passers-by on the street barely glanced in our direction. That was the beauty of New York City. Cosplay and fake sword fights on a cathedral lawn didn't stand out to them any more than a hot dog stand.

Gayla's idea to fake an indie movie scene was brilliant. I was able to wield my sword in broad daylight without drawing any unwanted attention. Tate and I carried the scene all the way over to the door that led down to Rasputin's office below the cathedral. And once we had enough distance between us and the street, we stopped the acting.

Bravo. A familiar voice rang out in my mind, drawing my gaze up into the tree branch hanging over the small path we stopped upon.

"Al?"

In the feathers. He hopped down the branch a little closer to me. *Where have you been? I couldn't find you after the convention. Is that... did you go to Agartha and get the Firelake blade?*

"I did. There's a lot to catch you up on, but it'll have to wait." I cast my eyes back to the door.

You're going to see Rasputin, aren't you? Want me to come?

"No. I've got to do this alone. Stay with the others. I'll be back soon."

Tate and Gayla regarded the owl with uncertainty. His head swiveled to take them in before he focused his yellow eyes on me again. *Be careful.*

"I will." I faced my friends next. "Promise you won't follow me in there. He's dangerous, and you guys don't have the same protection I do." I notched my chin toward the sword in my hand.

"Cross my heart," Gayla said.

Tate wasn't as quick to respond. After a brief moment of hesitation, he pulled off his mask and stepped forward, cupping my cheeks in his palms and sending a wave of fire through my body from head to toes. Bringing his face just inches from mine, he whispered. "I love you, Everly Gordon. Come back to me alive, okay?" He kissed me before I could answer.

The rest of the world melted away in the short time our lips touched. Then all too quickly, he was gone. The flame he'd placed in my heart was still a raging inferno, though. Our love through this bond was a powerful thing, and greater strength coursed through my veins as I pulled open the door.

With one final glance to my friends, I turned to face the darkness lurking beneath the cathedral. The hall I entered was quiet. I focused on the mosaic of light from the stained glass along the walls, trying to keep my nerves at ease. But it wasn't necessary.

Every step I took was more sure than the last. My heart drummed a steady beat that only grew louder and more confident the closer I got to the basement door. And as I twisted that knob and descended the stairs, it had all but turned into a war song.

Athena was awake, and she was out for blood.

I marched through the dimly lit halls of the basement toward Rasputin's office and paused outside the door. The blade burned hot in my hand, ready to strike. His door was cracked, so I lifted my foot, ready to kick it in, but it swung open instead.

A tall, hooded figure in a long faded black robe greeted me. His smile pulled his long, unkempt beard, and he gestured for me to enter.

"Come on in, Everly. We've been waiting for you."

CHAPTER 3

MY FIRST URGE WAS to slice through Rasputin's neck with my blade. But a decapitation would be bloody and brutal, and it wouldn't serve my purpose. I needed to find Driskell. Rasputin was a means to an end.

I inhaled deeply, hoping the cool damp air of the basement might soothe my inner Athena's bloodlust, then dropped my chin in a bitter greeting to Rasputin. "Where's Driskell?"

The old man stepped back to reveal his nearly empty office. Empty, except for the chair in the center of the room that held Driskell, strapped down to its rigid back. A gash above his left brow was covered in dry, crusted blood, and the skin around his eye was swollen and purple. He was filthy and fatigued, and though he couldn't speak around the gag shoved into his mouth, his raging glare said enough.

"Untie him. He's coming with me."

Rasputin laughed—the sound garbled like he had a throat full of dusty gravel. "Oh Everly, you know it's not that easy."

I'd expected him to refuse, but at least I gave him the chance to make a better decision. Now I didn't have to feel bad about plunging my blade into his old body. I lunged, but he was gone before I reached him.

His voice came from behind me next, the humor gone from his tone. "It would be impolite to murder your host before we have a chance to speak."

I spun around, pushing the heat in my chest through my arm and into the sword, flinging my power through the blade at the old man. But again, he disappeared. A large chunk of rock came loose from the wall where the blast from my sword landed, sending up a cloud of dust as it slammed into the floor below.

My inner warrior was roaring now, ready to destroy. And I could. I could wreak havoc in this small basement office. I could bring the whole cathedral down if I wanted to—I felt the power bubbling up inside me. But I needed Driskell, and I wouldn't risk losing any other innocent lives that may be in the building as well.

Sensing my hesitation, Rasputin continued. "You are here to see if this man can interpret another piece of the prophecy, yes?"

"I am here to rescue an innocent man from a monster."

"Harsh words from such a lovely mouth." Rasputin exaggerated a grimace. "Especially considering this *monster* may be able to help. Would you like me to interpret the tablet for you?"

"I want you to let Driskell go." I refused to confirm or deny that I was in possession of the tablet. The less Rasputin knew, the better. Though I suspected I wasn't fooling him at all.

He walked casually over to the chair where Driskell was seated and placed his hand on his captive's shoulder. Driskell winced and tried to pull away, but he was bound too tightly to move an inch. "We've discussed this before, but I'm not sure you understood. I want to help you. I have been training up an entire army of humans, Keepers, and everything in between. We have dedicated our lives to the very thing you were created for."

"Is that how you think of me? As your *creation*?"

The barest flick of his brow betrayed Rasputin's confusion.

"You didn't think I'd figure it out, but I did. You impregnated my mother, thinking that we could join together and destroy the Keepers once my powers came into effect. My mother knew—she tried to keep my powers hidden, probably out of fear that you would find me and use me as a weapon against the world. Well, unfortunately, you didn't consider the fact that abandoning me as an infant would destroy any hint of loyalty I might have had to you. I may be the Deliverer, but I'll only deliver to you what you deserve." The fire burned so hot in my chest that I could see my actual glow. A soft white light emanated from my arms, leaving no doubt that my words were true.

I was the Deliverer. And I was prepared to kill my father.

Rasputin's expression remained solid. For about ten seconds, there wasn't a sound to be heard. But I didn't fear his reaction. I didn't fear anything.

I also didn't expect him to smile. Rasputin's eyes crinkled in the corners as he threw his head back and laughed—a full belly laugh—so hard I thought he might choke on his own spit.

"I'm not your father," he said at last, once he'd regained his composure. "Though it is precious that you see me as a father figure."

"You act like you know so much about me... if you're not my father, then who is?"

"Wouldn't we all like to know..." A slow grin pulled his mustache wide.

A strange combination of relief and despair rushed through me at the news that Rasputin wasn't my dad. I was glad to not be the daughter of a villain of course, but I had no other likely guesses. This power I possessed was unlike any other.

And if we weren't related, then why was Rasputin so careful not to hurt me? He'd lashed out at everyone around me, but he had yet to lay a finger on me.

As though he could read the frenzied thoughts racing through my mind, Rasputin took a small step forward. His voice was gentle when he spoke again. "Everly, I want to work with you. I see you for who you are, and we have the same goals. The Keepers have grown far beyond their purpose. Their thirst for power will destroy us all if you don't stop them. With my power and army behind you, you can fulfill your destiny. It's meant to be. Hand me the tablet and I will prove it to you. I will show you what it says."

"No." I spat my answer through gritted teeth.

His smooth façade cracked for only an instant, but it was enough for me to see the anger boiling inside. I suspected it took a great amount of self-control for Rasputin to stop himself from attacking me and taking the tablet by force.

It was certainly more self-control than I had. The hilt of my blade grew hot in my hand, begging me to use it. And who was I to deny an ancient call to action?

Power surged through my limbs and I thrust my weapon toward the old man. I felt the blade make contact with his shoulder, but then he was gone. I whirled around, ready to strike again, but the room was empty aside from Driskell and me.

"We weren't finished yet!" I called out, not sure if Rasputin was invisible or somewhere else completely. I turned in a slow circle, readying myself for the instant he reappeared. My chest was burning, white-hot flames itching to be released. Rasputin had lived for too long. It was clear he wasn't going to provide me any additional information. His usefulness had run dry.

He must have known it too, because he didn't return. After a solid minute of panting and searching the space for any signs of him, I was brought back into my right mind by the sound of Driskell grunting through his gag. With a final look outside the office, up and down the hall, I accepted that Rasputin had gotten away.

Thankfully, he'd left Driskell here for me. I made quick work of removing the gag and untying the ropes that bound him to the chair. He was shaky on his feet, but he could walk.

"Are you okay?" I asked, scanning him for any additional injuries.

"I am now." He coughed into the crook of his arm. "But I would like to get out of here."

"Right." I wrapped my arm around his back and guided him back to the exit. "Let's get you back to Millie."

CHAPTER 4

TATE AND GAYLA SWOOPED in to help me carry Driskell's weak body back to the limo the moment I emerged from the cathedral.

"Are you hurt?" Tate asked.

"No, but Driskell has seen better days." We pulled him into the backseat of the limousine and Millie wasted no time checking him over.

I felt Dom's scrutinizing gaze as Jeeves veered the vehicle back onto the street. She frowned when I met her eyes, finally voicing the scene she saw play out in my mind. "Rasputin got away."

I nodded. It was easier than recapping everything, so I opened my mind wide to her. There was pity in her eyes when she finished taking it all in, and I looked away. As tough as I may have appeared, Rasputin's confession about not being my father cut deeper than I expected it to. I just wanted to know where I came from.

An hour later we all gathered back in Millie's study, including Devon who had zapped back in with Sean by his side as soon as they heard Driskell was found.

Al had followed us back to her place as well, flapping through the air above the New York City streets as we drove. I opened the window to allow him entry to our meeting. There was no use hiding his existence anymore—everyone had either seen him fighting the Manticorians after the convention or heard about it by now. The only one who raised a brow at the appearance of my little owl friend was Rossel, and he wasn't going to get an explanation.

After a hot shower and sandwich sent upstairs from Pierre, Driskell filled us in on what happened the day he was taken. I was right about his kidnapper. It was Peter Bratton.

Peter had entered Porta Maris with the very true confession that he had been removed from his position in the Atlantean guard. He forgot to mention, however, that he was working for the Manticorians now.

Driskell had tried to fight back when Peter sneaked into his room during the night, but he wasn't as strong. Peter was a brute of a man, and it was his giant hairy fist that did the damage to Driskell's eye. He knocked him out, and Driskell found himself in Rasputin's basement office when he awoke. He'd been there for two days before I arrived.

Sean's face reddened at Driskell's recount of the story, but I suspected it was more out of anger than embarrassment. He'd never had a great relationship with his father, but any traces of love that remained had been completely obliterated after Peter's stunts in Atlantis and at the convention where he killed Tate's father.

He turned toward the old man. "I am so sorry, Driskell. And my words may not mean much, but I swear to you I will make it right. My father will pay for this."

"I appreciate your concern for me." Driskell scratched his nose. "But everything turned out fine, and we don't need to speak of it anymore. Besides, I know the real reason you all were so eager to rescue me. Go ahead. Bring out the tablet. I want to know what it says just as badly as you do."

Millie gave a small nod, so I moved for the cabinet where we'd stored the latest piece of the tablet. It had been calling to me since we got back to Millie's place, like it knew we were ready for its message. And it was ready to reunite with the other pieces.

As I retrieved the newest piece, Millie disappeared into her bedroom, where the other half of the tablet was stored. I knew that joining the pieces together would create another rush of power, and I hadn't been ready for it yet. I wanted to know what it said first. But after Driskell interpreted it for us, there would be no use keeping them apart any longer—especially if I was to go with Rossel to Olympus after this.

There was a collective silence in the room as everyone watched the small piece of stone pulse in my hand. I felt its power as strongly as I felt the sword's energy in my other hand. It was an extension of me, of my power. The prophecy was ready to come alive.

I held it out for Driskell, unwilling to let it go. He didn't dare touch it, which was wise. It would have surely been too much for him.

The old man squinted as he leaned in to take a closer look, and the rest of us in the room held our breath. Driskell's eyes moved rapidly back and forth over the ancient symbols, the wheels turning in his head. And finally, the corner of his mouth quirked.

"What does it say?"

He scratched his nose again. "Well, it says you're going to kill the Keepers."

"What?!" My heart raced. That had been the rumor, of course. But standing in a room full of family and friends, I didn't want to believe it. I was okay with destroying their system, or eliminating their power. Destroying the concept of the Keepers was perfectly fine, but killing them? Nope. "What does it say, *exactly*?"

"It's only a corner piece, so we're working with fragments of thoughts here. I can't be sure until we have the rest of the tablet."

"Hand me the other half," I said, setting down the sword and holding an empty hand out to Millie. She stood near the door, wearing heavy-duty rubber gloves that extended all the way to her elbows. The top half of the tablet pulsed wildly in her hands, looking like it could explode with energy at any moment.

The instant it touched my hand, I had no choice but to push the pieces together. They demanded to be reunited. A blinding light filled the room and my chest felt like it was cracked open and welded shut again with the burning flame of power. If this was only three-quarters of the tablet, I worried that once it was complete the full power of the prophecy may kill me.

But after several long seconds the light faded, and I was still alive, if not a little unsteady on my feet.

Woah, Ev. Al's voice in my mind was the only thing I heard. *You don't look human at all anymore.*

He was right. I looked down, surprised that I was able to see my own aura. Not only was I glowing, but my skin had taken on a pearlescent quality. And if it was strong enough for me to see, I wondered how different it must look to everyone else in the room.

Their open mouths and wide eyes told me it was quite a sight. I shook them off, refocusing on Driskell. "Will you read it?"

He cleared his throat and began.

"The daughter of sea and sky,
together with the one who

ignites her heart in her
centennial incarnation
shall form a white braid of
the powers that bind.
The Deliverer alone can wield…"

He paused, looking up at me below heavy brows. "This is where the new piece starts."

"Got it." I was on the edge of my seat. "Please continue."

"…the sword
…and fire to
…hunger for
…Keepers shall perish
…the Deliverer
…will unite as one
…before and
…shall be."

A quick glance around the room revealed that everyone else was just as confused about it all as I was. Everyone except Rossel. His features were pinched as he fought an internal battle he couldn't win. At last, he met my eyes. "May we leave now?"

"Shouldn't we try to figure out what this means, first?"

He clenched his jaw. "It's not complete."

Dom stepped forward and reached for my arm, but she stopped short of touching my strange glowy skin. "I think what he wants to say is that he can help you get the full story. The final missing piece is in Olympus, and I'm thinking Rossel can bring you right to it."

We turned back to the man, trying to read his dark, calculating gaze. He revealed nothing. And though the logical part of my brain begged me to keep my distance from him, I couldn't deny the steady beating of my heart, drumming out a rhythm that urged me into motion.

The glow across my skin brightened as I mentally relented to my inner warrior's command. I had no other choice. My fate was sealed by the prophecy, and I would have to find the last remaining piece. It was what I was created for.

"Is she right? Will you take me to the missing piece?" I reached for my sword, already knowing the answer and preparing for the trip to Olympus.

He said nothing again. The curse would strike him if he tried to speak of it, but I knew. I knew this was the final leg of my journey—an adventure

I could have never imagined for myself.
   It was my destiny to change the world.

CHAPTER 5

THE PLAN WAS FOR Devon to teleport us to the nearest Olympian portal, but I wasn't ready to jump up and leave immediately. First, we needed to develop a plan for those who would stay behind.

"I can't help but feel like this is the beginning of the end." I leaned in to Tate's side, and he wrapped his strong arm around my shoulders, pulling me in even closer. His presence steadied me; it helped me think more clearly. I didn't know what to expect in Olympus, and Rossel couldn't give me any clues. But there was definitely a sense that everything was coming to a head.

"It's got to be about Rasputin and the Manticorians, right? Surely the prophecy doesn't mean that *all* of the 'Keepers shall perish' at my hands..." I sat up again and looked around the room at all the faces of those who had supported me through the weirdest time of my life. And Rossel. He was there, too, though he definitely didn't land in the support group.

Dom shifted uncomfortably on her feet. "We can only hope that's the case. There are definitely some bad eggs in all the Keeper territories. But we're not all power-hungry like Rasputin."

I watched Rossel as Dom spoke, and the twitch of his mouth didn't escape me. There was more he wanted to say, but he probably couldn't. Not without being struck dead by the curse he was under.

My heartbeat morphed into a steady war song as the conversation continued. With the full tablet, my sword, and my soulmate, I knew I would be unstoppable. I desperately wanted Tate to accompany me to Olympus, but it was impossible. He wasn't of Olympian descent, and there was no way King Baerius would authorize another Keeper leader's entry into his territory.

Besides, Tate had issues to sort out with his own territory. The Agarthians were divided among themselves, half wanting Tate to continue to lead them and half under the illusion that Osborne would be better in the interim. Idiots. Osborne wasn't good for anything.

But more than all of that was the impending sense of doom I felt in my bones. A war loomed over us—greater than any the world had ever known. And I had somehow become the face of it. I only hoped we could keep it at bay until after I'd acquired the last piece of the tablet. Then I would unleash what Rasputin had coming to him.

"Let them know," I whispered to Tate. "If it's true that I'm gonna destroy those who have let the power go to their heads, then we need the ones worth saving to keep their distance from me. I want to deliver the good Keepers to safety, and I don't know that I'll have enough control over my power when it all goes down."

"What about us?" he asked. "You can't expect us to stay away." The others in the room murmured their agreement and leaned in close, awaiting my response.

I swallowed. "It's probably best if you all keep your distance from me, too. I don't know what I'm capable of. And I won't know until it's too late."

Al fluttered over to the couch. *I can't do that. I've sworn an oath to you. I will be by your side, no matter what. And if it kills me, it would be a great mercy. I've lived for thousands of years. I'm ready to go. There is no greater cause worth sacrificing myself for than this.*

His feathery white body blurred through my tears. "Thank you."

Dom stepped forward next. "Let me guess, the owl isn't leaving?"

I bobbed my head, trying not to cry.

"Well neither are we."

Gayla joined her, crossing her arms over her chest. Sean was next, hands balled into fists at his side. He was ready for a fight. Millie and Devon stepped up behind him, each looking fiercely determined not to back down.

And Tate... the look in his eyes almost undid me right there on the spot. "You know I'm not going anywhere. Besides, you need my power." He leaned closer, his lips brushing my ear as he whispered, "almost as badly as I need you."

I prayed Dom wasn't reading the thoughts going through my mind right then, but Rossel cleared his throat before I could go too far.

"Alright." I took a deep breath. "But let it be known that I tried to save you all. And look out for each other while I'm gone. Al is really useful at keeping tabs on people. And owls have access to Olympus, right? As messengers?"

"That's right." Dom nodded. "So we should be able to reach you if anything goes wrong here."

"And I'll have your back up there." Gayla grinned and took my hand, pulling me away from Tate. "Sorry loverboy, but I don't think she'll let go if I don't make her." She winked, and my heart warmed at this ragtag group of Keepers—representing all the different races and uniting together for one cause. These were my people, and I would do whatever it took to save them.

I sheathed my sword into the belt Millie had pieced together for me, and threw my messenger bag over my shoulder. I wasn't sure if bringing the tablet with us was the best idea, but I couldn't bear to leave it behind. I didn't want it out of my sight. And something told me we were going to need it where we were going.

"Are you ready, then?" Devon and Rossel approached me and Gayla, looking a lot less afraid than I felt. My friend squeezed my hand, a gentle reminder that she was in this with me. And it was only then that I realized I didn't know exactly where we were going.

"Where is the Olympian portal located?"

"The most famous is atop Mt. Olympus, of course. But it would be difficult to get you all there in one trip." Devon looked a little ashamed that he wasn't strong enough to do it. But he'd been working so hard to find Driskell for the last several days that I was happy he could get us anywhere at all.

"It's fine, though. Because the Mohonk portal is way nicer anyway." Gayla looked at me over her shoulder. "Have you ever been to the Catskills?"

We landed on a clear flat cliffside overlooking a scene that could have been displayed on a painting. In fact, I could've sworn I'd seen this exact image on a puzzle at Hobby Lobby—probably titled *Autumn Radiance* or something equally enchanting. It was an explosion of reds and yellows and oranges on trees surrounding the most picturesque little lake. A castle-like resort sat nestled quietly off to the side, a cherry atop the natural beauty of the Hudson Valley.

The Mohonk Mountain House was a prime example of what the humans viewed as an elite getaway for the wealthy. If only it were that simple. They'd lose their minds if they knew what kind of secrets were really held within its historic walls.

"Ah, takes me back to my childhood." Gayla sighed.

"You're still a child." Rossel huffed and turned toward a tall stone tower behind us, his shoes crunching heavily on the rocky cliff as he stomped away. A couple of humans stood in front of the old structure, snapping pictures with their cell phones. They scattered when they saw Rossel coming. I wasn't the only person he creeped out.

"This is where I've got to leave you," Devon said. "Be careful up there, and come back to us as soon as you get the missing piece."

"I'll keep her safe." Gayla stepped forward, a look of sincere determination drawing her pretty mouth into a hard line. "Promise."

"Come on," Rossel called from over his shoulder. We said goodbye to Devon and followed Rossel up a couple of worn steps and into the tower. A plaque on the front of the stone monument said it was built a hundred years earlier as a memorial.

"He was Olympian," Gayla said as I read the name on the memorial plaque aloud. "He bought this land as a retreat for our people, and they added the portal to Olympus shortly after he died. It gets a little touristy at times, but the humans generally know when to stay out of our way."

One look at Rossel's chilling glare was all I needed to understand what sent the humans running. If it weren't for that steady war song in my chest, I'd probably want to run, too.

It only took a moment for us to find ourselves alone inside the old stone memorial tower. An empty fireplace sat against one wall of the first floor—large enough for all three of us to fit inside. As we neared it, I saw the tell-tale shimmer of a Keeper portal, invisible to mortal eyes. It wasn't nearly as glamorous as the painting portals in Agartha, but it was a step up from the Atlantean portal at the bottom of the ocean, I supposed. At least there weren't any sea monsters here.

Rossel closed his eyes and inhaled deeply, and I couldn't help but wonder what he was so afraid of on the other side. Wasn't he the king's right-hand man? *His* nerves ignited *my* nerves, and Gayla's steady presence was the only thing preventing me from running after the humans. I could do this. I had to do it.

"Get your sword ready," Rossel said. Then he yanked me through the wall.

CHAPTER 6

OLYMPUS WAS REALLY... *white*. Like, shockingly white. It looked a lot like how I'd imagined it would be to skip across the tops of the clouds when I was a little girl, but much less joyful. No, Olympus didn't bring me any joy at all. All I got from this ethereal land was a hefty weight of foreboding.

The portal spat us out onto a platform at the top of a white marble staircase. Clouds and a thick purple haze in the sunlight made it difficult to see what lay below, but I had a good guess Mount Olympus was somewhere down there, back on the mortal earth miles underneath us. Though it was evening down there, the sun shone brightly on us above the clouds.

The platform was at one end of a ridge of rough, pale mountains. A towering white stone acropolis reigned high at the opposite end of the ridge, and a pale golden path led from our platform to its enormous white columns. Its commanding presence told me it was probably the Olympian palace, where King Baerius dwelled. The ridge curved around what I assumed to be a city in a valley at the base of the peaks, but it was obscured by a thick mist—a glowing shroud of mystery.

Rossel looked left and right, his movements jerky and disjointed. There was a panic in his otherwise empty, black eyes. Remembering his words from before, I wrapped my hand around the hilt of my sword.

We didn't see a single soul as we carefully made our way down the golden path toward the palace. After several minutes, I relaxed my grip on my weapon, content to take in the sights of Olympus—or what little I could see of it anyway. The cloudy mist covering the city in the valley emanated a pale lavender glow—the auras of its people. It was the only way I knew there was life here at all.

"Is this how you saw it play out in your vision?" I asked Gayla. I was grateful to still be standing, though I didn't quite understand how I'd been able to enter the territory without being stricken by the curse. Dom's theory about my white aura must have been true. In some way, my power must be like a braid of all three Keeper races, allowing me access here.

Gayla nodded, cheerfully. "Yep. You walked right in, like one of us. I told you there was nothing to worry about."

She had just barely gotten the words out before a large stone flew up through the mist and landed squarely in the center of Rossel's forehead. I ducked just in time to dodge another one. Gayla cursed loudly and yanked me to the ground, where Rossel's body was now sprawled on the golden pavement. His white hair was spread like a fan above his head, and he groaned, reaching for his forehead. A thin trail of blood dripped down from the spot where the rock had made impact.

"Get up!" Gayla shook him violently, but it did no good. Rossel had been hit hard, and he wasn't going to be able to get up again any time soon. It was a wonder he was still awake. He had to have been concussed at the very least.

"We've got to run," my friend said, turning frantically back to me. "The king's guards may be using stones now, but they won't be as nice when they discover you here without the king's approval."

It made sense. And the mortal girl from Oklahoma would have done just that—run to save my life. But I wasn't just a mortal anymore. And I certainly didn't plan on running.

Credit to Gayla—I saw the instant she realized I wasn't backing down. Her resolve hardened, and the flame of power in my chest burned hotter when I saw that she would remain by my side. I wasn't alone in this. And I wasn't fighting just for myself. I was fighting for Gayla, who had never been given the opportunity to choose how she lived her life. I was fighting for all the Keepers who had been forced into lives chosen for them—lives without any real purpose other than increasing the power of the leaders already in place.

No more. I would deliver them from the shackles that had bound the Keepers for thousands of years. It was time to put an end to this.

I wheeled around just in time to see the first of the Olympian guards emerge from the ridge, stepping through the mist. Her hands were raised, and a bevy of rocks hung in the air before her, ready to be launched toward us. I'd dealt with telekinetics before, but never such a large number of them. More guards came up from the mist then, probably fifty of them in total.

They weren't all telekinetics. Some held real weapons—swords and bows with glowing arrows nocked and ready to fire. Many of them were aiming for Gayla and me, but I was surprised to see just as many taking aim at Rossel.

If the king had somehow discovered Rossel's plan to help us find the missing piece of the tablet, then of course he wouldn't be happy about it. This was the kind of royal secret that was never intended to be released. The prophecy was a rumor that the Keepers had spent millennia trying to keep quiet. I didn't know why I hadn't considered the situation from Rossel's position before.

It had been so easy in Atlantis, and even Agartha. I was a fool to think it would be just as easy here in Olympus.

The first guard pushed both hands forward, sending the rocks soaring toward us at inhuman speeds. Good thing I wasn't human...

My ancient instincts kicked in before I could even process what I was doing. The rocks slowed until they hovered in the air a few feet from us like a swarm of giant gnats. Certain they weren't going to start flying toward me again, I took a deep breath and looked around. Time had stopped. Frozen. I was the only person aware of my surroundings.

I could already feel the pressure in my chest. There were too many of them. Or maybe it was because we weren't on earth anymore. But the amount of power it took to sustain the pause was greater than I'd experienced before. I wouldn't be able to hold them off for long.

I moved Gayla first—getting her far from where the rocks would strike. Then I started pulling weapons from the other guards. But as I worked, the pressure continued to grow until my ribs felt like they might crack under the strain. Knowing I had only seconds left, I changed my plan and began kicking guards back down the ridge. One at a time, I placed my foot squarely in their chests and knocked them to the ground. I'd almost finished when the last string of power snapped and time shifted back into motion.

There were startled gasps and yells as the guards all tried to reorient themselves. Several were a ways down the mountain, bruised from their falls. The others were just confused.

I could feel the power building up inside me again, my skin growing hot. Stepping forward, I raised my sword and called out to the guards. "Back away and no one else has to be hurt. You can't stop the plan that is in motion. But you can get on the good side of history before it's too late. Lower your weapons and halt your power. It's time for Deliverance."

An obnoxious slow clap thundered out from down the ridge. "Bravo, little girl."

The guards parted, clearing a narrow path through which the king of Olympus stepped forward. He was large and unattractive for a Keeper, with thinning white hair that he wore long to distract from his receding hairline. He was overweight, but not soft—a man who had once been a trained warrior but had long since passed his athletic prime. I didn't remember how many hundreds of years he'd been leading the Olympians, but it was certainly long enough for him to grow comfortable on his throne and let his appearance fall by the wayside.

His entrance had distracted me, and I didn't notice the heat in my chest fizzling out until it was too late. King Baerius was known for having a very rare power. He had the ability to drain other Keepers of their individual powers. Even, as it appeared, the powers of the Deliverer. I tried to gather up whatever wisps of might remained and flung them into the Firelake blade, but nothing happened. It had become an ordinary sword, just a piece of metal like any other. And I was as weak as a mortal.

"Seize them all!" the king bellowed.

CHAPTER 7

MY POWERS WERE GONE, but Baerius couldn't touch my will to survive. I swung my blade, my arm reverberating from the impact it made with one of the Olympian guard's shields. It was heavy and awkward in my hand, reminding me how much of my might came from my immortal soul rather than raw skill.

But that didn't stop me from fighting.

"Baerius, wait!" Rossel cried out from behind me. I couldn't turn and look at him because any lapse in my attention would provide the guards an opportunity to capture me, but it didn't sound like Rossel was putting up much of an effort.

A flash of platinum blond hair and a fierce yell told me Gayla wasn't backing down, at least. But she was unarmed and just as powerless as me. We weren't going to make it very far against this army of Olympian guards.

"Don't you know who this is?" Rossel shouted again, desperately trying to get the king's attention. "I've brought you the Deliverer."

"Of course I know who she is. Do you think me a fool? What I don't understand is how you thought you could sneak her into our territory without being caught."

The guard I fought against pushed me back with his shield, using my loss of balance as an opportunity to strike. The impact should have sent my own sword flying from my grasp, but thankfully the blade refused to leave me. Even as my grip loosened, the weapon remained steady in my hand.

Whoever wields the blade is invincible. Tate's words rang out in my memory, bringing me a small sense of comfort as another guard jumped into the fray and the two expertly secured my arms behind my back. They might be able to capture me, but they couldn't take me down.

"Drop your weapon," one of them snarled.

"Make me."

The second Olympian tried. *Foolish man.* He reached for the blade, and though my power no longer surged through the steel, the blade's power remained intact. His scream was pure agony over the sizzle and pop of burning flesh.

King Baerius raised his hands. "Stop." He eyed me closer then, stepping forward eagerly as he finally realized what I held. "You have the Firelake Blade."

It wasn't a question, so I didn't give him confirmation. The blisters on the palm of his guard were answer enough. He reached out a hand as though he wanted to take hold of the weapon, but Baerius knew better.

"You see, Your Highness. My men could not eliminate her with the blade. We had to find another way to lure her here to you." The quiver in Rossel's voice wasn't lost on me. The normally harsh and cruel man was afraid of the king.

"I see." Baerius stared at me a long moment before turning to Rossel. "It brings me great relief to know that you did not betray me as suspected."

My stomach turned. I knew the idea of Rossel joining our side was too good to be true, but it still stung. I was more angry with myself for trusting him than I was mad at *him*, though. He was just doing what wicked Olympian snakes do. I should have known better.

"Release the seer." Baerius waved a hand in Rossel's direction, then focused on Gayla. "Not this one, though. I suspect her intentions were less than honorable."

Gayla's lip turned up at the king and I felt a surge of pride at seeing the fight in her. Unfortunately, it wouldn't be enough. "Lock her in a holding cell until her father arrives. He'll deal her a punishment far worse than I could. And as for our *Deliverer*..." He cocked his head to the side as he took me in again. "Bring her down to block thirty-three."

"But that's where—"

The king's hand shot up, silencing the guard who had dared to object. "Do as I say. No questions."

The guard's grip on my arms tightened as Rossel was released by the woman who had bound him during the fray. I instinctively fought back, jerking my body hard away from the man's grip. But another came. Then another. A rope was spinning around me, moving effortlessly through the air by Olympian magic rather than manpower. I stomped on the toes of the man who held me, eliciting a yell, but his grip stayed firm until my arms were securely bound behind me. Thankfully they didn't think to remove my bag before strapping my arms down. The tablet was tucked safely by my side, hidden away in my bag under the ropes.

"What about the blade?" A female guard gestured toward my sword.

"Leave it," Rossel said. "The thirty-third block is the safest place for it. No other man can take the blade, lest he die."

The king grunted his approval, but he clearly wasn't happy about it. Gayla was dragged away, yelling the entire time about how she would be back, swearing that she wouldn't allow them to get away with this. And Rossel...

The man simply stared at me with those hollow, black eyes. I'd expected a smug smirk, perhaps. Maybe even a little taunting. He'd gotten me just where he wanted me—in the hands of his leader. They couldn't kill me now that I had the blade, but there were certainly other ways to punish me. This block thirty-three place didn't sound particularly pleasant.

But there was no victory in Rossel's expression. His jaw was hard set, his shoulders tense. And some sixth sense told me this wasn't over yet. Logic screamed that I had been betrayed by the man, but something about the look on his face kept a flicker of hope alive inside me.

It was the last thing I saw before a thick canvas sack was yanked over my head. Then my feet were lifted off the ground, suspended in the air by an invisible force as the Olympians carried me wordlessly across the ridge.

There was no use fighting against the Olympians' unseen powers. I'd be better off reserving what little energy I had left for when I met solid ground again. Baerius couldn't remain by my side forever, and when he left I knew my powers would return. Then I would be nobody's prisoner.

It was a long time before we reached the Olympian palace. I'd been transported through the air, across the ridge for probably half an hour or so before the party stopped. Orders were whispered just out of earshot, then a door was opened. The guards' heavy footfalls sounded like they were now on tile rather than the rocky golden pathway across the ridge. We were inside.

Baerius barked more orders—nothing useful—and most of our party was dispersed, leaving only the king, what I guessed to be two or three guards, and me. I didn't hear Rossel leave, but I couldn't tell if he was still with us or not. The man was stealthy, even when he wasn't trying.

The guards marched through the halls of the palace, and it felt like we'd gone around three corners when I heard the distinctive sound of stone scraping on stone. We paused until the sound stopped, then I was plunged down into cold, dank air. The feeling on my skin reminded me of an old basement, and through the cloth sack over my face, I watched the light fade to darkness. My heart thudded against my ribs, amplifying the hollow feeling beneath my sternum where my power should have been burning hot. Even the hilt of my sword felt lifeless and cold in my hand.

There was a creaking of metal and no time to brace myself before my body hit a hard stone floor. I bit down on the yelp that tried to escape, refusing to appear weak in front of the king. And the moment I realized I was free from the guards' invisible tether, I struggled back to my feet—the movement difficult with my arms still bound by the rope. I bent over, shaking my head to rid it of the cloth sack then jerked my face upward, inhaling a deep lungful of the musty air.

As I did, the lock on a door clicked shut.

Rossel stood with two guards and King Baerius on the opposite side of steel bars that kept me enclosed in a small empty prison cell. Three of the men looked at me, watching to see what happened. But Rossel's attention was fixed elsewhere. He stared thoughtfully into the cell beside me.

A thick stone wall prevented me from seeing who or what lay behind those bars, but it was certainly important judging by the concern etched across Rossel's face.

Baerius didn't address me when he finally spoke. "Keep her here until we can put together a plan." A greedy smile overtook the king. "I have some arrangements to make."

Rossel turned toward me, dipping his chin in a movement so small I thought I could have imagined it. Then he followed the king and his guards down a long hall leaving me with nothing but a cold floor and a racing mind.

How was I going to get out of this?

CHAPTER 8

AS SOON AS THEIR footsteps faded, I got to work. They'd had no choice but to leave me with my blade, and I had every intention of using it. I twisted the weapon in my hands, careful not to drop it. With my power dormant, the sword was nothing more than a piece of metal. Thankfully, it appeared to keep its own power—it didn't scald me like it had the others, but I couldn't put it to use until the after-effects of being near Baerius faded.

I needed my powers to return.

Even a basic sword was useful though. Finally getting it into an upright position, I slid the blade up and down across the ropes that bound my arms. The movements were small and stilted, but I didn't stop until the rope was broken. The rope fell to the ground and I paused—the faintest sound catching my attention from the cell next door.

It was the last cell in the hall, the only one we hadn't passed when the guards brought me down here. Until I knew what I may be dealing with in there, I didn't want to give the other prisoner any reason to think I was up to something. But the noise didn't come again.

Once my breathing stabilized, I silently opened my bag to ensure the tablet was still safe inside. It was there, but even the stone seemed to have its life drained. There was no glow. No pulse. No inexplicable draw keeping it close to my side.

That's when I realized Baerius wasn't here anymore, but his power remained active. I stepped closer to the bars of my cell, running my hands up and down the cold metal, fingers prickling at the contact. The prison must have been infused with the king's ability to absorb my power. And with my power gone, the tablet and the Firelake blade were merely stone and steel.

Which meant my power ignited them just as much as their power ignited me. It was a symbiotic relationship, and the only thing missing was the final piece of the tablet. With the prophecy restored, I suspected even Baerius' power wouldn't be able to suppress me.

The thought reignited my hope. I had nothing to fear. I was the Deliverer. It was my destiny to save the world. Pressing my face to the space between the bars, I called out, emboldened by a feeling of invincibility. "Hello? Is anyone else in here?"

"Everly?" There was some shuffling in the cell next door before a slender arm reached through the bars closest to my cell. I could barely see it in the darkness of the hall, but I knew who it was. "Everly, is that you?"

My mother's hand grasped at nothing in the air. I watched it like it was a part of someone else's story playing out on TV. I felt the emotion. I saw her—flesh and bone—alive. I heard her voice calling for me. And still, it took me a second too long to believe that it was really her.

She called my name a third time before I came to my senses and realized this wasn't a movie. This was real life. My life. And my mother was alive. I'd found her at last.

I rushed forward, shoving my own arm through the bars and grabbing her hand. We said nothing at first, just squeezing the only pieces of each other we could reach. A tear ran down my cheek, falling to the dusty floor below with a tiny splash.

"I can't believe you're here," I whispered. "Are you hurt? What have they done to you?"

"Nothing. I'm fine, really. Better than fine actually, now that I know you're okay." She squeezed my hand, and the familiarity of her touch made my heart swell.

"We've got to get out of here."

"We can't. I've been trying for weeks. Baerius has enchanted the cells. We have no power here."

"We don't." I pulled my hand away and stuck my sword through the bars in its place. "But there's still some life left in this. As long as I have it, they can't hurt me. And I am willing to do whatever it takes to get us out of here, even if that means leaving a few Olympian bodies in my wake as we leave."

"Everly!"

"I've seen a lot in the last few months, mom. I fought off the Kraken, reached the bottom of the Firelake in Agartha, slept a night in Porta Maris, and won a battle against the Manticorians. I may have even found my soulmate. Eliminating a few Olympian guards who are threatening our lives won't be an issue."

She said nothing in response. There was no sound but her stifled sob.

"It's okay, mom. I know who I am, and I know what I have to do. I'm sorry you got wrapped up in this. I know you didn't choose this for yourself. You have nothing to do with the prophecy. But mark my words, I will not let you be collateral damage. I will deliver you from harm, just as I'll deliver the rest of our people."

Her arm disappeared back through the bars and I heard her body slide down the stone wall. "The prophecy? *Goodness.*" Her breathing intensified. "I can't believe I never put it together..."

"Put what together? What do you mean?"

"It makes sense," she said softly, still sorting through her thoughts. "I never understood how it was possible. But this..." She inhaled deeply and spat out her next words at rapid-fire. "Everly, your father—"

A coughing fit cut her short. My mother heaved, choking and physically ill by the words she could not speak. The curse. It was still active, and I had not yet heard the full story.

"It's okay, mom." I tried again to calm her. "You don't have to say anymore. I'll figure it out soon. I'll get us out of here, and we'll get all the answers." My voice dropped to a whisper. "Then I'll save the world."

My mother couldn't tell me anything about how she got to Olympus. I still had no confirmation of who had kidnapped her or why, but she didn't have to tell me. I knew Rossel was responsible. I'd known since I first spoke to him on Gayla's yacht. But I never expected to find myself here with her. It was both a blessing and a curse.

Since she couldn't say much, I caught her up on what I'd been doing and what I'd learned, instead. She tried to stay strong, but her sniffles would break through from time to time. And I lost track of how many times she apologized. She'd told me she was sorry almost as many times as she told me how proud of me she was.

The guards didn't return, not even to bring us dinner. Maybe it was better that way. We eventually drifted off to sleep, hands clasped through the bars outside of our cells. My arm was numb from the odd angle when I awoke some number of hours later.

My body stilled, certain I'd heard something. It sounded like footsteps, but there was nothing but silence punctuated by my mother's restful breathing now. I strained my ears, listening intently until I'd convinced myself it was only a dream. Carefully pulling my arm back inside the cell, I stretched my achy muscles.

That's when I saw him, hooded in black, visible only by the pale skin framing his black eyes. "Rossel."

He stood near the far side of my cell. It was dark, and the man moved quietly, hidden in the shadows. Whatever he was doing here, he didn't want it to be known by any other Olympian eyes. He put a finger to his mouth, then rustled in his pocket until he pulled out a key.

He leaned close, placing his face next to an opening between the bars of my cell. Part of me wanted to use the proximity to punch him in the nose, but my curiosity won out. He wouldn't be here in disguise, in the middle of the night, unless he was doing something to benefit us. King Baerius wouldn't have it.

I stepped close enough to hear his whisper. "There's something I need to show you. If I let you out, will you follow me?"

"Are you going to lead me back to the king or other uncertain death?"

He frowned, unamused. "No. It's..." He hesitated, shaking his head slightly. "It's just something you'll have to see. I can't tell you any more."

It was the final piece of the tablet. It had to be. Rossel wasn't permitted to discuss the prophecy. The curse prevented him from it, as I'd seen back at Millie's place. My pulse rushed loudly through my ears as my excitement grew.

"Yes," I whispered, nodding eagerly. Our discussion had awoken my mother. I heard her get to her feet on the other side of the stone wall, and I longed to see her face. "But she's coming with us." I jerked my chin in the direction of her cell.

"Of course." Rossel's agreement came as a surprise, and doubt flickered again in my mind. It was too easy. Was this a trap? No, surely not. If he wanted to hurt us he would have done it in broad daylight, to the delight of the king. Besides, even if he tried my blade would protect me, and I would protect my mother.

Once we were out of this enchanted prison, Baerius' power would no longer drain us of our own. My mother could teleport us away after I secured the tablet. And I had no doubt that I would be able to defeat anyone nefarious who crossed my path once the prophecy was fully intact.

With just a simple click of the lock, I was free. My mother stepped out a moment later, and I threw my arms around her. She was a bit thinner than when I'd last seen her, but she otherwise seemed to be in good health. I breathed her in, enjoying the feel of her arms—the feeling of home. We weren't home, though. This place wasn't safe. Rossel cleared his throat impatiently, reminding me of the urgency with which we needed to escape, and I reluctantly pulled away from my mother's embrace.

"There's a secret exit this way." Rossel turned with a swish of his black robe, and we had no choice but to follow him.

CHAPTER 9

WE PASSED A NUMBER of empty cells before we reached the exit for block thirty-three, the enchanted part of the royal prison where my mother and I had been held captive—a place unknown to the majority of Olympians. A spark reignited in my chest the moment we passed through the archway back into the dank halls of the palace basement. I inhaled, mentally fanning the flame of my precious powers.

A staircase ahead probably led up to the main part of the palace, but Rossel didn't take us to it. He stepped into a small alcove in the wall and pulled on a low, flickering lantern that hung there. The stone wall creaked and groaned loudly as it opened to a narrow space beyond, and Rossel hurried us through, panic flashing in his dark eyes. "Move quickly." He urged us ahead, pushing gently against our backs.

Once inside, the wall began creaking back into place. There was an instant where I feared Rossel had locked my mother and me into a dark antechamber by ourselves—prisoners again. But just before the stone wall reached its original position, he leapt inside. "Hurry!"

Rossel quickened his pace, moving to the front of our group. Even as he ran, I noted how his feet didn't fully touch the ground. He was a strange creature—wise and infuriating, cruel and deliberate, mysterious in all the wrong ways—and hopefully the answer to all of my questions. My mother and I looked clumsy in comparison, chasing him as he glided through the dark halls.

A thin, half-rotted wooden door spat us out of the building and into the palace grounds. From the outside it appeared to be nothing more than an abandoned old servants' entrance, but I felt the energy humming from the frame as we passed through. It was likely enchanted as well, permitting only those who the king approved to move over its threshold. And I wondered again if we were the ones being duped by Rossel, or if he had truly turned against the King of Olympus. If the latter was true, he either expected to lose his life as a result of his next actions, or he knew everything was about to change.

Rossel led us to a worn switchback path that winded down the steep side of the ridge behind the palace. At first I thought he was leading us into the city, but we were on the wrong side of the ridge for that. As far as I could see, this was the edge of the territory—the end of Olympus. At the bottom of the ridge there was nothing but the night sky.

We didn't have to go far. After a short hike the path jutted off to the right. Just ahead lay a large mouth to a cave, illuminated within by a soft white light. An eight-foot-tall black wrought-iron gate stood firmly in front of the entrance, but I didn't know whether it was intended to keep something vicious inside the cave, or to keep nosy explorers like us out.

My power was back in full force now, the heat in my chest drumming along with my pulse. I searched for the draw I knew I'd feel once we came into close proximity to the last piece of the tablet, but it wasn't there. We'd have to go inside to find it.

I moved for the gate, turning once I was within arm's reach to find that I was alone. My mother stood beside Rossel, several paces back. The color had drained from her face, and both of them looked like they were going to be sick. I couldn't imagine what kind of horrible beast must have dwelled inside to have both of them looking so ill.

"Are you guys coming? Or should I do this alone?" I pulled the blade from my belt, its weight a comfort in my hand. Leave it to the Olympians to hide the tablet behind some deadly mythical creature. Whatever monster hid inside this cave, it was no match for my full power backed by the protection of the Firelake blade. I dared it to try to hurt me.

Rossel and my mother exchanged a disconcerting look.

"I can do it. In fact, maybe it's safer if you guys wait out here. The tablet will call to me when I get close." I raised my weapon. "And I don't fear whatever is in there."

"It's not that." My mother's eyes glistened in the moonlight. "Everly, you should know that—" Another coughing fit cut her off. Rossel frowned in her direction before focusing his black eyes on me.

"I'll open the gate for you. The tablet is not there, but..." He rubbed at his neck. "Just hurry. You have about an hour before this opportunity will be gone, and I'll be killed if we're caught."

Rossel stepped forward and took hold of the large lock on the gate. With the twist of a long, unusual looking key, the lock clicked open and he gently pulled the gate open and gestured for me to go inside.

I hesitated at the opening, staring into nothing and wondering where the pale light emanating from deeper inside was originating. There was only one way to find out. Placing one foot in front of the other, I took my time walking toward the bend in the cave, cognizant of the power that grew hotter in my chest with every step. Something big was about to happen. I knew it. My inner warrior knew it. Even the sword in my hand seemed to ready itself.

I'd considered the possibility of many kinds of beasts, each more dangerous than the last. Something so hideous that the Olympians had no choice but to hide at the edge of the territory in a cliffside cave, trapped by iron bars. What I didn't consider, was that it would be an old man.

He stepped around the bend before I reached it, backlit from the glow deeper within. Shadows obscured his features, so all I could see was his long white hair, matted and unkempt. He was slightly hunched, placing his weight on the staff he held in his right hand. It was a smooth, crooked stick with a glowing purple orb at the top.

"Make it count," Rossel said, and the gates clattered shut behind me.

The sound drew the attention of the old man away from me. Then, with a shocking burst of youthful energy, the man ran forward. I lifted my sword, ready to defend myself, but he shot right past me toward the gate with a snarl. As he passed I realized he was much younger than I'd originally thought. His hair was white, yes. But his jaw was hard, pale skin taut, deep brown eyes lit with a fire inside.

"Matilda Gordon!" The man's baritone voice was deep and strong as he yelled for my mother. There was a familiarity there, but it wasn't a friendly one. Outside the gate, she dropped to her knees, tears in her eyes as she raised one hand toward the man.

"Callan."

He roared, losing all control of his sanity as he grabbed the bars of the gate in his hands and shook them violently. The metal clanged against his strength, and it felt like the whole cave rocked with his anger. "They told me you would return. Face me. Enter so I can rid the world of you once and for all."

A sob escaped my mother's throat. Who was this man, and what kind of beef did he have with my sweet mom?

She didn't answer him, turning her gaze back to me instead. The man followed it, facing me with a fury in his eyes that made my chest burn. I adjusted my grip on the sword and straightened my shoulders.

"Who are you?" The man, Callan, pointed his staff at me, the purple globe on top glowing even brighter now. It looked like there were webs of violet lightning exploding within the small glass ball. With every flash of the tiny storm inside I saw an equally explosive flash of anger in the man's eyes.

The light brightened his face enough for me to better make out his features. He had strong cheekbones and a sharp jawline. He was handsome for a lunatic. He leaned heavily on his little walking stick of a staff for someone who didn't really need its assistance. And I knew he didn't need it because I'd seen him run and practically tear the gate apart. He was strong and able-bodied, even if his mind was a little worse for the wear.

"My name is Everly Gordon." I stood a little taller. "And I am the Deliverer."

His chest rose and fell three times before he finally lunged for me.

CHAPTER 10

I INSTINCTIVELY BROUGHT MY arms up before me, blocking the man's attack. His staff came flying toward my face, but I lifted my blade, causing the wood to crack and splinter into two pieces with the force of his strike. The man still had a death grip around the piece with the orb, which was almost blinding with its increasingly bright purple glow.

It looked more like a dagger now, with sharp splinters where the other end had snapped off. The crazed look of a madman lit up his eyes as he lunged for me again, making every effort to stab me with the wood.

He was easily a foot taller than me when he stood to his full height, and he must have weighed twice as much. There would be no way for me to defeat him without my inner Athena rising to the surface. And I knew she was in there—I could feel the white-hot power surging through my veins. But it was just out of reach somehow. I urged it into the blade, ready to slay the man with its might, but my power wouldn't budge.

"Don't hurt him!" My mother's voice cut into my brain, my face twisting as I tried to process her words. She was worried about *him* being hurt? Fat chance. The man had backed up several paces and leaned forward, looking every bit like a bull ready to charge me.

I steadied myself, lifting the sword again. Power or no power, I wasn't planning on taking it easy on him. He was trying with everything he had to destroy me, and he'd said my mother would be next. There was no way that was gonna happen.

I swung my blade toward the man's neck just before he reached me, but my aim was impossibly off. There was no way I could have been so far off of my target—even without my inner power. But the blade seemed to resist the man, pushing back against my might so that it made impact with his staff-turned-dagger instead of flesh and bone.

The purple orb shattered, filling the room with a blinding light before it went dark. Glass shards flew in every direction, scratching across my skin and creating a glittering carpet of sharp edges where the fragments landed on the cave floor. And the man who had been mid-attack just... stopped.

He straightened, rubbing his head with a grimace, and then looked at me. Confusion twisted his features before we both turned our attention on Rossel and my mom, who were very loudly vomiting uncontrollably outside the gates.

"Tilly!" The man rushed over and gripped the gates again, but his anger was gone, replaced with a frantic kind of concern for my very sick mother.

My grip loosened on the sword, certain that the man was no longer a threat. Of course, my sword seemed to have known it all along. My only guess was that his behavior had been linked to the glass orb atop his staff somehow. With it broken, he was a completely different man.

That didn't mean I was ready to put my weapon away just yet, though. I dropped it to my side, adjusted my bag to the other shoulder, and cautiously joined him at the gate. He eyed me again as I stepped up to him, but there was no malice there.

"Mom, are you okay?"

I ignored the sharp intake of breath beside me as the man studied me more closely. I was more concerned with my mother, and even Rossel, as they dry-heaved outside. It seemed to be slowing, though. And after another minute, my mom stood, eyes wet and hair disheveled. At least she wasn't sick anymore.

"I'm fine, sweetheart." She smiled. "Better than ever, actually. And you?" The question was for the man, not me. "Are you back with us, Callan?"

The man still appeared thoroughly confused. He ran a hand through his tangled white hair, looking back and forth between my mother and me. "Is this your daughter?"

Rossel finally got the lock on the gate open again, and they entered the cave with us. My mom stepped right up to the man, biting her lower lip as she slowly nodded.

Callan's eyes widened. "Is she..."

My mother nodded again.

Callan put a hand to his face, looking me over. "She's... she's *beautiful*. She looks just like you. I can't believe I almost hurt her. I can't believe I almost hurt *you*!"

Full of anguish, he turned back to my mother. A tear spilled over her lower lashes as she pulled the man into an embrace, resting her cheek on his shoulder. "It wasn't you." She stroked his hair as she consoled him. "It was the curse. You had no control over your actions."

Understanding began to dawn on me, but I needed to hear it before I'd truly believe it. Callan. This man. Was this my father? I turned to Rossel, but he avoided eye contact, shifting uncomfortably on his feet. Unsurprising. He didn't strike me as the affectionate type.

I, too, gave my mother and the man a moment to reconnect before at last they pulled away and faced me. "Is the curse broken, then?" Callan asked Rossel.

The seer nodded, gesturing to the fragments of glass. "The curse was shattered with the orb. Tilly and I have forcefully emitted what remained from our systems, and we should be able to speak freely now." He glanced at his watch. "But I urge you to hurry. We're down to half an hour before the guards do a sweep of block thirty-three. Once they discover the women missing, we'll have mere seconds before Olympus is shut down at the borders. He'll kill us all to prevent the information from spreading."

"I'm sorry to interrupt." I stepped forward with my hand in the air. "But would anyone care to fill me in on what is going on here?"

My mother smiled. "Everly, meet Prince Callan: lost heir to the Olympian throne. Your father."

CHAPTER 11

MY FATHER. A PRINCE. And an Olympian one at that. It was impossible. The different Keeper races weren't able to bond without being killed. What made my mother and Callan any different? How had they survived the curse?

The shock must have been evident on my face, because my mother tilted her head with a sad smile. "I know it's hard to believe, darling. The truth is, I didn't understand how it was possible either, not until you told me that you were the one written about in the prophecy. But it makes sense now."

"You'll have to explain it to me too, then. I'm almost as lost as she is." Callan sent an uncomfortable glance in my direction. He didn't know about me. He'd had no idea that he was a father. And though we were mere strangers, a broken piece of my heart was smoothed over with the knowledge that he hadn't deliberately chosen to leave me as an infant. He'd never had the chance to know me at all.

"You'd best start at the beginning," Rossel said with a frown. "But do be quick."

My mother nodded. "It began about twenty years ago. I had just been promoted to work with Maxwell as a messenger for the leadership of Atlantis. It was an important role, and I took my work very seriously. It was my job to relay messages to Mt. Olympus in Greece. It's the largest portal to the territory here, and since I couldn't teleport to Olympus itself, I would stop there and find a guard or an owl to carry our news the rest of the way. It was there that I met Callan.

"He was being trained up as the next heir to the Olympian throne. As his father's only living child, there was never any question for his future. He'd completed his studies and was beginning his rotations with the different Olympian specialties in the mountain. And I didn't realize it at the time, but I fell in love with him the moment I laid eyes on him."

Callan's cheeks reddened slightly, the adoration in his eyes clear as he listened to my mother's story.

"We became fast friends during his time there, and we continued to communicate when he left the mountain for his next rotation. We sent messages back and forth from Olympus through the owls, and we would secretly arrange to meet up any time he was permitted to return to the earth's surface. But one night, everything changed."

"The Millenial Gala." Callan rubbed his chin, trying to hide a smirk. Now it was my mother's turn to blush.

Rossel grunted his disapproval, but my mother continued, unfazed. "The ambrosia was flowing that night, and everyone was in high spirits, as Keepers always are at the turn of a century. But this one was extra special. It was a new millenium. Callan and I snuck off away from the crowd, and months of pent-up chemistry were finally unleashed. We couldn't help ourselves, though we knew what would happen."

"The curse?" I asked, trying to shake the image of my mother and this man *unleashing their chemistry*. Ew.

"Yes. We knew the risk, and we were willing to take it. A lifetime without each other wouldn't have been worth living anyway."

I knew how she felt. Hadn't I had the same thoughts with Tate? If Callan and my mother were soulmates, there was no way they would have been able to resist each other forever. The draw to one another was too strong. It was out of their control.

"But the curse never struck." She stared into the distance, lost in a memory.

"It was something far worse than a curse," Callan added. "We were caught. By my father."

"No!" My jaw dropped. "What did Baerius do?"

"He called me," Rossel said. "He was furious. You see, he has legions of seers to help prevent this kind of thing from happening. None more highly trained than myself."

"You couldn't have prevented it," I said. "Not if they were destined to be together."

"I know." Rossel shook his head. "And I didn't try because I knew the truth from the very beginning."

We all turned to look at him, waiting with bated breath for him to elaborate. He paced silently, mouth twitching as he tried to find the right words to say.

"Well, what *is* the truth?"

Rossel stopped. "There was a prophecy made thousands of years ago. The exact wording has been muddied as it's been passed down over the years, but all Keepers knew the main point of it: their time in power would come to an end at the hands of one called The Deliverer. The oracle who delivered the prophecy had given a bit more description of this Deliverer, claiming the being was to be pieced together from all three races—Atlantean, Olympian, and Agarthian. But no one knew when or how this Deliverer would come into power.

"The kings of the time were terrified at the prospect of losing their kingdoms. Their identities were wrapped up in their power. They would be nothing without their titles and their rule over Keepers and humans. So they broke the tablet upon which the prophecy was written and scattered the pieces across the territories and into the tundra where no one could possibly put it back together. Then they brought together the most powerful people of their nations to forge an unbreakable curse. They determined that if they could prevent the races from bearing mixed children, they could prevent the Deliverer from ever being born.

"And it was so for thousands of years. Many, many Keepers have been killed by the curse. Those who bred with mortals also suffered, as their offspring were murdered under the guise of being fractured souls. But really, all the death and destruction was a direct result of the rulers' own greed—the very thing the Deliverer was sent to destroy."

The information was coming at me like water from a firehose, and I feared I might drown under the pressure of what happened and what had to be done.

"But the curse didn't strike them," I said to Rossel. "My mom and Callan survived."

"That's right. Because it was their destiny to conceive you—the Deliverer."

Callan shook his head. "I am Olympian, and Tilly is Atlantean, but that's only two of the races. You said the Deliverer was to be all three."

"A white braid of power," I whispered. My heart raced as the pieces all came together. "Daughter of sea and sky. But I can't do it alone. I'm supposed to work with the one who ignites my heart. My soulmate. The Agarthian prince."

"Titus?" My mother's eyes widened.

"Tate." I couldn't hide my smile as his name crossed my lips. "He's the third strand of the braid. The one who completes me."

"And he is technically the king now, not a prince." Rossel glanced at my mother from the side of his eyes. "I'll fill you in later." With his attention back on me, he finished his story. "Anyway, I saw you in a vision, and I knew their illicit relationship was the beginning of the end for the Keepers. I tried to warn the king, giving him the opportunity to right his kingdom before he faced your judgment. But he wasn't interested in that. He didn't know that the damage was already done—that the child was already conceived. He separated the young lovers to prevent the Deliverer from being born, locking his son away in this cave and ordering Matilda's arrest. But she vanished before he could catch her. So he cursed us instead, binding the spell to the globe you destroyed. We were not able to speak of the relationship or the prophecy, and Callan was cursed to thirst for the blood of his ex-lover. He had no control over himself, driven mad by the proximity of the globe that he was spelled to protect in here."

"I went into hiding for almost twenty years." My mother's features were pinched with regret. "I bound my powers, and suppressed yours before they ever emerged. I wouldn't let them take you. But after so many years, the pressure was gone. Baerius presumed me to be dead, and you were determined to get out of Oklahoma. I knew I couldn't keep you under my roof forever, so I thought I'd let you stay with Millie, where she could watch over you. But I never got a chance to explain myself to her, either. Once we saw that portrait of you in Rossel's gallery, I knew you were still in great danger."

"I had to take her." Rossel's eyes were vacant as he stared off into nothingness. "I had to take your mother back to Olympus. And when Baerius discovered you, he ordered your death, but he didn't want to be connected to it. Since we knew you did not have a pure soul, we thought the easiest way to have you eliminated would be to hire the job out to the Agarthian hunters. Thaddeus, specifically, was falling from honor and needed a job this size to stay in the king's good graces. If he didn't capture your soul, his father would banish him from Agartha forever. He'd shamed the family by choosing a hunter's work over his royal education. So the king needed him to earn the kingdom's trust by strengthening the alliance between Agartha and Olympus. He had to carry out this job for Baerius."

"But you didn't know we were soulmates?"

Rossel shook his head. "Once I realized it, I looked into the prophecy further. Eventually I came to the realization that this was exactly how fate had intended it to be. You were the daughter of sea and sky, as you said, and Thaddeus was the third piece of the braid. He was the missing piece of your heart—your soul. And you were complete. The Deliverer--the very same I saw in my vision twenty years ago. So I went to Agartha to help you."

"And here we are." We all stood silently for a moment, allowing the facts to sink in. "So what do we do now?" I asked the old seer.

"Now we retrieve the final piece of the prophecy."

CHAPTER 12

"HOW MUCH TIME DO we have before the guards circle around and find us missing from our cells?" I shoved my hand into my messenger bag, feeling the familiar smooth surface of the tablet, which responded to my touch with a warm pulse and a jolt of energy surging through me.

"If they haven't discovered it yet, it will be only minutes." Rossel frowned.

"Then we need to get out of here." My mom took Callan's arm in her hand and gestured for Rossel and me to join them. "Quick, everyone grab hands before—"

Her body was slammed backward, pinned to the cave wall. She grunted as the wind was knocked out of her, but she was still conscious.

"Before the guards find you here?"

I spun around to find the deep voice had come from the head of Baerius' guard. The large Olympian man was flanked by two other men. One of them had his hands raised, his invisible power holding my mother high on the wall where she wouldn't be able to teleport us out of here. That wouldn't stop her from leaving on her own though. *Please mom, save yourself.*

I stepped in front of Rossel and Callan, knowing that I was invincible with the blade. And Baerius wasn't here, which meant our full powers were at our command. As a seer, Rossel wasn't much help in the way of combat, but I realized I had no idea what Callan could do. My father. He was big, if nothing else.

The guard to the captain's left lifted his chin and two throwing knives hovered in the air before him. There was no time to think. I had to act before those blades came flying in our direction. The captain turned his gaze to me with a sneer and I got the sense that he was in my head, reading my thoughts the way Dom could do.

Blade in hand, I channeled all of my energy into the steel and swung it into an arc in front of us at the same time the guard unleashed his knives. Miraculously, the motion created a shimmering, translucent shield that the knives bounced lifelessly off of. The guard pulled them back to him through the air, and the captain's sneer faded. "You can't hold the shield forever, little girl. And as soon as King Ba—"

With another swipe of my arm, I released the power in front of us and aimed it like a dart to the man with the knives. It hit him square in the chest, knocking him to the ground with a loud cry of pain. I didn't know if the shot would kill him, but I couldn't be concerned with that right now. I had two more angry guards to fend off.

The captain turned his head just a fraction, but that minor lapse in attention was all it took for Callan to leap out from behind me. He wasn't aiming for the captain, though. He had his sights set on the man who had my mother pinned. Callan lunged, slamming the guard's body to the ground and wrapping his meaty hands around the Olympian's neck.

The captain had noticed him by then, and lifted a dagger, ready to slam it down into Callan's back. I lifted my own blade, ready to strike the captain before he could hurt Callan, but my mother beat me to it. She stepped through reality, teleporting herself from the cave wall to the captain in an instant. Grabbing his hand with both of hers, she turned the blade toward him and slammed it down into the man's chest before he could even register what happened. The whole thing took less than half a second.

My mouth fell open, awestruck and dumbfounded by what I had just witnessed. My mother had always been a spitfire, but I had no idea what she was really capable of. This woman was a warrior. Strong. Deadly.

"Let's go," she said, rubbing the captain's blood off of her hands and onto her grimy pants. "We've got to get out of Olympus before they realize what happened."

"You go. Get to safety. But I have to get the last piece of the tablet. We're so close now, I can't leave until it's safely in my hands."

"I'm not going without you." She turned to Rossel. "Where's the tablet?"

"I don't know. That's why we came for the prince."

We all turned to face Callan. "You think I know where it is? My father hasn't spoken a word to me in twenty years."

"That may be true," Rossel said. "But in the training of your youth, they must have discussed the kingdom's secrets with you. Is there a vault, or some other space reserved for royalty only?"

Callan shook his head and paced back and forth three times. "Not that I recall. But if I know my father, he won't let it far from his sight. Especially now that the Deliverer is here, it wouldn't surprise me if he kept it on his person at all times."

"He doesn't have it on him. I would have felt it calling to me," I said.

"Then it's probably in his private study." Rossel frowned. "Which makes it virtually impossible to retrieve."

"I'll get us in there." My mother extended her hands, but Rossel shook his head again.

"You can't. The king's study is directly off of his bed-chamber. His rooms are all protected against messengers and any powers other than his own. I can't even drum up a vision in there."

"Then we'll go by foot." I stepped over a fallen guard, moving for the cave entrance before anyone could object. To my surprise, no one argued against me. They all fell silently into line behind me.

Outside the cave, Callan paused and took in a deep lungful of air. He looked up, lost in the stars, and I wondered how long it'd been since he had been out in the open. What kind of a father would do this to his own son? How could Baerius have locked him up and driven him mad, his future destroyed all for the sake of Baerius' own power? He had to be stopped. And I was just the girl for the job.

"We've gotta keep moving." It pained me to pull Callan away from his first taste of freedom, but there was no time. He could enjoy this world he'd missed out on after I acquired the tablet. I continued the trek up the winding path back to the palace on the ridge, stopping just before we reached the top at the sight of an old friend.

Al's wings were brightly illuminated in the moonlight. *You guys look rough.*

"Thanks," I muttered. I wasn't in the mood for Al's jabs.

But you're gonna look even worse if you don't wait here for a minute. There's a gaggle of guards up here. Give them time to pass around to the other side of the palace. I'll let you know when the coast is clear.

"A gaggle? Really?"

Do you want me to count them for you?

I rolled my eyes and glanced over my shoulder to tell the other we needed to hold off. Rossel already seemed to know. His eyes flicked from me to the owl and back again. "More guards?"

I nodded. "He'll let us know when it's safe to continue." Then I turned back to Al. "Any word from the others?"

Tension is still growing in Agartha. Loverboy may have to go soon, but he's determined to wait until you're back. The others are just as impatiently waiting for your return.

"Tell them we'll be back soon. We'll be coming in hot with the tablet any time now. But they may want to start spreading the word soon, if they haven't already. Tell them to warn the nations. The Deliverer is coming. We're on the brink of war, and only the pure of heart will survive it."

That sounds intense.

"It is intense, Al."

Alright. The guards are gone. Be safe, and I will return to help you as soon as I can. Al fluttered up into the air. *Go get 'em, Tiger.*

We emerged topside on the ridge, the territory eerily silent in the mist below. The Olympian acropolis towered over us, a harsh but beautiful old structure, white against the dark sky. And within it lay king Baerius, breathing what I hoped would be his last few breaths.

CHAPTER 13

"YOU SHOULD WAIT HERE. I have the Firelake blade. He can't hurt me, even if my powers are suppressed. But you..." My voice trailed off, unwilling to speak aloud what could happen to them if they were caught by Baerius.

"We are definitely not waiting here." My mother stepped forward with that maternal look that I could never argue against. I may have been the Deliverer, but my mom was scary when she meant business.

Callan and Rossel stepped up too, and my heart warmed at this strange fellowship we'd formed. We were a bunch of oddballs, and I loved it. If the four of us could unite, there was hope for the world after all.

"Okay." I took my mom's hand. "But promise me that if things get ugly in there you will take these two and get yourselves outta here. You can't save me if the king captures you. You'll be better off joining up with the others on earth for a concerted attack."

"I promise," she said. "But I don't intend to let it get that far."

We marched onward, tiptoeing around the giant columns that stood sentry on either side of the grand entrance. "There will be guards just inside the main doors," Rossel warned. "We should find another entry point."

"We're already here," my mother said. "I'll take care of it." Then she was gone. Thirty seconds later she reappeared, slightly out of breath. "Clear."

We cautiously swung open the main doors to find two guards knocked out on the floor. My mother didn't so much as pay them a second glance as she continued onward into the large foyer. It was then that I noticed we weren't alone.

"Gayla!" I ran forward to my friend who was chained to a chair in the center of the large space. Her eyes were glued to my mother, her fear evident. "It's okay. That's my mom."

"I know." Her already raspy voice had gone a few notes deeper. "I've seen her before."

That was right. Gayla had seen her locked up in a vision long ago. But her somber expression now had me wondering if that was the only vision she'd seen.

"Rossel, do you have a key to these locks? Let's get her out of here."

"No!" The color drained from Gayla's face and I'd never seen her look so serious. "I'm not injured. My father thought public humiliation was the only way for me to atone for my mistake in joining forces with you. I'm a symbol for the rest of the Olympians—a reminder of what happens if we disobey the king. But they won't physically hurt me."

"So what? We're not gonna leave you here. It won't matter what the people think of their king soon enough anyway. The whole territory is about to come crashing down." My chest burned hot as I spoke the words. Athena was ready for war.

"No." Her voice was firm. "Leave me here. I saw what would happen if I were to go with you. I can't."

I looked at Rossel, but if he'd had a similar vision, he wasn't mentioning it. I believed her, though.

"What happens, Gayla? How does this end?"

She pinched her lips together for only a moment before shaking the memory of the vision from her mind. "It doesn't matter what I saw, because we're doing it differently. You all need to go. Get the tablet. I'll create a diversion and try to hold them off for as long as possible, but you need to hurry."

"Is it in Baerius' study?"

"It is. But the king is not in there—not right now anyway. He's visiting one of his... *mistresses*." She shuddered. "Get in the shadows by the stairs. There's an alcove in the wall behind the tapestry that hangs there. Hide until I can get the guards out of the way."

We did as she said. I held the tapestry away from the opening as the others filed in, and just before I swung in myself, Gayla's shrill scream pierced the air. I paused, turning to see what kind of trouble she faced, but she was still alone. She mouthed the word *go*, then screamed again.

I tucked myself into the nook at the same time heavy footsteps came bounding down the stairs. Gayla continued her shrieking until one of the guard's booming voices yelled at her to shut up. "Quit your screaming and tell us what happened!"

"Over here, Leo!" A woman's shout echoed from farther away—near the front doors if I had to guess, where the other guards' bodies lay unconscious on the floor.

"You better get to explaining. Quick." The first guard growled at Gayla, and I gripped the hilt of my sword even tighter, ready to pounce if I needed to spring into action. More footsteps came toward us now, guards from across the palace grounds converging to see what all the screaming was about.

"It was the Manticorians!" Gayla's voice was shrill and full of terror. She really was an amazing actress. "There were three of them. They tried to break in but saw the guards and ran down toward the city instead. You have to stop them! Now! They're going to destroy Olympus!"

"Why didn't they hurt you, too?"

"I'm not exactly a threat like this am I, you buffoon!"

The guard grunted and Gayla gasped as I heard skin smack against skin. The pressure continued to build in my chest, and I was seconds away from stopping time and eliminating every one of those arrogant Olympian guards. But the female guard was urging them to go investigate. "Come on. If there are only the three we can stop them before they do any damage."

There was a moment of silence, broken only by Gayla's soft cry.

"Someone needs to warn the king." The male guard said.

"Pleeeease..." Gayla sobbed loudly. "Just go! My sister is in that city!"

The guard huffed then called out some orders to the others who had gathered. The footsteps thundered toward the door, and before long the room grew quiet again. Gayla's cries stopped abruptly before her voice cut through, steady and strong. "Go. Now."

We didn't delay. I led the way up the stairs, where Rossel took over at the front of our pack. He took us down a hall and up another flight of stairs until we reached the king's personal residence. Pausing for just a moment outside the rooms, the old seer looked as if he were sending a prayer up to the heavens before he finally twisted the handles and eased the heavy wooden doors open.

The king's rooms were dark. It was quiet inside and there was a chill in the air. I guessed he probably hadn't been here at all tonight. But that wasn't my concern. I only cared about one thing, and I could feel its presence the instant we stepped over the threshold.

Ignoring the others, I moved deftly through the rooms—past the foyer, through a sitting room, and straight into the king's bed-chamber. Power pulsed violently through my veins, increasing with every step I took. I scanned the small space until I located the door that concealed the tablet. A faint blue glow crept through the cracks around the edges of the door, and the rest of the prophecy in my bag physically compelled me to reunite it with its missing piece.

Reconnecting the other three pieces had caused bright, almost violent events. A part of me worried that this final corner could create a catastrophic reaction. "Stay here." I turned back to Rossel, Callan, and my mom. "The tablet won't hurt me. It can't. But I don't know what it might do to you. Plus, you can be my lookouts. If you hear Baerius coming, don't wait for me. Get yourselves out of here before he can zap your powers. I'll be fine. I promise."

They exchanged unspoken words through the worry creases around their eyes, but eventually my mother agreed. "Be safe, darling. I love you. We'll see you in a minute." There was no confidence in her last statement, and I realized that they feared what could happen when the prophecy was pieced back together almost as much as I did. After all, they were Keepers—perhaps the very Keepers I was destined to destroy.

I wanted to hang back for a moment longer and give them a proper goodbye. I couldn't come close to thanking them enough for the sacrifices they'd all made to get me here, but I wanted to try, at least. Unfortunately, the tablet had other plans. As though I was under its ancient spell, my feet began moving, one in front of the other until my hand gripped the cold metal knob of Baerius' study door.

CHAPTER 14

I BARELY NOTICED THE room's furnishings. My attention was solely focused on the glass case in the center of a round wooden table in the center of the king's study. Within that clear box glowed the final piece of the prophecy. My lifeblood. *Mine.*

My arm was swinging the blade before I had time to consider any other plan. The metal crashed through the glass with ease, sending shards flying throughout the space. I exchanged my weapon for the piece of stone, laying the blade on the table as I gripped the electrified piece of the tablet. My other hand plunged into my bag, and like magnets, the missing piece pulled itself to the rest of the prophecy.

The explosion of light that resulted from the bond was blinding. I fell to my knees, overcome with an indescribable sensation of the power. It felt like it cut through my skin, lightning dancing up and down my spine. My chin was jerked upward, and though I couldn't see anything, I heard it. An ancient tongue whispering to me in another language of hisses and slurs. The words were nonsense but the meaning was clear.

Obey.

I didn't have time to consider what the command meant. In a violent blink, the light went out and my body collapsed into a pile on the floor.

"Get her up!" The bellow of King Baerius jerked me back into the present. My head lifted—not of my own accord—and I watched myself climb clumsily back to my feet like some kind of out-of-body experience. But I was still in my head. I just wasn't in control anymore. I wanted to yell. I wanted to grab my sword and fight, but I could do nothing.

"Bring her here."

My vision was still clouded from the earlier brightness of the tablet, but I saw the shape of two men against the far side of the room. One was large and commanding. Baerius. The other was smaller, barely older than a child, and timid. Had they been there the whole time? I supposed I wouldn't have known it. I'd only seen the tablet—nothing else.

I watched with horror as my feet moved toward them, the tablet still gripped in my hands. It was perfect. Whole. Smooth. And the writing etched into its surface glowed with an ancient power. The prophecy was complete, and I was delivering it straight into the hands of the king of Olympus. I was pretty sure that was not the original intention of my title. But alas, I could not stop.

The heat in my chest had fizzled down to nothing—barely a pilot light flickering inside. He'd subdued my powers and somehow taken control of my actions. "Hand me the tablet."

No! I wouldn't. Again, I tried to yell, fanning the tiny flame that still flickered deep inside my chest. Where was my inner warrior when I needed her? And why had I set down the Firelake blade when I needed it the most?

I realized then that Baerius wasn't speaking to me. He was speaking to the small young man beside him. With a jerk of the boy's chin, my hands extended toward the king. I wasn't under the king's control... I was under the boy's!

Baerius reached for the prophecy, greed gleaming in his eye. And it brought me more than a little satisfaction to hear his cry of pain upon contact. *That's a good little tablet. Scald the hands of the big bad king.*

His lip curled, baring his teeth at me as he clenched his fists, fighting off the pain."Get the manacles, boy."

My muscles tensed, ready to run. I had to get out. I had to warn my mother and Rossel and Callan. If I couldn't save myself, I could at least try to save them. But my feet were cemented to the floor, lips glued shut.

The young man turned and wrestled with something on the shelf behind him, and there was a sadness in his eyes when he faced me again. He glanced down at my hands, still holding tight to the prophecy, and lifted his chin. I raised them toward him, and he easily shackled my wrists together. The metal was cold, and it tingled against my skin. "Don't panic," the boy said quietly. My muscles relaxed at his command. "I won't hurt you."

Obey. The ancient tongue slithered through my mind again. But I didn't want to obey! Nothing about this was going according to plan.

"The manacles are imbued with my power." A cruel grin spread across Baerius' face. "You are nothing with them on. You have nothing, and you can do nothing. So don't even try. Tomorrow we'll come back for the blade and your real training can begin. But for now, I need you to set the prophecy back on the table where you found it."

I tried to give him the most stubborn look I was capable of. I would not obey this king. But he waved at the boy. "Go on. Make her do it."

My feet moved forward, and though my brain shouted for my hands to stop, they betrayed me by resting the tablet back on the round table in the center of the room, right next to my blade. I longed for them, and they for me. Even with Baerius' magic-draining shackles, I could feel the draw between me and the ancient relics. But there was nothing I could do.

"I knew from the moment I saw Rossel's painting that you were a much larger threat than he gave you credit for. But I believe we can change fate. There is no need to destroy this magnificent world we've built. In fact, I think we can make it better. And now that you're mine, there is nothing I can't do. No man is greater than I am." Baerius stepped in front of me, obstructing my full field of vision.

"My granddaughter, the Deliverer. What a gift! Thank you for making me the most powerful man who has ever lived. Together, we'll rule the earth!"

DELIVERANCE

CHAPTER 1

A PETITE OLYMPIAN SERVANT girl set a small crystal bowl on the table in front of me. Its contents smelled divine—a combination of apples and cinnamon and cream. It was the most beautiful bowl of oatmeal I'd ever seen. But it was still... just... oatmeal. And even worse—it was *Olympian* oatmeal. I'd rather have Pierre's golden raisins.

The girl curiously lifted her dark eyes to inspect me more closely, and I clearly imagined tossing the bowl and all of its contents violently into her pretty little Keeper face. She took in a sharp breath and jerked her head backward. Served her right... getting into my mind unwelcomed like that. I had no patience for these telepaths Baerius kept trying to sneak by me.

She scurried out of the room and I turned my attention to my other companion. "May I eat, Chaz? Or would you like to control my spoon as well?" I hated the sarcastic, bratty tone I'd taken on, but between Baerius' spies and his little puppeteer, I was out of patience. Yet, there was nothing I could do.

It had been three weeks since the tablet was restored. Three weeks since Baerius cuffed my wrists and took me as his prisoner, compelled to obey orders given by his youngest accomplice, Chaz. I didn't know how Chaz's powers worked, only that I couldn't refuse his commands. He was my Geppetto.

But the little puppet-master wasn't the only force vying for my attention. Something new had been created the day the tablet was restored. Something bigger than life. And it had taken up residence in my head, whispering only one word, day after day.

Obey.

I rolled my shoulders back and cracked my neck, trying to ignore the ancient tongue hissing in my ear. But I couldn't get rid of it any more than I could clip the strings binding me to Chaz and whatever whims the king had him force upon me. Thankfully, I hadn't been compelled to do anything offensive. Yet. But there was a storm brewing.

I picked up my spoon, eying the cuffs that adorned my wrists. They were gold, inlaid with diamonds and pearls. They were lovely—really too beautiful to be as sinister as they were. Like the bars of the prison below the palace, these cuffs were also imbued with Baerius' power, which meant mine was totally useless as long as I wore them. And I would likely wear them forever... because *Chaz* told me to.

Chaz, the sixteen-year-old punk kid who refused to make eye contact with me. Even as he sat across the breakfast table listening to my sarcastic jabs, he dutifully pretended I wasn't there. I had to wonder what kind of dirt Baerius had on the kid, because it was clear that Chaz wanted to spend time with me as much as I did with him. In other words, we both would have rather been anywhere else.

I shoveled in a mouthful of oatmeal, angry about how delicious it was. I was angrier still about the small part of me that had grown almost comfortable in my time as a prisoner of Olympus. I'd had three weeks of good food, a plush bed, and a bathtub the size of a small swimming pool. It would have been a vacation if not for the two hours I spent with Baerius every morning after breakfast.

But that time was good for something. It was a reminder to stay vigilant. I had to remember that I was the Deliverer—destined to save the world from oppressive Keeper rule—not Baerius' pet.

Chaz's gaze fell upon me as I stared into my bowl. I could feel it on me, but I knew if I tried to meet his eyes he'd immediately look away. It was the same game we played every morning. I mouthed off. He feigned indifference. And when he thought I was distracted, he'd let his curiosity get the best of him.

But our game was interrupted this morning by the abrupt entrance of an Olympian guard. "Where's the king?" he demanded.

Chaz lazily gestured over his shoulder with a thumb. "In his study. What do you need?"

"I need to speak with him," the guard grumbled.

"You can leave your message with me." Chaz crossed his thin arms over his chest, daring the man to object.

"It is of the highest importance. I'm not going to leave a message with some—" The guard bit his tongue before he said something he might later come to regret. "Please just ask him if he will see me."

"No can do." Chaz took a slow bite of his own oatmeal, waving a hand in front of his mouth to cool off the too-hot spoonful. He took his time swallowing it down then sipped his apple juice. And just before the red-faced guard blew a gasket, Chaz finally finished his thought. "The king specified no visitors this morning. Again, you can leave your message with me or try to catch him later this evening."

The guard huffed, his patience officially at zero. "Please tell his Majesty that we were unsuccessful in New England. We'll try the west coast of North America next."

Chaz mumbled something indiscernible through another huge bite of oatmeal, accompanied by a thumbs up. That was all the confirmation the guard needed to know that his message would get through, and he clearly didn't have the patience to put up with Chaz's teenage attitude any longer. He turned on his heels and stomped back out of the king's suite.

I had to admit, I kind of respected the kid's total disregard for authority. I just had to find a way to turn it against the king, instead of only the king's men.

"So they still can't find Rossel and my mom, huh?" I couldn't hide my smirk. Not that Chaz saw it, anyway. He went right back to ignoring me the second the guard left the room. All signs that he had any personality at all vanished when we were left alone again.

He was working so hard to keep his distance from me, speaking to me only when Baerius commanded him to control my actions. But why? Was he afraid of me… of the powers Baerius had under his control? Or was he afraid that he might agree with me if he allowed himself to hear me out?

I hoped it was the latter. Maybe it was time to change my approach. Instead of lashing out at the boy who pulled my strings, perhaps I should work harder to get him on my side.

CHAPTER 2

THE DOOR TO BAERIUS' study burst open at nine-thirty on the dot, the same as it had every other morning of the last three weeks. He didn't even bother to greet us anymore, which was totally fine in my opinion. The less I had to speak to that horrid man, the better.

The king bounded past Chaz and me in the dining room, straight to the private back entrance of his rooms. We silently stood and followed the man. We knew the drill. After breakfast every morning came two hours of training in the king's private courtyard with just the three of us.

I fought against it the first few days, much to the chagrin of the quiet voice in my head. But it was no use. Baerius and Chaz could make me follow them anyway. It was easier to save myself the effort and humiliation of losing that battle every morning. Plus—I really hated the feeling of Chaz's compulsion taking over me. It wasn't nearly as pleasant as when the Agarthian sirens did it.

We made our way down the stairs and out into the open air. It was a crisp morning, but the sun was bright. The air smelled of honeysuckle, and there was a faint breeze. Again, it would have been lovely under any other circumstances.

Obey.

I get it, okay? Shut up! I silently snapped back at the ancient tongue. It loved to remind me to behave myself. Often.

Who peed in Baerius' coffee? He looks grumpy today. I had to hide my smile at the third voice in my head. That was the other reason I'd quit fighting with the king about coming outside to train every day. This was the only time I was permitted to leave the king's rooms. Once Al discovered me here, these became my favorite two hours of the day. I only wished I could speak back to my favorite little owl without fear of being overheard by the king.

I kept my eyes away from the wall where I knew he was perched. He kept to the shadows, out of sight. But even if Baerius did notice him sitting up there, he wouldn't think anything of it. There were owls all over Olympus. It was how the Olympians communicated with their people on the earth's surface.

Al didn't usually say much, but I knew he was watching. Listening. Waiting. He mentioned one day that my aunt and friends were working on a plan to rescue me, but he didn't offer much in the way of details. And with Baerius and Chaz around, I couldn't ask. But I wanted to... desperately. Nonetheless, seeing his feathery silhouette morning after morning was one of the few things that kept my hope alive.

They were going to save me. And once they did, I would destroy Baerius. Though it was strange how I thirsted for revenge against *Baerius* rather than the young man who actually held the control over me. I glanced at him then, and found him squinting into the shadows where Al was perched.

Chaz had noticed the owl on more than one occasion, but if he suspected that Al was with me, he didn't say anything. It wouldn't have surprised me if the kid knew a lot more than he was letting on. After all, he was always within a few feet of the king. He was all teenage angst and attitude on the outside, but I could see the keen intelligence glistening in his eyes. Maybe that's why he chose not to look directly at me. I might ruin his act.

And I didn't want to ruin his act. Why? Well, I wasn't entirely sure I could explain why. I just knew that a boy that smart, with such a unique power, didn't have to be indebted to anyone. If it weren't for the protection of my blade, I might even fear him. Something told me there would come a day when Chaz would bow to Baerius no more. And when that day came, I wanted him on my side.

Snap out of it, girl! Al's admonishment cracked through my mind, and I looked up into the stern glare of King Baerius.

"Don't tell me you're going to pull this garbage again." The king's jowls looked extra droopy when he was angry. "You know I can force you if you won't act on your own. So I'll ask you one more time... pick up the blade."

I bit down on a sharp retort and obediently walked over to the small wooden table where my blade lay beside the fully restored tablet. The prophecy pulsed erratically as I approached, and I wanted to pick it up and cradle it. Soothe it. It was mine, and I hated every second that we were apart.

But I couldn't touch it. The only reason it was here was because Baerius refused to let it out of his sight. I'd been compelled to place it inside a glass case so that he could handle it without being burned, and now the man carried it with him everywhere like a toddler with his blankie. I couldn't wait for the day I would shatter that case and all of Baerius' dreams along with it.

I picked up the blade, relishing the half-second I could feel its power before the cuffs on my wrists cut it off. Instantly, Chaz's control latched onto my brain like steel claws that I couldn't shake off. Every day it was the same. We would come out here to practice the elaborate charade of unity between the Olympian king and me, with a constant grip on my mind in case I chose to defy the king's commands. Which I did. Often.

His plan was to use Chaz's control to wield my power, hoping the world would believe we worked together. He knew I alone had the ability to command Keepers across all three races, and he desperately wanted that power for himself. Again, he was blinded by his greedy need for power. And I couldn't stand for it.

Obey.

The tablet's glow grew brighter at the silent command. And while I normally shrugged it off in annoyance, today I considered it. The prophecy was for me. It was clear in what I must do. And if it told me to obey, perhaps there was a good reason for it.

I looked at Chaz, who immediately flicked his gaze away from me, and a plan began to take shape. What if I *did* obey? What if I made the king believe I was giving up and joining him? What if I played nice with Chaz and got him on my side? Together, we could strike the king when he least expected it, and he would be no match for my power and Chaz's combined —especially if Chaz could somehow prevent the king from suppressing mine.

The boy met my eyes then, his stare so intense that *I* had to look away this time.

King Baerius stepped closer to me. Too close, in fact. I could see the spittle balancing delicately in the corners of his mouth as he barked commands at me. But I bit my tongue, relaxed my expression, and focused on what he wanted me to do. Today was going to be different. Today I would obey.

"Aim the sword at your target. Good. Now when I say go, I want you to blast it with the sword's power."

The sword depended on me for power, just as I depended on it. It couldn't do anything as long as I had these cuffs around my wrists. Baerius knew that, he just chose not to believe it.

But instead of mouthing off as usual, I aimed my weapon, summoned all the energy I had in me, and watched with wonder as a tiny spark lit off the tip of the blade.

The king's jaw dropped. "It worked! I knew we could get it to work if we just kept at it. Now do more."

"I'm not sure I can, *Your Majesty*." I forced his proper title through my teeth, because what I wanted to call him certainly wouldn't win me any points. "It is my power that activates the blade. It won't work while my power is suppressed." I raised my wrists in the air, watching the sunlight sparkle in the diamonds.

The king glanced at Chaz who gave the tiniest of nods. "I will remove one cuff, but don't even think about trying anything foolish. Chaz here will have you incapacitated by your own hand should the thought even cross your mind."

I'd suspected Chaz was also a telepath, but that confirmed it. How though, could this boy read minds and control them at the same time? No one was so powerful. That kind of capability simply didn't exist. Then again, the ability to control minds wasn't supposed to exist on its own, either.

The cuff on my left wrist clicked and fell to the ground. I flexed my fingers, enjoying the feel of the air on my skin, which looked pale and thin where the cuff had been. Chaz's mental grip tightened in my head. A warning. But I didn't intend to act against the king, no matter how much self-restraint it took not to. I had other goals today. Violence didn't win friends.

The voice of the tablet hissed through my mind again. This time—for the first time—it said more than one word. *Good. Obey. Patience. Your time is coming.*

I whipped my head back to see the prophecy flashing wildly in the morning sunlight, but Bearius and Chaz both appeared to be none the wiser. Had I imagined that, or was I finally on the right track to fulfilling my destiny? Either way, I wasn't backtracking now.

It looked like Baerius and I were about to become very good friends.

CHAPTER 3

WITH A HEALTHY DISTANCE between me and one of the cuffs, I felt like I could breathe again. I hadn't realized just how much of my essence was being sucked dry by the gorgeous piece of metal. I was only halfway unbound, but I felt like a brand new woman.

And to the king's great delight, I was able to summon quite a bit more power with my one free arm. He laughed and cheered, clapping his meaty hands together with every new step we took in the right direction. And I obeyed. Every command, every heart-breaking word he uttered about me joining his side—I accepted them. Fighting back was useless. But if I could gain his trust, or at least lead him to believe he was still in full control, perhaps I'd find an opportunity to strike.

Our typical two hour training session stretched well into the afternoon that day. Baerius couldn't get enough. He was drunk on power—my power—and giddy over the possibilities my obedience presented. A sweaty sheen glistened across Chaz's forehead and my arms shook with fatigue when Baerius finally called it quits for the day. I plastered a smile on my face, blinking innocently at the man when all I really wanted to do was turn the blade on him and end his life with a single swipe of power.

Obey.

Al was gone when we finished our training. I wasn't sure how much of my act he'd seen, but I could only hope he knew my intentions. Surely he knew I could never team up with Baerius.

The king picked up the glass case containing the prophecy and tucked it under his arm, practically skipping back into the palace. Chaz and I followed more slowly, each of us drained from the strenuous work of the afternoon.

Baerius called for a messenger as soon as we reached his rooms. "It's time," he said to Chaz. "We'll continue practicing for another week or so, but I can't wait any longer. Are you prepared to move forward with our plan?"

The furrow in Chaz's brow was almost imperceptible. Baerius may not have noticed it, but it didn't get by me. "Yes," the boy said. "I'm ready."

The messenger knocked timidly on the door, and the king ushered him in with great enthusiasm, shoving a scroll and a pen into the young man's hands. "Take notes," he ordered, then began listing a long series of actions the messenger was to take—plans for an event the king was planning. It would require the help of many different heads of the Olympian council.

"Let's make it a gala. We'll usher in the beginning of our new era in style. It will be a party so grand, they won't be able to refuse the opportunity. I want it to be the biggest event of our time. Bigger than the annual convention. Every Keeper of every race should be in attendance. Do you hear me, boy?"

The young man nodded, desperately jotting everything down as the king droned on.

"Excellent." Baerius clapped his hands together after naming eleventy-million more action steps. "Now scurry along. And as for you two..." He turned back to face Chaz and me after the messenger left. "We've got one week to come up with the most dazzling speech and presentation these people have ever heard. I want every knee to bow to me before the end of the party. And I need you to make it happen. Now get your dinner. We'll practice some more after the meal."

And so it went for the next week and a half. I didn't think Baerius would be able to pull off an event of that kind of magnitude in such a short amount of time, but he had his whole territory scrambling to please him. I heard bits and pieces of the planning updates in between our training sessions, but that time was rare. Any time we weren't practicing our act for the gala I was trapped in my room, being measured for gowns or shaved, plucked, and prodded by some female attendants until I fit the image Baerius was going for.

My appearance wasn't the only thing he wanted to fit his ideal. Now that he was convinced he had me under his control, Baerius worked me non-stop, perfecting my every movement under Chaz's control. He wanted to dazzle the crowds with my power and fluff his ego with my praise and deference to him. He wanted them to believe he owned me. That my power was his power, and they were no match for us.

I was a prize for him to show off, like a magician with a caged tiger. But just like the tiger, I was only biding my time. Baerius could go on believing he had me under his control, but once we were on stage in front of Keepers from across the globe I would bring his plan crashing down. I was no one's pet, and I would never bow to the king of Olympus. I would bow to no man. Ever.

Chaz gave me the side-eye the evening before we were to go back down to the earth's surface, and I quickly wiped any coherent thoughts from my brain. I'd gotten used to repeating my new mantra anytime he was around. *Obey. Obey. Obey.* He probably thought I was some kind of deranged robot zombie, but I didn't care. I was just one day away from my freedom.

Not only that, but if all went according to plan, I was just one day away from having the tablet transcribed by Driskell and learning the full prophecy. After that, who knew what I would be capable of...

It was definitely worth it to play my role for just a little longer.

Another messenger met us in the king's rooms after our final evening session in the courtyard. Chaz and I were on our way to our individual bedchambers for the night when she entered. "The storm master is ready, Your Majesty."

I slowed my steps, curious to hear why the woman's voice trembled with her message. Chaz slowed as well. I expected a push in my back or the claws of his control to urge me back into my room, but he didn't seem to be in a rush. Together, we paused in the hall, listening to the woman's report.

"Excellent," Baerius rasped. "And how are the mortals taking it? Has it been reported and the area evacuated?"

"Yes, Your Majesty. Mostly. There are always some who don't follow the mortal leaders. But the storm master has assured me that they won't be a problem. He is prepared to make landfall at your command."

"What are they talking about?" I whispered to Chaz.

"Shh." He leaned toward the antechamber where they spoke, and it struck me that he was outright eavesdropping now.

"Tell him to proceed. Let me know when the humans have been taken care of, and I will make my descent. Please ready the guards. Have the first order go down to the mount as soon as it's clear, and let them know I won't be far behind." Baerius chuckled. "I've waited my entire life for this day, and it's finally here."

"Yes, Your Majesty."

The messenger's footsteps left the king's rooms, and Chaz yanked open my door, shoving me inside before Baerius caught us listening in the hall. He waited with me until the king retreated into his own bedchamber.

"What's he gonna do, Chaz? Is he talking about killing humans?"

Chaz's jaw hardened. He shot me a dirty look, then left my room with a huff, not bothering to answer my question. I was left alone, with nothing but the sound of my breathing. But my blood grew hot, my heartbeat pounding out the war song I'd kept suppressed for too long now. My left hand tingled with power—not even half of what I could do, but would it be enough? I channeled all of my energy into my free hand and with all the power I could muster, I flung it at the cuff on my right hand. I had to get out of here.

It bounced off in a blinding flash of light. My wrist burned as though I'd been branded by the metal, but the cuff remained firmly in place. It wasn't even singed. With a cry of frustration, I slammed my fist into the door and instantly regretted it.

Now burned and sore from the impact, I shook out my fingers and twisted open the knob. I couldn't just stand by while Baerius murdered humans with some storm master. I had to stop this. If that meant I'd be his captive for a while longer still, then so be it.

My anger grew with every step I took toward Baerius' bedchamber. I wasn't sure how I intended to stop him, only that I had to try. Perhaps the tablet could help me. Or the blade. He kept both locked away in his study. I just had to get my hands on them.

But I never made it to his private rooms. Chaz's door opened as I passed, and he once again pulled me silently inside. "Get off!" I jerked my arm away from him, but immediately felt his power take control in my brain, holding me to the spot.

"Go back to your room."

"But the humans!"

"I've got it."

He spoke the truth. Miraculously, I saw it play out in my mind's eye like a movie projected from his brain to mine. The few people who refused to evacuate before the oncoming storm were hunkered down in their homes. This wasn't a place I was familiar with, but the village they were in had a distinctly European look. And I *felt* more than saw Chaz's power take control in their minds, convincing them to get out of town.

"He won't hurt them if they get away," Chaz explained. "The king just needs them to leave so he can make his grand entrance."

"You're helping them?" My jaw fell open, anger subsiding. It seemed he had a hint of a moral compass left, after all. "Thank you."

"Don't thank me." Chaz's features pinched together, bitterly. "Now get back to your room, like I said."

This time I obeyed. I had no other choice. But at least I knew the humans were safe. And maybe...just maybe, I still had a chance to win Chaz over to the good side.

CHAPTER 4

"GET UP."

I groaned and pulled a pillow over my head. "Shhhh... You'll scare the dolphins." My voice was raspy in a half-sleep state.

"I said get up. Now."

My dream evaporated into thin air as the metal claws of Chaz's control took hold in my brain and wrenched me from my bed.

"Hey! You don't have to be such a—"

The claws twisted and I clamped my mouth shut. He could physically control me, but he couldn't stop me from finishing that thought in my mind. Knowing he could hear it, I threw in an extra silent insult for good measure, but Chaz ignored me.

He forced me into my en suite bathroom, where one of Baerius' attendants waited beside a running shower. The room was full of steam, and the attendant girl smiled kindly, urging me to get in. The door slammed shut behind me, with Chaz on the other side. He didn't go far, though. I could still feel his presence in my mind.

"What's going on?" We normally enjoyed breakfast and a morning training session before our showers. And I certainly didn't require any help getting clean.

"His Majesty has asked me to help you get ready. You'll be earth bound in about an hour."

Oh... *oh!* That's right, today was the day! I rubbed the sleep from my eyes, suddenly much more motivated to get ready. I was going back to the earth's surface today. This was it: my chance to break free from Baerius and step into my calling as the Deliverer. I grinned at the girl and wasted no time hopping into the steaming water, my mind racing wildly with ideas.

She provided me with "comfortable travel clothes" after I dried off, which looked more like uptight business clothes in my opinion. The pants were wide-legged slacks—a light camel color with golden threads woven in. The shirt was a form-fitting classic white button-up, and the nude heels added a couple of inches to my height. This was an interesting development. Maybe Baerius would try to take control of the other Keeper leaders in a formal meeting of the heads before the gala. I'd have to adjust my schemes for that.

One quick blow dry and a touch of make-up later, I was back in Baerius' main living space. Chaz waited there alone, similarly dressed for what looked like a business event. I quickly tried to clear my mind of any thoughts relating to bringing Baerius down and joined him on the couch.

"Where's the portal?"

Chaz grit his teeth together. I didn't think he was going to answer me at first, so it took me by surprise when he finally spoke. "We're not using the portal."

"No portal? How else are we supposed to get back?"

The door to Baerius' bedchamber opened before Chaz could answer, and the king's humming voice echoed down the hall until he joined us. He was followed by a pair of attendants who held the Firelake blade and the prophecy—both encased to prevent any accidents—in the air with their power. The grin on his face twisted my stomach. "Rise and follow me. It's time to make history."

Twice as many guards as usual stood outside the entrance to the king's rooms. With them was another man—perhaps the oldest looking Keeper I'd ever seen. He wore his hair long, and his beard was even longer. Upon our exit, the man nodded at the king, barely dipping his chin. He seemed disinterested, or maybe he was simply too hunched over to pay the king proper respect. The ancient looking man was surprisingly spry, however. He marched in line with the rest of us as our large group descended the stairs through the palace and congregated behind the large stone building near the cliff where we'd rescued Callan.

My eyes drifted toward the path that led to his cave, a breath hitching in my throat. I'd waited a lifetime to meet my father, but the opportunity came and went before I had a chance to let it sink in. Now he was gone again, and I still knew next to nothing about the man. I was only certain that he was Olympian. And a prince. The son of my wretched captor.

I turned back to Baerius, and the nausea already turning in my belly twisted even further. I hated that I was related to him—this man who wanted to control the world. The man who was so desperate for power that he locked up his only son for years, driving him mad. And the same man who tried to have me killed. But that was before he found a way to control my power.

I looked back at Chaz then, surprised to find that he was already watching me. *Shoot.* I needed to do a better job of keeping my thoughts empty around him.

"My scouts have reported that the coast is clear. Would you do me the honor, Silas?"

The old bearded man nodded, and Baerius curled his fingers, gesturing for Chaz and me to join him and his attendants at the cliff's edge.

"What's happening?" I whispered to Chaz.

"The storm master is sending us to earth in style." The boy's jaw was hard, and if I didn't know any better I'd think there was a hint of fear behind his stoic expression.

"The storm master." I repeated Chaz's words, taking a closer look at the old man called Silas. His eyes darkened—the sign of an Olympian summoning his power. My pulse quickened as I watched the man, barely breathing as I anxiously awaited his next move.

My attention was so narrowly focused on the man that I didn't notice the mist of Olympus coming to life, rolling across the ridge and up from the valley below. I didn't see how it gathered and swirled around our legs, picking up in intensity, until my feet were lifted from the ground. It thickened into a dense cloud, defying the laws of physics as it pulled me closer to Chaz, Baerius, and the two attendants who pulled the prophecy and blade into the sky alongside us.

Then, with a flick of his wrists, old man Silas proved his title of storm master to be true. The cloud that had formed beneath us surged forward off the cliff, and we were falling to the earth's surface miles below. It happened so fast I couldn't even summon a scream. I froze in place, eyes locked onto the king, whose laughter thundered through the sky. And when I didn't think things could get any worse, a blinding flash of lightning surged out from our impossible chariot, bringing Baerius' laughter into a crazed frenzy.

To my great surprise, Chaz reached out and gave my shoulder a soft squeeze, reminding me that I wasn't alone. Though it did little good, because his face was frozen into a similar look of terror. My only consolation was knowing that the Firelake blade was near. I was shackled and controlled by the king, but the blade would prevent my untimely death, at least.

And there was no way Baerius would risk my life for the sake of a grand entrance. Not when he was so close to everything he'd ever dreamed of. He needed *me* to get what he really wanted.

It wasn't long before the hair whipping around my face stilled and the cold gusts of stormy air slowed to a strong breeze. We were maybe a hundred yards above the ocean, moving toward a stretch of coast lined with narrow streets and low buildings. The village was nothing too impressive, especially compared to the blue silhouettes of towering mountains not far beyond it. And I knew right away where we were going. It was as though a piece of me recognized this land. We were headed for Mount Olympus.

More lightning flashed from our cloud and thunder cracked through the empty village with a deafening boom. Leaves and branches littered the ground, and the grim realization struck that our little storm master had been busy long before we got here. This must've been the village I saw through Chaz's mind last night. Hopefully he got the people out to safety before the storm landed.

Enormous gusts of wind blasted across the world below, and the sound of shattering glass filled my ears as debris flew wildly. But still we barreled forward, carried on a storm cloud driven by a power-hungry maniac of a king. The mountains drew closer and closer still, until my scalp tingled where my hairs stood on end. There it was: Mount Olympus in all its glory. It seemed like a portal would have been an easier method of travel, but as we finally approached the mountain's summit I knew why Baerius had chosen to arrive in the clouds.

Hundreds—no, *thousands*—of Keepers stood around the base of the mountain, all staring up with wide eyes and open mouths as we descended upon them. Some of the Olympians bowed. One man's voice carried through the air with shouts of "*Zeus!*" And maybe that was it. Maybe Silas the storm master contained the soul of Zeus, with the power of lightning at his command. You'd think that would automatically put him in charge of the Olympians instead of Baerius. But perhaps even the soul of Zeus was no match for the king's cunning and ability to repress others' power.

None of that mattered now, though. Not as we landed gracefully atop the mountain, my shaky legs barely keeping me upright as the cloud dissipated into mist. The attendants trembled beside me, arms wavering as they held the cases containing my blade and the tablet suspended in the air. Even Chaz looked pretty shaken up.

Not Baerius, though. He stood tall and led us toward a flat vertical expanse of stone at the top of the mountain. The views were incredible from this height. I could have stood there drinking in the sights for hours if I didn't have a king to destroy and a world to save. But duty called, and so I followed.

The rock face shimmered as we approached. "After you." Baerius grinned, and my stomach knotted. But it wouldn't be long now. I stepped through the shimmery surface and prepared to fulfill my destiny.

CHAPTER 5

I DON'T KNOW WHAT I expected to see on the other side of the rock wall, but it certainly wasn't this. The business attire suddenly made more sense as I surveyed the sleek interior of a conference hall as nice as anyone might find in a New York City skyscraper. All that was missing were the windows.

It was basically the opposite of what the inside of a mountain should look like. It smelled of plastic and office supplies, and harsh fluorescent lighting shone off of the slick tiled floors right alongside the reflections of hundreds of irritated Keeper faces.

Olympian guards stood in a line along the walls of both sides of the space. In the left half of the room was a group of Atlanteans, tall with red and brown hair and blue-green eyes. Maxwell, Gloriana, and Anasasha huddled at the center of their troop of Atlantean guards. Though her parents scowled in my direction, Anasasha looked more hurt than angry. It was a look of betrayal. I wanted to shake my head and tell her the truth. *Hold on, it will all make sense soon.*

But Anasasha was the least of my worries. The right half of the room was filled with Agarthians, and noticeably absent from the group was their interim king. My heart dropped. Where was Tate? Was he okay? I scanned the crowd, searching for those familiar golden eyes, but I knew he wasn't here. There was no tingle. No tether joining our hearts together. No Tate.

"Welcome to the summit of the mount." Baerius spread his arms, chest puffed out with bravado as he grinned at the crowd before him. "Thank you all for joining me on such short notice. This gala shall be one for the history books. But before it begins, let us convene in the main conference room. We have much to discuss before the crowds arrive."

The Olympian guards surrounded Baerius as he moved deeper into the space. My blade and the prophecy still hovered in the air behind him, held by the power of his attendants, but there were several additional guards surrounding them now. I suspected he wanted to show them off to the Atlanteans and Agarthians, but he was still afraid of losing the precious objects, and rightfully so. There was never a bigger target on anyone's back. But I knew they would be safe. After all, the only person who could touch them and live to tell about it was me.

I stepped in line to follow the king, but Chaz cut me off. "You're not invited."

"What do you mean?" I looked back at Maxwell, as though my own leader might be able to speak up on my behalf, but he very purposefully avoided any eye contact with me. They were going to meet—probably about me and my power—and I wasn't even invited.

"Let's go," Chaz said, ignoring my question. I felt his control lock into place, and decided now wasn't the time to fight against it. I needed to save my energy for when it would make the largest impact. I'd wait for the gala. Besides, there was still a chance I could get Chaz on my side if I played my cards right. I hoped there was, anyway.

I obeyed, falling into step beside him as he led me to an elevator in the center of the mountain. "I had no idea this place was here." The doors opened with a ding. "I mean, I knew Mount Olympus existed, of course, I just didn't know it was more than a mountain. Have you been here before?"

"No," Chaz grumbled, looking straight ahead. He mashed a button and the elevator began to drop a moment later.

"Where do you normally hang out on earth? Do they have, like, Keeper high schools or something?"

He pressed his lips together and didn't answer again. This whole *make-friends-with-Chaz* plan was failing hard and fast. Though I don't know why I expected anything different. He'd been cold towards me ever since we met. I could put up a fight against Baerius on my own, but it sure would help if Chaz would join me. Without his help, I'd have to obey the king's orders and only hope that my friends would see my distress and somehow come to my rescue. That is, if they were even here. Tate's absence admittedly had me pretty shaken up.

"Look," I said as the doors opened and Chaz stepped out into another hall. "I'm sorry that you hate me. I don't like being stuck together anymore than you do. But this might be the last day for the rest of eternity that I'm not known as the 'girl who destroyed the world.' And I suspect it's the last day of *your* freedom, too. I'll shut up if you want, but like it or not, we're in this together. I just thought we might as well try to be friends."

Chaz stiffened and his control in my brain wavered for the tiniest of an instant. "I've never been to the earth's surface before."

"What?!" I whirled around to face him. "This is your first time? And Baerius dragged you down here on a storm cloud without even giving you a chance to get acclimated?"

He frowned and kept walking. I followed of my own accord, before he had to force me and remembered why we were stuck together to begin with.

"Well, maybe after this is all over I can show you around," I offered, trying once again to make peace with the kid before Baerius put us on display.

"There won't be much to see." Chaz ran a keycard through a slot on the wall and a door clicked open. He gestured for me to go inside.

"Why do you say that?"

"Call it a hunch." He frowned. "The current war is bad enough. I'm afraid after tonight's announcement things will only get worse. Everyone wants power, but no one knows how to handle it when they get it."

"What war are you talking about?" Something clenched in my chest, my subconscious reacting to what I already knew deep inside.

"Your Agarthian prince's war. You wondered why he wasn't here... that's why. Agartha has no king, just as Baerius intended. He's allowing them to fight amongst themselves while he slides in as ruler over all the Keepers."

"You mean to tell me that Baerius is the one instigating this war in Agartha?"

"I mean to tell you nothing." Chaz clamped his mouth shut and closed the door, locking me in a room alone. "Your attendants will be by to get you ready before the event." His muffled words grew quieter through the door as he walked away.

I yanked on the handle, trying to pull it open, but it was locked from the outside. I was trapped—a prisoner again, with nothing to do but wait until I helped bring the world crashing down later tonight.

CHAPTER 6

THE ROOM LOOKED LIKE something from a contemporary design magazine. It was large and sparsely furnished, with straight lines and flat gray surfaces. Even the bed was nothing but hard planes. It looked about as soft as a slab of granite.

A line of light drew my attention to the far wall. A thin strip of an opening, barely wide enough for me to stick my fingers through, ran horizontally across the smooth stone surface of the wall just higher than my head. I ran over to inspect it and realized that it was a cutout, an open air window of sorts, or maybe just a vent just large enough to let in a sliver of light.

I grabbed the first thing I could carry—a small wastebasket under a sleek desk—and pulled it over to the cutout. Turning it upside down, I stepped on it like a stool and lifted up onto my tiptoes until I was eye level with the opening.

The walls of the mountain were probably three feet thick. Even if the opening was large enough for me to stick my arm through, I wasn't sure I'd be able to reach all the way through to the other side. Such a narrow slit in the mountain would be completely unnoticeable from the outside, which was obviously Baerius' intention for the design. And we were thousands of feet in the air, far from any hiking trails. It would be impossible to find any help up here. But that didn't stop me from trying.

"Hello? Is anyone out there?" A cold breeze was the only thing to answer, so I tried again. "Please! Anyone! Can you hear me?"

Everly?

I squinted, shifting back and forth on my toes to try and get a better view. Was my desperation playing tricks on me, or was that... "Al?" I was almost afraid to say his name out loud. Afraid to hope for the impossible. But a flutter of white feathers confirmed it was him a moment later. "Al!"

Quiet, or someone will hear you! I swear in the thousands of years I've known you, you have never been good at keeping quiet. It's like you were created without the ability to be stealth.

"Okay, I get your point! I'll keep quiet," I whisper-yelled through the slit. "Now can you get me out of here?"

He flapped his wings at varying speeds, dropping enough to peer inside the cutout before lifting up again so that all I could see were his cute little owl feet. *I don't see a way.*

His feet disappeared. I waited just a minute, expecting him to come back. And when he didn't return, panic surged up into my throat hot and fast. "Al? AL!"

Shhh. My goodness you are loud. I was just searching the rocks out here to find a way in.

"Well, what did you find?"

Nothing.

Ugh. I kicked the wall out of frustration and nearly sent my trash can step stool toppling over. Quickly readjusting to peek out of the crack again, I spotted Al perched on a piece of rock jutting out from the side of the mountain. He looked tired. "How did you find me? Did you fly all the way here from New York?"

Of course not. I'm an owl, not a passenger jet. Devon brought me when we received Baerius' command—er, invitation.

"Devon! Does that mean Millie and my mom are here, too? And the others? What about Tate? Have you seen Tate?" I lifted higher onto my toes as though it would give me a clearer view of the ground below, but I could barely see anything through the narrow slat in the thick stone walls.

They're uh... yes. They're here. Everyone except Tate. But they're caught up with something right now.

No. "Where's Tate? Is he alright? Is he at war? I heard the Agarthians were fighting over who should rule. What is happening out there?" I had so many questions, and Al just wasn't talking fast enough. I had to get out of this place!

He shifted on his feet and turned his head in a very owl-like fashion to peer down at something near the base of the mountain.

"Al? What is it? What do you see? Are they okay? Please tell me what's going on!" That panicky feeling began to surge up through my chest again.

Things have gotten tense since Baerius called for the meeting here. Yes, Tate is fighting to maintain control over his people, though things haven't gotten physical yet for the most part. The rest of the Keepers are talking all across the globe. And we fear they're not the only ones joining us here for this little soiree. Unfortunately, I believe the Manticorians are on their way too, even as we speak.

Of course they were. Rasputin wanted my power as badly as Baerius did. He'd made that clear. But I had successfully evaded him and his army of witches once already. Surely I could do it again. I'd get away from Baerius, too. They could fight amongst themselves for all I cared. I just wanted to get a hold of the prophecy so I could finally understand what I needed to do to take action.

"That's okay," I said, more for myself than Al. It didn't sound as though Tate was in danger, and though the people were tense, everyone was still safe for now. "I'm not afraid of Rasputin. We'll handle him when he gets here. Do you know where Driskell is?"

He's at the base of the mountain with the others. They're spreading word of what is to come—trying to prepare the other Keepers to stand up against Baerius when he attempts his transition to power.

"Great. Listen, I've got to get out of here. Will you have my mom or Devon please zap up here? I know where the tablet is. Baerius has it, and my blade, too. But if we can just get them and have Driskell interpret the full prophecy for me, I know I'll be able to put a stop to this. Even Rasputin will be running from me once I have my power back. I've felt it, Al. It's... it's impossible to describe how much power lies within that tablet."

I believe you. But it's also impossible for anyone to teleport themselves into your room. The wards surrounding you are thicker than the stone walls.

"There's got to be a way!"

I'm sorry, but there's not.

I pounded the wall with a fist, frustrated again that I couldn't find a way out of this. "We'll have to wait for the gala, then. Please let my mom and the others know, no matter what they see me do in there, I'm on their side. We're gonna get through this. We have to. And Al?"

Yeah?

"Please find Tate. I'm gonna need him here."
I'll do my best.
With a flutter of white wings, Al was gone.

CHAPTER 7

I SPENT THE NEXT hour trying everything within my power to break off the remaining cuff on my wrist. I rubbed it on the corners of the furniture, bashed it against the stone walls, and even called upon the soul of Athena to help me destroy it. But Baerius' block on my power was too much. Athena was asleep, and I was trapped.

Every step I took pacing back and forth in my large, empty room took me one notch closer to insanity. I was losing my mind thinking of Tate and the others working so hard to stop Baerius from taking control. And meanwhile, I just waited patiently, playing along like a good little girl and waiting for them to force me to betray our people.

And all for what? Did I really think I would be able to resist his control once he had me on stage at the gala? I couldn't even get the stupid cuff off of my wrist! Chaz was nowhere close to joining me in taking Baerius down, and there was literally no way for me to resist the control he enacted in my head. He could make me do anything. Anything at all. And I was powerless to stop him.

Completely lost in my thoughts and despair, I hardly noticed the faint knock on my door until it opened with a whir and a click, and three Olympian attendants stepped inside. One carried a long garment bag. One dragged a suitcase on wheels. And the third held a pair of throwing knives. *Delightful.*

"It's time to get you ready for the big event." One of the girls smiled while the others got to work laying out cosmetics and hair irons across the desk in my room. She hung the garment bag on the door frame and unzipped it. I began to object until I saw what hung inside that bag.

It was a gown—resplendent in glittering gold. I knew that gown. I'd seen it before, painted in glorious detail on a portrait of myself in Rossel's gallery. *Deliverance.*

Chill bumps dotted my arms and my heart skipped a beat. This was the night Rossel saw in his vision—the night everything would change. *No pressure.* Biting down on my objection, I decided to go back to my original plan. I would continue to play along and pray that an opportunity to break free would present itself when the time was right. It was my destiny, after all. I was so close now.

I sat quietly as the attendants did my hair and makeup, never once asking to see the mirror. I knew how I would look. I had already seen the finished product in Rossel's painting. Surely the king had as well. Did he know the dress they'd picked out for me tonight? Had he done it intentionally, believing he was part of the plan all along?

Perhaps he was. I knew I wouldn't have much choice in the matter either way. The Deliverer didn't get to choose her own destiny. It was chosen for me.

There was no way to tell if Chaz recognized the golden dress or not when he picked me up from my room a short while later. He was straight faced and stoic. And I worked hard not to betray what I knew as I fell into place beside him on the way back to the elevators.

We dropped down, down, down, neither of us speaking a word as the elevator plunged us deeper into the base of the mountain, or maybe even further below ground by the feel of it. We fell lower into the earth for what felt like ages before the doors finally opened with another ding.

Thousands of people stood on the other side. Not people—*Keepers.* They were all dressed up in formal attire. Suits and gowns of every color, from every culture across the world painted a dizzying landscape before me. The room seemed to tilt and sway as the Keepers moved from conversation to conversation, each lost in their own individual importance.

The air felt heavier here. Enchanted. It had to be. Of course Baerius wouldn't risk any harm coming his way on the biggest day of his life. But where was he now?

I scanned the crowd in search of him, but landed on a pair of green eyes instead.

"Excuse me." Anasasha grabbed me by the shoulder and pulled me away from Chaz, sending him a dirty look before settling her scrutinizing gaze on me. Chaz lingered nearby, watching—and most definitely listening—but mercifully he didn't come after us. Neither did Anasasha's guards, who towered over my sixteen year old puppeteer.

"What are you doing?" Her tone was laced with that betrayal I'd seen written on her features earlier. "My father says you're teaming up with Baerius? That you're trying to hand all power over to him? That's not what we agreed on. That's not why I helped you escape from Atlantis. You were supposed to save me—save us all—not doom us."

I risked a glance at Chaz, who pretended to be distracted by some dirt on his shoe.

"I'm trying." My voice was barely a whisper. Then I mouthed *trust me*, hoping it might get past Chaz. But Anasasha only frowned. Why should she trust me now?

Changing tactics, I decided to ask her about my friends, instead. If there was anyone who would have pinned Sean down the moment he entered this place, it was Anasasha.

"I haven't seen them."

"None of them? Not even Millie?" My voice quivered with disbelief. Al said they were coming. They should have been here by now.

"Not yet." Her expression softened slightly. "But they'll come. Everyone has to. Those invitations you and Baerius sent…" She shook her head. "Well, let's just say they are impossible to refuse." And with a scowl she turned away again, motioning for her guards to follow.

"Was there some kind of a spell put on the invitations?" I asked Chaz after they were gone.

He said nothing, leading me through the crowd of Keepers across the ballroom. There, at the opposite side of the room, was a stage. And on that stage sat a throne—the throne from the painting.

Hope surged through me again. *It's there. Wake up, Athena. It's time for war*. I searched desperately for the power I knew I still held inside, but Bearius' control over it was too strong. I couldn't break through.

There he was, grinning arrogantly with his hands resting on the back of the throne—*my* throne. I didn't want him to touch it. Didn't want him to look so smug and unshakeable up there on that stage. Didn't want to see the cases holding the prophecy and the Firelake blade resting on the table behind him. They were mine. All of it was *mine*.

A set of double doors on the left of the stage slammed open as I took it all in, and I didn't know which was more shocking: seeing Rasputin stride confidently onto the stage, or seeing the wide grin spread across Baerius' old face at the sight of him.

The Olympian and the Manticorian shook hands like old friends, then turned their eyes to Chaz and me as we approached.

"Hello, Everly. It's a fine evening for some Deliverance, wouldn't you say?" There was an unmistakable gleam in Rasputin's eye. "And Chaz, you are looking fine this evening as well."

Chaz dipped his chin. "Thank you, uncle."

Uncle?

The shock must have been evident on my face, because Baerius roared with laughter. He gestured out at the ballroom full of Keepers who finally began to take notice of the man who had just entered the room. Nervous murmurs worked their way through the crowd, but not a single soul tried to do anything, despite facing the leader of the Manticorians on the stage before them.

The king spread his arms wide. "Shall we begin?"

CHAPTER 8

CHAZ FOUND A SHADOW along the wall next to the stage to hide himself in, but I wasn't so lucky. I watched my feet take a step toward Baerius. Then another. I tried to open my mouth, but my lips were sealed shut, replaced with a forced smile. My arm reached up to give a small wave to the nervous crowd, and I hated Chaz in that moment.

I hated him for making me appear so human. I hated him for his relationship with Rasputin. I hated him for fooling me into believing he still had a modicum of kindness in his soul when he so clearly planned on helping Baerius take over the world all along.

And I hated him for controlling my every movement so precisely that I couldn't even turn to give him a glare.

Every eye was on me as I took my place between Baerius and Rasputin, grinning like a fool. Inside, I was screaming. My skin crawled in their presence. They were cruel, disgusting old men and I wanted nothing more than to break open the case that contained my blade and end them here and now. But I couldn't. I could do nothing but play their game.

Obey.

Even the ancient words of the prophecy whispering through my brain felt like a betrayal. I didn't understand any of this. And I would not obey. Not if I could help it. I struggled against the invisible chain locked around my free will and the cuffs binding my power, but it was no use.

The words Baerius used to address the crowd hardly registered in my mind until I heard a name that was one step too close to the people I held dear. "Titus, King of Agartha, accepted the new order immediately. He is so invested in making this work that he joined up with Rasputin and myself several weeks ago to ensure our success. You may have thought him gone, but he was only working hard for his people. Titus, why don't you come on out and speak to your people... to *our* people?"

Chaz allowed me to look at the doors to the side of the stage where Rasputin had entered earlier. They opened again to reveal Tate, and a collective gasp filled the room. My heart thundered raucously against my ribs at the sight of my beloved. But no, this wasn't Tate. It was Titus, his identical twin, and something was wrong. Titus' eyes were glazed over and almost vacant behind the smile plastered across his face.

Titus moved to the front of the stage and began to speak some dribble that was obviously written by Baerius. It was so rehearsed, so robotic in nature, that I wondered how anyone in the crowd could possibly buy into this load of garbage. Cutting a look over to Chaz, I realized that I wasn't his only puppet. His eyes were focused on Titus, mouth moving ever so slightly with the words he was forcing Titus to speak.

His words were bone-chilling. He was essentially handing the keys of Agartha directly into Baerius' hands, citing the prophecy as his motivation. They'd twisted a tale of power so great that no one could stand up to it, and my blood curdled at the looks of the Keepers as they twisted their faces in horror at me. I was an abomination. A beast. I wasn't here to deliver them, I was here to enslave them under the rule of Baerius. A new era. A new order. No matter how they phrased it, the people knew this was the beginning of the end. And it was all my fault.

Obey.

But why? Why would I obey this? This was against everything I'd believed all along.

"So now we have the Manticorians." Baerius gestured toward Rasputin. "We have the Agarthians, and we have the most powerful Atlantean, known better as the Deliverer, all joined together with me and the Olympians. The time has come, my good men and women, to unite under one accord. And it is with great honor that I accept the role of Imperial Leader over all the Keepers and above all of mankind."

The crowd had been quiet until now. They were willing to hear Baerius out until he propped himself up as the leader of them all. Now the Atlanteans, especially, began to bristle. Heads shook and murmurs rose until one brave soul called out, "Why should we believe you? This girl looks like nothing special. I bet you just placed some kind of an illusion on her aura to make it appear white."

"Yeah!" another man yelled. "The Deliverer is a myth. There is no prophecy!"

Shouts of agreement rang out around him, but Baerius only smiled. This was the moment he'd been waiting for. This was his chance to parade me in front of them all like a cheap party trick.

"Come." Baerius wiggled his fingers and my traitorous feet stepped forward.

Taking my hand in his, Baerius raised our arms and swept his free hand in front of me like I was some overpriced piece of jewelry displayed on the home shopping network. "I have proof, and I will show you under one condition. If I can prove that what I say is true, Maxwell must concede his power to me and the Deliverer. For he will soon discover that he is no match for us. If he does not concede, we can—*and will*—easily take Atlantis by force. And I'm sure none of you wish to begin a war." Baerius looked over at Titus who was still grinning like a dunce off on the side of the stage. "Not another war, anyway. So do I have your word?"

He'd been prepped on this in their earlier meeting, but obviously Maxwell had yet to agree. To put him on the spot in front of most of the Keepers on earth was uncalled for. Baerius truly stooped to the lowest of tactics to get his way, and I hated him even more for it.

If Maxwell did not agree, he would be guaranteeing a war on his people. If he did agree, he'd look like a gullible push-over. His people would feel betrayed and he would be hated forever, going down in history as the weak man who helped Baerius rise to the top. There was no easy way out of this for him, and Baerius knew it. The entire room held its breath waiting for Maxwell's response.

"Read us the prophecy. Prove that you can even decipher its words, then share them with the rest of us," Maxwell said. "Once we hear it, I will agree to concede if you can show proof that she is who you claim. But I will set the terms. I will determine what kind of proof will be acceptable only after we hear the prophecy in its entirety."

Baerius turned to look at Rasputin, who gave a subtle nod. Satisfied, Baerius turned back to the crowd and clapped his hands together. "You have a deal."

Rasputin's menacing chuckle made my hairs stand on end as he moved back to the table with my precious artifacts. The brick of dread in my belly grew even heavier when he called me over to join him.

I resisted. Or, I tried to resist. But my feet moved forward. I flung as many silent insults at Chaz as I could come up with, but of course it didn't matter. He had complete and utter control over me. Cursing the boy would make no difference.

"Now you see," Baerius said, "the prophecy has been put back together. It was formed from the original four pieces that were broken and scattered thousands of years ago. And until now, it was impossible to bring them back. Only the Deliverer could do so. And now that it is whole, only the Deliverer can safely touch the object." He nodded to me and I reached for the first case—not of my own accord.

Though it wasn't my choice to unleash the tablet from where it lay hidden inside the enchanted case, I couldn't deny that I wanted it. I needed to feel its power coursing through me again. My heartbeat picked up into a frenzied symphony as I unclasped the locks and allowed the lid to fall open.

The tablet's glow filled the room. I hadn't seen it unleashed in its full glory since the first night I'd pieced it back together. It was beautiful. And the entire room must have felt its power, judging from the gasp followed by an awed silence. Even my inner Athena seemed to stir, despite Baerius' cuff on my right hand.

And even though I knew better, I couldn't help the hope that flickered again at the sight of it. It only grew when Baerius asked me to lift the tablet before the entire room. The stone immediately began to pulse in time with my heart beat, rushing faster and faster as the tablet's power poked and prodded around Baerius' restrictions. It was looking for a way in, and I desperately wanted to help it break through.

Not yet. I perked up at the ancient whisper. 'Not yet' was certainly better than 'never' or its favorite 'obey.' And it was enough to let my hope surge free as Baerius spoke again.

"Rasputin, will you please read the words of the prophecy aloud for our audience, here?"

"Wait!" Maxwell stepped forward. "I want someone else to read it. I don't trust him." He stepped up on the stage beside Baerius and faced the crowd. "Can anyone else decipher the meaning?"

I scanned the crowd, searching for the bushy brows and beard of Driskell. It hurt more than I cared to admit that he wasn't there. Not just because I wanted him to read the prophecy, but because I thought he cared enough to help me out of this. Driskell and Millie, Sean and Dom and Gayla, Tate, my mom and... dad. None of them were here. None of them came to save me. Even Al was gone.

And there wasn't another soul in this entire giant ballroom—not another soul in the entire mountain—who was able to read the old language. None other than Rasputin. But I would know if he was lying. I knew what three quarters of it said. If he got that part right, I would have to trust that the rest of it was correct as well.

"Fine." Maxwell's shoulders dropped and he waved his hand at Rasputin in defeat. "Tell us what it says."

I turned to offer Rasputin a better view of the prophecy in my hands, and the tablet seemed to dim slightly as he looked upon its face. Greed flared in his eyes, and his lip curled as he began to read the words aloud.

"The daughter of sea and sky,
together with the one who
ignites her heart in her
centennial incarnation
shall form a white braid of
the powers that bind.
The Deliverer alone can wield
the power of the sword
with grace and fire to
destroy those who hunger for power.
The Keepers shall perish at the hand of the Deliverer,
and the world will unite as one,
as it was before and
evermore shall be."

The room paled and an invisible fist clenched around my heart, which grew uncomfortably hot in my chest with unleashed power. It was right. Rasputin read the words correctly. I knew it in the marrow of my bones. But that's what terrified me.

Was I really sent to destroy the Keepers? All of them? And if so, how did Baerius expect this to turn out? This wasn't good for anyone here.

"So you see?" Baerius grinned. "We have the Deliverer in our midst. But thanks to me, she has agreed to let us live. We shall not perish at her hands so long as you all agree to bow to our rule. What will it be, Maxwell? Shall we count the Atlanteans as friends, or foes? Allies or enemies?"

CHAPTER 9

THE GALL OF BAERIUS never ceased to amaze me. His plan was all making sense now. He'd enlisted Chaz to control me for... forever? So that he could use me as a means of gaining control over all the Keepers as well as all the humans of the world. He was twisting the words of the prophecy, and making the other Keeper races fear for their lives if they did not follow him.

It was written as plain as day: *The Keepers shall perish at the hand of the Deliverer*. The words made me nauseous. I couldn't kill them. Not all of them. So in that way I supposed I was glad Baerius had dampened my powers. I certainly wasn't about to thank him for it, though.

And Chaz... poor kid. I didn't like him, but that didn't mean I thought he should have to devote his next thousand years to keeping me under control. He was as much a slave as I was.

"We still need to see proof that this girl is the Deliverer." Maxwell didn't make eye contact with me. He couldn't bring himself to look in my direction. And who could blame him?

"As you wish." Baerius only widened his sick smile. "What would you like to see?"

Maxwell's brows furrowed as he considered the request. "The prophecy, assuming that it is the *real* prophecy, says, 'The Deliverer alone can wield the power of the sword.' But I see no sword."

"Ah!" Baerius raised one finger in the air, triumphant that Maxwell was still unwillingly playing right into his hand. "Allow me to show you the Firelake Blade."

Again, the entire crowd gasped. Chaz's grip on my mind tightened, and I carefully placed the tablet back into its case, then reached for the blade's case beside it.

I heard its song, strong and true, the moment I unbuckled the clasps. It felt good in my palm. The weight was perfect, the hilt cool and solid beneath my fingers. My hand came alive with the contact, and the only thing that seemed to keep my power under control was the cuff around my right wrist, siphoning nearly all my strength and all the ancient power the sword provided to me.

Chaz willed me to spin around and raise the blade high overhead. The crowd cowered slightly at the sight of it. Again, they had to have felt its power. There was no question that this was no ordinary blade.

"As the stories say, this is the most powerful blade in the history of the world. Nothing compares to it, and only the most noble can wield it, for its owner becomes invincible with its strength. Our Deliverer here went to the depths of the Firelake to retrieve it. Only she could survive such a feat, and only she can wield the blade's power now. Show them." Baerius inclined his chin toward me.

He then pointed to a giant crystal chandelier hanging over the center of the ballroom, and I dreaded what I knew came next. With my sword held awkwardly in front of me—the best my inexperienced puppeteer could make me do—I felt the flicker of power buzzing in my chest. I tried to hold it back this time, even as the ancient tongue of the prophecy again urged me to *obey*. But I was powerless against the cuff and Chaz's claws in my brain. I flung my power through the blade, and with a vivid flash of light like a bolt of lightning, it shot across the room and struck its target with stunning precision. The fixture exploded like a firework, and shattered crystals rained down upon the horrified crowd below.

The room came alive with shouts and screams as the Keepers dodged the falling pieces. I knew it wouldn't kill them. They could recover from surface wounds quickly, and there were plenty of Atlantean healers in the room to assist those who required extra attention. But I still hated that I'd caused them any pain at all.

Baerius, however, cheered with glee. It was exactly what he wanted. "There you see it! Only the Deliverer can wield such power!"

After the chaos calmed, the Atlantean leader stepped forward again. "Such theatrics! It's a nice story, but that's all it is. A story. The Firelake Blade is a myth. You cannot prove to me that this is it with your flashing lights and explosions." Maxwell's skin was growing increasingly red and blotchy, like a rash creeping up from the collar of his shirt.

"Try to take the blade and see for yourself." Baerius smirked. "No one else can so much as lay a finger on it. Only the Deliverer has what it takes."

Maxwell hesitated for only the briefest second before stepping forward. I wanted to pull my sword away or shout for him to back up. The blade had always been powerful, but now that the prophecy was completely restored, I wasn't sure just how much damage it would cause if Maxwell attempted to take it. It could be deadly.

But of course Chaz wouldn't allow me to offer any warning. I simply grinned and held the blade politely in front of me, offering it up to Maxwell like a prize.

"Sir! Stop!" One of the Atlantean guards stepped out from the crowd. "Please allow me to try. If it truly is the Firelake blade, you could be badly injured or worse. Let me do this for you."

I could see the pain in Maxwell's expression as he considered the guard's offer. But at last, he relented. "Thank you, Boudreaux."

The guard stepped forward, his Adam's apple bobbing as one shaky arm reached toward the sword. To his credit, he did not hesitate. He fought through the fear that gripped him and wrapped a full hand around the hilt before his body started convulsing and he fell to the floor.

The skin of his palm was still smoking after he landed, and the smell of burnt flesh stung my nostrils. I swallowed down bile, sick with myself for not stopping the man from what I knew was going to happen. But I couldn't. I turned to place the blade back inside its case, and angled my chin just enough to see Chaz's pale face, taut with emotion. He wouldn't look my way. Good. I hoped he was sick with himself, too.

Baerius on the other hand couldn't have been more pleased with himself. He joined me as a cluster of healers rushed forward to tend to the Atlantean guard. Rasputin surprised me by stepping up on my opposite side. And as though they'd rehearsed it, each man took one of my hands into his and lifted their arms, creating what appeared to be a united front between the three of us.

"The Manticorians shall bow to you, Deliverer." Rasputin's voice was chilling and quiet, though it still somehow filled the room.

"As shall the Olympians. And I thank you for entrusting me with the power to rule, Deliverer. I shall carry out your commands to the fullest as the Imperial Leader." Baerius squeezed my hand, urging me to play along as though I had any choice in the matter.

Titus reappeared then, still completely glazed over as he dropped to his knees before us and bowed his face all the way to the ground. "The Agarthians surrender all control to you, Deliverer. Through the leadership of our Imperial Leader, Baerius, we shall obey."

Something about the way he said 'obey' triggered a sleeping part of my brain. I couldn't place my finger on it, but I felt something shift into motion.

There was only one Keeper race left. I looked at the ashen-faced leader of my people. Maxwell's eyes were deep with sorrow. Full of regret. He inhaled and opened his mouth to speak, but the doors at the back of the ballroom slammed open before he had a chance to get a single word out.

Osborne entered the room, glowing with hellfire as two Agarthian elementals stood on either side of him, covered in flames. "Before you say another word, I want to see for myself that this Deliverer is truly who you claim she is. Let me have a crack at her and we'll see if she's really invincible with that blade."

CHAPTER 10

I SHOULD HAVE FEARED Osborne's words. He'd essentially told the entire room that he was going to try to kill me. And the Firelake blade would protect me in theory, but could I really sustain myself without full access to its power? There wasn't a chance Baerius was going to release my cuff and let me off my leash.

So yeah... I should have been terrified. But I wasn't. Because the instant the doors flew open, I felt it. A tingle started in my toes and quickly spread —faster than the flames that engulfed Osborne's guards. My body came alive with an electric sensation, and the invisible string tied to my heart was pulled tight.

Tate was here.

I couldn't see him, but I knew it was true as much as I knew I needed oxygen to breathe. And I didn't fear Osborne, because I knew that if he really did have bad intentions for me Tate would have destroyed him before he ever got this far. Plus, Osborne didn't have the same venom in his tone that he usually reserved for me. And the fire reflecting in his eyes wasn't focused on the stage at all. He was looking at Titus.

"We've done our part. What more proof do you need?" Baerius did little to hide his rising irritation. "She is the Deliverer. You can try to best her, but your life will be lost as a result. Is that a risk you are willing to take?"

"Yes." Osborne took a step forward

"Foolish man." Baerius shook his head, but to my surprise, he stepped aside, opening me up to whatever attacks Osborne threw my way.

The Agarthians moved closer, and the flames dancing across the skin of the guards grew brighter and hotter with every step. I'd never seen anything like it. I knew they existed, but the only elemental Agarthian I'd ever seen use her power was the girl with the wind back at Columbia. And if I thought her wind was scary, these fire-wielders were in a whole different ballpark.

Every eye in the room was trained on them. Even Chaz watched them closely, hopefully so that he could help me dodge or block their attacks and stay alive.

"She needs the blade," Rasputin said. "Give her a moment to retrieve it before taking aim."

Osborne nodded his agreement and I went back to the table. The Agarthians took turns tossing fireballs back and forth between them like they were playing a game of catch. The Keepers watched them on pins and needles, just praying one of the balls wouldn't drop. It wasn't until I turned my back on the crowd to get the blade that I noticed the doors to the side of the stage were cracked open.

My heart jolted in my chest. Tate? It had to be him! I glanced quickly at Chaz who was already trained on the doors. I didn't know if he'd read my thoughts or the thoughts of whoever stood in the hall beyond, but I wouldn't let him hurt Tate.

Chaz turned to me then, with the strangest look on his face. He gave a subtle shake of his head and looked back at the Agarthians with the fireballs in the ballroom. The door cracked open even further, and to my surprise, it was my mother's face I saw. She grinned before pulling herself back into the darkness on the other side. Then Tate appeared.

I froze, unable to breathe. All I could hear was the rushing sound of my own blood pumping through my ears. I was overjoyed... but also horrified. What would Baerius do to Tate when he caught him here? Or worse— what would Chaz have *me* do to him?

He put a single finger up to his lips, then he, too, disappeared back into the darkness. My heart was still thundering in my chest as I stood in shock, completely forgetting what I'd been doing before I saw his face. But Chaz's claws dug into my brain, moving my hand toward the Firelake blade, then spinning me around to face the crowd. They were still so absorbed in the circus act by the fire-wielders, that they hardly noticed my delay.

I stepped forward, back to where Baerius and Rasputin created a gap for me in the center of the stage. They moved further to the edges, leaving me exposed there alone. But the blade felt sturdy in my palm, and I prayed that it would be enough to defend me, even without access to my full power.

"Are you ready, then?" Osborne's sneer didn't pack as much punch as it had before.

"Yes." My feet moved me into more of a defensive pose, but it felt unnatural and staged. So fake. I imagined Chaz was probably copying something he'd seen from a TV show. The fireballs now blazing in the palms of Osborne's guards, however, were definitely not fake. I refocused on the very real threat in front of me, once again trying to wake up that inner goddess of war.

Come on, Athena. I could really use your help here.

All three of the Agarthians narrowed their eyes at me, and Osborne's voice slid into the sing-song timbre of a siren. "Lift your hands in the air and don't move. This will only hurt a little."

Obey.

I did as he said, but not because his glamour worked its magic on me. On the contrary, I felt none of Osborne's power at all. I did it because somewhere in my soul I knew the tablet's words were important. I had to obey.

Just at the edge of my periphery, I saw movement from Baerius and Rasputin. They lifted their arms into the air, and Osborne's fire boys each turned to face the men. Osborne still watched me, but there was no malice in his expression. He gave a quick jerk of a nod, and the audience gasped, refocusing their attention behind me.

"What is the meaning of this?" Baerius shouted. He dropped his hands, using his own power to squelch the glamour Osborne had placed in his mind. The Agarthian guards launched their fireballs then, but Rasputin was able to erect some kind of shield to block them before they hit their targets.

"Seize them!" The king and his men rushed forward to Osborne.

I stood there dumbly, watching in a stunned silence until a firm hand on my shoulder grabbed my attention. I whipped around and finally saw what had shocked the crowd a moment before. My mom grinned, tears glazing her lashes. Behind her stood Callan, Rossel, and Millie. But there was no sign of Tate.

CHAPTER 11

"WE'LL HAVE TO RUN. I can't teleport you." My mother moved urgently toward the doors.

I started to follow, but Chaz and his stupid brain claws stopped me in my tracks. I turned to glare at him, but he was already walking this way. His jaw hung slightly askew as he looked past me. Past my mom and Rossel, straight at Callan.

My father smiled at the boy. "Hey, Chaz."

Chaz's eyes flared wide with disbelief, but it was only temporary. He quickly regained his composure and shot a furious look in my direction. "You can't go. Not yet."

As much as I hated to admit it, I knew he was right. I couldn't leave with Titus and the other Keepers still in danger.

"*You.*" Baerius snarled and pointed his thick finger at Rossel. Osborne and the guards had been apprehended and he'd only just now realized that another crowd had joined us via teleportation behind his back. "You're dead."

My mother quickly grabbed Callan and Rossel, who took Millie's hand, and the four of them vanished. Baerius roared. Pride surged in my chest for my clever mother. She acted quickly—too fast for Baerius to enact his power over her. Now I just needed her to stay gone. She wouldn't be so lucky a second time.

A buzz shot up my spine, lighting me up from the inside out. I knew who it was immediately, I just had to find him. There! Standing in a group with Devon, Sean, and Gayla, Tate was reaching for his brother. Devon must have teleported them in while Baerius was distracted by my mother.

Titus looked confused. He was obviously not in his right mind, but whether that was from drug use or something Rasputin had done to him, I couldn't be sure. Tate spoke quietly to him, urging him to his feet and into the center of the group. The next moment, they were gone. All of them but Tate.

His golden eyes locked on to mine, and a triumphant smile spread across his face. My goodness he was a beautiful creature. I'd almost forgotten. But even if he were ugly as mud, I would still love him with every ounce of my soul. Our tether yanked tight in my chest, and heat blossomed beneath my sternum.

Now.

Wait, what? Surely I'd misunderstood. Did the tablet really just say...

NOW!

I leapt forward, shielding Tate with my body before Baerius could hurt him. The king curled his lip. He began to speak, but movement just to the side snagged his attention before he could. My mother reappeared there with Callan and Rossel. Millie wasn't with them this time.

"Enough!" Baerius bellowed loud enough to shake the room, and everybody froze. For a moment I feared he'd sucked out all the power from every Keeper here. But a flicker of a white hot flame burned in my chest, and I knew he couldn't snuff it out. Not anymore.

Two Olympian guards emerged from the crowd at Baerius' command, and in a matter of moments they'd rounded up my mom's crew with invisible ropes, holding them together in a tight cluster. But rather than killing them on the spot, Baerius arrogantly decided to use their disobedience as a teaching moment for the others in the room.

"You want to know what happens to those who choose to fight against their new Imperial Leader and the Deliverer?" He looked at Chaz from the corner of his eye—no doubt signaling for the boy to puppet me forward. Only Baerius didn't know that Chaz's claws were gone. I was unbound. Part of me wondered if Chaz was even aware. "Well, let me show you."

Tate joined my side, leaving my skin practically sizzling where his arm brushed against mine. And that flame in my chest was so hot now that I could barely contain it. Any more power and I would have to forfeit myself to it, allowing it to fully consume me. But as long as Tate was by my side, I could hardly care. And I wasn't about to let Baerius ruin things again.

He pointed two fingers at a new pair of Olympian guards, giving them their cue to take aim at my mother and the others. He never saw me coming. I lunged forward, slicing through the air with my blade and creating a shield to protect them. The electric blasts from the guards rebounded, scattering across the room and singeing the walls where they finally made impact. The other Keepers in the room screamed and ducked for cover, but no one was hurt.

"What are you doing?" The king failed to keep an even keel to his tone. He looked from me to Chaz. "They've acted against the new order. They must pay for their crimes with their lives."

"There is no new order," Tate said, loud enough for the whole room to hear. "Maxwell has yet to concede. And as the interim ruler of Agartha, I decline to subject *my people* to your rule, either."

Baerius' cheeks were red hot, and I had to fight the urge to strike him down. "You are nothing, Thaddeus. Titus is alive and well. Everyone saw him. He gave his allegiance on behalf of Agartha."

"He was under duress."

"He was no such thing!" Baerius' voice boomed throughout the ballroom. "Guards, seize this man. Kill him and the rest of them as well so we can get on with our evening!"

"Don't you dare." My voice was barely more than a whisper, but not for a lack of courage. I was fearless. Baerius' threat against my soulmate ignited something inside me that couldn't be tamped down. And though my words were soft, the promise underlying them was clear to everyone in the room. I was out for blood.

The guards instantly stilled, choosing to obey me rather than their king. It was a wise move, especially considering they'd all just heard a prophecy that they would perish at my hand. But Baerius was enraged.

"I said kill them!" He stomped his foot like an insolent child.

"Control yourself." My voice took on an otherworldly tone. It was like the ancient tongue of the prophecy now mingled with my own words, and the warning was clear. "Calm down Baerius. Let's not get hasty and murder your only son." I looked at Callan—the father I still hoped I'd one day get to know.

"My only son?" Baerius barked out a humorless laugh. "He's dead to me already. He betrayed me long ago, and today he has chosen the side of our enemies. The same rules apply to him as everyone else here: go against the new order and face imminent death. But don't fret over my lineage, Deliverer. Callan is not my only son."

"He's not?" I looked at Callan, but he wasn't watching me anymore. He was looking at Chaz. No... *Chaz?*

My sixteen year old puppeteer turned to me, answering my bewilderment with a look of solemnity. *Is it true?* I thought, hoping Chaz was listening in. He gave a subtle nod. But how? He'd called Rasputin 'uncle.' He couldn't also be Baerius' son.

Please, Chaz. Stop this. You know it's not right. There has already been too much death, too much blood on your hands. You know Baerius won't stop. We've got to put an end to this.

"Of course he's not." Baerius said, answering my earlier question. "But even if he were, it wouldn't matter. *You* will inherit my throne, my dear. Together, you and I are going to change the world, just like we've discussed." Baerius stepped closer and leaned down, twisting his brows into a quasi-look of concern. "We're a team now. We just have to remove those who stand in our way. Those people lied to you. They've betrayed you since birth, holding you back from your true destiny. Haven't you had enough? Please, let's stop them now so we can rise to our fullest potential. You and me, granddaughter. We can do it. Together."

Tate placed a reassuring hand on my back, reminding me that I wasn't alone. And that single touch was all I needed for my power to explode into action. My inner Athena roared to life. My chest burned white hot, and my limbs felt like they were on fire.

So I relented. I gave in and allowed my natural instinct to take over. The blade came to life in my hand. I lifted it before me and like a flash of light it cut through the air, slicing through the tender flesh on Baerius' neck and silencing the entire ballroom as the king's head rolled across the ground.

I froze, unsure of what had come over me and terrified of what would happen next. For three long breaths everything remained silent. Then the ballroom erupted with shouts of victory.

CHAPTER 12

THE REMAINING CUFF BROKE free from my wrist and hit the ground, but I didn't even hear it clatter over the riotous shouts of acclamation that filled the grandiose space. There was movement all around, overwhelming and choking me. But Tate's touch once again brought me back to the present.

"You did it, Ev." There was no condemnation in his tone. There was nothing but respect and love. But how could he love a monster like me? I was a murderer.

"You did what had to be done." Chaz approached me on the other side. A strange mixture of emotions cycled across his face, and I wasn't sure what he planned to do next. After all, I'd just killed his father—the man he'd teamed up with to put all of this into motion.

And even though he'd kept me locked under his control and forced me to play along with Baerius' sick games, I wasn't mad at him. Some sixth sense—maybe it was Athena—made me take compassion on the boy.

"Well done," a thickly accented voice croaked in my ear. I whipped around to find Rasputin grinning at me. He didn't appear upset by the act of horror I'd just committed, either. "You are magnificent, my Deliverer. Now that the true threat is out of your way, it's time for you to rise up." His hands were on my shoulders, and he was guiding me back to the throne.

Tate looked like he might lash out at the man, but I gave a subtle shake of my head. I wanted to hear what Rasputin had to say. I still didn't trust him further than I could throw a stick, but he'd been the one who insisted I take my sword. He was possibly related to Chaz, and he still showed no signs of wanting to injure me. There was nothing in it for him anymore, so the least I could do was hear him out.

Rasputin sat me on the throne and took a spot by my side. "What do you think?" he asked the small group who had joined us on the stage. Tate, my mother, Callan, Rossel, and Chaz all looked at me with wonder in their eyes.

"Remarkable." Tate turned to Rossel. "It's just like the painting."

My golden gown glittered under the stage lights. Despite the fact that I'd just beheaded a man, I was spotless. And I'd never felt more alive. The power of Athena coursed through my veins with the pulse of the prophecy. I felt every ounce of ferocity I'd seen painted on my face that day back in Rossel's gallery. *Deliverance*. But what did that mean for me, exactly? What was I supposed to do now? I still had so many questions.

Chaz approached, reading the thoughts running through my mind, no doubt. "Baerius spoke the truth. He was my father. And yes, Rasputin is my uncle."

"Then that makes you *my* uncle."

Chaz shrugged. "Yeah, I guess so."

"But how is that possible? The curse doesn't allow the races to mix and produce offspring."

"When Baerius saw that your mother and father successfully bore a mixed race child, he wanted to attempt it for himself. He took several women from Agartha and Atlantis as his concubines and called upon Rasputin's expertise in the dark arts to keep him safe from the curse. Somehow, they found a way for him to survive. The women weren't as fortunate, however, and the experiments never worked. But Rasputin had an idea."

"I offered my sister." Rasputin stroked his beard, grinning like he'd won a Nobel Prize. "The elixir I created took time to work in the woman. I fed it to her for three years before allowing Baerius to take her. She grew ill after Chaz was conceived, but we were able to keep her alive long enough for him to be viable outside of the womb."

He killed his sister to help Baerius produce a mixed race Keeper. The realization repulsed me. But it made me look at Chaz with a new understanding. We were more alike than I knew. "So you're half Olympian and half Agarthian?"

Chaz nodded. "I inherited telepathy from my Olympian genes and glamour from my mother's side. Combined, the two were stronger than they could ever be on their own. And that's how I have the powers you know now."

Rossel spoke next. "Baerius commissioned me to locate you as soon as Chaz's powers came in over the summer. He was ready to find you and kill you once he saw my vision on canvas. But when Thaddeus proved to be unsuccessful in taking your soul, he decided to take matters into his own hands. He called upon Rasputin again for help."

"But you must understand, my magnificent girl, that I never planned to submit to Baerius." Rasputin dropped to his knees and reached for my hand, but I moved it away. "I knew all along that he would never succeed. It is *you* who must rule over us all. They are ready to serve *you*. And I will help you with every step, my lovely. I will guide you."

"I don't want your help." I stood from the throne, heat surging through me. "And I don't want to rule. I'm sick of the battling for power. The curses and the bickering. The pointless rules. I don't want any of it."

"Then let us stop it." Rasputin slid an arm around my shoulder and my blood boiled even hotter. I felt Athena raging up inside, but I didn't want to let her out again. If I released her another time I may never be able to rein her back in again. "You already have the allegiance of Olympus and Agartha. Just convince Maxwell to serve you, and you can take your rightful position and put an end to anything you see unfit. You have my word that the Manticorians will help you with anything you need. Even the impossible, as we did for Baerius."

My stomach twisted at the reminder of what he had done. My grip tightened around the hilt of my sword, and I took a deep breath to calm myself.

It didn't work.

Faster than lightning, I grabbed the front of Rasputin's robe and pressed my blade against his neck. It took every ounce of restraint I had not to push the blade any farther. Athena was ready to finish him the way she had Baerius, but I didn't want to be known for violence and death.

He wants your power, the tablet whispered through my brain.

And I knew it was true. Rasputin was no good. He was never good. But I couldn't kill him like this.

He vanished, just as he had done in his basement when I rescued Driskell from him. And he reappeared behind Chaz, using him as a body shield. His eyes glowed with an eerie red-gold hue as he whispered into Chaz's ear. The boy, my uncle, flicked his gaze up to mine and I saw the moment his decision was made. His lip curled, and he ducked down while simultaneously shouting, "Now!"

Rasputin fired a shot of darkness at me, something that looked like pure shadow—dark enough to suck the rest of the light from the room—and the power within me stopped time. My breaths were heavy as I surveyed the situation. How did I get here? And more importantly, was there a way out of this without getting anyone else hurt?

I looked at the crowd and the terror etched onto each of their faces. I looked at Chaz, and again, somehow I knew this wasn't his fault. He wasn't bad. He wasn't encouraging Rasputin to fight. He was encouraging *me*, asking me to kill his uncle. Was that the only way for me to keep everyone safe?

The words of the prophecy echoed again through my mind: *The Deliverer alone can wield the power of the sword with grace and fire to destroy those who hunger for power.*

Hunger for power.

Like Baerius.

Like Rasputin.

Not all of the Keepers had to perish—only those who had gone mad with their hunger for power. I knew what had to be done.

I placed myself squarely in front of the blast of darkness. Closing my eyes, I breathed in deeply and counted to three before setting time back into motion. Then my instinct took over. My sword slashed through the air, creating a shield for me and perfectly reflecting the blast right back to its source. It all happened so fast that Rasputin didn't have time to react. The shadow struck him squarely in the chest, and his screams rang out through the mountain.

I ducked along with the other Keepers in the room, none of us sure how to react other than to cover our ears and wait for the wailing to end. The floor and walls and even the earth around us shook at the sound. I'd never heard anything so bone-chilling, so soul-rattling in my entire life. It was dark and deep—a kind of magic I couldn't even imagine. I didn't *want* to imagine it. Whatever power Rasputin used to fire that shot at me was composed of all the darkest things this world had to offer. Pure evil.

And when the noise finally subsided, we all opened our eyes and dropped our hands to find nothing but a pile of ash where Rasputin once stood.

CHAPTER 13

ONE BY ONE, THE Keepers dropped to their knees.

"Wait, no." I turned to Tate and was blown away by the adoration in his eyes. "What are they doing? Make them get up."

"They're paying their respects. You just single-handedly eliminated the two greatest threats to our kind." Then he dropped to his knees as well, before taking my hand and tenderly kissing the back of my knuckles. It was so heart-wrenchingly sweet and tender that I almost lost it.

But no, I couldn't lose it here. Everyone was watching. Nearly every single Keeper on the earth was in this room, bowing down before me. My mother knelt beside Callan with tears of joy streaming down her cheeks. Even Rossel bent his long limbs into a bow of respect.

Chaz was last, but he, too, fell to the ground. He didn't have to. He could have easily taken control of my mind and made this event turn out any way he wanted it to. Chaz could wield my power as his own. He was the only other person capable of bringing the place down. But I knew he wouldn't. It was that sixth sense again. I didn't need to attack Chaz. If anything, the kid could probably use a friend.

"Thank you, everyone. But please get up. I am nobody special." Nobody moved, so I said it again, louder. "Please? Please stand."

Maybe you should demand it as their new ruler.

"That kind of defeats the pur—" I spun around. "AL!"

My owl was perched on Gayla's shoulder. Dom stood beside her, grinning from ear to ear. Behind them were Devon, Millie, Sean, and Driskell. They must have teleported in during all the chaos with Rasputin.

"You guys made it!" My free hand flew to my mouth, as though I could cover the crack in my voice that revealed just how weary I was. But this wasn't over yet. I had to think. What was I doing here? How was I supposed to deliver these people from the chains of the law they'd been bound by for thousands of years?

The tablet pulsed on the table, as if it were answering my question. I stepped forward, running my fingers over the smooth stone and carved symbols before picking it up and hugging it to my chest. Lava flowed through my limbs, firing me up from the inside out. I stepped forward, and feeling more confident now, raised my voice so that everyone in the room could hear me.

"You heard the words of the prophecy. They're true. I am the Deliverer. But I am not here to take your lives. I'm not here to rule over you. You don't need a ruler. Can't you see? We are much stronger together than we could ever be apart."

Something snapped between me and the tablet. Some invisible string was cut. A thousand memories rushed through my brain—speeding by in flashes and whirs like a bullet train. I couldn't keep up. I saw thousands of years of history playing out before me. All the knowledge of souls past, condensed into one feeble brain. It was too much.

My legs swayed under me, but I stood strong. It was only a moment before the feeling passed. And though I couldn't pick out specific memories, the knowledge of the ancient world became clear to me.

I took a moment to catch my breath before beginning again. "This is how it was always meant to be. This is why we were created. Our power combined is what the world needs to stay whole. We were united in the beginning, but greed and a hunger for power divided us. The races were cast apart—thrown into distant corners of the world.

"Bearius was wrong about a lot of things, but he was right about this: it's time for us to reunite. Not under any ruler, but together. As one. The rules that you have lived by all your lives have done nothing but separate us more. It's foolish. Even the humans have been hurt by this struggle for power. No more!

"I am here to deliver you from these chains that are holding you back. May every curse be broken. May every soul be freed. May the fractured be restored, and may we all find peace with the ones our souls crave. Mark this day as the day the world changed forever—for the better."

The tablet seared my fingers. It was hotter than fire and bright as the sun. The only light in the room that could rival its glow was my aura, which had become almost blinding during my speech. I released the prophecy, surprised to see it hanging in the air as if by a string. Then I reached for the Firelake blade, and I swung.

The tablet shattered. There were no solid pieces of it remaining—only dust. Bright, glowing dust, as fine as powder, rained down on heads of every Keeper in the mountain. The people rose to their feet again, awe-inspired gasps filling the large space.

And when I turned around I was face to face with a strange man I'd never seen before. He was shorter than me, dressed in a flowing white gown with feathers sticking up from one side of the golden band wrapped around his forehead. I didn't recognize him until he spoke.

"I have arms."

I laughed. "Yes, Al. You do. And legs. And... skin."

We stared at each other for a moment before the man rushed forward and wrapped me in an embrace. Though I'd never seen him in human form, there was something comforting in the hug. My soul knew him, and after thousands of years tag-teaming through this world together, it was only right that we saw each other face to face.

Finally, I pulled back. "How?"

"How what?"

"How are you a human instead of an owl?"

"You broke the curse."

"You were cursed." I took in a breath and held it. Of course he was cursed. How else did I think an owl was speaking to me? And how many others had been cursed over the years? "How long?"

"Twelve thousand years." Al ran a hand through his hair. It wasn't even streaked with gray. Time must have stopped for him while he was an owl. And it dawned on me how miserable it must have been to be stuck in bird-form for twelve thousand years.

"Who would do that to you?"

"Well... *you did*."

Thank goodness Tate chose that moment to wrap his strong arm around my waist, because I might have fainted otherwise. "I would never!" I said as he guided me toward the rest of the group on the side of the stage.

"You did." Al smiled, sadly. "But it was well deserved."

"I suspected as much," Driskell said with a twitch of his mustache. "I'd read stories about the curse, but no one ever believed them to be true." He laughed, but it sounded more like a cough. "Go on, then. Tell us what happened."

Al sighed and nodded. "We lived as you said, together as one united front. And we watched over the mortals, as was our duty. But some of us got a little too eager to use our power. We grew great nations, technologically advanced and beautifully created. And the bigger they got, the more our greed grew. More was never enough. We were insatiable. And that's how the territories were divided. I ruled Atlantis in those days. It was my fault we were cast into the bottom of the sea. And you—well, you were always destined for greatness. All of you."

I looked around the small circle of friends. No one seemed to understand what he meant. Even Dom and Chaz, with their mind-reading capabilities, looked perplexed.

"You see," Al said. "Your souls were connected then, just as they are now. You—" he pointed at Gayla. "You saw the fall of the Keepers before it happened. And likewise, you saw our return to glory. But you didn't know just how long it would be, only that Everly here would be the one to bring us back together.

"You were so angry." Al dropped his chin before meeting my eyes. "You were furious with me the day Atlantis fell into the depths of the sea. But you knew one day justice would be restored. And you cursed me—turning me into an owl so that I could never go below the water to enjoy the nation I worked my entire life to create. I have nearly forgotten what Atlantis even looks like now." He paused, staring off into the distance as if trying to imagine it.

"I'm sorry," I whispered.

"No, no. No apologies." He waved a hand in the air and snapped back to the present. "The other part of the curse was for me to follow you and protect you until the day the Keepers were restored. I played a major role in our destruction, and the only way to redeem myself was to play an equally major role in our redemption.

"That meant thousands of years of looking after you and keeping you safe. But I couldn't mention the prophecy. I couldn't mention your role. You had to come to that on your own. One wrong move and it could have changed our world forever. So my memories of that day were erased." He looked at Chaz. "Erased by you."

"Me?" My sixteen year old uncle was astounded.

"Yes. And the memories weren't restored until now, when the tablet was shattered. Things were different back then. Our powers were stronger. More varied. As you now know, great things happen when the races work together. Great powers are created through our bonds. And I very much look forward to seeing our world restored when the Keepers unite again."

I blew out a breath through my lips. "Wow. That's a lot." I looked out at the crowd. Their excitement was palpable. The air was thick with anticipation and hope for our future. "So just to be clear, everything I said is okay? That's how it's supposed to be?" I spoke the words from my heart and I passionately stood behind them. But to believe that it could be a reality was almost more than I could ask for. No curses, no rules on bonds or soulmates, no separation of the territories, freedom for the fractured souls...

"That's exactly how it's meant to be." Al smiled. "Thank you. You have delivered us from twelve thousand years of punishment, and the world will be greater for it."

I never could have guessed the afternoon would end like this. We were all exhausted, but as I looked at the faces around me—my mom and dad, new friends, a long-lost uncle and an owl-turned-man—my heart was full. We were an unlikely group. A very strange family indeed. But these were my people. This was *my* family, and I wouldn't have it any other way.

Tate wrapped his arms around me from behind and whispered in my ear. "Come on, Ev. Let's tell everyone the good news." He spun me around to face him, never releasing me from the protective circle of his arms. The kiss that followed was gentle, sweet, and far too brief. But he was right. There would be time for more kisses later.

My only job now was to tell our people that they were finally free.

EPILOGUE

THERE WAS A POUNDING on the door. "Everly!"

"Just a minute! I'm... *busy*." My words came out muffled against Tate's mouth. I felt his lips pull into a grin over mine and I couldn't help but kiss him again.

"Yeah, I know exactly how busy you are. You have until the count of three before I'm busting in."

"Tilly." My father's voice was soothing. "She's a grown woman. Give her just a minute."

"She may be grown but she's still my daughter. *One!*"

"Maybe we should continue this later." Tate gave me one more lingering lock with his magical lips before sitting up.

"*Two!*"

I groaned and sat up next to him, running a hand through my hair to smooth it out.

"*Three!*" True to her word, my mother barged into Millie's study, where Tate and I had snuck away for a few minutes before the dinner party. She put her hands on her hips and tilted her head. She had that mom-look down pat. "You think you can get out of silverware duty to sneak away and make-out without getting caught? Think again."

"Sorry, Ms. Gordon." Tate stood and shoved his hands innocently into his pockets, giving my mom a respectful nod in the process.

"It *is* a great make-out couch." Gayla popped her head into the doorway. "If I had a nickel for every time I caught Devon and Millie in here..." She cringed and shook her head. "Anyway, Pierre said dinner will be served in about five minutes. You guys better wrap it up." She winked and disappeared back into the hall.

We followed after her, stopping just long enough for Tate and my father to shake hands. "It's been a while, Thaddeus. Good to see you again. How's the underground?"

"Better than ever, sir." Tate grinned. "We had our first council meeting a couple of days ago. Surprisingly, I think Osborne is going to do a pretty good job as the Agarthian chairman."

"You bet your tail I am." We rounded the corner into the dining room and nearly crashed right into the smug-faced ex-hunter. He clapped Tate on the back and stepped aside so we could find our seats for dinner. There were so many of us tonight that Jeeves had to put both leaves in Millie's already huge dining room table.

"Gang's all here!" Gayla beamed in a fuschia dress that would have revealed way too much of my gangly limbs, but it looked fabulous on her, as everything always did.

And she was right. Everyone I cared about had shown up to celebrate tonight. It had been three months since the gala where we almost lost everything. Three months of spreading the word to every Keeper who couldn't make it that night, letting them know the Deliverer had come through. Three months of tearing apart old systems and working to build them back stronger. Three months of getting to know my father and his huge heart and dry sense of humor. Three months of showing Chaz what life on earth looked like.

We'd made lots of progress, but it wasn't all easy. Dom smiled at me from across the room and helped Titus into his seat, scooting him up to the table. She'd dropped out of Columbia after that fateful day. She said she couldn't sit in a classroom while she knew there were so many Keepers out in the world struggling to make sense of life now that their curses had been lifted.

She and Chaz started a small, private clinic using their unique views into other people's minds to help them overcome their trauma. Titus was Dom's first client, and perhaps the most challenging. We still weren't sure of everything Rasputin had done to him while he was held captive, but the damage had definitely left a mark. Dom made it her personal goal to help him heal.

She'd also helped Sean's dad, Peter. And Chaz had taken in a few of the fractured and reformed Manticorians who had been running from the hunters for ages. The Hall of Souls in Agartha was empty now, the pools gone dry. We weren't sure where they'd all gone, but I hoped with my whole heart that they'd somehow been restored. They were free now, in any case.

Millie and Devon sat at the head of the table, while my mother and Callan took the opposite end. The rest of us spread out in between. Osborne, Gayla, Chaz, Tate and I sat on one side. On the other side sat Driskell, Dom, Titus, and my favorite new couple: Sean and Abby.

They were the first openly Keeper-human couple that I knew of. Sean hated the attention it brought him, but I couldn't have been more proud of him. And if there was ever a human who could stand up to the criticism of some of the old-school thinking Keepers, it was Abby. She already knew so much about our world that she slid into place seamlessly.

Even Gayla had finally come around to accepting Abby. Her days of pining over Sean were long gone. Besides, she'd found a much more capable sparring partner in Osborne. They swore they hated each other, but it was quite a smoldering hatred, if you asked me. It reminded me a bit of the way Tate and I used to jab at each other before we discovered we were soulmates.

He reached under the table to take my hand, and my heart swelled. Thank goodness we'd gotten over that whole hating business. This love stuff was way more fun.

Jeeves came into the room, refilling our glasses before Millie's new maid brought round the salads. He was in on the secret now, too. We hadn't gone fully public to the mortals yet, but I figured it wouldn't hurt to let our favorite humans know what we were. Especially Pierre. He needed the fear of my power to light a fire under him when he got to running at the mouth sometimes.

The sound of a spoon clanging against a glass silenced the room. All eyes turned toward Callan as he stood at his end of the table.

"Oh, hey. That was louder than I thought it would be." He set down his cup and ran a hand through his hair, looking uncharacteristically flustered. Focusing on me, he began speaking again. "Everyone take just a minute to look around this room. Look at this crazy group we have gathered around the table. Who would have ever imagined us here together?"

We all traded looks and smiles. Tate gave my hand a gentle squeeze.

"I certainly never imagined I'd be so lucky to have friends like this." Callan looked down at my mother, and his eyes crinkled in the corners.

His love for her was written all over his face. It was the kind of look men gave their leading ladies in all the romcom movies my mom and I used to binge. And it was her real life now!

"And I never imagined I'd have a daughter." He looked at me again. "To get to know you, Everly, has been one of the greatest joys of my life. You are a remarkable young woman, and I thank you for allowing me to enter your life. But I have just one more small request to ask of you, if you don't mind." He swallowed and looked back at my mom. "How would you feel if I asked your mother to marry me? Officially?"

I gasped and looked at my blushing mother. Her eyes were glistening as she awaited my answer. "It's okay by me, but you'll have to ask her."

"I was hoping you would say that." Callan smiled and dropped to one knee, taking my mother's hands into his. "Tilly Gordon..."

The musical chime of Millie's Scottish doorbell and two loud barks interrupted him, followed by a loud voice and some hushing out in the hall. A moment later Rossel and Al came through the dining room doorway, followed by two very worked up mastiffs.

Rossel looked supremely annoyed, but it was Al they were after. He must have still smelled like an owl on some molecular level, because Tiny Tim and Lemondrop couldn't stop drooling and licking their chops like they were about to dig into a turkey dinner anytime he was near.

"Shhh. Down!" Al kicked out a leg then looked up with wide eyes once he realized what he'd just interrupted. "Oh dear. So sorry we're late." He hurried into the room followed by Rossel, who held a canvas with a giant bow wrapped around it.

Callan cleared his throat, but my mom grabbed his face in both hands and kissed him before he could speak again. "Yes, I will marry you!" she exclaimed when she finally came up for air. Then she kissed him again while we all whooped and hollered.

"You guys need to take that to the couch in Millie's study," Gayla said with a laugh.

Jeeves jumped at the opportunity to grab a couple of bottles of champagne, and as he retrieved the flutes Rossel stood and offered his canvas to my mother. "I wanted to be the first to offer my congratulations."

She took the painting into her hands and tears immediately filled her eyes. "Is this a vision?" she asked with a shaky voice.

He nodded, and the first salty tear made a wet trail down my mom's cheek. "It's beautiful, Rossel. Thank you so much." She spun it around to reveal a painting of her and my father, sitting in rocking chairs on the wrap-around front porch of my old Oklahoma home. In her arms was an infant delicately wrapped in a yellow blanket.

A mom *and* a dad, and now a baby brother or sister? My heart couldn't get any fuller.

We spent the rest of the evening giving toasts and laughing until tears streamed from our eyes. It was a night I would cherish for the rest of my life. We would have more challenges, of course, in between our moments of joy. The hard stuff never really disappeared completely. But when you had a life full of people who would go to the ends of the earth to help you see those challenges through, what more could you ask for?

Thank you so much for reading Everly's story. I hope you enjoyed it! If so, would you please be so kind as to leave a review on Amazon? Even just one or two words would be wonderful! Your reviews are one of the main ways new readers find my books, and I truly do appreciate every single one!

And if you're looking for another great series to dig into, may I suggest The Ember Society series? It's got a dystopian near-future society, handsome rebels, charming Leaders, and a whole lot of action and adventure. You can get the first book here: From the Dust

Or sign up to get email alerts from me for every new release, with a hefty dose of good deals on ebooks sprinkled in there for you as well! Get AR Colbert's emails HERE.

A DEEPER LOOK

SCYLLA AND CHARYBDIS (2- The Unseen): In Greek mythology, Scylla is the daughter of the sea gods, a once beautiful water nymph turned monster like her many sisters. She is described as having six heads atop long necks, with mouths full of sharp teeth. She sat on one side of the strait of water separating modern day Sicily and the southern tip of Italy. Any ships that sailed too closely would have six men snatched off the boat—one in each of Scylla's mouths.

Charybdis sat on the other side of the strait. She was said to be a minor goddess of the tides. Some believe she was once beautiful, turned into a monster by Zeus. Others believe she was born a monster. In the ancient stories, she created a giant, deadly whirlpool three times a day. Any ships that sailed too closely would be dragged below the depths of the sea, never to return.

Ambrosia (2- The Unseen): You've probably heard of ambrosia—the food/drink of the gods. Many believe it provided them with immortality. Others suggest it might have just been honey. In the world of the Keepers, it is a special ingredient that grows only in Olympus, high above the earth's surface. It does not provide immortality, but it offers some healing powers and a feeling of pure bliss upon consumption. This feeling might cause humans to believe they are immortal, and they will stop at nothing to obtain the high that it provides once again. While not quite as addictive for Keepers, it can still be dangerous when consumed in excess.

Monkshood (3- The Apothecary): (also known as wolfsbane) is as lovely as it is deadly, with the entirety of the plant containing toxins. When boiled or steamed, the toxicity is reduced to a level where therapeutic effects can be enjoyed, including a reduction in joint, muscle, and nerve pain. But higher doses can cause numbness and tingling, altered heart rates, and gastrointestinal issues. Too much of the herb will induce respiratory paralysis and/or death.

Alma Mater (3- The Apothecary): This statue (as well as the others mentioned in the story) truly stands on the campus of Columbia University. Although there have been many controversies and lore surrounding the statue, she is mostly benign. And there is, in fact, a tiny owl hidden in the folds of her robe!

Rasputin (3- The Apothecary): Grigori Rasputin is a man shrouded in mystery and wrapped in rumors. Supposedly a mystic, prophet, and healer, he was a close mentor to the last imperial family of Russia in the early 1900s. Rasputin was murdered in 1916 in perhaps the biggest controversy of his life. Some say that he would not die even after several strong doses of cyanide and a gunshot wound to the chest. He had to be shot again much later, after he was already presumed to be dead, then his body was thrown into a half-frozen river.

Saint Anthony's Hall (4- In Pursuit): While described as a literary fraternity, the St. A's chapter at Columbia is the original and perhaps most mysterious chapter of this collegiate society in existence. This elite, and extremely exclusive frat has seen its fair share of scandal and controversy over the years, but one thing is certain: only the wealthiest of the wealthy will ever know what secrets truly lie within the walls of Saint Anthony's Hall.

Tantalus (5- Unraveling): this figure from Greek mythology was known for several sins, including cutting his son into pieces and serving him as dinner for the gods. The Keepers, however, remember him for another deed. He was said to have been invited to dine among the gods, or the Olympians, according to Keeper history. But Tantalus abused their hospitality and stole some of their ambrosia, intending to serve it to his people and give mortals everlasting life. He was punished by standing eternally in water as high as his chin that he could never drink, with fruit hanging above his head that he could never eat.

Manticore (6- Old Man on the Sea): The Manticore was a mighty mythological creature described as having the head and face of a man, the body of a lion, and the tail of a scorpion. Some describe it as having wings as well. It was cunning and nearly impossible to defeat. The beast was said to be greedy for human flesh, using tricks to lure men to it so it could devour them with its three rows of sharp teeth.

The Flannan Isles Lighthouse (6- Old Man on the Sea): The lighthouse on Eilean Mor of the Flannan Isles off the coast of Scotland is home to a real life mystery. One night in 1900, three keepers of the lighthouse disappeared without a trace. Some speculate a storm washed them out to sea, while others report journal entries that suggest otherwise. The mystery was never solved, and the island continues to attract the attention of wanna-be sleuths to this day.

Chronos (7- Finding Atlantis): Chronos was a Greek god often depicted with a long white beard and a scythe in his hand. Philosophers referred to him as Father Time. Some myths claim the god consumed his own children, the way time also consumes all things. Though he was technically a Titan, not an Olympian, they all fall under the same umbrella when it comes to the world of the Keepers.

Soma (8- The Water Princess): Like ambrosia, soma is known as a sacred drink of the gods from ancient Indian texts. It was said to elicit divine visions and offer immortality. For the Keepers in this series, it serves a more recreational use.

Bimini road (8- The Water Princess): The Bimini Road is a collection of stones that can be found off the coast of North Bimini Island in the Bahamas. The stones are lined up like a path or a wall running a half a mile long, but they are buried under the water. Some say they are a natural formation, but with their straight lines and even spacing, many speculate that they are the man made remnants of an old road, possibly one that once led to the lost world of Atlantis.

NEW BY AR COLBERT:

EYE OF THE FATES, Fateborne Trilogy #1:

He's fated to die by the hands of his betrothed, and the kingdom shall succumb to darkness.

Kidnapped at birth, Vaeda has spent her life among the Moirai, carefully watching over the mortal realm and guiding her subjects toward greatness or death as the fates see fit.

When the fate of a mortal prince shifts, Vaeda sees the future of his kingdom falling to the dark mages of Caligo. The only way to prevent evil from overtaking the entire realm is to break the number one rule of the Moirai: take fate into her own hands.

But Vaeda isn't the only one looking for the prince. Theilen, cast out from the kingdom to live among the dragons, has waited his whole life to avenge the death of his parents. Vaeda might just be his ticket back into the kingdom. He only has to stay on her good side for a short time.

Vaeda doesn't know Theilen's true intentions. And she doesn't know why she's drawn to the gruff, slightly feral beast of a man. All Vaeda knows is that she can't allow him to sidetrack her from her real mission: Save the prince. Save the kingdom. And get out before she gets in too deep.

✓ A fresh twist on mythology ✓ Magical world-building ✓ Slow-burn enemies to lovers romance

About the Author

AR COLBERT IS A wife, mother of two, and life-long daydreamer from central Oklahoma. She believes in the magic of a good story and would love nothing more than to spend the rest of her days getting lost in books. Her other hobbies include baking, cheering on the Oklahoma State Cowboys, and obsessively scrolling through Zillow.

You can follow her online on Goodreads, Facebook, or Bookbub to learn about new releases.

Other books by AR Colbert:

The Fateborne Trilogy *(Romantic Epic Fantasy)*
Eye of the Fates
Heart of the Fates
War of the Fates

The Ember Society Series *(Dystopian Adventure)*
From the Dust
From the Earth
From the Embers
From the Flames
From the Ashes

Printed in Great Britain
by Amazon